Alex & River

USA TODAY BESTSELLING AUTHOR

KENNEDY FOX

Alex & River

BISHOP FAMILY ORIGIN, #1

USA TODAY BESTSELLING AUTHOR

KENNEDY FOX

ALEX & RIVER
Bishop Family Origin, #1

Includes: *Taming Him,*
Hitching the Cowboy, & Catching the Cowboy

This special edition Bishop family origin collection consists of three books from the *Bishop Brothers World.*

Taming Him
Alex & River

Hitching the Cowboy
Riley & Zoey

Catching the Cowboy
Diesel & Rowan

Bishop Brothers World

The parents get their stories in the first generation,
the *Bishop Brothers* series.

Their children get their stories in
the second generation, the *Circle B Ranch* series.

GRANDPARENTS
Scott & Rose Bishop

PARENTS
Evan Bishop
John Bishop
Jackson Bishop
Alex Bishop

KIDS
Riley
Maize
Elizabeth
Rowan
Ethan
Mackenzie
Kane
Knox
Kaitlyn

Reading Order

Each book in the Bishop Brothers World can read as standalones but if you wish to read the others, here's our suggested reading order.

BISHOP BROTHERS SERIES
Original Bishop Family
Taming Him

Needing Him

Chasing Him

Keeping Him

SPIN-OFF'S
Friends of the Bishops
Make Me Stay

Roping the Cowboy

CIRCLE B RANCH SERIES
Bishop Family Second Generation
Hitching the Cowboy

Catching the Cowboy

Wrangling the Cowboy

Bossing the Cowboy

Kissing the Cowboy

Winning the Cowboy

Claiming the Cowboy

Tempting the Cowboy

Seducing the Cowboy

Taming Him

ALEX & RIVER

He's sexy, charming and has a panty-melting smirk.
She's swearing off men.
Two weeks on the beach is what they both need—
no strings attached, no expectations, no broken hearts.

Alex Bishop is your typical cowboy.
Charming, sexy, and wears a panty-melting smirk.

Working on the ranch helped build his solid eight-pack and smoking body. He's every girl's wet fantasy and he knows it too. After wining and dining his dates and giving them the best night of their lives, he always sends flowers and calls the next day—even if it's to say, *let's just be friends.* His mama taught him manners after all and his southern blood knows how to be a gentleman. Still, that isn't enough to tame the wildest of the Bishop brothers.

River Lancaster has finally met the man of her dreams. Too bad after six months of romantic bliss, she finds out he's married. With a broken heart and blind rage, she books herself a ticket to Key West, Florida. Who needs a man when there's an all-you-can-drink margarita bar, anyway? That's what she tells herself until she bumps into the right guy who can make all those bad memories disappear. *Even if it's only temporarily.*

Two weeks on the beach is what they both need. No strings attached, no expectations, no broken hearts. Too bad the universe has other plans—one that'll change the entire course of their lives in just nine short months.

It's not a silly little moment
It's not the storm before the calm
This is the deep and dyin' breath of
This love we've been workin' on

"Slow Dancing in a Burning Room"
-John Mayer

PROLOGUE

River

TWELVE YEARS AGO

Rounding the corner into the hospital room, I see Rylie lying in bed and immediately rush to her side. She's hooked up to machines and oxygen, and though it's common for her, it still feels like a stab to the gut when I see her like this.

"Riles," I whisper, holding her hand in mine and squeezing three times. "Can you hear me?"

With a nod, she squeezes my hand back three times. She slowly tilts her head down and tries to open her eyes. The medication makes her sleepy, and she can't always stay awake even when she tries.

"Love you, baby sis," I tell her like I always do. She'd normally reply with, "Love you too, big sis," and we'd both smile.

My father catches up to me and stands on the other side of her bed. "River," he says in a deep scolding tone. "What'd I say about running?"

"Well, had I known she was in here earlier, I wouldn't have ran to get up here as soon as I could," I tell him, returning the tone. My father had just picked me up from school and told me Rylie was back in the hospital.

"I already told you there was no need to take you out of school. She's just running a fever," he says so casually as if having a fever while being treated for cancer was no big deal.

Rolling my eyes, I hide my disapproval and focus on Rylie. "What's the doctor saying?" I read the monitors, too familiar with what the numbers represent.

"He's running more tests," my mother answers, walking into the room with a Styrofoam cup of coffee. She's wearing big sunglasses, most likely to hide the bags under her eyes. Mom stresses more than she sleeps, and Dad works nonstop. It's Mom, Rylie, and me most of the time, and even though I love my dad, I wish he was around more for our sakes during times like these.

Dad walks toward Mom and gives her a quick peck on the cheek before he starts digging around in his pockets for his keys. "I have to get back to the office; call me when there's news, okay?"

"You're leaving?" I glare.

"I left work early today, River. I have to finish some things up."

"But Rylie's sick." I say the obvious, furious that he'd leave us at a time like this.

"I know, sweetie." He steps toward me and presses a kiss to the top of my head as if I'm a baby, but I'm not. I don't need his coddling anymore. I'm a freshman in high school who's watched her nine-year-old sister battle leukemia for the past two years. "I'll work as fast as I can," he says before rushing out of the room.

I recognize the disappointment on my mother's face immediately. It's always the same thing. Rylie spends more time in the hospital than she does at home, and having him here would give us comfort, but he leaves that role to Mom instead. She always plasters on a fake smile and pretends to be strong for Rylie and me.

The doctor comes in not long after with Rylie's chart and tells us they'd like to keep her overnight for observation. She more than likely has an infection, which triggered the fever.

"Until we locate the source of infection, we'll keep her on oxygen and monitor her stats," he tells us. "The nurse will move her to another floor in a bit."

"Thanks, Dr. Potter," my mother murmurs.

The bare hospital walls, the cold air, the cream-colored floors—they're all I've seen the last three years. Rylie got sick over two years ago, and we were in the ER at least once a week until she was officially diagnosed and they started chemo treatment.

"I'm going to call your dad," she tells me before standing up and leaving. I can see the distress and exhaustion all over her features. Mom quit her job and has been Rylie's caretaker since the beginning. She and Dad never go out anymore—at least not with each other—and if they aren't fighting about bills, they're fighting about his long hours at the office. I've overheard some of their conversations and sometimes wonder if Dad wishes he could leave us and find another family. Mom's accused him of cheating, and though he never denies it, he just tells her she's crazy.

The tension is thick when things are rough like this. Before Rylie's diagnosis, they both worked full-time but always made sure to be home in time for dinner so we could eat as a family. We'd talk to Mom about our day, and Dad would ask about homework. It was predictable, but it was nice.

How easy it is to take life for granted until it throws a curve ball and changes the entire course of it.

I hate seeing Rylie like this. She doesn't deserve this, and I'm often angry that she's the one having to go through it and not me. I'd take her place in a heartbeat. She was only seven, and though she annoyed me on a daily basis, I loved her so much. Mom used to tell me stories of how I'd beg them for a baby sister, and when they got pregnant, I was so excited. Growing up together wasn't always rainbows and sunshine, but I knew I was lucky to have her in my life.

I press the back of my hand to her cheek and feel how cold it is, even with a low-grade fever. These hospitals are always cold, and I hate it. Doing what I always do when Mom isn't around, I crawl onto the bed next to her. I'm always careful of her lines, but then, at least, I can give her some of my body heat and comfort her.

"Let me know if I'm hurting you, okay, Riles?" Even though my voice is just above a whisper, when she squeezes my hand back again, I know she heard me.

I rest my chin on top of her head and hold her close to me before closing my eyes and sending another prayer up. "Love you, baby sis."

A nurse comes in an hour later to move her to another floor.

Once she's settled, Mom tells me Dad is coming to pick me up soon.

"Why can't I stay here?"

"You need to eat some dinner and finish your homework," she says with little emotion.

"'I'm not leaving!" I shout. "I'm staying with Rylie."

Dad arrives twenty minutes later, ordering me to come home with him for the night.

"I'll bring you back tomorrow. Let's go. *Now.*"

I kiss Rylie's cheek and squeeze her hand three times. When she squeezes mine back, I smile and promise her I'll be back as soon as I can. When Rylie is kept overnight, Mom always stays, but Dad never does.

The next morning, I call Mom before school, and she says she doesn't have any updates yet. I make her promise to call the school if anything changes so I can know right away, and even though she agrees, something in my gut tells me otherwise.

After not hearing any word from Mom all day, Dad picks me up and drives us straight to the hospital. He's eerily quiet during the ride over. That could mean anything since he's not much of a talker anyway, but something isn't settling right in the air.

"What is it, Dad?" I finally ask as he searches for a parking spot in the hospital garage.

"Nothing, River."

I narrow my eyes at him, wondering why he's lying. As soon as he parks, I jump out of the car and run the entire way up to Rylie's room. Doctors and nurses swarm in and out, all holding charts and double checking her monitors.

"Mom, what's wrong?" I pant, catching my breath.

She's wearing her sunglasses again, but I know she's choking up before she even speaks. "She's septic." Her words barely leave her mouth before one of the monitor alarms starts going off. It's her heart monitor. The doctors have talked about sepsis previously during other visits, so I know it's a life-threatening complication of an infection.

"She's flatlining!" a nurse calls out, and they all rush around.

I've never felt this kind of panic in my life, and I've had many reasons to up to this point but watching her heartbeat flatline on the monitor has me gasping for air. I can't seem to catch my breath between the tears and screaming.

Dad's arms wrap around me from behind, holding me tight to his body as I scream for Rylie. Hysterically, I watch as they use the defibrillator and shock her chest.

I still remember the way her hair smelled. She was obsessed with everything pink and strawberries, so anytime I smell something fruity, I immediately think of her.

Watching Rylie battle for her life was painful. During her good days, she'd smile up at me, and I swear she was stronger than me through it all. She always made sure I was okay, which was crazy because I wouldn't be okay until she was cured. Even then, I'd always fear the worst anytime she'd get a fever or a cold.

Memories flash through my mind of everything we went through for all those years, and when it was time to choose my career, I knew without a doubt what I wanted to study. Hell, I'd been experiencing it for years. The rest was just textbook stuff that I knew I could learn, but being at someone's side while they were in their most delicate state was something I knew I could and wanted to do.

I went to nursing school, more determined than ever to soak up any and all information. Mom and Dad fought and grew apart and eventually divorced. Our family was broken, but I wouldn't let it take me down. Even when I failed to stay strong, thoughts of Rylie always kept me focused. What she endured proved she was always the strongest of us all.

Part One

CHAPTER ONE

Alex

I watch the early morning fog roll over the hills as I walk across the pasture toward the barn. There's something about waking up before the roosters crow or the sun rises that gets me going. Maybe it's because ranch life is ingrained in me, but I wouldn't have it any other way.

"What the hell?" Dylan shouts, carrying grain in buckets for the horses. I glance down at his boots and can't help but laugh as he stands smack dab in the middle of a steaming pile of fresh shit. He groans as he slides his boot across the wet, dew-soaked grass, but there's not much hope for his boot.

Dylan's mom and mine have been best friends since they were both kids, so we met when we were in diapers and have been inseparable ever since. Every summer since high school, he's worked for my father until it became a full-time gig. He's become my partner and sidekick around the ranch, though he's definitely not the greatest influence. He's always up for anything regardless of the consequences, which has gotten us into plenty of trouble over the years.

13

"You should be happy you didn't trip and fall face first in it," I tell him, chuckling. "It makes for a pretty shitty day."

"Sounds like you've fallen a time or two." He snorts, knowing damn well I have. Dylan struggles with smearing the crap off the sides of his boots because his hands are full.

"One time, after tripping and being covered in cow shit, Jackson refused to let me go change. Basically, had to stay like that for the entire day. Eventually, it dried, but I swore I could taste it in my mouth for days."

"Jackson can be such an asshole," Dylan says with a laugh.

"It must be a Bishop thing." I chuckle.

Once we're inside the barn, we dump the feed into tubs for the horses in each stall, then head down to feed the pigs, chickens, and cows. By the time we finish, the sun is barely peeking over the horizon, and I know we need to get a move on if we're going to finish our tasks on time. Though feeding the animals happens every day, what we do afterward that changes on a weekly basis and is usually discussed over breakfast with my father every Sunday morning.

Dylan and I make our way to the east side of the land where we'll be replacing fences along the property line. It's physically laboring work, but I don't complain. I enjoy the hard tasks even when it feels like it's going to kill me. I was born and bred to be a Bishop, and I've been helping my parents around the ranch since I could walk. One day it'll be my and my three brothers' responsibility to manage, but for now, we all have our own tasks to focus on to keep everything running smoothly.

We drive down the old county road along the pasture, and from a distance I can already see a group of workers pulling metal pipes from the back of a lowboy and laying them on the ground. As soon as we park and walk up, I can tell Evan, my oldest brother, is in an agitated mood just by the attitude and stink face he's wearing. His hair is a blond mess as pieces stick to his forehead and cheeks from the sweat.

Evan spends most of his time working at the hospital, but on his days off, Dad drags him out to help on the ranch. *You're still a Bishop*, Dad likes to remind him, so Evan puts in his time when he can. He's nothing more than a pain in my ass anytime he's around. He's years older than me, so we didn't grow up together and bond like my older brothers did, but I still enjoy giving him hell when he serves it to me.

"Who smells like shit?" Evan asks over his shoulder as he carries the post hole digger across the way so we can get started.

Dylan glares at me. "Do you think he can really smell it?"

Bursting out into hearty laughter, I shake my head at him and throw him his work gloves. "I have ever since you stepped in it."

I stand by and watch Evan crank the driver. When he rams it into the ground, Dylan and I begin mixing cement. After each hole is dug, we slam the six-foot pipes in the ground and make sure they're level before adding cement to set them in place.

"So I got some good news," Dylan tells me as he fills the hole with the rock mix.

"Yeah? Mallory wants you back?" I like to give him shit about his ex every chance I get because I warned him about her. Several times, in fact.

"Hell no. I wouldn't take her back again."

I glare at him in denial and snort. "That's what you said last time," I remind him.

"Shut up," he fires back. "Honestly, after I found out how many times she cheated on me, I wouldn't even fuck her with *your* dick," Dylan states, laughing in disgust.

"Fuck you. My dick takes offense to that. I don't make village bicycles a habit," I say matter-of-factly, slamming a pipe into the ground.

"That's 'cause you *are* the village bicycle." He chuckles at my expense, and I groan. He's damn lucky my hands aren't free at the moment to slap that shit-eating grin off his face. He clears his throat and tips his chin up. "Everyone with a tight pussy and big rack step right up!" he hollers, raising his arms up for emphasis. "Come and get a ride on the Wild Stallion, Alex Bishop! Six-foot something, dirty blond hair, and a smart mouth to boot! He may be a cocky son of a bitch, but don't worry, his mama taught him right. He'll wine and dine you before fucking you till you forget your own name! Now ladies, who's first?"

I snort at his pathetic performance, shaking my head but not entirely disagreeing with his words. "Yeah, well, everyone knows a stallion can't be tamed." I smirk, lifting my cowboy hat and repositioning it on my head while Dylan rolls his eyes.

We get back to work, and that's when I remember his announcement earlier.

"So, asshole, what's your news?" I ask as we continue to work.

"Oh so, remember that big giveaway contest at the fall carnival last month?" he asks with a knowing grin on his face.

Narrowing my eyes, I think back on it. "Yeah, the romantic Key West getaway?"

Dylan continues to nod. "That's the one! Guess which lucky bastard won?" He gloats.

"Don't tell me that bastard is you?" I mock.

"Fuck yeah, it is! Two weeks all expenses paid! As long as the boss lets me take off, I'll be packing my bags to set out into the sunset with all the beer I can drink."

"That sounds like the most pathetic country song I've ever heard."

"Sorry I don't have a line of women waiting to jump my saddle, so I'd rather go alone than miss out on a free vacation."

"Ya sure you don't want to call Mallory?" I tease him again.

Dylan drops his shovel, and as soon I glance over at him and realize he's charging at me, I start running in the opposite direction. He has the same look on his face like the time he tried to kick my ass in seventh grade when he caught me kissing his longtime crush, Summer Sanders. *What can I say?* She came onto me first.

Luckily, the only thing he has on me is speed. As he tackles me to the ground, I'm quick to put him in a headlock before he can throw the first punch. Struggling to get out of my grip, we both freeze when the motor of the pole digger stops. Seconds later, Evan pulls me up by my collar and glares at me.

"Dylan might not be able to take you in a fight, but if you don't get to work, I'm going to kick your ass from here to San Antonio and back," Evan threatens before I push him out of my way. Considering we live in Eldorado, that's a three-hour ass kickin', and I don't fuckin' think so.

"Just because I'm your little brother doesn't mean you're my boss. So, pull out the stick that's wedged in your ass and worry about yourself," I snap at him, walking back over to the metal pipes and cement mix.

Looking over my shoulder, I see Dylan is curled over laughing his ass off.

"Shut up, asshole!" I yell back at him.

He quickly runs and catches up with me. "You started it by bringing up Mallory." He slams his shoulder into mine.

I smile, not denying it. I live to give him shit about her. Mallory's the epitome of a snobby, rich girl who thinks she's a Southern belle who's above being nice to anyone who works for a living. Yeah, I didn't exactly like her, so I bust his balls about her every chance I can. Getting tackled and caught by Evan? Totally worth it.

"Well, you know how cranky Evan can get sometimes. He's probably gonna tell Dad we were fucking around again. Asshole," I say. "Maybe if he got laid every once in a while, he wouldn't be such a prick," I mutter under my breath, shaking my head.

"Mr. Bishop doesn't care as long as we get our work done. You know that," Dylan reminds me, and although he's right, Dad won't think twice about putting me in my place if he thinks I'm not doing my fair share around here.

"So anyway, before I was rudely interrupted." Dylan snickers, glancing back at Evan as we pick up another bundle of pipes. We carry them across the way before dropping them on the ground, causing a loud clang.

"Since the trip is for two, I thought you could come with me," he says, shaking out his arms from carrying the heavy iron.

"Wait, hold up," I say, stopping him from continuing and furrowing my brows. "You want me to go on a romantic two-week getaway with *you*?" I ask, glancing over at Evan who's painfully holding back a smirk. I narrow my eyes at him, then turn my attention back to Dylan.

"Well, it won't be a damn date, cowboy hotshot, because honestly, you ain't my type. However, considering the trip is free and bound to be crowded with single girls, I thought we could go together. Plus, I ain't got nobody else to take, so if anything, come be my wingman. Help me find a woman." The corner of his lips curls up, and I know exactly what he's thinking. "*Partaaaay,*" Dylan adds, confirming my thoughts as he waves his cowboy hat above his head and dances in place.

Shaking my head, I laugh at his antics, but before I can give him my answer, Evan clears his throat.

"You two ain't going nowhere till this fence is built. I can promise you that," he snaps, adding himself to our conversation.

"Worry about yourself. Dig your holes and mind your business," I snap.

"Shouldn't you be at the hospital saving some lives or somethin'? You're slowin' us down anyway."

Evan huffs, knowing he hates when I bring up his job at the hospital. It's a reputable career, and I know he's worked hard to become a doctor, but he's the first male Bishop in decades to pursue something outside of the ranch life. I wouldn't be doing my Bishop duties if I didn't feed him shit about it every chance I got.

"Keep runnin' your mouth, I'm going to be takin' a life today." He directs his eyes toward Dylan. "Maybe two."

The rest of the afternoon passes by quickly. As I drive us back to the main house, my shoulders tighten from driving poles into the ground and dumping cement nonstop for hours. Dylan and I are exhausted, but we'll be working on that damn fence for the rest of the week. Quite honestly, I'm still salty that I have to work on it in the first place, and it's all because of Jackson.

A few months ago, he threw a huge party, which quickly got out of hand when he started driving around in his Jeep. He'd been drinking and being more of a dumbass than usual when he decided to go off-roading and lost control, slamming straight into the barbwire fence. The next day, we spent the whole damn morning rounding up the cattle that escaped. Jackson was the only one amused by the whole situation, said it was the best one-eighty turn he'd ever done in his mud-covered Jeep.

Dumbass. Although according to Mama's gossip, he got plastered because of a girl. I highly doubted it because Jackson Bishop didn't do serious relationships—or relationships at all—but then she mentioned Kiera's name. It all made sense once I heard that, and I forgave him just a little.

Kiera Young and Jackson have known each other since they were babies. Her parents and ours were friends, and we've spent a lot of time on their ranch just as much as she has on ours. She was like an older, annoying sister to me, but not to Jackson. He's always had a thing for her but never grew the balls to admit it or even tell her. We all know she feels the same, but she continues to date other guys, pissing Jackson off and causing him to drink and act a damn fool. They're both too stubborn and continue this vicious cycle of denying their feelings.

After months of planning, Dad decided to replace the barbwire fence along the county road. If someone crashed into it again, only their vehicle would get damaged, and we wouldn't risk losing our cattle again.

Dylan's excitement brings me back to our conversation. "I've never been to Key West before, so as soon as I won, I did some browsing online. If it's half as fun as it looks, I might never come back! The nightlife, the beaches, the views," he rambles on. "You're gonna thank me that I dragged your ass along." Dylan beams as we head back to the main house.

"I haven't agreed to go yet," I remind him. "Depends if we can get off work or not. Might need to smooth talk Dad a little first," I say, knowing that if we don't get ahead of schedule, we'll never get approval to both take off for two weeks. "Or maybe a lot. Duties have to be done rain or shine, and if I'm not there, that means someone else has to do it."

"I'm gonna go buy him a bottle of Crown Royal Reserve." Dylan chuckles.

"To butter him up or get him wasted?" I laugh.

"Both," Dylan tells me.

I park the truck in the driveway and see Mama unloading groceries from the back of her car. Dylan and I rush out to help her.

"Mama, you shoulda called me," I scold. "I would've come sooner." I reach into the trunk, trying to grab as many bags as possible. Dylan stands next to me, doing the same, so we don't have to make a second trip.

"I knew you were busy. It's no big deal," she says sweetly, walking ahead of us to hold the front door open.

As soon as I enter, I see Jackson sleeping on the couch with his boots on, snoring loudly. After I set the bags down on the kitchen table, I walk quietly into the living room, and Dylan follows behind silently.

I get real close to his face, watching his chest rise and fall and wait for just the right moment before yelling, "FIRE!"

His body jolts up, his feet kicking in the air. With beet red cheeks, his eyes gaze over the living room. "What the fuck, Alex?" he barks, scrubbing his hands over his face.

In no time, Mama comes storming from the kitchen with a wooden spoon in one hand and glares down at Jackson.

"I've got a bar of soap with your name on it if you keep using that language in my house, young man," she scolds, fearlessly.

I cross my arms over my chest and smirk.

"Mama," he begins, but she's quick to shut him up.

"Hush. Get your boots off the furniture, too." She walks away before Jackson can argue some more.

"Wakey, wakey, asshole," I whisper, just loud enough for him to hear.

As soon as Mama is out of sight, he brushes his fingers through his hair, trying to process what just happened. "You bastard," he mutters to me. "You nearly made me shit myself."

I scoff. "Good. That's payback for me having to work on replacing that damn fence today. You should be out there fixing your own damn mess," I tell him.

"Oh sure, then you can be the one to train the horses and do all the guided tours for the guests at the B&B."

I grimace at the mention of the Circle B Bed and Breakfast that he helps manage on the ranch.

"That's what I thought," Jackson mocks. "Be glad you were building fences, little brother." He says the words with venom laced in his tone. I know Jackson loves working on the ranch, but there's working with horses, and then there's working with people. In Jackson's case, he's better off working with the horses.

As soon as he stands up from the couch, Evan comes bursting through the front door with a scowl on his face. "I owe you," Evan hisses with a finger pointed directly in Jackson's face. "Do you have any idea how much work replacing that damn fence is?"

I clear my throat, satisfied to see Jackson getting what he deserves. I glare at him, but all he does is smirk.

"Both of you need to chill out," Jackson says with a laugh, not taking either of us seriously.

"Boys!" Mama yells from the kitchen, breaking the tension in the room.

It's like she has a sixth sense about us and tends to break up fights before they can truly begin.

Evan rolls his eyes before walking toward the kitchen. Dylan and I follow closely behind him, leaving Jackson in the living room, unharmed—*this time.*

As soon as we round the corner, I see Mama throwing the breaded chicken into a pan, then placing homemade cornbread into the oven. Before speaking, she rinses her hands, dries them off, and then wipes her blonde hair from her eyes with the back of her hand.

Looking directly at us, she puts both hands on her hips as she always does when giving an order. "Now listen, I don't want to hear no bickering tonight, ya hear?"

"But—" Evan tries to interrupt.

"No!" She's quick to cut him off. "I don't want to hear it. Your father will be home any minute, and I want us to have a nice dinner together," she states sternly, then turns back around to give the chicken in the hot sizzling pan her attention.

Quietly, the three of us help unpack the grocery bags. We set everything on the table before Mama directs us where to stock it all. After growing up in this house, I know where most things belong, but she has a "system" that she makes us abide by.

Just as she's mixing the homemade mashed potatoes, John—Jackson's twin—and Dad walk through the back door. I hear the clomping of his boots against the wood floor before I see him. Once they're in the kitchen and see us all, he places his hat on the table before glancing over at Evan. "Y'all finish placing the poles?"

"All are set with cement. Just need to paint tomorrow," Evan tells him.

"Good," Dad says, walking to the fridge and filling a cup with ice and water.

As Mama tells us to set the table, Dylan tells everyone bye.

"You sure you don't want to stay? I got plenty for you too," Mama tells him.

"I'd better get home. If I miss dinner again this week, my mother may disown me," Dylan explains, shrugging.

"Yeah, we know how mamas can be." I look over at Mom with an overly sweet smile on my face.

"Yeah, you'd better get going then." Mama gives him a side hug, and he leaves.

Mama finishes up dinner while John and I set the table. We carry in the dishes of chicken, potatoes, and cornbread and set them on the long wood dining table that's a family keepsake.

Once everything is ready, we all take our seats and sit around the table like a big, happy family. Dad says grace as per tradition, then Mama plates his food. Once everyone has what they need, John makes small talk about the B&B and how booked it is for the next eight weeks. Dad then informs us about the hay bales that need to be picked up from the fields on the east side of the property and stored in the barn. This is how most dinner conversations go when I stay. The Bishops are workaholics and talk shop all day and night.

I'm nervous about asking Dad for time off, but I know that if I'm going on that trip in a couple weeks, I need to tell him in advance. That's the only bad thing about working for your parents. They aren't afraid to say no.

"Dad," I mumble over all the voices. As the table quiets, I continue. "You think it'd be possible for me to take a few of my vacation days soon?" I ask. It's so still in the room, all I can hear is Jackson's loud ass chewing.

"Hmm," he says, barely looking up at me. "When're ya thinkin'?"

I glance at Mama for a moment, wondering if she'll back me up or not. "About two weeks from now."

He nods as he continues shoveling food onto his fork. "For how long?"

I clear my throat, swallowing hard. "Um, well. I'd need two weeks."

"For what?" John asks, but his question gets ignored.

Dad shakes his head without even taking a second to think it over. "You know we still have things to do before the holidays and—"

"Scott," Mama interrupts Dad by using his first name, which always means business. "I think it would be perfectly fine for you to take off, son." My brows shoot up into my hairline, shocked at her words. "Alex works hard and deserves a break. Besides, Jackson can rearrange his schedule so he and Dylan can take care of your daily chores till you get back."

"Seriously?" Jackson groans, glaring at me.

"Well, actually..." I swallow hard before continuing. "Dylan needs off, too. There's a trip we'd like to go on."

"Absolutely not," Dad snaps, taking a sip of sweet tea. "That's far too much to rearrange. I can't have two men out at the same time." His words are final, and I know there's no point in arguing.

Mama clears her throat, an obvious signal for Dad. He looks over at her, and they hold a silent conversation as Mama purses her lips and raises an eyebrow. When she gets that look on her face, we all know it's her way or the highway, even when it comes to Dad.

He clears his throat before taking another sip of his drink. "We'll handle it," he finally mumbles, but I can tell he isn't happy about it.

Jackson mouths a, "You suck," to me when I look at him, and all I can do is smile because I'm going to Key-motherfucking-West for two weeks, and there's nothing that asshole can do about it.

Can't remember the last time I even had a vacation, and at this moment, I make a vow to myself that this trip will be one to remember.

After we help Mama clean up the table, I pull out my phone and see Dylan's already sent me a text.

DYLAN
Well? Any news yet?

ALEX
Hope you're ready to be my ride-or-die!

DYLAN
Seriously?! We can go?

ALEX
Yep! Pack your bags because we're about to give Key West some Southern cowboy hell!

CHAPTER TWO

River

"River!" My name is called as I rush down the hallway toward the blaring sound of the beeping alarm. As I round the corner, I realize it's coming from room 448. McKenna Black's room. Mrs. Black is screaming my name, urging me to hurry. My aide, Jenny, is already inside the room waiting for me.

I memorize all my patient' files word for word. I know their personal information and their medical history. It's part of my job at Milwaukee Children's Hospital where I treat sick kids in the PICU—pediatric intensive care unit. No matter how long they've been here or how short their stay is, my photographic memory allows me to remember every detail of their conditions and treatment plans.

"What's her O2 level?" I ask Jenny as I silence the alarm. She rambles off the baby girl's stats, and I immediately unwrap my stethoscope from my neck so I can listen to her heart.

"She's seizing," I say aloud before rolling her little body to the side.

McKenna is only five weeks old and in a fragile state after being diagnosed with bacterial meningitis. She's been here for a week and is on a twenty-eight-day antibiotic treatment, but side effects like this from the medication or illness are common with these types of infectious diseases.

"*What*? She's seizing?" Mrs. Black cries from the end of the metal crib.

"Call Dr. Weasley," I order Jenny. "She's going to need anti-seizure medicine before it happens again."

"River, what's going on?" Mrs. Black cries out again, her voice filled with panic.

Before I can explain, Jenny speaks up. "Dr. Weasley isn't here."

I wave my hand in the air. "Whoever's on call then. She needs something before it gets worse."

"Worse? Why? What's wrong?" Mrs. Black is frantic, concern evident in her voice. She's in constant fear of her daughter's life, and it breaks my heart. It's something I see here every day.

I watch as her stats start to level out and breathe out a sigh of relief.

"She's okay, Mrs. Black," I face her and say softly. I try to get to know my patient's family as best as I can because it helps put their minds at ease and builds trust as we give the best treatment possible. "It was a tonic seizure. I'm going to have the doctor prescribe some medication to prevent it from happening again."

"Wh-what's that?"

"It's where her body stiffens and muscles spasm. It's most likely caused by the infection, and although not uncommon, we want to control it and make sure it doesn't happen again. Otherwise, it could make things worse."

"Worse?" She gasps. Shit, I should've left out that part. I always try to be honest and up-front with the family, but I know sometimes I have to leave out things that will only cause more concern.

"The infection that's in the spinal fluid leading to her brain can cause seizures depending where the infection is, but the seizure subsided, and her stats are already normalizing, but the meds will help stop it from happening again. Okay?" I place a hand on her shaky fingers that are gripping the crib rail.

She nods, keeping her eyes locked on McKenna. Her tiny little body is covered in PICC lines, an oxygen line, a feeding tube, and artery lines in both of her cute, chubby thighs. Her face is swollen from the fluids, and her tiny arms are in casts so the lines stay in.

It's a sight no parent should ever have to see, but in the PICU, it's an everyday occurrence.

Hours later after McKenna gets her medication, I finally take my break. I work twelve-hour shifts on rotation and have been on my feet for ten hours straight. As I'm sitting in the cafeteria about to stuff my face, Natalie plops down across from me.

"You look like hell."

"Should've seen me before I fixed my hair and makeup." I reach for my coffee and take a long sip. "I can't feel my feet, and I'm pretty sure my ankles have swelled to twice their normal size."

"Isn't your shift almost over?" She looks down at the time on her phone. "You're taking a late break."

I nod, agreeing. "Had to wait for the on-call doctor to prescribe some medication for my patient and then once I administered it, I wanted to wait to make sure she was stable. Her mom was upset, and I didn't feel right leaving."

"You know your aide could've stayed with the patient's mom so you could leave for twenty minutes," she reminds me. Natalie works in radiology and is constantly telling me to take care of myself, or I'll burn out, but I can't help it. I love my job and my patients.

"I'm fine, *Mom*," I tease.

"You need a vacation," she says matter-of-factly. "Get some sun on your pasty ass."

I snort. "Sure. Vacation for one!" I roll my eyes. "And your ass is probably as pasty as mine."

"I sunbathed nude on the rooftop all summer, so joke's on you." She smirks.

"Thanks for that." I wrinkle my nose. "Didn't need that visual."

She rolls her eyes, and I laugh.

"But seriously. You could use a vacation. Or a distraction. Find a hot guy and bang his brains out." She waggles her brows with a sultry smirk.

Still chewing my food, I burst out laughing and shake my head at her. "Banging random men isn't going to change the fact I gave the last six months of my life to a man who 'forgot' to tell me he was married." I suck in a deep breath and exhale the anger that's been weighing on my chest for the past three weeks since finding his wedding ring hiding deep in his dress pants pocket.

"Oh, screw—what's his face anyway…" She scrunches up her face in disgust. She never liked him much anyway based on the few times they met. "*Asshole.*"

"Andrew," I fill in for her, feeling bile rise in my throat at saying his name aloud.

"Andrew. Asshole. Same thing, really." She curls the corner of her lip. "Screw him. Go on a single's cruise and find yourself some hot man meat!" The tone of her voice is serious, which terrifies me.

"Hot man meat?" I arch a brow. "We graduated from middle school over a decade ago," I inform her with a teasing grin. "The only hot meat I want near me is a big fat turkey." I smile, getting excited about spending Thanksgiving with my family next month up in Eagle River where I'm originally from. I moved down here for college, and once I got hired at the hospital, I made it my permanent residence.

"Okay, so no singles cruise." She frowns.

I give her an eye roll, then reach for my purse. I dig around inside until I find my prescription bottle. Once I open it and grab a pill, I toss it down my throat and swallow it with a big gulp of water.

"What's that?" she asks, tilting her head to read the bottle as she takes another bite of her carrot stick.

"It's my STD medication. A parting gift from Andrew," I deadpan. She starts choking on her carrot, and I nearly die of laughter.

"River! That isn't funny." She smacks her chest as tears form in the corner of my eyes.

"Oh my God. The look on your face was priceless," I say, wiping tears from my cheeks.

"You're seriously a bitch. You deserve an STD after that." She scowls.

Once I've controlled my laughter, I shove the bottle back in my purse. "Don't be so dramatic. My doctor prescribed it for my sinus infection; thankfully, it's almost gone now."

"Oh my God!" She slams her palm down on the table, the loud bang echoing through space. I jump at her unnecessary spasm.

"Jesus, Natalie," I scold. "Nearly made me pee myself."

She points a finger in my face. "You deserved it." She smirks. "Anyway. I just got the best idea. Adam and I are going to Key West soon for two weeks. You should totally come!"

I furrow my brows at her like she's crazy. "I'm not going on a couples' vacation with you and your boyfriend, Nat. That'd be weird."

"No way. We'd have a blast," she insists.

"I'd be the third wheel," I correct.

"Hardly. Adam plans to go fishing like every morning. You can keep me company on the beach drinking margaritas and checking out the local eye candy. Then when he's back, the three of us can find fun stuff to do like snorkeling or sailing."

"That sounds fun, it really does, but I can't just tag along on your couples' trip. I'd feel like such a burden."

"Girl, stop it. Adam and I are basically an old married couple. Truth be told, I'd have more fun with you hanging around anyway. Once Adam starts talking about fish and worms, and God knows what else, I start to fall asleep."

"Oh, so now you want me to be your buffer. This is sounding better and better," I muse.

"What's it matter?" She grins. "Just come and enjoy the sun and the beach and the water and forget about the STD married asshole man."

"For the record, I don't have an STD, Natalie!" I whisper-shout.

She waves me off as if it's irrelevant.

"Just think about it, okay? You can book a separate room at the same resort. We can head down to the pool and have breakfast together and read books by the beach, and then when you get yourself drunk enough and find a hot, *single* man, you'll have a room all to yourself for slutty banging time."

I groan at her words but laugh at the eagerness in her tone. She's nearly begging at this point.

"I don't know. Two weeks? I doubt I'll be able to get off work in such a short amount of time." I pick at the remaining food on my tray, thinking it over.

"You work nonstop, River. You deserve a vacation." She stands up and grabs her baggie of carrot sticks. "Just think about it." She winks before walking away.

As I finish the rest of my shift, the thought of spending two weeks on the beach and how nice it'd be to get away for a bit invades my mind. Once I finish charting and clock out, I walk to the bus stop near the hospital and wait.

Digging my cell out of my purse, I turn it on and see I have a few new voice messages. As soon as I hear Andrew's voice, my body tenses.

Hey, baby. I miss you. I know you hate me right now, but I promise I can explain—

I delete the message before he can continue his lies. I click on the next one.

I can't stop thinking about you, River. Please come back to me. I'll—

Delete.

Any guesses who voicemail number three is from? *Asshole.*

Shoving my cell back into my purse, I stand as the bus comes into view from down the road. Within moments, another bus passes and drives through a puddle only to splash muddy water on my shoes and uniform. The gentleman standing next to me steps to the side, glaring at me as he takes in what a mess I am.

Oh my God!

I'm completely drenched, except my hair. Not that it matters because it looks like a bird set up home there anyway. It's early October in southern Wisconsin, which means the temps have dropped into the forties and fifties. Stupidly, I wasn't wearing my winter jacket, and now I'll sit on the bus freezing my ass off.

Once I'm home, I strip off everything before I enter the kitchen. The ride across town was complete hell, and I'm cold to the bone. My shoes, scrubs, and bra find their way to the floor. My roommate is a girl I went to college with years ago, but she's never home. Sasha spends most nights at her boyfriend's place, which makes being her roommate easy. As long as she pays her half of the rent, I don't care if she's home or not. The only complaint I have is how she leaves her cat, and I'm constantly feeding and watering him since she seems to forget that responsibility.

"Hey, Leo," I coo as he jumps on my bed, begging for some kind of attention. I pet him briefly before grabbing my towels and heading to the bathroom for a shower.

The hot water feels amazing and soothes my tense muscles. My legs and feet are sore from walking so much today, and I can't wait to climb into bed with my Kindle. But as soon as I turn off the water and wrap a towel around my body, I hear noises coming from the hallway.

First, pictures are falling off the wall. Next, I hear giggling. Then more smacking against the wall.

What the fuck?

Tightening the grip on my towel, I open the door and peek out. Long brown hair falls loosely down Sasha's back, and her legs are wrapped around a man's waist as she dry humps him against the wall.

Blinking, I'm shocked to see her home at this hour on a Tuesday night, considering I know she works early in the morning. But then I look over at the guy she's sucking face with, and that's when I realize it's not her boyfriend.

It's Asshole.

By the time I get to work the next day, I'm still in shock. Suffice it to say, I had a shitty night's sleep. Not because I found my roommate with my ex, but because Andrew is loud in bed. Once I started thinking about it, I understood why he was that way. He was overcompensating for his teeny weenie by insisting he loved eating pussy more than making love.

I roll my eyes so hard at the revelation.

No guy needs to make that much noise while feasting between your legs. The woman should be the loud one; if he's doing it right, anyway.

After texting Natalie on the way to work to tell her what happened, she insisted it was a sign. A sign I needed to go to Florida with them, and after hearing his voice and seeing his nasty face, I could use a vacation more than ever.

During my break, Natalie and I meet up again.

"I can't believe he left you a voice message and then hours later ended up in your apartment with Sasha," she says for the third time, just as shocked as I was.

Well, there's a club she can join because I can hardly believe it either.

"Yeah, he probably thought I was her, considering I have bleach blonde hair and she has dark brown hair. It'd be easy to get us confused." I snort.

"God, I'm so glad you broke up with his nasty ass. I should send Adam over there to kick his butt." She starts to get all worked up.

"Natalie," I say, covering her hand with mine. "I appreciate the sentiment, but Adam would hurt himself before hurting Andrew."

She scowls. "Hey, he's muscular."

I chuckle. "I know he is. I wasn't saying he isn't, but Andrew ate steroids for breakfast, so no one stands a chance. He's a fake, liar, and cheater, and not worth anyone's time or energy."

She frowns. "I'm sorry you had to find that out the hard way."

I shrug, lowering my eyes to the floor. "Live and learn, right?" I blink and meet her gaze. "Besides, he left his six-thousand dollar watch in my room." I grin.

"Holy shit!" She gasps. "What kind of watch costs that much? It better come with fifty-five hundred dollars and a male stripper on the side."

Bursting out laughing, I'm easily reminded why Natalie and I are friends. She always finds a way to make me smile in the worst of times.

"Some hoity-toity designer, but it was a gift from his job when he got promoted last year."

"Oh, boo for him." She wiggles a finger down her cheek to mimic a tear. "You should pawn it instead."

I snap her a look. "That's a little vindictive."

"Or…" She snaps her fingers. "It's being resourceful and now paying for your *well-deserved* vacation. Think of that as a *real* parting gift." She starts to hold up her fingers. "He cheated, lied, and now screwed your roommate in the same apartment as you. That dirtbag deserves a lot worse."

I can't argue with her, but I don't feel right pawning it. Though, he doesn't exactly deserve to have the watch returned to him either.

Or does he?

After my shift, I head home and sit on the edge of the bed. Deciding to take the high road, I grab the watch from my nightstand and stare at it. It really is a nice-looking watch. Too bad he doesn't know a good thing when he has it. He should know better than to leave valuables lying around.

Thankfully, he and Sasha were gone this morning before I left for work because I'm not sure what I would've done. Thinking back to the night before and hearing them in the room next door boils my blood even more. I'm so pissed I wasted my time on him. I replay moments of us together and realize all the signs pointed to this. I should've known from his sketchy behavior and random phone calls. I shouldn't have been so naïve, and I almost can't believe how vengeful he is. Fucking my roommate and knowing I'd be home was just a low blow. That bastard.

I take his watch and place it on the kitchen counter. A moment passes, and I stare at the shiny gold band and diamonds on the face. Searching through the drawers, I find a meat tenderizer—well suited name, too—and grip it firmly in my hand. Raising it above my head, I lower it and slam it against the watch. I do this over and over, groaning and grunting until only tiny pieces are left.

Whew! That felt fucking great.

Next, I find an envelope, shove all the remaining pieces inside, and before sealing it, write him a little note.

Hope you think twice before wasting someone's TIME again.
Love, River
P.S. Fuck you.

Feeling satisfied, I write his business address on the front and shove the envelope into my purse, so I can mail it first thing in the morning before work.

Looking around my apartment, I realize all the anger and resentment I've been harboring, and it makes me really consider Natalie's offer.

I grab my phone from the nightstand and type out a text to her.

RIVER

Okay, you win. Send me the info for the resort. I'm going.

CHAPTER THREE

Alex

Dylan and I finally finish up for the day and double-check that we've completed everything Dad's given us to do over the past two weeks. Ever since I asked for two weeks' vacation, he's overworked us, but we've not complained once. The fence is finished, hay is baled and stacked, and we even dug out a ditch on top of our regular morning duties. We've started work before sunrise and stayed out past sunset, but it's been worth it because I plan to take full advantage of this trip.

"Jackson was volun-told to drive us to the airport in the mornin'," I remind Dylan as I drive him back to his truck parked near the cattle barn.

"Good. Don't wanna leave my pickup in the parking lot that long," he says. "I'll be here around five, so we've got plenty of time to make it to the airport."

"Just be prepared for Jackson to bitch the entire drive." I smile, knowing how irritated he is that he has to do our work on top of his own, but that's payback for the fence incident, so I don't feel bad about it.

After dropping Dylan off at his truck, I head home, knowing I still need to finish my laundry and pack. I've been putting it off because I have no clue what to bring to Florida. My closet is full of Wranglers and work shirts. I have some Oxfords for when I go out, but I'm sure those will stick out like a sore thumb on the beaches of Key West.

For the last few years, Jackson and I have lived together in an old ranch hand house we remodeled. Since then, Friday nights have been known as Whiskey Fridays. He and a bunch of his friends listen to country music, shoot off their rifles into the fields, and drink like it's the last few bottles of whiskey left on Earth.

As soon as I walk through the door, Jackson strolls over to me and places his arm on my shoulder with a wide, drunken smile.

"Now the fun has arrived," he shouts to a room full of people who then lift their glasses in the air with a loud round of hollering.

He pours me a glass and hands it to me. "I have to pack," I tell him with a smug smile on my face, realizing he's already drunk his limit, and the night is still young.

"Come on, little brother, you can do it later," he reassures, clinking his glass against mine. "After the shit show of a day we've had, drinks are in order!"

I look down at my clothes and hands that are stained with oil. For most of the day, Dylan and I worked on a damn truck that decided to break down while we were in the middle of hauling hay from one barn to another. Oil was everywhere and made a big fucking mess. We did nothing but fix shit all day. Not one task was completed without a mini disaster, which meant we were out way after the sun set to finish everything, but that's common 'round here.

One thing leads to another, and soon, Jackson and I are sharing a bottle of Jack Daniels. A few of the guys who live in the ranch hand quarters are singing with the radio at the top of their lungs. By the time I drink the last bit of whiskey, I realize I've totally screwed myself.

"I gotta go to bed," I tell Jackson. "Don't forget you're driving us to the airport tomorrow, too."

Alcohol and exhaustion swim through my veins, which isn't a good combination.

34

"It'll be fine," Jackson says with a wave of his hand, stumbling over his words and not concerned about anything. The words of a true drunk.

I smile, pat him on his shoulder, and tell everyone good night. Even though the music is blaring and everyone in the house is loud as hell, I manage to remember to set the alarm and fall asleep in no time.

The morning comes early, and my head is killing me from drinking way too much. I already know today will be rough. Looking over at the clock, I realize Dylan will be here in about ten minutes. I grab my suitcase from the closet and shove clothes into it along with my toothbrush and deodorant. Procrastination mixed with Jackson's peer pressure got the best of me again. I'll just buy whatever I forget at the resort because I don't have time to overthink it.

Just as I'm slipping on my blue jeans and boots, I hear a knock on the door and know it's Dylan. I walk through the house and see Jackson asleep in the recliner in the corner of the room. After I rub my hands over my face to try to wake myself up, I open the door. Dylan steps in and laughs.

"Whiskey Fridays." He knows the aftereffects all too well.

"Unfortunately," I say with a groan. I walk back toward Jackson and shake him, but all he does is groan and slap my hand away.

"You're supposed to drive us to the airport," I remind him.

"He's probably still drunk," Dylan says, looking at Jackson who's still wearing his clothes from yesterday, including his boots.

"Without a doubt," I mumble, walking to the kitchen to make some strong coffee. I lean against the counter and wait for the coffee to drip into the pot as I grab a few ibuprofen from the medicine cabinet.

"I assume Jackson isn't bringing us to the airport." Dylan stares at Jackson who's snoring loudly.

The coffeemaker beeps as I grab a travel mug. "Mama's gonna kill him today if she finds out he didn't drive us down there," I say, pouring the coffee.

"I wouldn't mind seeing that." Dylan chuckles. "Mrs. B on a rampage isn't a force to be reckoned with."

I nod. "She's the scariest when she's pissed. Even Dad won't mess with her when she gets that way. It's fine. I'll drive my truck since Jackson has the extra key. I'll have him and John drive there and pick it up later, so it's not sitting down there for two weeks."

Jackson snores himself awake, and he sits up, forcing his eyes open. "Shiiiiiiiiit."

"What?" I ask, feeling a little more like myself after the coffee warms my veins.

"That's what I feel like." Jackson tries to stand but stumbles and trips over his feet.

Dylan and I nearly fall over laughing. That's what he gets for making me drink with him. Misery loves company, my ass.

"You're not driving us anywhere." I chuckle as we watch him struggle to pick himself up off the floor. "Sit back down before you hurt yourself."

"If the room would stop spinning, I'd be just fine," he groans, finally sitting his ass back down.

"We've got to get going or we're gonna miss our flight." Dylan checks the time on his phone. "Ready?" He gives me a big cheesy grin because we both know I'm not.

I double-check my suitcase really quick, refill my travel mug, then holler, "Goodbye," to Jackson before stepping out the front door and walking toward the truck.

Dylan grabs his suitcase from his truck and throws it in the back before we both get in and head to the airport. Our drive isn't too far—a little over an hour—but we have to get on one of those little planes I hate before connecting in San Antonio. Once we're at the airport and parked, I can see the sun rising in the distance. We check our bags and sit at the gate while we wait for our departure to be announced.

"Nervous?" I look over at Dylan.

"Nah, just ready to get there and relax," he says, but I can see he's sweating beads.

I hate the small planes, too, but luckily, we'll only be on it for about an hour.

After we board and the plane takes off, I feel a little more relaxed. By the time I get used to feeling every little bump, we land in San Antonio and head to our next gate. My head is killing me again, so before we board the next plane, I buy a pack of ibuprofen and a bottle of water then say a little prayer and hope it goes away before we land in Key West.

It's confirmed—Jackson is a bad influence.

The next plane is bigger, giving us more room to stretch out our long legs. My head isn't throbbing as badly anymore, and I can actually take in the view from the small window next to me.

"So yesterday after work, Mama had me run to the grocery store, and guess who I ran into?" He gives me less than a second to guess before continuing. "Gretchen Garcia. Dude, she's still so pissed at you." He starts cracking up. "I wonder how many women have you on their hate list right now. I can count about six without even thinking about it too hard." Dylan chuckles again.

"Hey, it's not my fault they don't understand the concept of casual sex. It's not like they didn't know that up front when I said I wasn't looking for anything serious. I'm always honest. I use my manners and am polite, so if that's not good enough for them, then that's on them. They know what I have to offer before anything happens. Every one of them says they're okay with it, and then afterward decide they aren't. They always think they can change my mind or that they'll be the 'one' to change me, but nothing's going to change the fact that I don't want or have time for a relationship. I ain't lookin' for anything other than a little fun. But I guess that's what being honest gets me," I tell him with resentment in my tone. Gretchen knew all of that, too, before we ever hooked up. Not my fault my words fell on deaf ears. And considering we hooked up over a year ago, she needs to get over it.

"Well, either way, she said she wanted to cut off your balls and feed them to the pigs," Dylan says with a teasing grin.

I adjust myself. "I knew she was crazy but damn. I need my balls."

"I promised her I'd relay the message if she promised not to cut mine off."

I burst out into laughter. "Smart."

After a while, I close my eyes and end up falling asleep until the plane lands. Relieved to be back on the ground, I look out the window again. Besides all the water surrounding us, I also notice how bright and sunny it is. We're definitely not in Texas anymore. Even though I have no idea what to expect, I'm more psyched than ever to be here.

We deplane and retrieve our suitcases before taking the shuttle to the resort we'll be staying at. I actually feel a lot better since sucking down those ibuprofen and getting in a short nap, so now I can't wait to get settled and explore the city and beaches.

As we get closer to the resort, I'm completely taken aback by the view. Palm trees and tourist shops line both sides of the street. People walk with smiles on their faces as they shop and take photos. They all look so damn happy to be here. I catch glimpses of the clear-blue water behind it all, and as we get closer to the resort, I notice beach chairs and cabanas along the beach. This is just the kind of vacation I need.

The shuttle parks outside of the hotel, and we grab our luggage and step out. As we're standing in front of the hotel, I look over at the people walking in and out of the hotel, and then over at Dylan and I realize we stick out like a sore thumb. Cowboy hats, boots, and plaid shirts—we're Texas twins right now in the same getup, and I'm sure our accents aren't going to do us any favors.

Walking in, we chat about what we want to do tonight and wait in line for reception. Once we're waved up, we walk up to the woman and greet her with a loud *howdy*. The corner of her lips tilts up as she eyes our Stetson hats before asking for our information. Dylan gives her his name and slides his ID across the counter. She continues to type on her keyboard, only briefly glancing at the two of us before going back to the screen. As soon as she makes eye contact and hands over Dylan's ID, I give her a smile and a wink. She tries to hide the blush that hits her cheeks behind the computer screen, but it doesn't work.

"Mr. Hart, how many room keys would you like?" she asks, chewing on her bottom lip.

I look over at Dylan and whisper, "Wait, did we get separate rooms?"

"About that…" He laughs, then looks back at her. "Two, please."

The woman clears her throat and slides our room keys across the counter. "All meals and beverages are included with your stay, along with nonmotorized water sports. You do have a couple's massage that you'll need to schedule by using this number here," she says, pointing down at the brochure before placing the keys inside.

Since Dylan thinks this is so damn funny, I decide to play along by wrapping my arm around him and pulling him to my side. "Honey, when would ya like to schedule those? In the morning perhaps?"

Dylan elbows me hard in the side, and I can't help but laugh. The woman smiles at us sweetly.

"The elevators to your suite are right down the hall to the left. In the morning, breakfast is served from six to ten. If you have questions or need anything, just dial zero."

"Thank you, ma'am," Dylan and I both say in unison before walking toward the elevator, dragging our luggage behind us.

"This is going to be interesting," I mumble as we pass guests in their shorts and swimsuit tops.

"You embarrassed that poor girl," Dylan tells me as we step into the elevator, and I hit the button for our floor.

I shrug, holding the rail as we shoot upward. "She was looking at us like we were real-life cowboy lovers. Thought I'd help her fantasy a little."

"This is why girls like Mallory threaten your balls," he teases as we get off the elevator and walk to our room. As soon as we slide our keycard and step inside, I'm shocked to see how large the place is. It's as big as one of the cabins the ranch hands live in at home. There's a giant bathroom, TV room with chairs and couches, and a separate room that leads to the bed. The windows lining the wall overlook the ocean, giving us an amazing view of the beach.

I can't help but laugh when I see a champagne bottle in an ice bucket and red rose petals spread across the bed. There are even towels at the end of the bed folded in a heart shape. "This is a perfect touch; don't you think, sweetheart?"

Dylan looks at the flower petals and laughs so hard that he nearly chokes.

I pull my phone from my pocket and snap a quick picture.

"Gonna show Jackson what he's missing out on." I laugh as I send him a text.

"Yeah, I'm sure that'll make him jealous." He snorts.

Checking the time on my phone and seeing it's already nearing late afternoon, I ask, "So what if I find a chick I want to bring back to the room?"

Dylan removes his boots and sets his hat on the dresser. "I thought about that, too," he admits, brushing his fingers through his messy dark hair. "Maybe we come up with a code phrase or something, so we know not to walk in on each other? I've decided I'm going to be more like you on this trip."

"Gonna get your dick wet finally?"

39

He scoffs. "I meant a no-strings-attached kind of thing. Just having fun. Be completely up front with women without the pressure of what it means."

"About time you let loose. You've been single way too long. So if and when we decide we want to bring someone back, we just text each other the phrase."

"Okay, so what's the code word?" Dylan asks.

I contemplate for a moment before thinking of the perfect one.

"I've got it: Cowgirl—after my favorite position." I flash him a smug grin as he thinks it over.

"Reverse cowgirl." He shakes his head, laughing at me, but reluctantly agrees anyway. "You're such a dirty bastard."

I pop the cork on the champagne bottle and pour us both a glass before handing him one. "C'mon, you know you're dying to find a girl to ride you bareback like a stallion!" I slap a hand on his shoulder just as he tips the flute back, and he nearly chokes on the liquid.

"Well, if someone catches a glimpse of our phones, at least they'd have no idea what the hell we're talking about." Dylan takes another swig from his glass.

"And that's why we're friends," I tell him, clinking the edge of my glass against his. "Now, let's go have some damn fun and show Florida how cowboys really party."

"Okay, but first..." He tilts his head back and finishes off his champagne. "...let's go shopping and find some different clothes," Dylan suggests.

I look at my Levi's and boots. "Yeah, good idea." I smile then take the final sip of my drink. "Then we show them how to party!"

CHAPTER FOUR

River

I can't believe I'm really doing this.

After begging my supervisor, she put in the request for my time off and made sure our boss approved it. She knows I'm a hard worker and work nonstop, and after giving her the sob story of Asshole, she sympathized, having had her own experience with a married man. God, the men here just suck.

Not that I'm expecting the men in Florida to be any different because let's face it, downtown Key West is party city. But at least now, I have zero expectations. Don't get too close. Have fun. No rules.

Yep. That's going to be my life for the next two weeks.

And I couldn't be more excited and nervous about it. The last time I ever did anything spontaneous was back in my sophomore year in college when I ran through the commons area topless in the middle of January. My nipples nearly froze off, but it was for some club I was in. We were protesting something, but I can't even remember what it was now. So obviously, I lived it up during my college years.

Actually, I studied nonstop. Nursing school is no joke and definitely not for the weak. I almost quit five times, but I wouldn't let it defeat me. More determined than ever, I graduated with honors with a 3.8 GPA.

I smiled as I boarded the plane, feeling brave for taking this step. Thankfully, it was a direct flight from Milwaukee to the Key West International Airport. Natalie and Adam left yesterday, but all the airlines were booked, so I had to fly out the next day. I didn't mind though, because I planned to read during the flight anyway.

"Going for business or pleasure?" a deep male voice asks next to me.

Blinking, I look up and see a man sitting next to me who I hadn't even realized was there. I had taken my seat by the window first and buried myself in my book right away. He was dressed in a sharp, black suit and looked to be a tad older than me.

"Um, I'm going for a vacation. So pleasure, I guess." I flash a small smile. "You?"

He brushes his fingers over his black tie. "Business." He confirms my thoughts, his attire giving it away.

"Well, maybe you'll get a few moments to enjoy the beaches. I hear they're amazing," I say, making small talk because I'm not really sure what else to say. I spend my days with children and hard-ass doctors, so I almost feel rusty when it comes to communicating with people outside of my job.

"Yeah, not a lot of time for beaches on work trips." He smiles wide, showing off his perfectly white teeth.

"Oh, that's a bummer."

"Well, I might be able to squeeze in some extracurricular activities...if you're interested." His voice goes silky smooth, yet his tone makes me shudder. Then he winks, sealing his offer.

Is he seriously hitting on me right now?

"No thanks," I blurt out, uncomfortably. "I'm meeting a couple friends there, and we'll be busy." I flash a weak smile that I hope gives him a hint.

He digs into his pocket, making me wonder what the hell he's up to next. Pulling out a business card, he flicks it at me and smiles. "Well, if you change your mind and have some extra time, hit me up."

Reluctantly, I grab it and crumple it in my fist.

"Sure," I mutter, nearly hugging the window to keep my distance. Just as he shifts in his seat, my eyes gaze down to his hand, and that's when I see it. That rat bastard. "How sweet of your wife to share you. Too bad she doesn't realize what a skeez you are." The words come out harsher than I intended, but even so, I don't even feel bad about it.

Without saying a word, he turns his body away from me. Coward.

If this is what being out in the dating world is like, then count me out. I'd only met Andrew on a rare evening out with a friend for her birthday. She'd gotten so wasted, I had to help her walk outside and hail a cab. I nearly slipped on my heels—that I hardly wore—and both of us were about to face-plant when Andrew grabbed my waist to keep me steady on my feet. He'd just so happened to be walking out of another bar when he saw us stumbling and ran to help.

It was one of those damsel-in-distress moments, and if I'd been thinking clearly, I maybe wouldn't have wasted the last six months on him. However, he saved us both, helped me get my friend in the cab, and before I followed behind, he asked if he could have my number. I figured he'd never call anyway, so I gave it to him. He surprised me when he called the following day and asked me out.

Completely smitten, I'd fallen for him hard and fast. I kept pushing away any signs that I was being paranoid and kept telling myself that I was lucky to even have a guy like him interested in me. I wasn't naturally an insecure person, but after a few failed online dating attempts, I decided there was no way decent men exist anymore. Up until three weeks ago, I thought Andrew was the exception.

But it seems married men can't seem to keep it in their damn pants no matter what state I'm in.

Relieved when we finally land, I grab my luggage after deplaning and stop for a coffee before hailing a taxi. By the time I'm in the cab, I already have Natalie on the line to let her know I'm here, and she nearly popped my eardrum with her excitement.

"Oh my God, River! It's gorgeous here, isn't it?" She releases a dreamy sigh into the phone. I can already picture her lying out poolside with a drink in hand. "Adam decided to go looking for some good fishing spots for tomorrow morning, so it's just me, the sun, and my Bahama Mama."

I chuckle, loving how relaxed she sounds. This is just what I needed right now.

"Well, I can't wait to join you. Once I check in and settle into my room, I'll change and meet you down there," I tell her, looking out the window at the touristy views.

"Perfect! I'll have a drink waiting for you!"

The warmth is the first thing I notice when I get out of the cab. The wind brings a nice breeze my way as I walk through the doors of the hotel, reminding me I'm no longer in Wisconsin. It was cold and gloomy this past week, so this weather is definitely a welcome change.

As soon as I walk in, I take in everything from the bright blue color palette to the ocean views all along the back through the windows. It's something straight up from a magazine. People walk around with their oversized beach bags, sunglasses, and flip-flops. It instantly brightens my mood.

"Hello, welcome to the Hyatt. Can I help you?" the receptionist greets me, and I'm more than happy to say, "Yes, yes, you can!"

Once I'm all checked in, she directs me to the elevators, and soon I'm scanning my keycard into my room. I ended up with a corner room, which at first, I was hesitant about because I wanted all ocean views, but as soon as I walk in, I see I'm not the least bit disappointed.

With the wraparound balcony and two sets of sliding glass doors, it looks like the ocean is *in* my room. The entire half of my wall is taken over by the sliding doors and the perfect beach views.

"This is heaven," I mutter to myself with the biggest smile I've had in weeks.

Once I give myself the tour, I unpack my luggage and dig around for my swimsuit. I'm never been more eager to wear the damn thing, which considering all the winter weight I put on last year, says a lot. When I'm at work, I wear scrubs and clogs, so this is a change I don't mind.

I change, find my swimsuit wrap and pull it over my body. Grabbing a towel, my key, and bag, I head out ready to find Natalie and one of those umbrella drinks.

"Oh my God!" Natalie screams, jumping out of the chair as soon as she sees me rounding the pool. "I can't believe you're actually here!" She wraps her arms around my neck and squeezes. "Perfect timing, too! I just ordered another drink and got one for you."

"Great, thanks! It feels a little unreal that I'm actually here," I say, squeezing her back. "Thank you for inviting me," I continue as she releases me. "Or rather, thank you for forcing me to come." I grin.

"What are friends for if not to give you a little push when you need it?" She smirks, grabbing my bag in one hand and leading me over to her spot.

"I can't believe how beautiful it is, and I've only seen the airport and lobby so far." I pull my cover off and start digging into my bag.

"Well, look at you," she teases, eyeing my body. "I haven't seen that much skin on you since that time I walked in on you changing."

"That's because you have no boundaries," I remind her, chuckling.

"No doubt you'll definitely find a Florida hottie during this trip." She waggles her brows. "Big ta-tas, curvy hips, slim waistline."

"I'm starting to feel a little violated now," I mock, adjusting my swimsuit top to make sure it's covering all appropriate boobage and nipples.

"Okay, well, I'm just saying. You have nothing to be embarrassed about." She takes a long sip of her drink, and I give her a look that says otherwise.

"I can't wait to go down Front and Duval Streets. I looked them up on YouTube, and they look like a lot of fun," I say, kicking off my shoes.

"We have lots of time to explore, but today is the perfect pool day." She sighs, getting comfortable in her chair. She leans back with her large sunglasses on her face and tilts her head up to the sun.

"I hope you put sunscreen on," I tell her, pulling some out of my bag.

"I came to Florida for a tan," she says matter-of-factly, adjusting herself deeper into the chair.

"And melanoma?" I raise a brow even though she's not looking at me. She groans.

"C'mon, sit up," I order. It'll take me five seconds."

"Yes, Nurse River." She winks. "That sounded way dirtier coming out than it did in my head."

I roll my eyes and laugh. She does as I say, and when I finish, she motions for me to turn around so she can spray my back and arms. When she's done, I spray my face, chest, stomach, and legs. This Northern girl is as white as they come, but that doesn't mean I want to risk it either.

Once I'm settled, I sprawl out on the chair with my own pair of oversized sunglasses and a topknot on my head. I grab my phone and turn on some tunes just as a gentleman comes over with a tray of drinks.

"Your drinks, ma'am," he greets, handing the first one to Natalie, who hands it to me and then takes the other for herself. She smiles at him before handing him a tip, and we both thank him.

"This is the life." I chuckle before taking a large sip. "Drinks just taste better when they get delivered to you by the pool."

"You said it, sister," she quips. "Especially when the cabana boys aren't that bad to look at." She tilts her sunglasses off her nose and eyes him as he walks away.

I laugh. "I'm sure Adam wouldn't think so."

"Are you kidding?" She chuckles. "He basically dragged me down here and told me to have a 'good time,' if you know what I mean." She smirks.

"You two have the weirdest relationship I know."

"Nah, it works just fine. Looking at other people is what we use to keep things hot in the bedroom." The playful tone of her voice lets me know there's more to the story, but I have no desire to dig for further information.

"Good to know." I smile even though she's not paying attention to me. Natalie and Adam have been together for as long as I can remember, so it doesn't surprise me that their relationship is the way it is. As long as he takes good care of her and treats her right, I keep my nose out of it.

Sipping my drink till it's halfway gone, I set it down before adjusting myself on the lounge chair and lie back. The sun heats my body in no time, and I almost fall asleep when the cabana boy arrives with another round of drinks.

"When did we order those?" I ask, taking the glass off the tray.

"I have them on a schedule for every hour." Natalie beams.

Smiling, I shrug and take a sip. "Ooh, this one tastes different."

"I ordered Bermuda Triangles. It sounded more tropical."

I laugh at how serious her tone is and take another sip. "These taste like trouble."

"Oh, trust me, they are. These got me in so much trouble during Frat week my sophomore year, I swore to stay away from them forever."

"That lasted long." I grin.

"Vacation is an exception," she states matter-of-factly. "And bonus, I don't have to get up tomorrow and give an oral presentation for a psychology exam."

My head falls back as I burst out laughing. Natalie was always known for being the life of the party, whereas I always had my face buried in a book. Nursing school nearly killed me. There was no time for ludicrous parties or getting so drunk I couldn't function the next day. Even though nursing school certainly made me want to.

The following morning, I wake up stretched out in my king-sized bed with a slight headache. Though I only drank two of those Bermuda Triangles, we didn't stop there. After we soaked up the sun, Natalie dragged me to the hotel bar until Adam came and tore us away. He walked me to my room before leading Natalie back to theirs.

Rolling over, I check my phone on the nightstand and see a text waiting for me.

> **NATALIE**
>
> Continental breakfast in the lobby! Meet us there at 9!
>
> **NATALIE**
>
> AND MIMOSAS!
>
> **NATALIE**
>
> To cure that hangover you probably have, you lightweight ;)

I smile and laugh at her messages. Natalie has always known how to keep things entertaining.

Once I've showered and dressed, I make it down for breakfast just on time. Natalie and Adam are already at a table waving me over.

"Good morning, sunshine," she says with a bright smile.

"Does she always wake up this perky?" I direct my eyes toward Adam as I take a seat.

"Only on days I don't have to work or when I wake up in paradise," she answers for him with a dreamy sigh.

"I thought you'd be out fishing already?" I reach for the mimosa already set in front of me and take a drink.

"I was."

"He was."

They both speak in unison like a lovesick couple who finishes each other's thoughts and sentences.

"I was on the water by five. Came back to check on Nat and have breakfast with her before I head back out."

"I expect you to catch us enough fish to last all winter, okay?" Natalie teases.

"Don't forget the lobster and crawfish, too," I add.

"Yeah, I'm on it." He winks.

"Well, I'd better grab something to eat to soak up this alcohol before I end up like Nat during Frat week." I wink in her direction as Adam tilts his head to give her a side-eye.

I eye the buffet like it's the best thing I've seen all year. It's full of pastries, fruit, and yogurts on one end, and hot items on the other. I grab a few pieces of sausage and a spoonful of scrambled eggs before heading over to the other side.

As I'm walking toward the fruit platters, I notice a couple guys with full plates making their rounds from the hot and cold sections. They're acting like they haven't eaten in days. I smile internally at the thought of these two bulky guys eating enough for four. They definitely aren't from around here. Though they're both good looking, I find myself eyeing the blond guy. He's got the palest blue eyes, and his shirt is stretched across his muscular and wide chest. Not half bad actually.

The guy speaks in a very noticeable Southern accent, and suddenly I'm finding myself a little flushed at the thought of him saying my name with that accent.

"Dude, these ain't nothing like Mama's pancakes, but they sure smell good."

"Yeah, I can tell the maple syrup isn't homemade either, but I can't complain when we're in the Keys." They both chuckle as they continue piling food on top of food.

And they live with their mama. Great. I always know how to pick 'em.

I've dated a man, or rather *boy*, who was highly dependent on his mother, and as much as I like a guy to be respectful to his mom, being a mama's boy isn't the quality some think it is. In fact, it became borderline annoying.

Just thinking about how my ex would have to text his mother goodnight after we had sex sends shivers down my spine. Maybe that makes me the weird one, but there needs to be a healthy balance.

I take my seat with Natalie and Adam a few tables away from where the Southern men are sitting while trying to shake the images of my ex from my head. Natalie's discussing how she swore she saw a Kardashian sister in the bar last night, and Adam's pretending to add to the conversation by throwing in some 'uh-huhs' and 'mm-hmms.'

Just as I stab a sausage link and shove it into my mouth, I feel a shift. Natalie looks up over my shoulder with wide, dreamy eyes, and I know somebody is standing at my side.

"'Scuse me, ma'am?" I hear the Southern accent and immediately feel the hairs on my neck rise.

I chew as quickly as I can and swallow it down, nearly choking when I try to speak. "Uh, yes?"

Up close, he's even bigger looking. Well over six feet tall, and I can almost see his ab muscles through his shirt.

"I was wonderin' if you could help settle an argument between my friend and me?"

I blink up at him, mouth gaping open. "Sure." I clear my throat, realizing what he's doing. I've heard dozens of pickup lines start just like this. It usually ends up being something super cheesy. By the smirk on his face, I'm almost willing to bet him and his friend are arguing about how pretty I am and want me to say which one I'd go on a date with.

"Well, my friend over there said there was no way you'd find me good-lookin'. I told him there's no way you'd be able to resist my Southern charm

49

and undeniably sexy abs, so since we can't seem to agree, I figured I'd come right to the source and ask myself." He stares intently at me for a moment, licking his lower lip before he sucks it in briefly as I remain dumbfounded. "So whaddaya think? Is he right?" He gives me one of those smug, I-think-I'm-God's-gift-to-women winks before showing a slight preview of the abs he felt so inclined to mention.

Natalie snorts in the background, laughing while covering her mouth with her hand. Adam's grinning and shaking his head as if he's thinking, *poor bastard*.

"Hm…" I decide to play along, tilting my body around him to get a look at his friend. Dark hair, light eyes, and I can tell he's muscular too. When our eyes meet, he tips his head at me with a wide grin. Then I direct my eyes to the guy in front of me and act like I'm giving it serious thought. Clearing my throat, I gaze my eyes back up to his with a confidence smile. "Tell him I've seen better."

Natalie can't contain herself anymore and totally loses it. His friend overhears my response and starts laughing.

"Damn. That hurts," he teases, placing a hand on his chest. The corner of his lips tilts up into a small grin.

"Sorry, but I'm sure there's plenty of ladies around here that'd be happy to mend those wounds." I wrinkle my nose at him to soften the blow. He bows his head down, slouches his shoulders, and begins to slowly walk away back to his friend.

"You think *I'm* attractive, though, right?" the friend shouts from his table, and the blond guy punches him in the arm to silence him.

"Jesus, they're relentless," I mutter so only Natalie and Adam can hear.

"Oh, c'mon! Give 'em a bone," she quips.

I roll my eyes at her in response and pop a piece of fruit in my mouth.

"You know the only way to get over a guy is to get under another one," she teases, her voice carrying throughout the entire room.

I nearly choke on a grape and almost have to give myself the Heimlich.

"Natalie!" I whisper-shout. "Swear to God, I can't take you anywhere."

Adam's smiling and trying to hide his laughter behind a forkful of food.

"This is *your* fault." I point my finger at him. "You just let her roam around free without any kind of restrictions or *muzzle*."

"Don't look at me," he defends. "You knew her before I did, which means you let her be this way long before I came around."

I chuckle in defeat.

"What happened to having fun on this vacation?" Natalie ignores us and changes the subject. "Those were some cute Southern guys who wanted to show you how to ride their mechanical bull. I bet you can last all eight seconds even."

Choking again, I give up and put my fork down. "I've gotta stop eating around you. I never know what will come out of your unfiltered mouth."

"I bet he's hung like a horse, too," she states dreamily, looking past us toward their table.

"And I bet if you asked nicely, they'd even let you ride them bareback." Adam adds fuel to the fire, getting another laugh out of Natalie.

"You two suck," I say, pointing my fork at them.

My eyes land on a woman walking in our direction. She's all legs, long dark hair, and tan. She's a dark-haired Barbie, wearing one of those teeny bikini tops as a shirt with a pair of booty shorts, though the word "shorts" is questionable since I'm pretty certain her ass cheeks are hanging out. She rounds our table and heads directly for the two Southern men.

"Howdy," the blond says, looking up at her with bright eyes.

"So last night was fun," she tells him, her voice all high-pitched and annoying. The guy nods in agreement as his eyes scan up and down her body. "Call me if you want to do it again." She reaches into her back pocket to grab a piece of paper and hands it over to him.

The guy takes it and unfolds it. "Sure thing, darlin'." His accent is even more noticeable when he says that. Damn, it's kinda hot too. Before the woman walks off, he winks at her with a smile that can only mean he'll be calling her soon for another hookup.

The dark-haired guy is smirking and shaking his head.

"Nice." I mutter my annoyance at the fact that he was literally just hitting on me, and five seconds later he's drooling over this chick.

Better yet, why do I care?

"What's that?" the blond guy asks, startling me when he raises his voice loud enough for me to hear. "You jealous already? I didn't even sleep with that one…" He smirks, then winks as if that's his seductive trademark.

"Wow, I'm shocked by your willpower. Better catch her and remedy that then." I hold back rolling my eyes, which is my own trademark when I'm annoyed.

"Nah. I'm not impressed with the local cuisine. I'd rather try something...new and interesting. Any suggestions?" He arches a brow, giving me every opportunity to mock him.

Natalie's about to burst a vein with how hard she's trying to hold back her laughter.

Swallowing, I hold my stance and play his little game. "I'd suggest you stick to what you know, so you don't get bitten. Or worse."

"Damn," the dark-haired guy blurts. "She's my new favorite person." He chuckles, and the blond elbow jabs him. "She shot you down and put you in your place. You'd better marry her, or I will."

I snort. "I'm leaving now." I stand, taking my plate, and push in my chair.

"Okay, but don't forget we have a couple's massage at ten!" Natalie shouts. "Unless you'd prefer Mr. Southern 'n Dirty accompany you?"

I wave a hand up in the air and salute with my middle finger.

CHAPTER FIVE

Alex

The sun feels like it's burning my skin straight through the window as I roll over in bed. Last night, we stumbled back to our suite, and since we drank and sang karaoke all night, I forgot to close the curtains—hell, I'm lucky I even made it to the bed at that point.

Just as I sit up, my head pounds hard and loud like the beat of the music at the club. Drinking so early after we traveled all day was a bad decision on my part, but Dylan was all for it, as usual. We aren't letting any part of this vacation go to waste.

I stand and walk to the bathroom only to catch a glimpse of myself in the mirror.

You look like shit, I think to myself, needing to clear my throat that's sore from all my loud singing. Favorite song of the night: "*All My Exes Live in Texas*." I chuckle because they do.

The world's spinning, and I place my hand against the wall to steady myself before I face-plant on the floor. I stumble to the mini fridge to grab a bottle of water and realize I don't see Dylan anywhere in the room. Opening the door that leads to the sitting area, I find him sleeping on the couch with his legs and arms hanging off the side. He's too tall for that small couch, and it makes me laugh, even though it hurts my head when I do. He's trying so hard to be comfortable, it's comical. We might be a hungover shitshow, but we showed Florida how to really party—Texan style.

Last night, after we bought some swim trunks and flip-flops, we changed clothes, grabbed a quick dinner, then went down to the cabana bar by the water where country music was blasting loud and proud. Five shots of tequila and a few beers later, we were dancing and singing, and now today I'm paying for it.

Just as my stomach growls, Dylan rolls over off the couch and lands flat on his ass. He rubs his hand over his face, and I can tell he feels as bad as I do.

"Ugh," he moans, trying to get up but fails miserably. Walking over to him, I hold out my hand to pull him off the floor. As he stands in front of me, I see bright red lip prints all over his face.

"Last night must've been good." I chuckle, plopping down on the couch and leaning my head back.

Dylan looks at me confused before walking to the bathroom. Once he flicks on the lights, I hear him mutter, "What the hell?" I know he's referring to the lipstick on his face and neck. "All that and I slept on that damn miniature couch alone!"

My stomach growls again, and I know the only way to fix this hangover is to eat something.

"I'm hungry," I tell him as I force myself to stand and go to my suitcase. I slip on a T-shirt and a pair of jeans.

"Me too," Dylan agrees.

Just as I walk toward the door and slip on my flip-flops, Dylan falls in line behind me. He's still wearing his clothes from yesterday but doesn't seem to care.

We take the elevator to the ground level, walk through the lobby, and head straight to the room where the continental breakfast is served. The smell of sausage and bacon fills the room, and my mouth instantly waters. Not wasting any time, Dylan and I stack food on our plates like we always do, yet with the selection in front of us, we keep adding as if we haven't eaten in a week. Pancakes, sausage, bacon, fruit—hell, we got a little of everything.

Before we sit, I notice a pretty blonde at the buffet. As soon as I make eye contact with her, she looks the other way, pretending as if I don't exist. Dylan and I end up sitting a few tables away from where she and her friends are.

"You should go talk to her. You're eyeing her more than the eggs on your plate," Dylan encourages with a smirk.

"Nah," I say, pouring syrup over my pancakes and cutting into them.

"Dare you," he whispers with a mouthful of food.

Now there's one thing a person shouldn't ever do, and that's dare a Bishop.

I eye him, knowing there's no going back on it now.

"Unless you're chicken," he teases before he begins clucking at me.

After I finish chewing my food, I try to listen to their conversation because if it sounds important, I'll have to take a rain check. Dare or not, Mama always taught us boys not to interrupt important discussions. Once I realize her friend is chatting about a celebrity, and everyone at the table looks tuned out of the conversation, I take it as my cue to walk over.

Standing behind her, I catch the slight hint of her strawberry-scented shampoo. Her friend peers up at me and smiles, and I throw out some cheesy pickup line that always works when hitting on girls in trashy bars.

She looks over at Dylan then back at me, and that's when I see a hint of blush hit her cheeks. I'm talking loud enough so he can hear our conversation, and I quickly look over my shoulder at him. All he does is shake his head and laugh.

Once I'm completely rejected by her, I pretend to be hurt and walk back over to Dylan who's laughing so loud other people in the dining area are staring at us.

"Damn. She's a savage. I like her," he says with a shit-eating grin. Moments later, I see Miranda or Mazie—whatever her name is—bounce up to our table with a devilish look in her eye. I take full advantage knowing the blonde girl is watching even though she rejected me just moments ago.

Miranda or Mazie hands me a piece of paper, and once I see it's her phone number, I look up and wink, knowing I have no intentions of actually calling her. But I'm a gentleman after all, so of course, I smile in return. We had a good time last night at the bar drinking and dancing, but that's as far as things will go.

I watch her walk away, and when I look up, I see the blonde girl glaring in my direction. The opportunity to taunt her is too good to pass up when I see her muttering under her breath.

Just as I take a huge bite of my pancakes, the redhead that was sitting with the blonde girl who just rejected me walks over to our table with a beaming smile on her face.

"Hey, I'm Natalie, and this is my boyfriend, Adam," she says, waving her hand to the guy standing next to her. "And that girl at my table you were talking to is my friend River."

Smiling, I quickly swallow down the rest of my food. "Nice to meet y'all. This is Dylan, and I'm Alex."

"River likes to play hard to get, but she's totally single." She flashes a wink. "Just in case you were wondering," she adds, then continues, "and she'd probably murder me if she knew I told you that."

Now I'm the one laughing. "Probably, but I can keep a secret."

"Okay, good. Thanks." She grins. "Well, I hope we'll see you around the resort."

"I'm sure you will. We're here for two weeks," I add, giving her a smile.

"Us too!" Natalie squeals. "Wait, are you single?" She furrows her brows at me. "Want to make sure there isn't a wife, girlfriend, or fiancée waiting for you at home."

Dylan snorts. "Ma'am, his middle name is single."

I glance at Dylan, but Natalie doesn't seem to notice.

"Well, that's great news." Her eyes light up, and I can tell she's already trying to play matchmaker. It's not the first time I've seen that look on a woman's face, and I'm sure it won't be the last.

"Babe, we gotta go. The boat leaves in twenty minutes," Adam reminds her.

She nods at him with a smile then looks back at me. "We'll totally see you around."

Once she walks away, Dylan scoffs. "Seriously? I swear, it's so easy for you. She's already trying to hook you up. What a nice friend." He grins.

I continue to stuff my face. "Basically, but she's just trying to play matchmaker. I already know what type she is—overly flirty and sweet, but a loyal friend. And I sincerely appreciate her giving me the scoop on her pretty friend. The info might come in handy."

After Dylan rolls his eyes then basically licks his plate clean, he sits back in his chair and pats his stomach. "Might need a wheelbarrow to get me out of here."

"Wasn't like Mama's cooking, but it hit the spot," I admit, overly full too. Dylan and I finish our juice before we stand and stretch. Thankfully my head stopped pounding, and I feel like a new man after eating.

"Whatcha wanna do today?" Dylan asks just as a man with a stack of bright yellow flyers walks through the hotel lobby and hands us both one.

"Stand up paddleboarding, windsurfing, jet skis, kayaks, snorkeling, and an all-day pass is *only* $149. But wait, for just $59.99 more, we can add a sunset cruise with a romantic dinner."

"You've got the creepy infomercial voice down," I tell him with a chuckle. "I saw some people on those board things yesterday. It looked like fun."

"Yeah and the weather outside is perfect. We should do it. The rental place is right around the corner." Dylan folds the paper and shoves it into his pocket.

"Let's get ready and head over there."

After we go to our room and change into swim clothes, we walk down to the water sports shop, just like the flyer says. Before we leave the hotel lobby, I glance around for River but don't see her anywhere. That woman is officially on my radar. Her smart mouth and the way she responds to me is intriguing, and I'd be lying if I didn't admit I was curious. After I shake the image of her round ass walking away from breakfast this morning, I realize Dylan is talking to me.

"What do you want to do first?" he repeats himself, annoyed.

"Let's start at the beginning of the list and work our way down."

As we walk a few blocks, we see the big yellow signs pointing to the shop.

"Hey, welcome!" a high-energy woman says from behind the counter when we enter.

"Howdy, ma'am," Dylan and I both respond in unison. It's easy to blend in with the tourists in our board shorts and flip-flops, but the moment we open our mouths, people know we're not from around these parts. Though we've been here less than twenty-four hours, Key West is a culture shock to us. It's much different from the rolling hills, cactus, cows, and ranch. Reggae music plays in the background, and seashell wind chimes rattle in the breeze.

"Have you ever been on a paddleboard before?" The cute woman walks around the counter as we look at the different boards and paddles lined up against the wall.

"No, ma'am," Dylan says, putting the Southern accent on real thick, and I'm pretty sure she's about to melt in his palm.

"Please don't call me ma'am. I'm twenty-two years old, not eighty," she tells him with her eyebrow raised. "I'm Trish."

"Nice to meet you, *Trish*," Dylan says in a low raspy voice. Right about now, if he was wearing his cowboy hat, he would've tipped it.

She blushes. "I have a class in ten minutes to teach beginners if you'd like to sign up," she tells him with a flirty smile playing on her lips. "We'll meet right over there by the flags." She points to the bright blue flags out by the kayaks on the shore. The shop is walking distance from the water, which'll make carrying everything convenient, considering the boards are so bulky.

Dylan looks over his shoulder at me for approval, and I nod my head at him with a smirk.

"Yeah, we'll sign up." He pulls out his credit card and pays.

We happily walk to the beach with our boards and paddles while the sun beams down on us. A slight breeze wisps through the palm trees, and it feels as if we're in actual paradise on Earth. I take off my shirt and throw it on the beach, trying to enjoy the warmth while I can. In a month, the temperatures in Texas will drop below forty before lunchtime, so warm days like this will be few and far between.

"She was cute, don't you think?" he asks, removing his T-shirt too.

As soon as I get ready to open my mouth and give him some shit, Trish comes bopping toward us in a small bikini. After a quick explanation of how to mount the board, she starts giving extra attention to Dylan, allowing her eyes to linger a little too long on his chest and abs. I encourage him with every innuendo she throws his way.

"Get on your knees." She points at the board that sits on top of the sand. "This is a very important *position* especially when you need a break from…" She licks her lips, and Dylan waits on edge for her to finish the sentence.

"…standing," she says with a wink.

Considering we're the only two in the class, I'm starting to feel like the third wheel.

"I agree," he says with a smirk, eating up everything she's saying. I'm trying really hard to keep my scoffs and eye rolls to myself.

Once we've practiced a few times on the sand, she tells us to take our boards to the water, which is as calm as can be. We mount our boards how she taught us, and at first, we both look like baby cows learning to walk for the first time—all wobbly and trying not to fall on our asses.

But before too long, we're both standing and paddling around.

After an hour, Trish lets us know the beginner's lesson is over and releases us to the ocean alone but tells Dylan now that if he wants another lesson, she'd be happy to give him a one-on-one. Knowing Dylan, he'd be more than happy to take her up on that offer, but he wouldn't leave me alone, so he tells her maybe another time.

Without further hesitation, we head back into the water, but paddle farther than before. From a distance, the people lying out on the beach look tiny, and I know it's time we turn around.

"Race you back?" I ask Dylan, and he happily agrees to the challenge.

"Loser buys drinks tonight," Dylan calls out, confidently.

"Deal." We line our boards up and then count down before we both take off.

We're laughing and talking shit, and just as I start to pass Dylan, he takes his paddle and swings it at me, but misses and falls off his board.

"Cheater!" I yell back at him, waiting for a rebuttal. I'm halfway to the shore when I turn around and realize he's not on his board or floating in the water. Panic rushes through me, and I start yelling his name before diving from my board back toward him. I swim as hard as I can, searching for any sign of life when I finally find him sinking lower into the water.

Seconds feel like minutes as I wrap my arm around Dylan's chest and pull us up above the surface. I swim as fast as I can back to shore with one arm. Before I make it to the shore, a few people take notice and run into the water to help me carry him. I'm freaking the fuck out as Dylan lies on the sand on his back, blue in the face and completely unresponsive.

Like an angel, River comes running from out of nowhere and immediately goes to work on Dylan. Without hesitation, she checks his pulse and begins chest compressions as hard and fast as she can. It all happens so quickly that I can barely think, and I feel so helpless as River directs her ear to his mouth to check if he's breathing. Someone behind me cries out on the phone, and I realize the woman is on the phone with 911. I'm completely speechless watching River work like a pro. She tilts his head back and pushes air into his mouth twice before going back to chest compressions. A moment later, Dylan begins to move.

"He's breathing!" River exclaims, rolling him over onto his side, and I watch as he coughs up water. The crowd that gathered around us breathes a collective sigh of relief as Dylan blinks up at us.

Just as he comes to, the paramedics arrive, and once River explains what happened, they begin the process of inserting an IV with fluids into his arm and ask Dylan how he's feeling. He responds while they place an EKG monitor on his chest and clip a thing onto his finger.

"What's that for?" I ask, nodding my head at it

"A pulse oximeter so we can see how much oxygen is in his blood and make sure he's getting enough air," one of the paramedics answer.

"The normal range is between ninety-five to ninety-nine percent, so he's a little low right now, but that's common given the circumstances," the other paramedic adds.

More questions are asked as to what happened, how long was he underwater, how long it took for him to start breathing on his own, and River and I answer the best we can as they load him onto a gurney and recommend he see a doctor for follow-up tests.

"I don't need to go," Dylan says softly, trying to sit up. "I'm just fine," he insists.

"You should," I hear River tell him. "They need to make sure you're okay, and that I didn't fracture a rib or anything." She smirks at him, and he actually decides to listen to her.

As Dylan's pushed into the ambulance, I climb in behind and sit on the bench next to the gurney. The paramedics strap in and we take off to the hospital. On the way, all I can think of is how his mama is going to kill me as I replay every moment in my head.

One minute, he was being an asshole trying to cheat by knocking me off my board, and the next I'm dragging his unconscious body to the beach because he nearly drowns. It seems surreal, actually. I couldn't find him, and when I did, adrenaline pumped through me so hard I rushed back to shore as fast as possible.

Once we arrive and Dylan is unloaded, they immediately move him to a private triage room as we wait for a doctor to evaluate him.

"What the fuck happened?" I ask when we're finally alone, emotion thick in my voice.

"I don't know," Dylan tells me, making eye contact. "I was never a strong swimmer."

I run my fingers through my hair. "How have we been friends for forever, and I never knew that? Why'd you agreed to get in the water then? And why the hell did you go out that far?" I'm throwing question after question at him because I don't know what else to do. I've never felt fear like that in my entire life. "You could've died, Dylan. Do you know what your mama would've done to me if that had happened? I would've blamed myself forever," I scold a little too sternly. My face softens, and I let out a long breath. "I'm glad you're okay. You scared the shit out of me."

Dylan smiles. "Not getting soft on me, are you?"

"You're a dick," I spit out just as a female nurse walks in, holding a file in her hand.

"Mr. Hart," she addresses sweetly. "How are you feeling?"

Dylan sits up in bed. "Better. I'm breathing," he jokes.

"That's great to hear. Just to be completely transparent, the doctor wants to do chest X-rays to double-check there's no fluid in your lungs or anything. Otherwise, you could get pneumonia, and that can be very serious," she continues to explain. "The X-ray technician will be here in the next few minutes with their portable machine to do testing. But before then, do you have any questions for me?"

Dylan glances over at me, then back at the nurse. "How long do I have to stay here?"

"The doctor will follow up with you on that after the results come in, but normally it's recommended you stay overnight so we can monitor your oxygen levels and make sure everything stays normal."

Dylan huffs, and I can tell he's unhappy with that answer. After the nurse exits the room, he starts his bitching.

"I'm a walking party foul! All I wanted to do was a have a good time and now look at me. Being pumped full of shit and having to get X-rays of my lungs…" Before he can finish his rant, the technician walks in, and I'm asked to wait in the hallway.

I sit in the waiting area and find myself becoming more antsy with each tick of the second hand on the clock. Standing, I walk to the window and stare out at the blue sky and thank my lucky stars that Dylan is alive. It was such a close call and frightening as fuck. Sure, I've had to deal with some shit on the ranch, like cuts and bruises, dying animals, and snake bites, but there's nothing like watching my best friend lie unconscious. Before I'm allowed to fall too deeply into my thoughts, I'm told I can go back into the room.

I enter, and we sit there for at least an hour listening to the beeps of the machines before a doctor finally enters with a file in her hand and a smile on her face.

"Hi, Mr. Hart. I'm Dr. Jacobs. I've had a chance to review your X-rays," she states sweetly.

"Howdy," Dylan greets in return.

She opens the file and grabs the films before placing them onto a screen, and the X-rays light up when she clicks a button. "Your lungs look clear for the most part. This cloudy area down here…" She outlines the area with the end of her pen. "…somewhat concerns me, so just to be on the safe side, we're going to keep you overnight for observation. I'd like to continue monitoring your heart rate and oxygen levels and keep you hydrated with the IV. I'll order another X-ray in the morning just to be sure, and if everything looks clear, you'll be discharged." She flashes a hopeful smile, though Dylan looks displeased.

Dylan forces out a smile so as not to be rude.

Dr. Jacobs smiles back at him. "Do you have any questions for me?"

"No, ma'am. Thank you," he tells her.

"If you need anything till then, you can press the call button, and the nurses will be happy to help. Don't hesitate to reach out, especially if you start feeling any differently," she says before leaving the room.

We sit in silence for a few moments, and that's when Dylan groans.

"Suppose that means you won't be texting the code word tonight." I chuckle, breaking the tension, but he rolls his eyes instead.

"On a serious note, after I'm moved to my room, you should go back to the hotel where you can actually sleep comfortably. I don't want you to be a prisoner in the hospital, too."

I stare at him. "Are you sure? I'll stay here with you. I don't mind."

"Yes, I'll be fine," he insists. "I'm gonna try to get some sleep so I can live it up the rest of the time we're here. I don't think what happened has completely set in yet, but I feel exhausted, and it's barely five."

I nod, not wanting to argue with him because I can only imagine how he feels. Though I don't feel right about leaving him here, I don't argue with him. An hour passes and Dylan is finally moved to his room. I go with him, and when we enter, I'm almost grateful he doesn't want me to stay. It's small and stuffy, and there's a chair in the corner with a blanket draped over the arm. A nurse closes the blinds and tells Dylan the kitchen will close pretty soon. He smiles and nods, but I can tell he's too tired to eat.

"If you need me before tomorrow, don't hesitate to call me. Also, text me when you get discharged, okay? And don't be too damn stubborn while you're here."

"I'll let you know," he says.

As I walk toward the door to leave, Dylan calls my name. "Alex."

I turn around and look at him. "Yeah?"

"Thanks for saving my life."

I smile. "Really glad you weren't a statistic, man. Next time, no fucking water sports." I point a finger at him as if I'm scolding him. "Honestly though, without River, I don't know what would've happened." I shrug, hating to admit that and terrified of the what-ifs.

"Well, from the sounds of it, both of you saved my life. I owe you one," he says sincerely, pulling the blanket up to his chest and releasing a yawn. "You better not tell my mama."

"I won't. I'll see you tomorrow," I say as I exit.

After a taxi ride across the island, I arrive at the hotel and head up to the room. As soon as I get in the room, I jump in the shower and wash the day away before changing into some jeans and a button-up shirt. I grab one of the miniature whiskey bottles from the wet bar and slide the balcony door open. I plan to soak up the late evening breeze and forget about what happened. From a distance, I can see the calmness of the water and hear the wind blowing through the palm trees.

Glancing around outside, I scan the bar outside near the pool, and that's when I see her.

River.

She's smiling and chatting with Natalie, and I find myself watching her play with her long locks. I notice a few little things, like how she throws her head back when she's truly laughing. One can only imagine the conversation they're having after all the excitement today, and Natalie seems like the kind of friend who constantly gives her shit regardless if she saved a man's life or not. There's no telling what they're discussing.

I let out a small chuckle and realize I never properly thanked her for stepping in without hesitation and saving Dylan.

That changes *now*.

CHAPTER SIX

River

After the day's excitement, I need a drink. Or ten.

I've saved many lives before; hell, I've worked on a child's chest, pumping and giving him CPR while the mother screamed and cried and called me every curse word in the book. I've also had many experiences with life-threatening emergencies, even before I was in nursing school, but the Dylan situation definitely made me nervous.

"Look at the hero walking in," Natalie teases as soon as I take the seat next to her at the bar.

"Stop," I groan. "I can't escape it."

"Of course not! You're the town hero!" she mocks, lifting her shot glass up victoriously before tilting her head back and shooting it down her throat.

I give her a look that tells her to tone it down a notch.

No one could've anticipated what happened with Dylan today. Over the years, I've found when emergencies arise, I don't give myself time to even think before rushing into action. As soon as I saw that blond guy pull Dylan out of the water, I knew something was wrong. I hurried over and immediately saw how pale he was as he lay motionless on the sand.

The entire scene has been running on repeat through my mind nonstop. Relief flooded through me when he finally came to, and I assume he's going to be okay now, or at least I hope. I'm thankful he agreed to go to the hospital because you never know what other issues can arise from situations like that. That alone eased my mind because there have been many instances of others not being so lucky after nearly drowning.

"Hey, you're that girl who saved that guy on the beach today!" the bartender shouts loud enough for everyone in the pool area to hear.

Natalie responds before I can. "She sure fucking did!"

I glance at her and scowl, not wanting the extra attention.

"Drinks on me, pretty lady," he says with a wide grin. "What you did was amazing."

I force out a smile. "Thanks. I'm a nurse, so it's just instinct," I respond, trying to brush it off so he stops talking about it.

"So what can I get you? You deserve one!" he insists.

"She needs sex on the beach!" Natalie hollers before I can speak, *again.*

"Nat!" I scold.

"Oh, sorry. I meant, she'll take a Sex on the Beach." She looks over at me and winks. All I can manage is to shake my head at her and laugh.

"You got it," the bartender responds, reaching for a clean glass.

"Fruity drinks get me drunk way too fast," I complain, just loud enough for Natalie to hear me.

"That's the point," she states matter-of-factly. "Unless you plan on staying sober this trip?" She grins.

"Not if you're going to be this way the entire time." I chuckle, and she's too drunk to even realize that was a burn directed at her.

Moments later, the bartender serves me my drink and winks before walking to the other end of the bar to help another customer.

Natalie holds up her drink before I can even take a sip of mine. "To River!" she shouts, making Adam and me hold our drinks up, too. "For being a kick-ass nurse!"

Okay, I can drink to that, I think to myself before clanking my glass with theirs and taking my first sip. It's strong as fuck, but luckily, my room isn't far.

Adam knows how Natalie gets when she's in party mode, so he knows she'll need some assistance getting back to their room tonight, which is why he takes it easy and only drinks a couple. I haven't seen her this way in a really long time, but I know she works hard and doesn't let loose that much anymore. At least not since our early college days.

"River," I hear a rough and deep voice say behind me. It's one I recognize.

"Alex!" Natalie squeals before I even have a chance to turn around. "How's your friend?"

"He's doing fine. They kept him overnight for observation."

Inhaling a deep breath, hoping I don't look too tipsy right now, I straighten my posture and turn around to face him.

"That's good," I sincerely say in response to Dylan's condition.

I don't know why, but things feel awkward between us. We barely spoke on the beach today mainly because there was no time. I didn't even know his name until just now, yet he knows mine.

"Can I sit?" he asks, nodding his head toward the empty seat next to me.

"Of course, you can!" Natalie answers.

"I think we should take a walk," Adam says, sensing the awkward tension between Alex and me and grabs Natalie's hand.

"Ooh, I've always wanted to take a walk on the beach. It sounds so romantic," she slurs against his chest after he steadies her.

I chuckle, while silently thanking Adam because no telling what embarrassing things Natalie would say in her current condition.

After Alex takes the seat next to me, he gets the bartender's attention and orders himself a beer then places money on the counter.

"So you didn't stay with him?" I ask, facing the bar again.

"I offered, but us Southern men are stubborn when it comes to our pride," he explains with a smirk on his face. "I told him to call me when he's discharged so I can bring him back. I'm sure he'll be itching to party."

"As long as he stays far away from the water," I add, smiling.

The bartender takes his money off the bar while shooting me a wink.

"So I don't think we've formally met," he states, holding out his hand. "I'm Alex Bishop."

Swallowing, I place my hand in his. "River Lancaster."

"That's a beautiful name," he tells me, moving my knuckles up to his lips and placing a soft kiss on them.

"Thank you," I whisper.

We stare into each other's eyes, and he keeps my hand in his. Somehow, I'm stuck in his trance, and I don't know how to get out. He's a beefy guy, solid and muscular, and I've never seen a man like him before. Most of the guys I've dated were gym rats, but I can tell he's not. His body was built from hard labor.

"Here you go, bud," the bartender interrupts with a sneaky grin on his face as he sets the beer down. The intense moment fades, and he gently releases my hand.

"Thanks." He tips his head to the guy and brings the glass to his lips. I find myself watching his every move before blinking and tearing away my gaze.

He sucks down half his drink before setting it down. Turning toward me, his eyes lock on mine and pin me to him. "So I actually never thanked you for today. I was scared shitless and you doing CPR ultimately saved his life. I don't know what I would've done without you."

A blush surfaces at his compliment, which is insane since I do this type of stuff every day at work. I tell myself it's what I do, it's in my nature, but to hear those words from him has my heart racing.

"So thank you, River. Sincerely. Those words hardly do justice to how thankful we both are that you were there today."

His words are so soft and tender, his accent making the words even sweeter.

I release a small smile and lower my eyes before blinking and meeting his again. "You're welcome. I didn't think twice about it and would do it over again if I had to."

"That's what makes you so amazing." He winks.

"I'm actually a nurse," I admit. "I've had lots of training." I shrug as if it's not significant.

"That makes a lot of sense actually," he says, nodding. "You were so calm, and when you spoke to the paramedics, you used all the technical terms."

"Yeah, they kind of beat those into you during nursing school."

He laughs, reaching for his beer again. I grab my own drink and take another sip.

"Where you from?" he asks as we easily fall into conversation.

"Wisconsin," I answer. "Milwaukee, actually."

"Oh, wow." His eyes widen. "Aren't you known for being the beer state?"

"Dairy, actually, but beer is basically its own food group up there." I shrug and smile.

Laughing, he nods as if he agrees.

"Or I guess you could say the frozen state considering we have some of the coldest winters."

"Is that why you're here? To escape the cold weather?"

"Oh, it's not even that cold yet. Still had highs in the forties when we left."

"Fuck." He shakes his head. "That's too damn cold for this born-and-raised Texan."

"I guessed Texas."

"That obvious, huh?" He smirks, and I playfully shrug.

"Actually, the coldest times are between January and March. It's usually in the negatives with the wind chill, but that's when the ice freezes on the water and becomes thick enough for people to go ice fishing. They build these ice shanties and carve a hole in the ice, so they can sit around and fish for hours."

"And y'all do that for fun?" He raises a brow, skeptical.

"Yup." I laugh, nodding. "Snowmobiling, snowboarding, skiing. All that stuff. But that's not until January usually, sometimes even February. Right now, it's just cold and gloomy, not yet ready to give up fall even though winter is right around the corner."

"I bet that brings lots of dumbasses into the hospitals up there."

"Well, yes it does, but I actually work at the children's hospital in the PICU."

His eyes narrow as if he's not sure what that entails.

"I work with sick kids who need around-the-clock care and treatment."

"Wow…" His voice is soft. "That has to be a tough job."

I nod, agreeing. "It is. But I love it. As bad as it can be, it's also very rewarding. Many of the kids have been there a while as they await transplants or getting treatments for life-threatening illnesses. I get to know them and their families quite well. It's always disheartening when a child isn't getting better, but it's part of the job." I shrug, taking a gulp of my drink to get ahold of my emotions.

"I can tell how passionate you are just by the way you talk about it. And especially how you ran to Dylan's rescue without a second thought."

"I am. I've wanted to be a nurse since I was a teen." I basically already was to my baby sister by the time I was twelve.

My drink is completely gone, but I keep sucking on the straw, and Alex has already ordered his third beer when Adam and Natalie come strolling back by.

"We just wanted to let you know we're heading to our room," Adam tells me, holding Natalie's hand tightly as if to keep her from roaming away.

"Are you two getting along?" Natalie speaks up, making things awkward again. "He's single, River. Don't worry, I checked for ya," she says nice and loud, flashing a very obvious wink my way.

"Thanks," I mutter, sliding off my stool and tossing my purse over my shoulder. "Let me help Adam get you back to your room before you tell everyone here I have daddy issues and a broken heart, m'kay?"

"I would never say that," she whisper-shouts in a very serious drunken tone, forcing a laugh out of me. "Don't worry, Alex. River's totally normal and is a goddess in and out of the sheets." She winks at him, and she doesn't know how to wink with alcohol in her system, so she's basically just blinking harshly at him like a witch trying to put a spell on someone.

"Okay, time to go." I grab Natalie's other hand and start to follow Adam.

"Bye, River!" Alex calls out, grabbing my attention.

I blush for some unknown reason and wave back. "See ya!"

The first five days in Key West have certainly been interesting. After meeting Alex and Dylan on Monday, we haven't seen much of them since then. We've run into them during breakfast, but then Natalie and I have kept busy shopping and exploring the streets as well as tanning and drinking by the pool. I'm sure they've been busy themselves, but Alex has still been on my mind for some reason.

I can't deny that he's good looking, and his accent definitely alerts my senses, but there's something else I can't quite put my finger on. However, knowing my history with men, it's probably not a good thing. Even if he is single, we're from two different worlds. What would be the point of getting involved with someone who lives hundreds of miles away?

The fact that I'm even thinking about this makes me want to slap myself. *It's gotta be from all the sun,* I tell myself. *Or the abundance of alcohol.*

Either way, I'm quick to push those types of thoughts from my head. There's no time for men in my life right now, especially after Asshole wasted half a year of it.

"Tonight, we're going to a pub on Duval Street!" Natalie tells me as we sit for lunch.

"I think I need to detox for a night," I whimper, waking up with a headache for the fourth morning in a row.

"No, tonight's different!" she insists, and I resist rolling my eyes because she says that every time. "It's ladies' night, which means we drink for dirt cheap! Plus, there's a local live band, and I really, really want to hear them play. Please!" she begs pathetically, yet it works.

"Being the third wheel was cute the first time, but now I'm just looking pathetic as fuck," I tell her, groaning at the thought. I stab a piece of chicken with my fork and stuff it into my mouth. Considering the drinks have been nonstop, I need all the food I can get to absorb the alcohol.

"Oh, I'm sorry. Did you come to have fun and drink, or did you come to wallow like an old lady?" she scolds in a motherly tone. When she catches me roll my eyes that time, she continues. "That's what I thought. You can be responsible and shit when we get back home. Until then, we live it up!" She raises both arms above her head like we're on a roller coaster.

"Okay, I'll go, just put your damn arms back down." I chuckle around my forkful of food.

"Invite Alex and Dylan," she tells me again, as she has for the last three nights. I've already told her my concerns and reasons for not wanting to get too close, but she waves it off and reminds me I'm here to have fun.

I head back to my room and get ready for the night. Natalie ordered me to wear my best dress, which isn't hard considering I only own one. Working nonstop doesn't give me a lot of time for going out or dancing, but this little black number has paid for itself in drinks time and time again.

Once I've showered and finished my hair and makeup, I slip it on and pull out my heels. I'm not sure exactly what kind of bar this is, but if there's dancing and a band, I can only assume I'll need to dress up.

I'm used to throwing my blonde hair up into a ponytail or bun while working, but tonight, I decide to leave it down and curl it in loose waves. I take a look in the mirror and barely recognize myself but smile at the reflection anyway.

A knock on the door grabs my attention, and as I walk toward it, I grab my purse and phone off the table before opening it.

"Girl!" Natalie squeals, barging her way in. "Hot damn."

She gives me a once-over, and I do the same to her. She's wearing an emerald cocktail dress that complements her fiery hair and pale complexion. She looks damn good, but Natalie always does. Walking over to the full-length mirror attached to the closet door, she reaches into her purse and digs out her lipstick.

"This color would look amazing on you. Come here," she orders, opening the lid and twisting the bottom till a bright red color appears.

"Holy shit, that's bright," I tell her, wary of putting it on. "What color is that?"

"It's called Hooker Red, but don't let the name scare you. It's actually really pretty on."

My eyes widen, and my brows rise. "Why don't I trust you?"

She chuckles, then pulls me to her till we're both in the mirror's view. "Just shush and trust me, all right?"

"But I don't trust you." I laugh, pulling away, but she grabs my wrist and pulls me back again.

Giving in, I let her put the Hooker Red color on my lips, and when she turns me around to face the mirror, I actually don't hate it.

"Told you," she gushes.

I playfully scoff in defeat and smile. "You got lucky." I point at my black dress that would match any color anyway.

"Okay, let's go! Adam's waiting for us in the lobby."

Even though the bar isn't that far, we take a taxi because I'll be damned if I'm walking in these heels. I don't need to go back to work with a sprained ankle, or worse.

"Oh my God!" Natalie squeals as we exit the backseat. "How cool is this?"

People are piling out of the bar, hanging out on the streets, and the music is so loud it could probably be heard from the beach. This is definitely going to be a wild night.

CHAPTER SEVEN

Alex

Hanging out with River and talking to her really opened my eyes to the kind of person she is—kind, caring, sweet. She didn't hesitate for a second to come to Dylan's rescue, and I find myself so intrigued by her that I want to know even more—if she'll let me.

"Did you harass the nurses all night?" I tease Dylan while we're in the back of the taxi.

"More like, they harassed *me* all damn night. When I'd finally fall asleep, they'd barge in, flick on the light, and say they needed to check my vitals. The first time, I was like okay, no big deal. But by the fourth time, I told her to get the hell out of my room."

I snort, shaking my head at him. "You did not."

"I sure as fuck did. Couldn't get no more than fifty minutes of sleep before they were waking me up, and when four a.m. rolled around, I was over it."

"Damn. Now, I'm glad you made me go back to the hotel last night. Otherwise, I'd be a cranky asshole like you." I grin, adjusting my ball cap.

He wrinkles his nose and doesn't respond. Once we're back to our room, it's just past noon, and I'm starving.

"Should we find someplace to eat?"

"Sounds good to me. Let me grab a quick shower first to get this hospital stank off me."

I grab the remote and flick on the TV while he showers. The first few days in Key West have definitely been interesting ones, and even though it got off to a rough start with Dylan's near-drowning, I know we aren't going to let that ruin our time here. In fact, Dylan's ready to party more now than ever.

Over the next few days, we continue exploring the island and even take one of those bus tours. I keep a lookout for River but don't see her at the pool, bar, or beach. I'm partially worried she left, but then I remember Natalie saying they were here for two weeks too.

"Stop," Dylan groans as we walk around the historical parts of the Keys.

"What?" I ask, not bothering to look at him.

"You keep looking for River."

That grabs my attention. "What are you talking about? I'm looking at all the…" It's then I realize I have no idea what I'm looking at. "This historical building."

He scoffs. "You idiot. This is the Hemingway House."

Blinking, I look around and realize he's right when I see the sign. We've been walking around and taking buses to different areas, but I've also been so lost in my head I hadn't realized where we were.

"I knew that."

Looking up at him, he rolls his eyes and keeps walking as I follow behind.

"Okay, I was looking for her," I finally admit, catching up. "I haven't seen her since the bar on Monday night, and I kind of want to see her again. Is that so bad?"

"See her or bang her?" he teases, knowing my reputation.

It takes me a minute to really think about it. "Well, I wouldn't say *no* if she offered, but I really liked talking with River and just being around her. I don't know, she has this vibe I'm gravitating toward. It's hard to explain," I confess, feeling more confused than before. I don't typically hang out with girls unless it's to get her into my bed.

"I should've known," he says as I fall into step with him, and we make our way back to the hotel.

"Known what?"

"That you'd get hung up on the first hot girl you saw—who's way out of your league, by the way—even though there are probably hundreds for you to pick from, and now I'm gonna hear about it for the next ten days."

"Okay, asshole." I punch him in the shoulder. "I do not get hung up on girls. Wanting to chat up a girl is no different than when I meet a girl in a bar back home," I lie, mostly to convince myself, but Dylan knows me way too well to know I'm bullshittin' through my teeth.

"Fine, then prove it. Let's go out tonight, hit up a busy bar or somethin' and find a girl to hook up with."

"You're telling me to go sleep with someone to prove to you I'm not hung up on River?" I confirm, realizing how insane it sounds. But what's crazier is how much she intrigues me, and we've only just met. If I'm going to hook up with a chick during this trip, I want it to be her.

Any other time, I'd be all over a dare like this. I'm not about to admit that to him, though.

"Pff, easy." I swallow, not wanting him to see through my lies.

After grabbing a quick bite, we go back to the hotel and get ready for the night. I'm more determined to prove to myself that I *can't* be hung up on River than to prove Dylan wrong. I can do this. I can find a chick and bring her back and fuck her brains out. Hell, it should be second nature by now.

"You ready?" Dylan calls out an hour later.

"Almost," I tell him.

I finish up and step out of the bathroom, dressed and ready to head out. Deciding to leave my ball cap off, I comb my fingers through my hair until it's tousled, then I decide to wear my black cowboy boots with my relaxed fit jeans.

"'Kay, I'm good to go."

Dylan and I walk down Duval Street, knowing it has the best nightlife near the hotel. We've learned a cab ride back is cheap since most of the bars are within walking distance, but when you're tipsy and can't walk straight, it feels like miles.

"Don't forget our deal," Dylan reminds me as if I need reminding.

"Yeah, yeah. I know."

He slaps a hand on my shoulder. "Good. Don't forget the code word either." He flashes a shit-eating smirk.

We head into the bar we've visited the last couple of nights and order our first round of beers. The streets are packed with tourists, and my hope for seeing River again diminishes.

"Hey, mates!" Liam, a guy we met the other night, greets us just as we order our second round. He has a girl hanging off his arm tonight, though. He's from Sydney, which was pretty obvious once we heard him speak.

"Hey!" Dylan and I both say. "How's it goin'?"

Before Liam can respond, the girl speaks up. "Oh my God! I love your accents!" she squeals.

"They sound like you," he tells the girl, but she dismisses him with a wave.

"Texas, right?" she asks in an overly flirty tone.

"Yes, ma'am," Dylan answers. "Where you from?"

"Ontario," she replies with a wide smile. "I'm Jessica, by the way. I just love the south. I'm completely infatuated with it."

The girl's hand loosens out of Liam's arm, and soon he's shrugging her off and ordering himself another drink.

"Did you find your girl yet?" he asks me while Dylan chats with Jessica, or, rather, Jessica chats up Dylan.

I frown. "No. I'm starting to think it's hopeless." I shrug, pretending it's no big deal.

"Oh, for fuck's sake," Dylan interrupts with a groan. "You told Liam about her, too?"

Liam grins and nods.

"Not really," I start to explain. "He asked why I wasn't out on the dance floor, and I said I was trying to find a girl I met the other night. That's all."

"River," Liam adds. "Guess we'll need to put together a search party soon." He chuckles.

Dylan shakes his head disapprovingly. "Well, he's been given a new mission tonight," he tells Liam and Jessica. "Find a girl to bring back to the room to prove he's *not* hung up on her." He jabs his elbow into my side.

Liam's eyes widen as he takes a pull from his beer. "Really, mate?" He turns and looks at me for confirmation.

I shrug and purse my lips.

"If he brings a girl home tonight, where does that leave you?" Jessica asks slyly, directing all her attention back to Dylan.

Tuning them out, I turn toward the bar to order another beer. If I have to go through with this dare, fuck if I can do it sober.

"What if you end up finding her, after all?" Liam asks, sitting on the stool next to me without concern that Jessica is now all over Dylan. Apparently, he's not bothered by it.

I shrug, not really wanting to answer that. "What if I don't?"

"You won't know, but I bet if you do, you'll regret sleeping with someone else." His words go straight to my gut.

"I've only regretted sleeping with two women in my entire life," I tell him matter-of-factly. "One was because she *forgot* to tell me she was engaged—and I don't sleep with women who are spoken for—and the other because she turned out to be bat-shit crazy. She left me thirty-four voicemails within twenty-four hours, and because that wasn't enough of a hint to leave me the hell alone, she showed up at my door."

Liam starts cracking up laughing. "No!"

"Not only that, she shows up wearing an oversized trench coat with a bottle of whiskey."

"A trench coat?" He looks confused.

"Yep, and when I told her I wasn't interested, she opened her coat and was completely naked." I take a pull from my beer, shaking my head at the memory.

"Holy fuck. Naked?" Liam continues to laugh. "How'd you talk your way out of that one?"

I hang my head and shake it.

"No..." he slowly says. "No, mate. Don't tell me..."

I close my eyes and reluctantly shake my head. "Yep. I blame the whiskey, though."

"So then what happened? How'd you get rid of her?"

I pinch my lips together, realizing it probably wasn't the best story to share with a person I barely know, but what the hell. It's not like I'll see him ever again once we leave.

"Walked her to the door the next morning, told her I'd call her, and then changed my number."

Liam is dying with laughter, completely losing control.

"Then when I saw her at the diner in town two months later, she walked up to me with an entire pie and smashed it in my face in front of everyone."

"Oh, fuck." Liam continues his fit of laughter.

"Then to top it off, she grabbed my hot cup of coffee and poured it in my lap."

Dylan finally breaks away from Jessica long enough to show his interest in our conversation. "You talkin' 'bout Crazy Carly?" He grins, and when I confirm it, he starts laughing along with Liam.

"Crazy Carly?" Liam asks. "Sounds fitting."

"Way, way too fitting," I agree, grabbing my beer and finishing it.

We hang out with Liam and Jessica for another hour before we decide to take off and find another bar. Loud music comes from both directions, but we head toward the bar where a live band is playing.

"You're going to run out of time," Dylan teases. "However, some girls are probably desperate enough to go back to the room with you tonight." He chuckles.

"Fuck off." I push him slightly as we enter the bar. "I don't need a babysitter, so why don't you find your own girl for the night."

"I was trying to get Jessica, but I felt like I'd be stealing her away from Liam."

"Nah, I don't think he cared. Seemed like they'd just met anyway."

"Really?" His brows raise. "Well, then I'm going to go back and find her. You sure you don't mind if I leave?"

I shoot him an irritated look. "No. Go. Just make sure to check your phone or text me if you head back to the room. I don't need to see your white ass again."

"You got it." And with that, he turns around and heads out.

Relieved I finally have him off my back, I step inside. The live music is loud as fuck, but within a few minutes, my ears adjust, and it's not so bad. I can't help it, but I glance around with hopes that my luck changes.

I head up to the bar and order another drink, and just as I turn around to face the band again, I see *her*. Blinking several times to make sure I'm not imagining it, I take a few steps closer to confirm.

She's in a short, tight black dress and her beautiful blonde hair is down around her shoulders in loose waves. I only got a glimpse of her side profile, but I'm damn certain it's her. After a minute, I realize she's not alone. Natalie and Adam are next to her, and a guy I don't recognize has his arms around her waist. My heart races and my feet gravitate toward her before I can stop myself.

"River," I lean down and shout, hoping she can hear me over the music.

Startled, she quickly turns and when she realizes it's me, her eyes and smile widen.

"Alex!" she shouts back. "Hey!"

Natalie, Adam, and the other guy all turn around at the same time.

"Alex! Yay!" Natalie shouts. She attacks me and wraps her arms around my neck. "Where have you been?"

"We've been out exploring and partying," I respond. "Haven't seen you guys around in a few days," I say, hoping I sound casual, but I can feel the energy buzzing between River and me. Lowering my eyes, I keep them locked on her. "What have you guys been doin'?"

"Beachin'!" Natalie offers in her tipsy voice.

I grin and nod. "Can I buy you a drink?" I ask River, keeping my attention on her. The guy's grip tightens as he pulls her to his side, and my teeth clench.

"She's with me," the guy speaks up, his voice weak and pathetic.

Blinking, I take one look at the dweeb before bringing my eyes back to River. She lowers her head as if she's not sure what to say or do.

"River," I drawl, grabbing her attention. "Is that right?"

She pulls her lower lip between her teeth and bites down.

"Dude, what's your problem? I said she's with me, so back the fuck off." The guy's voice gets louder, and River visibly cringes.

Taking that as a sign, I grab River's hand and pull her out of his grip. "Not anymore. Get lost, asshole."

I lead her the other direction before the guy can even respond. She clings to me as if her life depends on it and when we reach the bar, I swing her around until she's facing me.

"Who was that?"

"Brant...*something*," she answers with little confidence. "We met earlier, a few hours ago, I guess."

My brows raise. "And he already held his claim on you?"

She sighs. "I guess, I mean…I was dancing, and he just started getting closer and closer, and because Natalie demanded I have fun tonight, I was trying to let loose." She shrugs almost as if she's embarrassed about it, and I feel bad for asking.

"Well, we can still have fun tonight." I grin, and she flashes a wide, genuine smile up at me.

"Sounds good to me."

I order us a round of drinks, a beer for me and a cocktail for her. We sit at the bar and chat for at least thirty minutes before Natalie and Adam find us. River is tipsy from already having a few drinks tonight, but Natalie is past the point of tipsy.

"You two are so damn cute together!" she squeals, wrapping her arm around River and squeezing. "Seriously!"

"Okay, Nat." River laughs. "Time for you to be cut off," she says, eyeing Adam.

"Guys, I mean it!" Her tone is so serious, it's hard not to laugh. "River's been talking about you nonstop," she directs toward me, and River's face immediately turns red. "Alex this and Alex that. It was getting to the point where I was about to send her to rehab."

"Oh my God." River's eyes squeeze tight before she opens them.

"Is that so?" I grin.

"I *maybe* mentioned you a couple of times," she admits, the red deepening on her cheeks.

Leaning down to her ear so only she can hear me, I whisper, "It's really fuckin' adorable when you blush."

She sucks in her lower lip, shaking her head up at me. "Don't be getting a big head now," she teases.

Thank God Dylan isn't with me because I know he'd be telling her the same damn thing right now.

"I'm going to take Natalie home," Adam interrupts. "River, do you want to ride with us in the cab?"

"Um…" she contemplates while Adam looks up at me, giving me a warning look.

"If you want to stay, I'll make sure she gets back safely," I promise, making sure Adam can hear my sincerity.

"That okay with you?" Adam directs the question to River, making sure she's comfortable with staying.

"Yeah, I'll be fine." She smiles.

"You two would make the most beautiful babies." Natalie hums, wrapping her arms around River's neck and lazily dropping her head on her shoulders. "Just don't have babies before I do, okay?"

"No worries," River says, confidently. "You two can make all the babies you want."

Natalie giggles, and Adam carefully wraps his arms around her and leads her away.

I chuckle as we both turn back around. "That girl knows the definition of having a good time, doesn't she?"

River laughs, nodding. "She's drunk so much, she'll still be drunk when we get home."

We continue chatting, and I order us another round because I don't want this time with her to end. The live band is still jamming, and the crowd fills in even more.

Just as the band starts singing a John Mayer song, I notice River's eyes light up.

"Oh my God, I *love* this song!" she gushes, and it takes me less than five seconds to decide to pull her out on the dance floor.

"Come on," I say, grabbing her hand and helping her off the stool.

She lets me lead her to the middle of the room, and soon our bodies are fused together as our hands wrap around each other.

"'Slow Dancing in a Burning Room' is my absolute favorite," she tells me as we rock back and forth.

"I can't say I'm familiar with it, but I can see why you like it."

"He gets a bad rap in the tabloids, but he's talented as hell," she says, her chest moving more rapidly against mine. She looks up at me with bright green eyes filled with lust, and I know she's thinking the same thing I am.

"Maybe he's just one of those misunderstood types." I grin.

She smirks. "Aren't all musicians?"

The longer I listen, the more I understand the meaning behind the lyrics. The guitar acoustics are rad as fuck, but it only adds to the melancholy of the song. The steadiness of the beat really gives me that visual of two people being together, yet they know their relationship is coming to an end, and it's only a matter of time before it burns out.

"The lyrics are kind of depressing," I say, moving her closer to me.

"They really are," she agrees. "You can hear the heartbreak in his voice."

"It's tragic," I add.

She blinks, giving me those sultry eyes again, and I can no longer hold back. I cup her face in my hand and watch her for a moment, just staring into her eyes before I lean down and press my mouth to hers.

Her lips move against mine, parting so I can slip my tongue through and kiss her the way I've been dying to since the first time I saw her. My other arm tightens around her waist, holding her possessively as I inhale her scent and taste her.

River moans against my lips, encouraging me even more. My hand slips around to the back of her neck, and when her head tilts up, I deepen the kiss further. She tastes sweet and fruity, like the drinks she's been ordering, but that's not all. She has a fresh and clean scent that I inhale as my tongue twists with hers.

She grips my shirt in her fists, pulling me against her as close as we possibly can be. Taking control, she runs her hand up my body until it reaches my hair and tugs, eager to feel and taste me with the same fervor I have.

The song is ending, and I know people will soon notice us making out hardcore on the dance floor. It's not that I really care about people seeing us, but I want to do so much more than kiss her. *So* much more.

"River…" I whisper against her lips. "We should…"

"Yeah," she interrupts before I can finish. "Want to come back to my room?" she asks, and I don't know why, but I'm a bit shocked. I was going to say we should stop so we don't give the entire bar a show, but she has something much better on her mind.

"Uh, yeah." I step back slightly just as the song ends and notice how red and swollen her lips are. Yeah, I like that look on her. "I'll close out our tab if you want to grab us an Uber?"

"Sure, I'll schedule one right now."

Taking her hand, I lead us off the dance floor and get the bartender's attention and pay. Once it's settled, I grab my phone to let Dylan know I won't be coming back to the room tonight. As soon as I unlock my phone, I see he's already texted me.

DYLAN

REVERSE COWGIRL, BITCH!! Don't even think about coming back here, asshole!

Shaking my head, I laugh at his message. Guess going back for Jessica paid off.

Poor Liam.

ALEX

I'm not even surprised, you fucker! I'll be at River's for the night anyway.

ALEX

P.S. You're paying housekeeping to do an extra thorough cleaning tomorrow.

"Ready?" River asks, grabbing my hand. "The Uber is here."

Shit, if she only knew. I was fucking ready days ago.

CHAPTER EIGHT

River

I've barely scanned my keycard and opened the door before Alex's mouth and hands are on me. The moment I saw him tonight, something inside me ignited, a deep desire I'd been fighting to acknowledge. Perhaps getting some of that liquid courage helped me realize I wanted him as much as he wanted me.

I cling to him as he kicks the door shut and pushes us deeper into the room. He's pulling at my dress while I undo his belt buckle and tug at the button of his jeans. Soon I'm standing in just my bra and panties while he kicks off his boots. As he cups my breast, our mouths crash together. Strong arms wrap around my waist as he pulls me up and my legs instinctively wrap around him.

"Alex!" I squeal with laughter as he walks us closer to the bed.

He plants my ass on the mattress, and I lean back just as he stands and wraps his hands around my knees. Flashing me a mischievous smirk, he pulls my body toward him until my ass is on the edge of the bed, nearly hanging off.

Leaning over me, he closes in and presses another kiss to my lips. "I hope you don't mind, but tasting you earlier has me dying to taste another part of you." He winks, making me melt at his words.

His large hand slides down my stomach and cups my pussy over my lace panties. Just the sensation of him touching me has my back arching, and I'm already desperate for more.

"I can feel how wet you are already." He teases my clit with the pad of his thumb. "You want it, don't you?"

I bite my lip and nod—wanting him is an understatement at this point.

"Say it, River," he demands, his eyes locked on mine. "I won't do anything without your permission."

"Yes," I whisper, my hand reaching out to wrap around his forearm. "Yes." I dig my nails into him, showing him just how badly I do.

The corner of his lips tilts up, satisfied with my answer. He kneels, spreading my legs wider until they wrap around his neck. Kissing along my inner thigh, he continues rubbing circles on my clit as his mouth moves closer to where I need him.

"You liked me that day we first met, didn't you?" he asks, my mind spinning and unable to concentrate. "You pretended not to."

"No," I disagree. "I thought you were an egotistical ass."

He smiles against my leg, and I know he's amused.

"I seriously doubt that," he mocks, reaching closer to my clit. His tongue replaces his thumb, and soon, he's sucking on it through the thin fabric of my panties.

My hand fists the sheets as my eyes roll to the back of my head. I feel the strokes of his tongue along my slit and back up to suck my clit, then he repeats it several times over. The fabric just adds to the intensity, but I want to feel him against me.

I reach down with one hand and pull my panties to the side, letting him know exactly what I want. He takes my cue and wraps his hands around my ass and squeezes before sinking his tongue deep inside me.

Moaning, I use my free hand to fist his hair and keep his head anchored.

The last time I had a guy pay me this kind of attention was…hell, I don't even know how long. That's how long it's been. Most guys don't believe in foreplay, or maybe they just don't care to put in the effort. Not Alex. He's already devouring me, and I'm seconds away from exploding.

"Oh my God," I moan, the muscles tightening around his tongue. "Yes, right there!"

He flicks his tongue, swirls it around my clit, and inserts two fingers inside. *Oh God.* This guy is too fucking good. There's no way I'm going to survive him. No fucking way.

I'm on the edge when he increases his pace and pushes in deeper, his lips flicking and sucking and when he curls his finger and reaches that spot, everything tightens, and I scream.

My entire body rocks and shakes, and I've never felt anything like it from a guy going down on me. He keeps up his pace as I ride out my release, and once my body relaxes, he presses a quick kiss to my thigh. When I finally peel my eyes open, he's sucking on his fingers. *Those two fingers.* Holy fuck, that's hot.

"I knew you'd taste good, but goddamn. That should be the flavor of the fucking day." He winks, and it's hard to hold back my laughter.

As he stands looking like a Greek God, I watch him lower his jeans and kick them off along with his shirt. He's just in his boxer shorts, and my eyes lower to the very noticeable tent he's sporting. I'm staring at it so hard that I'm completely taken aback when he grabs my waist and flips me over on the bed. My legs are still hanging off the edge, so I crawl forward until I'm centered and on my elbows. He waits until I'm situated but then slaps a hand across my ass cheek.

"These aren't needed," he tells me, pulling my panties down my legs and tossing them aside. "And I think you'd be more comfortable without this." He reaches for my bra, and I chuckle a little when he starts cussing. "The fuck?"

I laugh again at how puzzled he sounds.

"The hook's in the front," I finally explain.

"Ahh, I was just about to find some scissors and cut the damn thing off."

"Figured you'd be a pro at ripping off bras," I tease as he leans down and wraps his arms around my chest.

"You're kind of damaging my ego here." I can tell he's smiling as he struggles to find the hook. Moments later, he finally unlatches it.

"Good. It could go down a few notches," I quip as I help him slide it off my arms.

"Ooh, you're even sassier when you've been drinking." I turn my head just in time to see him smirk. "Or have you just been holding back on me?"

"Get off your high horse, cowboy."

"Really? A cowboy joke?" He arches a brow as he cups my bare breast and squeezes. He begins to massage and flicks the nipple, getting it hard. My eyes close, and before I can stop myself, a moan releases. "That's what I thought, city girl."

He slaps my ass again, making it tingle. Lowering his body, he brings his mouth down to the small of my back and presses light kisses up my spine. I moan at the contact and the way his erection presses against my ass. He rocks his body against mine, letting me feel how hard he is, and it's pure torture because I want him. *All of him.*

"Alex…" I plead, his mouth sucking on my earlobe. He brushes my hair to the side and devours my neck.

"Yes?" he whispers.

"Fuck me. *Please,*" I beg. I *fucking* beg because that's how worked up he has me.

Pathetic. But I can't help it. Between the alcohol buzzing through my veins and the heartbreak I'm trying to get over, I'm desperate to feel him inside me.

Desperate for him. Desperate to forget.

He smiles against the flesh of my neck. "How do you like it, baby?"

I hadn't expected him to ask me that, but if I was honest, it was nice to actually be asked. Lord knows, Asshole never did or put my needs and wants first.

"Hard," I answer, hoping I don't sound pathetic in my plea. "And rough."

"Fuck, River…" he growls in my ear. "That's the hottest damn thing I've ever heard. You sure you're up for that?"

I turn my head and grin. "You sure *you* are?"

He presses his lips to mine briefly before pushing off the bed and reaching for his jeans. I hear him digging for a condom in his wallet, and thank God he came prepared. I'm on the pill, but I'd rather be safe than sorry and bring an STD back home.

Looking over my shoulder, I wait in anticipation as he slides his shorts down and sheaths himself. Placing a knee on the bed, he spreads my legs before grabbing my hips and pulling me up slightly until our bodies meet. Once I feel the tip at my entrance, I arch my back and rest up on my elbows as he rocks his hips and thrusts inside. I inhale sharply as I feel him inch by inch.

"Goddammit, River," he growls, gripping my hips with both hands.

We've barely moved yet, and I can already tell he's thick. His size is impressive, not that I'm really surprised. It's not until he pulls out and thrusts back in again that I can really feel the length and girth of him, stretching me every time he enters inside me.

"Oh my God," I whimper, my head falling down between my shoulders. He increases the pace, digging his fingers into my hips deeper as he thrusts harder and faster. "*Yesyesyes…*" I mutter.

One hand slaps my ass again as he continues fucking me from behind. God, it feels so good at this angle, and he fucks so damn good, too. His body towers over me, and his lips press against my neck as he moans and cusses in my ear.

"Fuck, River, fuck," he growls before biting down on my shoulder.

We continue that pace until he pounds so hard into me, the buildup becomes too much, and I moan out his name. The way my body tightens, I'm shocked he holds back his own release.

"Hell if I'm done with you yet," he tells me, flipping me over onto my back. He hitches my knee up as he slides back inside, thrusting harder and harder.

I dig my nails into the flesh of his arms, biting down on my lip until I can no longer hold it in. Moaning, I tell him how close I am and beg him not to stop. I'm so close, which seems impossible since I rarely orgasm even once during sex, but three times? That had to be some kind of record.

"C'mon, baby," he encourages, bringing his mouth back to mine. "Come on my cock again. It's fuckin' hot."

*Oh my God…*the thought barely comes when I feel it ripping through me. My pussy tightens more than before, and I feel his body jerk above me.

"God. That's so perfect," he tells me, wrapping my hair in his fist. "You're so perfect."

I can tell he's close now too.

"Let me ride you," I say, wanting to watch him come like he's watched me.

"Fuck, yes." He grins.

I straddle his legs and press my palms to his chest as I slide over his length and feel him harden the deeper he goes. His lips tilt up when I start moving my hips, and even though he's already worked my body into a blissful state, I give him everything I can. First, his hands are on my thighs, moving my hips faster, and then he rests them behind his head as I rock my body against his, desperate to feel him come undone.

"Christ, River…" he growls, his eyes closing as his head tilts back. "Fuck. Fuck. *Fuck*." He moans, grabbing the back of my legs again and squeezing them with all his strength as I feel him release inside me. The look on his face is pure fucking bliss, and I can't believe how hot he looks right now. He groans and curses, arching his hips deeper inside me as he continues chasing the high.

"Holy shit," I mutter, feeling an orgasm hit me unexpectedly. We ride the wave together as he pushes himself up and wraps his arms around my waist so he can press our mouths together. I welcome his lips on mine as we slowly come down. All that can be heard is our rapid breathing.

His hand on my cheek keeps us still, and we're both relaxed and completely sated. I feel his breaths against my lips while he presses our foreheads together. That was the most intense night of my life, and even though I know we're both only here on vacation to have fun, I can't help but think that's how sex is meant to be, and I've been missing out.

If that's the case, my expectations just doubled.

"You're really beautiful, you know that?" Alex whispers, breaking the silence.

"Thank you." I smile lightly as a blush surfaces. I don't know why him giving me a compliment after what we just did embarrasses me, but luckily, it's too dark for him to notice.

"I'm going to clean us up and get some water before one of us passes out from dehydration." He smirks, pressing his lips to mine before moving off the bed.

"Considering how much we drank tonight, it's actually possible considering seventy-five percent of Americans suffer from chronic dehydration and don't even know it." I lean back as he walks toward the bathroom, and I smack myself in the head. I am so lame.

His chuckles echo from the bathroom, and I want to die from embarrassment. Grabbing an oversized T-shirt, I slip it on and start fussing with my hair. It's a complete mess, but considering it's sex hair, I kind of don't mind.

When he returns, he's holding a cup of water and a towel for me. I thank him and gulp down the water before climbing into bed next to him. He eyes the old T-shirt and tells me to remove it because sleeping naked is the "best thing ever," and I'm too satisfied to argue, so I shrug it off and climb into bed next to him. Way too exhausted to analyze the fact that Alex is sleeping in bed next to me, I let him wrap me up in his arms and hold me until I fall asleep.

Oh. My. God.

It's the only words my brain forms as my eyes flutter open and my head begins to pound. I'm thirsty and desperate for a glass of water. The sun blares through the windows and patio door and announces it's morning. Groaning, I roll over, and the first thing I see is a bare muscular chest and that sexy V that leads to one of the happiest places on earth.

Oh. My. Fucking. God.

I blink hard to confirm I'm not dreaming, and when he rustles, I know I'm not.

The images of our drunken night together come in quick flashes, and that's when my mini freak-out happens because hooking up on vacation wasn't really on my things-to-do list. Even if Natalie was very persistent on it being the *only* thing on my list.

All my insecurities about men and dating come rushing through me, and I think *what the hell did I just do?*

Thinking back, I try to remember how this happened. He had me the moment our eyes met, and somehow, he's now asleep in my bed. The only things I can blame is the tequila, loneliness, and that deep Southern accent that's sexy as sin. What a dangerous combo. However, if I'm pointing fingers, then Natalie gets her fair share of the blame too, just for encouraging this.

I can't remember the last time I had a one-night stand but can definitely see why I haven't made it a habit. It's awkward as fuck. Do I continue lying with him and assume everything is fine or do I get the hell away before he can reject me first? As I'm contemplating my options, I realize we're in my hotel room, so escaping before he wakes isn't even a choice. Trying to stay calm, I close my eyes tight, hoping he'll disappear, and I won't have to make any decisions, but when I peel them back open, no such luck.

Knowing I can't lie here any longer while my mind races, I decide to jump in the shower with hopes that when I get out, he'll be gone. Surely, he's done the one-night stand thing before and he'll know that is his cue to leave.

However, as soon as I move, a large arm wraps around my bare waist and pulls me close. My eyes widen when his length presses hard on my back. When he smiles against my ear, I nearly melt into him, forgetting all the warning alarms that are going off in my head.

I'm not doing this. I can't do the pretend couple thing. Not after everything I've gone through in the past six months. I'd be stupid to let myself get attached again, even for only a week. All I can think is, *he has to go*. I need time to process my thoughts, process what happened, and where we go from here. Maybe I'm making this more complicated than it needs to be, but one-night stands are not in my repertoire. Somehow, I can hear Natalie's voice tell me that they are now, and I should just have unadulterated fun for the last week we're here.

"Good morning, beautiful," he whispers in a deep, rough drawl. All the little hairs on my neck stick up, and a shiver rushes through me. One night and my body responds to him like it's found its other half. Last night was good. No, it was fucking *amazing*, but that doesn't change anything. It can't.

Regardless, my body is heating up again just by the way he feels pressed against me. Stupid, traitorous body—betraying me again, like it did with Asshole.

His strong hand trails across my hip and stops on my stomach. I still and pretend I'm asleep, but he knows I'm not when my breath hitches at his contact. Soft lips kiss my neck, trailing across my shoulder and up toward my jawline. *Fuck.* My eyes flutter closed, but then I blink them open and realize I have to stop before his hand or mouth trails any lower. I turn my body and look up at him. Deep blue eyes stare seductively into mine, and I swallow hard, knowing what I have to do so I don't lead him on or give the wrong idea. Last night was fun, but that's all it can be now—a memory.

"I'm sorry, Alex." I sit up, pulling the sheet up to cover my bare breasts.

He smiles. "For what, darlin'? You have nothing to be sorry for. Not even for the way you screamed my name and buried your head in the pillow."

My eyes widen, a blush creeping up my neck and cheeks. "I think you should go," I tell him, keeping my composure, trying to make it less awkward than it already is.

Placing his hands behind his head, he takes me by surprise when he lets out a big hearty laugh. "Before breakfast? I could grab us some plates from the continental breakfast downstairs and bring it back up, so we can refuel." He flashes a wink as if to indicate refuel for round two, *or three.*

I purse my lips. "Umm, I don't think that's a good idea." I use a gentle voice to lessen the blow.

Alex sits up, and he's basically face-to-face with me. Smiling, he tucks loose strands of hairs behind my ear and rubs his thumb across my cheek before standing. "I'm in room 5513 if you change your mind, sweetheart." The confidence in his tone makes me think he doesn't really think I'm going to let him leave or he's pretending that being kicked out doesn't bother him.

My heart flutters, but I ignore it. Why does he have to be such a gentleman? Pushing him away and getting this reaction is making me feel guilty, but I'm not sure why.

As hard as it is, I can't take my eyes off his sexy ass as he walks across the room, buck naked. Confidence oozes from him as he grabs his clothes and puts them on.

Looking over his shoulder at me, he smiles. "Last chance to stop me." He winks, and it almost has me second-guessing my decision. I'm half-tempted to say the hell with it and pull him back into my bed, but I stay silent instead.

It's better this way. At least that's what I tell myself as he flashes another smile before leaving. As soon as the door closes, I lie back in bed and let out a long sigh. I lie there for a few moments, thinking over the events of last night and how Alex—basically a stranger—worked my body and made me feel so damn good. After a while, I peel myself out of bed, not wanting to waste the day. Refusing to let my thoughts get the best of me, I get up and walk to the shower. I turn on the hot water and step inside. My body is sore, and each time I move, I can feel exactly where Alex had been. He marked his territory, and as much as I don't want to admit it, it was some fucking good sex—okay, admittedly, it was the best sex I'd ever had. It's no secret the man knows his way around the bedroom.

As I'm washing my hair, I can feel how sore my arms and legs are. Jesus. The man was a savage.

The glass door of the shower fogs up, and I take that as my cue to get out. I grab a towel and wrap it around my body and take another one for my hair. As I walk toward my suitcase, I hear my phone vibrating on the nightstand. Picking it up, I see several texts from Natalie.

> NATALIE
>
> Seriously, you're not awake yet? It's 9am!

> NATALIE
>
> Is someone having Texas sausage for breakfast?

> NATALIE
>
> I'm dying over here. I need the deets!

> NATALIE
>
> I swear this is the last text I send, but I have to make sure you're alive. Adam is leaving to go fishing, and I need to drink away this hangover.

Her messages make me smile, even if telling her is going to be a whole debacle, and she's going to want intimate details. I check the time and realize it's been over an hour since she sent them.

As I finish towel drying my hair, I think back to the last time we got rid of our hangovers by drinking more. We were freshmen in college and went to our first frat party. The next morning, we woke up and drank shitty Bloody Marys until we couldn't taste the cheap vodka anymore. As I sit here with a pounding headache, it actually doesn't seem like such a bad idea.

> RIVER
>
> I'm alive. I think. Where are you?

Her text bubble instantly pops up.

NATALIE

Finally! I'm having brunch at the hotel restaurant.
Best eggs beni I've ever had. Come meet me!

RIVER

Order me the same. I'll be down in a sex.

RIVER

I mean *sec.

NATALIE

I know what you've got on the brain. ;)

Rolling my eyes at her last text, I lock my phone and grab my keycard before heading to the elevator. I'm halfway hoping I don't run into Alex, not after I all but pushed him out the door this morning. The guilt of how I acted is starting to build, but I have a good reason.

Once I step off the elevator and walk into the restaurant that overlooks the beach, I see Natalie. Her fiery red hair gleams in the sun, and as soon as she makes eye contact with me, she smirks.

"I think you're actually glowing—and *not* because of the sun," she says before taking a bite of her eggs.

"I don't want to talk about it," I tell her just as the waitress arrives with my plate of food.

She rolls her eyes at me. "You're no fun. When did you become such a prude?"

"Apparently, I'm *not* fun. I'm beginning to think there's something wrong with me."

"By the smug-ass look on your face, it seems like it. Did someone piss in your Cheerios this morning? Was it something he did? Was he an asshole toward you?" Her face is full of concern. "Do I need to kick his tight Texan ass to Kentucky?"

Her protective words make me grin, but I shake my head. "No, no. Nothing like that. The opposite actually. He was an absolute gentleman this morning, and I'm sure if he would've gone home with anyone other than myself last night, it would've continued on this morning. But instead, I asked him to leave."

Natalie's mouth falls open. "What?" she shrieks loudly, not realizing

95

how loud she's being when I shush her. "Why? Don't you know how vacation flings work? Did I forget to teach you that?"

I glare at her, not responding to that comment. I turn to my plate and take a few bites of my Eggs Benedict and the hollandaise sauce basically melts in my mouth. "Oh my God, Nat. You were right. This is to die for."

"Nope. No, I'm not going to let you change the subject on me like that. Not this time. I'm not falling for it," she states matter-of-factly.

Groaning, I knew I wouldn't be able to distract her for long. "Apparently not. Why don't you enlighten me?" My tone is laced with sarcasm that isn't lost on her.

"You're supposed to lock yourself in your room with Mr. Southern 'n Dirty, and you don't leave until your vagina falls off or your plane flies out. And sometimes the sex is so mind-blowing it's worth missing a flight. Trust me." She wiggles her eyebrows, making me smile. Being around Natalie helps me relax a bit, and I'm so grateful she's my best friend who knows what to say to help me out of my funk.

"I'll keep that in mind the next time I see my vag lying on the floor." I can barely get the words out before I burst into laughter.

"Seriously, though, Riv. Let loose for once. Let your hair down and give yourself permission to enjoy yourself. You've been taking care of people for almost your entire life. It's time for you to finally take care of River and just have fun. When we get back to the tundra, then you can go back to being guarded and uptight in your fancy scrubs." She flashes a teasing smile, but her tone softens at my reluctant facial expression before continuing. "Just promise me you'll try to have a good time the rest of the week." Natalie gives me a small smile, and I can't deny her when she's being this sincere.

"Okay, fine. I promise to *try*. Just for you," I tell her between bites of toast, hoping I can push away my reservations because I know she's right. I've put people first for as long as I can remember without really thinking about what I wanted.

"Good. Just remember, though, what happens in Key West stays in Key West." She winks.

And I honestly hope she's right.

CHAPTER NINE

Alex

Waking up with soft skin pressed against my chest and legs tangled with mine immediately makes me smile. Inhaling her scent, I press my lips to the flesh of her neck and whisper in her ear. Just as she turns over and I look at the beautiful woman lying next to me, her eyes flutter open.

At first, River smiles with almost drunken happiness, then as reality sets in, her brows furrow. Sitting up in bed with wide eyes, she pulls the sheet to cover her breasts. When I look at her, I think she might actually be in shock that I'm here. She glances at my chest, then looks up at me. "I think you should go."

Tilting my head, I search her face, waiting for some sort of smile or anything that gives her away, but nothing does. We both know she enjoyed last night just as much as I did, but when she keeps her serious stance, I take that as my cue to leave. The dream of her quickly turns into a nightmare as she acts confused by me. This is the same woman who nearly begged me to come back to her room last night, isn't it?

Standing, not giving a fuck that I'm naked, I search around for my clothes that are not-so-conveniently scattered around the room. I feel her watching me, and when I look over my shoulder to meet her eyes, blush hits her cheeks. Knowing I'm getting to her, even if it's just the slightest bit, is cute. It makes me want to kiss the fuck out of her, but if she wants to play hard to get, I'm game. A Bishop always gets what he wants, and I want—no —*need* more of her, especially after our night of pure ecstasy. And I know she secretly wants me too, even if she's not ready to admit it just yet.

Being together was more emotional than I could've ever expected, so I understand why she's pushing me away. While we were together, I found something I'd been missing with other hookups. Deeper feelings surfaced than I'd ever experienced before. From seeing her that first time at breakfast, to her coming to Dylan's rescue on the beach, to spending hours chatting and drinking together—it's already felt like more than any of my previous flings. In that short amount of time, we've built a connection that even I don't understand. It's frightening, but exhilarating all at the same time, and I'm ready to dive in head first to see where it goes. We have a week to experience each other to the fullest, and I'll be damned if I allow precious time to be wasted. Sometimes a person has to put their cards on the table, call the bluff, and make a bet, even if the odds are stacked against them. I have to know if this is just a stupid vacation fling or if there's potential for more between us. Our story could already be the lyrics to a stupid country song.

After I'm dressed, I give her a wink, taking one last long look at her— knowing deep down it won't be the last time we're together—before leaving. The connection we shared was almost too much. It's intoxicating and feels like it will completely swallow me whole or break me—I'm not sure which one it is yet. We may barely know each other, but something about her pulls me to her, like an invisible lasso. She's holding the rope and calling the shots.

Hunger takes over as soon as I leave her room, so I take the elevator down to the coffee shop in the hotel lobby and grab a few muffins and a giant coffee to take back to my room.

To know I've actually been snubbed is a strange sensation. Not often has that happened to me; actually, I don't think it ever has. I'm usually the one pushing girls out of my bed in the morning, and oddly enough, it makes me want her that much more. The chase makes it that much more interesting and fun, as crazy as that sounds. For a moment, I slightly understand Crazy Carly then try to forget the stupid thought as I ride the elevator to my floor.

Before I slide my keycard, I pound on the door like I'm the police and wait for some sort of noise on the other side. Since there's no answer, I assume the coast is clear and enter.

"Fuck!" I shout. "It stinks like nasty sex in here." Just as the words leave my mouth, I see rustling in the bed, then Jessica's head pops up like a prairie dog.

"Howdy," I tell her, taking a bite of my blueberry muffin, feeling slightly bad for being an asshole. As I chew the dry ass muffin, all I can think is how much better Mama's are. Even my sister, Courtney, could put these nasty bricks to shame. In Key West, the biggest disappointment is the cooking.

Dylan groans and pulls the blanket from over his head, giving me a death glare. "Go away!"

"No, sir. The night's over. Time to get up. It's nearly ten in the morning. Going back to work is gonna be a bitch if you keep sleepin' in late," I tell him matter-of-factly, turning my back as Jessica tries to slyly slip on her clothes without revealing too much. Poor girl has to take the walk of shame, and the look of it is all over her face. It's always easier to sneak out before the other person wakes, that's one-night stand basics, but even I didn't follow the basics this morning. As I take the last bite of the first muffin, I hear lips sucking and smacking each other and groan.

"Get a room," I say with a laugh.

"I've got one!" Dylan throws a pillow my way.

"Get *another* room," I correct myself, just as Jessica walks around the bed to grab her purse.

"Bye, Alex," she says as she sashays toward the door, blowing Dylan a final kiss before she leaves.

Just as she walks out, I turn and look at Dylan. "You're dirty as fuck."

He sits up in bed, rubbing his face. "I know. What was I thinking?"

"You weren't. I don't remember her looking quite like that last night." I try to think back, but honestly, the only thing on my mind right now is River. Her body against mine. The way she tastes. She's like a poisoned apple and has already made her way through my veins. I can't stop thinking about her, and it's been less than an hour since I left. Goddammit.

"Beer goggles. Those sneaky bastards will make a two a ten. You'd think I'd learn my lesson by now," Dylan says with a grunt. "No wonder Liam was so willing to push her off on me."

"No regrets, though. Right? I'm sure she's a nice girl." I bite into the last muffin, and when my stomach gurgles, I regret eating them, but finish it anyway because this hangover isn't going to cure itself.

"I swear, if you wouldn't have shown up, she may have never left. Which is okay, I guess. But to me, she seems like a psycho. You know the phrase: a freak in the sheets? Well, that's her times ten. I'm not gonna go into detail, but if for some reason I go missing and don't make it back to Texas, she's suspect one."

"Damn, dude," I say with a laugh, but he looks at me a little too seriously for my liking.

"I need a shower." He doesn't even wait for me to reply as he walks into the bathroom—bare ass and all—and shuts the door.

After he's showered, Dylan decides he needs to eat. I'm so full of sugar the thought grosses me out, but I go anyway, secretly hoping I run into River.

"Gonna tell me what happened last night?" Dylan asks with a shit-eating grin on his face as we leave the hotel and walk down the sidewalk.

"Nah. I'm good."

He punches me in the arm, and I'm half-tempted to punch his ass back.

"So you found your girl, and she turned out to be a psycho, too?" Dylan leads us into a burger joint a few blocks away. Every blonde I see in the distance makes my heart race, but it's never her.

"No. She's not a psycho. She's actually pretty fucking perfect. Maybe a bit guarded, but perfect nonetheless. And that's where the problem lies."

Dylan orders himself a double cheeseburger, and we sit at a huge window that overlooks the beach. I stare out, watching people walk up and down the white sand having a good time.

"Because Cowboy Prince Charming found his Princess Cowgirl and all she left was her boot on the stairs at midnight?"

"No wonder you're single," I tell him, stealing a fry from his plate, hoping to change the subject.

"I have little sisters. Give me a break. Disney and princess shit is something I've had to deal with for years. So I guess things didn't go as planned, then?"

I give him a look that tells him he's right.

"This just keeps gettin' better and better." He continues eating, not taking his eyes from me, waiting for me to spill the beans.

"Or worse," I correct. "After one of the best nights of my life, I was kicked to the curb like a stray dog," I finally tell him.

Dylan laughs so hard I'm concerned I might have to give him the Heimlich. I'm beginning to think he's a serious liability on the island. After he catches his breath, he shakes his head.

"I've always heard that *Karma's a Bitch*, but now I might actually believe it. Alex Bishop has finally met his match. Perfect. Can't wait to watch how this plays out."

"You're a dick," I mutter as he cleans his plate. "A nasty dick at that."

"I learned everything I know from you," he says as he stands to dump his tray in the trash.

I let out a laugh. "So what you're saying is I've created a monster. *Great.*"

Most of the day passes, and we spend it exploring other parts of the island. I'm no fun because all I want to do is go back to the hotel, pound on River's door, and ask her if we can talk. The more I think about this morning, the more bothered I become. Call me a hypocrite because of my track record, but it all feels wrong.

Once we've basically explored every inch of the west side of the Keys, and I grabbed some tacos from a food truck, we decide to Uber back to the hotel. Just as I see the hotel in sight, my palms become sweaty and my heart races. I have to figure out exactly what I'm going to say to her because I *will* see her again.

"Apparently, there's a volleyball tournament on the beach tonight at six. Wanna go play?" Dylan asks.

"Do you think it's a good idea? I'm afraid you'll break something or hurt yourself." I joke with him, though I'm halfway serious.

"You only live once, right?" Dylan smirks as he thanks the driver and gets out of the car. We enter the hotel lobby and round the corner only to find Jessica waiting impatiently by the elevators with a big smile on her face. Dylan turns and looks at me with wide eyes, and all I can do is laugh.

"You chose it." I smirk, patting him on the back and giving an encouraging push toward her. I should be a good friend and save him, but I don't because it's funnier this way. He deserves it for all the shit talking he's done today, and at least, he'll have a good story to bring home.

"We actually have plans tonight." Dylan turns and looks at me.

"Nah, we don't." I give her a wink as his face turns blood red.

"See, that means we *can* do the boat tour and watch the sunset!" She shrieks in excitement.

When I make eye contact with Dylan, he whispers, *"I'm going to kill you,"* before he's whisked away to the beach for a romantic afternoon. He's too much of a gentleman to tell her no, and if he's learned everything from me, then I'll take that one as a compliment.

Considering I'm alone and the night is still young, I make my way through the lobby, past the pool, toward the cabana bar that overlooks the beach. I order a beer and stare out at the water as the sun begins to set in the distance. Chatter echoes from the pool, and I'm lost in my thoughts before I realize my name is being called in the distance.

Just as I turn, I recognize the voice.

Natalie.

"I'm really sorry my friend is such a sour puss," she says with a smile. She's alone, and her mouth is the color of the blue drink she's sipping. Drunk Natalie just might be my ticket to finding River.

I smile and pretend like I don't know what she's talking about, but I'm sure she already knows everything. I'm not the kinda guy who kisses and tells because some secrets are better left buried, and Mama raised a gentleman.

"I'm going to fix this, I promise," Natalie says before flashing me a wink as she stuffs her phone into her pocket and waves bye before I can ask any questions. Curiosity gets the best of me as I watch her walk away.

I don't know what she's up to, but I kinda like her style.

She's fierce with a side of no fucks given.

CHAPTER TEN

River

I feel completely relaxed after Natalie and I had massages this afternoon. The masseuse really worked out the kinks of having rough sex last night. Afterward, we parted ways, and I went up to my room where all I did for the next few hours was lounge around. I decided to read one of my romance books because someone should get a happily ever after on this vacation even if it's living vicariously through fictional characters.

About halfway through my book, I decide to take a nap, and it felt good to actually do nothing for a change. Instead of meeting Natalie and Adam for dinner, I decided to order room service and stay in, hoping to detox my mind and body of everything Mr. Southern 'n Dirty. Reading a steamy romance was probably not the smartest choice to help me forget about last night, but I don't think I could ever forget...even if I tried.

Once my food arrives, I sit up against the headboard and flick through the TV channels, inhaling my food in the process. I stop once I come across an old black-and-white western. Just the sound of the man's deep, gravelly voice has my mind back on that damn cowboy. I turn it off and finish my dinner in silence, but everything in my head goes back to him and the way he cherished my body. Gah! It's ridiculous.

The sound of a text has me shaking him out of my head, and after I grab it, I see it's from Natalie.

NATALIE

Meet me at the cabana bar past the pool ASAP. It's really important!

RIVER

On my way. Is everything okay?

My instincts take control as I slip on a sundress and flip-flops. I quickly pull my hair up into a messy ponytail before grabbing my keycard and phone. I can't help but wonder if there's something wrong. When she doesn't respond to my message, I grow more concerned. Did she and Adam get into a fight? Or worse, *did they break up*? Different scenarios flood my mind, and without another thought, I rush toward the cabana.

When I step outside, the warm breeze brushes across my skin, and I can't help but glance at the plum-colored sky as the dark orange sun falls below the horizon. Everything about this island is incredible, and I'm definitely going to miss seeing its beauty once I'm back home and surrounded by the cold and snow.

Music flows lightly through the crowd, and I immediately search for Natalie's red hair once I reach the pool area. People surround the bar, so I move closer to see if I can spot her on one of the stools. Worry consumes me when she's nowhere to be found. I glance over the nameless faces, and though I'm in a crowd of people, it doesn't stop me from seeing *him*. And when I do, he's looking directly at me.

For a moment, I contemplate turning around and pretending I didn't see him but find it hard once our eyes and bodies are locked together in a trance. It's as if we're the only people on this whole fucking island. My phone vibrates in my hand, breaking the tension, and when I glance down, I see it's another text from Natalie. I quickly unlock my phone, hoping everything is all right.

NATALIE

Don't hate me, but you needed a little push.
Love you!

I let out a hard sigh when I realize this was all a sham so I'd jump out of my comfy bed and come down here where she must've known Alex was waiting. I grind my teeth, already planning to give Natalie an earful when I see her tomorrow.

By the time I look up from my phone, Alex is gone. The glass he was drinking from now sits empty along with the vacant barstool. For a split second, I'm slightly disappointed that he left, but I know I shouldn't be. I'm half-tempted to text Natalie back and rub it in her face that her stupid plan didn't work after all.

Annoyed, I turn around and immediately bump into Alex who's now standing directly in front of me. The smell of him suffocates my senses—pure man mixed with the ocean breeze. My body remembers every single touch and kiss. Swallowing hard, it takes everything I have to look into his baby blue eyes and keep a straight face.

"Looking for someone?" he asks nonchalantly with a smirk on his face.

Inhaling a deep breath, I keep my composure. "Actually, I was meeting Natalie," I tell him, unable to move as if I'm glued to the ground. He actually laughs, which confirms my suspicions about this all being a setup. I narrow my eyes at him, and he shrugs unapologetically.

"Hmm. Doesn't look like she's here." He pretends to look around, then his eyes fall back on me.

Being this close to him forces heat to permeate through my body, and it feels as if hot flames are licking my skin from head to toe. Blinking and clearing my vision, I finally get a good look at him, and he smiles before taking my hand and leading me to the beach.

"Wait, what are you doing?" I ask, but I don't pull away.

He chuckles, not answering my question, and we walk pass the cabana until we're standing in white sand staring out at the water.

"We need to talk." He finally turns to me, and when I face him, he glides his hand along my cheekbone before brushing a loose strand of hair behind my ear.

Knowing this isn't a conversation I should have, I shake my head, dismissing him. My messy ponytail is loose and starts to fall out, and I quickly try to adjust it.

"Yes, ma'am," he drawls, adjusting his ball cap. "Don't be stubborn." He notices me fussing with my hair and pulls the band out of my fingers, causing it to fall around my face.

Opening my mouth to give him a piece of my mind, I barely get a word out before he palms my cheeks and his lips crash into mine. Soon, his fingers are threading through my hair, and I can't help the small moan that escapes. I feel as if I'm falling into a bottomless pit as our tongues twist together. The beach and sand and everything surrounding us melt away, and it's just us. By the time we break our embrace, we're both gasping for air, for some sort of relief. The intensity of the emotions behind his kiss is almost too much—too soon—and it makes me want to run and push him away. It's what I *should* do anyway. It's the smart thing to do, but when I meet his eyes again, I'm incapable.

"You were saying?" he asks against my mouth.

"Don't be a smartass." I can't help but smile and chuckle against his lips.

"Just felt like you needed a reminder of last night, ya know, in case you'd forgotten." He releases his hold on me but slides one hand down the length of my arm and threads my fingers with his.

"Uh, no. I actually have a *great* memory, so I don't forget much at all," I retort, remembering every inch of his hard, sweaty body against mine.

"Good to know. Well, I'll just come out and say it then. I had a real fucking good time last night, and I'm pretty sure you did, too. In fact, I know you did, several times. I'd hate for us to stop hanging out, because like I said, last night was a fuckin' good time. So if you plan to spend the rest of the week playing hard to get, I'd just like to know so I can make sure we're on the same page. Otherwise, we can go ahead and continue where we left off last night." He winks, brushing his fingers across my bare arms, causing goose bumps to cover my skin.

Swallowing hard, I try to steady my racing heartbeat. I should've known a guy like Alex Bishop wasn't going to let me off easy, especially with the way I kicked him out this morning.

"Trust me when I say I'm not the girl you want." I'm trying to convince him, or maybe myself, but either way, he doesn't let me continue. His finger reaches up and softly covers my mouth, stopping me.

"You don't know what I want, River." His voice is low and sincere, but his demeanor is serious as he searches my face. "And you're wrong."

All the words I wanted to say to him disappear with a single breath, and I'm left speechless. I'm insanely attracted to him, there's no doubting that, but the last time I allowed myself to get caught up in a guy is the very reason I'm here on this vacation—to escape the drama men seem to bring into my life.

"You can't deny there's something between us—a connection. I can't quite put my finger on it, but I felt it the first time I saw you, and if my instincts are right, you did too."

I nod in agreement but don't offer him anything else just yet.

"But if I go back to Texas knowing I didn't try my hardest with one of the prettiest and most stubborn women I've ever met, I'll live to regret it. And I'm sorry, darlin', but I don't like to regret anything in my life. So, as I said, we can go about this the hard way or the fun and easy way. I'm even willing to play all the games you want, but we're runnin' out of time here. So I'm going out on a limb and cutting to the chase." He tilts my chin, so our eyes are locked. "I haven't stopped thinking about you since that first time we met, so while we're both here, why don't we explore this connection we have?"

My heart beats rapidly in my chest, and I feel like I'm dreaming because his words are perfect—a tad *too* perfect. I'm tempted to pinch myself just to make sure I'm not. Being my typical logical and cynical self, I can't help but have questions and concerns. But just as I get ready to voice them, I dig deep and ask myself, *what do I have to lose?*

Nothing.

"Please say something, River," he demands.

"I'm sorry. It's just… I need a little bit of time to think about this. I've been burned before, and I can't just jump into your bed because you're good-looking and say all the right things at the right time with that damn accent. It's all confusing to me," I blurt out, needing to catch my breath. "It's like there needs to be rules or something, but how can there be rules when we only have days left of our vacation? Oh God. Now I'm rambling. I'm making this more difficult than it needs to be, aren't I? Like always. Spoiler alert?"

Alex cracks up, a sound I could actually get used to hearing.

"I like rules, sweetheart. How about this? I'll promise to always make sure you come first. When you beg to be fucked harder, I won't hesitate for a minute. But I'll also take you out because I'm not a complete asshole. I'd love to go out and explore the city together. No strings attached, just fun."

"Just fun?" I confirm, my brows rising.

He nods. "And to be fair, you haven't jumped into my bed...yet. But I can check my schedule for tonight." The smile on his face grows as the heat hits my cheeks.

Instinctively, I bite my bottom lip while last night replays in my mind. I could do *just fun*, right? I mean, I've never done casual before, but Alex sure makes it sound really good.

"I'm not asking for marriage here. Just a week together. Then we can go our separate ways and continue living our lives with only the memories we made. I can guarantee you'd enjoy making memories with me, darlin'. This sizzling tension between us is electric, and if we don't get each other out of our systems, we're both going to explode," he adds, just as a couple of drunk people stumble close to us on to the beach, invading our privacy.

"This fucking sand is so hard to walk in," the whiny girl complains as the guy she's with falls down laughing.

"Babe! Babe! Help me up. Dammit. I think there's sand in my underwear." The guy holds out his hand, but she's not strong enough to lift him and tumbles onto his chest. I hear lips smacking together and clothes rustling, and I turn my head away from them. I'm somewhat thankful for the interruption because my head is in overdrive right now.

"I think that's our cue to go," I tell him, stepping farther away from the couple.

"I'll walk you to your room." He wraps his arm around my waist, holding me close as we head toward the hotel. Just as we walk into the lobby, I see a brown-haired girl hanging off Dylan's arm, but he doesn't look happy about it.

"There you are." Dylan huffs. "I've been texting you because I forgot my keycard," he says to Alex.

"Sorry. I've been busy," Alex tells him, nodding toward me.

"Hey, River." Dylan acknowledges me with a smile and a head nod.

The woman looks me up and down, but then she smiles wide when she notices how close Alex and I are standing to each other. "Hi, I'm Jessica."

"River," I reply.

Alex hands Dylan the card, and we all ride the elevator together. I have to hold my laughter back when Dylan tells Jessica his head hurts and he's going to call it an early night. The elevator stops at their floor, and the two of them exit together, but I have a feeling she won't be staying long.

"Did he really just use the headache line?" I ask, laughing.

"Totally did, but she's persistent, so I wouldn't be surprised if she pulls some extra-strength Tylenol out of her purse then tries to ride him like a bull."

The elevator stops on my floor, and Alex walks me to my door. Before leaving, he places a soft kiss on my lips. "Think about it, okay?"

I smile and nod.

"Have a good night, River. Sweet dreams." He winks, leaving me breathless.

"Night." I scan my keycard, and once I'm inside, I lean against the door, my legs feeling like jelly as I slide down.

What the actual hell just happened?

My mind is racing, and I need to talk my thoughts out with someone. Pulling my phone from my pocket, I text Natalie and make sure to give her a dose of her own medicine.

RIVER

Nat. I'm back at my room. Can you meet me here? It's really important.

NATALIE

I'll be right there. Give me a few minutes.

I change back into my comfy clothes and sit on the edge of the bed. The room service menu is still open from when I ordered dinner earlier, and if I'm going to really think about Alex's offer, I'm going to need reinforcements. I decide to get the double chocolate cake I passed on before. After calling in my order, I lie flat on the bed and stare up at the ceiling, letting my mind wander to all kinds of places. Twenty minutes pass, and when I hear a knock on the door, I fly off the bed to answer it. However, I'm shocked when I see it's room service with my dessert instead of Natalie.

Sitting on the couch, I cross my legs, and before I can take a bite of the most heavenly chocolate cake I've ever seen, there's another knock on the door. Dammit, it better be Natalie this time. I open it, and she's standing there with a giant red drink, and I swear a whole pineapple is stuffed inside.

"What the hell? Did you have to crawl here or something? What took you so long?" I scold her before realizing how tipsy she is already.

"Sorry," she slurs, stepping inside the room. "Adam distracted me, and then I had to wait forever for my refill."

Shutting the door behind her, she follows me to the bed.

"I was about to send the search team out for you," I tease, deciding to let her off the hook.

"Is everything okay?" she asks, knowing damn well what she did to me earlier.

I give her a smile. "I'm fine. But you deserve a mouthful right now after setting me up like that."

Laughing, she sets down her drink on the nightstand, then grabs my plate and proceeds to eat my chocolate cake.

"A mouthful of what?" She wiggles her eyebrows and smirks.

"Ew, no!"

"What?" She swallows the bite of cake down. "I was talking about this delicious cake."

"Right." I roll my eyes.

"Okay, I'm sorry I set you up, but I saw Alex in the lobby earlier and could tell he was looking for you before he went to the cabana. Whatever you two have is so obvious, and I knew if he could get one more opportunity to talk to you, he could help you see it, too." She flashes a smile that tells me her plan was sincere, albeit manipulative. "Chemistry like that means the sex is bound to be out of this world," she adds.

"Well...you're right. I can't deny there's something there," I say honestly. "He laid it all out for me and said we should have fun and basically get each other out of our systems because we enjoyed being with each other," I explain to her, and the smile on her face grows wider.

"I like where this is going." She nods her approval.

"That's crazy though, right?" I ask, knowing I'm asking the wrong damn person right now. She's totally Team Alex. "I just keep second-guessing it and thinking how wrong it'll go."

"Oh, honey. Casual sex is healthy," she schools me. "In fact, you're a nurse. You should know that." She chuckles.

I roll my eyes but smile. "It's the emotional stuff I'm struggling with, especially after Asshole. How do I just turn that off?"

"You do it like you do everything. You've gathered all the facts, and you know the expectations and outcome, which means there'll be no surprises." Her words are convincing, even though I don't really need it. Being with Alex even for the week would be an experience of a lifetime. A very *fun* experience at that. "Hell, if I were single, and he was offering me no-strings-attached sex, I'd be naked the entire time and order room service between the sex marathon and sleep. In fact, the only time I'd see that beach is when my body was pressed up against that balcony window."

I burst out laughing, my head falling back as I take in her words. I can't deny how fucking great that all sounds.

"Let your inhibitions go, River. It's just sex. That's it. Fuck him out of *your* system, then go home and add the memories of it all to your rub club."

I think about her words and really let them sink in. "See, that's why I keep you around. You're blunt with no filter."

"I know! What would you do without me?" she asks, reaching for her drink and taking a sip.

"Have a full piece of cake left," I tease.

"You love me! So you know what you've got to do, right?"

I nod with a smile. "I think I do."

CHAPTER ELEVEN

Alex

DYLAN

We're going out to find a bar and go dancing.
Wanna join?

I shake my head at his dumb ass.

ALEX

Guess that headache went away quickly.

Taking the elevator back down to the lobby, I decide to grab a drink from the cabana until they're out of the room.

DYLAN

Fuck you. Beer will solve that.

ALEX

Beer Goggles. Good idea, man.

DYLAN

Yeah, whatever. You comin' or not?

ALEX

Nah. Gonna grab a drink by the pool. Go have fun with the future Mrs. Hart.

DYLAN

That's not even funny! Damn, I thought you gettin' laid would soften you up.

I blow out a breath of frustration.

ALEX

Text me if you're not coming back tonight so I don't worry she's kidnapped you.

DYLAN

Yeah, I will.

Finding a seat at the bar, I order my usual and watch the people around me. Looking out at the water, I think about all the stuff I still want to do on this trip—jet skiing, snorkeling, parasailing. Lord knows I'm not risking Dylan in the water again. I'd love to do them with River, but now I'm overanalyzing everything I said to her and wondering if I pushed too hard.

I've never had to convince a girl to be with me, but maybe that's why I'm so damn intrigued by her. She's more than just a chase, and I know it would only be for the week, but fuck if she hasn't consumed my mind since day one. But why wouldn't she? Beautiful, intelligent, compassionate about her work. She's the whole damn package.

And as long as I take my own advice and keep to the rules, what could possibly go wrong?

The sun has long set, but I walk down to the beach anyway. Lights from the hotel illuminate the beach just enough so I can see where I'm going. These views are stunning—something I'll sure miss. Sitting on the white sand, I find it so peaceful out here. Most of the tourists are barhopping by now, but some of the hotel guests are still partying by the pool.

I stare out at the water for almost an hour before finally getting up to head back to my room. Adjusting my cap, I spin around and gasp when I see River standing there.

"Hi," she says softly, tucking her hair behind her ears. She's not wearing the sundress she was earlier but seeing her in leggings and the oversized sweater is pretty freaking adorable.

"Hey." I take a step toward her. "What are you doing here?"

She blinks and lowers her eyes before looking up at me. She's nervous.

"I was looking for you."

Smiling wide, I reply, "Well, you found me."

She swallows before inhaling a deep breath. "I was thinking you could maybe help me out with something."

Confused, I furrow my brows and nod. "Sure."

My eyes are drawn to her lips as she licks them. "What you said has me thinking that this trip is really a once-in-a-lifetime vacation for me, mostly because I work a lot and don't travel much, but it's made me realize I should take full advantage of it while I can."

So far, I'm liking where this is going. "Okay?"

"So maybe you could help me accomplish a vacation bucket list?"

I tilt my head, encouraging her to continue.

"I've never had a one-night stand with a stranger I met on vacation, so I can mark that off."

"Glad to have helped." I chuckle.

"But maybe we could add more. Sex in a public place, skinny-dipping, sex on the beach, a threesome."

"A threesome?" My eyes widen, shocked.

"Kidding!" She laughs, her smile reaching her eyes. "Well, just about the threesome. Not about the other stuff."

Taking another step, I close the gap between us and cup her cheeks. "I'd be honored to help you fulfill a vacation bucket list, but on one condition."

"What's that?" Her big green eyes look up into mine, making me smile at how beautiful they are.

"I get to take you out. Sex with you is great, no doubt, but let's make the most of this bucket list. Let's go on adventures and experience as much as we can with each other. What do you think?"

"I think you have yourself a deal, cowboy."

Grinning, I pull her lips to mine and devour her mouth. I slip my tongue inside and kiss her the way I've wanted to all damn day.

I reach down and grab her hand, leading her off the beach.

"Where are we going?"

"About to mark an item off that list." I look over my shoulder and wink.

Luckily, there's a little convenience store near the hotel, and when we step inside, I lead us directly down the aisle where the condoms are stored.

"A twenty-four pack, really?" She chuckles when I grab the largest box.

I press her against my chest and lean my mouth down to her ear. "Darlin', I plan to fuck you against every possible surface, which means I need to stock up." I wink, and she blushes. After I pay, I lead her back toward the beach.

Since it's dark out and the hotel lights only hit certain areas on the sand, I look for a shady spot and walk us down to one of the empty lifeguard huts.

"Turn around," I order, unbuttoning my jeans. She wraps her hands around a post and looks over her shoulder at me.

Fingering her leggings and panties, I pull them down to her ankles. "From now on, dresses or skirts only."

She nods, grinning.

I grab a condom from the box and slide it over my erection that's been hard since the moment she agreed to this arrangement of ours. Aligning our bodies, I grip her hips and pull them toward me. Dipping my head down, I taste her neck and kiss along her jawline.

"Spread your legs, River," I growl, and she immediately obliges.

Grabbing my cock, I position it against her and thrust inside. Her head falls back against my shoulder as I pull out and push back inside deeper.

"Oh my God," she whimpers, her eyes sealing shut. I remind her to hold the post and keep her legs spread wide.

I wrap my hand around her throat, keeping her head tilted back so I can watch the pleasure on her face. It turns me the fuck on as I keep up the pace and fuck her hard.

"Christ, River," I growl in her ear. "You're so tight from this angle."

She moans, and I tighten my grip on her. The beach is empty, but the cabana bar isn't that far away. Luckily, the music will drown us out, but knowing anyone could see or hear us has me pounding into her deeper and faster.

"Shit, Alex," she groans, struggling to catch her breath. I can tell she's close, so I slide my hand down and rub circles on her clit.

"Come on my cock, baby. I wanna feel how tight that pussy gets," I encourage.

Within moments, her entire body is shaking as she rides out her climax. She tightens around my throbbing cock, making it impossible to hold back my own release.

"Fuck," I mutter against the flesh of her neck. "River."

We're both panting as we come down from the high, my cock still deep inside her.

"That was really fucking hot." She breaks the silence with a satisfied smile on her face.

"You have *no* idea," I tell her, pulling out to dispose of the condom.

I kiss her shoulder before spinning her around and taking her mouth.

"You feel way too good. At this rate, I'm not sure I'll ever get enough," I tell her honestly, which also scares the shit out of me. I've never felt like that before, but I don't allow myself to dwell on it now.

"You have seven days to give me your best, cowboy," she teases, licking her swollen lips. "Let's not put them to waste."

I all but haul River up to my room and text Dylan to stay the fuck out tonight before I'm slamming back into her sweet body. This time, she's bent over the chair that overlooks the beach. My hand is wrapped in her hair while I pound into her over and over again until she screams out my name.

I know I'll have dreams of her voice when I'm back home, but for now, I'm bottling it all up.

We fall asleep a tangle of arms and legs and wake the next morning when a loud knock disrupts us.

"I think Dylan wants his bed back," River says in a sleepy voice, laughing.

"Yeah, he's gonna be pissed knowing we fucked on it." I chuckle, tilting her chin up so I can give her a quick kiss before I look for my clothes.

"Hold the fuck on," I shout at his persistent knocking. I slip on my jeans before opening the door for him. "Are you on fire or something?"

He barges in within seconds, looking like he's just escaped prison.

"Jessica," he offers as I close the door. "She's like a vulture, yet I can't stop sleeping with her." He turns toward me, his face all flushed. "What the fuck is wrong with me?"

He starts undressing, but I clear my throat and nod my head over to River.

"Oh, shit." He pulls his jeans back up. "Hey, River."

She tightens her grip on the sheets pulled against her chest. "Hey, Dylan."

He turns toward me with a wicked grin plastered on his face. "Guess you had a good night after all."

"Sure the hell did." I slap a hand on his shoulder, giving him an obvious signal to get the hell out. "Go back to Jessica's room."

He shrugs my hand off and winces. "I swear to God, that girl has no off button."

"You like her," I tell him, knowing it's obvious. Dylan wouldn't screw around with a chick he didn't at least like a little. He's just not willing to admit it.

"I'm getting in the shower," he says, walking to the bathroom, dismissing my statement. He looks over his shoulder and adds, "And get the hell out of my bed, you motherfucker."

Grabbing some clothes, River and I head out and walk to her room where we can shower and get ready. Since we were so rudely awakened, we take advantage and mark another bucket item off her list—morning shower sex.

"Want to go parasailing today?" I ask over breakfast. Her friend, Natalie, is spending the day with her boyfriend, so I finally get River all to myself.

Her eyes light up as she talks around a mouthful of food. "Yes! I've been wanting to try it!"

Over the weekend, River and I do a handful of water activities as well as lounge on the beach and find new and fun places to have sex.

I can't deny how happy I am being around her and being able to experience all this new stuff with her. Not only is she willing to be spontaneous and adventurous with me, but she's also fun as hell. I love hearing her laugh and squeal with excitement when we try something different. She's also in great shape and keeps up with everything I throw at her.

By Tuesday morning, the strong realization that we only have days left haunts me. I push those thoughts away, not wanting to ruin the time we do have. We spent all morning in my bed, ordered room service and showered, then spent all afternoon in her bed. Dylan's still pretending he can't stand Jessica, yet we still switch rooms so they can have their privacy.

"We've successfully checked eleven things off the vacation bucket list," River tells me over dessert. We finally left her room and went to dinner.

"Oh yeah? What's left?" I ask, taking a bite of our strawberry cheesecake.

She looks up at me and grins mischievously. "Skinny-dipping."

Taking the final bite, I leave some cash on the table and grab her hand.

"What are you doing?" she whisper-shouts as I lead her through the restaurant and out the door.

"Condoms," I say, smiling at her over my shoulder.

Once we've restocked, I lead us to the beach. The sun has just set, and there's only a handful of people left lounging on the sand.

"Take off your clothes," I order.

She looks around, a blush rising to her cheeks. "Are you sure we won't get caught?"

I kick off my shoes, pull off my shirt then my shorts. "No." I smirk. "Hurry."

Quickly, she removes her sandals and sundress, standing in only her panties and bra.

"I'm nervous." She bites her lip, contemplating on removing the rest.

"It looks like you're wearing a swimsuit," I tell her, appreciating the way her undergarments hug the curves of her body. "But it's called skinny-dipping, not swimsuit-dipping."

She chuckles, looking over her shoulder once more.

"Want me to help?" I arch a brow.

I'm on my knees before she can respond and slide my fingers into her lacy panties. Luckily, we're near a palm tree and can use it as a shield for now.

"What are you doing?" she squeals when I slide a finger inside her.

"Helping you relax." Once her panties are removed, I spread her legs and press a flat tongue along her slit. She whimpers, fisting her hands in my hair as I coax an orgasm out of her. She doesn't disappoint and gives me exactly what I want. "That's it, baby."

I stand, wrapping an arm around her waist and pressing her to my chest. My hand cups her cheek, and I kiss her. "Ready now?"

Sated, she nods. I step back, giving her room to remove her bra. I remove the last of my clothing, my hat and boxers, and soon we're both standing naked.

"On three," I say, grabbing her hand and facing her. I start counting, and on three, we run from the edge of the beach all the way into the cool water. Hearing her laugh as we make our way is music to my ears. I love hearing her sweet laugh.

I wrap my arms around her waist, so we're chest to chest. Pressing my lips down to hers, I hold her face as I kiss the fuck out of her. My tongue slides inside, and when we walk deeper into the water, she wraps her legs around my waist making it easy to carry her.

"I'm going to miss this," she admits as our lips part briefly.

"What's that?" I coax, hoping she'll say what I'm thinking.

"The ocean and beach." She smiles looking up at me. "And you."

My lips twist up into a smirk, happy that she's enjoying our time together as much as I am. I bend down and kiss her once more. "Me too."

We swim farther into the water until it's to our chests and no one can tell we're naked.

"So how was your first skinny-dipping experience?"

"I'd give it an eight out of ten," she teases. After every new adventure we've done, I've asked her, and she'd rank it.

"What'd make it a ten?" I ask, moving us closer together.

She purses her lips as if she's thinking about it. I watch as she looks around, eyeing the beach to see if we're still alone.

I feel her hand slide down my stomach until she firmly grips my length in her palm. "River," I warn, knowing we don't have a condom way out here. She's going to get me all worked up without being able to do anything about it.

"Shh…" She shushes me with a devil grin. She steps closer before giving me a wink and sinking down into the water.

"What the hell?" I ask, though she can't hear me now. But it doesn't matter because the moment I feel her mouth wrapped around my cock, I know exactly what she's doing. The water is usually clear, but without the sunlight, I can only see the top of her head.

"Oh my God," I groan, arching my back and hips. "Fuck, River." I fist her hair in the water and help control her movements. She bobs her head up and down, sliding her tongue along the vein of my shaft. Who knew a blow job could feel this fucking good under water?

She stands up, slicking her hair back and catches her breath. Before I can say anything, she sinks back into the water, and I feel her stroke my dick between her breasts. *Oh, fucking hell.* The girl has great fucking tits, too. I only wish I could see the way she looks right now.

Switching between her mouth and breasts, she works me up so goddamn good, I know I can't hold back much longer. When she stands up to take another deep breath, I stop her and plant her back on her feet.

"We have to go. Right now." I grab her hand and lead us to our clothes.
"Why?"

I look at her over my shoulder, and she laughs as soon as she sees my pained expression.

"Got it," she says.

Once we're dressed, we waste no time and head straight to her room. Within seconds of entering, I have her flat on her back on the bed. I devour her pussy as she wraps her thighs around my neck. Fuck, I love the way she tastes. So damn sweet.

"Alex," she pleads, kneading her fingers into my arms as I insert two fingers inside her tight body. "More."

I love the way she begs for me. It encourages me to increase the pace until I feel her climax on my tongue, and when she does—I fucking lose it.

Ripping off my jeans, I grab her ankles and place them on top of my shoulders as I slam into her. She cries out as I thrust deeper and harder, and when I feel my own release building, I quickly pull out and stroke my cock till I come on her stomach.

"Shit," I mutter, as I collapse on the bed next to her.

"What?" She's panting, trying to catch her breath.

"I forgot to put on a condom." I face her, brushing my hand along her cheek. "I lose all control around you, River." Which is the damn truth. I know the deal we made and how this isn't anything more than a vacation fling, but that doesn't stop the swelling in my chest anytime I think about her.

She gives me a small smile, completely sated and relaxed. "Well, I'm on the pill and take it religiously," she tells me, easing my nerves "And after my last boyfriend cheated on me, I got myself checked out and was clean."

"I've always used a condom," I tell her. "I'm clean."

"Good, then we don't have anything to worry about." She smiles, looking up at the ceiling as her eyes flutter closed.

Once we're cleaned up and dressed, we lie in bed. "So what kind of dumbass would cheat on you?" We talked about some personal stuff, but mostly, we've treaded carefully. I think both knowing this is only a short-term thing, we've been trying to prevent getting too close. However, I can't imagine any guy stupid enough to cheat on a girl like River.

She groans, biting her lip. "Technically, I was the mistress."

My brows shoot up. "Wow."

"Yeah, I know. Then once I left him, he banged my roommate."

"You're kidding." I couldn't believe the audacity.

"I wish. He completely blindsided me. Split personalities or something, because I didn't see it coming."

"Which I bet made it that much harder when you found out, huh?" I hold her tighter, pissed that any guy would put her through that much pain.

"Oh, yeah. Hence this trip." She sighs.

"I'm sorry."

"Don't be. It's not your fault." Shrugging, she snuggles closer to my chest and wraps her arm around me.

"Well, I'm sorry it happened to you. Send him my way, and I'll give him a genuine Texas ass kicking." I grin, though I'm serious. Assholes like him deserve it.

"He's not worth it," she says, confidently. Her strength is admirable, but I hate to think how he made her feel.

"I'm going to think of it as a blessing," I tell her, matter-of-factly. She looks up at me puzzled. "His stupidity led you to me." I tuck a piece of wild hair behind her ear. "You wouldn't be here if it weren't for him."

She nods. "You're right." Smiling, she holds her fist up as if she's making a pretend toast. "To Asshole: for being a cheating dirtbag and putting me in the arms of the sweetest and sexiest cowboy I've ever laid eyes on!" I hold a fist up to hers, and we bump them together.

"Good riddance, Asshole!" I wrap my arm around her body and press my weight on top of her.

Giggling, she gazes up into my eyes. "I couldn't think of a better way to celebrate."

CHAPTER TWELVE

River

Natalie and I are having mimosas at the hotel restaurant Friday morning when Alex approaches our table. He presses a kiss to my cheek before taking the chair next to me.

"Good mornin', ladies," he says, taking off his ball cap and setting it down. I have a feeling he does that a lot back home with his cowboy hats. He's always a proper gentleman, making sure my needs are met before his, and being super polite—yet not too polite in the bedroom.

Too bad there's none of that Southern charm in Wisconsin.

"Morning!" Natalie beams, the smile on her face gives away what she's thinking. We've barely seen each other since the weekend, but as she's said over and over, she more than understands.

"Where's Dylan?" I ask when he doesn't take the other chair like I expected.

"Buried in Jessica probably."

I laugh, knowing he's more than likely right. We've hardly seen Dylan either, not that Alex seems to even mind.

The waitress comes over and takes our orders. Adam left early for one last fishing trip since he and Natalie fly out tomorrow night. My flight isn't until Sunday, giving me only one more night with Alex since he and Dylan leave Saturday afternoon.

The past few days, we've explored more of Key West, checking more items off my vacation bucket list—or rather adding items so we could check them off—and the more time we spend together, the harder it's going to be to leave him.

"I can't believe I have to go back to work on Monday," Natalie whines. "Maybe I could convince Adam to move down here instead. I'm sure they could use a radiologist at the hospital or something." Her tone is serious, though I know she'd never leave her family.

"Doubtful." I chuckle. "He's too much a country boy. He'd miss his ice fishing and snowboarding."

Her shoulders fall. "Damn. A girl could get used to this beach lifestyle."

I grin, agreeing. "It's definitely going to be hard going back to twelve-hour shifts after this."

"Damn, you work long hours," Alex states. "I'm usually up around four or five a.m. to feed the animals before starting on the day's chores, but Dylan and I fuck around most of the time." He chuckles, and I have a feeling he's being humble about how hard he actually works.

"Twelve hours minimum," I add. "Then sometimes I don't even get a break until the end of my shift, which means my feet are swollen and I look like I've just ran a marathon."

"That's intense," he says, studying my features.

"I'm sure you're used to those long hours, too," I say. "Don't ranchers work till the late afternoon or something?"

"Oh, yeah. It just depends. Every week can be different, especially at the Bishop ranch. My older brothers, Jackson and John, live on the ranch, too, so we're supposed to split up the duties."

"I can't even imagine living on a ranch," Natalie blurts out. "Being constantly dirty and smelly and oh my God, the heat. That's a double hell no from me."

Alex chuckles. "You city girls."

I grin, not denying he's right. I love my job, and at least I get to work indoors.

Moments later, our food arrives, and we dig in. Alex talks more about the family ranch and his brothers. It's very family-oriented, which actually sounds nice. But there's no denying we're from two completely different worlds.

"So you've talked about different aspects of your job, but I don't think you told me what made you want to become a nurse in the first place," Alex says, curiously, and though his question isn't out of line, it does come a little unexpected.

Natalie lifts her face right away to watch my expression and waits to see if I need an out. I don't let her give me one, and even though talking about Rylie never gets easier, I don't avoid it either. Hiding what happened to my baby sister won't change the past.

"I ended up spending a lot of time in hospitals when I was eleven or twelve. As sad as it sounds, it became my second home for a few years. I met a lot of nurses and doctors and started learning more and more about it as I got older," I begin.

"Were you sick?" His brows squeeze together.

"No, I wasn't." I swallow, lowering my eyes before looking back up. "My baby sister, Rylie, had leukemia, and after she was diagnosed, I didn't leave her side. Every doctor appointment, ER visit, or chemo treatment—I stood next to her because I didn't want her to be alone."

"Oh my God, River. I'm so sorry." He reaches over and squeezes my hand. The tears surface, but I blink them away.

"It was horrible," I admit. "I watched her deteriorate and become a lifeless version of herself."

"Is she okay now?" he asks, and even though I anticipated that question, it does nothing to my aching heart.

I try to find the right words as I respond. "No. When I was fourteen, she ended up in the ER for the millionth time and contracted an infection that took a turn for the worst. She became septic, and her organs rapidly shut down."

"She didn't make it," he says softly, his voice somber. He closes his eyes.

I cover his hand and squeeze three times. He couldn't have known, and I know he feels bad now for bringing it up.

"Alex," I whisper, and he opens his eyes.

"I'm sorry."

"It's okay," I tell him. "I like talking about Rylie, even when it's sad."

He wraps his arms around my shoulders and pulls me close. "You became a pediatric nurse because of her."

"Yeah. I knew I wanted to be around children, and as weird as it sounds, it makes me feel closer to her. I want to do good by her, make her proud."

"By the sounds of it, I'd say she'd be very proud." His smile is genuine.

We turn our heads, putting our attention on Natalie who's staring dreamily at us with tear-filled eyes. "I'm not crying." She wipes her cheeks.

I laugh through my own tears. "Me either."

"Me either," Alex says in a thick voice, making Natalie and I both laugh.

We finish our breakfast and part ways with Natalie so she can start packing.

"So…" Alex begins as we walk hand in hand along the beach.

"Yeah?"

"What do you want to do for our last night here?"

I was hoping he wouldn't bring it up actually and that we would just continue the way we've been without saying it aloud that he leaves tomorrow.

"I'm not sure. Do you have any ideas?"

"I do, but I'm not sure if you'll approve or not."

I give him a side glance. "Why? Is it some weird kinky shit that's going to have me tied up with a gag?"

He narrows his eyes at me, almost scared. "What kind of romance books are you into?"

I chuckle.

"I guess it's a little more than just our casual sex agreement. But I figure I'd risk it anyway because what's the worst that can happen? Not like you can call it off now." He smirks when I look up at him and winks.

"So what you're saying is it's a romantic gesture?"

"Yeah, I would say so, but I saw the ad for it and think you'd really enjoy it. One last vacation bucket list item to check off." He stops and turns so we're face to face now. "Whaddya say?"

Smiling up at his hopeful face, I couldn't deny him even if I tried. "Lay it on me, cowboy."

Alex and I spent the afternoon in my bed, both of us wanting to memorize every inch of each other. I love his rough and bossy side, but I also really like his sweet and passionate side too. Alex makes love as good as he fucks.

Later that night, he tells me to get dressed because he's taking me out for dinner. We end up at a nice steakhouse where he orders us wine, and we talk about anything and everything.

Once dinner is over, we travel to another part of the island, and in the distance, I can see exactly where he's taking me.

"A hot air balloon?" I exclaim, my smile widening from ear to ear.

"Yeah, you ever been on one?"

"Hell, no! Oh my God! This is so exciting!" I wrap my arms around his shoulder and tightly hug him. "It's perfect," I tell him. *The perfect way to say goodbye,* I think to myself.

"I was hoping you'd say that." He grins against my lips.

As soon as we're inside the bucket, the instructor talks a little about what to expect. I'm so giddy, I mostly tune him out. Before long, we're floating toward the clouds.

The view is incredible as I look out with Alex's arms wrapped around my waist. His chest is pressed against my back as he holds me, and it's the most romantic thing I've ever experienced.

"The sunset is amazing," I say when he rests his chin on my head. "No view will ever be able to compare now."

He dips his face and buries it in my hair, inhaling the scent of my shampoo. His lips linger down to my ear where he presses kisses along my neck. "Agreed," he says, though he's not looking at the sky.

He's looking at me.

The hour ride is over too soon. I'm dreading the descent because we'll be back on land where time exists. Up in the balloon, we floated above the horizon, over the beaches and water, and it was as if time stood still.

"Thank you," I tell him as he holds my hand and leads me back to the hotel. "Definitely my favorite on the list."

"Even more than patio sex?" His brows rise, teasingly. A couple nights ago, Alex turned into a caveman and pressed my body up against the patio glass door and took me from behind. And if that wasn't the hottest damn thing ever, he then opened the door and bent me over the railing. I could see people down at the pool below us, and the fact that any of them could look up and see us had me hot all over.

I chuckle and shrug. "Okay, I guess it's a tie then."

He brings our hands up to his mouth and kisses my knuckles. "I can deal with that." He winks.

When we're finally in my room, the mood is somber, both of us knowing what's to come tomorrow. Neither of us want to bring it up again, and the tension is thick in the air. It's obvious this week together turned into much more than just a fling, but that doesn't mean anything can change once we leave. We aren't from the same worlds, and another broken heart would be inevitable at that point.

Nerves take over my body, and Alex can sense my apprehension.

"River." His voice is deep and thick with emotion. I look up at him and see it in his eyes. He's sad, too.

"Yes?"

Wrapping his hand possessively around my neck, he brings his mouth down to mine and slowly kisses me. He takes the time to really explore my mouth and savor the taste. I cling to him, gripping my fingers in his shirt and holding him to my body. We mold together effortlessly.

"I'm going to miss you," he says, breaking the kiss. He rests his forehead against mine, and the deep breathing between us is all that can be heard as he waits for my response.

Swallowing, I do my best to keep my emotions at bay. "You're supposed to be the strong one," I tease, choking back tears.

He flashes a small, gentle smile. "Let's not waste our last night together being sad, okay?"

I nod against his forehead. "Okay."

Slowly, he strips me of my clothes. His movements are calculated but not rushed. Taking his time, he studies everything about me, placing it all into his memory. He kisses my neck before moving down to my shoulder and collarbone. My head falls back as I welcome his mouth on me, burning his touch into my skin.

Alex roams his hands around my waist and pulls me close. I grab his shirt, needing to feel his skin on mine. Pulling it over his head, he doesn't waste a second before crushing his mouth back down. Our bodies mold together, hunger and desperation taking over our senses.

I wrestle with his belt and undo his jeans. A throaty moan escapes his lips when I pull his boxer shorts down and palm his cock. I want to memorize everything about him—the feel of his skin, the length of his hardness, the way his lips burn into my neck. It's perfection.

Alex makes me feel like the only girl in the entire world, and I've never felt like that before. I know what we have is based on variables—being on vacation with limited time, meeting a sexy stranger, and knowing that whatever happens can only happen *here*—but that doesn't mean I haven't let thoughts of *what-if* escape me.

We were, in fact, slow dancing in a burning room.

It's only a matter of hours before we leave everything we shared behind.

I push all those thoughts away, not wanting to think about it. Not tonight, anyway.

Moaning at the way his mouth devours mine, I absolutely love it when he palms my cheeks as if I'm the most precious and important thing to him —at this moment, at least. After he removes the rest of his clothes, he pushes us to the bed, and I adjust my body till we're lying in the middle of the mattress and his body towers over mine. Though I've seen his naked body all week, I'll never get tired of looking at him. He's rock solid all over, has one small tattoo on his chest, and a small happy trail that leads all the way down to his glorious cock. Both of his ears are pierced, and with his blond hair and blue eyes, he's the very definition of a Southern playboy. Always the smooth talker with his dirty words, yet he's charming and polite. Everything about Alex Bishop screams perfection, and I've been the fortunate one to have his complete and undivided attention during this trip —something I sense many other women don't get from him.

Even though it feels like it's been a real-life fantasy, no one can ever take this week from me. It's one I'll hold in my heart forever, and once we leave this place, that's where it'll stay stored.

"River…" his deep voice murmurs against my lips.

"Mm?"

"You're so beautiful," he tells me—something he's told me often, but not always believed.

I peel open my eyes and see him looking down at me with a small, crooked smile.

"You are too."

His fingers brush over my lips softly, and when my breath hitches, he paints my mouth with his. Alex continues to devour me all night long, taking his time and building me up over and over again.

I've left scratch marks all over his back and arms, no doubt. His teeth and lips have left bruises—the good kind—over my neck, shoulders, and chest. I love feeling the scrape of his teeth along my back when he takes me from behind as if he can't get enough of my skin against his.

He takes me slow, pushing inside me with firm thrusts, but doesn't rush. Building me up ever so slowly yet pounding into me deeper as I ride out my orgasm. His fingers lace with mine as he brings my arms over my head and chases his release. As my thighs wrap around his waist, I dig my heels into his ass and push him inside deeper. His face twists as he howls out a guttural moan, his entire body tightening as he comes. It's the most beautiful thing I've ever seen, and now that I have the vision of Alex coming permanently etched into my memory, I don't know that anything could ever come close to topping it.

Afterward, he always rubs his palm along my chest and stomach. He massages my breasts, flicking and sucking on my nipples, and runs his fingers along my hipbones. Tonight, he doesn't disappoint, but rather, he holds me tight to his chest and rests his palm on my racing heart as if he's storing the beats of it to his mind.

Later, we take a shower together, and he pins me to the wall and kisses every inch of my body. The way he cherishes me is something I know I'll miss.

Once we're fully satisfied and back in bed, he keeps me wrapped in his arms and legs and holds me there until morning.

"Alex?" I whisper, wondering if he's awake or not. His breathing has picked up, but he hasn't moved.

"Hm?" he finally groans.

"What time does your plane leave?" I cringe at the words, but I know if he doesn't get up, he'll more than likely miss it.

"Whenever I get there."

I chuckle at his arrogance. "Oh, you must be a personal friend of the pilot."

"Yep." He rolls me over, and I see a cocky grin on his face.

"Have you packed yet?"

"Nope." His eyes aren't fully open, but he doesn't seem to be worried about it.

"Has Dylan?" I furrow my brows, wondering how the hell these two guys even made it here in the first place.

He yawns, stretching his arms over his head. "No idea."

I purse my lips together, narrowing my eyes. "Okay, well do we have time for breakfast? Or do you want help packing?"

"Oh, there's always time for breakfast." The corner of his lips curls up into a mischievous grin, and it takes me a second to realize what he's doing when he pulls the covers back and kneels between my legs.

"What are—"

He wraps my thighs around his neck as he digs his fingers into my ass and presses his mouth between my legs.

"Alex!" I squeal and laugh, then moan and scream because he licks and sucks, circling my clit with his tongue, and then presses a finger inside as the orgasm builds and releases around him.

"Sorry, darlin'." He winks, licking his lower lip. "They do say breakfast is the most important meal of the day."

Once I convince him to get up and dressed, I walk with him down to his room. As soon as we walk in, it looks like a bomb went off. Clothes, bedsheets, shoes, towels, food, and room service trays are spread out all over the floor.

"Dylan, you sick fucker."

I chuckle when I see girl's clothes spread all over the floor, and the air reeks of sweaty sex.

"Go away." We hear his mumbles from the patio.

"Ah, shit," Alex groans, rubbing a hand along his scruffy jawline.

"Hey, Dylan," I call out, making sure he knows I'm in here, too.

"He looks in rough shape," I whisper, making sure only Alex can hear me.

"Yeah, he doesn't do goodbye very well."

I pull in my lips. *That makes two of us.*

"You want me to leave you guys alone to pack and…maybe throw him in the shower?"

He wraps a hand around my waist and pulls me into his side, kissing the top of my head. "We have to leave at three to make our flight." He checks the time on his phone. "Come back at one?"

"Sure, that'll give me time to start packing my own shit." I tilt my head up and kiss him.

When I shut his door behind me, realization hits that it's the final time I'll be in there.

I text Natalie and tell her I'm heading over. She also leaves this afternoon, so I figure I'll keep myself busy for the next couple of hours by helping her pack.

"Oh, River." She frowns the second she sees me. I step inside and wipe my eyes.

"What?"

"I hate that we're leaving, but I hate even more knowing you and Alex are going your separate ways."

I hear the shower running and know we have a few moments of privacy till Adam is done.

Shrugging, I sit on the edge of the bed. "We both knew what we were getting into. One week, no strings or attachments, no expectations."

"Even I know that's a bunch of bullshit," she blurts out.

"This was your idea, Nat," I remind her, eyeing her.

"I know, but I didn't know he'd turn around and be Mr. Perfect."

"It's because we're on an island, sipping margaritas, and living on the beach. That's not real life," I say, trying to convince myself more than her. "Even if we lived on the same planet, you know the moment we'd get back home, shit would hit the fan. It always does."

"You sound so cynical," she spats.

I arch a brow, knowing I have every right to be. Shrugging, I play it off because I don't want to talk about it anymore.

"Did you two have a nice night together at least?"

I smile, thinking about it. "Yeah, we really did. It was a great way to say goodbye." I look up at the ceiling, knowing if I see her face right now, it's going to make me an emotional wreck.

"Are you going to exchange numbers?" she asks, drawing my eyes back to her.

"No, that's part of the 'no strings and casual sex' agreement. Why draw something out that's only doomed to fail? I'd rather take all these great memories and hold onto them than taint them with trying to make it work. Because let's be honest, we live hundreds of miles apart, and I doubt we could 'just be friends' after a week like this."

"That just makes me so sad, River. I wanted you to come here and have no-attachments sex, but I hadn't expected the guy to be...well, Alex."

"Yeah, damn those Southern cowboys," I mock. "All charming, sweet, and polite."

"And in bed?" She wiggles her brows.

"Definitely not polite." I smirk. "Always the gentleman, though."

After I help Natalie and Adam pack, we say our goodbyes. They're going to grab lunch before heading to the airport, so once they're off, I head back to Alex's room.

When I walk down the hall of his floor, I see his door is propped open, and when I get closer, I see it's housekeeping.

I look around for him or Dylan, but when I step in, a woman is stripping the beds.

"Hello," I say, shyly. "Are the two guys who stayed in here around, do you know?" I feel silly for asking, but I have no idea where else they'd be.

"No, ma'am."

"Okay, thank you."

Where the hell would he be? He knew I was coming back.

Swallowing, I walk out and head up to my floor. Once I'm at my room, I see a piece of paper taped to my door with my name written on it. I open it up and see it's the scratch paper we used to write out my vacation bucket list. After deciding that we were going to follow one, Alex and I had handwritten one out. He must've had it in his pocket.

River,

We got a notification that our flight was canceled, and the only flight available back to San Angelo was right now or we'd have to wait till Monday. We had no choice but to take this one, and I'm so sorry I have to leave like this. I looked in the lobby and around the bar, before coming back to your room to double-check if you were here. But we have to go now.

I don't want this to be the way we say goodbye, so please call me. (325-555-2539).

Love, Alex

P.S. For what it's worth, you were much more than a no-strings-attached-vacation-hookup. You made these last two weeks memorable in every sense of the word, and I'll never forget it.

Oh my God.

My feet feel frozen to the floor as I scan the note again. *He's gone.*

I feel my heart racing, and I blink out of my trance before running back to the elevator. Maybe he's still down there. I have to at least look.

Searching the lobby, pool, and bar area, it's confirmed. He's gone.

Go to the airport, a thought pops into my head. And for a second, I consider it, but then push it away. Calling him and hearing his voice or seeing him one last time isn't going to change anything. In fact, it'll only make things worse. Saying goodbye wasn't going to be easy in the first place, so maybe this is the way it had to be.

As I walk back to my room, thoughts of last night surface and how wonderful and magical it all was. Those are the memories I want to remember. Like I told Natalie, *that* was the perfect way to say goodbye. Anything else would only deepen the wound.

Part
Two

CHAPTER THIRTEEN

Alex

THREE MONTHS LATER

The rain won't stop coming, and by the looks of the forecast, the rest of the week will be exactly like today. I'm cold, wet, and miserable, and no amount of rain gear helps me stay dry. By the time Dylan and I break for lunch, we're soaked from head to toe.

"This fucking sucks," Dylan complains as we slosh through the mud toward the truck. Once we're inside, the rain pounds so hard against the windshield, I can't see shit. I put the truck in reverse, and the wheels do nothing but spin. No amount of pressing the gas pedal is getting us unstuck at this point. I look over at Dylan, and he's pinching the bridge of his nose.

"Guess we're walking back to the house. Dammit," I hiss between gritted teeth.

I keep the truck running and try to warm up my frozen hands.

"Let's call Jackson to come get us in the Jeep. It has 4-wheel drive at least, and we won't have to walk over a mile in this crap. It's cold as hell out there."

"Good idea," I say, grabbing my phone from my pocket. Jackson's probably doing nothing right now anyway, so I don't even feel guilty bothering him. During the day, he usually trains horses and takes guests trail riding, among other things. When the weather is shit like this, he doesn't really have much to do.

ALEX

Hey, the truck is stuck and we need a ride back. Can you give us a lift?

JACKSON

Busy.

ALEX

Don't be an asshole. We're stuck at the barn in mud to our fucking knees.

Just as I'm about ready to call John, he texts me back to let me know he's on the way. Bastard just likes to make me sweat.

"He's coming. Thought he was gonna let us deal with this shit on our own," I tell Dylan, shoving my phone back into my pocket.

"If he did that to us, I'd kick his ass. Or tell your mama. I think the latter would be worse, though. Mrs. Bishop's wrath is frightening as fuck!"

Chuckling while agreeing, I lean my head against the seat and watch the rain slide down the windshield. It's a nice distraction but doesn't keep my mind from wandering.

It's been three months since Key West, and I haven't been able to forget the time I spent with River. At the oddest moments, I'll think about her and wonder what she's doing. I'll relive our last day together over and over, wondering why she never called me. I knew the deal and that it was just supposed to be a vacation hookup, but I hadn't expected her to bulldoze into my heart the way she did. It hadn't been like anything I'd ever experienced before and knowing she chose to end things the way she did has me obsessing over every little detail.

If I dig deep, I can almost smell her shampoo or hear her laugh. My heart aches when I think about how she really left everything we shared back on that island. I could've sworn there was something more between us than just the physical stuff. I felt it and know she did too, whether or not she wants to admit it. Hands down, I would've taken a million-dollar bet that she would've called me as soon as she read my note. To her, we were nothing but two lonely strangers and a vacation bucket list.

"You're thinking about her again, aren't you?" Dylan smirks, giving me shit like he has almost every day since the plane landed in Texas.

"Something like that," I groan. When I talk about her, it makes all the memories I've buried over the last few months rise to the surface. How the hell did I end up in this state of mind? Women don't usually affect me like this. But River was different. She was a bad girl pretending to be good, a thief who stole my heart without warning. The intentions of giving it back never existed, and what makes it worse is I never saw it coming. I never saw *her* coming. Being completely blindsided by the memory of her soft kiss, warm touch, and everything we experienced is no stranger to me. Now that's all that remains. *The memories of us.*

"You're doing it again. You get this look on your face every time you have River on your mind. It's kinda disgustin'. Like a love sickness or something." He pretends to throw up in his mouth.

"I don't wanna hear about it, considerin' you're still talking to Jessica—who lives in New York, by the way—every single night. So disgustin' is your middle name."

Dylan takes a deep breath, getting ready to tell me where to go, but before he does, a fist bangs against the passenger window. We both jump, and Jackson's on the other side laughing his ass off as the rain pours around him in buckets. Once we're out of the truck and in the Jeep, that's when the shit talkin' really begins.

"The truck was all fogged up like you two were makin' love in there," Jackson teases, putting the Jeep in reverse, slinging mud everywhere. "Only thing missing was that palm print on the window like in *Titanic*."

"Fuck off," I tell him. "Dylan's not really my type anyway."

"I'll never let go, Jack. I mean, Dylan," Jackson continues.

"More like, I'll never let go, *River*," Dylan adds.

I turn around and shoot daggers at him. If looks could kill, his ass would be dead in the back seat.

"Good one. I'm almost certain that Alex has cried himself a roaring river over the last three months because at this point, I'm not sure she's actually real." Jackson has been antagonizing me about her, too.

"You motherfuckers can drop dead."

The biggest mistake I made when I got home was telling Jackson about River, but I couldn't help it. I needed someone to chat with other than Dylan, and I wanted another opinion to make sure I wasn't losing my fucking mind. Unfortunately, Jackson's unsolicited advice was to fuck a different woman every night for two weeks, and he guaranteed that'd get her out of my system and off my mind. Knowing that would never work—that no woman could replace River, nor would I want to do that—I swore I'd never ask him for female advice again. And I shoulda known better, considering he's hung up on Kiera, even though he'd never admit it.

Jackson drives fast down the dirt road that's turned to mud as if he has somewhere to be. I hold on to the oh-shit handle and can hear Dylan being knocked around in the back as Jackson creates his own path to Mama's house. Jackson can't stop laughing as Dylan and I huff at his horrible driving. By the time he drops us off close to the porch, we're ready to fall out of the Jeep.

"Thanks, man," I tell him as I get out, and he gives me a head nod before spinning out, slinging mud all over us. I flip him off, hoping he'll see me in the rearview mirror, though I doubt he cares.

"I kinda wish we would've walked now. I thought I was gonna die," Dylan admits. I pat his shoulder and nod.

"Or next time we call John. He doesn't have a death wish."

Jackson and John may be twins, but they're as opposite as they come. Aside from their identical looks, their personalities are what set them apart. Jackson lives every day as if he's turning twenty-one for the first time while John is the more sensible and responsible one. Though if you asked anyone who knew the Bishop brothers, they'd say I was more like Jackson, whereas John and Evan were similar in personality traits.

Before walking inside, we remove our boots and dirty jackets and leave them on the porch. No need to set Mama off by wearing filthy clothes inside her immaculate house.

As soon as we walk in, I can hear Dad and Mama chatting in the kitchen. Smells of cornbread fill the house, and it makes me hungry.

"Hey, Mama," I say, leaning over and giving her a kiss on the cheek as soon as Dylan and I enter the kitchen. "Got the truck stuck again."

"Son, why don't you call it a day?" Mama asks.

"Because there's work to be done," I tell her politely with a smile.

Dad drinks a glass of milk, and when he finishes, he wipes his mouth and makes eye contact with me. "That's enough for today, son. Not too much more can be done in this weather. Waste of my damn time, if you ask me. If it's a mess outside tomorrow, then we'll pick up on Wednesday."

"Yes, sir." I glance at Dylan, knowing we're going to have time to do whatever we want after we feed the animals tomorrow morning.

"You boys be back here around six. Chili should be ready by then. It's perfect for this cold weather." Mama pats me on the back with a grin. "Tell your brothers, too."

"Yes, ma'am. We'll be back."

Just as we head out of the kitchen, Mama calls me back. "Will you bring these treats over to John before you head home? Tell them to set them out for the B&B guests since they'll be stuck inside the next few days."

Though it's a little out of the way, I agree with a smile knowing I'm not on anyone else's schedule today. Instead of getting my truck dirty, I grab the keys to the old Jeep parked in the barn beside the house. It's not the fanciest vehicle on the ranch, but it's better than the work truck we drive around, and it has 4-wheel drive, so no chance of getting stuck again.

"I'm not heading home in this bullshit. Hopefully, a few hours from now it'll let up," Dylan says after we put on our boots and run to the Jeep. We try not to get any wetter but fail miserably. We drive slowly to the bed and breakfast, and when we finally get there, I see the parking lot is full of vehicles.

After I park on the side of the building, I grab the sack of treats, and we bolt to the side door. Guests fill every empty chair available while others huddle around the fireplace though it feels like it's a hundred degrees inside. Glancing around, I spot John who's standing behind the counter reading a hunting magazine.

"Mama told me to deliver these to you. She made them for the guests and all that."

"Again?" John asks, grabbing the bag and peeking inside.

"You know how she gets. When she's bored, she bakes. By the weight of it, probably a hundred cookies in there."

"Well, she sure knows how to butter 'em up," John says, walking behind the bar and looking for something to put them in.

"Butter them up or fatten them up? I'm not sure which one anymore," I say with a laugh. John nods in agreement as he places the cookies in a basket and sets it on top of the counter.

"So what y'all doing today in this lovely weather?" A tinge of sarcasm hits John's tone as he glances outside the bay windows.

"Day drinking," Dylan responds with a smirk.

"Hell no. We can't be showing up for dinner completely wasted. Mama will murder us." I shake my head at Dylan, and all he does is nod. I narrow my eyes at him. "Seriously, no."

"We'll see," he teases.

Guests spot the cookies, and they take them by the handfuls. Everyone is all smiles, and I wonder if Mama made special cookies by how happy they are eating them.

"I'm going home, I guess. Oh, Mama's making chili. Be there at six. Let Jackson know too," I tell John. He gives me a nod before Dylan and I head out. We ride in silence across the property. Once we get to my house, we run inside and kick off our boots.

I walk to the kitchen and make myself and Dylan a turkey sandwich because we didn't get a chance to eat. "You can borrow some of my clothes if you want so you don't have to sit around in those nasty wet ones. I'm going to shower," I tell Dylan once I finish eating.

As I walk away, I catch him grabbing a beer from the fridge and realize he wasn't kidding about day drinking. He tips it and opens it with a shit-eating grin. Shaking my head, I continue down the hallway to the bathroom.

While I'm in the shower, thoughts of River flood my mind again. Why didn't I ever ask her for her number? Why didn't I insist that we keep in touch? The more I think about it, the more I want to kick my own ass. Once I dry off and get dressed, I head into the living room where Dylan is chatting it up with Jackson, who's wearing shorts and cowboy boots, looking more ridiculous than normal as he drinks a beer.

"You know Mama is expecting us at six, right?" I tell him, glancing at the bottle.

"Yeah, John told me...so?"

I don't dare argue with him while he digs his own grave. Instead, I plop on the couch and watch TV. I'm so lost in my own head I couldn't tell you what's going on.

"I'm going to look her up on Facebook," I tell Dylan, loud enough for only him to hear.

"No, it's not a good idea. Like I've told you before, if she wanted to talk to you, she'd call you. Simple as that. You're just setting yourself up to be let down. So why even go there?" Dylan hounds me much like he has before, but I don't give in this time. "Don't. Give me your phone." Dylan holds out his hand.

I flash him a look and refuse to give it to him. "But what if she lost my number? Or what if she lost her phone? There are a million different scenarios that could've happened. I know what we had was more than just a fling. I know it was," I tell Dylan.

"A hundred days later and you're still hung up on her. That pussy must've been good. That's all I'm saying," Jackson adds from the kitchen.

"Shut the fuck up, Jackson!" I yell back at him, not needing his side comments.

He stalks into the living room and sits on the couch next to me, grabs the remote and flicks through the channels. Pulling up my Facebook app, I look at the ridiculous picture I have on my profile of Dylan and fishing. It's been way too long since I've been on my profile, so I decide to check my friend requests first to see if maybe she looked me up and friended me. There are women in there, but not the one I want.

My mind drifts to the first time we had a real conversation. Dylan was still in the hospital, and I knew I had to speak to her. After formally introducing ourselves, I was lost in her trance as she grabbed my hand and we sat there together, frozen in time. That was the first time I felt the electricity soaring between us. Her touch was like fire and set my body ablaze.

Sucking in a deep breath, I type her name into the search bar and wait for her profile to load. I scroll through several River Lancasters until I find her. As soon as I see her sweet smile, I'm frozen in place. I click on the profile picture of her and Natalie and can't help but swallow down my heart as I see the tight black dress she's wearing. They're both smiling big, and by the decorations that fill the background, I can tell they were celebrating New Years. *Damn.* I wish I would've been there to kiss her as the clock struck midnight.

My finger hovers over the friend button. I suck in a deep breath, and it takes everything I have to close out of the app instead. As hard as it is, I force myself to leave our relationship exactly where it started and ended—in Key West.

A week passes and the rain does too, but the pastures hold water in some places, so it's still a sloppy mess. After work, I go home and shower before driving into town and to the Main Street Diner. I'm in the mood for breakfast for dinner, and the diner has the best bacon and eggs in town. I might even splurge on a big slice of pie. Mama is busy baking for the ladies at church, and we've learned not to even ask about food when she's baking for a purpose. So, instead, I decide to do my own thing.

As I drive across town, a stupid thought crosses my mind to message Natalie instead of River. She was tagged in River's profile picture on Facebook, and I know if I messaged her, she'd at least be supportive, I think. She was always so eager for River and me to hang out, so I can't imagine much had changed. However, the more I think about it, the more I realize how insane that sounds, even in my head. I don't want to seem desperate or like a stalker, but ever since I found her online, it's bothered the shit out of me.

Walking into the diner, I glance around and see Mrs. Betty shuffling behind the counter, so I take a seat in her section because I know she's always been good at giving advice. The woman has been working here since I was a kid, and she's good friends with Mama, plus she always has the latest town gossip to distract me with. Sometimes, when I've got a lot on my mind, I'll come down to the diner and drink coffee for hours. I always leave full and with a grin on my face.

Mrs. Betty instantly greets me with a smile and a steaming cup of coffee.

"So, did you talk to your lady, yet?" is the first thing she asks me. After hearing Dylan and me talking about River one night over dinner, she stuck her nose right in and told me to stop being a foolish man and track my woman down. I left out the part about River and my no-strings-attached sex-only deal, so of course, she thinks I should go to the ends of the earth to find her.

"No ma'am," I say, taking off my baseball cap and setting it on the bar. "I'm not going to contact her. I've decided that if she doesn't want to talk to me, then I don't want to talk to her either." My mood is sour, but I can't help it. It's been controlling my life these past three months, and it's driving me crazy. I can't keep on living like this.

"That's too bad, honey. Personally, I still think you should just go for it. What if she's having the same conversation with herself at this moment? You don't want to look back on your life when you're old like me and realize you didn't fight for love—real love—none of that made up stuff. I don't care about distance; love always finds a way. Trust me on that, sweetie." She flashes me a wink.

I give her a smile but don't speak.

"What do you have to lose?" she adds.

"Apparently nothing but my mind." I sigh as she hands me a menu even though I always order the same thing. I don't bother opening it but give her my order instead.

"Good for you," she says with a sweet smile when I add a slice of pecan pie to my order. She doesn't press me on River again, which I'm grateful for.

Time passes and before long Mrs. Betty is sliding my food across the bar top toward me and refilling my coffee. The eggs practically melt in my mouth, and the bacon is cooked crunchy just like I like it. As Mrs. Betty refills my coffee again, she's smiling, and there's something telling about that smile of hers.

"So tell me again what your dream girl looks like," she says, her smile still lingering.

I finish chewing, not talking with my mouth open, and tell her as I have before.

"She's tall. Blonde. Has a cute button nose and a smile that's so contagious, she could make a whole room smile along with her. She's kind and passionate, and you can tell she really cares about others' well-being

145

just by hearing her speak about her job. When she laughs really hard, her eyes light up like emeralds. Mrs. Betty, she's the most beautiful woman in the world. But don't let her fool you, she's as stubborn as a mule too," I say, chuckling on the surface, but anger is burning through my veins. Angry that I let myself fall for her, something I never do with *anyone*, and angry that I was so duped into thinking the connection we had was mutual. And mostly, angry that I can't seem to get over it.

I look up at Mrs. Betty and catch her glancing around, a mischievous grin plastered on her face. "Well, I have a good feeling things are going to change for you, sweetie." She pats my hand before walking away.

Once I've finished, she gives me my pie in a to-go box and the check. I tell her thanks and that I'll be seeing her soon before putting a twenty down on the counter. As I stand, I grab my coffee cup and finish the rest before placing my cap back on my head. I feel good about my decision. Fuck her for leaving things the way she did. I wasn't ready to say goodbye, but she made that choice for me, so it's time to let go. I need to move on.

"Bye, Mrs. Betty," I call out, walking toward the exit.

"Bye, Alex." She winks.

Pushing the door open, I barely get one foot out before I hear my name being called behind me.

"Alex." I'd recognize that voice anywhere. My eyes widen, not willing to believe it's actually *her*. Not after all this time. Not after I'd just convinced myself to let go.

All the hair on my neck stands up, and when I turn around and see River's face, mixed feelings from lust to rage surface.

She's only standing a couple of feet from me, her scent intoxicating my senses as soon as I step back into the diner.

Looking up at me with her bright green eyes and blonde hair pulled into a side braid, she sways on her feet nervously.

Swallowing hard, I pin my eyes to her as my jaw clenches.

"What the fuck are you doing here?" are the first words to spew out of my mouth. They come out harsher than I intended, but considering everything I've been through, it's not entirely unmerited.

In fact, I think it's more than deserving.

CHAPTER FOURTEEN

River

"What the fuck are you doing here?"

His words sting, but I'm not exactly sure what I expected. After not calling him for three months, now here I am in Texas looking directly at a man who seems heartbroken and pained to see me again.

Not that I could blame him entirely. I can only hope he'll forgive me, but I wouldn't exactly blame him if he didn't.

Seeing him after all this time has so many mixed feelings and old memories surfacing. The moment I saw him walk into the diner, I knew it was my chance to approach him. I had planned on calling him once I was settled into my room to ask if we could meet up, but him being here brought us face-to-face much sooner than I'd anticipated.

I'd been sitting here for the last two hours thinking of what I'd say when I finally saw him again, thinking about how I'd explain why I didn't call or why I was here now. The more I thought about it, the more I lost the courage to reach out to him.

I had needed more time. Guess fate had other plans. It was now or never.

"I came to see you," I finally respond, my bottom lip trembling at the way he's looking at me. He's angry, *so* angry. I can see it. Hell, I can feel it steaming off his skin.

He pulls his cap off his head and brushes a hand roughly through his hair. The same locks I used to fist my own fingers through not too long ago.

"Can we go somewhere to talk?" I ask once he doesn't say anything. He's just standing and staring, and I can tell his mind is running a thousand miles an hour.

Before he can respond, someone walks in through the door, bumping Alex and pushing him forward right into me. The guy mutters a weak, "Sorry," and keeps walking. Meanwhile, my heart beats faster and harder now that Alex's arms are wrapped around my waist to steady me.

"Sorry." His voice is just above a whisper, and as he stands only inches away from me, it feels like we're the only two people in here.

I watch his throat as he swallows hard. This isn't how I wanted us to reunite, but regardless, I came here on a mission and am going to tell him what I came all this way for.

"Yeah, let's talk." He nudges his head toward the door, and I follow him out, so we're not in the doorway of the diner anymore. "Where are you staying?" He faces me and asks when we're several feet away from the entrance.

"Uh, this countryside bed and breakfast. I rented a car and was just about to head over there before I saw this diner and decided to stop and eat first." I don't admit that I stopped to grab a snack just twenty minutes before that.

The corner of his lips tilts up in a mock grin. "Of course." He fidgets with his hat and hair some more. "That's my family's B&B," he tells me, and when I lower my eyes, covering the guilt over my face, he snorts. "I'm betting you knew that though."

I nod before slowly looking back up at him. "I wasn't sure if you'd give me a chance to explain, so I figured the closer I was to you, the better chance I had."

"*What?*" he growls, whipping his head. He pulls his brows together, looking more pissed off than before. "You honestly thought I'd turn you away? You think that little of me?"

I shrug, feeling worse. "No, I just wasn't sure what state of mind you were in since—"

"Since you chose to end things without giving me a damn chance to say goodbye?" he interrupts, his voice deep and rough. "Or since you neglected to call me to at least say that you didn't want to keep in contact? Or since you left things up in the air without giving me *any* kind of explanation? Do you know what I've been through these last three months wonderin'? Is that really what Key West meant to you? Because then I guess I read the entire situation wrong."

He's mad, obviously, but this is why I wanted us to meet somewhere private. Maybe I shouldn't have stopped him and let him walk out so I could mentally prepare better. God, I'm such a fool for coming here. I blow out a breath of frustration, reminding myself I came all this way for a reason and wasn't leaving until I laid out all my cards on the table.

"Okay, I fucked up!" I shout, taking him by surprise. My hormones have been uncontrollable these past few weeks, but instead of apologizing for my outburst, I continue. "I know I should've called to say goodbye the right way, but I was *scared*. Our time together meant more to me than I wanted to admit at the time, and I was scared I'd get hurt again if I let you in. But then I started to fall for you anyway. The only way to get over you was to try and forget it all happened, but I never could. I'm sorry, but—"

He steps toward me, closing the gap between us, and cups my face with his large hands as he tilts his head to the side and presses his lips over mine. His mouth cuts through my unspoken words, but I welcome it because the moment I feel his body close, electricity radiates from me.

Gripping his shirt in my hands, I pull his chest to mine and inhale his fresh, manly scent. I can tell he just took a shower, yet there's something so rugged about him. God, he kisses so passionately and with purpose. He holds my face like I'm the most precious thing in the world, and when a moan escapes his lips, I know we've lost ourselves in each other. I can't deny that this is the reaction I'd been hoping for, even if we did have a lot to discuss still.

"Alex..." I sigh against his mouth. Our lips part and he rests his forehead on mine, my heart pounding.

"Let's go. I'll take you to the B&B, and then we can talk."

I nod as he grabs my hand. "Oh wait. Should I grab my luggage?"

"Yeah, I can bring you back into town tomorrow to get your rental."

"Is that safe? What if someone tries breaking into it or steals it?" My question puts a wide small on his face before he bursts into a fit of laughter. "What's so funny?"

"Darlin', you're in small town Texas. No one wants to break into your Prius."

"Oh," I mutter, feeling stupid. "You can take the girl out of the city, but you can't take the city out of the girl, I guess." I shrug, lowering my face to hide the blush that's rising over my cheeks.

He chuckles, holding out a hand as I dig for my keys. Once he pops the trunk and grabs my suitcase, he slams it shut and leads me to his truck. My eyes widen when I see he drives a nice black Ford F-150.

"I'm slightly relieved to see you don't drive one of those decked out and lifted trucks with orange and yellow flames on the side," I tease when he opens the door for me.

He gives me a puzzled look.

"What? You Texans are obsessed with your trucks." I slide into the seat and reach for the buckle.

"Damn right we're obsessed," he jokes, adjusting his hat. "This one is even the Texas Edition." He smiles, proudly.

"Texas Edition?" My brows lift. "I'm definitely not in Wisconsin anymore."

Grinning, he shuts the door and walks around to the driver's side. The tension is still thick in the air, yet I'm so relieved even though we have a lot to talk about.

"So, how'd you end up finding me anyway?" he asks once we're on the road.

"Bishop, ranch, Texas. Not hard to Google." I shrug. "The property is huge, and I had no idea if you lived on the ranch or not, so I took a chance staying at the B&B, hoping I'd be able to find you."

He licks his lips as he focuses on the road ahead of us. "Well, guess you didn't need to look hard. Small town perks."

"Yeah. Guess so." I slouch into my seat, my nerves feeling shot already.

He glances over at me before speaking up again. "I looked you up on

Facebook but didn't have the courage to friend request you. Figured I'd look needy or some shit since the ball was in your court and you didn't take it." He shrugs, the guilt crawling up my skin. "Saw your profile picture, though. You looked real pretty and happy."

I blush, both sad and pleased he thought to look me up. "Thank you. Natalie and Adam threw a huge New Year's Eve party."

"I figured it was. Natalie looked pretty smashed." He laughs.

I laugh with him and nod in agreement. "Yeah, after she threw up on my shoes, Adam proposed. Then she drank some more to *celebrate*." I don't tell him I hadn't been drinking that night at all and had been thinking of him nonstop.

"They got engaged?"

"Yep. Finally. They've been together since college."

"Wow, tell her I said congrats."

"I will."

The silence fills the air, and when I look out my window, all I see is country. Miles and miles of rolling hills and crispy brown grass. The sun is setting, painting the sky a pretty yellow and orange canvas. Texas is glowing, and I take a moment to take in the scene of the afterglows on the horizon.

"This is so different from city life," I murmur as he drives through the winding roads that are starting to make me nauseous. "So weird to me."

"I'm sure. It's the only life I know, though. I couldn't live anywhere else," he admits, and my heart aches.

After a fifteen-minute drive, we turn down a gravel road until I see a giant house set in the distance with every light on inside. As we slow to a crawl, a large black post with a sign that reads CIRCLE B RANCH BED & BREAKFAST embellished with a bird on top comes into view. It's surrounded by a bed of wild flowers and adds to the rustic feel of the whole ranch. Once I found this place online, I did as much research as I could and discovered that everything about the ranch life fascinates me. It's obvious the whole community is very family-oriented, considering a majority of the ranches and land are passed down from generation to generation. You don't see that much where I'm from.

"It looks even better in person," I say as he parks right in the front.

"Wait till you see it in the early morning. The sun shines and brightens up everything. Mama's worked obsessively on all the flowers, and John and Jackson take turns with the horses and trail riding. John manages more of the business aspect of it, too."

"I can definitely see the appeal." I smile, taking it all in. Alex jumps out and walks to my side to open the door. "If you're interested in riding, we could set something up."

I tuck my lips into my mouth and stop the words that so desperately need to come out.

"Sorry, I didn't mean to rush anything. Just figured while you're in Texas, might as well enjoy some of it."

"No, it's fine." I shake my head. "I mean, maybe. I'm only here for a few days."

The smile drops from his face, and I feel bad for disappointing him once again.

After he grabs my suitcase, Alex reaches for my hand and walks us up the large staircase that leads to a gorgeous house with tall colonial columns and a wraparound porch. Planters and rocking chairs line the porch, and I make a mental note to come out here and sit later. It looks so cozy, and I haven't even stepped inside yet.

"I'll get you checked in. My brother is probably still here, so just a warning." His tone hardens, and I wonder if he's mentioned me to him.

"Okay."

"John," Alex says to a tall, brooding man. He's Alex's opposite with dark blond hair that's longer on one side. Scruff covers his chiseled jawline, but his eyes are the same—soft and kind. He's taller and leaner where Alex is beefy and muscular, probably since he does more laborious work.

"Mama send you again?" he asks with annoyance in his tone. "I already told her—"

"No, she didn't." Alex cuts him off before he can rant. "I have a friend checking in."

His eyes noticeably shift from Alex to me, lowering down my body then back up to my face.

"What'd you do?" he accuses with a strong Southern drawl, crossing his arms over his chest. "Is your house too full of the Delta Gamma Sorority sisters again?"

I arch a brow, pinching my lips together as John gives him shit. I look back and forth between the two and can tell they must do this often.

"Fuck off," Alex spits back, then clears his throat when he realizes his voice was a tad too loud in a house filled with guests. "Just check her in," he demands. "River Lancaster."

Something flashes over John's face, recognition maybe, but his shoulders relax, and he smiles. "River, yes. We've been expecting you."

"What room is she in? I'll take her." Alex's deep voice is possessive, and I can't deny how much it turns me on to hear it again. How much I hope to keep hearing it from now on.

"She's in the Violet room," John tells him, reaching for the key. "Make sure to show her everything. And how to call down if she needs anything."

"Yeah, I got this. Thanks."

Alex takes my hand and leads us to a staircase. I look at everything as we walk down the hall toward my room. It's all so stunning. Definitely has that country charm with a modern flair.

"The Violet room? Does that mean everything's going to be purple?" I tease.

Alex unlocks the door and opens it for me to walk through first. "No, Mama named all the rooms after dead family members."

"Oh, well that's not morbid at all."

Alex sets my suitcase down and shuts the door behind him. I look around, appreciating all the little touches of flowers, candles, and décor pillows.

"Okay, so before John murders me, here's the booklet on the property. They serve breakfast between six and nine and come hungry because you'll want to try everything. And I mean *everything*. This is homestyle country eatin' down here, none of that city processed pumped-with-steroids food shit."

I chuckle, grabbing the book out of his hand. "Okay, I will, but I draw the line at grits." I don't dare tell him that just about anything can set off my nausea so there's no guarantee I can keep anything down.

"Oh God. Don't let anyone hear you say that." He chuckles. "We're serious about our grits down here. Sugar grits, cheesy grits, salt and pepper grits; there's a grit for every meal, trust me."

"Duly noted." I flip through the book and browse over the details about the ranch, the horses and trail riding, the side by sides and everything their little town has to offer. It's perfect for what I need right now.

"I love it," I say, setting the book down and glancing around the room. "Pretty sure it's bigger than my entire apartment."

"No, thanks," Alex grumbles, shaking his head at the thought.

The silence between us is awkward, but I don't even know how to begin this conversation.

"Do you need anything right away? John's your bitch, so just let me know."

I smile and laugh. "No, I'm okay. Thinking I should shower off the travel smell and change."

"I can wait if you want," he says sincerely, appreciating how he's not rushing me to talk.

"You don't mind?"

He closes the gap between us and cups my face, making circles with his thumb across my cheek. "I've been waiting three months, River. I think I can wait another twenty minutes."

I lean into his touch, loving the way it makes me feel when he does that. Smiling, I step away to grab my suitcase and head into the bathroom. Even though I'm wearing a sweater and it's covering my stomach, I'm still feeling overly self-conscious. Nerves are taking over, and the courage I felt earlier is long gone. I know I need to tell Alex the truth, but knowing I'm about to change his entire life has my heart thumping right out of my chest.

As I shower, I think of how I'm going to tell him. I could just rip it off like a Band-Aid and blurt it all out. That sounds the easiest. I'd rather gradually ease into everything I need to say. Then there's the fear that his reaction is going to burst the bubble I've been so content hiding in.

I can do this, I remind myself. It's a familiar chant I've had to tell myself a lot over the past several weeks.

Once I'm out of the shower, I wrap a towel around my body while I dig for my heartburn pills. It comes out of nowhere and is usually strong enough to make me sick.

"Hey, Alex," I call from inside the bathroom, peeking my head around the door.

"Yeah?"

"Would you mind grabbing a white bottle from my purse? I'm not dressed yet." I clench my eyes the second the words come out, knowing he's already seen me naked.

"Sure." I hear him chuckling, probably thinking the same thing. His mouth and hands have been all over my naked body.

I step back inside, digging out my hairbrush and deodorant. Next, I look for something comfortable to wear, which consists of leggings and loose shirts because that's all that fits me now.

After a solid minute of waiting, I peek back out. "Alex?"

No response.

What the heck?

Once I finish getting dressed, I throw my hair up into a wet, messy bun and walk out to where I set my purse.

"Alex?" I call again. When I round the corner, I see him standing frozen facing away from me. Finally, he turns around. His eyes are wide, and his face has gone pale. "What's wrong?"

I step closer, finally seeing the stick he's holding.

"Is this yours?"

Planting my feet, I lick my lips and release a deep breath. "Alex..." I breathe out, hating that none of this has gone as planned. I totally forgot I put it in there. I don't know if it's common for pregnant women to keep their tests, but I'd been in such shock and denial the first couple of weeks, I stuffed it in there as a reminder. "Is this yours?" His voice is louder with anger in his tone as he stares me down.

I blink when he steps closer, invading my space. He holds the stick firmly between his fingers, demanding answers.

"Yes. It's mine." I swallow hard.

"You're pregnant." His words are soft, defeated almost.

"Yes."

He stays silent for a moment, and I can tell he's putting all the pieces of the puzzle together. "That's why you're here."

"Yes," I say with a breath. "I didn't think it was something to tell you over the phone," I add honestly, though I'd definitely thought about it at first. Just thinking about coming here and seeing him again had me nauseous for days.

"It's mine?" A pleased grin forms on his lips.

Relieved at his smile, I laugh. "Yes, you dummy."

He falls to his knees and wraps his arms around my waist, pressing his cheek to my stomach. My head bows while I wrap my arms around his neck, tears forming in my eyes.

This man. He never ceases to amaze me.

"Thank you," he says against my shirt.

"For what?"

Looking up at me, I can see the emotion written all over his face. "For coming here. Telling me. Letting me be a part of this."

"Trust me when I say it wasn't an easy decision."

He stands up and wraps a hand around my neck, pulling me closer. "Whatever it was, I'm just happy you're here now. I wanted to be really pissed at you the second I saw you, but I couldn't. Not for long at least. I don't know what it is about you, River, but you just make me want to be a better person. You were all I thought about, and once I finally saw you, I couldn't resist kissing you again. Knowing you could very well walk away with my heart, it was worth the risk."

I feel so guilty, knowing I should've contacted him sooner, and I regret pushing him out of my life like I did. These last three months have been a whirlwind while deciding what to do. I went back and forth with my options, wondering if Alex would even want to be involved or if I'd be better off raising the baby on my own. The conflict consumed me for weeks, battling between my emotions of being able to have Alex back in my life and be a family or learning the hard reality of him rejecting us both. Ultimately, Natalie helped me realize I had to tell him face to face because it was the right thing to do—regardless of the outcome. I'd been sick for weeks, so I wasn't even sure I'd make it on a plane, but I knew I'd regret not telling him if I didn't.

It wasn't just about him and me anymore.

We now had a baby to consider.

CHAPTER FIFTEEN

Alex

I've barely processed all this information, but I don't care. The girl of my dreams is right here, in my arms, telling me we're having a baby.

And that changes *everything*.

"There's more," she tells me.

I just want to hold her again, lie in bed with her, and hear her tell me she's staying.

"There's a lot we need to discuss," she clarifies.

I nod in agreement.

Locking my fingers with hers, I lead her over to the bed and sit.

"Do you know when the baby is due?" I ask.

"End of July."

It's mid-February, so that means we still had time to figure everything out, which, if I had it my way, that'd be moving her ass here to be with me permanently.

"Do you know the gender?"

"Not yet. It's too early."

"Okay. Well—" I think of how to proceed, but River is quick to interrupt.

"I had this whole speech planned out, but everything I've been trying to plan has basically backfired, so I'm just going to come out and say it. I found out I was pregnant when I was eight weeks, so right before New Year's. I didn't drink that night, by the way. I was Natalie's personal assistant in making sure she didn't vomit in her sleep and choke to death. Since then, I've had a doctor appointment and ultrasound. I heard the heartbeat and even got an ultrasound picture."

"Really?" My eyes widen. "Can I see?"

She smiles, proudly. "Of course."

Retrieving her purse, she digs out an envelope where she's stashed the pictures. She hands them over to me, and my heart beats wildly.

"I've never seen an ultrasound photo before, but I already know it's the most perfect blob I've ever seen. She already looks so much like you." I grin, studying the pictures.

She bursts out laughing, her head falling back between her shoulders as she releases a sweet, throaty sound. "It's the sac, you fool. It's too soon to see details. However…" She points her finger down at the photo. "You can see the tiny arm and leg buds."

"Wow." I sigh. "I can't believe it."

"Are you panicking?"

"No, the opposite actually. I always imagined I would if a girl told me she was pregnant, but with you—not one bit."

She sucks in her bottom lip, gazing up at me with her stunning emerald eyes. "Honestly, it took me a couple weeks to really grasp that I was pregnant. I was shocked, to say the least, since I was on the pill and we used condoms. However, I'd been taking an antibiotic for my sinus infection, and apparently, it canceled out my birth control."

"It can do that?" I gasp.

"Oh yeah, and I feel really stupid because I should've thought of that, but then we were using condoms, almost every time, but there's still a small chance they're not effective."

"Jesus."

"Yeah, I know." She sighs, and I can tell her mind is racing. "So that brings me to why I'm here, aside from telling you the news of course. Once I found out, I contemplated on what my next step should be. I thought about just raising the baby on my own and being a single mom because I thought dropping this huge bomb on you would be too crazy for you to handle. Not that you can't handle it, just that people don't typically expect to start a life with someone they were just randomly hooking up with on vacation…"

My eyes burn into her as she continues to nervously ramble on, and as much as I want to tell her to stop—that this isn't too much for me to handle —I allow her to continue. "Anyway, once I finally came to terms with it, I decided I'm definitely keeping the baby. I wanted to come and inform you out of respect, but basically, tell you I don't expect anything from you. We live completely different lives, so you can be as involved or not as you want, no pressure."

What? Was she seriously thinking I'd walk away from her? From our baby?

"What?" I blurt out. Was being delusional a symptom of pregnancy? It had to be if she thought I'd let her get away again.

"Well, it's just I live in Wisconsin, and you live here, and like you said, you never want to leave Texas, so the only thing I can think of is to—"

"Move here," I blurt out, interrupting her words.

She blinks, looking up at me. "What?" Her voice is soft, almost a whisper.

"Move here, River," I plead. "I want you. I never stopped. Let me take care of you. Let me provide for our baby."

Her breath hitches, and I can tell she wasn't expecting that kind of a reaction from me. "I have a life back home, and what if—"

"*We* can have a life here. Why not?"

"I'd be lying if I said the thought hadn't crossed my mind, knowing that'd be the most logical and smart choice, but how? We're basically strangers. How are we going to raise a baby together?"

"Well, I wouldn't say we're *strangers* exactly." I grin, and she flashes me a mock smile. "Okay, listen." I take her hand and hold it gently in mine. "I've thought of nothing except you for the past three months. I've been angry, sad, furious, heartbroken…and I had just talked myself into moving on and getting over you. I couldn't continue to live with the fact that things ended the way they did." She visibly cringes, and I feel bad for bringing it up at a time like this. "However, that same day you walked back into my life and told me I'm going to be a father. If that's not fate, River, then I don't know what is."

Her lips part but no words come out. She closes her eyes, and I know she's trying not to cry.

"River…" I whisper, tilting her chin up so she'll look at me. "We can do this together. Let me do this *with* you."

Her chest moves as she inhales a deep breath, and I know she's already been considering it. "I don't want to be a relationship out of convenience, Alex. I wish I could say I have enough confidence to just let us be together, but it'll always be in the back of my mind. Then what if we try, and it doesn't work out? How are we going to raise a baby together then? And how would this even work, given our history? Do we date? Do we start over? Do we pretend we didn't spend any time apart and continue where we left off? What if—"

"River!" I press my finger to her lips, needing her to stop rambling because it's all nonsense. Her insecurities are nothing she needs to worry about, and I honestly can't even believe she'd have them.

"I. Want. You." I pluck her bottom lip with the pad of my thumb. "I wasn't lying when I said I haven't thought of anyone except you, which you should know, never happens to me. Trust me when I say I've been driving my brothers and Dylan insane talking about you nonstop." I chuckle, and she flashes me a small smile. "So, to answer your questions, *what if* everything works out? What if I show you and prove that we can make this work, however you want to do it, but I'm not letting you go this time. Do you hear me? I stupidly left last time without telling you my honest feelings, but I'm not going anywhere now. We're having a *baby*."

She leaps off the bed and wraps her arms around my neck, sniffling in my hair as I hold her tight to my body. I feel the tiny bump of her belly press against me and smile.

"River," I whisper into her hair before pushing her back, so I can see her face. "Stay. *Please*."

She wipes her fingers under her eyes and clears her throat before sitting back down. I don't rush her, but I can see she's thinking hard, probably contemplating every outcome, the way she always does. Her eyes meet mine, and my heart pounds so hard that I feel as if it may beat right out of my chest. Putting everything out there and asking her to stay is a big and risky move on my part. I know that, but as long as we're together, I have no doubt we can make this work. As our breaths mix with silence, it feels as if all time is standing still as I wait for her answer. But that's what I do. I wait patiently.

"Okay," she finally says above a whisper, her eyes bright and glowing. "I will."

"Okay." The permanent smile on my face doesn't falter. She's just made me so fucking happy.

"But I'll need to go back and pack up my apartment. I'll have to let my job know and put in my notice." I smile wider when she tells me that. "This isn't going to be easy, Alex. Everything about this is a huge adjustment and moving will just add to it. In fact, now that I'm saying it aloud, it actually sounds really crazy. Like we should both probably be evaluated for jumping into this." She half-laughs to herself.

"River, baby. I don't need easy. Hell, I want crazy and everything that it entails. As long as it's with you."

She smiles, adjusting her top. "Okay. Well, prepare yourself."

I grin, ready to do whatever it takes. "I can fly back to Milwaukee with you and help pack or move if you want. Maybe over a weekend?"

"Nah, it's fine. I can hire movers for all of that. I just need to grab the essentials before they pack it into the truck."

I lean in and cup her cheeks, needing to taste her lips, but right before I can, she presses a hand to chest and stops me. I blink, trying to read her face.

"What? Is this where you tell me you want to see other people?" I tease.

"Shut up!" She laughs, smiling. "I think we need to set some ground rules first."

My brows raise. "More rules? Didn't those rules get us into our current situation?"

She narrows her eyes at me, hiding a smirk. "I just don't think we should jump right back into bed together." Before I can comment, she hurries and continues. "And yes, I know that's how we got into our current situation, but nevertheless, if we want a chance at having a real relationship, we need to give it a fresh start."

I crease my brows, twisting my lips up. "A fresh start as in what? You want me to court you?"

She bites her tongue and shakes her head. "Just because I'm pregnant doesn't mean I don't want a genuine relationship. What we had in Key West was a vacation fling based on sex. If this is going to work, we need to start over."

"You expect me to just start over as if everything we shared never happened?" I ask, perplexed.

"Well no, I mean, the feelings and our connection can't be altered. But I want us to really get to know each other, and we can't do that while our hormones are hyperactive on sex. We need to set some boundaries."

"Boundaries, okay. Like what?"

"Sex is off the table."

"Yeah, I got that." I roll my eyes, smirking. "What else?"

"We take things slow. Go out and talk. I'd love to meet your family and learn about the ranch and just get to know you as you."

I can't even be mad about her no-sex rule because honestly, that sounds like fucking heaven. I've never wanted a girl to stick around longer than a night, and knowing that River wants this to work as much as I do makes every grueling day we were apart worth it.

"Okay." I smile. "I think I can work with that." I press my lips to her cheek and groan as I inhale her fresh, clean scent.

This might be harder than I anticipated.

I suck in a deep breath and let it out slowly through my nose. River watches me, and I turn my head to meet her eyes that seem to see straight through me.

"What are your plans tomorrow?" I ask, my nerves getting the best of me.

She laughs. "I'm having breakfast between six and nine. Other than that, my day is free."

"Great. We're having lunch with my parents."

After I kiss River good night and tuck her into bed, I walk downstairs. As my foot hits the bottom step, I see John is getting ready to leave for the night. Christopher was actually on time to relieve him from staying too late, for once. We walk out together, and I'm in a weird state of mind. Noticing, he pats me hard on the back.

"Want to talk about it?" he asks as we stand on the front porch. His breath comes out as smoke because the temperature is dropping again. I've chatted with John about River over the past few months. He knows our history and how infatuated I've been with her ever since. There's no telling what he's thinking, especially with her showing up on a whim and staying at the B&B. "I'm so fucking happy she's here," I tell him. As we watch the late fog roll in over the ground, I try to find the right words to explain what's going on.

"I didn't piece together it was her, or I would've given you a warning when I saw the booking. But I'm happy if you're happy. I just can't help but wonder why she's here exactly." John is as smart as a whip, and I know I won't be able to end this conversation without telling him the truth.

"River came to tell me she's having a baby. *My* baby. So, I guess you're gonna be an uncle to another little one." I glance over at him and watch his eyes widen.

"I'm. Well. Damn, I'm shocked," he finally spits out. "Out of us all, I swore Jackson would be the one to knock up someone." It comes out as a laugh.

"Yeah, I did too, honestly." I chuckle. "But you know, I'm actually over the moon about it. Maybe it's not the traditional way, but I think everything is going to work out just fine."

He pulls me into a brotherly hug. "I'm happy for you. I'm going to spoil the shit out of that little one."

Our laughs echo across the pasture.

"So now what?" John tucks his hands into his pockets and starts walking toward his truck as I follow him.

"She's moving here. We're gonna raise us a Bishop, *together*. Here. The best place in the entire world for a kid to grow up, honestly." As the words leave my tongue, pure happiness covers me. Never in my life would I have expected this, but River makes me want to go from zero to fifty in a heartbeat. I'm just happy I'll be holding her hand on our next adventure.

"Better tell Mama," he warns. "I'll pretend like I don't know."

"Good." I give him one last smile before I walk to my truck, but once I'm inside, I sit there and stare up at the room where River is sleeping. Yesterday, she was a thousand miles away, and today, she's within arm's reach. Dreams do come true and good things happen to good people. With anyone else, it would have been a curse, but for me, having a baby with River is nothing short of a blessing.

I sleep like shit. Tossing and turning knowing my woman who's carrying my baby is at the B&B drives me fucking crazy. I want nothing more than to drive over there, crawl into bed with her, and never let her go. Ever.

But we're taking it slow.

And I'm going to try to hold back the reins as best I can, but fuck, I've missed her so much; it's going to take all the willpower I can muster to be the proper gentleman.

If I continue to lie in bed staring at the ceiling as memories and fears rush through my head, I'll drive myself to drink. And we all know that drinking at four in the morning is a terrible idea. So instead of continuing the insanity, I get up before the roosters crow and get dressed. Considering it's in the mid-twenties this morning, I dress in thick layers. Just as I'm pouring coffee into my thermos, Jackson stumbles in.

"What the holy fuck?" I glare at him. "Where the hell have you been all night?"

His face is full of smeared red lipstick, and his hair is disheveled. What confuses me the most is the hay stuck to his clothes.

"Don't worry about it, little bro," he slurs. Jackson's a hard worker, so I rarely have to get on him for that, but hell if he isn't a hot mess most of the time.

"Please tell me you weren't fucking in the barn again? Romping in the hay like an animal. You do realize it's cold as hell outside right now?" I arch a brow, wondering if he has a death wish or if he's just crazy.

He laughs, plops on the couch, kicks off his boots, and closes his eyes. "Why do you think I came home? Now if you don't mind, I'd like to catch a few z's before I have to be at work in two hours."

"You did it to yourself. Hope she was worth it," I add, knowing his schedule is full of horseback riding today.

"*Totally* worth it," he says, rolling over onto his side, dismissing me with his middle finger.

After I place the lid on my coffee, I grab my cowboy hat and walk out shaking my head, trying to put all the pieces of the puzzle together. River is moving to Texas. She's having my baby and going to be living *here*. Holy shit. I have a lot of things to figure out in just a few weeks.

Cranking the truck, I let it warm up before I drive across the property to go check in with Dad. The man never sleeps, and I'm sure he's up drinking coffee already.

As soon as my parents' house comes into view, my nerves get the best of me. Today, I'm going to have to drop the bomb on them about River and the baby. Dad won't say much—I can read him like a map—but Mama will be a different story. Thinking about her reaction makes my stomach twist because it will either be really good or really bad.

I turn off the engine of the truck, and as I walk to the porch, I look up at the sky and can still see stars. The Milky Way is almost as bright as the moonlight, and I smile thinking about all the stars I wished upon over the past three months. Somehow, I roped the moon and got my girl.

Pulling my keys out of my pocket, I insert the right one into the door and swing it open. Just as I suspected, Dad is already up drinking his morning coffee. As soon as he sees me, he checks his watch, confused to see me at this early hour.

"Mornin', Dad."

He looks up at me. "You're up early today."

"Yes, sir. Couldn't sleep, so thought I'd get started a little earlier than usual if that's okay."

Sipping his coffee, he nods. "It's never too early to work."

Somehow, I knew he'd say that. I grab the keys to the work truck off the hook by the door and give Dad a quick wave. Before I completely walk away, I turn around.

"Dad, can we do lunch today, around twelve?"

Tilting his head, he narrows his eyes at me. I know it's a little out of my norm, but this needs to be talked about today, and I won't be able to relax until they both know what's happening.

"Everything okay?" he asks, curiosity in his tone.

"Life is grand, Dad."

"Sure. Twelve it is. I'll tell your mother to prepare somethin' good considering hell has frozen over outside." I smile, knowing that this weather is definitely something Southerners aren't accustomed to.

After I walk out, I'm able to breathe just a little easier, but I'm still a nervous wreck. Mama's always wanted grandkids, though. Luckily, my sister, Courtney, broke the ice with her pregnancy announcement not too long ago; however, my situation is a little less traditional. Nevertheless, Mama will have to get used to it because what's done is done. I'll need to think and plan what I'm going to tell them exactly; fortunately, I have a few hours to think about it.

To keep my mind busy, I get started with the day. I'd usually wait for Dylan, but I can't today. The busier I stay, the better.

After the animals are fed and before I head back to the barn to meet Dylan, I call the B&B and leave a message for River at the front desk. I'm sure John will guarantee the message is delivered when he arrives.

Lunch is at 12. I'll pick you up.

And I can only hope the next eight hours pass by quickly.

CHAPTER SIXTEEN

River

For the first time in months, I slept like a baby. The temperature was perfect, and the bed was as soft as clouds. Sleeping late isn't something I typically do because of my early work shifts, but it was nice to get a few extra hours, especially after traveling.

I lie in bed, the fluffy quilt surrounding my body, and I can't help but smile. Everything finally feels like it's going to be okay. I felt uneasy during the plane ride over and wondered if Alex had moved on.

What if I would've shown up and he was in a relationship with someone else or was back to his routine of random hookups? Luckily, I had a fallback plan for either scenario. I would've told him out of respect, but then left and carried on to raise the baby on my own, expecting nothing in return. I knew I could do it, albeit hard, but I was a strong, educated woman who was resourceful. I'd be ignorant to come all the way down here without some kind of backup plan, but I didn't need it.

To know Alex waited for me and had been thinking of me as much as I'd been thinking of him, even when we agreed to leave it all in Key West, means more than he'll ever know. We shared something magical and meaningful on that island, something I hope wasn't brought on by bucket lists and beaches, but only time will tell.

Being able to see the reaction on his face and how happiness radiated from him when he found out he would be a father confirmed I did the right thing after all. I'll never forget that moment for the rest of my life—no matter what. He could've pushed me away. He could've argued with me or told me to fuck off. Instead, Alex embraced me like a long-lost lover and looked at me like I was his whole world.

The feelings that swirl through me as I think back on it are so intense my eyes water, and a tear rolls down my cheek. I swipe it away, cursing my damn emotions that have been getting the best of me the past few weeks.

I stand and stretch, adjusting my top that is now tight against my belly, then walk over to the large window and open the sheer curtain that allows the right amount of morning sunlight to leak in. I stare out and take in the beauty that I'm definitely not used to seeing back home. The land goes on for days, and as much as I want to go explore, I remind myself that I'll have plenty of time. The thought excites me while another one catches me off guard. Am I really moving to Texas?

After I shower and get ready for the day, I walk downstairs and see a large buffet area set up with breakfast platters just as Alex mentioned. Before I can even make my way over to the plates, John walks up holding a folded piece of paper.

"Mornin', ma'am," he says with a big grin.

Southerners are so damn polite; I just want to bottle them all up. "Morning."

"Did you sleep okay last night?" he asks. I know he's making small talk, which I actually don't mind. I want to get to know everyone in Alex's family as best as I can.

"I did, thank you. I think that bed is better than the one I have at home." I tuck my hair behind my ears, and when I look over at the buffet table, John realizes he's stalling.

"Oh, sorry. Make sure you try everything on the buffet. It's all delicious and from my mama's recipes."

"I'll do my best." I grin, keeping the thoughts to myself on being nauseous in the mornings and how some of their country style food is foreign to me.

"Well anyway, Alex left a message for you." He hands me the slip of paper.

"Thank you." I smile, and he gives me a head nod before walking away to help a guest check out. The more I look at John, the more I notice how similar their mannerisms are.

I open the note and recognize the Circle B Ranch emblem on top.

Lunch is at 12. I'll pick you up.
—Alex

Looking at my watch, I see it's only a little past nine, which means I have a few hours to get my mind right before I meet his parents. My nerves are stretched thin, and I can only hope they like me. Given the circumstances of how Alex and I met and got pregnant, I'm not so sure that's a formula for a great first impression. However, I am having their grandbaby after all, so hopefully, they'll warm up to the idea quickly. I feel like a teenager again, meeting the parents of a boy I like and all that.

I grab a plate and put a few items on it. As I walk down the buffet line, I see stuff that looks a little scary. The woman next to me is pouring white gravy on top of biscuits, and the thought of it grosses me out. I grab some fruit, bacon, a blueberry muffin, and a large cup of orange juice—all of which I recognize and pass all the Southern delicacy like buttermilk pancakes with icing, grits, and cornbread.

There's a lounge chair by a window across the room, and I decide to sit there and eat my breakfast. As I stare out the window, I take a bite of a blueberry muffin, and it's so damn delicious that I'm tempted to snatch up the rest of them and stuff them in my purse so I can eat them throughout the day. However, I find some self-restraint and stop after my second one. I feel the juice in my belly. The sugar always makes the baby toss and turn. It's the weirdest, but coolest feeling ever.

Just as I'm getting ready to place my empty plate in the dishpan, John walks in with a big cheesy smile.

"Howdy," he says.

"You were right. It was delicious." I give him a smile in return, hoping he didn't see I only put fruit and muffins on my plate. He stops in his path and crosses his arms over his chest, then looks me from top to bottom. He narrows his eyes and takes a step forward until he's close.

"Is that right?" He studies me, which is odd because we just spoke not twenty minutes ago. "So, where you from?" he asks with a side grin plastered on his face.

I laugh. "Wisconsin. Is it that obvious I'm an outsider?"

He grins before taking off his cowboy hat and tipping it, keeping his eyes on me. "Welcome to Texas, sweetheart. If you need anything, be sure to let me know. I'd be more than happy to show you 'round."

Before I can respond to his strange comment, I hear shouting coming from behind him.

"Jackson!" When I glance around, I see John walking toward us. My mouth falls open, and I'm so damn confused that I don't even know what to say. That's when I realize they're not even wearing the same damn clothes.

"There's two of you," I finally manage to get out after the initial shock passes. "I forgot. Alex told me once."

John chuckles, smacking a hand on his shoulder. "This is Jackson, my asshole brother. Sorry, it can be kinda confusing when you don't know we're twins. And he's such a dick, he'll pretend he's me, especially around pretty ladies."

"I'm much better looking though, right?" Jackson winks. But honestly, they look identical. There's nothing different about them, so telling them apart is going to be difficult as hell.

"Stop, dickhead. This is *River*," John tells him. Recognition flashes across Jackson's face, and I can tell they have one of those bonds where words aren't needed as they hold a silent conversation.

After a minute, Jackson finally laughs and slaps his leg. "You're a real person. I wasn't convinced." He looks me up and down again. "But *now* I understand."

I playfully roll my eyes. "Well, I hope whatever's been said about me is all good."

"Oh yeah, totally. Just have an obsessed Bishop, which is damn right annoyin' when you're on the other end of that conversation. If I had to hear about that vacation one more time, I was gonna kill Alex."

I laugh, nervously. Slightly weirded out that Alex talked about me so much. "Sorry about that. There's probably a club you could join. My friend back home was front and center for most of it."

"Is that so?" The corner of his lips tilts up. "She single?" He wiggles his brows.

John elbows him in the gut at the same time I laugh. "Sorry, no."

"Damn. Go figure." Jackson shrugs, and the silence between us becomes awkward. "Not to be rude, but why are you here now?" Jackson looks at me somewhat confused.

John clears his throat as if he knows what's going on. "Don't you have work that needs to be done? Actually, I need you to help me with something."

Jackson shakes his head, and somehow, John steers him away. "Nice meeting you, River!" Jackson says as he turns around.

Well, that was…interesting. My heart begins to race as I think about meeting his parents again. Everything's happening so fast that my head is spinning trying to process it all.

I make my way back to my room and try to decide what I'm going to do until lunch. My rental car is still sitting at the cafe so going to town to explore isn't an option. Instead, I grab my Kindle and decide to read and relax. First impressions are so important to me, and even though I'm trying to distract myself and read, I can't comprehend anything I'm reading because I'm overly anxious.

After an hour of fidgeting and not being able to get comfortable, I grab my jacket and decide to go outside and explore the land. I walk through the common room and head toward the backdoor. Everyone is bundled up like it's freezing, and it makes me laugh considering most of them are decked out in scarves and boots. This is considered warm for me, but I feel like a heater now anyway. I know it's common in pregnancy, but I could live without the hot flashes.

As soon as I open the door and stand on the back porch, a smile touches my lips. It's a cool forty-five degrees outside, and I'm actually happy there's no snow and negative temperatures. It's great for around the holidays, but once February hits, I'm over it. Sucks walking and driving in it, so this is definitely a nice change.

The rolling hills are so beautiful as I look out. I allow my feet to guide me as I take the steps down the porch and head toward the stables.

Curiosity gets the best as me as I walk down the path and decide to step in. As soon as I get closer, I can smell the horses and hay. It's not something I'm used to smelling, making me feel like I'm really in the country. Many of the horses are wearing coats, which makes me giggle. As I continue walking through the stable, some of the horses poke their heads over the stall to greet me. I pet a few of their soft noses, and they nip at me, hoping I'll feed them something, I'm sure.

Just as I'm about to make my way through the other side of the stable, I hear my name being called. Turning, I can't help but smile when I see Alex stalking toward me wearing tight pants and boots, a heavy jacket, and black cowboy hat. He's as country as they come, definitely different from what he looked like in Key West. However, it's pretty damn sexy. I take a mental picture of how rugged he looks with the scruff on his jawline and messy hair under his hat. As soon as he's close enough to touch me, he wraps his strong arms around me and kisses my forehead.

"Mornin', beautiful," he says with a sexy gruff in his tone. "Sorry, boundaries. I know. It's going to be hard, though. Just a warning."

"It's okay." The smile on my face might be permanent.

"I couldn't wait to see you. We're not finished for the day yet, but since I started earlier than Dylan, he said he'd cover until after lunch." He loosens his grip on me and swings his arm around my shoulder and leads me toward the other entryway. Once we step outside, I see several trails that lead out in different directions.

"It's so peaceful out here," I say, taking everything in.

"These are the trails we have for horseback riding and for the Ranger side by sides, which are basically beefed-up golf carts. The blue trail goes to a pond. In the summer, it's surrounded by wildflowers and a cute family of ducks. The red trail leads to a beautiful lookout point, and the green trail is for easy riding. It's usually the ones we take the kids on. They're all loops and circle back here. I'd love to take you one day. Have you ever been horseback riding?"

"No, but I've always wanted to, though. Bucket list item," I say with a smirk.

A knowing grin fills Alex's face. "Darlin', start making a Texas bucket list, and we'll check them off one by one."

Hearing him say that sends tingles down my spine. I don't know what it is about this man, but it feels as if no time has separated us at all. We're easily falling back into the same Key West rhythm we were in, but the reality is, it's not just him and me anymore. We're having a baby together, which is a forever commitment, and just thinking about all of that scares the shit out of me. He notices me tense and squeezes my hand but doesn't say anything.

"You know what I *would* like to do?" I smile wide.

Smirking, he lifts his eyebrows. "What's that, sweetheart?"

"I want to take a tour of the ranch. This place is huge. I looked it up on Google, and I just can't imagine what hundreds of acres even looks like."

"Right now?" he asks.

"Whenever you have time. I think it'd be fun."

Alex grabs my hand and leads me back through the stables. We walk past the horse corral to a big red barn that looks like it should be on a movie set. Sliding the large door open, he takes a step to the side and I see 4-wheelers and the beefed-up golf cart things he was talking about.

"I've got all the time in the world for you."

How can he consistently say all the right things at exactly the right time? The past few weeks I've felt horrible, and I've hated the way I've looked, but being around him changes all of that. Alex looks at me with so much fire in his eyes, it almost burns my skin. Just being around him, smelling him, staring into his eyes is making my hormones go haywire. At this point, I might need more self-control than he does because my body remembers every single kiss and touch, and it's been craving him since I left Key West. Pregnancy hormones are way worse than Key West hormones, especially since I already know what I'm missing.

He watches me watch him. As he steps closer, he brushes his fingers across the softness of my cheek before giving me a sweet smile. "A complete tour would take days. We have to be back for lunch in two hours, and Mama doesn't accept tardiness. You'll learn that, though. If you want, we can see a small portion of it right now. We can take the blue trail. They're not going to be riding for a few more hours anyway."

I nod eagerly. "Yes. I'd love that."

Alex grabs a set of keys from the wall and leads me over to the side by side parked in the front. I climb in, and as soon as I sit down next to him, he places his hand on my thigh, and I place my hand on top of his. We both glance at each other and smile.

"Hold on," he says, pressing on the gas, and we zoom out of the barn, drive around the stables, and make our way down the trail.

"Just remember: baby on board." I nod my head down to my belly. "No major bumps or anything."

"Don't worry. I got you." He winks.

A few minutes into the trail, Alex speaks up again. "I should probably tell you more about my family before lunch. Mama and Dad have been married since they were eighteen. High school sweethearts and all that. Got married young, had babies young. Mama's strict, but she loves with everything she's got. Dad's a tough one to crack, but over time, he'll warm up to you. They're both set in their ways, but with five kids, they've had to juggle a lot. I think I mentioned my siblings before, but just a reminder in case you forgot. I'm the youngest of the boys, so I get shit on a lot for it." He shrugs with a sideways grin. "Then there's John and Jackson, the twins."

I chuckle to myself, thinking that reminder would've been nice a couple hours ago. "Yeah, I met Jackson this morning."

He gives me a sideways glance at the tone of my voice. "Don't worry. John put him in his place." I chuckle.

"Good. So, then there's my sister, Courtney, who ironically is also pregnant. But with triplets."

"Triplets?" I gasp, and my eyes go wide. "I can't even imagine."

"Yep. She and her husband, Drew, tried for a couple of years before seeing some fancy fertility doctor and ending up with three babies. They live in California but come and visit when they can. Oh, speaking of doctor, my oldest brother, Evan, is a doctor."

"A doctor?" I ask, surprised. I really thought they'd all be involved with the ranch in some way, but I know a doctor's busy schedule.

"Yeah. He's a hardass and super smart. He's the only one of us boys who decided he didn't want the rancher life, but Dad makes him come and help on his days off," he explains.

"Sounds like there's never a dull moment with the Bishops." I chuckle. "So thanks for the twin warning ahead of time, by the way. I was really confused this morning when I was talking to John, or I thought I was anyway, and it ended up being Jackson. He had no idea who I was and hit on me until John intervened." I place my free hand in the pocket of my jacket because the wind seems colder now that we're speeding up.

"That motherfucker," he mutters. "Yeah, he does that. *A lot*, actually. Drives John fuckin' nuts, but Jackson lives for a laugh especially when it comes to making any one of us uncomfortable. Sometimes he likes to wear the same clothes as John, and it makes John so mad. But it's pretty funny. Mostly because I get to witness it."

"I don't know if I'll ever be able to tell them apart," I add over the roaring of the engine.

He chuckles. "Most people have that issue. But John is the quiet one. He's more sensible, and Jackson likes being an asshole. John is an introvert whereas Jackson is loud and proud, and overly flirty with every woman he sees. No matter her age. They may look the same, but they're complete opposites in personality. You'll figure it out sooner than later, trust me. Jackson doesn't know how to shut up."

"That's good information, actually." I chuckle. "Jackson definitely gives off the party vibe."

He looks over at me with a knowing look. "You have no idea."

We continue down the trail and begin climbing a large hill. By the time we make it to the top, Alex turns off the engine and gives me time to look out. It's magical how the land goes on as far as the eye can see. It almost seems like a mirage, and the silence is so relaxing. There's no rushing cars or city noise; it's so quiet that I can hear the wind rustling the grass.

"Wow," I whisper.

"You've not seen nothing yet." Alex turns on the Ranger and presses the gas. We roll down the other side of the hill and drive into a valley. Time seems to stand still as we continue forward until a large pond comes into view. Trees surround it, and there are a few picnic tables under the trees; I can imagine people having lunch out here. Once Alex cuts the engine, we get out and walk toward the pond. The blue sky and clouds reflect upon the water, and I feel like I could stare out at this view all day long. I can't wait to see it with wildflowers surrounding it, just like Alex described.

We stand next to each other, and I turn and look at him.

"Are you afraid?"

He licks his lips, and his face distorts. "Not even for a second," he replies, confidently. I wish I felt like that, but nevertheless, I'm relieved by his answer.

"I'm scared, Alex. I'm worried about this pregnancy. I've witnessed so much working at the children's hospital, seeing babies suffer, watching their parents cry and fall to pieces. Hell, I saw it with my own eyes with my sister, Rylie, and what it did to my parents. Everything's going to change, and all I can think about is what if this baby is sick or worse. The thoughts are so overwhelming and now being here with you..." I pause, inhaling a much-needed deep breath. "It's all so much."

Grabbing my hand, Alex turns me toward him and tilts my chin up. Staring into his blue eyes, I notice how they're the same color as the sky above us. "I'm here, darlin'. There are going to be plenty of *what-if* and scary moments, but all you need to know is that I'm here. We'll do this together, and everything's gonna be all right."

He kisses me softly, and I melt into him. My body relaxes, and I believe every word he says. Maybe if we're together, everything really will be okay.

We spent too much time at the pond, so instead of going straight back to the B&B, Alex drives us to his parents' house using a different trail. The property is so large that I'm lost and turned around because all the trails seem to connect to each other. My nerves are on fire again as we drive past another barn and he parks the side by side close to the back steps of a large country home. It's got a wraparound porch just like the B&B. When we walk inside, even though my heart is racing, it feels and smells just like home—a home I always wished I had.

"Mama," Alex yells out as soon as we walk in.

"In the kitchen," she responds. I stop and take a quick breath, preparing myself for the possible outcomes. My stomach starts to twist in knots, and I know it's not from the pregnancy this time.

CHAPTER SEVENTEEN

Alex

B y the look on River's face, I can tell she's nervous. Before we walk into the kitchen, I stop and hold her sweet face in my hands.

"You have nothing to worry about." I try to offer her some sort of comfort even though I've been pushing my own nerves below the surface. "Trust me, okay?"

She nods. "I trust you."

I grab her hand and lead her down the hallway toward the kitchen. Mama pulls sugar cookies from the oven and sets the hot baking sheet on top of the stove. She wipes her hands on a dish towel and turns around with a smile on her face that immediately fades when she sees River standing next to me.

Fuck. I know what that look means.

"Hey, Mama." I walk up to her, giving her a kiss on the cheek, then turning to River.

"This is River. River, this is my mama, Rose," I say, introducing them with a big smile on my face, hoping it spreads like wildfire. I almost introduced her as my girlfriend, because it sounds right, but I didn't want to cross the line or make the situation more awkward than it needs to be. Mama's never seen me bring a girl home, and I now realize this is going to be a lot harder than I expected.

"Hello," Mama says, looking her up and down before smiling.

"Hi," River says sweetly. "It's nice to finally meet you."

Mama nods and turns back to her cookies, placing each one on the cooling rack so they don't continue cooking on the tray. Just as I'm about to say something, Dad walks through the back door, placing his cowboy hat on the table.

"I'm starving," he says, pulling out a chair and sitting.

"River, this is my dad, Scott." I grab his attention to us.

"Hi," River says to him.

"Howdy, River." He stands and holds his hand out to shake hers.

"Alex didn't tell us he was bringing a guest, so let me grab you a place setting." Mama gives me a sideways glance, and I know she suspects something.

"Sorry, Mama," I apologize, knowing she doesn't like surprises. Oh well. She'll find out soon enough now.

We take our seats at the table across from my parents, and I try to make small talk, but the tension in the room is steadily growing. Mama serves baked potato soup in big bowls with tons of cheese and bacon on top.

River and I thank her, and once she sits down at the table with us, we hold hands and say grace. I look over at River who flashes a nervous smile, but she has nothing to worry about. I'll be with her through it all.

"This is the best soup I've ever eaten," River compliments after a few bites, and Mama offers a soft thank you.

"So you want to tell us what's goin' on?" Mama directs her question at me, and Dad pops his head up, wanting to know too.

I grab River's hand under the table and interlock my fingers with hers. "Well, turns out you're going to be grandparents to another little bundle."

Mama glares at me. Dad's face stays exactly the same, no reaction surfacing. The silence seems to drown on.

"How did this happen?" Mama asks, looking back and forth between

River and me. I can almost taste the venom in her words even though she tries to cover her disdain with a smile.

"Well, it's kind of a long story. We met in Key West when Dylan and I went last October." I don't want to go into details about our relationship and our vacation hookup agreement. Mama would never approve of my past lifestyle, which is why she isn't privy to that type of information.

"Well, son, I have to say I'm quite shocked right now. I feel blindsided by this whole situation," Mama says to River and me. And I understand. It's a lot to take in. I'm not a child, but Mama has always had high traditional expectations.

"What does this all mean, exactly?" Dad asks.

"I guess it means I'm gonna be a father," I reply.

Dad chuckles softly. "You two raisin' the baby together?"

"Yes, sir."

Mama sets her spoon down in her bowl and pushes it away. After wiping her mouth with the napkin from her lap then setting it on the table, I get the hint that lunch is over. Maybe bringing River here and dropping the bomb this way wasn't the smartest idea. Maybe I should've told Mama alone so I could get her real reaction, and we could talk it through. The whole situation backfired, and I can sense how uneasy River is by the tightness of her grip. Before getting up to leave, I thank Mama for lunch and tell Dad I'll be back to work after dropping River off at the B&B.

As I go to walk out, Mama calls me back. I place a hand on River's shoulder and tell her I'll meet her outside.

"If you weren't a grown man, I'd slap you right now," Mama says with her arms crossed over her chest. Fuck, I haven't seen her this pissed since she caught me stealing the tractor for a joyride when I was ten years old.

"What's your problem? You always said you wanted grandkids. Now you're going to have one close to you, and you're being rude. You didn't treat Courtney this way with her big announcement," I tell her and instantly feel terrible for playing the comparison game.

"Your situation and Courtney's are completely different. Courtney is married and settled. You, on the other hand, decided to knock up a stranger and bring her here, then expect me to welcome the news with open arms. Maybe you should've thought this through. Are you sure it's even yours?"

"Mom!" I scold her quick judgment.

"I'm sorry, but this is going to take me a while to process. Where does she live? Is she moving here? It's obvious the poor girl doesn't know anything about our lifestyle and has a lot of learnin' to do. And that's gonna need to change real quick. You know my motto, son: can't stand the heat, get out of the kitchen."

Good lord. If this is how fast she's blurting words out, I can't imagine how fast her mind is racing.

"Well first, yes, River *is* moving here from Wisconsin because I want to take responsibility for my baby, and we're going to be together. I know this is out of your traditional values, but what's done is done. You can be on board with it or not, but this is happening, and there's nothing you or anyone else can do about it but accept it." I search her face before I walk away, but I don't wait for her response because I'm pissed, and she knows it.

Before I walk outside, I put on a fake smile because I don't want River to be upset. We climb inside the side by side and drive across the pasture.

"She doesn't like me," River says on the way back to the B&B.

"She doesn't *know* you. I'm sure she'll fall in love with you. I have no doubts about it. Just gotta give each other a chance," I say confidently, and I truly believe that. It's just going to take a little adjusting for everyone. "Mama will come around."

"I hope so." She bows her head, chewing on her bottom lip.

I drive us around to the back and pull the side by side in the barn at the B&B. We sit in silence for a moment before I turn and look at her. "I'm sorry for that. I truly expected a different reaction from them both."

Sweetly, she places her hand on top of mine. "It's okay. I honestly didn't know we were telling them about the baby right away. I thought maybe I'd meet them first, and then you'd mention it later when I wasn't around to feel their wrath." She falls silent.

"I'm so sorry. Stupid decision on my part, but I think Mama already had it figured out. She's as smart as a whip, and not much gets past her. Though you're the first girl I've ever brought to lunch, so I should've expected her to suspect something. I was just so excited for them to meet you, I didn't think it through."

"It's fine. At least they know, and we can move on, I guess." River isn't happy, and I hate knowing I disappointed her.

We get out and walk toward the back porch of the B&B, and I don't want to leave her, not in this state, but I have to get back to work, or I'll never hear the end of it. Just as the thought crosses my mind, I get a phone call. I pull my phone from my pocket and see it's Dylan.

"Yes?" I answer.

"Where the fuck are you? I need help getting this hay in the middle barn loft. I can't do this shit alone. I need you to go pick up the trailer and bring it over so we can load this shit and be done with the day."

"I'll be right there," I tell him.

River turns and looks at me. "Is that Dylan?"

I nod.

"Tell him hi for me!" River says, and she's smiling again—thankfully.

"I heard her," he tells me. "Tell her I said hey and that your ass needs to leave right now before I drive over there and drag you back."

All I can do is laugh. "Okay, okay. I'm heading that way. Give me fifteen minutes."

I walk River inside, up the stairs, and to her room. Yawning, she sits on the edge of the bed, kicking off her shoes. There's nothing more I wanna do right now than pull her into my arms and hold her until the sun goes down. It's barely past one, and I'm sure she's exhausted from everything we did today.

"So I guess we have a lot of planning to do. When does your plane leave?" There are so many questions to ask, but I feel like I have zero time to get them all out, especially with Dylan waiting for me.

She lies back on the bed. Her blonde hair surrounds her face, and she looks so damn beautiful. She folds her hands over her belly, and I smile at the small bump forming on her petite frame. I blink hard making sure I'm not imagining any of this because since I saw her at the diner, I've been in a dream state.

"Tomorrow at twelve. I didn't initially plan to stay very long. Get in, get out type of thing because I didn't know what your reaction would be. Plus, I have to be back to work on Wednesday." She props herself up on one elbow and looks at me with so much passion in her eyes I'm forced to hold myself back. She has no clue what she does to me with just one glance. I ball my hands into fists and tell myself I can't do the things I want to do. But if I could, I'd lay her down, make sweet love to her, then fuck her really good for making me wait this long.

"Okay," I say, my eyes wandering up and down her body. "Oh, we're planning a surprise birthday party for Mama next month, so my entire family will be there, and I'd really like you to be there, too."

River sits up straight. "I don't know if that's a good idea, considering she hates me."

I sit next to her, needing to touch her in some way, just to make sure she's really here. I face her and grab her soft hands in mine.

"It's a really big deal. Mama's turning fifty. All my aunts, uncles, and cousins are coming. Even the ones who have to travel from hours away. I'd really love for you to meet everyone, so we can share our news. Don't know the next time we'll all be together again."

She chews her bottom lip, stewing it over. "Well, I can't make any promises, Alex. If I can, I will, but I have to go back to Wisconsin first and make arrangements. Pack up my apartment. Find a moving company. Put in my two weeks' notice and see if a transfer close is even available before coming back here. I don't even know where I'm going to stay or what I'm taking with me. There's so much up in the air right now that I don't feel like I can commit to anything, even if it's a month away. A lot can happen in such a short time, so I just don't want to disappoint you." I can hear the worry in her voice.

"Darlin', don't worry about anything here. I promise I'm going to work on all that and have it settled before you come back. And let me say, the sooner, the better. I honestly wish you didn't have to go back at all."

She nods, her green eyes meeting mine, and I can't stop myself any longer. I pull her to my chest, my mouth magnetized to hers. River sighs against my lips, and her body melts into mine as we kiss slowly and passionately, not rushing. I want to take all the time I can with her because this moment seems too good to be true. When we finally break apart, her chest rises and falls, and I watch as she swallows hard.

"Sorry," I whisper, knowing I've crossed her boundaries once again.

What we had in Key West, that insane connection, is still here and is as strong as ever.

Smirking, I stand. "I have a feeling I'm going to be apologizing for doing things like that a lot."

"We're supposed to be taking it slow, remember?" She chuckles.

I shrug. "I know. But it's hard when I finally have what I've been missing all these months," I admit.

"Yeah, what's that?" River raises an eyebrow and studies me.

"*You.*"

Before we can get too caught up in each other, my phone vibrates in my pocket, and I realize I've lost track of time again. I reject the call. Dylan needs to find a little patience and give me a fucking break.

"Dylan and I will get your car from the diner and park it downstairs for you, so you don't have to leave any sooner for the airport than you have to."

River stands, digs in her bag, and hands me the keys. "That'd be great considering I have no idea how to get to the diner from here. Since my flight leaves at noon, I should be there around ten."

"I wish you didn't have to go," I tell her and watch her face soften.

"It won't be forever," she reminds me as she hands over the keys. Leaning forward, I kiss her on the cheek before telling her goodbye— something I already hate doing.

"I'll come back after work if that's okay."

"I'd love that," she says, walking back to the bed. "I think I'm going to read for a while and maybe take a nap until you come back."

"Okay, darlin'. Sweet dreams." I smile before walking out. As soon as I'm in the hallway, I send Dylan a text and let him know I'm on my way to get the trailer then I'll meet him. All I get in return is a middle finger emoji.

It takes me no time at all to drive to the middle pasture where the large storage barn is. Bales of hay are plopped on top of each other in the entryway, and I back in the old work truck and trailer. Slamming the door shut, I get out and yell, "I'm back, asshole!"

"'Bout damn time!" he says, throwing another bale of hay from the loft above. It hits the ground with a thud, causing dust to rise. I put on my gloves and begin loading them on the trailer until it's full. It's backbreaking work, but I welcome the distraction.

Once we've got the truck packed down, Dylan climbs down the ladder.

"So, how's Daddy doin'?" he teases. When I told him earlier, he wasn't shocked at all, but it hasn't stopped him from giving me shit and making daddy jokes all damn day. I don't imagine that will stop anytime soon, either.

"Shut the hell up," I tell him as we climb into the truck.

"How'd it go today?" He turns the heater on full blast and places his hands over the vent.

"Mama wasn't happy about it. Shoulda probably told her alone."

"She'll get over it, though. Remember that time Jackson thought he knocked up that preacher's daughter? Remember how angry she was? I thought she was gonna grab a shotgun and hunt Jackson down."

I chuckle, completely forgetting about that. "Yeah. I remember now. But she was pissed because she heard it through the grapevine *at church* and not Jackson's mouth. So it's kinda different."

We drive down the rock road, kicking dust up in our wake, and head over to the B&B to unload the hay into the stables. Considering the group of riders will be back within the hour, Dylan and I make quick work of it and stack hay in the feed room until it's full. After we're done, we drive around the property and drop hay for the horses and cows. It takes more time than I predicted, but that's to be expected when there's so much land to cover.

Before we call it quits for the day, I ask Dylan if he'll ride with me to get River's car. Rolling his eyes, he agrees. We drop the work vehicles back at the barn and take my truck to the diner. The sun is setting in the distance, and I know we don't have much time before darkness falls. Fifteen minutes later, we're pulling into the parking lot. When I see Mrs. Betty inside wiping a table down and getting ready to close, I decide to step in really quick.

"Hey, honey!" she says with a big wide smile.

"Hey, Mrs. Betty." I give her a hug. "Can I order a piece of chocolate cake to go? Actually, make it two."

"Sure thing." She walks around the counter and cuts two huge slices and places them in boxes, then bags it. I hand her a twenty and tell her to keep the change.

"You always spoil me," she tells me. "Is that for your lady?" Her eyebrows raise as she waits for my answer.

"Yes, ma'am. The other piece is for Mama."

"I'm sure there's a story behind that one. You'll have to come see me sometime this week and fill me in," Betty says just as someone walks up to pay their check. I promise her I will and make my way out the door.

"I'm not driving that," Dylan says, pointing to the Prius. "My dick may actually fall off if I even sit in that thing."

I hand him the keys to my truck. "Hopefully your dick will be okay with that."

Unlocking the car, I walk over to it and shake my head, understanding why Dylan was so reluctant. As soon as I open the door and attempt to sit, I search around the seat to slide it back so my legs have more room. Once I've adjusted the seat and mirrors, I press the button to crank it but can't hear the engine. I don't have to search around for the lights because they turn on as soon as the engine roars to life. Seriously, what is this futuristic shit? I put it in reverse and step on the gas, and it moves, but I'm not convinced the damned thing is even on.

The whole way back to the ranch, I can smell her shampoo, and it causes my mind to wander back to the beach. That really was a trip of a lifetime that changed both our lives forever.

I turn onto the country road that leads to the ranch, and Dylan follows close behind me. Instead of going straight to the B&B, I turn on the long driveway that leads to my parents' house where Dylan's truck is parked. When I get out with a to-go box and plastic fork in my hand, he looks at me confused.

"I'm gonna be a while. I have to talk to my Mama before going to see River. I have an apology to make for being disrespectful."

Dylan hands me my keys and walks toward his truck. "You better apologize then. Mama can make your life heaven or hell, and you ought to know by now you get more bees with honey than vinegar."

"Story of my life. See you tomorrow!" I tell him as I walk up the sidewalk that leads to the front door. Before stepping in, I inhale a deep breath, say a little prayer, and hope I can smooth this over. Pushing my ego to the side, I turn the doorknob and enter.

Mama is sitting on the couch with a blanket on her lap watching one of those cheesy movies on the Hallmark Channel that always fades to black.

She glances at me then focuses on the TV.

"Hey, Mama," I say sweetly, sitting next to her on the couch.

"Hey, baby." She speaks, but she doesn't look back at me. The tension in the room is so thick, I could cut it with a knife.

"I'm sorry for being short earlier. You raised me better than that." I hand her the piece of cake and fork.

She opens the box and immediately smiles. "Trying to sweeten me up with Betty's cake? Your father taught you right."

Before she even asks, I walk to the kitchen, pour a big glass of cold milk, and return to the living room. "I just want us to be okay. That's all. I don't like going to bed angry. Something you taught me a long time ago."

"Sit," she demands, taking the milk willingly. "Listen to me, son. I love you no matter what. Okay? I'll always love you and your brothers and sister. Knowing that you're all going to start having kids of your own makes me realize that you're no longer my babies, that you're growing up, and moving on."

I open my mouth to speak, and she lifts her mighty finger to stop me.

"I always wanted you all to have a better life than I had. Than your father had. I wanted you to experience everything you possibly could, but most of all, I want you to be happy."

"Mama, I'm so happy. I'm the happiest I've ever been in my life right now. And that's why it's so important to have your acceptance. I want Dad's approval, too. It hurts me to know that you're disappointed in me or in the situation or that you don't like the woman who's carrying your grandbaby."

She takes a bite of cake and closes her eyes as she chews. Betty's cake is the best in six counties; even Mama knows it.

"Honey, I don't know her. How can I not like someone I don't know? I just thought you'd settle with some sweet Southern girl who has the same values as us, not someone from a different world. But I've had to realize that's not my choice, that's *yours*. However, I was shocked today. It took me by surprise that's all. Out of all my sons, I didn't think you'd be the one to be in this situation right now. If anyone, I thought it'd be Jackson, honestly."

That makes me laugh because she really has no idea. Jackson talks a big talk, but he doesn't walk the walk. He's a loose cannon on most days.

"I know, Mama. But I thought you'd be happy to hear I'm doing the right thing. We're going to do this together and be a family, which strangely enough, is all I want. She came here to tell me she was pregnant and keeping the baby but didn't expect anything from me, just thought I deserved to know. I begged her to move here so I could be involved. She's leaving the only life she's ever known to be with me because that's the best chance we have of having something real."

She blinks, taking in everything I've just said, and her shoulders visibly relax. "Do you love her?" she asks.

It takes me less than a second to respond. "Yes, Mama. I think I do." Memories of us together flash through my mind. The way River's face looks when she laughs and how pretty she is when she's sleeping are all I can think about. I try to imagine my life without her in it, and it's just not possible. "I've never felt this way about anyone in my life."

The corner of her lips tilts up. "That's good enough for me, son. Come here," Mama says, setting the cake on the coffee table. She opens her arms, and I fall into them.

"I love you, Alex."

"I love you, too, Mama. I always will."

CHAPTER EIGHTEEN

River

Instead of taking a nap, I sit on the back porch and read for hours. In Texas, they seem to eat before five o'clock, and I hadn't realized I was hungry until someone mentioned dinner was being served. Somehow, I clear a plate of pot roast and mashed potatoes like I haven't eaten in weeks.

After dinner, I read until dark. I had to know what happened at the end of my book regardless of my eyes being tired. Not knowing what time Alex would return, I decide to crawl into bed for the night because I'm exhausted. I don't know how long I've been sleeping when I wake to the door of my room slowly being cracked open. The moonlight streams through the window, and I'm groggy as I turn to see Alex walking inside.

"Hey, sweetheart," he says, softly.

"Hi." I barely get out. I hadn't realized how damn tired I was till now. He doesn't turn on the lights, but instead, he sets a Styrofoam box and plastic fork down on the small dresser next to the bed. As he steps closer, I can smell him. He smells like hay and leather all mixed with sweat, and it's a scent I'd like to bottle up and bring back to Wisconsin with me.

"I'm going to take a shower if that's okay," he whispers close to my face, brushing the hair off my forehead and pressing a soft kiss there.

I nod, closing my eyes, and drift in and out of sleep as I hear the water run in the bathroom.

Just as I'm falling deeper into sleep, I feel him crawl into bed next to me. The warmth of his body from the shower feels good against my skin as our bodies mold together. He holds me like he's never letting me go, and when his hand brushes against my stomach, I smile, then tense up when all the memories of us in bed flood in.

"I just want to hold you," he says against the softness of my neck, and it feels like home. For the first time in months, I feel complete with Alex next to me, and that thought scares me. Whatever's going on between us has to work. I want it to work, but the possibility of it not is still there. I push the thoughts out of my head, and when I hear the low sound of his heavy breathing, I know he's asleep. It doesn't take long for me to follow him to dreamland.

I wake up in the early morning and wonder if last night was all a dream because Alex is nowhere to be found. The Styrofoam box is still in place, so I know it wasn't.

Checking the time, I realize breakfast is still being served and take the opportunity to go downstairs to get more of those delicious blueberry muffins. As soon as I see them, my mouth instantly waters. I grab two and sit in my favorite chair by the window.

Just as I'm stuffing my mouth, a man walks in wearing dark blue scrubs with an ID badge pinned to his top. He must be the older brother, Evan—the doctor. I watch him as he walks to the counter and speaks with John. He shares similarities to Alex with the same dark blond hair and build, and those same bright blue Bishop eyes. However, Evan's face is more aged, and

I can tell he's the oldest of the brothers. His jawline is cut with darker scruff, and the stress from his job is evident in his features.

I don't realize I'm staring until John points over at me. Lifting my hand, I wave and try to swallow down the huge bite of muffin I took. Evan makes eye contact with me then walks over. The way he's looking at me like he knows all my secrets makes me nervous as hell. Cocky confidence must be a Bishop thing because they've all got it.

Evan doesn't ask before he sits in the chair across from me.

"I'm Evan. Alex's older brother," he says, formally introducing himself.

"Hi, I'm River. Nice to officially meet you," I tell him, wondering if he's an asshole doctor because if I had to judge him by his looks and the way he carries himself, I'd say he was. He has that brooding and serious look down.

"I'm just going to cut to the chase." He looks at his watch then back at me. "I know about you and Alex. I also know you're a pediatric nurse. You know I'm a doctor. See what I'm getting at?"

I continue eating my muffins because I have no clue what he's insinuating but pretend like I do.

"If you're really moving here and need a job, I can put in a good word for you, if you're interested. Alex said you were worried about finding work here, but we're always looking. We can use all the help we can get at the hospital, especially on the children's floor. Not many people with your experience move to Nowhere, Texas, so we're always shorthanded."

Well, these Bishops just get straight to the point, don't they?

I swallow down the muffin. "You're offering me a job?"

"Well, I don't do the official hiring, but one phone call and you'd have an interview within an hour. Mostly just to make sure your references pan out and that you are who you say you are. Then there'd be official paperwork for you to fill out and all of that, but if you want it, then yes, I could help make it happen." His words make my head spin because I hadn't decided what I'd do for work yet or if I'd wait till after the baby was born.

"Wow...I don't know what to say."

"Think about it and get back to me. No pressure. Just wanted you to know the option is there."

"I will, thank you." I smile, feeling the stress melt away. I love my job and working with kids, and knowing I'd be leaving it behind is a hard reality to swallow. However, if I could continue some of that work here, I wouldn't feel so useless and dependent on Alex.

"Get settled and learn the area and people, and if you want to wait till after the baby, the job will still be here for you."

I'm shocked to the point of almost being speechless.

"Working with kids was a dream, so I really can't imagine doing anything else."

"We don't have a pediatric hospital—just a ward—so it's not as large as you're probably used to, but they could use a nurse with your experience. In fact, they *need* someone like you. It's a nice community, and even though you're not one of us, you'd eventually fit right in," he teases.

I smile, chuckling. Evan isn't anything like I'd expected, but that could change. The last three minutes have been strange, to say the least.

"I don't know what to say..." My mind is racing from information overload on top of everything else.

"No worries. Just think about it. I don't need an answer now."

"Okay, well thank you. I certainly appreciate it."

He winks and checks his watch. "Sorry, I'm going to be late for my shift if I don't get going," he says, standing. Before he walks away, he turns and looks straight at me. "Oh, nice meeting you and congrats."

All my words have vanished. I remember Alex saying his brother was a doctor, but I didn't realize he had so much pull at the hospital. His words keep replaying in my mind. The hospital needs *me*. That's all I needed to hear to help me solidify my decision. Sure, the children's hospital in Milwaukee needs me too, but it's not dire. There are handfuls of other nurses who are just as well versed as I am. But moving here would be different. It'd be more intimate at a smaller hospital. And I don't think he'd lie about needing my experience. After I finish eating, I go upstairs, grab my cell phone, and call Natalie. I have to talk to her now. Considering she's off today, I know she's awake and probably doing nothing.

"Nat!" I say as soon as she answers, my excitement building.

"What? Is everything okay?" she asks, and I can tell she's walking.

"Yes, it's great. I have so much to tell you." I sit on the edge of the bed. "Alex wants me to move to Texas."

"Oh, my fucking gosh! That's so great, River! See, I told you! Sorry if I'm breathing heavily; I'm climbing the stairs to my apartment because the elevator line was too long."

"So his brother is a doctor..." I add.

"No fucking way. A *hot* doctor?" she asks, her tone rising in pitch.

"I am *not* answering that, soon-to-be Mrs. Adam Mathews. Anyway, he says he can help get me a job at the hospital on their children's ward. This shouldn't be this easy, right? Like I'm starting to second-guess everything."

She laughs. "I was wondering if old skeptical River was going to come out and play."

"Ha-ha." I roll my eyes even though she can't see me. "Actually, it's not been that easy. I met his mother yesterday, and I don't think she's too fond of me. She was nice, but the way she looked at me, I just got the feeling she wouldn't blink twice if I caught on fire."

I hear Natalie unlock a door then I hear it click closed. "Mothers don't like *any* girlfriends. Do you think Adam's mother loved me when we first met? Hell no, she didn't. She thought I was the devil who was taking away her only son. Just gotta kill her with kindness, and you'll grow on her. Remember you're always the second woman. *Trust* me on that." Natalie laughs, and I remember some of the stories she'd told me when they first started dating, and it helps me relax slightly about my situation. It's been so long since I've been in any sort of real relationship that I forget these types of things are normal.

"Thanks, Nat. Oh, don't forget to pick me up from the airport around five tonight."

"Yeah, babe. I know. I'll be there. Just hope you don't get delayed. The snow won't fucking stop. I feel like I'm in a frozen winter hell."

I can't help but smile. "Don't jinx me, dammit! I'll text you as soon as the plane lands or if I get delayed beforehand. I'd better go pack because I have to get going soon if I'm going to make it there on time." I look at the clock and realize I have to leave in an hour.

Natalie squeals. "Can't wait to see you!"

We say our goodbyes, and I start packing my suitcase. I grab all my toiletries from the bathroom and make sure I don't leave anything behind, even though I'll be back soon. Just as I glance over, I see the Styrofoam box that Alex set on the dresser last night. My keys are sitting right next to the fork. I open the box and see it's a giant piece of chocolate cake. Smiling, I decide I'm taking it to the airport with me and eating it while I wait for my plane.

After everything is packed, I roll my suitcase down to the car. The airport is a little over an hour away, and I should leave soon, but this time, I'm not going anywhere without telling Alex goodbye. Once my foot hits the bottom step, I see John rushing toward me. He grabs my suitcase and carries it to the car for me like a perfect gentleman.

"You coulda called me. I would've been happy to help you with this."

"I know, I know. I'm just used to doing most things by myself and forget to ask. Thank you so much, though," I tell him as he loads the suitcase in the trunk before shutting it.

Just as I turn around, I see Alex walking and looking straight at me.

"Safe travels, River. We'll see you real soon," John says then walks back inside, giving Alex and me some privacy.

"Hey you," Alex says. His clothes are dirty, and he even has dirt on his face and hat.

"What the hell?" I look him up and down, lingering a little too long on his *package*. Those tight pants are giving away his secrets, and I can't help but glance down.

He lifts his hat and scrubs a hand over his face and hair. "The cowboy life is rough." A sexy smirk plays on his lips as he notices where I was looking. His hair is disheveled, and he looks so damn sexy as he stands in front of me.

"I knew you'd be leaving soon, so I wanted to give you a proper goodbye and get your number; something I shoulda done a long ass time ago," he says, pulling out his phone and unlocking it. I grab it and program my number into his contacts, then text myself so I've got his too.

I can't help but think how ironic and strange it is that we're just now exchanging numbers.

"Please text me when you land so I know you made it back okay. And call me when you get home so I can at least rest easy tonight knowing you're safe," he says softly as I hand him his phone.

I smile. "I will." And this time, I mean it. "Promise."

Even though he's dirty, he wraps his arms around me tightly, not wanting to let go, and it's something I welcome. "Bye, River. Come back to me soon."

"I will. I'll keep you updated on everything, too. I'll give you a timeline as soon as I get my life situated," I tell him as he loosens his embrace.

"If you need any help with *anything*, just let me know." Alex leans in, pulling my bottom lip into his mouth, and sucks on it. He runs his fingers through my hair and kisses me, and my hormones go haywire as I taste him. When we break apart, I realize that's the goodbye we should've had in Key West.

A week has passed since I've been home and taking care of business. I'm nervous and have asked myself at least a thousand times if this is the right decision, but each time I speak with Alex on the phone, my heart reminds me it is.

After doing some research and pricing moving companies, which was way out of my budget, I decide to list all my furniture online instead. Then I'll pack and ship a few boxes of things I want to keep, then donate the rest. Luckily, I don't really have that much, considering I didn't spend a lot of time in my apartment except to sleep and eat.

Once I returned from Key West, I kicked out my roommate because she kept bringing Asshole around, and I didn't want that kind of negativity in my life anymore. I planned to move into a one-bedroom apartment, then found out I was pregnant. Now, I'm grateful I'd been downsizing.

There are only two things left to do before everything is wrapped up in Wisconsin: give my parents the news and say goodbye to Natalie.

My parents live up north, so I call them and ask if they can drive down to meet me after lunch. Even though they're divorced, I want to tell them together in person.

I'm almost ready to start a new chapter in my life, as odd as it feels. Everything's happening so quickly, which might be the norm when it comes to Alex Bishop, but that's yet to be determined.

My job was very understanding and allowed me to take the rest of my vacation days instead of working the final two weeks. Leaving was hard, but I took my time saying goodbye to my patients. It was bittersweet.

After I eat a quick bite, I take a bus across town to a coffee shop where I asked my mother and father to meet me. I'm nervous, but I don't expect either of them to beg me to stay or anything. Since Rylie's death and their divorce, they haven't been the same. Even when I was around, they acted like I was invisible.

It's been years since the three of us have been together, and for once, this is a good reason. Or at least I hope that's what they'll think.

When I walk in, they're sitting at a table, pretending the other isn't there. They're not holding a conversation or even looking in the same direction, which kind of hurts my heart.

"Hey, you two!" I say, trying to lighten the mood.

"Hey, River. How've you been doing?" Dad asks, standing up to greet me with a hug.

"Good. Really good," I tell him, giving Mom a hug next before I sit down.

"That's great, River," Mom adds.

"How was the drive? Traffic okay?"

Dad purses his lips. Mom narrows her eyes.

"Traffic was fine," Mom finally answers. Geez, you'd think I asked them to perform a rain dance ritual or something. I know their marriage ended badly, but it's been years. You'd think that hostility would've diminished by now.

"Well, I'll just cut to the chase since you both have to drive back tonight. I'm sure you're wondering what's going on," I say, inhaling a deep breath.

My heart begins to race, and I know I need to spit this out, but it seems like I'm walking through thick honey and can barely move.

"I've decided to move to Texas in a few weeks."

They both stay quiet for a moment until finally, my father speaks. "What prompted this decision?"

"Well..." I pause, wishing I would've bought a bottle of water because my throat is as dry as the Sahara. "I recently found out I was pregnant, and the father lives in Texas. We're going to see where things go between us, but I also want the baby to have him in his or her life."

Tears of happiness stream down my mother's face. "River," she says in a hushed tone. "We're going to be grandparents." She looks at my father, and his eyes meet hers as if he's seeing her for the first time in a decade.

"Hell, had I known getting pregnant was the trick, I would've tried it back in high school," I tease.

"That's not even funny," Mom scolds, but I laugh anyway.

"I wish you weren't moving so far away," Dad adds. "We'd like to be involved too."

Guilt washes over me because I didn't think they'd care that much, considering they haven't wanted to be involved in my life in a long time.

"You can always come visit. We can text and FaceTime too. I'm sure you'd love it there. No snow. Horseback riding. All the typical Texas stuff: cowboys, cacti, and horses." I smile, knowing their love for winter sports trumps anything Texas could offer.

Dad lets out a sigh.

"As long as you're happy, sweetie. That's all that matters. If moving to Texas to be with this man is what you want, I fully support your decision."

"I do, too, baby," Dad confirms. My shoulders relax, and it feels so good to get it all out.

"Does he treat you right?" Mom asks.

I grab her hand with a lopsided grin. "Yes, Mom." I sigh. "He treats me like a queen."

"You deserve to be," she says with a smile on her face.

"You really do," Dad adds.

For a moment, I feel my emotions bubble over. I'm halfway shocked when tears stream down my face because their reactions shined light to a dark corner of my heart. After the conversation is over, we exchange hugs and goodbyes, then Dad leaves, and Mom follows behind him. I take the bus to Natalie's apartment and try to replay everything that happened today.

As soon as she opens the door, she pulls me into a big hug. Out of everything that's here, Natalie is who I'm going to miss the most. She's my best friend and has been for as long as I can remember. I hope and pray distance doesn't affect our friendship.

"Come in," she tells me as she releases our embrace. I don't hesitate before stepping inside.

I walk in and smell cookies baking, and I know she made them just for me. Sitting in the recliner, I prop up my feet and lean back. "You're making chocolate chip oatmeal cookies again, aren't you?"

"Of course, I am, Mama. They're your favorite." She smiles and sits on the couch. "How'd your parents take the news?"

"Surprisingly well," I admit, and I'm still kind of shocked by their response.

"That's great, River. They don't really have a choice other than to accept what's going on, you know?" The oven beeps, and Natalie quickly gets up and takes them out. She grabs a spatula, places a few on a plate, and pours two large glasses of milk. She spoils me. Before Adam gets home, we talk about everything—about me moving, her coming to visit, keeping in touch, FaceTiming, and how I have to keep her involved in every aspect of the pregnancy. We lose complete track of time reminiscing, and when I realize hours have passed, I decide it's time for me to go.

Natalie pulls me into a big hug, and we squeeze each other so tight it almost hurts.

"I'm going to try not to cry," she says.

"No tears. This isn't goodbye forever. We're going to chat all the time," I remind her.

She chokes back tears, and I do too. Sucking in a deep breath, I somehow find the strength to walk away.

"Text me when you get home," she says as I step onto the elevator.

"I will!"

She waves goodbye just before the doors close, and I wipe the tears away.

I guess it's really all settled now. There's nothing else holding me here.

CHAPTER NINETEEN

Alex

"Shut the hell up!" I yell at Jackson as he irritates me from his bedroom.

"You're the one who's forcing me to move out," he retorts as he carries boxes outside to his truck.

I laugh when he walks back in and flips me off with both hands.

"I'm paying thousands of dollars for you to leave. You've wanted your own place for a while anyway. It's not going to take that long to finish that house. Dad already told you that."

Since River will be here tomorrow, I've been trying to get everything settled, and Jackson's deadline to get all his shit out was yesterday. Being the asshole procrastinator he is, he waited until the very last minute to pick up the remaining boxes. This whole process hasn't been the easiest, considering Jackson and I split the cost to have this house remodeled.

Unfortunately, he's been giving me shit ever since Mama suggested it. I was surprised when she did, but luckily it was her idea, so Jackson caved and did what she wanted. But until the house is fixed up and remodeled, Jackson's staying with John, who isn't happy about the whole idea.

After a few more trips to his truck, Jackson comes back in breathing heavily. "That's all of it."

"Thank God." I sigh, relieved.

He takes a few steps forward, and at first, I think he's going to punch me, but instead, he gives me a big brotherly hug. "Better be glad I love you."

"Don't get all mushy on me," I tell him, and he laughs.

He looks down at his watch. "Gotta go. John's gonna be home, and I want to meet him at the door wearing the same clothes."

"You're such a prick."

He laughs and gives me a sarcastic thumbs up. "Not many people have a twin they can fuck with. Gotta take advantage of it every chance I get."

I shake my head, and when I hear the rumble of his truck in the distance, I let out a deep breath. The house almost looks empty without his shit all over the place, but that'll give River a blank space to make this place her own. I just hope she accepts living with me since I haven't officially asked her yet. I wanted to make sure she was standing in front of me when I did.

Not wanting to push her limits, I had an extra bedroom set from the B&B moved and set up in Jackson's room since River decided to sell her furniture. I wish I could sleep next to her instead, but I'm not rushing things, just as she wanted. The more I thought about us while she was in Wisconsin, the more I realized she was right about taking it slow. I plan to spend all the time I can getting to know every little thing about her. I want our relationship to have a solid foundation, considering she already has my heart.

It's almost been two weeks since River left, and today, she's finally coming back to me for good. I wake up, feed the animals, finish my day, and clean up before heading to the airport to pick her up. It's close to five p.m., and I'm exhausted, but just knowing she's on her way gives me an energy boost. During the hour it takes me to drive there, I do nothing but think about her and our future. It's all still hard for me to believe.

I sit in the chairs that line the wall and wait for her plane to land. The airport is tiny, so when I finally see a small plane slow and stop, I know she's here. My heart pounds with happiness, and I can't wait to hold her in my arms again. As soon as I see her, looking as pretty as ever in a pair of black leggings, a sweater, and snow boots, I stand to greet her. Almost immediately, she spots me, and a smile fills her gorgeous face.

Walking over to her, I can't help but smile too. I'm tempted to pull her into my arms, but I remind myself of those boundaries she asked for previously. It was impossible the last time she was here, repeatedly crossing those lines, but I'm making a solid effort now. If I want us to have a chance at making this work, I know I need to keep my distance, so we *can* start fresh.

She wraps an arm around me for a side hug, which I gladly accept. Whatever pace she leads, I'll follow from now on. Grabbing the carry-on bag from her hand, I walk beside her to the truck, making small talk.

"Nice boots," I say with a laugh, buckling up. Once we're both settled in our seats, I back out of the small parking lot.

"They're not shit slingers, but they made sure I didn't fall on black ice. I'm so happy to see sunshine. You have no idea."

"Sunshine? Is that my new nickname?" I tease, and she gives me a sideways glance with a grin.

As I drive us back to the ranch, I'm able to breathe a little easier knowing she's finally here—*home.*

"How was the flight?" I ask as we turn onto the old dirt road.

"Sucked. I hate those little planes. They're horrible. Thought I would need the barf bag, but I saved myself from the embarrassment and held it back," she admits. "Perks of being pregnant!"

"I can only imagine." I grab her hand as I park the truck in front of my house. She turns and looks at me with wide eyes.

"Where are we?" she asks.

I look at her and kiss her knuckles before I speak. "We're home."

River's mouth falls open, and I smile. She gets out of the truck, and I interlock my fingers with hers as we walk up the steps that lead to the modest farmhouse. Before we walk in, I stop her at the door.

"You can say no, but first let me just say this. I thought maybe living together would make the most sense for us, seeing that you're having a baby and all. That way we can raise him or her together and see where things go between us. If that's moving too fast, just let me know. But I did kick Jackson out, so you can have his room."

"Seriously?" she asks.

I nod and open the door, hoping that's a good reaction. She walks in and looks around, the smile on her face not faltering.

"Give me the grand tour, please," she says, reaching for my hand. I take it and never want to let it go. Her skin brushing against mine feels like home as we walk through the house.

"This is my bedroom." I open the door, and she steps inside, sucking in a deep breath.

"So this is where the magic happens?" She turns and looks at me with an arched brow.

"Only if you want it to."

She licks her lips as I eye her. I notice her breathing harder but decide to just tease her until she can't handle it anymore. Pulling her out of the room, I walk her around the rest of the house. "Here's the kitchen, a bathroom…"

When I open the door to Jackson's old room, her eyes light up. All the bedroom furniture is set up how I imagined she'd want it. "And here's your room."

She walks to the bed and her hand smooths the handmade quilt my grandmother made. "I can't believe you did all this for me."

"I'd do anything for you, River."

She bites her bottom lip, and I'm so tempted to lay her down on that bed and break it in properly. She doesn't even know how beautiful she is right now, and I want nothing more than to tell her as she looks up at me with seduction in her eyes. I remember that look in Key West and know it oh so damn well.

"There's more," I say, breaking the silence before I strip her clothes off and make sweet love to her. She follows me as I take her to the room where we kept our pool table, but now it's empty except for an old rocking chair. "This is the baby's room. I didn't paint or anything because I thought maybe we could do it together."

"Wow." Her eyes light up. "It's perfect," she whispers, walking around the empty space. "Thank you for doing this. I honestly didn't expect any of it."

Once River explores the space, she comes back to me and wraps her arms around my waist, pulling me close to her. I inhale the scent of her hair, and I want her so damn bad it almost hurts. Eventually, she takes a step back, creating space between us.

"So, you're okay with this arrangement?" I finally ask. "Sharing a house and setting up a nursery together?"

"Yeah, definitely." She nods, taking it all in. "It'll be like we're... roommates," she adds with a grin. "However, the last roommate I had slept with my ex-boyfriend, so hopefully you'll be better than her," she teases.

"I can promise you I won't be sleeping with anyone's boyfriend," I joke with her. "But don't walk around nude because I don't know if I'll be able to hold myself back. And if you'd like to save a horse and ride a cowboy instead, you just let me know," I tell her with a wink.

Her breath hitches and blush hits her cheeks. It's so damn cute when I catch her off guard. After shaking off my words, she finally speaks and changes the subject.

"You have a really nice house."

"It's *our* house now."

"Why are you so perfect?" she asks.

"Trust me, I'm not." I shrug. "But you make me want to be."

"See, that's what I'm talking about. You always have something sweet to say."

I chuckle, giving her a smirk. "Do I?"

"You know you do!" She laughs and playfully slaps my chest. "You've got this charm thing down to a science."

I can tell she's happy being here. All the stress from traveling has already melted away, and it's easy being here with her like this.

We're still standing in the baby's room, and she takes a step back and looks it over again. "We should paint it a neutral color like yellow. When the sun rises and sets, it will make the room glow even more when the windows are open."

"Whatever you want, sweetheart," I say, placing my hand on her shoulder. Right now, I know what true happiness is. There's no other place in the world I'd rather be than with River, and when she turns and looks at me with a sweet smile on her face, I know she feels the same way.

"Are you hungry?" I ask, knowing she's bound to be after traveling. It's nearly six thirty.

"Did you hear my stomach roar?" She giggles.

"Nope. But come on, we'll go to Mama's."

When her eyes meet mine, my heart does a flip-flop in my chest. I'm constantly at war with myself, telling the devil on my shoulder that I can't kiss her or make love to her, and bending her over the couch and fucking her senseless ain't gonna happen anytime soon. My body remembers Key West like it was yesterday, and I wish we could fall into the same step we were in before we left. I want to go from zero to sixty in five seconds with River, and just being around her for this short amount of time is a constant reminder of where we are right now—taking it slow. This is already proving to be harder than I ever imagined, but Mama raised a perfect gentleman, and when she wants me, she'll let me know—hopefully.

We walk to the truck and drive down the old country road until my parents' house is in view. Once I've parked and we get out, I lead her up the porch, but she stops me before we walk inside.

"I'm nervous," River says.

"Don't be, darlin'. Mama's expecting us." I open the door for her. As soon as River walks in, my cousin Benita jumps out of her chair and says hello. Her face lights up when she sees me following behind. She runs up to River and gives her a big hug like they're longtime friends.

"I'm Benita! It's so nice to finally meet the pretty lady who's been stealing my cousin's heart. I'm so excited for you guys! I heard the news last week." Benita glances over at me as she hugs River. I relax because when Benita is around, everyone seems to be in a good mood. Her energy is always high, and she's loud and doesn't give a shit about anything. I seriously love her like my sister.

"I didn't know you were gonna be here," I whisper, giving her a hug.

"Well, my mama wanted me to drop off some dishes that were left at church last Sunday when they had their ladies luncheon. Also, I came to sneak some pictures from your dad for the party this weekend. Mama put me up to it by saying I was Aunt Rose's favorite, so she'd never suspect anything. She still has no idea about the party," Benita whispers, pulling a handful of pictures from her coat pocket.

River turns and looks at me, giving me a big smile when Mama yells for Benita and pulls her away from the conversation. We walk toward the kitchen, and I lean forward and whisper loud enough for her to hear. "You're beautiful."

She turns, and I can see how nervous she is.

"Everything is going to be okay," I tell her, placing my hand on the small of her back, trying to give her a dash of confidence considering our last visit didn't go over so well.

When we enter, I see Mama already set the table and has burgers cooking on the stove.

"Hey, son," Mama says to me, then smiles at River. "How was your flight, dear?"

Mama's in an extra good mood tonight, but I think that's because Benita's here sprinkling her happiness everywhere.

"It was fine, minus the fact that I nearly take up two seats now. Glad to be back in Texas, though, with no snow," River says, real friendly like.

Mama pulls french fries from the pan and places them on a plate with a paper towel to soak up the excess grease. She adds cheese to the burgers, sets out buns, and works around the kitchen like a natural.

"Hi, Mr. Bishop," River says to my father as he sits at the table.

"Hey there, River. How are you?"

"Great, thank you," River tells him as she sits across from him at the table. Benita begins to talk River's head off about the area and how she wished she could make snow angels at least once in her life. She has us all rolling with laughter because the way she words stuff sometimes is so over the top. Benita's busy talking about babies and everything else when John, Jackson, and Evan all come rushing in one after another.

"You're late!" Mama scolds. They all sit down, and Jackson starts blaming John.

Dad whistles real loud, stopping everyone from talking over each other, and all I can do is laugh. It's always like this when we get together and has been for as long as I can remember.

I look over at River, giving her a look that says *welcome to being a Bishop!*

"So, River," Evan speaks up first, "I heard you saved Dylan's life in Key

West." I swear to God I'm going to punch Dylan in the mouth for telling Evan anything about Key West.

Mama's eyes dart toward River, and I can tell she's curious and even a little impressed.

"Yeah, I guess so," River says quietly, and I know she doesn't want the attention. "He nearly drowned. Apparently, he wasn't a good swimmer, so when I saw Alex pull him out of the water, I knew something was wrong."

"Why in the hell was he in the water?" Jackson asks.

"Because he's an idiot," John tells him.

"We were paddleboarding," I clarify. "He just went too far and fell off."

"Oh, so you were both being idiots." Jackson laughs, and I roll my eyes at him.

"Well, he would've drowned if River wouldn't have been there to give him CPR. I think it was the moment I fell in love with her." I grab her hand, and she tenses but continues to smile. Maybe I shouldn't have said that in front of everyone, but it slipped out, and it's the truth. It was the moment that I knew she was unselfish, caring, and an angel. It was the first real moment that brought us together.

Benita lets out a big *awwww*, and the room fills with conversation again. After we're finished with dinner, Benita and River help Mama pick up all the plates and wash them. I can already tell they're going to be friends, which makes me so damn happy because Benita lives close and can relate to the mom stuff.

"You didn't bring the twins tonight?" I ask Benita about her toddler boys, Reagan and Beau. "Haven't seen them in a while."

"Nah, left them home with Aaron for a bit. It was his turn to chase them around the house." She laughs.

"Twins?" River gasps, glancing at me. "And you said Courtney's having triplets, right?"

"Yep."

"You sure you're only having one?" Benita teases. "Multiples run in the family."

River's eyes go wide, and even though Benita's joking around, it's always a possibility that one of us Bishop boys could have twins. My money's on Jackson, though. After the shit he puts us through, he deserves five sets of twins.

When River starts yawning, I know it's time to go. She's had an emotional jam-packed day, and I'm sure she's exhausted. Just as I stand to tell everyone we're leaving, Benita stands and says she better get home and rescue Aaron before he loses his mind. Taking it as our cue to leave, we all split at the same time, exchanging hugs and goodbyes.

Once outside, the cool air touches my cheeks, and River turns to me. "Is that really when you fell in love with me?"

I lick my lower lip, thinking back to our time together. "There's a handful of moments when I knew I was falling for you. Moments I didn't want to admit to myself at first."

She smiles as I lead her back to the truck. "Is this real life?" she finally whispers as I open the door for her. She climbs in and buckles up.

"As real as it'll ever be," I tell her, backing out of the driveway.

As we drive home, I remind River about the details of Mama's birthday. "You came back just in time. It's this Saturday. Benita and Mama's sisters planned the whole thing, but everyone's coming since it's a big one. Benita's a sweetheart and would do anything for anyone, but party planning is right up her alley. The twins slowed her down, but now that they're older, she's back at it."

"I honestly can't imagine carrying two babies."

I nod and laugh. "We're lucky, considering everyone's popping out multiples in the family."

Pretending to wipe sweat from her forehead, she giggles. "Dodged a bullet there."

"Well, there's always next time." I wink.

"Funny," she deadpans.

"You sure we're only having one baby though, right?" I ask because stranger things have happened.

"I'm positive. I *think*. Now you've got me stressed that there could be two babies in the oven."

I chuckle loudly. "Guess we should book an appointment with the doctor soon."

"Shut up." She laughs. "Seriously."

"Okay, okay." I grin.

"That reminds me, though. I'll need to find a doctor here."

"Shouldn't be too hard considering there are only two baby doctors at the hospital. I can ask Evan for a referral."

"That's okay. I can call. Or give me Evan's number and I can talk to him myself. I'm sure the last thing you want to discuss is mucus plugs and stretch marks."

I glance at her and see her biting down on her lip to prevent a laugh from escaping.

"I bet Benita would love to have you around as she decorates the church for the party." I slyly change the subject. "I can text her and ask if you'd like."

"That actually sounds like a lot of fun. I really like her already. She's nice, and I can tell she's got a kind heart. I really like everyone, actually. I don't know how your parents handled all you boys, though."

I can barely contain my smile. "We were a handful; that's for sure. You'll have a good time tomorrow, and I'm sure Benita will enjoy hanging out with someone who's under fifty." I laugh.

We park and walk inside, and I notice she's yawning more frequently.

"You should go to bed," I suggest, sweetly.

"You're right. I'm exhausted." She smiles with a cute, sleepy look on her face. "Come tuck me in, cowboy."

She walks to her room, and I follow behind her. I watch her hips sway, and all the things I want to do hit me with full force. I want her so badly, I have to adjust myself and force my eyes to the ceiling instead. When she turns around, I pretend I'm just fine. I lean against the doorway and watch as she climbs into bed.

"Alex," she says, "thank you again for everything."

Walking toward her, I brush my fingers across her cheek, stopping myself before my lips meet hers. "Thank *you* for everything. Good night, darlin'."

After I turn off the light, it takes everything I have to walk to my room. All I want to do is crawl into bed with her and hold her.

As I lie in bed, the only thing on my mind is River and how even after three months of being apart, she consumes my mind as if no time had passed at all. Even after everything we've been through, she still has no idea what she continues to do to me. That's going to have to change, but after I get rid of these boundaries.

CHAPTER TWENTY

River

"River!" Benita calls, waving me over. "I wanna introduce you to the ladies."

I set down the bags and walk over, smiling wide. Between having breakfast at the diner and shopping at Dollar General, I'd already met handfuls of people from this small town. I'm actually surprised there are some I haven't met at this point.

"River, this is Mrs. Hattie and Mrs. Savanna. They're Aunt Rose's choir friends."

"It's great to meet you both," I say, reaching out to shake their hands.

They ignore my hand and wrap their arms around me instead. "Oh, River. It's such a pleasure to meet you."

"You're just so darling. Look how big you are already." Their eyes dart down to my belly, making me feel self-conscious. I'm only in my fourth month, but at my last doctor appointment, I measured just right.

"Oh, um, thank you." I find myself a little taken aback by their sudden affection. I'm starting to learn people hug down here a lot. "It's nice to meet you."

"We heard the rumors, and to be honest, we weren't sure what to believe. That Alex isn't exactly known to settle down."

"I don't think any of those Bishop boys are actually." Mrs. Hattie snickers.

"Okay, well we better start setting up, or we'll be here all night," Benita interrupts, saving me from this awkward conversation. "My mama's in the kitchen prepping some of the food if you two wanna go help." She directs them away, and I mouth a, *"Thank you,"* to her.

"Sure, no problem. See you girls later." They smile sweetly, and I force another smile out, grinding my teeth.

"Don't put too much stock into small town gossip. You can't escape it, but most of the time it's hogwash anyway," she says, trying to comfort me. I have a lot to learn living here—their mannerisms being one. You hug someone you just met in Milwaukee, you risk getting mugged or shot.

"Well, where should we start?" I ask, walking back to the bags we brought in.

This morning, Benita picked me up and took me to the Main Street Diner where I officially met the infamous Mrs. Betty. Once we were full of eggs and pancakes, we went shopping. Something new I learned today: Dollar General is the only store in town. At first, I cringed when she told me that's where we were headed but quickly realized it's nothing like the one back home. We stocked up on plates, plasticware, cups, and napkins—all color coordinating to Rose's favorite colors, red and blue.

We just about cleared out the decorations aisle. Balloons, streamers, confetti, table centerpieces with "50" on them, and tablecloths.

"What do you think?" Benita had asked me when the cart was piling over.

"It looks like Uncle Sam threw up in here." I chuckled.

"Perfect then. Aunt Rose loves the Fourth of July!"

I hadn't realized just how much stuff we got until we unpacked all the bags and everything is sprawled out on the table. "Geez." I laugh.

"Yeah, I go a little extra on parties. Something you'll have to get used to." She winks.

I narrow my eyes, curious to what that means. "Don't think you're having that baby without a proper baby shower." She points a finger at my belly with determination.

A baby shower? I hadn't even thought about that.

"I-I don't know." I wrinkle my nose. Honestly, I'd feel guilty taking anything from Alex's family. I just met them, and I don't want it to seem like I'm taking advantage.

"Oh, it's not optional." She grins.

I can't help but laugh. Shrugging, I change the conversation. "Okay, so tablecloths and centerpieces, I can figure out, but where do you want the balloons and streamers to go?"

For the next hour, we work together on decorating the tables and setting up the buffet line with the plates and plasticware. Centerpieces and confetti are sprinkled down the middle of the tables. Next, we work on the streamers. Benita stands on a ladder and attaches them to the middle of the ceiling until three blue and three red pieces are hanging down to the floor.

"Aaron will be here soon, so he can help us twist these and stretch them across the room. It'll look awesome once all six are spread along the ceiling," she explains, stepping down. I can envision it already and know it'll look great.

"I love it." I smile. "What about the balloons?"

"Hmm…" She thinks for a moment before her eyes light up. "What if we blew them all up and found a way to attach them to the ceiling, like with a net or something? Then when she walks in, we pull a string that releases them at the same time!" The excitement in her tone is short-lived when Aaron comes strolling in with their twin boys.

"That'll never work," Aaron says, setting the boys down so they can run over to Benita. She wraps her arms around them and smiles.

"Don't underestimate me," Benita warns without taking her eyes off the twins. I love how they cling to her as if she's their whole world. When they finally turn around, I see the resemblance of Benita and Aaron in both of their features. "Daddy has a fishin' net I'm sure I can borrow. Tack it up and attach it to a string so once it's pulled, the balloons all come down."

Aaron keeps his stance, crossing his arms over his chest and pouting. "There's no way that's going to stay, babe. Trust me."

She narrows her eyes and scowls. "Nope. I'm callin' Daddy." She reaches for her phone before looking up at me. "Oh, River, this is my stubborn ass husband, Aaron. Stubborn Ass, this is River, Alex's...lady friend."

I snort, shaking my head at her description. Though she's not really wrong either. We aren't putting labels on our relationship at this point since we're taking things slow, but I'm definitely more than just his *friend*.

"It's nice to meet you," I say, wondering if he's the shaking hands or hugging kind. He steps toward me and takes my hand.

"You too. I've heard a lot about you."

I blush. "It's all probably only half true," I joke, and Aaron laughs.

A few moments later, Benita is off the phone and smiling wide. "Daddy's comin' to help. You and the boys can go play out back since you don't believe in me."

Aaron groans as if he's been through conversations like this before. "C'mon, boys. Let's leave Mommy to drive other people crazy for once."

"Okay, you two are kinda made for each other," I tell her once they're out of earshot.

"I know." She beams. "Though he drives me up a wall, I love him so much."

"All good men do, honey," one of the ladies I met earlier says from behind us.

We continue decorating, and twenty minutes later, Benita's dad arrives with all the supplies we'll need to make a balloon dropper. After she introduces us, he puts us both to work. I take the opportunity to sit and start blowing up the red and blue balloons. We also picked up a few that had "50" scattered over them. I'm nearly out of breath when Benita announces the net is ready.

"Oh my God!" She claps her hands. "It's going to be epic."

"Should we try it out first? Put a few in there and test the string?" I ask.

Benita's dad releases a loud humph. "This ain't my first rodeo, darlin'."

"Oh." I feel bad for doubting him now.

"That's not what she meant, Daddy." Benita comes to my rescue. "Better be sure than find out tomorrow." She grabs a few of the balloons and climbs back up the ladder to stick them inside. "Want to pull the string, River?"

"Sure." I walk toward her, and just for fun, start counting down from three.

"Three...two..."

"One!" Benita yells, and I pull the string. "Yes!" she instantly cheers when the net releases and all three balloons fall.

"Told ya." Her dad snickers, and I chuckle.

"You did great, Daddy. Thank you!" Benita sets it back up, so I can start tossing the balloons up to her. Takes us a good five minutes to get all the balloons packed, but once it's done, it looks awesome.

"That was a great idea," I tell her, looking around the dining hall and seeing how amazing everything turned out. The buffet table is set up minus the food. All the round tables are decorated. The streamers are twisted and hung up, and so is the balloon drop. "Well, you weren't lying," I say after giving the room another once-over. "You're definitely extra."

Shortly after, Alex surprises me when he walks in with a bag from the Main Street Diner.

"I thought Benita might be working you to death and you'd be hungry." He smiles before kissing the top of my head and sitting down next to me at one of the tables.

"Oh, you're a smart man." I smile, reaching for the bag, and moan when I see a juicy cheeseburger inside.

"Hey, where's mine?" Benita teases, peeking inside the bag.

"You're not eating for two," he retorts.

"Oh, so only when I'm pregnant you'll get me food?" I look at him, sucking in my lower lip to hide the smile.

"Dug yourself that one," Aaron blurts.

I chuckle, taking the burger out and taking a bite.

"Everything looks great in here." Alex looks around. "A bit much for a spaghetti dinner though." He laughs.

Benita reaches over the table and whacks him one. "We worked hard, thank you very much. Aunt Rose is gonna love it."

"She is," Alex confirms, narrowing his eyes on the balloon dropper.

"Benita risked her life for that," I joke.

"Well, Daddy helped." She grins.

I continue stuffing my face when everyone stops and stares at me. "What?" I ask around a mouthful of food. Once I swallow, I look at Alex. "Do I have something on my face or something?"

"Nope."

Turning my head toward Benita, I ask, "What? Do you not eat burgers down here or something?"

"No, you're just eating like you haven't eaten in a week," she teases. "It's cute. You're pregnant."

"I'm just worried I didn't bring you enough," Alex jokes, and I scowl at him.

"You both suck. Picking on a pregnant woman. Shame on you."

They laugh, and I finish my burger in two more bites.

"My sister wants me to FaceTime her, so I can show her the hall and meet you."

"Now?" My eyes widen. I'm hot and sweaty.

"Yeah, that okay?"

I wipe my mouth and feel around my head for how messy my hair is right now. "Sure, if she doesn't mind that I look like a hot mess right now."

"She's almost seven months pregnant with triplets; I can guarantee you she feels more of a hot mess than you do," Benita says.

"Okay, well that makes me feel better."

I know I'm not meeting Courtney face to face, but I'm nervous. I want Alex's family to like me, and since he only has one sister, I'd really love if we could have some kind of relationship, too. Especially since our kids will be cousins.

"Hey!" she shouts, waving. Alex has his phone aimed at both of us when he makes the call.

"Hi," we both say in unison.

"This is River." Alex points the phone directly at me. "And this is my annoying little sister, Courtney."

"Hey!" she scowls. "I don't know how you put up with my brother, but bless your soul for doin' so."

I laugh, already loving her personality. "Yes, please pray for me."

"I got your back." She winks.

"So how are you feeling?"

"Um, pretty much like I'm carrying triplets." She half-laughs, half-sobs.

"I can only imagine. Geez, makes me feel bad for complaining about the heartburn."

"Yeah, let's talk when you can't see your feet or vagina anymore."

I nearly choke and die laughing, especially when Alex's face turns red and Benita chuckles.

"I like her," I tell Alex.

"Yeah, I had a feeling you two would hit it off."

"You break her heart, Alex Bishop, I'm taking her side," Courtney warns.

He rolls his eyes, adjusting the baseball cap on his head. God, I love when he wears that hat. It's the one he wore in Key West, too. It's dark gray and worn to shit, but there's just something about how it looks on him that makes me want to jump his bones.

Oh God. I need to get those images out of my head. We're not having sex, at least not for a long time, even if my hormones are going wild for him.

"It was great to finally meet you, River. Tell Alex to give you my number so we can text, okay?"

"Definitely! It'd be nice to chat with a girl Bishop for once." I grin. "Bummer you can't be here."

"I tried to talk Drew into flying there first class, but it was a hard no." She pretends to pout.

"Well, as a nurse, I'd have to agree with your husband on that one." I smile.

"I know." She sighs. "All right, now give me the grand tour of Mama's party," she tells Alex.

He takes his phone and walks around the hall, showing her the decorations, the buffet table, the balloon drop, and the centerpieces. I hear her aahing and oohing, and it makes me feel good about helping Benita get things done today. I'm slowly getting closer to his family, which makes me feel better about uprooting my life and moving down here.

"Well, the boys are getting into everything, so we better get going," Benita says. I stand up, and she wraps her arms around me—always the hugging down here. "Thanks again for your help."

"No problem, but it doesn't feel like I helped that much."

"You did great. My mama ran out to pick up more food from the grocery store. If she asks, we went to get the boys ready for bed."

"Sounds good."

"We're heading out too," Alex interrupts. "Haven't seen my girl all day."

My heart beats a little harder.

We exchange goodbyes, and when Alex and I walk out to his truck, he grabs my hand and leads me to the passenger side.

"I was thinking we could take a little detour before going home. Whaddya think?"

"I think I'm okay with that." I grin as we get in and buckle.

He drives us down a country road that takes us out of town. I love watching out the window because everything is so open, and the land goes on for miles. It's easy to see why Alex and his brothers love it out here so much. A rush of emotions overcomes me as I think about raising our baby in the same small town community where Alex was raised. The baby will be cared for and watched over by so many who love him or her. A warm feeling rushes through me.

"You okay?" Alex reaches for my hand and squeezes it three times.

Turning to look at him, I can't contain my smile. "I'm great." I squeeze his hand back.

Several minutes pass when Alex drives the truck off road and parks at a lookout area that gives the most breathtaking view of an ongoing prairie and rolling hills.

"Where are we?" I ask.

"Found it four-wheeling one day. It's a great place to view wildlife. Just far enough from the road, so they don't get spooked. Sunset is the best time to come up here."

I check the clock and see it's at least another two hours till then.

"It's so peaceful," I say, sinking into my seat as I stare out at the vastness. "Makes me think about how busy city life is, speeding along, always having somewhere to go. There's no time to stop and take in the fresh air and just breathe. So much is taken for granted rushing through it."

"I couldn't agree more."

We sit in silence, and it's not even awkward anymore. Being comfortable with Alex has never been an issue, but the sexual tension in the air is always lurking between us. Not that it isn't now, but both knowing that we're taking things slowly takes away that pressure.

"A deer," Alex whispers, pointing to the right.

"Wow." I smile. "The only deer I've seen in Milwaukee were on the side of the highway."

"That's morbid." He laughs. "What about where you grew up?"

"Eagle River," I say. "I lived in town, so I never saw any close up like this."

"Weird," he murmurs.

"What?"

"That some people don't see wildlife like this. There's turkeys 'round here sometimes too."

"Well, there's petting zoos, but I don't know if you can really call that wildlife anymore."

"Yeah, don't get me started on those."

I chuckle.

"Told you. It's a different world down here." The closest town barely has a population of two thousand people. There's a church, grocery store, Dollar General, small health clinic, feed mill, gas station, diner, and school. Everyone knows everyone, and the old ladies who sing at church run the rumor mill. It's absolutely nothing like home, which terrifies yet comforts me. It's the ultimate fresh start.

He turns his body and faces me, reaching for my hand again. "Do you think you'll miss it?"

"Wisconsin?"

"Yeah. Where you grew up. Your home? I don't want you to resent moving here for me even though I'm really, really happy you're here." He flashes a small smile.

I contemplate how to answer. "Well, there is something about city life. It's definitely not for everyone, but it's exciting. It's always busy, something to do, and someone to talk to. There are touristy parts of Milwaukee, but not where I worked and lived. I guess if I wasn't used to it, I'd hate it. I moved there for college first from a small, boring town, so the city life was exciting at first. However, it's hard to compare to a place like Texas."

"That's because Texas fuckin' rocks." He smirks.

"I made a lot of great memories there, but I know I'll make great ones here, too."

"Good, I hope so." He brings my hand to his lips and places a soft kiss. "I'd really like that, too."

"Can I tell you a secret?" I ask, swallowing hard at what I'm about to admit.

"You can tell me anything."

It takes me a moment to collect my thoughts, but I know I'll feel better once I get this off my chest.

"I know I've told you about my sister, Rylie, and how having a baby scares me because of the what-ifs and complications than can arise."

He nods, keeping his eyes planted on mine.

"On top of those fears, I'm terrified I'll be one of those parents with no maternal instincts. I know my mom did the best she could, given the circumstances, but between my dad's distant attitude and their divorce, I didn't have the best example. I know the basics of parenting, but that's all textbook stuff. I love working with kids and helping them through their illnesses, but in an effort to avoid getting too attached, I've always blocked a part of that getting too close connection out of my brain. It's like they drill it into your head in nursing school. Learn the facts, don't get too close, do what you need to do to diagnose and treat your patient. It's why so many of our doctors are great. They keep a healthy distance because if you got emotionally invested in every child you lost, you'd be an emotional wreck."

I finally take a breath, letting Alex catch up on my rambling. He's listening so intently, which I absolutely adore about him, but now I'm afraid I've scared him.

"I'm an emotional dud," I add.

"You are *not*," he finally says. "Keeping an emotional distance so you can do your job right and loving your child are going to be two completely different things."

"How do you know?"

"Because I've seen how you've opened up to me in the short amount of time we've known each other. I've seen the effort you put in to get to know Mama and my dumbass brothers." He grins. "I've seen your friendship with Natalie. You're not giving yourself enough credit."

His words sink in, and I hope he's right. I know I'll love this baby no matter what, but the insecurities continue to weigh on me. I think about the times Rylie looked so helpless, and how badly I wanted to fix it all for her but couldn't.

"After Rylie passed, I shut down. For a long time. I think part of that still haunts me. Then when I started nursing school and my clinicals, I dug back to that time and shut down that part of my brain, so I could emotionally separate myself from getting too close. Focusing on the facts and patient

217

treatments was my way of keeping those feelings at bay. My professors would praise me for how well I handled certain situations, and the more I heard it, the more I kept it below the surface. I don't know. Now that I'm saying it aloud, it all sounds so stupid."

Before I can drop my head, Alex catches my chin and tilts it toward him. "It's not stupid, River. Nothing you feel is stupid. I'd be lying if I said I didn't carry my own burden of insecurities. I'm scared shitless to be a father. I still can't believe it, but I know when the time comes, as long as you're by my side, there's nothing we won't be able to figure out."

"You really think so?"

"I do."

"This kid is going to have the most obnoxious uncles." I laugh.

"They really are." He chuckles, and soon we're both laughing hysterically.

"It's hard not to think about Rylie at times like this because I want nothing more than to be able to talk to her about everything. About you. About her being an aunt. I know she was sick, but she had so much life in her. Had so much life to live that she was robbed of. It's not fair." I close my eyes when the tears start to surface. I hate crying in general but even more now that I'm pregnant. The emotions are ten times more intense.

Alex doesn't speak. Instead, he crawls over the center console and wraps me up in his arms. While he holds me, I cry against his chest until the tears dry out.

CHAPTER TWENTY-ONE

Alex

I never want to let River go, not when she's giving me her heart and opening herself up to me. The emotions she shared were raw and deep, and I knew she'd been harboring those feelings for a while. After we drove home, I thanked her for sharing herself with me and reassured her I'd always be there for her, no matter what. That's one promise I intend to keep.

The next morning, Benita picks up River, and they head straight to the dining hall to make sure everything and everyone are in place. Considering most of my family can't keep a secret to save their lives, I'm more than shocked when I pick up Mama, and she has containers of muffins packed and ready to go.

"What's this for?" I ask as she hands them over to me to carry.

"I made dessert for the spaghetti benefit. No one even mentioned that, so I thought I'd surprise everyone and bring my famous muffins." She smiles, actin' real proud of herself.

I try hard to hold my poker face because the moment she realizes she baked muffins for her own party, she might die laughing or at least everyone else will.

"Where's River?" Mama asks politely.

"Benita asked her if she'd help, and she agreed." I smile, actually telling the truth.

Mama's pleased with that answer. "That's real sweet of her."

After I place the muffins in the backseat of Mama's Cadillac, I open the door for her.

"Patsy told me a ton of tickets were sold for the benefit. That makes me so happy," Mama says with a big smile, climbing in. On the drive over, I play along, and she doesn't suspect a thing, chatting about how much money they're gonna raise. The story Aunt Patsy and Aunt Charlotte came up with is flawless, and I can't wait to see the look on Mama's face when she realizes everyone's really there to celebrate her birthday.

As we pull into the parking lot, Mama smiles big, excited to see it jam-packed with cars. People are parked on the grass, and some are lined on the street, and I'm almost shocked by how many people showed up. But it's a small town, and there's not too much more for people to be doing on a Saturday afternoon.

She looks over at me as we unbuckle. "I don't think I made enough muffins."

"Mama, they aren't even expectin' dessert. I'm sure it'll be fine."

She nods. "You're right. I just don't like people goin' without."

We get out of the car, and I grab the muffins then follow behind her. The temperature is perfect, and the sky is blue without a cloud in sight as we walk across the parking lot toward the entrance. Making sure to be a gentleman, I open the door for her, and she walks in. The room is packed full, and people yell, "*Surprise*," just as balloons fall from the ceiling. At first, Mama is confused because she really believed the lie, then she immediately puts the pieces together. She never really makes a big deal about her birthday, and over the years we haven't either, so it's bound to be a shock to her for so many people to care. Covering her mouth with her hands, her emotions take hold, and she holds back tears of joy as Benita, Patsy, and Charlotte all walk up and tell her happy birthday.

"I shoulda known you three were up to somethin'," Mama tells them with hugs. "But I have to admit, you got me. I even made muffins!" She turns and points at the containers I'm holding. I smile, and Benita takes them from my hands and carries them to the kitchen.

Across the room, I see River is laughin' to the point of tears and sitting next to her is Jackson who's obviously running his mouth. Whatever he's saying to her is probably about me and embarrassing as fuck. By how John keeps rolling his eyes, I know it is.

I walk toward them, trying to break up whatever is goin' on, but it doesn't really work. As soon as I make it to the table, River swallows down her laughter, but the big smile on her face doesn't falter. Honestly, Jackson can keep talking, especially if whatever he said makes her this happy.

"What's so funny?" I lift an eyebrow at her, and she snorts.

"Nothing, *cow patty*," Jackson says with a smirk. Now I know why John had that reaction. It's the story that'll never die, apparently.

"And he walked around with cow shit on his ass all day and had no idea. He looked like he shit himself. Even went to town like that." Jackson pats his leg, overly amused with himself.

"River, if you keep encouraging him, he'll *never* stop talking!"

"There was another time Alex decided he was gonna be a big rodeo star," he continues.

I walk over to River, grab her hand, and pull her away.

"Wait, I wanted to hear that story," she says with a grin.

Mama walks up to us, and I give her a big hug. "Love you, Mama. Happy Birthday!"

"Happy Birthday, Mrs. Rose," River says.

Unexpectedly, Mama pulls her into a hug. "Thank you, hon. Thanks for helping set up too. Benita told me. It's beautiful. The decorations. Everything."

"You're welcome." River hugs her back while looking at me over Mama's shoulder with wide eyes. I give her a wink and a grin. It may have taken a little while for Mama to start coming around to the idea of us being together and River having my baby, but I think everything's gonna be just fine.

Soon Aunt Patsy announces it's time to eat and everyone starts lining up and grabbing plates. I take it as my opportunity to introduce River to aunts and uncles, cousins, and family friends. Considering there are so many people here, and our family is so large, I don't imagine she'll be remembering anyone's names, which is okay. We fill our plates with food and grab big glasses of sweet tea, then sit with Benita, Aaron, and Dylan.

River instantly starts chatting with Dylan like they're old friends. "Not been in any large bodies of water lately, right?" River kids.

"No, ma'am. I'm staying away from all beaches and lakes unless I'm in a boat." Dylan laughs, continuing to make small talk.

Just as Dylan starts talking about Key West to Benita, River takes a huge gulp of sweet tea and starts coughing. "What the hell!"

"What?" I ask, sipping my tea.

"How do you drink that? It tastes like overly sweetened toilet water."

The three of us burst into laughter. "No, it doesn't. It tastes like a delicious honey drink." I clink my glass with Dylan's, and we drink it down like it's the sweetest nectar in the south. She pretends to throw up in her mouth a little.

"You better get used to it, River. Us Southerners drink sweet tea by the gallons," Dylan tells her.

"I'd throw up because apparently, I don't have the taste buds for it. Can you get me a bottle of water, pretty please?" River turns and asks me sweetly.

Dylan looks at me like I'm whipped, and maybe I am, but I don't hesitate to get up and grab a bottle of water. When I sit back down, River's laughing at Benita's twins who are too busy playing with their food instead of eating it.

"They're so cute," River says.

Benita winks, then fixes Beau's hair that's sticking up in all different places. "You'll have one of these in about four months. You're going to have the most beautiful baby; I know it. It's fun to imagine what he or she will look like. Do you want a boy or a girl?" She tilts her head and looks at River and me.

"Maybe we'll just have one of each," I joke, but River doesn't laugh.

"I swear, I'm going to hurt you if you keep joking about us having twins."

Benita chuckles. "You're not big enough for twins. No way, especially not Bishop twins. You'd be twice as big and twice as miserable. Aunt Rose talks about how they all weighed ten pounds each, like big ass turkeys."

River stops eating and glares at me. "You were an eleven-pound monster baby? Oh my God."

"Oh yeah. Mama's been taking it out on us ever since. Ask Evan," I tell her.

"Twins. Giant babies. Anything else I need to know?" Her eyes meet mine, and she laughs nervously.

"Nothing I can discuss in front of our current company."

Benita rolls her eyes. "Thanks for sparing me."

As soon as Mama's finished eating, Patsy carries in one of Mrs. Betty's famous chocolate cakes from the kitchen with candles lit. Everyone starts singing "Happy Birthday" just as the cake is placed down in front of her. Mama looks around the room at all the family members and friends, and I can see tears on the brims of her eyes ready to spill over. Dad places his hand on her shoulder with a big grin. She's so damn happy that it's contagious, and there's not a face without a smile in the entire room.

"Make a wish!" I hear Jackson yell from the back of the room, causing everyone to laugh just as Mama leans over to blow out the candles. As soon as she does, we start clapping and hooting and hollering.

"Real quick," Mama says, holding up her hand getting everyone's attention. The room quiets, and she stands and speaks. There's a softness in her tone as she makes eye contact with each person in the room. "I just want to thank every single one of you for comin' out to celebrate my birthday. This is a day I'll never forget for the rest of my life. Thank you from the bottom of my heart."

Chatter fills the room, and Aunt Patsy immediately leans over and cuts the cake then slaps it on plates and hands them out. River and I take a slice and walk to a table that has pictures of Mama from over the years spread around.

"Wow, your mom is beautiful," River whispers then looks at a photo of her and my father together in high school. "They were so young. Wow! You look just like your dad."

I place my hand on the small of her back. "A lot of people say that. Especially the older ladies that thought my dad was a looker back in the day."

She snickers. "I can't imagine growing up here. Reminds me of a movie.

Cowboy hats, horses, ranch life, and your parents are a real-life Southern love story."

I burst into big, hearty laughter, and all I want to do is pull her into my arms and kiss the fuck out of her. "You're too cute."

Tucking hair behind her ears, she looks up at me. The constant pull between us is becoming too much. When her eyes meet mine, everything that surrounds us disappears. In a room full of people, it's just her and me, and I know she feels it too. With one single look, River causes my heart to race, my head to spin, and my body to react.

"You two are plain ol' disgustin'," Jackson says, walking between us and breaking our trance to look at the photos on the table. He's eating his cake real loud with his mouth open like a savage.

"Do you always just appear at the exact wrong time?" I ask, slightly annoyed by him.

"I try my damnedest!" He chuckles, and somehow River and I escape his presence without him noticing too much.

Just as we're about to walk back over to Mama, my phone vibrates in my pocket, and I see it's Courtney trying to FaceTime me. I instantly answer it, and it's so loud in the building that I can barely hear a word she's saying, so I walk her over to Mama and hand over the phone. They exchange I love yous and I miss yous then she hands the phone back.

"Tell River I said hi!" Courtney shouts, and River pops her head into view.

"Hey, Court!"

I have no doubt that if Courtney lived closer, the two of them would be the best of friends. So far, everyone in my family seems to adore River and especially now that Mama seems on board.

"Take care of my dumb brother," Courtney teases with a laugh.

"I'm the smartest brother you have," I tell her defensively, and she just giggles.

"I'd say you're the biggest pain in my ass. Always annoyin' the hell out of me when we were kids."

I narrow my eyes at her. "You're right. I can't even argue about that one."

After we end the call, I pull River close, just needing to be by her. John and Evan walk up to say their goodbyes, and I can tell the party is coming to an end because the room isn't as loud.

"Are you ready to go?" I ask River quietly.

"I thought I'd help Benita clean up," she says, looking around at the mess that's left over.

Confetti is sprinkled everywhere, and it looks like a party train wreck happened with all the streamers and decorations. It'd take Benita a good hour to clean this up alone.

"That's a good idea, and she'd probably appreciate it."

After we help Benita clean the dining hall and all the tables are put back in the storage room, River and I make our way home. It's barely after five in the evening, but we're both exhausted. As soon as we walk through the front door, we both plop on the couch and let out a sigh of relief. The day was busy and full of fun, but it's good to sit in quiet for a minute and decompress after being around so many people.

"I think I need a shower," River finally says. "I just feel...sticky."

"Welcome to Texas, darlin'." I smirk.

River stands, and I can't help but look at her cute little tummy. She notices and gives me a smirk with a quick little eyebrow raise. "Do you want to see?" she asks.

Her question takes me off guard for a moment, but I look back and forth from her belly to her eyes and nod. "Yeah."

Slowly, she lifts her shirt and reveals the cutest little bump. "It almost doesn't look real."

"Trust me, it's real." She chuckles. "The skin is stretching and itching like hell though. Not to mention all the stretch marks that are starting to form." She sighs, curling her lip in disapproval.

I reach for her hand and pull her between my legs. I place a palm on her tummy and press a soft kiss on top. "Stretch marks or not, you're the most beautiful woman I've ever laid eyes on." I wink, meaning every word.

Biting her lip, she pulls her shirt down before she walks to the bathroom.

Damn, she's so sexy. I close my eyes and imagine her straddling me on the couch. Just the fantasy of her has me adjusting myself. It's to the point where being with her is no longer a want. It's a burning need that's poisoning my mind with dirty thoughts.

As the door to the bathroom opens, I turn my head, and soon she's

225

stepping out with a towel wrapped around her petite body. My mouth slightly falls open, and I have to force myself to close it. My eyes don't leave her until she walks into her bedroom.

After she's dressed, we warm up leftovers and eat in front of the TV like an old married couple. Once we're finished eating, River lets out a big yawn.

"I think I'm going to lie down and read my book," she says with excitement in her tone. "I left off on this one chapter, and now I have to know what happens next."

"Oh, what kind of book?"

Her eyebrow ticks up. "Romance."

"Dirty romance?" I tease.

"Let your imagination wander then go ten steps past that."

"Oh, that's *real* dirty," I tell her as she walks to her room.

Taking off my boots, I place my feet on the couch and flip through the channels, not able to focus on anything until I hear River calling my name.

"Yeah?" I instantly stand and go to her, not even waiting for a reply.

When I walk into her room, she's lying there with a sweet smile on her face. Her blonde hair surrounds her head, and she looks so damn sweet.

"Everything all right?" I ask.

"Yes, come here. Hurry. I think I felt our little peanut flutter," she says, waving me over.

"Really? Will I be able to feel it too?" I sit on the edge of the bed, and the heat of her skin touches mine.

"Oh, I felt it again." River places my hand on her belly, and I almost feel the air still around us as my hand feels her soft skin. We both sit in silence, waiting.

"I don't feel anything," I tell her in a hushed voice.

"Keep talking. It happens every time you say something like he or she's excited to hear your voice!"

I smile at how happy she is. "Okay. So once upon a time, there was a Bishop kid."

"There it is again! Keep going," she encourages, but I don't know what to say.

My eyes flicker to her Kindle, and I pick it up and begin reading out loud.

"*I love it when you're a greedy whore, sugar lips. Your cunt is so tight and wet and tastes so fucking good. Your body just aches for my cock.*" I gasp, laughing. "River! What the hell is this book you're reading?"

She begins laughing as a hint of blush hits her cheeks, and I continue because I love hearing the sound of her laugh.

"*He rubs his thumb down my pussy and back up again before circling my rosebud between his fingers. He knows it drives me wild, and he won't stop until he feels me come once again.*" I cough, needing to breathe a moment. "Woman. This is some kinky shit. But I kinda like it."

I take a deep breath, and as I get ready to continue, she stops me.

"Okay, okay. Don't read that anymore. It's not appropriate for the little one. But every time you talk, I feel movement. I think he or she likes the sound of your voice. It's good for the baby to hear you talk because then he or she will recognize it after their born."

I grab her hand in mine and squeeze. "I can start reading your books to you every night if you want me to."

"Oh my gosh, no. But then again, it did sound pretty sexy in that accent of yours. Especially when you say 'sweetheart'."

"What was that, *sweetheart*?" I lick my lips, wanting, no—*needing* to taste her.

"Oh, there it is again!" She presses my hand harder on her stomach.

"I can't feel anything yet. But wow. Just knowing there's a life growing inside you right now is making me feel... I can't explain it. It's indescribable. Grateful? Excited? Whatever it is, I'm just so fucking happy I get to experience it with you."

Her green eyes meet mine as we share this special moment together.

We're going to be parents, and every single day it becomes more real.

CHAPTER TWENTY-TWO

River

A s Alex and I walk outside hand in hand, I inhale the fresh, crisp air while it's still breathable in the morning. Early May temps in Texas feel like August in Wisconsin. Hot as hell. And it's only going to get worse.

It's been over two months since I moved, and although there have been many perks to being here during the Wisconsin winters, I'm starting to think I won't survive the Texas summers. My body isn't used to this heat so early in the year, and I've debated stuffing bags of frozen peas in my shirt and shorts.

"Are you excited?" I'm nearly bouncing to the truck. "I can't wait for you to see the baby on the 3D ultrasound."

"Explain to me what that means again?" He opens the door for me and helps me inside. Now that I'm over six months pregnant, and my growing belly is much more noticeable, Alex has definitely been extra protective. A quality I definitely like in him.

Once he rounds the front of the truck and hops inside, I explain. "Well, it provides three-dimensional views of the baby, and you can see all their little features in great detail. A regular ultrasound you can see the outline and sometimes the small facial features, but with a 3D ultrasound, it's like seeing the baby right in front of you. It also provides better analysis of the assessment."

"Oh, I think I've seen one of those before. Makes the baby look like an alien," he cracks, starting the engine. Immediately, I crank on the air because being pregnant is a self-heating oven as it is.

"It does not." I slap his shoulder and scowl.

He looks over at me and winks. "I'm just kiddin', babe." He shifts his baseball cap around and leans over the center console for a kiss. "It'll be the cutest alien baby there ever was."

"Stop it." I crack up laughing at his cuteness but lean in for a kiss anyway.

"So, are we going to find out the sex? Everyone keeps asking me, and I just keep saying it's a boy."

"You're telling people it's a boy?" I chuckle. "What if it's a girl?"

He shrugs, keeping one hand on the steering wheel while he holds my hand in the other. This is as much as we touch, but my body begs for more. I keep holding back, trying to remind myself that we can't rush this like we did the first time. Even though he's been a complete gentleman, it's getting harder and harder to deny the fact that I need him.

I want to strip off his clothes and ride him like a mechanical bull.

Oh God. Now I'm starting to sound like Natalie.

"If it's a girl, I guess she'll be wearing a lot of blue," he teases.

"No way. Pink and purple."

He snorts. "Yeah."

"Then I guess we better settle it today and find out."

"Fine by me." He shoots me a wide smile.

We could've found out when I was twenty weeks, but with the hospital being an hour away and a severe case of morning sickness that day, I ended up canceling my appointment. Since there's only one radiologist available, I had to wait for the next opening, which is today.

"Have you thought of any names?" I ask him when we finally hit the highway.

"Not really. Unless you like Bruno?"

I furrow my brows at him and curl my lip in response.

"That's what I figured. Then nope. Have you?"

"A few, but nothing that's really stuck."

"Well, we have some time to figure it out."

"I guess, but it's going to fly by quick. We have less than three months left. But knowing the gender will help. Then we only have to brainstorm for one gender."

"My money's on it being a boy." He looks over at me and grins.

"Well, knowing my luck, and the fact you have three brothers, I wouldn't take that bet." I chuckle. "Probably is another wild Bishop boy."

"Yee-haw!" Alex shouts.

We arrive at my appointment with five minutes to spare and end up getting in right away. I'm so anxious I can barely contain myself. I've also had to pee for the last half hour, but having a full bladder helps get the best images.

"Doctor Granger asked for some measuring stats, and once I get those, we'll take some pictures of your baby, okay?" the tech tells us as I settle into the seat.

Alex sits next to me, holding my hand and eagerly watching the screen that's hung on the wall across from us.

"The detail is unreal," he whispers. I smile and nod. It really is.

"That's definitely a Bishop nose," I say, laughing.

The tech continues measuring the head, heart, and length of the body. When an ultrasound is performed at twenty weeks, it's a little easier to measure everything, but itching close to seven months means the baby has less room to stretch.

"I think I see it," Alex announces, narrowing his eyes on the screen. "Yup, it's definitely a boy!"

The ultrasound tech pulls her lips in to hide a smile, but I can't.

"That's a leg, you fool!" I laugh so hard, the tech has to stop the wand until my stomach stops moving.

"Oh, come on," he groans. "Here I thought I produced a legend."

I snort and take a deep breath, so the tech can continue.

"This is why I can't take you places," I tease.

He smirks and flashes another wink. Hell. Doesn't he know what those do to me? Or shit, maybe he does, and that's his plan.

After another five minutes, the tech tells us she's finished measuring everything. I see the heart beating rapidly and smile. "Everything looks okay?"

I know she's technically not supposed to say anything since the doctor has to look at the scans first, but she flashes me a grin that reveals what I need to know.

"Everything looked really great."

"So what's the gender?" Alex asks, looking back and forth between me and the screen.

"You really wanna find out? Are you sure?"

"I do, but only if you want to."

I bite down on my lip, contemplating, but decide I do want to know. "Yeah, let's find out!"

The tech moves the wand around until we can see between the legs, and as soon as the baby shifts a little, I see it.

"You see the baby's two legs moving right there?" I point to one side of the screen as we get a view from behind the baby.

"Yeah?" He tilts his head.

"See that thing between it?"

The tech snaps a pic and freezes the frame.

"Wait..." Alex says, narrowing his eyes. "Is that a—"

"That's a penis!" the tech blurts out.

"It's a boy? It's a boy!" Alex jumps out of his seat still holding my hand. My head falls back, laughing at how excited he is right now. "I knew it!"

"Yes, you did." I smile.

He leans down and cups my face before pressing his lips to mine. It's not a quick kiss like we've been sticking to, but one that lingers. It's sweet and passionate, and if we didn't have an audience right now, I'd be tempted to deepen the kiss.

Once we break apart, the tech prints out the pictures and tells us congratulations.

"Thank you," I say before she walks out of the room to give us privacy.

"I can't believe it." Alex sighs.

I grab my clothes so I can change.

"Okay, but we aren't naming him Bruno," I warn.

He snorts, giving me one of his irresistible looks. "We'll see."

Once we're back in the truck, I snap pictures of the ultrasound photos with my phone so I can send them to Natalie and my mom. I add the words "I'm a boy!" to the message and hit send. I promised to keep them updated as much as I can, but there's always so much going on, I often forget. I want to surprise Alex's family and tell them in person.

"Before we go to the mall, I need to find some food," I tell Alex as he pulls out of the parking lot. Since my appointment was this morning, we planned a whole day while we're in the city. I need a few things for the nursery yet, and now that we know it's a boy, we can start gathering more stuff.

He looks at the clock and then back up at me.

"Yes, I know I just ate before we left, but I'm hungry again." I grimace.

He lifts a hand up. "I didn't say a thing."

I throw him a faux scowl. "You didn't have to. I can read your body language pretty well, cowboy."

He smirks, keeping quiet.

"We need to find a gift to send to Courtney and Drew, too. I feel awful they're up there all by themselves now. I wish we could've flown up there with your mom and Benita last week to visit them in the NICU." They could only stay a few days to meet the babies and visit. Since the babies are preemies, they'll be in the hospital at least for a couple months, which I know is hard.

Courtney went into labor ten days ago and had a C-section. Two boys and a girl. All three are in incubators and breathing machines until they gain more weight. I've seen a lot of babies in the PICU and NICU, and it was always devastating to watch the parents cry and beg to hold them. It brings me to tears just thinking about it.

"Babe, what's the matter?" Alex notices the shift in my mood and grabs my hand. "Why're ya cryin'?"

"I'm fine." I swipe the tears away. "Hormones make me way more emotional than I should be."

"We can FaceTime Courtney later if you want? Check on them."

I nod. "Yeah, if she's up for it, I'd love that."

I know Courtney and Drew have friends in California, but there's just something about being stuck in a hospital for hours and days at a time that can drive a person mad. I've seen it too many times to count.

"We should get Courtney and Drew a gift for just them and then something for each of the babies for when they come home."

"Sounds good, sweetheart."

Courtney and I grew pretty close over the past several weeks. Ever since Mama's surprise party, we've texted and FaceTimed to chat about our pregnancies and all the cute baby clothes they were stocking up on. They decided to wait on having a baby shower until the babies were born and back home, so I hope Alex and I will be able to visit when that time comes.

After we stopped to refuel the truck, we stop for food to refuel my belly.

"What are we looking for exactly?" Alex asks when he drives around for a parking spot at the mall.

"Well, we need a crib for starters. A changing table. Dresser and nightstand. Some kind of bassinet. Clothes. Diapers. Humidifier—"

"River," Alex blurts, grabbing my hand to stop my rambling. "If you'd just let Benita and my mom throw you a shower like they want, we could get everything we need and more."

I give him a look; the same one he gets every time it's brought up. "You know how I feel about that."

"About them wanting to shower you with gifts?"

"About taking advantage of their generosity. I barely let Natalie take me out for my birthdays. I just don't feel right taking gifts from people."

"Think of it as them showering the baby with gifts instead."

I flash him another look when he finally finds a parking spot.

"Hey, it's what Southerners do. We throw parties and give gifts. Sometimes all at the same time. Hell, sometimes for no reason at all. Not accepting it is an insult."

"So, you're saying if I don't let them throw me a party, they're going to be insulted?"

"Yes. They enjoy that kind of stuff. They *live* for that kind of stuff. Plus, it'll give you and Mama more time to bond."

I keep my lips tight and force out a smile. "Fine." I grit my teeth.

"That's my girl." He winks. "So we can head back home then?"

I scowl, tightening my grip on his hand. "No. We need a gift for Courtney and the babies, plus something blue so we can tell your family it's a boy. And maybe some new yoga pants because my ass is falling out of these."

He starts to snicker.

"Don't you dare laugh at me. Your huge baby is doing this to me."

"Considering all of us boys are well over six feet tall, my guess is he's going to be big too."

I sigh. "Might as well skip the newborn clothes and go straight to the twelve-month clothing."

"Let's find him a little cowboy hat, too." He grins. I say something smart but just seeing him all excited melts my heart.

We browse the mall for hours until my lower back starts to tighten. Looking down, I see my ankles are starting to swell, too, and that's when I know it's time to sit. We ended up finding matching green onesies for the triplets that read *I'm new here* on the front. Even though we got the zero to three month size, they won't be able to wear them for a while.

I found Courtney a baby journal so she can document everything that happens while they're in the NICU. I've always found that journaling helps me cope with stress and figured she could write in it while she's recovering from her C-section.

Then we found a blue onesie with a matching bib set that reads *I get my looks from my daddy* and plan to show it off to everyone to announce we're having a boy.

Alex was such a champ shopping with me today. He didn't complain once and even pointed out stuff that we should put on our baby registry. Sometimes I'd just stare at him and wonder how I got so lucky to be with a man who's this excited about becoming a father. Not that I wouldn't expect him to be in normal circumstances, but given our situation, I truly had no idea how he'd react to all of this. Considering I barely knew him, there were a handful of reactions I was anticipating, but none like this.

"You're really great, you know that?" I tell him when we're both standing in the nearly empty nursery.

He arches a brow. "You're just now figuring that out?" The corner of his lips tilts up, grinning.

I teasingly roll my eyes and move close. "Are you always this humble?"
"Very."

When I step into his space, he takes advantage and wraps his arms around my waist to pull me even closer.

"Pretty soon, my belly is going to be so big, your arms won't be able to fit."

"Nah. I have long arms." He flashes me a wink and tightens his grip.

I gaze up at him, my eyes telling him everything my mouth doesn't. He leans down and presses his lips to mine. They feel so good; I don't stop or push him away. Hell, I welcome them. I reach my arms around him, fisting my fingers in his shirt. My breath hitches when his lips move down my jawline and suck on my neck. My head falls back, encouraging him, and when he moans against my flesh, I nearly lose it right then.

His lips make their way back to mine, and as he cups my face, I feel the hardness under his jeans rub against me. It's been so long that I'm desperate to touch and taste him again, but I don't want things to change between us. The moment sex is back on the table, I know there will be that shift. Once those boundaries have been crossed, we can't ever go back. We're waiting, building our relationship from the ground up, and making sure what we have is something that can last. Jumping back into bed together can create a whole other set of problems that we don't need.

At this moment, though, I don't let those thoughts stop me from kissing him. His hand roams down my side and grips my ass, pushing my hips harder into his erection. Fuck, it feels so damn good. It makes me want him even more, and I'm ready to throw all our rules out the window because feeling him inside me again is the only thing I can think about.

My fingers cling to him as if my life depends on it. He reaches under my shirt and cups my breast, squeezing. A moan releases from my lips, and just as I grab for his jeans, his phone rings and interrupts our moment.

We break apart, both panting. Alex curses and pulls his cell from his pocket.

"Yeah?" he answers, annoyed.

I try catching my breath, adjusting my bra and shirt. Oh my God. That got out of hand way too fast.

"Fuck. Okay, I'll be right there."

He hangs up the call and looks at me with dreamy eyes.

"Sorry, that was John. He needs help with the horses quick. Apparently, a gate was left open, and they're roaming freely around the B&B."

I lick my lips and nod. "Okay. I'm going to get ready for bed."

He steps forward, closing the gap between us. "I'll be back as soon as I can." He kisses my forehead before walking out of the nursery.

Once I hear his truck rumble to life, I lean against the wall and slide down it. Shit, that was intense. And close. I was nearly ready to rip off his jeans and ask him to fuck me six ways to Sunday.

I'm not sure if Alex and I can ever recreate the intensity we had in Key West, but I know being around him always ignites a fire inside me. Anytime he's near, I can't deny it. One thing I know for sure—if his phone hadn't rung, the small shred of willpower that's been stretched to the max would've finally snapped.

CHAPTER TWENTY-THREE

Alex

The dining hall is covered in blue from top to bottom. I never knew so much blue existed. Between the tablecloths, decorations, balloons, and streamers, it looks like Cookie Monster exploded in here. Considering it's a baby shower planned by the Bishop family, I'm not even a little bit surprised.

"I'm so excited y'all are having a boy. The twins will have someone else to play with besides each other." I overhear Benita talking to River who's sitting on a chair in the middle of the room. She's smiling, but I know she secretly hates all the attention.

After talking her into letting Benita and Mama host her a baby shower, those two wasted no time in planning. Even after I told them to take it easy, Mama scoffed and told me since she wasn't able to plan Courtney's baby shower, this was her chance to do one right for her grandbaby. Of course, Benita didn't listen to me either. In the center of the room above where River is sitting are large alphabet balloons that read B-A-B-Y with blue streamers twisting along the ceiling.

As if that wasn't enough, Mama called River's mom, their official "meeting," and asked her to send some baby pictures of River. So there are framed baby pictures of River and me scattered all over the hall.

The buffet table is decorated with bright blue bottle-shaped confetti. Mama made her famous shredded beef sandwiches. Aunt Patsy made the potato salad, and Benita brought fruit. There's no such thing as a Bishop gathering without everyone bringing a side dish, so the table is jam-packed. And of course, sweet tea in a big ol' punch bowl. Fortunately, Benita snuck in a bottle of juice for River, so she doesn't have to pretend to like it for fear of being ostracized.

Everything looks way over the top, but what do I know? River's eyes lit up like the Fourth of July when she walked in; whether or not that was a genuine expression is yet to be determined.

Standing in the back with the other husbands, Dylan, and my three brothers, we watch as they pass River presents and squeal at everything she opens. River is wearing one of those sashes that reads *Mom-to-be* as well as a corsage with blue flowers and baby's breath. I had no idea what all the fuss was about until Benita schooled me.

Hell, I'm not even sure what half those items are she's opening.

"What is that?" Jackson leans over and whispers.

Dylan and I narrow our eyes, trying to figure out what the bag and tubes are. "It looks like some kind of bottle," I say with uncertainty.

"It's a backpack of bottles," Dylan adds.

"But the bottles have tubes on them." Jackson folds his arms over his chest as we all stand and analyze the mystery contraption.

"You idiots," Evan mutters.

Aaron snorts, shaking his head at us.

The three of us turn and look at them. "What?" I shrug.

"It's a breast pump," Evan tells us.

"Oh!" we say, accidentally grabbing the girls' attention.

"Everything all right back there, boys?"

"Just fine, Aunt Charlotte," I answer with a smile.

"Why don't one of you boys grab the cake from the fridge so we can serve that next?"

"I'll do it," John says, already walking toward the kitchen.

River continues opening each gift, and every time a new piece of clothing is revealed, they make her hold it up against her stomach oohing and ahhing as she forces out a smile. I can tell she's out of her comfort zone right now, but she's a real trooper about it all.

John brings the cake out, and Aunt Charlotte rushes over to check it.

"Well, what do you think, Daddy-to-be?" She smirks up at me.

"Looks great." I smile, looking at the blue-frosted cake she and Benita made.

Evan comes from behind with a cake server set. "Want me to cut it?"

"No!" Aunt Charlotte blurts out. "River and Alex need to stand behind it so we can take some pictures for the baby book."

"No one said there were going to be pictures," I groan.

"What are you, new? Of course, we're taking pictures."

River walks over after all the gifts are opened looking exhausted.

"Looks like we'll be set for a while." I chuckle at all the gifts sprawled out on the tables. Mama invited the entire family and most of the town. It was also her idea to make it a co-ed party, but I think that was just so she'd have us here to do the heavy lifting.

"I can't imagine one little baby needs all of that."

"Oh, that's because we know there'll be more babies coming down the road." Mama winks, intruding in on our conversation and then leaving like it's nothing.

"What did she just say?" River whispers, panic evident in her tone.

I shake my head at Mama as she watches me from the other side of the table. "She's still holding out hope we have more than one."

"Those Bishops do love to multiply," Mrs. Betty adds, who's been quiet all day, but the moment more babies come up into the conversation, she's all attentive.

"Well, let's see if I can even survive this Bishop." She points at me and everyone laughs.

Jackson walks toward me and pats me on the shoulder. "It's funny because it's true."

"If anyone's having multiples, it's you," I retort, shrugging his hand off me.

"Nope. I'm always packing."

River snorts and giggles. "So did Alex."

"Okay, well let's take those pictures so we can cut the cake," Mama interrupts flawlessly as she tends to.

We finish up the party with lots of photos and cake. As the guests eat, my brothers and Aaron and I load up all the gifts. Bags of diapers, clothes, and toys take over my back seat, then we put the bigger pieces in the bed of the truck. My parents bought the crib that River picked out as well as various other things but mostly just clothes that say *I love Grandma*. Aunt Patsy gifted us a swing and bouncy seat. Benita stocked us up on baby toys, diapers, and wipes, and told us she'd have lots of boy clothes to pass down to us as well. Between all that and all the other random gifts, there's no way we're going to need anything else for a while.

"Are you ready?" I ask River as she stands around and chats with the guests who haven't left yet. "Truck is locked and loaded." I flash her a wink.

"Yes! I need a nap." She chuckles. "You can put all the furniture together while I sleep."

"Or we could both nap?" I tease.

"Funny. Take me home, cowboy."

I love hearing her say that. *Home.*

"Yes, ma'am." I tilt my cowboy hat at her.

"Oh wait," she squeals, holding her belly. Benita, Mama, and Aunt Charlotte all freeze in place. "He just kicked really hard."

The three of them crowd around River in seconds, placing their hands all over her stomach.

"Where?" Benita asks.

"Over here by my ribs," she says, placing Benita's hand over the area. We wait for a few minutes, and when no more movement happens, they give up. "Maybe next time."

"All right, you kids." Mama walks over. "Get on goin' so we can clean up."

I thank her and kiss her cheek. She swarms River and hugs her. "Take care of my grandbaby in there."

"I will, ma'am." River smiles.

Grabbing her hand, I lead her out to the truck, and before opening the door for her, I push her up against it and kiss her deeply. One of those soul-crushing kisses I know she likes.

"What was that for?" she asks, catching her breath.

"Thank you for today. It meant a lot to my family. And to me."

She tilts her head. "You don't need to thank me. I should be thanking you and your entire family. I wished my mom had been able to come."

"Me too." I brush a piece of blonde hair behind her ear. "Hopefully, she can fly down once the baby's born."

"I hope so."

River and her mom have a complicated relationship, and I'm doing my best to tread lightly when it comes to it and how disappointed River gets anytime she brings it up. I understand that she's the one who moved away, but I wish her parents would make an effort to come and visit her at least.

I drive us home, and River nearly falls asleep before we make it there.

"I'm going to take a nap. Do you mind?"

"Not at all." I kiss the top of her head. "I'll bring everything in."

"Okay." She smiles before walking down to her room.

I jog back outside and grab as many of the gift bags in my hands as I can and carry them to the nursery. Just as I'm hauling one of the larger boxes in, I hear River calling out my name.

"Alex, hurry!"

I set the box down and rush down the hall until I'm in her room. "What is it? Are you okay?"

She's lying on her side with a hand resting on her belly. "Hurry, come here."

Walking over, she pulls up her shirt and reveals her stomach.

"He's kicking."

She grabs my hand and places it near her ribs. "Say something," she tells me.

"Like what?"

"Anything."

"Should I read another one of your romance novels?" I tease, but before she can respond, I feel a big kick against my palm. "Whoa!"

"You felt it!" Her eyes light up. "Keep talking."

"Uh…okay." I kneel on the floor next to the bed and place both palms on her belly. "Maybe I should tell him about the first time I saw you." I grin and shoot her a wink.

"He's a little young to be hearing about the birds and the bees, don't ya think?" She crooks a brow.

"Not the first time we did it. The first time I *saw* you," I clarify. "It was the morning we were both at the continental breakfast, and when you looked over at me and saw that I was already sizing you up, you blushed and looked away like I had creepy-crawlies all over my skin or something."

She chuckles, keeping her hand on top of mine. "That's not true. Don't be telling our son lies now."

"You said *our son*."

"Well, he is."

I can't stop the smile that spreads across my face. "I know. I've just never heard you say it aloud before."

Another hard kick.

"Dang, the little guy is strong."

"I told you. It's your voice."

"Yeah, he likes it." I wink.

"Must be that Southern drawl," she teases. "It's what got me."

My head falls back as I laugh. "Don't lie."

She shrugs. "Okay, you're right. It was the alcohol and the way your tight jeans hugged your ass." Grinning, she moves my hand up a bit farther, just under her breast.

"Well, I was drawn in the moment I saw your mama," I tell the baby, though I keep my eyes on her. She sucks in her lower lip as I continue. "She was wearing tiny little jean shorts and a tight top, so it was hard not to notice her. Then once I heard her speak and put me in my place, I knew I had to have her."

She chuckles, licking her lips. "You and I seem to remember the story differently."

"What?" I shriek, pretending to be offended.

"You were hitting on me with the cheesiest pickup line in the book. Then when that didn't work, you threw your friend into the water as a stunt to get my attention."

I know she's teasing, but I narrow my eyes at her anyway. "Don't believe her, son. The only reason she was on the beach that morning was because she was looking for me."

"Oh my God." She bursts out laughing. "Not true! Natalie and I were drinking and beachin'."

"Right. Just happened to be the exact same beach we were on."

She sinks her teeth into her lower lip, hiding the smile that hasn't faded since I walked in.

"But the moment I knew I really liked your mama," I speak to her belly again, "was the time I had her bent over, and she spread her thighs so wide…"

"Oh my God, Alex!" She smacks my shoulder, but for shits and giggles— and because I love getting a rise out of her—I continue.

"She was nearly begging for it, demanding I get inside her right then or else." I lick my lips and watch her blush, loving the way it's affecting her the same way it's affecting me. Hell, I'm going to need a cold shower after this. "So I spanked her ass hard and slid right in to home base."

"You're terrible," she says, shaking her head. "He's going to be scarred for the rest of his life now."

"Doubtful." I smirk. "He'll be watching way worse by the time he's ten."

"That's gross." She wrinkles her nose.

I wink at her before directing my words back to her stomach. "Then she came on my cock so damn hard, I felt her trembling from the inside. It was the hottest fucking thing."

Her breath hitches, and when I look up at her, I see desire in her eyes. Fuck, I should've thought this through, but seeing her lust after me the same way tells me she's close to cracking.

She swallows hard as she shifts her body. I stand up and lean down, tempted to kiss the fuck out of her like I want. Instead, I press my lips to her forehead.

"Enjoy your nap." I turn and walk out before I change my mind. "Gonna go take a cold shower," I mutter, adjusting my jeans because my cock is so goddamn hard right now.

After bringing in the rest of the boxes, I start working on the crib. I know River's dying to get the nursery set up, and since I'm home today, it's the only time I'll have since I'll be working in the pastures all week.

After two hours of cursing, the crib, changing table, and one dresser are all set up. All that's left is the nightstand and the swing. I decide to take a break and finish the rest after I get something to eat and shower.

I peek inside River's room and see she's sleeping peacefully. As I look at her belly, it still boggles my mind she's carrying our baby. Our son. There are days I'm overwhelmed with emotion that she's really here and that we're going to be a family of three.

Thinking back to those early days in Key West, I was a different man. I'd gone there ready to party and hook up with as many girls as I possibly could. Hell, I was sure I wouldn't be sober till the plane landed back in Texas, but one look at her, and everything changed. I don't know how or why, but they just did. Something brought us together in Key West at the same time, and I'll never question that fate. She's here, and she's mine.

As I step into the shower, visions of our time together haunt my mind. The words I said to her belly echo in my ear, and I can't help as I replay every instance we were together. Her plump ass, her tits bouncing, her pussy wet. Fuck. It's hard not to get worked up thinking about her.

My cock's hard and every muscle in my body is tense. I haven't fucked anyone since the day I met River, and this waiting game has been sexually frustrating, to say the least. I have no doubt in my mind that'll it be worth it, but that doesn't ease the need.

I palm my shaft and stroke it a few times, fantasizing about River being in here with me. Memories flood in from all the intimate moments we shared, and I'm desperate to feel those again, more than anything, but I know waiting is what's best. But fuck, being around her every day hasn't made that easy.

Tightening my grip, I pump myself faster as I place my free hand on the wall for support. Her gorgeous face, her sweet voice, her stunning eyes. Everything about her flashes through my mind as I envision making sweet love to her again. Those memories of us haunt me, fueling every stroke I make harder and harder until I have nothing left.

CHAPTER TWENTY-FOUR

River

"I miss you so much," I tell Natalie, standing in front of my phone so she can see how big my belly is getting. I've been trying to FaceTime with her as much as possible, so she can be involved, too. When we chat like this, it's almost as if she's here with me, which helps comfort the anxiety that creeps up every once in a while.

"You're the cutest pregnant woman I've ever seen! Nothing but belly. I'm not even kidding. I hope to look half as good as you when I start popping out Adam's spawns." Natalie's been gushing about how great I look during the entire call, and I find it quite comforting considering I feel like a blimp these days.

"You're just saying that because you're my best friend," I quip with a big smile, turning to the side. "Tell me about the wedding details. Did you set a date yet?" I lower my shirt over my belly and walk closer to the phone.

Her face lights up, and her tone goes up in pitch. "We're planning something for the fall, but no exact date yet. As soon as we set it in stone,

245

you'll be the first to know. I can't walk down that aisle without you up there next to me."

"You know I wouldn't miss it for the world. When do you plan to go dress shopping? Anytime soon?"

"Nope, not yet. You know how I am though." Natalie chuckles.

"Procrastination station."

We continue our conversation until I hear a horn honking outside.

"Shit. I gotta go, Nat. Benita is here to pick me up for lunch."

She waves her hand. "Already replacing me, huh?"

"Trust me when I say no one could *ever* replace your obnoxious loud mouth."

Placing her hand over her heart, she lets out an *aww*. We say our goodbyes, and I grab my purse, lock the door, and walk to the car. Benita is singing at the top of her lungs to Taylor Swift, and she's so into her vocal performance, she doesn't hear me knocking on the window to unlock the door.

"Shit," she says when she realizes and turns down the music.

"There's something about T. Swift that gets me all pumped up," she admits.

"Really? I'd think you'd be into that old-time country music," I say as I reach for my seat belt and buckle.

Benita playfully rolls her eyes with a smile. "I'm not a Southern cliché, River!"

I arch a brow, challenging her statement.

"Okay, maybe a little." She shrugs, and I chuckle.

On the way over to the diner, my stomach starts growling, and that's when I realize how hungry I am. By the time we park, I'm ready to eat a damn horse—the whole thing, by myself.

As soon as we walk in, Betty gives us a big wave from across the small dining area and walks over to us with menus.

"Hey, Mama," she says to me, patting my back. "You've been doing okay?"

"Yes, ma'am. I've been really great," I tell her.

She takes our drink order, and as soon as she comes back with them, we order our food. As Betty walks off, Benita excuses herself to call Aaron about the boys. I pull out my phone and take a photo of the diner and shoot it over to Natalie, so she can see how country it is with the western décor randomly placed on the wall.

Just as I get a text from her, Benita returns.

"Took you long enough," I joke, but she doesn't say anything.

I'm so into my phone, that when I look up, I don't see Benita sitting across from me. My smile instantly fades as the blonde woman glares at me with her fingers interlocked together on the table. She's staring, studying, and judging me. Her dark eyes scrutinize me as she narrows them.

"Can I help you?" I ask, returning the daggers she's shooting at me.

A fake smile touches her lips, but it never meets her cold eyes. "You must be the girl who snagged *him*."

My heart races, and I arch a thin brow at her. "What are you talking about?"

"Oh, let me formally introduce myself. I'm Carly." She holds her hand out, but I just look at it as if it's covered in mold, then back at her. I refuse to pretend to be polite, especially when I'm hormonal and hungry. After she realizes I don't have anything to say to her, she lowers her hand and continues.

"Pity you haven't heard about me. By our intense sexual relationship, I really thought I meant more to him. Who knew snagging Alex was as easy as getting knocked up? I might've purposely forgotten to take my birth control and actually had a chance. Nothing like an *accident* to help you rope someone for life. Amiright?" Her smile is more like a sneer, and the shade she's throwing at me isn't lost.

"Carly, is it?" I throw attitude right back at her. "You're probably too dense to understand this, but I'll talk slowly for you. Your words have no impact on my life, and the fact you have to spew hate to a pregnant woman you don't even know shows the type of person you actually are—not me. So if you're done, you can help yourself out." I shouldn't have fed her the attention she's obviously seeking, but she severely underestimated my tolerance for catty bullshit. The rage is building in her eyes, but before she can respond, Betty walks over and places extra napkins on the table. She looks over at Carly and then at me, feeling the tension in the air. "Is everything okay over here?"

"Perfectly fine," I tell Betty, and she searches my face, trying to read me. Unfortunately for Carly, I'm not easily intimidated because of all the shit

I've dealt with over the years, and the longer she sits here in front of me, the more pissed off I become. Betty walks away, but I see the skepticism on her face.

"Well, sweetie. You see, I was on my way out when I saw you sittin' here and just had to meet the talk of the town. The Northerner who's been able to tame the untamable guy who's broken more hearts than even he can count. But let me fill you in on a little secret," she hisses, leaning across the table and her voice drops even lower. "It's not just me who doesn't like you, honey. And trust me when I say there's a line of women ready to rip Alex's balls straight off for what he did to them. So the next time you're in the grocery store and a woman's giving you the side-eye, more than likely her heart was destroyed by Alex Bishop, too. It's how he is—the Bishop curse. He'll treat you real good, make you feel like you actually mean something to him, then when he's bored of you, he'll drop you like a bad habit. I'm sure it's just a matter of time until your time is up, too. Bet you'll find out soon enough since his commitment issues run deep. But maybe not, considering your *situation*. It's a small town, and he got around, just like the news of you, if you know what I mean." She gives me a fake ass smile just as Benita walks up fuming. I've never seen her this mad, ever.

"What the fuck is this?" Benita asks between gritted teeth.

"*Benita*," Carly says as she slides out of the booth and walks out of the diner.

I don't realize my hands were balled into fists until I feel my nails digging into my palm. It's been years since I've been this mad. I shake my head, not wanting to believe everything I just heard, but it's hard not to because he's told me from the beginning he doesn't do relationships.

"What the hell did she say?" Benita is so mad her hand is trembling.

I shake my head, but Benita encourages me to tell her.

"She basically said Alex is known for sleeping around, and he'll probably get sick of me, just like all of them. The line of them." My voice sounds weak.

Betty sets our food in front of us, and unfortunately, my appetite vanished the moment Carly sat down and opened her big mouth. Benita doesn't touch her food either.

"Is it true? Am I the town joke right now because I'm with Alex?"

Letting out a long sigh, Benita gives me a soft smile. "You are *not* the town joke. If she said that, she's a liar. They're all just jealous, River. And yeah, maybe Alex is known for his history with women, but that's because no one was ever good enough to steal his heart the way you did, and they resent you for that."

I take a bite of mashed potatoes, and they taste so damn good I can't ignore my food regardless of not feeling like eating.

"Do you think he's with me just because I'm pregnant, and he's the perfect gentleman, so he's forcing himself to do the right thing?" I know it's crazy to even think that considering how close we've grown these past few months, but I can't help thinking that maybe it's been too good to be true.

Benita gives me a look that tells me I'm crazy. "*Hell no*. Before you came here, you're all he talked about. He stopped dating. He stopped going out. He worked, slept, and refused to move on. It was River this, and River that. Key West this, and Key West that. It was sickening how obsessed he was with you and really annoying because it was *all the time*. He's not the man Carly knows. Alex has changed for the better, and it's all because of you. I know my cousin, and I know what love looks like. Trust me when I say there's a happy ending to all this that starts with a beautiful couple who is starting a beautiful family together." Benita grabs my hand and squeezes. I give her a small smile in return.

"Thank you. I really hope you're right." I let out a breath.

We continue with the small talk as we finish eating, but the mood is sour, and we both can feel it. Benita tries to make me laugh and smile, and she wins sometimes, but it doesn't stop the insecurities from bubbling inside me. Mrs. Betty knows something happened, too, and after we pay, she hands me a to-go box with a big slice of her famous chocolate cake because cake makes everything better. She gives me a big hug, rubs my belly, then sends me on my way.

On the drive home, I stare out the window, and Carly's words play on repeat in my head.

"Don't let it get to you," Benita says as she parks in front of my house. "If you do, she wins. She's a drama queen and attention whore who's just trying to get a rise out of you. Why do you think they call her Crazy Carly?"

I snort at that.

"Promise me you'll stop thinking about it," she pleads.

I give her a smile, not willing to make a promise I can't keep. "I'll try," I tell her because that's the best I can do in my current state. We exchange a hug goodbye, and I go inside and try to busy myself until Alex comes home.

Alex

As soon as I walk in, I can tell there's something wrong. The look in River's eyes is unsettled, and I don't like it one bit. I'm exhausted from herding cattle all day, but nothing can stop me from figuring out what's going on.

"Hey, Darlin'. Everything okay?"

She swallows hard as she sits on the couch and looks up at me. I stalk toward her and wrap my arm around her shoulders, but she doesn't lean into my touch the way she usually does.

"What is it?" I ask, concerned.

"Well, I met Carly today," she finally says.

That's all I need to know to understand the issue.

"*Crazy* Carly?" I ask.

"Apparently."

"You know we call her that for a reason, right? Because she's a psychopath. Ask Dylan if you don't believe me."

"Well, she told me things about you that have made me feel uneasy all day. Things that are true. About your past. How you couldn't settle down with anyone, basically. Everything she said played on all my insecurities, and it makes me afraid that you're not capable of settling down long-term. That you're going to get bored of the baby and me and want out because when all of this isn't new anymore, you'll realize it was a big mistake. It's nothing you've done, Alex, but I'm terrified you'll go back to your old ways."

I hold her cheeks in my hands and force her to look into my eyes. "No fucking way. *Never*. You'll be by my side as long as there's breath in my lungs and a beat in my heart. Do you even understand what you mean to me, River? What our unborn child means to me? I may've been like that in the past; I won't deny it. I have no reason to. I've been straightforward with you since day one and will continue to always be. I did some bad shit, I know, but I'm not that man anymore. Before Key West, I couldn't see a future with anyone—mostly because no one made me feel the way you did—but now I don't see a future without you in it. You and our baby are everything to me. If anything, you're gonna have to get rid of me, River, because I'm not going anywhere unless you want me to. Simple as that. Darlin', you've tamed me more than any woman ever could. You're the stars of my night, the love of my life, and the only person who has ever been able to steal my heart. I'll spend every day proving that to you. And you know what, sweetheart. It's yours. You can keep it. Because I love you, River Lancaster. I love you so damn much."

Her face softens right before my lips crash into hers with so much fervor that I'm blinded by the emotion in our kiss. I can't get enough of the way she smells and tastes or the soft moans that escape her lips as our tongues intertwine. As I consume her, everything she is, I'm greedy and need more. I want to go to the next level, but somehow, I find the strength to pull away. Our lips are swollen, and bodies are full of want and desire, but it's best if we don't go too far off the ledge because together we'll fall and destroy the boundaries we've worked so hard to keep. Just because I said those three words doesn't mean we fall into bed together. I respect her more than that.

By the time we catch our breath, she leans over and places her hand on my cheek, pulling me back to her greedy lips. "I love you too, Alex. I always have. I'm sorry I ever doubted you."

Her words rush through me in full force, and I've never experienced happiness on this level. To have the woman I love with every fiber of my being love me in return is the greatest high in the world. River leans forward and paints her lips with mine in slow, precise movements. With every breath, she encompasses and captures me, and I hope she never lets me go.

CHAPTER TWENTY-FIVE

River

"I swear to God, Natalie. I'm going to be pregnant forever." I groan, placing a bag of frozen peas on my neck. "And it's so fucking hot. Texas is hell. That's what it is. This ninety-something degree weather is for the damn birds." I'm going off, I know, but I'm so damn miserable.

"So I guess you're adapting to the heat," she teases.

"I hate you so much right now." I narrow my eyes at her, but my cell service sucks out here and keeps freezing during our FaceTiming.

"I know, babe. You hate everyone." She chuckles, clearly amused by my misery.

"How can I have another six weeks of this? That feels impossible. This baby is going to pop out of my belly button."

I hear Adam snort in the background, and just then Alex walks into the living room.

"Is it safe to come in? It doesn't sound very safe."

"Run, Alex! Run!" Natalie shouts when she hears his voice.

Alex laughs from behind me as he wraps his arms around my waist and kisses my cheek.

"Oh my God," I nearly scream, pushing Alex away. "What is that ungodly smell?

"Crap, sorry. Yeah, that's cow shit."

I look back at my phone and Natalie is losing her damn mind, laughing so hard I'm worried she'll pee herself. I pretend to sob and press my face up to my phone screen. "Help me. *Please.*"

"You made your bed, girl. Now lie in it. Or rather, lie in shit."

"You're the worst best friend in the world," I deadpan.

Alex chuckles, kicking his shoes off and unbuttoning his jeans.

"What are you doing? Natalie can see you," I remind him.

"Shh, don't stop him," she whispers before Alex can respond. "I wouldn't turn that away if his hair was on fire."

"You know I'm right here," Adam interrupts.

"Like she cares?" I joke. "Should've seen her at the beach googly-eyeing all the man meat."

I turn around and see Alex has tossed his jeans. Then he wraps his arm around his neck to pull his shirt off. Oh God, help me. I love it when he does that. The way he fists the fabric and shreds it off his back. I feel my ovaries combusting all over again.

"Sweet baby Jesus." Natalie's words interrupt my dirty thoughts.

My eyes widen, and that's when I take the phone and end the call.

"That wasn't very nice," Alex says with a sexy smirk on his face.

"You were two steps away from giving her the full strip show."

"Well, I didn't want to walk through the house with shit on my clothes. I was going to jump in the shower."

"You couldn't have done that in the kitchen?" I scold.

"I could've, but then I would've missed how flush you get when I take off my clothes." He winks, and I swallow hard to contain myself.

He walks out in only his boxers, giving me a perfect view of his ass. Damn him. He's doing this on purpose.

Later that night, we snuggle on the couch and watch a movie after dinner. I'm starting to really get used to this lifestyle of ours. Alex works a lot and sometimes really long days, but I love the feeling knowing he's coming home to me. He's always close by if I need him, and that security reassures me that everything is going to work out the way it's supposed to.

Ever since Alex told me he loved me two weeks ago, I can't get enough of it. We're continuing the no-sex part of our relationship, which is fine by me considering I look and feel like a whale. But our heated kisses tell me everything I need to know.

He's not going anywhere.

Crazy Carly and Jealous Jenna and Petty Penelope—or whoever was his past—no longer matter. I won't let his past come between our future.

I end up falling asleep on the couch and vaguely remember Alex carrying me to my room and tucking me into bed. His lips brushed along my cheek before I fell deeper into sleep.

"Holy fuck," I shout, sitting up in bed. A sharp pain stabs me in the back, waking me up from a dead sleep. Pressing my hand against my lower back, I trying adding pressure to where the pain is, but it doesn't let up.

"Shit," I mutter, shifting my body to see if that works. I've never felt this kind of pain before, and it feels much worse than just a regular back spasm.

I sit on the edge of the bed and try taking a few deep breaths. The stabs keep coming, stronger now, and I'm worrying it might be the start of labor.

"Alex!" I shout through the pain. I'm not sure he can hear me, so I say his name again. When I get no response, I reach for my phone and call him. I don't hear his phone ringing in the next room or him, so I somehow manage to get up and walk into the hallway. "Alex! I think the baby's coming!"

I thought for sure that'd wake him up, but since it's two in the morning, he's probably in a dead sleep. I knock on his door before walking in, another sharp stab riveting down my spine. "Fuck!"

Flicking the light on, I look around and see he's not in bed. The sheets are pulled back, but he's not here. "What the hell?"

I search the bathroom next, and it's empty. Then I walk into the living room and kitchen—nothing! Where the hell could he be in the middle of the night?

"Ah! Oh my God!" I lean over the kitchen table, panting and trying to breathe through the pain. About thirty seconds go by, then I'm able to walk back to my room and grab my phone. I call him again with no answer, then text him. My entire back feels like it's contracting, and I'm so goddamn pissed that Alex isn't here.

Why the hell would he leave in the middle of the night and not tell me when he knows I'm eight months pregnant?

I decide to call John next just in case there was another cattle emergency. When he doesn't answer, I call Jackson. "Fuck," I shout. Evan's phone is always on, but I hate to call him since he lives a half hour away. He probably works in a few hours, too, but after calling Dylan and not getting a response, I have no choice but to call him.

"River?" he answers, picking up right away. "Everything okay?"

"No," I whimper. "I think I'm going into labor, and Alex isn't home. He's not picking up my calls."

"What's wrong? Did your water break?"

"No, but I woke up with these really sharp stabbing pains in my back, and they last for about thirty seconds, but they take my breath away. They just came out of nowhere."

"How much time between when they stop and start up again?"

"Um…I don't know. A few minutes, maybe?"

"Okay, hang tight. I'm on my way."

I feel so unprepared even though I've been reading *What to Expect When You're Expecting* with Alex for the last couple of months. He surprised me one day when he came home and said he'd ordered it for me. I started reading it while he was at work all day, then when he'd get home, I'd recap all the highlights, so he knew some of the basics, too. I've worked with kids and babies for years, but it just feels so different when you know it's going to be yours, and you have to take this baby home and raise it.

Another sharp pain rips through me, and I swear they're getting more and more intense. I text Alex three more times before calling again and leaving another voice message. Finally, as my last resort, I call Mrs. Bishop.

"Hello?" she answers, sleep evident in her voice.

"Hi, I'm so sorry to wake you, but I can't find Alex. He's not answering his phone, and neither are Jackson and John. Do you know if there was an emergency or anything that he would've needed to leave for?" I ramble on as quickly as I can, then wonder if she caught any of that.

"River, darlin' is that you?"

"Yes, ma'am. I'm in a lot of pain, and Alex isn't home. Do you have any idea where he could be?"

She curses under her breath, and I hear her muttering her husband's name. "Scott, wake up. Did you send the boys out recently?"

A few silent moments pass until I finally hear his mumbled response. "No, why?"

"River's on the phone looking for Alex."

"No idea."

"Sorry, dear." Her voice is louder as she speaks directly into the phone. "Are you okay? Do you want me to come over?"

"Evan's on his way. He was the only one who answered."

"Okay, well you call back if you need anything or have any updates, all right? If I hear from Alex, I'll tell him you're looking for him."

I thank her before hanging up, and another sharp stab jerks my body off the bed.

"Holy fuck. This is intense." I lean over the bed, my palms flat and my legs straight as I breathe through it. Once it slows to an annoying, dull ache, I sit back down. I'm so goddamn mad at Alex right now. Where the fuck is he?

Anger boils through me as I think about his past and if I can really depend on him during times I need him the most. He promised me. Said he'd always be here for the baby and me.

Then where the hell is he?

I'm lying on the bed for twenty minutes trying to breathe through the pain when I hear someone walk in.

"Alex?" I sit up, but I'm disappointed when I hear Evan.

"No, it's me." Evan steps into my room, wearing his dark blue scrubs and carrying a bag. I wonder if he sleeps in those damn things, considering it's all I see him in.

"How'd you get here so fast?"

"Went eighty the entire way."

"You trying to kill yourself?"

"No, but I'm going to kill my brother. I called him ten times."

I groan. "Join the club."

"Show me where it hurts."

I point to my lower back and wince. "Radiates all the way up my spine."

"How have they been since you called me?"

"They've been feeling more intense, but that's probably because my blood pressure is skyrocketed with anger."

"That tends to happen when you're in pain, too. I'm going to find you a heating pad and see if that helps the pain. You're about thirty weeks?"

"Thirty-four," I clarify.

"Still too early," he states. "As long as your water doesn't break, you can stay here and wait to see if the contractions slow down. Once they're five minutes apart consistently for an hour, then it'll be time to get you to the hospital."

"You really think I could be in labor?"

"I don't know. Early labor signs are common, but you can't ever be too careful. My guess is Braxton Hicks, but I don't want to rule out early labor just yet."

Evan tells me to get comfortable in bed as best as I can and searches for the heating pad. Once he returns, he helps me adjust my body, so it rests on my lower back.

"How's that?" he asks after a few minutes.

"Good, the heat seems to be helping."

"I'm going to set my stopwatch and keep a timer on my phone. Tell me when you feel another contraction coming, and I'll keep track. If they don't let up, I'm calling your doctor."

I swallow. "Okay." As mad as I am at Alex right now, I just want him here. I don't want him to miss this. Though considering no one seems to know where he is right now, I can't help but worry about him too.

Fifteen minutes go by when Evan's phone rings. "It's John."

He picks up and answers. "Hey." Pause. "He did what? Oh, for fuck's sake." Another pause. "I'm with River right now. She was having contractions and couldn't get ahold of Alex." Another brief pause. "I'm going to kick his ass."

He hangs up, and I can tell it's not good news.

"Dylan's driving him back here right now. Jackson threw a party, and John called him to come handle it since he was out, then when John got back home, they were all drinking. Dylan, too, but he's sobered up enough to bring Alex back."

"Wait, what? They were drinking?"

"I guess." He shrugs.

Grinding my teeth, I bite my lip. So many questions swirl around in my mind, and the anger that formed earlier is now in full force. I can understand him doing John a favor and making sure the party doesn't get out of hand, but why the hell would he then drink himself knowing I'm home. He couldn't even consider sending me a text, so I knew where he was. He didn't even bother to check his phone to see that we've all been calling him! God. I'm so pissed.

"Another one," I tell Evan so he can start his timer again. Luckily, the gap between them has slowed down, but they're intense. He's been so nice to sit with me and talk me through all of this. He explained back labor and how some women get it worse than others, whereas some don't get it at all and suffer from cramps in their abdomen.

"Twenty seconds," Evan tells me once I motion that it's done. "They're not lasting as long, so that's a good sign."

"The heating pad really helps," I say, lying on my side with pillows surrounding me. "I think I'm going to be sleeping with this for the rest of my life."

He chuckles. "As long as you don't keep it on too long at one stretch."

"I won't."

Ten minutes later, we both hear a commotion coming from the side door. I hear Dylan mumbling as shit is being knocked over.

"For Christ's sake," Evan mutters, stalking out of my room and stomping down the hallway. Shit, he's just as pissed as I am.

"Are you fucking kiddin' me?" I hear Evan roar.

"Evan?" Alex asks, and I can tell he's wasted by the high pitch of his tone. His voice slurs, and he's chuckling at nothing. "What're ya doin' here?"

"Alex, I told you," Dylan pipes in. "Evan's helping River."

"Oh right," he says, lazily. "Is she okay?"

"IS SHE OKAY?" Evan shouts, making me jump. Holy fuck. "She's been in excruciating pain while wondering where the fuck you are. You know how to answer a goddamn phone?"

"Dude, chill," Alex snaps, and then I hear some stumbling.

"Are you fuckin' serious?" Evan growls. "Don't push me, Alex. I know you're wasted off your ass right now, but you fucked up, man."

"Let's just get him into bed, so he can sleep it off," Dylan suggests. I'm tempted to walk out there and give Alex a piece of my mind, but I doubt it'd make any difference right now.

"Yeah, get his ass to bed."

"Whatever," I hear Alex mutter.

"Don't come crying to me when River leaves your ass again. You did this to yourself." Evan's voice is harsh, and I wonder how things are going to change between us now. The pain shifts from my back directly to my heart. How could Alex do this to me?

"Shut the hell up," Dylan shouts. "Both of you."

I hear footsteps as Dylan walks Alex to his room next to mine. "I'm not undressing you," he says. "But I'll take off your damn shoes."

"Don't touch me. I'm fine," Alex slurs. "Let me talk to River."

"I don't think that's a good idea."

"She's my woman, Dylan. Get the fuck out of my way."

Evan's standing in my room, arms crossed and shaking his head. I hadn't even realized I was crying until tears start falling from my cheeks.

This is what I've been afraid of since the start. Completely heartbroken.

"River!"

He walks down the hall and stumbles into my room. Evan holds an arm out to keep him from falling. "She's resting," he tells him in a lower voice.

"What happened?"

"She's been having Braxton Hicks contractions. It's where the body starts practicing for labor—"

"Yeah, I know," Alex interrupts. "So she's not in active labor?"

"I don't think so. They've slowed down, and the heating pad seems to be helping for pain."

Alex walks toward me and drops to his knees so our faces align. He looks like absolute hell. He can barely keep his eyes open, and his face is pale. There's no doubt in my mind he's going to be sick as hell tomorrow.

"I'm really sorry, sweetheart." His voice is so low, it's almost torture to hear.

I inhale deeply as another jab comes, but I do my best to push the pain away.

"I could've been in labor, and you would've missed it," I say, softly. "I really needed you tonight."

He grabs my hand and hangs his head. "I let you down. I'm so, so sorry."

I squeeze his hand three times, but I don't plan to let him off that easy. "Why don't you go to bed and sleep it off?"

"No, I'm not leaving you again. I want to help."

"You're drunk," I remind him. "And Evan's here, so I won't be alone."

I feel his body tense up at the mention of his brother's name. Evan's a professional, and I trust him, but that's all this is. I've done my best to get close to Alex's family, but Evan isn't around as much as the others. However, after tonight I feel like I'm getting closer to him now, too.

"You sleeping this off is the only way you're going to help her," Evan interrupts. "I'll stay with her till the contractions stop."

Alex swallows, keeping his lips tight. "Wake me if anything else happens," he tells Evan when he helps him off the floor.

"Yeah, I will." Evan pats Alex on the back.

"I love you." Alex bends and kisses my forehead.

Another hour passes, and the contractions have dulled to almost nothing. "You can leave," I tell Evan. It's almost eight in the morning, and I doubt he slept much before I called him.

"I don't mind. I'll stay for another hour, then I have to leave for my shift."

"Evan…" My voice lingers, but exhaustion is starting to take over. "How are you going to work after being up all night?"

The corner of his lips curls up, amused by my question. He's leaning on the wall closest to my bed and has been for most of the night.

"What? You think you're the first girl to keep me up all night before a long day at work?" He winks, and I can't help but laugh at that.

"That's the most Bishop thing I've ever heard you say."

CHAPTER TWENTY-SIX

Alex

I've never sobered up so fast in my life. The moment I saw River in pain lying in bed, it was like the whiskey never happened. God, I felt like the biggest piece of shit as soon as I heard she was having labor pains. Had I known, I would've never gone over to John's house to check on things like he'd asked. I should've known better though. Jackson has a way of encouraging me to drink, and before I knew it, I was six shots and several beers in.

It's noon before I wake up, and I immediately feel everything I ate yesterday start to come up. Rushing out of bed, I whip open my bedroom door and make it to the bathroom just in time. I empty my stomach contents but still don't feel any better.

Fuck! Today's gonna suck.

I hear the door creak and footsteps walk in, and when I peek up, it's not River I see.

"Alexander Scott Bishop."

261

Mama.

She's pissed, to say the least. She taps her foot and crosses her arms over her chest. Her lips are in a firm line, and I know I'm about to get an earful.

I stand and grab the towel to wipe my face.

"What are you doing?" I ask, treading carefully.

"Came to see if my youngest son hit his head and suffered a concussion because that'd be the only excuse for your behavior last night."

Partying with Jackson and nursing a hangover isn't something new, but Mama hadn't known about that side of me. At least not the extent of it, so I know she's about to give me a lecture.

"I drank too much. I know, Mama. You don't need to scold me." I walk past her toward River's room. When I peek inside, I see she isn't in there. Mama follows as I walk to the living room then the kitchen next. "Where's River?" I start to panic, and when I look at Mama's face, I see disappointment all over her features.

"Benita drove her into the city, so she could get checked out by Dr. Granger."

"Fuck." I scrub my hands over my face and inhale deeply. I reach for a glass and fill it with water.

"She could have the baby any day now, Alex," she warns me, even though I already know this. "You need to be here. No excuses."

"Mama," I say, setting my glass down harder on the counter than I mean to. "I know. I fucked up, and I plan to make it up to her."

"Listen to me, son." She grits through her teeth, her tone grabbing my attention to her face. "First, you will watch your language around a woman, do ya hear me? Next, you'll be doing a lot more than making it up to her. You make things right, you get me?"

I furrow my brows, tilting my head. "Make things right?"

She nods, curtly.

"You want me to marry her," I confirm, exhaling. "Mama, it's not about me not wanting to marry *her*. It's about if she wants to marry *me*. I love River more than anything in this world, and I'd gladly spend the rest of my life proving that to her."

She flashes a relieved smile. "Good."

"But just because she's pregnant doesn't mean it's the right time to get married."

"Fine, but you apologize to her for your behavior last night and vow to never do it again. She'll forgive you. I see the love she has for you in her eyes. Your daddy has done countless things to piss me off, but I always forgive him. We're human, after all."

"I will, Mama. I promise. Last night was the first time in nine months that I drank like that. It's never gonna happen again." Nothing is worth losing River over.

She pats my cheek, a little too roughly, though, and smacks it. "Good boy. That's what I like to hear."

"Do you know when she'll be back?"

"I imagine in a couple of hours. So take a shower and get cleaned up. You have some groveling to do."

Three weeks have passed since River's Braxton Hicks started, and even though I royally fucked up that night, she's forgiven me. I've apologized countless times, but it's more than just telling her. I'll show her until the day I die.

I'm so grateful she's given me a second chance because I don't plan to leave her side ever again, and I'll do whatever it takes to prove that to her.

"So how're things going?" Dylan asks as we wrap up for the day. I'm covered in mud from working with the horses. It rained last night, and water pooled in the fields.

"Good, I think. River's miserable, though."

"Yeah, this summer's been a bitch. Especially this month," Dylan says.

"July is brutal. I feel bad she wasn't able to watch the fireworks last week." The central air has been cranked for weeks, and even though I offered to drive her out for the fireworks show and stay in the car with her, she was persistent on staying home.

"She's gonna go stir-crazy if she stays holed up all day and night," he tells me.

"Yeah, I know. On top of being hot as fuck, she can't get comfortable sitting or lying down, so she's not sleeping much. I read to the baby in hopes it'll help her relax enough to fall asleep, but she always wakes up a couple of hours later with back pain."

"That means it's gonna be soon." He pats me on the back.

"Doctor said she measured at three centimeters already, but that means it could be now or another two weeks. Honestly, though, I don't think River has another two weeks in her."

Dylan chuckles. "He'll come when he's ready."

I snort. "Don't say that 'round River. Natalie told her the same thing the other day, and she *growled* back at her."

"Good to know." He laughs. "Did you guys pick a name yet?"

"I think so, but we aren't revealing it till he's here." I smile, thinking of our talk a few nights ago. River had a list of names she liked and asked for my approval on which ones I liked best.

"Well, good luck." He gets into his truck, and I follow suit getting into mine. I need to shower badly. Once I'm cleaned up and eat, I plan to rub River's back and feet and anything else she needs. She's texted me about fifty times today, and even though the heating pad helps, it's not enough. I feel awful.

"River?" I call out as soon as my shoes hit the floor of the kitchen.

"In here," she shouts from her bedroom.

I quickly strip down to my boxers to avoid getting mud on the carpet. Setting my hat down, I brush a hand through my hair to remove the dust. When I round the corner and see her lying in bed, my shoulders fall.

"How ya doin', sweetheart?" I walk over and kneel beside her.

"I went walking today."

"In this heat?" My eyes widen.

"No, Benita picked me up, and we walked around the dining hall."

"Why?"

"It's supposed to help jump-start labor. Then I did squats and bounced on a big ball."

"Oh man." I suck in my lower lip to hide my smile. "Didn't work, huh?"

She groans. "Well, do you see a baby?"

I bite the inside of my cheek and shake my head. "Sorry, darlin'. He's just not ready yet."

"I'm thirty-seven weeks. That's technically full-term. He can come any day now," she whines.

"I know, but according to the book, you could go as long as two weeks over your due date."

She tightens her lips and scowls at me. "Fuck that book. I am *not* going another five weeks. I will pull this baby out myself if I have to."

Swallowing hard, I realize there's no reasoning with her right now. I know not to take it personally when she snaps at me like this. *Hormones,* I remind myself.

"I'm going to take a shower quickly, then how about I rub your feet for a bit?"

Her shoulders relax, and as she nods, she starts crying.

"River?" I hold her face in my hands and kiss the top of her nose. "Baby, it's gonna be fine. We'll get through this, okay?"

"Whoever said pregnancy was beautiful is a liar," she grumbles.

"If I remember correctly, you said those exact words last month."

She blinks and looks up at me, her scowl on point as she groans. Okay, probably not the best thing to say.

"Do you need anything before I hop in the shower? I'll be ten minutes tops otherwise."

"Could you get me some of that Butterfinger ice cream in the freezer?" she asks, wiping her eyes.

"Oh, um…I think you finished that off last night after dinner." I cringe, regretting not buying another pint when I was at the grocery store.

Her head falls back on the pillow as she mutters, *"Fuck."* I'd offer to run into town and buy her more, but I have a feeling she'd change her mind by the time I returned and want something else.

I quickly shower and scrub all the dirt off my skin. Being outside all day has me covered in sweat. I try to dry off throughout the day, but it's not easy keeping up with the heat.

Once I'm washed and dried, I walk back to my room and grab a pair of gray sweats and a dark blue T-shirt. I shake out my hair, and when I walk back to River's room, I see she's finally fallen asleep.

Oh, thank God.

I know she probably won't sleep for long, but she needs it.

Stepping into the nursery, I look around and smile. River's been working hard on getting it ready. All the baby clothes are washed and hung. The diapers and wipes are both stocked. She picked out the cutest crib bedding set with a ranch theme. Cows, horseshoes, and cowboy boots are displayed on the quilt. The sheet has cowboy boots and stars on it—perfect for our little guy.

Mama, Aunt Charlotte, and Aunt Patsy have all made us blankets. Benita made a special blanket, too, with *Bishop* crocheted on it. This baby is definitely going to have everything he needs and more. As the days tick by, I find myself more and more excited, but I'm nervous too. I haven't been around babies like River, but I like to think I'll catch on and already plan to be up with River when he wakes up for feedings or changings.

The rocking chair is in the corner next to the nightstand and lamp. I made some floating shelves for all the books we received and are displayed next to the chair as well. Everything's in place and perfect. I can't wait to hold him for the first time and bring him home *finally*.

After I grab myself something to eat, I peek in on River once more and am relieved when she's still asleep. I head to my room and decide to watch some TV and relax.

I'm dozing in and out, my head bobbing up and down when I hear footsteps in the hallway. My door slams open, and River walks in like she's on a mission. Her long, blonde hair is pulled up, and she's breathing heavy.

"What's wrong?" I pop up, looking at her. "You okay?"

"Take off your clothes," she demands as she starts pulling down her shorts.

"Wait. What?" I ask, jumping up.

"You heard me, cowboy." She kicks her shorts off and flings them across the room.

"River, what are you doing?" I tread carefully, making sure I'm reading the situation correctly.

"I want to have sex."

"Now?" I arch a brow. "I thought we were waiting, taking things slow and all that."

"Slow ended weeks ago. Any slower and my vagina is going to fall off." She's completely serious, but I'm certain this is the hormones talking again.

"Sweetheart..." I walk toward her, closing the gap between us and cup her face in my hands. "Don't take this the wrong way, because I absolutely want to make love to you, but I want to respect your wishes. Building our relationship from the ground up, starting fresh, and having a solid foundation. We don't have to have sex to prove our love to each other. I'm not going anywhere, I promise."

"It's time," she says softly.

"Darlin'…"

"Hey, you owe me."

"Huh?

"You said you'd do anything to make it up to me when you went out and got drunk that night."

I try to hide my laughter but fail. "River, you're acting like making love to you would be a chore. Trust me when I say I've had to pray for some serious willpower to stop myself around you. I've dreamed of making love to you again, so believe me, I fucking want to—desperately. But I want to make sure it's what you *really* want and not just because you're hoping it induces labor."

Her shoulders drop, and she pouts. "Damn, I forgot you read that book cover to cover."

I smirk. "Twice."

"Okay."

I bring our mouths together and tangle our tongues as we kiss deeply. She fists her hands in my T-shirt and pulls us closer. Fuck, she tastes good. I feel the way she arches her hips against me, and that willpower I was just talking about is diminishing by the second.

"River, stop." I pant against her lips.

"No." She wraps her hands around my waist, pushing my erection into her stomach. "Please, Alex."

Goddamn, is she *begging*? Fuck me.

"I want to make you feel good, sweetheart, I do. But I'm afraid after all this time waiting, I'm going to end up hurting you. Or the baby."

"You won't, I promise."

She reaches for my cock and begins rubbing it. Considering I'm wearing sweatpants, there's not much fabric between us.

"I'm so damn horny, Alex. My hormones are going insane."

I snort, pressing our foreheads together and moaning when she increases her pace.

"So take off your damn pants."

"River." I plead with my voice, though I don't want her to stop. Fuck, it's been way too goddamn long.

"TAKE. OFF. YOUR. PANTS," she demands slowly. Her eyes shift, and I watch the rise and fall of her chest. She's as worked up as I am, and I'm not sure I can deny her much longer.

"You tell me if I'm hurting you?" I look in her eyes and demand.

"I will," she vows.

"And darlin'?"

"Yes?" She swallows, her breaths growing shallower.

"As mad as I was that first time I saw you at the diner, I still wanted to fuck you so goddamn bad."

She licks her lips as she looks at me with hooded eyes. "Then what are you waiting for, cowboy?"

Wrapping a firm hand around her neck, our mouths crash together, and I carefully guide her to my bed. The only way this is going to work right now is if she's bent over the bed.

My lips trail along her jawline before lingering to her ear and pulling the lobe in between my teeth. "Turn around and bend over," I order.

She happily spins around and digs her elbows into the mattress, spreading her thighs wide for me. I slide a hand down her spine and carefully lower her as much as she's able without putting any weight on her stomach. She's hanging off the edge of the bed with her fingers gripping the sheets. Once I make sure she's comfortable in this position, I graze my hand down to her ass and pull her panties to the side until I can press a finger along her slit.

"Fuck, baby," I growl as soon as her wetness coats the tip. I rub along her pussy and find her clit. The pad of my finger circles it, and she immediately starts trembling. "You okay?"

"Yes," she pants. "I'm overly sensitive down there."

"I can tell."

My cock is rock hard and throbbing that it's becoming painful. I slide her panties down her legs before spreading them wide again. Once I remove my pants and shirt, I align my cock with her entrance and grip her hips, slowly guiding myself inside.

"Oh my God," River moans.

"Relax, sweetheart."

She does, and when her hips arch, I thrust in farther. "Christ," I hiss, grinding my teeth down. Her pussy feels like a vise grip as she clenches down on me, and I know it's not going to take long to get either of us off.

"That feels so good. Shit, really good." She rests her cheek on the bed, and her eyes roll to the back of her head.

Once I'm all the way in, I pull out and in again. Keeping my grip on her hips, I make sure to keep my stance and not lean over her like I usually would. Smacking of skin against skin fills the room along with our heated moans, but I can feel the orgasm building inside her. I squeeze her ass cheeks and spread them wide.

"Holy fuck," I growl, keeping up with her pace as she rocks her hips back and forth against me.

"Right there," she says. "Don't stop."

I thrust harder, chasing the release I know she's desperate for. My cock gives her what she's begging for, and when I wrap a hand around to her pussy and rub her clit, her entire body shakes as she screams moments later.

"Fuck." That was so damn hot. "*Goddammit*," I curse between my teeth as she tightens her pussy around my cock, and I can no longer hold back my own release.

My entire body jerks as I come inside her. I feel her muscles relax as we both come down from the high. Once I slide out, I help her stand up and turn her to face me.

She's flushed, and I love that I made her feel that way. Wrapping my hand around her neck, I bend down and kiss her lips. She moans softly, and I can tell she's relaxed and sated.

"Darlin', you're sleeping in my bed tonight," I say against her mouth, and she nods, happily. "In fact, you're sleeping in my bed every damn night."

CHAPTER TWENTY-SEVEN

River

The final two weeks of my pregnancy have been both heaven and hell. Hell, because I feel like a beached whale, and I'm sweating in places I never knew existed. It's the end of July in Texas, and I'm ready to claw my skin off.

Heaven, because being back in Alex's arms every night has been the only thing keeping me going with a semi-positive attitude.

He's kept his word and hasn't left my side, even though, at times, I enjoy the quiet time to myself. I know he still feels guilty about that night he went out and got drunk, but I'm over it now. He made a mistake, and he's more than learned his lesson. I believe him when he says it'll never happen again, and the fact that he'd given me a second chance without much thought after how things ended in Key West tells me the kind of person he truly is.

But that doesn't mean I can't enjoy the make-up sex in the meantime.

"River," Alex whispers against my hair. We're lying in bed together after a restless night. It's Saturday, so he doesn't have to rush off to work since he's off this weekend. I'd been up at least once every hour. Either because I had to pee or couldn't get comfortable.

"Mmm?" I murmur.

Before he can respond, his stomach releases a wicked howling sound. I chuckle, knowing exactly what he's going to say.

"Hungry?"

"*Starving*," he confirms. "What about you?"

I look up at him from the crook of his arm. "Do you even have to ask?"

He smiles, kissing the top of my head. "I'll go see what we have. Otherwise, we'll drive into town and go visit Betty."

"Sounds good to me. Except it might take me until lunch to roll off this bed."

"Let me help." He chuckles, standing up and reaching his hands out for me to grab them. He pulls me into a sitting position to the edge of the bed, and when I look down, all I can see is my huge belly.

"Thank God it's flip-flop season," I mutter, annoyed with how co-dependent I'm becoming. I hate asking him for help even though he reassures me he doesn't mind.

He tilts my head and presses a soft kiss to my lips. "You look beautiful, so stop whining."

I wrinkle my nose at him and scowl. "We'll see when I'm sweating and screaming through ten hours of childbirth."

"And you'll still be the most beautiful woman in the world." He winks.

"How do you always manage to do that?"

"What?" he asks, grabbing one of his shirts from the closet.

"Give me flutters every time you say something sweet and charming. Like you don't even have to try. The words just naturally fly out of your mouth."

He chuckles, pulling his shirt on before grabbing a pair of jeans from his dresser. "It's the Bishop way, darlin'. Just accept it."

I sigh, relaxing my shoulders as I feel anything but beautiful right now.

"I'm going to check the fridge, but I'm almost certain we only have a gallon of milk and a jar of Aunt Patsy's homemade jam." He heads out and walks down the hallway toward the kitchen.

"Okay, I'm going to attempt to get dressed. See ya in an hour." I groan.

Placing my palm down on the bed behind me, I start pushing myself up.

After some twisting and shifting, I finally manage to stand. I really underestimated what carrying a Bishop baby would feel like. I'm convinced all those pictures of those cute pregnant women in their last month on the internet are Photoshopped.

I wobble down the hallway to where my clothes are stored in my room. We haven't made the final transition of making Alex's room *our* room yet, but as soon as the baby's out and we're back home, I plan to turn it into a guest room of sorts. I want my parents, and eventually, Natalie and Adam, to come visit.

"Oh my God," I screech as I reach in my closet for one of my maternity shirts. "Dammit." I groan and let out a growl. I'm pretty sure I just peed myself.

Why does no one tell you this happens during pregnancy? I'm going to write one of those truths about pregnancy books because that sugarcoated shit they fed me was a lie.

I step back and decide I'm going to need a shower, but that's when I realize the liquid is continuing to run down my legs.

Wait.

My abdomen tightens as another gush of liquid lands at my feet. *Holy shit.* Oh my God. My water just broke.

I'd had some Braxton Hicks contractions over the last week, but nothing that was consistent. Now I'm sure this is the real deal.

"Alex!" I shout, stepping aside from the mess.

He doesn't respond, and I stand in complete shock. It's finally time!

"Babe, where are you?" I hear him in the other room.

"Down here, hurry!"

His feet rush down the hallway, and when he swings the door open, he spots my wide eyes and immediately comes toward me.

Before I can warn him, he steps in the mess on the floor and cringes.

"What the...?"

"I think my water broke," I finally tell him, blinking and meeting his eyes. "First, I thought I had peed myself, but then it just kept coming."

"Oh my God..." He steps in front of me, holding my face. "Does this mean it's time? It's *really* time?"

Nodding, tears surface, and my lip trembles. Now that the reality of having this baby is happening, I can't help feeling scared out of my damn mind.

"Sweetheart, don't cry." He wipes his thumbs under my eyes before pressing a sweet kiss to my lips.

"I'm nervous," I admit. "What if this baby is like…fifteen pounds and ruins my vagina for life?" I blurt out, and I can tell he wasn't expecting that by the way he chokes on his laughter.

"I will love our fifteen-pound monster and your vagina no matter what, okay?"

I smile and nod, though I'm not convinced about how my body is going to handle labor.

"Let's go have a baby."

We're packed and on the road in less than thirty minutes. I text Natalie, my mother, and Benita to let them know we're heading to the hospital. Alex calls Evan and says he'll let them know to be expecting us since he's already on shift. I doubt we'll see him till after the birth, though, since he works in the ER. Between calling his parents and his brothers, I've barely come to terms with the fact that I'm really in labor this time.

"How are you feeling?" Alex asks me, reaching for my hand and squeezing three times.

"The contractions are getting more intense. Worse than the Braxton Hicks because I feel it in my back and my stomach."

"Well, maybe that means he'll be here sooner than later."

"God, I hope so. I like to think I have a high pain tolerance, but then again, I've never pushed anything the size of a watermelon out of my vagina, so I guess we'll both find out."

He coughs to hide his smile, though I know he's trying to be supportive.

"Well, I'll be by your side the whole time."

"And I'm sorry if you were hoping I'd be one of those girls who wanted to have an all-natural birth, but I'm not. I plan to go as long as I can without any meds, but when it makes me want to cut off your balls, I'm getting the epidural," I inform him, wincing from another discomforting jab. God, it feels like my menstrual cramps are on steroids.

He shifts his body as if to guard his balls. "I'm on board for anything that saves my junk."

"Don't make me laugh," I beg, choking on my own laughter. "How much longer till we're there?" My head falls back on the seat, and as I hold my belly with one hand, Alex squeezes my other hand three times.

"Not too much longer. As long as there isn't traffic."

I groan, praying that I can breathe through this pain long enough to get into a room.

Within the hour, we're at the hospital and in the delivery unit. They set me up in a room with monitors and fluids. The contractions are intense, and when my doctor finally comes in to check me, I've only progressed to five centimeters, even though I've been at a three for weeks.

Natalie asks if she can FaceTime me and since I'm bored, I let her.

"Oh my God! I can't believe it's time!" she squeals as soon as I accept her call.

"He's already being stubborn," I groan.

"Just like his Mama," Alex blurts out, and I turn and scowl at him.

"Well, he's not wrong." She laughs.

"You're supposed to be cheering me up," I remind her. "Distract me. Talk to me about something else."

"Okay, well hmm..." She twists her lips, thinking. "Adam and I found a few houses we really like, so we're doing another private showing on one of them next week."

"Oh, that's exciting! Are you leaning toward one more than the others or is it a tie?"

"Well, the two we were looking at are one-bedrooms with a big kitchen. Then one we looked at yesterday is a two-bedroom, and though the kitchen isn't as big, the yard is really nice."

"Hmm...well are they priced around the same?"

"Yeah, pretty close, so we've been writing down pros and cons of each, but I think we're already leaning toward one." There's a hint of amusement in her voice, but I shrug it off as pure excitement. Now that she and Adam are engaged, they're finally settling down and buying a house in the suburbs of Milwaukee. Close enough so Natalie didn't have to drive far for work, yet not too close they had to deal with city noise.

I squeeze my eyes tight as a contraction comes to light, and Alex grabs my hand and rubs circles over my knuckles. "Breathe, baby," he reminds me.

Thirty seconds later, it passes, and I can breathe normally.

"You okay?" Natalie asks.

"Yeah, keep talking," I say as I grab the cup of ice chunks on the table next to me.

"Okay, so the pro is the extra bedroom, and the con is that it's an HOA neighborhood."

"Oh." I don't hide my disapproval. "You hate being told what to do, so maybe not." I chuckle.

"Oh, I know. But I think we could really use the extra bedroom, and it has everything else we need. So as Adam says, I need to put on my big girl undies and follow the rules."

I snort laugh.

"Wait. Why could you use the extra bedroom? You hate company." I narrow my eyes, confused.

"Well I mean, eventually we'll need it." She tries to cover her tracks, but I don't buy it.

"You're lying."

"Just tell her, babe!" I hear Adam shout in the background.

"Shut up!" she hisses.

"Tell me what?"

"It's nothing. I can tell you later. Today's your day." She smiles, guilt all over her face.

"Natalie..." I warn. "Shit." I wince again, feeling the next contraction rip through me. Once it's over, I go back to my phone. "You better tell me, or I'll withhold baby pictures from you!"

"You wouldn't!" She gasps.

Alex is next to me shaking his head.

"What?" I ask him.

"You really don't know what she's trying to say?" He raises his brows, and I follow his eyes down to my belly.

"What?" I screech, looking back at Natalie. "You're pregnant?" I sit up straighter. Her expression tells me everything I need to know. "Oh my God!"

"Yep, you're going to be an auntie!"

Tears start flowing down my cheeks before I can stop them, and I know I'm a hot mess right now. "Our kids are going to be close in age, and you're all the way up there."

"But we'll visit and vice versa. There's no crying during labor," she teases.

I chuckle, wiping my face. "When did you find out?" I ask, but before she can answer, a harsh contraction begins.

"They're getting closer together," Natalie states. "Are you getting the epidural?"

"Alex, press the call button. It's time." I squeeze my eyes shut and try to inhale and exhale slowly.

"Good luck, sweetie! Alex, FaceTime me when she starts pushing so I can watch!"

"Ew, no," Alex responds. "I'm staying above the waist."

"You better not!" she scolds. "You get down there and watch your son being born!"

"Okay, I'm hanging up now! Bye!" Alex presses the button before Natalie can retaliate.

"Do you two have any boundaries at all?" he mutters, but I can barely breathe to respond. "Okay, I'm paging the nurse right now."

Another thirty minutes go by, and I finally have an epidural and some relief. It felt like a couple of boxers were punching me down there, and now I feel happy as ever.

"I can't believe Natalie and Adam are going to be parents," I say, dreamily.

"I see the meds are working." He grins.

"Yeah, they are..." I rest my eyes and enjoy the comfort.

Alex

I sit next to River's bed and hold her hand as she falls in and out of sleep. I'm so relieved she doesn't have to feel her contractions anymore, but I know this is just the beginning.

Hours go by, and when the doctor checks River's progress again, she's only dilated to six centimeters.

"All of that, and I'm only at a six?" she whines to the nurse. She looks to be in her mid-thirties, and when I look down at her ID tag, it says Amelia.

"I'd suggest walking around, but you can't once you've had the epidural."

"I know," River says. "I used to work as a nurse up in Milwaukee," she adds.

"Oh, how cool. They have great hospitals up there. What brings you all the way down here?"

River points at her belly and then at me. Amelia chuckles.

"Well, then you probably know that these things take time. Rest as much as you can now because once you're at a ten, the doctor's gonna want you to start pushing."

"Great." She moans, her head falling back against the pillow. "Pushing alone can take a while."

"Up to two hours sometimes for a first pregnancy."

"Two hours? I don't think I even have twenty minutes in me."

Amelia pats her hand and smiles. "Let me know if you need anything, okay?" She directs her question at me.

"Will do, ma'am."

My phone is blowing up, so I start texting my brothers and Dylan back. I tell John to call our folks to give them an update before tending back to River.

"You want a foot rub?" I ask.

"Have sex with me," she blurts.

"River," I scold.

"It'll help me dilate. C'mon."

I laugh, knowing she's desperate to progress naturally and have the baby.

"I'm serious." She pulls on my hand, pouting.

"You can beg all you want, but there is no possible circumstance that will make me say yes to that right now. Also, I'm pretty sure that puts you at risk for infection since your water already broke."

"Argh," she groans. "That stupid book."

"Want me to read to you to distract you and pass some time?"

"Ooh yes. No, wait. That'll just make me want sex more. You'll have to find a thriller or something to read instead."

I click open my phone and begin searching. Once I find something she agrees to, I start reading aloud. She eventually falls asleep, and I step out momentarily when Evan knocks on the door just as Amelia comes back in with River's chart.

"How's it goin'?" he asks.

"Fine, I guess. Slow. River's getting anxious."

He pats me on the shoulder and pulls me in for an unexpected hug. "Proud of you."

"Thanks, but I'm not the one pushing out a Bishop."

He chuckles then makes a wincing face. "Well, text me if you need anything, okay? If you get hungry, I can bring you somethin'."

"Will do, thanks."

An alarm going off behind me grabs my attention and both of us come rushing in.

"What is it?"

Evan searches the monitors and answers. "The baby's heartbeat monitor. The heart rate is dropping."

"What? Why? What's that mean?"

Amelia clicks the button and mutes the sound. She's looking it over and tells us she's going to page the doctor.

"Is he okay?" River asks, panicked.

"River, let's move you to your side. Sometimes that helps."

Evan steps in and helps Amelia shift River till she's lying on her side. Amelia adjusts the monitor and continues watching it for several minutes until the doctor finally arrives.

"His heart rate went back up a tad, but it's not staying steady," I overhear Amelia say.

"River, I want to check you again and make sure everything's okay. The nurse is going to help you roll back over so I can take a look."

I squeeze River's hand three times once she's rolled onto her back. The doctor checks her progress, but this time her face drops when she looks back up at us.

"You haven't dilated anymore. I could give you a dose of Pitocin to help speed it up, but with his heart rate being inconsistent, I don't want to risk it."

"Why isn't she dilating?" I ask.

"The baby's not dropping, which makes me believe the cord could be wrapped around his neck."

"Oh my God," River screeches.

"Or his shoulders are too wide," the doctor adds. "He could be stuck."

"What does that mean? Now what?" I ask, trying to keep my voice steady for River's sake even though I'm panicking inside.

"I think the safest option right now is to start prepping you for an emergency C-section. If the cord is wrapped around his neck, it puts both you and the baby at risk," the doctor explains.

River and I both look up at Evan for confirmation. I trust the doctor, but getting my brother's advice is just as important to me. Evan nods and says he agrees it's the safest option right now.

The next ten minutes flash by in a blur. I didn't read much up on C-sections, stupidly assuming River wouldn't need to go this route, so I'm hanging onto every word the nurse tells us.

Before they roll River's bed out, I cup her face and kiss her. "I'll be right there next to you, okay?"

Tears fill her eyes, and I swipe them away. "I love you."

"I love you too," she chokes back. "Hurry up and meet me in there."

"I will." I wink before pressing my lips to hers once again.

Once she's rolled out of the room, I'm instructed to put a pair of scrubs over my clothes along with a scrub cap. Having Evan here is helping me stay calm, but inside, I'm freaking out. River's about to have emergency surgery to get our baby out, and I've never felt this terrified in my entire life.

"She's gonna be okay," Evan reassures me. "Doctor Granger is very skilled at what she does. River's in good hands."

"She fucking better be," I mutter under my breath. He leads me down the hall, and when Amelia steps out, she waves me inside.

"Good luck. I'll be out here waiting," Evan calls out.

I rush over to River who's spread out on a surgical bed with her arms out. "Hey, baby," I say softly, rubbing my hand on her head and dipping to kiss her forehead.

"I can't believe this is happening," she whispers. The doctor and nurses are already working on her, but there's a small sheet hanging above River's chest so we can't see anything. "I know this is a routine surgery, but I'm scared."

I want to comfort her, but at the same time, I'm as scared as she is right now. Regardless, I'll always put her needs before mine no matter what.

"Do you remember that first song we slowed danced to in that bar?" I ask, that night feeling like it was a lifetime ago already, yet I remember it so vividly.

She wrinkles her nose, then nods. "'Slow Dancing in a Burning Room'?"

"Do you remember what we said about the lyrics?"

"They were sad and tragic," she says.

"Yeah, and that was the night I made you mine. I knew the meaning behind that song, yet I wasn't willing to accept it was about us. A relationship ending that hadn't even started, yet we took the risk. And look where it's brought us now."

She smiles up at me, an oxygen tube running under her nose and still looking cute as hell.

"I always think of that night when I hear it," she admits.

"It's a night I'll never forget." I rub my nose along her hairline, desperate to kiss her.

"To think it was only nine months ago." Her eyes widen. "So weird."

I chuckle. "Crazy what can change in just nine short months." I wink.

"River," Dr. Granger calls out. "You're going to start feeling some pressure now, okay? I'll have him out in the next sixty seconds."

Holy shit. Sixty seconds.

"You're doing so good, sweetheart," I tell her, reaching for her hand closest to me.

"I hope he's okay." Fear evident in her voice.

I can tell she's starting to tear up, so I rub my finger along her cheek.

"Everything's going to be perfect," I promise, squeezing her hand.

"Okay," she says, barely above a whisper.

I can see the doctor's movement as the nurses all shuffle around, passing Dr. Granger objects and removing them from her hands. They're moving so fast, by the time I look down at River and back up again, she looks like she's elbow deep inside her stomach.

"A little more pressure, River," the doctor warns.

I give her hand three squeezes, and when I lean forward a bit, I see Dr. Granger removing some filmy stuff from the baby's face. I notice his face is blue, and that's when I see the cord is, in fact, wrapped around his neck.

My face drops, and River takes notice.

"Is he okay?" she asks nervously.

I watch the doctor wedge her finger between the cord and his neck. A nurse hands her a clamp, and within seconds, the cord is cut.

"Oh my God." I smile, relieved when I see his little mouth move. "You're doing great, sweetheart. He's almost out," I explain.

Within ten seconds, Dr. Granger pulls him the rest of the way out and is holding him up for me to see.

"It's a boy!" the doctor announces, giving me a wink. "Do you want to come cut the umbilical cord, Dad?" she asks me.

"Absolutely."

I take a few steps forward, and when the nurse hands me the tool, I grab it and cut where they tell me to.

The doctor holds him up higher over the sheet so River can see him. It's not for long though. Soon she passes the baby off to one of the nurses who starts cleaning him up right away.

Loud screams erupt from his little body, and it's the most perfect sound I've ever heard.

River

Watching Alex hold our baby is the most beautiful thing I've ever seen. He looks even smaller in Alex's big arms, but he came out at ten pounds, eight ounces and twenty-one inches long. So suffice it to say he wasn't a small baby.

"He looks so peaceful," I say, watching Alex rock back and forth on his feet. He's cradling him in his little security blanket while the baby sleeps soundly.

"I can't believe we made this." He looks up at me with pure happiness on his face.

"He definitely looks like a Bishop," I say. "Blond hair, square jaw, build like he's been ranching since conception."

Alex laughs, agreeing. I love how he can't take his eyes off him, watching him so proudly.

"He has your features, too," he tells me, though I'm not convinced. The baby looks like a Bishop from head to toe.

"Fatherhood already looks good on you. Go figure." I chuckle. "You've got that sexy dad look goin' on."

The corner of his lips tilts up as he shakes his head at me. "I think he's ready to eat." He walks over and brings him back in my arms. His little mouth is twitching, searching.

It's been two hours since they rushed me into surgery, and between stitching me up and cleaning him, it's the first intimate moment we've all had together as a family of three.

I slide my gown down and bring him to my chest. "I wish I'd been able to hold him right away."

Alex steps toward me and flashes me a sad look. "I know, darlin', but I'd rather have both of you alive and healthy."

"You're right." I look down at him and smile. "He's here now and healthy."

I FaceTime Natalie and then my mom and dad to introduce them to the newest member of the family. Later that night, Alex's family all come up and visit us. Mama is over-the-moon excited and can barely contain herself as she looks over my shoulder and stares dreamily at him.

"Are you excited to meet your uncles?" I coo, rubbing my finger along the softness of his cheek. "They're a crazy bunch."

"And it's about to get even crazier," Evan chimes in.

"Is Benita coming too?" I ask, wondering if we should wait to announce the baby's name or if she's coming later.

"She had to get the boys to bed, but she said she'd be coming first thing tomorrow," John tells me. Though it's disappointing she can't be here tonight, it's kind of nice just having Alex's parents and brothers here.

"So be honest," Jackson begins. "You named him after me, right?"

I snort, chuckling. Alex rolls his eyes.

"You want to tell them, darlin'?" Alex asks with an encouraging smile.

Everyone's standing around my bed, watching as I lay the baby on my lap, so they can all see him. "Okay, y'all," I start, purposely dragging out my Southern drawl. "Meet Riley Alexander Bishop."

CHAPTER TWENTY-EIGHT

Alex

THREE MONTHS LATER

Becoming a dad has been one of the greatest moments of my life. Just when I think I've got it all figured out, Riley surprises me, and I'm forced to adjust again. He's already smart as a whip and funny, like a true Bishop, and makes me so damn proud to be his dad every day. The amount of love everyone has for him is almost unfathomable, and with a single look, he had all the Bishops wrapped around his little pinky. Mama and Dad spoil him and demand to see Riley every single day, no excuses. Jackson, John, and even Evan become big ol' softies anytime Riley is around. They always fight over who gets to hold him first, but as soon as he shits, they can't pass him off to someone else soon enough.

The day Riley was born, I made a pact with myself that I'd always provide, protect, give love and advice, while being firm but fair, just like my father. Though only a short amount of time has passed since he entered this world, he's given me a new meaning to life. A once-selfish man has been transformed into a selfless one because of him, and for that, I will forever be grateful.

It took months, but we're finally on a somewhat normal sleeping schedule. Good news is Riley's already on a rancher's schedule, up before the sun and snoozing right after dark. After he's tended to each morning, it gives River and me a chance to drink coffee on the back porch before I leave for work. It's those quiet moments together that I've learned to treasure the most.

After returning from Natalie's wedding last month, I've had a lot on my mind. Mainly *forever* and what that really means. I met River's parents, and they were more than kind. However, everything River had told me about her past finally made sense. I understood why she was so apprehensive about us and not wanting to follow in her parents' footsteps of a failed relationship.

"Are you almost ready to go?" River asks, rushing around our room, completely distressed as she tries to finish getting ready. We're supposed to all be meeting at my parents' house for lunch.

"I'm ready," I tell her as I put on my boots. She walks from the bathroom, putting her hair into a tight ponytail, and no matter how much time has passed, I still find myself mesmerized by her beauty. I'm so fucking lucky to have her as mine.

Stalking forward in long strides, I pull River into my arms and kiss the fuck out of her. She smells like flowers and summer breeze, and I just want to strip her of her clothes and lie naked for the rest of the afternoon.

"If we weren't running late, I'd bend you over that bed," I growl in her ear.

She playfully slaps at my chest. "Mama doesn't like tardiness. Something you told me the first day I met your parents."

"You're right." I wink. "Let's go."

We drive over to my parents', and as soon as we walk in, Mama goes straight to Riley and pulls him into her arms and kisses his little cheeks. Evan and John walk in laughing about something and sit at the table. Soon, Jackson is rushing in—late, as always. We have lunch and talk about everything and nothing all at the same time. I look around, see everyone's smiles, and just know how lucky I am to have a family like this, a beautiful woman by my side, and a life worth living.

After we're finished eating, River helps clean up and chats with Mama. Soon Jackson is pulling River by the arm. "Time to go, sweetheart."

"Go where?" She looks at him like he's lost his fucking mind, which is a normal reaction considering. I stand in the doorway and watch as she glances at me with questioning eyes.

"Go on," I tell her with a smirk.

"Uhhh." She nervously laughs as Jackson tugs at her by the arm. At first, River is super confused and almost protests until Mama shoos her out the door and turns and gives me a wink.

River

"You are as stubborn as a damn horse. Come on, now. Do I have to coax you with a carrot?" Jackson jokes.

I narrow my eyes at him. "What are you up to?"

"Don't worry your pretty little face about it."

We walk down the steps of the back porch, and there's a side by side waiting with an envelope tied to the steering wheel. Confused, I untie it, open it, and pull out a piece of paper.

It's been exactly one year since Key West.
That vacation was the best.
Hills, trails, and prairies galore.
A body of water, flowers, and more.
Keep your eyes open, good luck navigating.
This is where the next clue is waiting.

286

I look over at Jackson who's smiling and shrugging his shoulders. The ranch is huge, and there are tons of picnic tables under trees, but I can only recall one body of water. Jackson jumps in the other side and allows me to drive.

"I might need oh-shit handles," he kids when I press on the gas, and we take off faster than I expected toward the blue trail. The cool breeze blows across my skin as we take hill after hill toward the pond Alex and I once visited. I'll never forget that day. I remember how the clouds reflected off the water of the pond and how he told me about the flowers that grew along the banks in the summer. At that point in my life, I was nervous as to what would happen between us, becoming a mom, and moving away from everything I ever knew. It feels like a lifetime ago, but then again, so does Key West. Jackson keeps talking shit about my driving the whole way over and has me laughing so hard that I purposely drive bad and run into every pothole I see.

We round the bend and drive into the prairie until the pond comes into view. I drive across the way until I see the picnic tables under the tree, but then I notice two horses tied to a post. Glancing over at Jackson, he laughs.

"Giddyup," he says.

I park the side by side and walk up to the horses where another envelope is tied to the saddle. I can't open it fast enough.

I never forgot about your bucket list.
To ride a horse is pure bliss.
Giddyup, sweetheart, let's get going.
From this location, you'll feel the sun glowing.
Stand at the top, and you can see it too
That's where the next clue is waiting for you.

There's a map of the property that's hand drawn with different points on it. There's a little X by the pond that says *YOU ARE HERE*.

"Wait," I say, reading the note again. "I have to ride a horse?"

"Why do you think I was volun-told to come along?" He bursts into laughter. "Mainly to make sure you don't hurt yourself or get lost."

I look at the large, intimidating horse and saddle. "I don't even know what to do."

Jackson walks over and explains the details of riding. "This thing around her head is a halter, and this rope is called a lead rope. I'll make sure to hold her steady for you just in case she wants to move as you're trying to get on. This is the stirrup. You'll stick your foot in here and hold on to the horn and pull yourself up. You'll fully swing your leg over the saddle then place it in the other stirrup. Once you're on, you'll grab these reins, and then it's as easy as driving a car. Move the reins left, the horse goes left, right she goes right, pull back and she stops. Her name is Willow. I know she's a big ol' girl, but she's gentle and one of the horses we put the kids on. So there's really nothing to be afraid of."

I'm pretty sure he could see the worry in my eyes. I look over at Jackson's horse, jet black, pawing at the ground with his hoof. "And I guess yours is the one the headless horseman rides? He looks like the devil," I say with a laugh.

"He's feisty, just like me. So we get along good. Better get going." Jackson holds Willow steady, and I stick my foot in the stirrup like he instructed. At first, I struggled, then was able to finally pull myself up on the saddle. I look down at him and can't believe I'm actually on a horse. "This is weird. I can't explain it."

"You get used to it. Hold the horn and the reins." Jackson unclips the lead rope and walks over to his horse and hops on like it's nothing. He looks over at me. "Come on. You're leading."

I reread the note again, trying to get comfortable on Willow and look at the map. There are several different places that could give me a view, but I have a feeling about this one. "The red trail to the lookout point. That's where we should go."

Jackson doesn't give me any clues, as I turn the horse and head toward the post that's painted red. Horseback riding is so different. This giant animal and I are as one as we continue slowly down the trail. I can't stop smiling and looking at my surroundings. This place is beautiful, and the sun is shining on my shoulders. It's so warm and covers me like a blanket. As I take it all in, I'm so grateful to be able to call this home and be able to raise our baby here.

"Ready to gallop?" Jackson asks, clicking his mouth and passing me up.

"Just hold on real tight with your legs and keep your arms down, so you don't look like you're flying away. Willow is a sprinter, and she's as fast as the wind," he says before going into a full run ahead.

I suck in a deep breath and barely kick, and Willow takes off. At first, I feel like I might bounce right off until she goes faster and we're moving in a smooth rhythm together, racing down the trail following Jackson's dust. I'm absolutely fucking elated as I hold on to the horn for dear life. This is freedom as the cool October breeze hits my face. At the end of the trail, where it splits into two, Jackson is stopped and waiting for me with a huge smile on his face.

"Now I know why you want to do this every day." I'm breathing hard, adrenaline rushing.

He gives me a quick head nod. "So which way now?"

I point. "Over there. At the top of that hill, where the lookout is."

"After you," he says, and I guide Willow down the trail, and Jackson follows. As we climb up a hill, I can see Mr. Bishop driving a tractor with a trailer full of hay bales. Once at the top, I pull the reins back, and Willow stops.

"Now, be careful getting off. Hold on to the horn, swing your leg over and touch the other side of the ground. She won't move on you, but make sure you don't stumble and bust your ass," Jackson tells me. He rides past me, grabs the reins, and I somehow manage to dismount without falling.

"Alex may have gotten himself a little cowgirl after all." He chuckles.

I flip him off where only he can see it, and he pats his leg, finding it overly hilarious.

My hair is windblown, and as I walk over to Mr. Bishop, he hands me another envelope with a big smile. I take a moment to fully take in the view. The land goes on for as far as my eyes can see, and it's so calm and beautiful out here.

How's the view, you'll have to let me know.
Take a good look before you go.
The leaves are changing,
the grass is turning brown.
Your next clue is in town.
Chocolate cake and pecan pie.
While you're there, tell Mrs. Betty hi!

I can't stop smiling. I'm pretty sure it may be permanent after this. Once I climb onto the trailer and sit on a bale of hay, I see Jackson lead Willow back down the trail we came from. The hay smells dry and sweet, and it reminds me of the first time I visited Texas.

We take an unrecognizable path, and I see parts of the property I've never seen. As we continue forward, I try to take it all in: the sunshine, the brown grasses, and the rumble of the tractor engine. I can't believe Alex would go through such a big effort to celebrate our one year of meeting.

Soaking in the scene, I can't help but think about everything that's happened over the last year. Though I was scared to death to become a mother, it all feels like second nature now. That unconditional love consumes me, and I never thought my heart could be so full. Between the love of my life and our baby, I'm living my greatest life possible.

I used to think love like that only exists in fairy tales, but every time I hear Riley's little coos, I know that's not true. Now, I can't help thinking back at my apprehension of being a mother, because it's one of the greatest joys of my life. Considering Natalie is pregnant, I've been helping her work through the mind fuck the hormones create too. Admittedly, I might not have it all figured out, but thanks to Google and all the mamas I'm surrounded by constantly, I can get answers quick. Alex was right; everything did work out just fine.

As I study my surroundings, I'm pretty sure we're on the other side of the property by the ranch hand quarters. Moving closer, I see several bunkhouses and vehicles parked around, so my suspicion is confirmed. The gate is open, and Mr. Bishop rolls through it then stops by a Jeep, with the top off, waiting for me. I get off the trailer and wave bye to Mr. Bishop.

He gives me a head nod and a quick wave and a smile before he pulls away.

The Jeep is still running, and I climb inside and take my phone from my pocket to navigate toward the diner since I have no clue where I am. Once the quickest route loads, I select it, then shift the Jeep into gear. I smile the entire drive over to the diner. Just as I put the Jeep into park, I see Evan standing by the door.

"I guess all the Bishops are involved in this little celebration," I say with a chuckle.

"Of course. A year is a big deal for any Bishop boy." He hands me an envelope, and I practically rip it open.

> Think back to coming to Texas, the very first day
> Where was it that you booked to stay?
> Go to the counter and grab the clue.
> There's a special surprise, waiting for you.

I look at Evan, and he's all smiles. "You better tell Mrs. Betty hello before you hightail it on outta here."

"Shit," I say, not even thinking about it. As soon as I walk in, Betty comes to me and gives me a big hug. "Happy one year!"

"Thank you! I was told to tell you hi! But I really gotta go."

She hands me a piece of chocolate cake in a to-go box, and I smile, but I have a feeling it was all to stall me. By the time I walk outside, Evan is already gone. I climb into the Jeep and head straight to the B&B. My heart is racing, and I'm so fucking excited that I'm smiling like a crazy person as I turn down the gravel road. The B&B comes into sight, and I can't get there fast enough but force myself to drive slowly. Once I park, I get out and run to the front door, open it up, and go straight to John. There are a dozen roses on the counter waiting for me with another envelope. I take a quick moment to stop and smell the flowers.

"Go ahead, River. Open it up," John encourages.

I swallow hard and do exactly what he says.

> This is the last and final clue

You know what you have to do
Meet me at Mama's in the backyard
Finding me won't be too hard.
I've got a surprise you'll never guess
I love you darlin', you're the best.

All I can do is laugh. Happiness like this should be illegal. I have no words as I tell my heart to stay calm because it's about ready to flutter out of my chest. There's too much excitement bubbling inside me as I grab the flowers and turn around.

"Wait up, I'm riding with you," John stops me before I make it to the door. I wave him on because I'm so damn impatient right now, I can barely contain myself.

We get in the Jeep, and I carefully place the roses in the back seat. It takes no time at all to arrive at his parents' house. As soon as I park and shut the door to the Jeep, my adrenaline spikes. John is nothing but smiles as we walk around the house. It takes everything I have not to run to the back like a kid.

Once we're in the backyard, I look everywhere for Alex but don't see him. At a closer look, I see a group of family members under the old oak tree and can hear them chatting and cutting up.

John and I move closer, and I can't see Alex, but I see Benita and Aaron, the boys, Mr. Bishop, Mama, Patsy, Charlotte, Evan, Jackson, Dylan, and John goes to join them. When I get about twenty feet away, everyone who's standing close together, moves out of the way, and that's when I finally see Alex. He's standing in a black tux and tie with messy hair and a sexy smile on his face. He's holding Riley in his arms who's also dressed in a little tux. When our eyes meet, the world around me fades away. My breath catches, and I feel like I can't take a step forward.

I glance around at everyone, forcing myself to walk toward him, wondering what the hell is going on. Just as I open my mouth to say something, Alex drops to his knee, holding Riley close to his chest. My hands fly to my mouth when I realize what's going on. Mama takes Riley from Alex's arms, and he waves me closer with a smirk.

"River," Alex says, digging inside his suit jacket. When he pulls out a black velvet box and opens it to show me the most beautiful ring I've ever seen, I don't feel like I can keep standing because my knees go completely weak.

"Meeting you a year ago has changed my outlook on everything. A life without you in it is no life at all, and every night, I thank God for you and Riley. I can't imagine a day without the two of you, and I never want to. You're the absolute best thing that's ever happened to me, and I'm so happy to call you mine."

Before he can even finish the rest of his speech, I fall to the ground and swing my arms around his neck, not able to hold back the tears that stream down my face. I have to kiss him, taste him, touch him.

"I love you, River."

"I love you so much," I say, my voice barely working. I don't want this moment to end.

"Please spend the rest of your life with me," Alex whispers across my mouth.

My eyes flutter closed, and it all seems like a dream. "Yes, yes. Forever."

For a moment, I forgot everyone was standing around watching us until Jackson yells out, "*GET A ROOM!*" We start laughing and pull away, and he wipes the tears from my cheek with his thumb before he slides the ring on my finger.

We all exchange hugs and congratulations, and I'm so overwhelmed, so damn happy, and completely ecstatic that I'll be a Bishop too. Today is the anniversary of our beginning, and it also marks the start of our forever. The excitement doesn't wear off, and then Mama tells me she's keeping Riley overnight. At first, I hesitate, but when Alex squeezes my hand three times, I agree.

"I want to be alone with you. I brought everything she could ever need for him while you were on your little treasure hunt," he whispers in my ear as we walk hand in hand toward the house. Benita is chatting about bridal parties and wedding showers, and when she asks me if she can start planning them, I tell her yes, because it makes her happy, and I know she'll go above and beyond because she's a party planning extraordinaire. She hugs me tight, and Aaron pulls her away with a chuckle.

"Welcome to the family. So excited I get to keep my honey bun overnight," Mama says, giving me a big hug. As soon as Riley was born, they turned Alex's old bedroom in the house into a nursery. It was a sweet gesture that warmed my heart, and I'm happy his parents want to be involved. She's a wonderful grandma and proves that every single day with her love.

After we say our goodbyes, I can't stop glancing over at Alex in a full tuxedo and tie as he drives us home.

"What?" He smirks.

"Nothing," I say with a smile, and he grabs my hand, looks at the ring that fits perfectly on my finger, and kisses my knuckles.

Once we park, and we're inside, nothing in the world can keep us apart. Our mouths gravitate together as waves of need wash over my body.

"God, I need you so fucking bad," he growls against my neck as his lips drag across my skin. Tracing the shell of my ear with his warm mouth, I lose myself in his gentle touch as his hand runs under my shirt and cups my breast. My head falls back on my shoulders, and I lose myself in his kisses.

Alex

Her skin tastes sweet, and I want to kiss every inch of her body, and tonight, I just might. To know River is going to be my wife, be my *forever*, makes me so fucking happy. I'm the luckiest man in the world, and each time I look at her, it's confirmed.

As I try to take off my suit jacket, she grabs my hands to stop me.

"Keep it on, just a little longer."

I smirk. "So you like this look?"

She wraps the tie around her fist and pulls my face closer to hers. "Sure do, cowboy."

Taking my time, I unbutton her shirt, watching her breasts rise and fall as I remove it from her body. Gently, I run my fingers across the tops of her breasts and reach behind and undo her bra. She watches me intently as I touch her, and it's so fucking intense. As the bra hits the floor, I dip down, taking her taut nipple into my mouth, swirling my tongue around the tall peak. River's eyes flutter closed when my hands slip lower, snapping open her jeans. I slide my hands into her panties and can already feel her arousal. Her breath hitches when I hook my fingers in her panties, and I slide them down along with her pants. Kicking off her shoes, she steps out of her clothes and stands before me naked. Stepping back, I take my time admiring every curve of her sun kissed body.

"Damn," I whisper, meeting her eyes, going all the way down to her cute toes and back up again. I take a mental snapshot of this woman who agreed to be my wife, my everything. "You're so fucking beautiful," I tell her, and she's all smiles.

"You are too." River stalks toward me, shaking her hips. Taking control, she takes her time removing my tuxedo jacket and tie and unbuttons my shirt. Her soft hands trace down my abs, and my breath increases. Not able to wait any longer, my greedy mouth is on hers. My hands are in her hair, and soon her legs are wrapped around my waist. Holding her ass tight as she straddles and kisses me, I walk us toward the bedroom. After I set her on the bed, she continues to watch me as I remove the rest of my clothes.

"I have to taste you first. Edge of the bed," I demand once I'm fully naked, and she smirks.

She doesn't hesitate, but I grab her ankles and quickly move her closer before dropping to my knees and placing her legs on my shoulders. As I dip my tongue into her sweetness, she lets out a long sigh, running her fingers through my already messy hair. I move my tongue up and down her slit, teasing her as much as I can. Immediately, her body responds, and I gently place a finger inside. As she moans, I watch as she grabs her nipples between her fingers and pinches. It's such a fucking turn on to see. I slip in another finger, giving her exactly what she desires. She's so fucking wet as I slide my fingers in and out in a slow rhythm while I apply pressure to her hard nub. River arches her back, writhing, as I apply more pressure and increase the pace. With white knuckles, she fists the comforter, pushing her body harder against me. Placing my hands under her ass, I pull her to me and drive my tongue deeper inside.

"Fuck," she pants, practically begging for release. "I'm so close."

Though I slow down, wanting the orgasm to teeter on the edge as long as possible, it doesn't take long before she's buckling beneath me. Her breath quickens, and her mouth falls open while she loses all control of her senses. As she rides the wave of her orgasm on my mouth, her moans are like sweet music to my ears. A crescendo of emotion as her body eventually goes still. I stand, and she moves her body up the bed until her head rests on the pillow. With a smile, she curls her finger, demanding I go to her, which I happily do. Kissing up her stomach, her breasts, her neck, I place flutters of kisses across her jawline until my mouth finally meets hers.

With hooded eyes, she looks up at me. "I love you, Alex."

"You have no idea how much I love you."

She grabs my face with her hands and searches my eyes. "I do."

Taking my time, I tease her opening with the tip of my cock. She opens her legs wide, begging to feel me, and I can't hold back any longer. In one long stroke, I fill her with my length. She's so fucking wet, so fucking beautiful, and it makes me hard as steel. Her fingernails scratch down my back, and she holds me tight as if she's never letting me go as we rock together in slow motion. Her soft pants against my skin cause emotions to swirl through me as I pump in and out of her.

"I want it harder, Alex. I need more."

"Mmm, whatever you want, darlin'." I grab her earlobe in my mouth and suck.

I don't make her beg, and I give her exactly what she wants. She screams out my name as I slam my cock into her, over and over again. I don't want this moment to end, but I know if I keep at this pace, I'll be crumbling to pieces soon. The orgasm quickly builds, and I force myself to slow so I can enjoy her as long as possible. As we continue to make sweet love, our hearts and bodies mend together as one. The emotions I'm feeling are almost too much as the orgasms sneak up. Another thrust, and I almost feel blinded by the orgasm. The intensity practically takes my breath away as I lose myself inside her. River is my everything, and without her there's nothing.

My heart is so full as she looks at me, her green eyes glimmering, completely satisfied, and I smile back. After we clean up, she crawls back into bed, and I pull her close, needing her skin against mine. As I hold her tight, she draws circles on my chest and listens to my heartbeat then wraps her leg around mine. We're a tangled mess, and I never want this to end.

"I can never get enough of you, River."

She props herself up on one elbow and smiles sweetly.

"Well luckily, we have forever," she says, glancing down at her ring before leaning over and tugging my bottom lip into her mouth.

EPILOGUE

River

SIX MONTHS LATER

Each day, Riley grows up more and more. He definitely has a strong personality but is an all-around happy baby. In nine short months, Alex and I have already watched him crawl for the first time, and even heard him say his first word, which happened to be "horse." I know once Riley starts walking, we'll be in trouble because he's already so independent, super curious, and wanting to do everything himself. We're raising our own little cowboy and couldn't be prouder.

With the exception of the day Riley was born, my wedding was the second most beautiful day of my life. Natalie and Adam flew down, and so did my parents. They all stayed in the B&B for almost a week, and I had a hell of a time showing them around the ranch and teaching them how we do things in Texas. I may be an implant, but I consider this home now.

After the proposal, we wasted no time on planning. The wedding was more than I could've ever imagined. The weather was perfect, which was needed considering it was outside. Since Alex's sister was married a few years prior on the ranch, the boys had plenty of practice with setting up giant tents and dance floors in the backyard. When the sun set, that's when the dancing and drinking really started. There were so many family members and friends in attendance, it felt like the whole town was there. All I have to say is the Bishops really know how to throw an epic party.

Looking back a few years ago, I never would've imagined this would be my life—a happy little family living on a ranch in West Texas. I didn't know what truly living was until I met Alex Bishop. My household is so full of laughter and love that it makes my heart burst with emotion. Though we didn't all get off on the right foot, Alex's family is everything I could've ever wished for and more. I'm the luckiest woman in the world, and each day that I hear my little boy giggle and feel my husband's touch, I know that's true.

Six months after having Riley, I decided to take Evan's offer and put my application in at the hospital. I was offered a position the following day and was happy to get back to a job I knew I loved, even though I knew I'd miss Riley tons. Mama Rose begged to watch him during my shifts, but she didn't need to beg hard because I know how much she loves and adores him. Riley loves his grandma so much and instantly smiles every time he sees her. They keep each other company while all the boys are out working too.

Alex and I decided to postpone our honeymoon because of our work schedules. However, we're planning to visit Key West again, and I can't wait to check things off the new bucket list we made. After the wedding on Friday, we said goodbye to our guests, then spent Saturday and Sunday alone at home as husband and wife.

Monday morning comes quick, and Alex and I rush around. After I feed and change the baby, I kiss Alex goodbye then take Riley over to Mama's house. She greets me with a smile at the door in her robe. I pass him off with a quick smooch, give her a big hug and thank you, then head to work.

While I drive to the hospital, all I can think of is how quickly the weekend went by. How everything these past six months have gone by so fast. The wedding events happened too quickly, and my head is still spinning at how magical and unreal it feels. As soon as the hospital comes into view, I let out a laugh when I think about Evan. A little birdy told me a rumor about him, and I can't wait to call him out on it because I'm pretty sure it's true.

I park and walk in, taking in the familiar smell of the hospital. No matter the location, they all seem to smell exactly the same—sterile, clean, and oddly enough, it brings me back to my childhood when we'd be in and out of the hospitals for Rylie. As I ride the elevator, I think about my baby sister. Though she's not physically here with me, I'll always carry a piece of her in my heart.

A smile touches my lips, but when I step off the elevator and see Evan, it grows into a shit-eating grin. My timing couldn't have been more perfect. He looks up from the chart in his hand and sees me walking toward him. Pretending to groan, he goes back to his paperwork.

"So...how was your weekend?" I keep the right amount of sweetness in my tone.

Evan glares at me. "How do you think it was?"

"If the rumors are true, I'd say it started off at a ten and dropped down to a one really quick." I chuckle.

Amelia, my labor and delivery nurse with Riley and who also became my partner in crime after I started working here, walks up smacking her gum with her eyebrow popped. "Rumors?"

Evan's uncomfortable with the conversation, but it's good for him to squirm every once in a while, and now that I'm family, he can't be rude. Mama's rule, not mine.

"Oh yeah. Juicy rumors, too. Apparently, Evan hooked up with some random chick the night of my wedding. Some friend of a friend and no one knows who this mystery woman is other than her name. Stelllllllllaaaaaaaaaaaaaa."

I watch as he takes a deep, annoyed breath and releases it slowly. I bet he's hoping I don't know the end of the story too, but he's not that lucky. There are no secrets when Jackson is around, and even he knows that.

"And apparently the morning after, he woke up and she was gone, along with every piece of the tux he rented. Underwear and all." I chuckle, biting down on my lip to keep my laughter under control. " Had to call every single one of his brothers to bring him a set of spare clothes." I'm laughing so hard, I can barely get the words out. "And the only person who answered his call was John. Apparently, there were some *pretty* desperate voicemails left." I glance at Evan who's wearing a scowl.

"Damn," Amelia says, her eyes wide. "Who does that?" She chuckles.

"Stella! He would've been better off wrapping a sheet around his waist and making a run for it. Because they're never going to let him live it down," I tell her. We're both bent over laughing, and Evan isn't amused, but we continue talking about it like he's not there.

"Don't you think I've gotten enough shit from my brothers about this weekend? Just *had* to bring it to work too. Go ahead, laugh it up. I'm glad I could amuse you both." Evan shakes his head before handing the file to a passing nurse.

Amelia and I continue poking fun when we hear Evan suck in a deep breath. I look up and realize the new doctor is stepping off the elevator with a lost look in her eye. Trying to make a good example, Amelia and I straighten up but continue giggling at Evan's expense.

"Who's that?" Amelia asks, looking back and forth between us.

"I'm pretty sure that's the new ER doctor they told us about last month. Dr. Emily Bell. She just finished her residency and has to work under Evan."

I look over at Evan who'll be training her considering he's the attending supervisor. Evan's been working as a emergency medicine doctor for several years and when Dr. Lockhart retired recently the hospital had to find a replacement.

Evan becomes stiff as a board, and I elbow him. "Lighten up before you scare the poor girl away."

He stifles a sarcastic laugh, and his entire demeanor changes as she stops at the nurses' station. I hear her ask for Dr. Bishop, and he rolls his eyes with a deep groan.

"What's wrong with you?" I ask him.

His jaw tightens. "That's *her*. That's the woman who stole my goddamn clothes," he says under his breath, shaking his head and scrubbing a hand over his scruffy jawline.

Amelia and I both turn our heads and get a good look at her. She's gorgeous, stunning actually. Her chestnut brown hair is pulled back into a long, sleek ponytail, and she's wearing a black pencil skirt so tight it could be painted on. Her cream blouse is tucked into her skirt, revealing a small waist. Her slender legs are accompanied by red heels at least three inches high. Black glasses frame her dark eyes and the deep red lipstick she's wearing says she doesn't take anyone's shit—the ultimate man eater.

As I glance back at Evan, I'm dying inside trying to hold it together. *What are the odds?*

"It was her?" I ask, confused. "Emily?" My jaw drops. "I thought mystery girl's name was Stella?"

"So did I," he says between gritted teeth, and now it all makes sense. Ultimate man eater confirmed, except she chews them up and spits them out.

Evan shakes his head and crosses his arms over his broad chest. The air in the room seems to dissipate and is replaced with thick awkwardness. Someone points out Evan, and she smiles then walks toward us. Once closer, recognition and maybe a hint of regret flash across Emily's face before she pushes the emotions away and continues forward.

Before she can even open her mouth, Evan speaks. "Emily? That's *real cute.*" Evan throws shade her way.

She sucks in a deep breath and releases it. "And you're *Dr. Bishop,* aren't you?"

Going to work just got *way* more interesting.

You can continue reading *Hitching the Cowboy* and *Catching the Cowboy* to get their kids' stories or you can read *Needing Him* to get Evan's story

Hitching the Cowboy
RILEY & ZOEY

Wedding bells are the last thing on twenty-two year old Riley Bishop's mind, but that's exactly what he hears after waking up in Vegas next to a woman he just met—his new *wife*.

He never saw her coming, but she might be worth the risk.

Zoey Mitchell is high on life, free spirited, and adventurous. However, learning she married a rowdy cowboy after a night of partying is not what she expected—even for her.

She's risking it all, gambling with her heart.

Deciding to give their instant marriage a chance, Zoey moves from her big city life to a small town Texas ranch. She has to know if their connection is based on more than just a wild one-night stand before announcing to her family that she got hitched.

One moment changes everything—*for better or worse*—and a secret could destroy them both.

And we'll build this love
From the ground up
For worse or for better

And I will be all you need
Beside you I'll stand

"From the Ground Up"
-Dan + Shay

PROLOGUE

Riley

My entire body feels as if I've been plowed down by a heavy ass tractor. Even trying to roll over makes me ache, and when I blink my eyes open, I realize I'm in my hotel room at the Bellagio in Las Vegas. The wide-open curtains allow the unforgiving sun to shine through the windows, blaring in my face.

"Fuuuuuck," I mutter as my head throbs, and I curse myself for how much I drank last night. Diesel, my best friend since grade school, turned twenty-one two days ago, and a weekend trip to Vegas was my gift to him. I'm fourteen months older and felt it was my duty to get him shit-faced in Sin City. Getting away was the only way to properly celebrate his birthday, considering we bust our asses working on the ranch six days a week. If he's feeling the same way I am, then mission accomplished.

Chuckling to myself, then groaning at how badly it hurts to laugh, I attempt to slide out of bed, but my arm is stuck under a body. Blinking, I realize a woman is lying against me.

With dirty blond hair and sun-kissed skin, she looks like a goddess sprawled out under the sheets that rest at her bare waist. Looking down, I see we're both naked, and flashes of last night flood my mind.

Zoey. Thinking for a moment, I'm almost positive that's her name. At least I hope.

I first saw her with a group of girls at a club when I dared Diesel to participate in an amateur stripper night. Miraculously, we ran into each other again, but now, she's here with me. My head pounds, but I try to ignore the pain as I recall all the details.

Oh God.

Glancing around, I check to make sure Diesel's not on the other bed nor on the floor. We're alone, thankfully. As carefully as I can, I pull my arm from underneath Zoey, but before I successfully slide from under the sheets, she rolls over and wraps an arm around me and snuggles in closer.

Holy fucking hell.

Her tits are on full display as she hikes a leg over my waist, brushing over my dick. Which is now hard, thanks to her.

"Good morning," she says in the sexiest sleepy voice I've ever heard. Without opening her eyes, she smiles and rubs her head against my chest, causing my heart to rapidly beat.

"Uh, mornin'," I reply, swallowing hard. Within a second, Zoey's eyes pop open, and her grin falls as she takes in the room and then me.

"Oh my God!" She looks down at our naked bodies and groans. "Oh shit." She gives me a small smile and shakes her head. "Sorry, I didn't mean it like that."

Chuckling, I rest a hand behind my head, and she removes herself from me. "It's okay. I didn't have the best first reaction, either. Zoey, right?" I feel like an ass for having to ask, but my memory is foggy as fuck. I know I drank a shit ton last night, but I'll never forget the way she squeezed her tight pussy around my dick.

She looks up at me, then grabs the sheet and pulls it to her neck, covering that sexy body I could stare at all morning. "Yeah," she confirms. "R-something?" She winces, then blushes, looking flustered as hell, which I find adorable. "I feel like a two-dollar whore. I'm so sorry. My damn head feels like someone pounded a hundred nails into it."

"Riley," I supply. "Don't be sorry, darlin'. Though, I would've happily paid more than a couple of bucks." I flash her a wink when she glances at me and chuckles at the reality of our situation. Sitting up, she wraps the sheet around her, and I can't help but admire how gorgeous she is. I might've woken up fuzzy, but the moment we fell into bed together will forever be burned into my memory.

And the...*wait*. I hold up my left hand and stare at the gold band around my ring finger. Memories flash through my head like photographs, nearly leaving me speechless.

"Uh, Zoey," I say slowly, repositioning myself.

"I'm just gonna find my clothes and do the walk of shame outta here. I'm sure you want your hotel room back," she says as if I was about to kick her out.

"Did we, uh...did we...?" I stutter as I remember the white chapel and Diesel's revenge dare.

"We both woke up naked in bed, so I'm quite sure we did..."

"That's not what I'm asking." I blow out a sharp breath and brush a hand through my hair. "Do you have a ring on your finger?"

Zoey immediately holds out her left hand and gasps. A simple but elegant gold band. She turns toward me and looks at my hand. "Oh God, I remember now."

"Was it really legal?"

"We signed a license and said vows, so yeah, I'm pretty sure we're legally married now." She sucks in her lower lip, then chews on it.

Before I can respond, the hotel door swings open, and Diesel walks in looking way too fucking chipper.

"Hey, lovebirds!" The door slams behind him, and Zoey and I both wince at the noise. "How are the newlyweds feelin' this morning?"

"Fucker," I grumble. "Did you seriously dare me to get married last night?" I grab the comforter off the bed and wrap it around my waist so I'm somewhat decent.

Diesel's booming laughter is all the confirmation I need. I'm gonna murder him in his sleep.

"Your mama's gonna kill you," he says, still chuckling. "And your grandma."

"Try both at the same time." I huff.

"Sorry to break up the honeymoon, but we gotta go. Pack your shit,"

Diesel says, rushing around the room and shoving his things into his suitcase.

"Now?" I gape, turning and looking at Zoey, who's grabbing her little panties off the floor. She seems embarrassed as hell, but I wish she wasn't. So adventurous and spontaneous, she brought out the best in me, and we had a blast together.

"Flight's in an hour, and we still gotta get there and through security. We'll be lucky to make it on time at this point," Diesel says, glancing at this phone. The time constraint is ruining my ability to talk to her about this, about us. I don't want to go, but fuck, I have to.

As Zoey picks up her bra, I round the bed and tilt her chin up so I can look into her eyes. "I'm sorry, I wish I could stay. But they're expecting us at work tomorrow, and it's a long drive from the airport to the ranch. Can we exchange numbers, at least?"

"Yeah, of course." She smiles. "We'll need to figure out what we're going to do." Her face drops, and I hate that I have to leave in such a damn rush.

"Or you could come with me?" I ask, feeling hopeful. "Try to get to know each other better." The words spill out before I can stop myself, but I don't regret them. She's unlike any other woman I've ever met.

"I-I can't. My sister's getting married next weekend, and my life is in Phoenix." She shrugs, holding the sheet against her body.

"Alright, I understand. I'll text you my address in case you change your mind." I smile, knowing the chances of that are slim. I walk to the nightstand and grab my phone. After she gives me her number, I text her so she can reach out as soon as she's home.

"Riley, we *really* have to go," Diesel urges.

"I'm going to get dressed so I can head out too." Zoey walks around me with her arms full and goes to the bathroom. Once the door clicks shut, I quickly slip on my boxers and dig in my suitcase for clean clothes.

"So, was it awkward waking up and realizing you guys eloped?" Diesel asks with a shit-eating grin on his face.

I glower, narrowing my eyes at him as I zip up my jeans. "You're an asshole."

Before he can respond, Zoey walks out in the same outfit she wore last night. I catch her staring at my bare chest, then she shifts her eyes away as she walks toward the bed, grabbing her phone and clutch. I hate that I'm being forced to dart out of here, and we don't have more than a couple of minutes together.

"Listen, Zoey..." I go to her as I slip my shirt on.

"It's okay, Riley. We don't have to do this."

Diesel opens the door with his bag in hand. "Riley, c'mon. We still gotta get a cab..."

"I'm sorry. Call me soon so we can figure this out, okay?" I lean in, cup her face, then kiss her cheek. "For what it's worth, I had a really fun night, *wife*." I flash her a wink, which causes her to blush. She shakes her head at me and smirks.

"Safe flight, *hubby*," she mocks. I stare at her, remembering the taste of her lips, the way she moaned my name, and how perfectly her body fit against mine. Our connection was instant, and while I didn't understand it, I couldn't fight it either. From the moment our eyes locked, I knew she was special. Turns out, the universe had bigger plans, bigger than either of us could have imagined. Or maybe Diesel's to blame.

"Riley! You have two seconds, or I'm leaving your ass in Vegas, and you can explain why you aren't at work in the morning to your family," Diesel walks out frustrated as hell, and I know damn well he would really leave me.

"Goodbye," Zoey says as I move away from her and grab my suitcase.

I give her an apologetic smile, then spin around to catch the door before it closes, leaving her behind and feeling like complete shit about it.

CHAPTER ONE

Riley

72 HOURS EARLIER

"Rise 'n' shine, motherfucker." Cold water to my face accompanies Diesel's loud voice, making me jump out of bed with fists swinging. Considering I'm barely awake, I miss, and he starts laughing.

Scrubbing my hands over my face, I see the faint hint of the sun shining through my curtains, then rush toward him as he walks toward the door.

"The fuck?" I push his back, forcing him forward into the hallway. "Gonna kick your ass for that."

"Yeah, right." Diesel chuckles, knowing damn well he has sixty pounds and five inches on me. He didn't get his nickname for being small. Built like a fucking house and loud as a diesel truck, he's had that nickname since middle school. "Besides the fact that you couldn't, you wouldn't hurt the birthday boy."

I snort, following him into the kitchen. "Your birthday was yesterday."

"But we're celebrating this weekend!" he shouts, and he's way too damn excited. "So technically, it's my birthday till we get our drunken asses back here on Sunday. Till then, it's fuckin' party time!"

"We still have a workday to get through," I remind him while pouring a mug of coffee. At least he managed to start a pot before waking me up by dumping water on my face. We've been roommates since he graduated from high school three years ago. Our house is on the Circle B Ranch that my family owns, and most of the Bishops live and work here in some capacity too. Diesel's originally a townie, meaning his family isn't in the business, and though he had no real experience, he applied to be a ranch hand like me. For some reason, my dad hired his ass, and we've gotten into more trouble than ever. Having been raised on the ranch, I live and breathe this lifestyle and don't plan on leaving anytime soon. Just like the generations of Bishops before me, I was born for this.

"Yeah, yeah," he grumbles, grabbing his to-go cup and taking a sip. "It'll go by fast since we have to leave by two. Are you even packed yet?"

"Almost. Not really sure what to bring, though. All I own are Wranglers, and I'm pretty sure cowboy boots won't be in style." I chuckle, remembering the story my mom told me about when she first met my dad. He showed up in Key West looking like something out of the Wild West, and my mother hasn't let him live it down ever since. Granted, I was conceived on that trip, which means the boots didn't throw her off that badly. Maybe I'll take them after all. Perhaps they'll be good luck.

"What's wrong with Corrals?" he asks, tapping the heel of his boot against the floor. "They go with my hat. My Stetson is a total chick magnet."

I snort and shake my head, grabbing my coffee as I walk back to my room to get ready for the day. Once I'm dressed and caffeinated, Diesel and I head to my truck. The sprawling ranch covers thousands of acres, so we still have to drive a good ten minutes to get to the workshop where we start and end each day.

By the time we arrive, my cousin Fisher is already there. His real name is Anderson, but we've called him by his last name since he was in junior high.

We always meet in the office to prioritize what needs to be done or fixed and make a game plan. The fridge is always stocked with drinks, and it's become a hangout for us between tasks or when it's hot as hell outside.

My dad manages the ranch's day-to-day routines and organizes most of the schedules. Uncle John has run the Circle B Ranch Bed & Breakfast since before I was born, but ever since he and my uncle Evan bought a run-down bar in town ten years ago, he's juggled both. After his oldest daughter, Maize, graduated high school three years ago, she's been helping out more and learning how to manage the B&B so John doesn't have to do it all on his own.

"'Bout time," Fisher smarts off the minute we walk into the shop. He grew up in California but has spent every summer here since he was a teenager. His mom, Courtney, is my dad's only sister. I was excited when she and my uncle Drew agreed to let Fisher help out on the ranch. He's an ass, but he works hard, which is helpful.

He gives me a pointed look. "I was about to call and chew your asses out."

"And I would've told you to kiss my white ass, Fisher," Diesel snaps, walking toward him. "We're thirty seconds late."

I chuckle because it's the same song and dance every morning. Fisher has a brother and sister back in Cali, and the three of them are triplets. When my aunt and uncle had been unsuccessful in getting pregnant, they tried IVF, then found out they were having three babies instead of just one. Fisher pretends he's years older and in charge, but Diesel relentlessly puts him in his place. We work year-round, and even though Fisher graduated from college last year, he hasn't found a permanent job yet, so he still helps during the summer. Grandma Bishop has told him he's hired to work on the ranch year-round, but he hasn't agreed to it. I think Diesel would lose his shit, though.

"The pig fence needs to be fixed today. After the storm a couple of nights ago, I noticed it got bent to hell and back. Think you two can manage getting it done?"

"Your fancy business degree doesn't make you my boss," Diesel reminds him. Opening the fridge, he grabs two bottles of water, then tosses one to me.

"Yeah, we'll go check it out after we feed the chickens," I answer before Fisher can respond. "We have to be done by one thirty, though, to get on the road by two."

"Oh, that's right. You're bailing this weekend." He grunts.

"Fuckin' right. Bye!" Diesel walks toward the door that leads to the equipment barn with his arm extended, flipping the bird. They haven't gotten along since Fisher stole his girlfriend Gretchen three years ago. Though they weren't "official," Fisher swept her off her feet. They've been together ever since, and she even moved to Sacramento to be with him and comes back to visit her family when Fisher works during the summers. It's been tense, and I'm constantly playing referee.

"Radio if you need anything else," I tell him before following Diesel out and shutting the door.

"I know he's your cousin and all, but I hate his city boy *I'm better than you* attitude," he says, jumping into the passenger seat of the side-by-side.

Taking the driver's side, I crank the engine and give him a moment to calm down. "You hate him because he's with Gretchen. Otherwise, he's not that bad," I tell him with a shrug, not wanting to take sides. What Fisher did wasn't cool, but Diesel wasn't exactly offering exclusivity either.

"Pfft," he huffs in response. "He can have that two-timing witch."

I smirk, knowing he doesn't mean it. He liked her a lot, and they'd been on and off for six months before Fisher strolled into town. She was hoping for some kind of commitment from Diesel, and he stupidly didn't offer it to her.

"We're going to Vegas. You'll have plenty of opportunities to find a rebound," I remind him, taking off and driving us toward the chicken coops. Once we're there, we collect the eggs, throw out feed, and place fresh hay on the ground and in the nesting boxes. Typically, one of my younger cousins would do this grunt work, but with less than a month of school left, they're all staying up late to study for final exams. I think it's just an excuse for them to get out of their morning chores. However, my sister, Rowan, who's three years younger, is coming home next week from the University of Houston, where she's finishing up her second year of undergrad studies in finance. When she comes home, she'll be able to help with some ranch chores, but she'll probably spend most of her time working at the family bar.

"I've had rebounds," he states proudly. "But it always comes back to bite me in the ass. There aren't enough options in this small town. And well, you keep telling me your sister is off-limits so..." He flashes a shit-eating smirk, purposely pushing my buttons.

"And I'll tell you again…" I warn, narrowing my eyes at him. Rowan turns twenty soon, and I know she's not innocent, but she's my baby sister, and I don't want Diesel's lips or hands anywhere near her. He's got a reputation when it comes to breaking hearts, and I don't need to kick my best friend's ass for hurting her because I will.

Once we're done dealing with the chickens, we drive to the B&B and deliver the eggs. It's a tradition to sit and eat before heading back out, but with our shortened day, we just grab a quick bite and refill our coffee. Before we make it out the door, my mom enters wearing scrubs, and she smiles at me.

"Hey, honey!"

"Hey, Ma. We're just heading out so we can get done early today." I wrap an arm around her, towering over her petite frame. She's been a nurse for over twenty-five years and commutes to the hospital in San Angelo, where my uncle Evan and his wife, Emily, work as doctors. "You leaving for work soon, or did you just come off the night shift?"

"I'll be heading in soon. Em and I are carpooling, but I wanted to say goodbye before you two kids left." She squeezes Diesel's cheek, which he hates but smiles through the pain. She's referred to him as her "bonus son" for as long as we've been best friends.

"We'll be back before ya know it, Ma," I reassure her, so she releases her hold on me.

"You better behave yourselves. I mean it." She jabs her finger in my shoulder.

"Yeah, Riley," Diesel goads, stuffing his hands in his front pockets and leaning back on his heels.

"I was mostly referring to you," Ma says pointedly.

"Me?" He brings a hand to his chest. "I'm an angel," he protests.

My mother snorts. "Please. I married a cowboy. I know all about you…*angels.*"

"I'm sure Dad was a complete Southern gentleman when you first met in Florida." I waggle my brows at her, knowing that'll make her blush and hopefully get us off the hook from hearing her "behavior" speech.

"Who was a Southern gentleman?" Grandma Bishop walks in, immediately pulling me in for a hug.

"Dad was when he first met Ma," I respond. "She's worried about us going to Vegas," I explain.

"I raised all my boys to be gentlemen, so he better have been!" she responds, then leans in and lowers her voice. "Though your mother showed up a few months later to announce she was expecting you, so perhaps he was *too* much of a gentleman if you get my drift..."

"Grandma!" I laugh.

"Oh my God." My mom groans. "Just do as I say and not as I do, okay?"

I grin. "You got it. No making you a grandma just yet." I flash her a wink, and her eyes go wide.

"I'm too young! And so are you!" She glowers at me, keeping her lips in a firm *don't push me* expression. My mom is sweet as candy, but when she means business, you don't mess with her.

"Promise, Ma. Plus, I'm gonna be rooming with this drunk. There won't be any inappropriate fornicating happening," I tell her.

"Don't use me as an excuse. What he meant to say is he'll have whiskey di—"

I jab my elbow hard into his ribs before he can finish his sentence. "Dude, my grandma is here."

"My apologies, Grandma Bishop. I should be more formal." He flashes a shit-eating grin at me before he continues, "Whiskey *penis*."

"And we're leaving now..." I roughly grab the back of his shirt and push his stupid ass toward the door.

"Bye!" He turns around and waves before I can open the door and shove him out.

"You're an asshole," I say as soon as we're on the porch.

"Your family loves me," he mocks, stumbling down the stairs.

Rolling my eyes, I follow him to the side-by-side so we can finish our shit and leave on time.

By two, we're packed and on the road, heading toward the airport. "Vegas bound!" Diesel shouts out the passenger side window, slamming his hand against the door.

"Why do I have a feeling I'm gonna have to watch you like a hawk this weekend?" I shake my head.

"Pfft. As long as neither of us comes back with an STD or a future baby mama, we'll be fine! Isn't the whole point of this *birthday* trip to celebrate

318

and get fucked up?" he counters in a snarky tone, making me want to smack his *you-know-I'm-right* grin off his face.

"As long as we come back in one piece." I shrug. "But I'm still not babysitting your ass."

"Deal!" He holds up his fist and bumps it with mine, but I'm still not convinced.

This might be the trip of a lifetime, or it might change everything—either are possible with two rowdy cowboys going to Vegas for the first time.

CHAPTER TWO

Zoey

The whole week has been a clusterfuck, and I can't wait until this weekend when I can go to Vegas and enjoy myself. After I graduated from cosmetology school, I rented a chair at a busy salon known for its crazy and outlandish styles such as rainbow-colored highlights and complicated updos. Though I work in Phoenix, our masterpieces look as if they should be in New York City.

Trina, a woman in her mid-fifties, arrives right on time and sits in my chair. I see her once a month because she's particular about covering her grays.

"How's your week going?" I ask once I've fastened the cape around her neck. She fills me in on all her family drama and the husband she's two seconds from divorcing. "Be right back. I'm going to mix your color, and we'll get started."

"I should've left him years ago," she says as I brush the dye onto her roots. "Cheating asshole wanted me as nothing but a trophy wife. Now he's got even more money, and I should take every red cent," Trina huffs. Listening to people's adventures is one of the highlights of my day, and considering everything I'm told, I should be paid as their therapist, not a stylist.

"If only I were your age again." Her eyes meet mine in the mirror, and it causes me to smile.

"What would you do?" I ask, actually intrigued.

"I'd do it all. I would live my life regardless of what everyone else wanted me to do. I'd move away. Be a free spirit. Spontaneous even. Travel more. Hell, I'd even get a dog," she tells me. "Maybe two."

"Dean's allergies are ridiculous," she complains with an eye roll. "We have an aquarium. It's about as far as it goes for pets."

Once I'm fully done applying her color, I set a timer and tell her to hold tight while I go clean out the bowl and brush.

"Just wait for the right man. Don't rush into anything," she warns when I return.

All I can do is smile because the only man interested in me is my dad's friend's son, and he's ten years older than I am. Benjamin and I have gone on a few dates, which I agreed to just to appease my parents, but that's about it. He's a hotshot doctor, an up and coming heart surgeon who's determined to take over the medical field with his smarts, charm, and good looks. He even gave himself the nickname "Life Saver." My parents are in love with him, and I'm trying to feel *something* but refuse to force it.

After I've rinsed out the color, then blow-dried and styled Trina's hair, she pays, leaving me a big tip. I adore her, and she enjoys spending her husband's money, so I have no complaints.

My next appointment isn't for two hours, so instead of staying in the salon all day, I decide to go out for lunch. Twenty minutes later, I stop at a sandwich shop downtown. Taking a seat outside, I eat, soaking up the Phoenix sun, wishing I could stay in this spot all day. As I'm taking my last bite, my phone dings with a text, and I pick it up and see a message from my sister, Summer.

SUMMER

Three more days and we're flying out! I CANNOT WAIT!

ZOEY

I know! I'm itching for a vacation.

I love taking road trips and seeing different places. Having schedule flexibility was one of the reasons I decided to do hair in the first place. I didn't want to be tied to a nine-to-five job and work for someone else. I needed the freedom to come and go as I please, and with my current position, I have that. Typically, every few months, I'll get in my car and drive somewhere I've never been before.

SUMMER

72 HOURS!

I smile at the thought of going to Vegas. Her best friend even scheduled a club crawl tour bus so we can easily barhop. Summer's been planning her wedding since she was five years old, including her bachelorette party.

Upon checking the time, I see I have a little under an hour until my next client arrives, so I go back to the salon and wait. The rest of the day flies by quickly without any cancellations, which is great, but it also means standing for hours without a break.

Even though I'm exhausted when I get home, I take the time to eat with my parents. My dad isn't home often for dinner, considering he's a doctor and usually gets called in even after long workdays, so I try to spend as much time with them as I can, though the conversation rarely goes in a positive direction.

"How's work going?" Dad asks as he scrolls through his phone. I've gotta give him props for even asking, considering I can't remember the last time he did.

"Great, actually. Pretty busy, but I can't complain." I keep my response short and sweet because I know what's coming next.

He sighs, displeased. "You're so smart, Zoey. You would make a wonderful physician. People adore you, and you have great people skills, just like Summer does. You two got that from me," he says with a small smirk. "There's still time to change your mind and go to school," he adds before stuffing his mouth. Not a week passes without a reminder from him about how great I would've been following in his footsteps.

Summer's a few years older than I am, and she's already graduated with a perfect GPA in pre-med and is working to become a doctor just like my father. Then there's me, who decided not to go to college or keep the family legacy of practicing medicine alive. Now they're convinced if I marry someone who they approve of—someone who comes from money or has money—then all will be well in the world, and as soon as that thought hits, my mother chimes in.

"So, how's Benjamin?" She looks at me with bright blue eyes, hoping I'll say exactly what she wants to hear.

"He's fine, I guess. Not sure." I shrug, hoping she'll drop the topic. "Haven't chatted with him in a few days," I admit and feel the disappointment streaming off her when she furrows her brows.

My father speaks up. "He's a great kid. You should really give him a chance, Zoey. Comes from a good family of doctors and is well mannered. Great at his job, which pays extremely well. He'll make a name for himself without a doubt. Hell, he's well on his way now, considering all the experience he's had in surgery."

Yes, because that's all that matters.

"He's also way older than me," I remind them just as I have several times before.

"Your father is ten years older than I am." Mom glowers. "I keep him young. Plus, marrying an older man means he's more mature and knows what he wants in life. No drama or games."

I nearly choke on my food and wish this conversation would end, so I change the subject.

"So, the Vegas trip is this weekend. Don't forget we fly out on Friday." I hurry and take a bite so I don't have to talk.

"You really need to be safe while you're there. Take pepper spray, and don't talk to strangers. Sometimes you're too friendly and will chat with anyone," Mom tells me as if I'm a five-year-old child. She's always so worried about me, probably because I'm nothing like her.

"I won't be alone. I'll have Summer and all her friends. We're not leaving each other's side," I tell her, hoping she'll finally get off my ass about it.

Dad breathes in heavily. "I don't know why Summer would plan something so childish. Most women do spa days or vacations in New York. Vegas is just...*trashy*." He gives me a pointed look, and his judgy tone can't be mistaken for anything else. He despises the idea.

"I even offered to pay for you girls to go to Bali for three days, and Summer refused," Dad grunts. I think it's the first time Summer has really gone against their wishes, and I'm actually proud as hell of her for doing what she wanted. Our parents tend to have a tight hold on us, especially me, and while I want to move out, I'm not sure how they'll react when I actually do. Though it's ridiculous, they're more focused on marrying me off so I'm "taken care of." I'm sure that's the only way they'll accept me leaving.

After we finish eating, Dad tells us good night, then heads toward the stairs. Since he has to be at the hospital at four in the morning, he goes to bed before the sun completely sets. I load the dirty plates into the dishwasher as Mom puts the extra food in containers. I'm being standoffish and just want to go to bed. I've had a long day.

"I know you get annoyed by us sometimes, but we just want the best for you, Zoey," she tells me as she closes the fridge.

"I know." I give her a smile, wiping off my hands on a dish towel.

"Will you please give Benjamin a chance? For us?" She's so hopeful, and I don't dare tell her no. "You two are perfect together."

I nod, not wanting to argue, and then give her a hug before going upstairs. All I've ever wanted is to make my parents proud, and the least I can do is try.

"Are you ready?" Summer asks from behind me. I've put off packing all week, and now I'm rushing since we have to leave in ten minutes to make our flight.

"Almost," I say, turning and shooting her a cheeky grin. She shakes her head, but a smirk crosses her lips. I'm known for doing things last minute, but this time, I really messed up. I stuff every sort of outfit I could ever need inside my suitcase, then zip it up. At this point, all I can do is hope for the best. Standing, I grab my shit and walk toward her, ecstatic to be spending the weekend with my big sister and her friends before she gets married.

"Mom and Dad have already given me the *be-careful* speech," I tell her matter-of-factly. "Along with the *don't do drugs, don't talk to strangers,* and *don't have sex.* In other words, don't have fun." I snort.

She smirks. "I've gotten warned too, but I'm not worried about it. What they don't know won't hurt them."

"It *is* your last weekend of being a single woman! I'm sure you could find a fling or two. What happens in Vegas, stays in Vegas. Amiright?" I joke. Summer's prim and proper most of the time; the exact cookie-cutter daughter my parents wanted. I'm the spontaneous and eccentric wild child. They don't know what to do with me most of the time other than try to force me to fit in their box. I've failed to follow their wishes, but it's not because I'm trying to rebel. I've almost come to terms with being the black sheep of the family. It's hard for them to understand me because I'm not like them and I'm not interested in the same stuff they are. I think on a different brain wave. I'm creative instead of analytical. I'd rather go with the flow than plan my entire life, and that's incomprehensible to them.

Summer chuckles and follows me as I struggle to carry my overloaded suitcase down the stairs. When I walk into the living room, nearly out of breath, my mother puts her book down and gives us both a sweet, practiced smile.

"Make sure to be responsible in Las Vegas. I've heard some terrible stories about that place," she warns, and worry is written all over her face.

"Just remember, Mom, this was all Summer's idea," I tease, taking the attention away from me for once. What they don't know is that she can drink us all under the table. She might seem perfect now, but she was a sorority girl in college, and I heard about the wild frat parties she attended. Just because she had good grades doesn't mean she didn't have the normal college experience.

"We better get going." Summer shifts the conversation with ease. "Love you, Mom. Tell Dad we'll be fine," she says, walking toward the front door.

"You two behave," Mom barks.

"We will," Summer and I say in unison.

Once we're outside, Summer pops the trunk to her car and helps me load the heavy ass suitcase. I see her carry-on inside.

"That's all you brought?" I ask, shocked.

She shrugs. "Don't plan on remembering anything that happens this weekend, especially not what I'm wearing."

My eyes go wide as I realize I might be in for more than what I bargained for, but I gladly accept the challenge. We listen to music as she drives us to the airport, excited to have the next few days of freedom. She gushes about her fiancé, Owen, who's her high school sweetheart. My father molded him into the son-in-law he's always wanted, one who has a career and can provide for his daughter. Owen went to med school and plans to follow in my father's footsteps. Luckily, she found the love of her life while she was a teenager. I'm probably doomed to die an old cat lady.

Once we park the car and make it to the entrance, I see her four best friends waiting impatiently. They're all beautiful and wearing matching bridesmaids' shirts. Avery hands me one that says maid of honor, and it has the same sparkly rhinestones on it as their bridesmaids' ones. I slip it over my crop top and give her a hug and a thank you. They're all Summer's age and treat me like their kid sister, but I don't mind. It's actually fun being around them, and I love how they bring out the wild side in Summer. She deserves this weekend more than anyone else I know.

Once we've checked our bags and made it through security, Avery and Chelsea drag us to a little cantina by our gate for pre-flight drinks. I try to pace myself, but it's useless when they keep ordering rounds of shots. By the time we're called for boarding, we're all two sheets to the wind and giggling about God knows what. Summer's grinning wide as we patiently wait for the attendant to scan our tickets, and I haven't seen her this happy in a long while.

After she got engaged, she became more serious, saying she needed to start acting like an adult. Essentially, she took etiquette lessons from my mother on how to be a good wife. It kinda makes me sad how manipulative they've been.

"Are you ready, sis?" Summer asks after we find our seats and buckle. Looking out the window, I feel my excitement nearly bubble over.

I turn and look at her with a huge smile on my face. "Ready to make memories of a lifetime!"

She squeals and so does the rest of the bridal party. Right then, I vow not to think about my parents, Benjamin, or anything back in Phoenix. This weekend is about experiencing Vegas and living life to the fullest.

CHAPTER THREE

Riley

Time zones confuse the shit out of me, especially when my internal clock is on ranch hand time—up at the ass crack of dawn and in bed before midnight. I left at four, was on a three-hour flight, and landed at five.

After we grab our shit, Diesel and I make our way to the hotel. Instead of renting a car, we use a shuttle to drop us off on Las Vegas Boulevard. I'm in awe as I look around at the buildings, bright lights, and all the tourists strolling the sidewalks. I can't fucking wait to go out tonight.

"Aw shit!" Diesel says, beaming. "We're gonna tear this place up. Ooh wee!" he yells, bringing attention to the two of us, not that we needed any. Considering we're both wearing cowboy boots and hats in the middle of the busiest street in Vegas, we're doing just fine without all that.

"Oh my God! A cowboy!" a drunk woman says, stumbling toward Diesel with her tits on display. "Can I take a picture with you?"

"Sure, sweetheart!" Diesel obliges, smiling big.

327

"Wait, is the accent real?" She looks at him suspiciously, and he eats up the attention.

"As real as your pretty face." He's laying it on good, making sure to thicken up his drawl.

"You're fuckin' ridiculous. Can we go now?" I ask, holding my carry-on suitcase like someone's gonna steal it.

"You're a cowboy, too?" Her eyes go as big as saucers as her friends giggle.

"Ma'am, I'm sorry, but we gotta go." I finally grab Diesel's arm and pull him away.

"You're such a party foul!" He whines all the way to the front counter of the hotel.

"The party can't start until we drop our shit off in the room. So quit your complainin'," I tell him before we check in and take the elevator to the top floor. When we enter the room, he opens the curtains, then walks out on the balcony to take in the view.

"Vegas! I'm gonna make you my bitch tonight!" he screams out into the vastness, and I chuckle at his obnoxiousness.

"I'm gonna shower. Try not to get into too much trouble in the next ten minutes, alright?" I open the minibar, find a little bottle of whiskey, and chug it in one big gulp. It burns going down, but I already know I'm gonna need a lot more than that.

"Big D!" I yell as I walk toward him. "You should go to the liquor store and get us some whiskey to pregame. I'll buy."

"In that case, I'm gettin' a bottle the size of Texas," he says as I hand him some cash.

"We're gonna need it," I tell him, walking to the bathroom.

"I'm on it." Diesel's out the door without another glance, and I step into the shower.

Chuckling to myself, I think about Diesel being on the Strip by himself and hope he returns in one piece because he's been raring to go since before the sun rose. Hell, I'm just hoping he makes it back. After I'm dressed, I wait thirty minutes before I call him, frustrated it's taking him so damn long. After he doesn't pick up or return my text messages, I decide to try to find him, and Google the closest liquor store. It's only a few blocks away, so there's no reason it should take this long.

As I'm walking down the street, I'm stopped by entertainers handing out fliers. I grab them and continue. Before I have a chance to enter the store, Diesel comes barreling out with two gigantic paper bags and lipstick smeared on his cheek.

"Seriously?" I ask with a smirk, shaking my head. "What'd you do? Bang her in the bathroom?"

Shrugging with a shit-eating grin, he hands me one of the bags.

"I don't kiss and tell."

Grimacing, I shiver at the thought. The bathroom is probably gross as hell. However, I wouldn't put it past him. Diesel glances down and snatches one of the neon fliers from my hand.

"Interesting." He studies it. "Amateur night at a strip club."

I give him a pointed look, and before he can even say a word, I dare him to enter the contest.

"No," he says, shaking his head. "There's no way in hell."

"Really? You gonna turn down a dare and finally pay up?" I taunt and burst into laughter when he scowls.

"I'm not dancin' half naked in front of a bunch of strangers," he whines. Ironic, considering he banged someone he just met in a restroom.

I shrug. "Alright..." I hold out my palm with a shit-eating smirk. "That'll be eight hundred bucks then."

"Piss off." He rolls his eyes, walking ahead of me.

"Should we resort to the old rules then? Drop your pants and get moonin'."

"I'll get arrested," he throws back. "That's just stupid."

"One or the other." I smirk, knowing I have him by the balls.

Diesel swallows, then narrows his eyes at me. "Fine. Let's go to this goddamn club, but just know, I'll get you back when you least expect it. And it will be monu-fuckin'-mental, Bishop. Just wait."

"Ooooh, fightin' words. I like it when you're all riled up. And you know I'm *always* up for a good challenge," I admit. Actually, everyone back home knows never to dare a Bishop. The tradition goes back decades.

Once we're back in our room, we crack open the whiskey and start drinking. I stand on the balcony and continue to pregame as Diesel showers. Eventually, he comes out dressed in his best, and we're already buzzed when we take an Uber to the strip club. Amateur night is for both men and women, but not surprisingly, the woman's prize is heftier. But if Diesel pulls it off, he could be five hundred dollars richer tonight, which could buy a lot of beer and lap dances—his words, not mine.

The parking lot is full of cars, and the line is fifty people deep. Our driver drops us off, and I'm grinning like an idiot. It hasn't left my face since he accepted the dare. I fucking live for making his life hell.

"I fuckin' hate you." Diesel groans, leading the way. Eventually, we make it through and meet a big dude guarding the door with a smug look, checking IDs. Diesel gets in free because he's participating in the activities, but I have to pay thirty bucks. Worth every damn cent to watch him embarrass himself.

"See, that's one perk," I tell him with a nudge in the ribs as I pull the money out of my wallet.

He narrows his eyes. "I need tequila for this."

I grin. "The first few are on me. You deserve it for being such a champ. Plus, you're gonna need it to shake your ass up there."

"I'm convinced you just wanna see my huge dick." He lets out a booming laugh as we walk through the club.

"Nah, I just wanna see what humiliation looks like," I counter. A long bar splits the room into two separate spaces, and the male and female performers are in different areas. I've never seen a strip club this large and have only ever been to one little hole-in-the-wall in San Antonio with a few friends. Vegas is magical.

We push our way to the bar, and two shots quickly turn into four. At some point, I lose count, but Diesel keeps them coming. When I look around at the crowded room, I notice a group of gorgeous women in the corner, obviously here for a bachelorette party. They all have sashes across their bodies, and one's wearing a bride-to-be crown. Sitting as close to the strippers as possible, they look up at the half naked man with googly eyes, giggling their asses off and throwing money like confetti. I can't help but notice one of the girls with blond hair and sun-kissed skin wearing the sweetest fucking smile I've ever seen. Damn, she's so beautiful, it nearly takes my breath away.

"Fuck," Diesel says, pulling my attention away. He stands and wobbles, and I realize we drank too much. We're doomed. Especially Diesel, considering he still has to put on the performance of his life. After two more shots, all the contestants are called to the far stage. Glancing at him, I nod toward his competition, who are all standing by.

"Imma get you back, Bishop," he tells me between gritted teeth, and I don't doubt him one bit. Diesel begrudgingly orders a beer to take with him and stumbles to the large group of participants eagerly waiting for instruction. He hates losing so much that, combined with all the liquid courage, I wouldn't be surprised if he actually tries to win.

I sit on the barstool, not able to stop grinning as Diesel makes his way behind the curtain. Trying to be somewhat responsible, I order a beer and pace myself while I wait for the show to begin. If he's stumbling around like a baby giraffe in heels—considering his tolerance is higher than mine—I'll probably fall flat on my ass if I don't sit for a while.

The lights flash and brighten, grabbing every person's attention in the room, and the wannabe strippers make their way to the front. Most of them look like total douchebags, and then there's Diesel looking like he fell off a horse with his cowboy hat and boots. The emcee, Nicole, introduces herself before explaining how this will work. Once she's done, Nicole sends out the first guy, and I watch, feeling secondhand embarrassment for the poor dude.

"And next up, we have Diesel! He said they call him that because he's big in *all* the right places. So hold on to your horses, this cowboy is ready to rock your world," Nicole says in a flirtatious tone.

Diesel walks onto a low-lit stage to Ginuwine's "Pony." It's one of the oldest, most cliché songs in the goddamn world, but I'm laughing so hard I nearly choke on my drink. He moves around like he's been stripping for a decade, and I'm convinced the bastard needs to join Magic Mike. All the women in the club are gathered around, ready to eat him up, and he's teasing them like he's the whole buffet. I swear I see their tongues hanging out.

Diesel takes it to the next level and calls up one of the pretty ladies from the bachelorette party to dance with him. Placing his cowboy hat on her head, Diesel slowly removes his clothes, piece by piece. She's absolutely mesmerized, tracing her fingers across his abs. My mouth falls open, and my eyes widen in shock when he slips down his pants and reveals a man thong.

"Jesus Christ. He's never living this shit down," I whisper as he sings the lyrics to the thirsty group who are ready to fuck him in front of everyone. As the song ends, fifty or more women scream out for more of Diesel.

"Well, it looks like someone's a professional," Nicole taunts as Diesel picks up his clothes and steps off the stage.

One by one, the other guys come out and do their thing. They don't compare or have the charisma Diesel exuded. After each performance, those watching aren't wooed and surprisingly continue to chant his name for an encore. When the last guy finishes, Nicole calls everyone back and has them line up on the stage.

"I don't think it's a surprise who's going to win this contest tonight," Nicole says as the audience continues to scream Diesel's name. Ridiculous as it seems, it's like he somehow put a spell on every person in the room.

"Diesel! Come get your money, honey!" Nicole finally says. "And if you want a job, you're hired," she tells him. Diesel takes his prize and grabs the mic to give his version of a corny acceptance speech.

"I just want to thank my best friend, Riley, who's sitting over there." The bastard points in my direction, and all heads turn and look at me. *Asshole.* "He's always wanted to see my package, so tonight, big boy, this one was for you," he tells me, then cups himself. I flip him off, and he laughs.

"Don't worry, y'all. I'm only into the ladies, so call me." He smirks and walks off the stage, then heads toward me. I turn around and order us both a beer because I'm gonna need it to get through the rest of the night with him.

"I can't believe you actually won," I say as he plops down on the stool next to me.

"Maybe I'll quit the ranch and move to Vegas," he teases, happily taking the beer to chug it.

"Yeah, and your mama would kill you," I remind him.

Looking over my shoulder, I catch sight of the beautiful blonde I saw earlier. This time, though, she's looking right at me, smiling and biting her bottom lip.

I fully turn around and mouth, "Hi."

She gives me a sexy wave with an eyebrow popped, and she's looking at me like I'm the sweetest piece of candy she's ever seen. I swallow down the lump in my throat, wanting to go to her but feel as if I'm standing in concrete. Girls like her don't exist back home.

Diesel's running his mouth about something, and I turn to tell him to give me a second because I need to find out every detail about her.

"I'll be right back," I interrupt, and he rolls his eyes. When I glance back, she's gone, and I'm left wondering if I'll see her again.

The next morning, I wake up with a slight hangover, but nothing a couple of ibuprofen won't fix. We're both starving, so we get dressed and go find breakfast. No matter how much I try to shake the thoughts of last night, I can't seem to get that gorgeous woman out of my mind. It feels as if she were a dream, some figment of my imagination. An electric current was pulling me toward her, and I've never felt anything like that before.

We eventually find a buffet, and Diesel fills two plates full of eggs, sausages, mini pancakes, and a tower of bacon. He's stacked like an NFL football player and eats like one too. As he's shoveling food into his mouth, chewing like a goddamn animal, his eyes go wide. He chews faster, nearly swallowing a sausage patty whole.

"Babes," he chokes out, looking past me with dreamy eyes.

"Babies?" I laugh, confused, but then see the group of women walk past our table.

One of them stops and takes a few steps back, staring at Diesel, who's grinning like a doofus. "Can I help you, ma'am?"

"Are you the guy from last night at the club?" She's intrigued. "Diesel, right? Oh wait, that's probably just your stage name, isn't it?"

He chuckles, and I find myself laughing too because most people only know him by that name. "It's whatever you want it to be, sweetheart."

She turns and looks at me for confirmation, and I nod. "Everyone calls him that back home."

"So, you're real cowboys, huh? It wasn't an act?" She glances back and forth between us, looking at our getup. Boots and ten-gallon hats are what we're most comfortable in.

"I'm a ranch hand in Texas," he admits. "But I'll be a cowboy if you want me to be," he adds with a wink.

I snort and shake my head.

"Hmm...I like you, Diesel," she says, pointing her finger at him.

"And what's your name?"

She lifts an eyebrow at him. "Summer."

"Wow, what a coincidence. That's my favorite season," he says in a heavy accent. All I can do is shake my head.

The conversation continues as Diesel lays it on thick, and from behind, I hear a sweet voice calling out. "Summer!"

Turning, I see the beautiful blonde from last night dressed in blue jean shorts and a shirt that shows her midriff. My mouth falls agape, and Summer notices.

"Zoey, come meet my new friends," she says with a grin.

I stand, fumbling over my words. "It's *you*," I say. "From last night."

Zoey smiles and tilts her head at me, then glances at Diesel. "Ahh, yes. You're Riley, right? The best friend who wanted to see his dick?" She snorts, and Diesel lets out a roar of laughter. I'm gonna kill him.

"I've seen his dick enough to last me a lifetime. He's my best friend, and roommate, and not a tad modest," I admit. "It's his prized jewel."

Diesel shrugs, and Zoey snickers. Before we can continue our conversation, the other girls call Summer and Zoey over to where they're sitting across the room.

"I guess we'll see you two later then," Summer says before turning to meet her friends. Zoey follows her, and they go to the buffet together. I can't stop staring at her.

"You in love or somethin'?" Diesel finally asks, looking at me like I've grown a second head.

"Shut the hell up." I scowl.

He stands and grabs the plate that actually has food left on it.

"Where ya goin'?" I ask, and all he does is look over his shoulder with a mischievous grin. I watch as he sits down at the table with the girls, loving all the attention he instantly receives. He waves me over, leaving an empty seat next to Zoey, making this way too easy.

Grabbing my plate, I sit down next to her, and I'm as nervous as a little boy around his first crush. For fuck's sake, I've never had someone—a stranger—affect me in such a way.

One of the girls speaks up and grabs Diesel's attention. "I'm Chelsea, by the way. You might not remember me, but you brought me on stage with you last night." She gives him a seductive smile, and I can tell she wants him, but I'm pretty sure half the girls at the table would fuck him at this point.

"I'd never forget a pretty girl like you. Of course I remember," he convincingly replies, but I know he was shit-faced and probably doesn't.

"So why do they call you Diesel?" she asks. "And I want the truth."

As if she set him up for a joke, he gives his canned response. "Because I'm big and loud like a diesel truck."

Zoey giggles, and it's the cutest fucking sound in the world.

"Is he always like this?" she asks, her eyes meeting mine, and I feel as if I'm falling into the abyss.

"For as long as I've known him," I stammer.

"Are you always like this?" She tucks a loose strand of hair behind her ear and blushes.

"Like what?" I look at her, confused.

"Adorably Southern," she states.

"Absolutely," I say without a doubt. A smile creeps across my lips, and I try to focus on my food, but I feel as if I've died and gone straight to heaven.

Maybe this cowboy hat is my good luck charm after all.

CHAPTER FOUR

Zoey

I can't believe the two guys from the strip club last night are eating breakfast with us. Admittedly, I only saw Riley from a distance, but I couldn't stop watching him. And here he is. Better looking than I could've ever imagined.

As he sits next to me, my nerves are in overdrive. Our arms randomly touch, causing jolts of electricity to stream through me. I don't know what it is about him, but I'm intrigued as hell. Maybe it's a combination of the cowboy hat and Southern accent, but he's also drop-dead gorgeous. Add in the deep voice, plump lips, and strong jaw…well damn, I'm a goner. Just by looking at his body, I can tell he works really hard. When he lifts his fork, I see calluses on his palms. I have so many questions, and I've never wanted to get to know someone as much as I do him right now.

I don't notice a ring on his left hand, not that it would matter. Lots of men come to Vegas and cheat, but Riley doesn't seem like the type. He might be around my age, maybe a tad older, but he acts mature or at least more so than his friend. Most of the guys my age back home are nothing but fuckboys who don't know their ass from their elbow—not relationship material at all.

Last night, Riley seemed so mysterious drinking alone. In their Wranglers and boots, he and Diesel stuck out, so it was hard not to notice him. If Summer hadn't been so determined to go to another club, I would've made my way over to him. Riley saw me too, and when our eyes met, it was as if time stood completely still. Everyone else focused on Diesel, but not me. There was something about the lonely cowboy, and I needed to know more.

After we finished barhopping last night, all I could think about was the hot guy from the strip club. What are the odds that we'd find each other again in this big ass city? Out of the two of them, I know Diesel's the troublemaker, and as he entertains my sister and her friends, I take the opportunity to chat with Riley. Being this close to him is making my heart race with nerves. Not to mention, he smells so damn good—a mix of man, leather, and a hint of cologne. I want to bottle him up and then eat him for dessert.

"So how'd you end up at a strip club?" I ask. "The real story." I meet his baby blues again, intrigued as hell about who this man is. He's dangerous in all the right ways. My hormones are in overdrive, and I try to snap out of it but can't. The attraction is too strong, and by how he's looking at me, I think the feeling is mutual.

"I dared him to sign up for the amateur contest," he tells me with a smirk, then shrugs.

"Why wouldn't he just refuse to do it?"

"Because he's too proud." Laughter escapes Riley, and it makes me smile. The man's as genuine as they come, but I have a feeling there's more to this story than he's letting on.

"And I thought you were a nice guy. Sounds like you're evil and played with his pride."

"Hey! My mama didn't raise no devil." He shoots me a wink, and it causes me to blush, which he seems to enjoy.

"That's too bad because I'm no angel," I quip, causing him to stiffen and nearly choke on his food. I grin, amused I can affect him just as easily.

Flirting with Riley is fun, though I'm not immune to him or his Southern charm.

"So where are you girls from?" Diesel asks.

"We're from Phoenix," Summer tells him.

"And where do you live?" I ask.

"Texas. Before you even say it, I know Imma walking, talking cliché."

This causes me to snort. "Just a little. I think it's mainly the hat."

Taking it off, he sets it on the table, revealing disheveled sandy brown hair, and I want to run my fingers through it. Dark facial hair grows along his jaw and chin, and I love how rugged it makes him look. His blue eyes sparkle, and I can't help but notice how his long eyelashes naturally curl up. Damn, he's the whole package. I'm at a loss for words as I look at him, admiring some of his best features. All this time, he's been hiding them under a gigantic cowboy hat. Heat rushes through my body, and I somehow force my attention away because I'm gawking.

My heart pounds rapidly in my chest, and I try to calm down so he doesn't notice.

"So what're you ladies up to today? Maybe we'll see you around?" Diesel randomly throws a wink to my sister's friends.

"Walking around and shopping, but later, we're going on a club bus tour," Chelsea tells him, leaning in close. She's ready to crawl in his lap.

"Is that right?" Diesel slaps his leg. "Riley and I are going on one too. Which one did y'all book?"

Summer chuckles. "It's the one from the Sin City tour agency. It leaves at nine in front of the hotel."

"Yeah, that's the same one we booked too. What a coincidence!" It's obvious Diesel's full of shit, but no one calls him out on it, which I'm okay with because I want to spend more time with Riley.

I lean forward and grin. "Wow, that's *very* coincidental."

"It really is, isn't it?" Riley smirks.

Avery, Chelsea, Naomi, and Julia are completely smitten by Diesel, and I have to hold back my laughter at how they're acting. Diesel doesn't seem to mind, though. If I didn't know better, I'd say he's actually enjoying them undressing him with their eyes. Though we all got a good look at what he had to offer last night when he took off his clothes.

"What do you like to do for fun?" Riley asks as I finish my food.

"Anything, really. I go with the flow, and I like being spontaneous. If it's not a planned adventure, even better. Love hiking and going on road trips too." After wiping my mouth with my napkin, I push my plate away.

"Spontaneous? I like that." The gruff in his voice has my entire body melting.

"What about you?" I turn my body toward him, giving him my full attention.

"I like horseback riding and camping, but I work a lot. We make the best with what we've got out in the middle of nowhere Texas, so we gotta create our own fun most of the time. Lots of pranks and dares and drinking," he admits, glancing at Diesel. "And keeping this one out of trouble and away from my little sister has become a part-time job."

I find myself smiling as he talks. I could listen to him chat about whatever he wants with that sexy Southern bedroom voice. "It actually sounds like fun."

"It can be, but there are some things that suck about being far away from a big city. The closest Walmart is hours away. Amazon is your best friend if you don't want to drive, and patience is key. McDonald's breakfast? Forget about it. Late-night craving for Taco Bell? Better learn how to cook. But I love it and wouldn't live anywhere else in the world. Texas is home," he tells me matter-of-factly.

"So no fast food or retail therapy? Wow. That's how I got through beauty school. It's hard to imagine not being able to get things instantly. Especially Starbucks." I try to picture it, but I've lived in Phoenix all my life with parents who'd buy me anything at any moment. I never really realize how privileged I was until now, but the simple life also sounds incredible.

Everyone has finished eating when Summer stands, interrupting the conversation. The rest of the girls do too, so I take it as my cue to get up. Riley and I push our chairs away at the same time, and we're mere inches apart. My breath hitches as I look up into his eyes and swallow hard.

"See ya around, Zoey," Riley says, taking a step back and putting space between us.

I nod. "Yeah, tonight on the bus."

A cheesy grin fills his face. "Oh right. It's a date."

"Not quite, but sure," I say, smiling. Summer interrupts our moment by looping her arm in mine and pulling me away.

"See you tonight, *Arizona*," Riley calls out a cute nickname, causing me to laugh, then heads in the other direction.

"Bye, ladies!" Diesel yells, and I watch Chelsea turn around and giggle.

We walk out the main doors of the hotel, and Summer smirks at me.

"What?" I finally ask, though I know I'm as transparent as glass.

"What were you and Riley chatting about? I could barely hear a word because of Diesel."

I roll my eyes. "Nothing much."

"He's cute," she blurts out. "*Really* cute, and he seemed interested in you."

A grin touches my lips.

She bumps her hip against mine. "You know he was."

"Okay, maybe he is, but he might as well be from another planet. He lives in the middle of small-town nowhere Texas."

As we wait to cross the street, I can hear Chelsea going on about Diesel, and her vulgar vocabulary makes me snort. She's dirty as fuck.

"Remember what you said, what happens in Vegas, stays in Vegas, right? I saw the way you two looked at each other. You should totally go for it." Summer gives me a suggestive look, and I laugh, almost shocked my sister is condoning this.

"What did Mom and Dad tell us again? Don't talk to strangers?" I remind her, chuckling at the ridiculousness of it all, considering we're not kids.

"Right, but they're not strangers anymore. We know their names and where they're from. Also, we had breakfast with them. So, they're our new friends at this point." She waggles her brows.

I smirk as we head toward the crowded strip mall. The six of us go through several shops, and for once, I'm glad I brought a huge suitcase because I hit up the sale racks.

Checking the time, I notice it's just past four. If we're going to make it to the tour on time, we need to eat before getting ready for tonight. We stop at the Hard Rock Cafe and have a nice dinner along with pregame drinks, then giggle our way back to the hotel. Summer's friends are the horniest bunch of women I've ever been around, and I can't believe they haven't corrupted her. Or maybe they have.

After Summer and I take our showers, we both stand in the bathroom fixing our hair while the other girls get ready in their room. She booked a nice room for just us and then got the other girls a suite to share. Summer's outdone herself with contoured makeup and bright red lips, and she looks absolutely gorgeous. I go for a more natural look with gloss and mascara, but we're both wearing dresses that hug our curves like a second skin.

Summer smiles as I finish up. "Nervous about seeing him again?"

"Do you think they're really coming tonight?" I'm not convinced they could get tickets because we booked this excursion months ago. It's a popular tour, and I wouldn't be surprised if it's full.

"Diesel seems like the kind of guy who'd sweet-talk himself onto that bus. He seems pretty resilient, and I don't think he'd take no for an answer from anyone," she quips.

"True." I suck in a deep breath and look at my phone, seeing a text from Benjamin. I groan, and Summer notices as I flip my screen face down so I don't have to look at it, but then it vibrates again. I remember my mother asking me to give him a chance, so I let out a huff and check it.

"What's he want?" Summer looks at me in the mirror as she applies another layer of mascara.

I let her read it for herself.

"Another date, huh? How many will this be now?"

"Four, maybe five? Honestly, I've lost count." *Because I don't care.*

"He seems like the perfect man. Has a great career, attractive, and comes from a nice family." She's basically repeating everything our parents say about him. "You should give him a chance. He could be really good for you, Zoey."

Wrinkling my nose, I disagree. "I have," I say with an edge in my tone. *How many times does a chance take?*

Summer looks at me in the mirror. "Sorry, sis. I'm not trying to tell you what to do. I just want you to have fun for the rest of the weekend and live in the moment during our girls' trip. Worry about all of that when we get back to Phoenix."

"Honestly, Benjamin's the last person I want on my mind at the moment," I admit.

"Because of the cowboys?" She waggles her brows.

I try to hold back any reaction but fail miserably when a hint of blush hits my cheek. "Cowboy. Singular. Chelsea has already claimed Diesel for herself."

Summer lets out a loud cackle. "She better be glad I'm getting married, because…"

She doesn't finish her sentence but instead looks off into the distance as if she's living out her fantasy with him right now.

"Eww, stop." I walk out of the bathroom and take a sip from one of the small bottles of vodka as I look out at the Las Vegas lights. I'm in awe as I stare at the busy streets and the sparkling buildings as the sun hangs low on the horizon. Riley comes to mind with his kind smile and witty banter, and I can't help but wonder if they're really joining us. I hope so. He's the distraction I need and want tonight.

Summer grabs two small bottles of rum from the minibar and hands me one. We unscrew the tops, tap them together, and drink.

"Tonight, we're gonna have so much fun." She pulls me into a hug.

"I just hope fun doesn't mean trouble," I say, only half-joking as she grabs more booze and leads me out of the room to meet the rest of the bridal party waiting downstairs.

CHAPTER FIVE

Riley

S eeing Zoey this morning at brunch was a pleasant surprise, and I'm not complaining. Though we'd briefly seen each other last night, actually talking to her today was electric. Our banter was effortless, and she's definitely not the shy type. Even though we're only in Vegas for forty-eight hours, I want to see her again.

The moment they mentioned their plans later, I knew the chances of running into her again were slim. Until Diesel blurted out that we'd booked the barhopping bus too. I wasn't sure if I should smack him for making us sound like stalkers or hug him for his genius idea. While our connection is strictly mutual attraction right now, I actually think she's quite interesting. Even though we'd spent less than an hour together, I'm already addicted to hearing her laughter.

Once we separated ways, Diesel and I walked down the Strip, found a casino, and gambled for a few hours. After we lost a few hundred dollars of Diesel's stripper winnings, we found other places to blow our money.

"I should get something for Rowan's birthday," I tell him as we arrive at a touristy souvenir shop. "Her birthday's next month."

"Yeah?" He pretends not to care, but he's not fooling me.

"Maybe I should taunt her with some shot glasses," I say with a snicker. She's turning twenty and won't be able to properly use them for another year.

"She'll throw them at you for getting her a shitty gift." Diesel deadpans.

"Good point. I'd rather not pick glass outta my face. T-shirt it is." She's always had a mild fascination with snow globes, so I look at those and grab one filled with glitter and displaying the famous Welcome to Las Vegas sign. Hopefully, she doesn't chuck that at me.

Once we're done shopping, we get more information about the drinking tour from the front desk, and somehow, Diesel sweet-talks the woman to get us added to the list.

"I don't know how you did that," I tell him, and all he does is grin.

"I just used my Southern charm. Works every time," he says, handing me the itinerary listing all the clubs we're supposed to visit. Guess we'll be getting shit-faced again tonight.

We go back to the room, drop off our bags, and get ready for the evening before going to eat because we have to be out front by nine. As I change, the thought of seeing Zoey tonight has my nerves in overdrive. I picture what she wore last night at the strip club and how beautiful she looked this morning in her T-shirt and shorts. Her bronze blond hair was in a messy bun, and loose strands fell around her face. Without even trying, she looked incredible.

The navy blue button-up shirt, dark wash jeans, and dress boots is one of the nicest outfits I have. I typically wear it to church, so hopefully no one will give me shit for being a cowboy cliché tonight.

"Look at you, pretty boy," Diesel taunts the moment I come out of the bathroom.

"Look who's talkin', Romeo." I grunt, scanning my eyes down his similar outfit.

Diesel chuckles, grabbing his wallet and phone off his bed. "I'm the birthday boy. I gotta look fuckable." He plasters on a wide, cheesy grin that causes me to snort.

"Yeah, yeah. Let's go," I say, getting my shit, then walking behind him out the door.

We find the meeting place for the tour bus, which is already booming with loud screaming and music. I've never seen anything like it and know tonight is definitely going to be one I'll never forget.

"I think this is it," Diesel says. "I call dibs on the bride-to-be." He waggles his brows before stepping up the stairs.

"Oh my God." I groan, following him. "Should've known this was a bad idea the second you blurted it out."

He pats my back as soon as we're on the bus, shoulder to shoulder with partygoers. "You'll be thanking me, man. Guaranteed."

"You guys showed up!" Summer shouts with a drink in her hand. She's wearing an obnoxious crown and sash like last night, but this time, she has a pink boa around her neck.

"Wasn't about to miss out on the bachelorette party." I wink at Zoey, then push my way through the crowd and sit down next to her. The seats line the windows to give everyone a view of the pole in the middle. Diesel immediately helps himself to the fully stocked bar in the back.

"You're aware a bachelorette party means girls only, right?" she teases, crossing her legs.

"Are you saying no boys allowed?"

"Not unless you're the strippers," Chelsea answers.

"Now *that* can be arranged…" Diesel stands and starts unbuttoning his shirt.

"Sit your ass down," I tell him, pulling on his arm. "We've all seen the show, and it's not that impressive. Never has been."

Zoey pulls back, giving me a look with her brows raised. "You've seen his strip show more than once?"

Diesel chuckles, not denying it.

"We grew up together. Just because the bastard's finally legal doesn't mean it's his first time drinking or stripping. Alcohol makes him loose."

"We're also roommates," Diesel says.

"Ahh…this is all making so much more sense." Zoey laughs.

"Let me grab you a drink before we get to the club. What's your poison?" I ask, making my way toward the bar. "No girly shit here, though."

Zoey rolls her eyes at my accusation. "Good, because I like the hard stuff."

I arch a brow. *Interesting.*

"Alright, I'll get us some shots then. Get this party started for real." I smirk, then walk up to the bartender and order. After he hands them over, I go back to Zoey and give her one.

"To a night we'll never forget…" she says in a slow, seductive tone that alerts my dick to how close she is to me.

"Cheers." We clink glasses, then shoot the booze down.

A night I'll never forget indeed.

Before we arrive at our first destination, Zoey and I are three shots in. With each one, she became more courageous, moving closer to me, and now, she's nearly sitting in my lap. Not that I mind, because there's obvious chemistry between us, one I wish I could explore for more than one night. But I'm taking whatever I can get.

The bus eventually slows in front of the first club of the evening. The perks of this tour include no cover charges or waiting in line, and we get full VIP access. Not too bad, considering the price wasn't outrageous. Every stop is ninety minutes long, and there's a set time and location to meet before the bus takes off again. If we're not there, we'll be left behind.

As soon as we're inside, we immediately go to the bar and order drinks.

"Do you dance, cowboy?" Zoey taunts, giving me a sweet, seductive look that's hard to resist. "Or is two-stepping more your thing?"

I smirk, admiring how damn cute she is. "Why don't we hit the dance floor, and you can find out for yourself, Arizona?"

She removes her straw and sucks down the rest of her drink. "Show me whatcha got."

Drake's "One Dance" blasts through the speakers, and I take her hand, guiding her out. The moment her back touches my chest, my hips move to the beat of the music. Pressing one hand to her stomach and grasping her waist with the other, we sway in sync as she looks over her shoulder.

"You've got some moves, who knew?" she teases, but I see the blush creeping up her neck and face.

The corner of my lips tilts into a knowing grin. She hasn't seen anything yet.

We continue to dance, our bodies rubbing together until Cardi B starts.

Zoey pops her ass out, then drops to the floor. Amused, I watch the private show she's giving me, though it's not really private, considering the swarm of people around us. But I know this is for me.

She continues moving her sexy little body, and when I find her hip, I pull her chest against mine and bring my lips to her ear. "You like teasing me, Zoey?"

"Maybe." She bites down on her bottom lip, then pulls it between her teeth. "Would you be interested if I was?"

A low growl escapes my throat. Is she fucking with me?

"Hell yes," I answer, pulling her closer as our eyes remain locked. We continue dancing until we realize it's been nearly ninety minutes since we arrived. I lost Diesel the second we walked in, but he's more than capable of telling time on his own.

Hand in hand, I lead Zoey back to the bus, and when we step on, I see Diesel working the pole, giving the party a show.

"Jesus Christ," I mutter, laughing and shaking my head at his poor attempt, knowing he loves the attention. "I think they saw enough last night."

"After you dared me, asshole," he spits, thrusting his junk toward Chelsea.

I sit, and Zoey snorts, taking a seat on my lap. "I'm picking the shots this time," she declares once we start moving.

"Be my guest," I tell her.

"Yeah, we'll see if you can handle it." She smiles as if she's up to something.

Moments later, she returns with two glasses, wearing a shit-eating smirk. "Ready?"

I eye it cautiously, not recognizing the light amber liquid. "What is it?" I ask, taking it from her and smelling it.

"Guess," Zoey says.

"It smells like you mixed a few liquors together, and you want me to puke my guts out later," I respond, watching her expression.

She shrugs, not denying it. "If you don't think you can handle it, then don't drink it."

Before I can respond, she shoots hers back, and after blinking a few times at what I imagine is a funky ass taste, she smiles. "Easy peasy."

"Might put some hair on that chest," Diesel goads.

"Shut the fuck up." I laugh, brushing a hand over the facial hair on my chin as I stare at the shot. It'll probably make me sick as hell, considering everything else I've drunk already, but I refuse to be a puss.

After counting to three, I sling it back. The burn has me wincing, and when I look at Zoey with wide eyes, I start coughing.

Zoey nearly dies of laughter and pats me on the back. "Wow, I thought you cowboy types would be able to take your whiskey, bourbon, tequila, vodka shot mixes without any issue."

"That was fuckin' disgusting." I cough again, setting the shot glass down. "There's no way you had the same thing."

"You're right."

Immediately, I grab her waist and pull her down onto my lap, causing her to release a yelp. "I'm gonna make you pay for that," I whisper against the shell of her ear. Her body shivers against me, and it's all the confirmation I need to know she feels what I do. Even though we just met, an electric current undeniably soars between us. I refuse to let this night go to waste and want to take advantage of every second I get with her.

When we enter the second club, we continue to dance and drink. Eventually, she mentions needing to find a bathroom, but I don't let her go alone.

"I'll join you."

Zoey gives me a weird look but doesn't argue. I'm a damn gentleman, after all. I hold her drink and wait in the hallway. Once she's done, I take her hand and lead her to the outside patio where we can sit for a minute.

"Is your sister gonna be upset that you're spending your time with me instead of her?" Even though she sits so close that our knees touch, I want her even closer.

Zoey sips from her straw. "Highly doubtful. The other girls are giving her plenty of attention. Not to mention your friend."

I smirk, knowing how much of an attention whore Diesel is. "Don't worry, he's actually harmless. He wouldn't touch a soon-to-be married woman."

"What about you? You have someone waiting for you at home?" she asks coyly, which causes me to grin.

"Nope. I work a lot on the ranch, and when I'm not, I'm helping at my family's bar. When I first turned twenty-one, I'd go out often, but work and family come first," I tell her honestly. I haven't dated since high school, but I don't mention that. I've had hookups, but it never turns into anything more.

"How old are you exactly?" she asks.

"I'll be twenty-three in July. What about you?"

"Twenty-one."

"Ah, so you're just a baby," I tease.

Zoey snorts. "You're less than two years older than me."

"But with life experience, I'm much, much older." I wink.

A Missy Elliot song starts playing, and everyone, including Zoey, loses their shit. "Oh my God, super old school! We gotta dance to this." She sets down her now empty drink and pulls me inside before I can protest, not that I would've.

Just as Missy tells us to get our freak on, Zoey wraps her arms around my shoulders, pulling our bodies flush. I hold her body to mine, then slide down to her ass, squeezing. People bump and grind all around us, singing obnoxiously loud, but my only focus is on her as I think about how gorgeous she looks in my arms. The look she's giving me tells me she wants more than just this.

The music fades, and another song roars through the club, and I have to taste her. Cupping her face, I capture her mouth, causing her to gasp as I slip my tongue between her beautiful, soft lips. I slow my pace, allowing her to push me away if she wants, but when she doesn't, I tilt her chin up and deepen the kiss.

"Mmm…" She moans as she twirls her tongue with mine.

"Fuck, Zoey." I kiss my way down her neck before finding her soft lips again. "Don't make those kinds of noises when I can't rip off your clothes."

Her eyes are open and on me in a second. Lust fills them, but I can't tell if my words offended her or if she's thinking the same thing. By the way her breathing hitches, I'm willing to bet it's the latter.

CHAPTER SIX

Zoey

By the time we're dropped off at the third stop, I'm beyond buzzed, though part of me thinks the alcohol isn't the only thing making me feel high on life. The moment Riley's lips touched mine, my world tilted, and I never wanted anything more than to get lost in his kiss.

I love how he can't keep his hands off me, the way my body responds when he's close, and the harsh feel of his facial hair against my soft skin. I want to scratch my nails down his back as our bodies rock in rhythm on the dance floor. His movements heighten my senses, making me wish we were alone so I could do inappropriate things to him.

There's a nice rooftop patio at the club, and it's where we all meet. My sister is happily plastered, and she has that glassy look on her face that tells me she's not feeling a damn thing. Tomorrow, we'll undoubtedly all feel like shit, but this is a once-in-a-lifetime trip, so I'm taking full advantage of letting loose while I can.

"You feeling okay, sis?" I ask with another drink in my hand. It doesn't even taste like alcohol anymore, and I've lost count of what number this is.

"Never. Better." She pronounces her words slowly and carefully, making us giggle.

"To Summer's last week of freedom!" Chelsea shouts, and we hold up our drinks and cheer.

"You excited to be tied down to one man forever?" Diesel challenges.

"They were high school sweethearts," I explain. "They're sickly in love!"

"He's always been the one," Chelsea slurs with a cheesy grin.

I adore him and am really happy they're finally tying the knot after all this time.

"Are you excited for the big day?" Riley asks. "Or nervous?"

"I'm only nervous about something not going right because our mother is a type A neat freak. A perfectionist. It's kinda annoying, even if she means well, but other than her stressing me out, I'm not at all apprehensive about marrying Owen."

Diesel claps his hands, grabbing all of our attention, as usual. "I just had the best fucking idea ever for your payback dare."

Riley groans, and I roll my eyes. "Of course you do."

"Payback dare?" I inquire as I sip on the last of my drink.

"Yeah, the asshole dared me to do that amateur stripper show last night, and now it's time for my revenge," Diesel explains, rubbing his palms together.

"This ought to be good," Riley provokes, putting both of his arms behind his head.

Diesel flashes a devilish smirk that even makes me concerned. "You—" He points at Riley. "And you—" Then he points at me. "Get hitched in Vegas."

I start laughing as do the other girls, but Riley just scowls and shakes his head at Diesel. What is it with guys always having to one-up each other?

"That's not a dare." Riley scoffs.

"You know what happens if you don't do it!" Diesel taunts. "Or do I need to remind you like you so nicely reminded me?"

"Uh…" I interrupt. "What exactly happens if you pass on a dare?"

"Don't ask—" Riley begins, but Diesel cuts him off.

"He—"

"Fuck off." Riley shoots him down again. "I'm not bringing Zoey into this."

"Well, let's ask the future Mrs. Bishop, shall we?" Diesel turns toward me with a shit-eating grin. "Don't you want to help this hunk of a Southern man, total gentleman, and from what I've heard—a great lay—go through with his dare so he doesn't have to pay a hefty fee? Or plan B— baring his ass to the whole city?"

"Oh my God, he said it…" Riley's head falls back on a groan, making me laugh at how embarrassed he is.

"So every dare you pass on equals showing your ass?" I ask.

"That was part of the original rules, but as we got older, we decided money was a better punishment. So if you don't do a dare, it costs fifty dollars for every year we've been friends. We've been best friends since I was five years old, so we're up to eight hundred bucks now," Diesel explains. "And your boy is cheap as fuck when it comes to dishing out cash, so he always does the dare instead of paying up. Neither of us has ever passed."

I snicker at the way they give each other shit. But then I look at Riley, who looks fucking irresistible. "Okay!"

"Okay, what?" he asks, furrowing his brows in confusion.

"Let's do the dare!" I jump up. "C'mon!"

Riley whips his head back and forth between Diesel and me. "For real?"

I hold out my hand, arching a brow. "Unless you'd rather pay up or moon us all?"

"Dude, you better marry this one before I do!" Diesel shouts, standing next to me.

Riley pulls me in to his arms and kisses me hard. "Lead the way."

We make our way down the Strip and find a 24-hour wedding chapel. The guy at the counter, Marcus, explains the package options, and we opt to buy wedding bands there. We don't go overboard or do anything fancy, so our ceremony is a quick five minutes with standard vows.

"I do," I say, smiling like a fool.

"I do," Riley repeats, grinning at me just as wide.

When we exchange rings, I'm shocked we're doing this. Then Marcus announces we're married, and Riley kisses his bride. *Me.* He wraps his hand around my neck and pushes our mouths together for a white-hot kiss. By the time we break apart, I'm seeing stars.

My sister and her friends cheer loudly as we walk down the short aisle hand in hand. Diesel's smiling like an idiot.

After we sign the marriage certificate, Riley scoops me up and kisses me.

As soon as our Uber arrives, Riley sets me down and opens the door for me. After we're inside, Riley shouts out the window. "Diesel, find somewhere else to sleep tonight!"

"Don't worry, I've been invited to the bachelorette suite!" he calls out with his arm around Chelsea. I nearly die of laughter because I can totally see the two of them hooking up.

The booze from the past several hours continues to rush in my veins as Riley leads me into his hotel room. We don't even bother with small talk. The moment the door slams shut, Riley pushes me against it and claims my mouth.

"Fuck, Zoey. I've wanted to do this all goddamn night long," Riley hisses against my ear as his hands make their way down my body and cup my ass. He grinds himself into me, and I feel how hard he is when he pulls me up. My legs wrap around his waist as he carries me to the bed.

"Tell me all the things you've wanted to do to me…" I prompt as he towers over me.

He growls. Fucking *growls* against my neck. I love the way his beard scratches my chin, and I wonder how it'd feel against my thighs.

"I want to taste every inch of you." His mouth moves down my throat. "Feel you tighten around my cock." His palm finds my breast, and he squeezes. "Hear you scream my name." His other hand slides up my leg. "Fuck you so hard you'll be feeling me all the way back to Phoenix."

"Yes. God *yes*. I want *all* of that." My head falls back.

"You realize you married me tonight?" He shakes his head with a sly grin. "You're officially Zoey Bishop."

"That has a nice ring to it," I say. "I quite like it."

"Good." He pulls off my dress. "Because I'm about to mark you as mine. My *wife*."

Hearing him say it aloud sends a shiver down my body. I know I've drunk my weight in alcohol tonight, but I can't find it in me to regret anything. At least not yet.

"Take off your clothes, *hubby*. I'm about to burst if you don't fuck me," I beg, pulling at his shirt because I need to see all of him.

Riley undoes a few buttons and then reaches behind his neck and swiftly removes it. My eyes widen at the glorious sight of him. *Holy mother of God.*

They make them real good down in Texas. Riley has abs like the models on the covers of romance novels. He's tan with hard chiseled muscle. He's definitely worked hard for what he has; every inch of him is solid. I'm drooling by the time he unbuckles his belt and starts removing his jeans because the muscular V has my entire body covered in goose bumps.

In only his boxers, he leans down again with his hands on either side of my head. "You look like you're about to eat me for dessert," he taunts, the corner of his lips tilting up. I was gawking and won't even deny it.

"You don't even look real," I tell him, pressing my palms against his chest, then sliding them down his stomach.

"I was about to say the same thing, baby. You're fuckin' beautiful, Zoey." He kisses me softly, and as soon as he pulls back, I already miss the weight of him.

Standing, he retrieves a condom from his wallet, then tells me to lie in the middle of the bed naked. Removing my bra and panties, I do as he says. Riley crawls between my legs, spreading my thighs apart, and inches closer to me.

Without wasting a second, Riley slides his tongue up my slit before he sucks my clit. A million beats of pleasure shoot through me, and the perfectly calculated pressure causes me to fist the sheets. My back flies off the mattress as he continues his delicious assault. Then he slides a finger inside, and my eyes roll back as a moan escapes me.

Riley twists his wrist and inserts a second finger, thrusting in and out as he flicks my clit with his thumb. It's the best pleasure I've ever experienced, and just when I'm about to beg him to let me come, it shakes through me like an earthquake. He knows exactly what to do as I ride it out, and when my legs fall to the side, all that can be heard is my panting.

"Holy shit," I gasp. "They teach you that down in the south, too?"

Riley chuckles, opens the condom, and takes off his boxers. My gaze slowly strolls down his body to the very thick and hard cock he's stroking. I watch as he slides it over his length, then climbs on the bed, hovering above me. Our eyes stay locked as he grips my hips and pulls me closer. Swallowing hard, I bite down on my lip as he gently enters. My back arches at the fullness, and I swear the room grows ten degrees hotter when he sinks deeper. Wrapping his hand around to grab my ass, he slowly slides out. When I hike my leg up his waist, he pumps in long and hard.

"Christ, Zoey," he mutters with uneven breaths. "You feel better than I imagined you would. *Fuck.*"

I lift my hips to meet his thrusts, and it's not long until we're both begging for relief. Riley cups my breast, then pinches my nipple, and I'm halfway to heaven when he moves his hand down and rubs my clit. "You like that, sweetheart? Because I'm only getting started with you."

"Yes…" I hum. "Oh God." My eyes flutter closed, and I'm moaning out his name as my body tightens. He leans over to capture my mouth with his, then slams into me over and over until I'm falling over the ledge once again.

Before I can catch my breath, he's losing himself too.

It's not long after we're sweating and panting that he flips me over and fucks me from behind, giving me the best sex of my life. Hell, the best night of my life.

I wake up next to a hard body pressed against me. I inch closer, not wanting to lose the warmth. Humming to myself, I smile at how content I feel. "Good morning," I say, nuzzling my face against skin.

"Uh, mornin'."

My eyes pop open at the deep and low voice as my smile falls.

There's a man in my bed! I glance around and realize I'm not in my room and then look at the person next to me. "Oh my God." Then I notice we're both naked. "Oh shit."

After I apologize for my reaction, he chuckles. I immediately pull away, grabbing the sheet with me. My mind is fuzzy as hell, and all I want to do is get out of here with the sliver of dignity I have left.

"Uh, Zoey…" I hear him as I sit on the edge of the bed, feeling like a hot ass mess. I probably look like one too.

The moment he mentions a ring, I hold out my left hand and gasp at the gold band on my left finger. "Oh God, I remember now."

The night comes back to me in flashes, and heat rushes through my body.

"Was it really legal?" he asks.

"We signed a marriage license and said vows, so yeah, I'm pretty sure we're legally married now," I respond, chewing on my lip. My parents are going to kill me. This is not good.

Riley's friend—aka the dare master—barges through the door, telling Riley they have to leave. My mind races a million miles an hour at the thought of having to figure this out because he lives in Texas. Somehow, we're going to have to fix this.

But then I remember the way it felt when he touched me. Kissed me. Held me and cherished me.

We only had one night, but I'd take that over a hundred crappy dates. Riley made me feel things I'd never felt before. Maybe it was the alcohol and the excitement of being in Vegas, but what if it wasn't? What if there could actually be something real between us?

Hell, now we'll never know.

After I get dressed in the bathroom and come back into the room, Riley's in front of me apologizing because his flight leaves in an hour and they're expected at work tomorrow. My sister is probably wondering where the hell I am too, though I know she wouldn't get on that plane to Phoenix without me. As much as I want us to have more time, I know it's not possible.

When he tells me to come to Texas with him and I explain why I can't, the thought saddens me. Part of me wishes I could while the other wonders how crazy we must be to even consider it after only twenty-four hours together.

Diesel is on Riley's ass, rushing him out the door. We have a few seconds to talk before he texts me his address and kisses my cheek.

"For what it's worth, I had a really fun night, *wife*."

The way he says *wife* sends a hot shiver down my spine.

"Safe flight, *hubby*," I retort.

Diesel has the door open and shouts for him again, irritation written all over his face.

"Goodbye," I say as he walks away.

He gives me one final look before he's gone for good, and I'm not sure I truly understand the mild heartache that rushes over me.

CHAPTER SEVEN

Riley

FOUR WEEKS LATER

Texas in the middle of June is hot as fuck. I rip off my shirt and chug half my water before putting my gloves back on and stacking more hay on the trailer. The main barn needs to be restocked, and that bitch work was assigned to Diesel and me today.

"Cheer up, buttercup! I know what'll make ya smile." He holds up a finger, and I roll my eyes.

Ignoring him, I keep working and tossing bales. Then his phone starts playing music.

"Meghan Trainor always makes me happy." Diesel flashes a shit-eating grin as "All About That Bass" blasts from his iPhone.

"Jesus Christ," I mutter and grunt, shaking my head at him when he starts moving his ass to that ancient song. Ever since I was served

357

annulment papers two weeks ago, he's been more obnoxious than usual, which is saying a lot.

"Oh, come on," he huffs. "Not even a little grin?" Diesel pops a brow, and I shrug.

"Can you get back to work now? I'm not getting paid to do your half." I throw a bale with more force than necessary.

I haven't been able to get Zoey out of my head since we left Vegas, and it's been no secret. I fucking hated that I left in a rush but was hopeful I'd hear from her after Summer's wedding. I knew she'd be busy with all the festivities, but then I received the surprise of a lifetime when the sheriff showed up at my house. With a frown on his face, it was obvious he knew what he was delivering. I had to beg him not to tell my mama because news travels fast in this small town. I could've messaged Zoey—hell, I was tempted after drinking too much that night—but I didn't. She made her decision, and I couldn't blame her. We barely knew each other, lived two completely different lives, and there was no reason to delay the inevitable.

I signed the papers and sent them back the next day.

"I have a whole playlist for you." Diesel keeps talking. "Fifth Harmony is next. Damn, those ladies can shake it."

"Am I supposed to know who any of these people are?"

Diesel gasps. Literally gasps.

Now that causes me to smile. Such a damn drama queen.

"You've been hanging around my little cousins too much. Or my sister." I turn and glare at him. His eyes widen as if he's just been caught. "Which one is it?" I pop a brow.

"Uh, which one gets me in less trouble?"

"Asshole," I mutter before turning back to the hay.

When we're done for the afternoon, we take the side-by-side to the B&B for a break. As we walk up the porch, I'm ready to punch Diesel because he never stops talking. I know he thinks it'll distract me, but it only pisses me off more. I shove him before walking through the front door. While my uncle John is probably at the family bar in town, there's usually a Bishop in here somewhere, so I try to be on my best behavior once inside.

Diesel groans when we spot Fisher in the kitchen. "'Sup?" he asks, making himself a plate of muffins and cookies. "Hay all done?"

"Would we be in here if it wasn't?" Diesel says before I can respond.

"Maybe you should've helped us for once, or are you too afraid of getting your city boy clothes dirty?"

"Actually, I've been on the phone all morning calling in orders and making sure the ranch has everything it needs for the rest of the summer, but if you think you're more qualified to take care of finances and inventory, be my guest," Fisher answers smoothly. "I'm sure I could handle moving around some hay. I'd even do it without whining too."

"Motherfucker," Diesel growls between clenched teeth. He's one step away from knocking Fisher out, so I grab his arm and pull him back.

"As entertaining as it'd be to watch you two punch each other's teeth out, there are guests in the living room who probably don't want blood splattered on them." I walk Diesel out of the kitchen. Before I can scold him, my mom walks in with my cousins Mackenzie and Elizabeth.

"Oh, there you boys are," Mama says, greeting me with a kiss on the cheek. "Diesel," she says firmly, giving him a light smack on the cheek. "Kenzie and Elle need some help hauling dirt to the gardens."

"Why can't Aunt Mila do it?" I ask since she's the one who tends to them usually.

"She's at the school today. A teacher called in sick," she explains. After Mila moved here to be with Uncle John, she opened a daycare center, but once their kids got older, she hired a manager so she could be home more.

"Sure, that's fine. Diesel would love to help. He needs some fresh air anyway." I smack him on the back and squeeze his shoulder, daring him to argue.

He shoots me daggers for putting him under the bus, but that's what he gets for not being able to keep his mouth shut around Fisher. My cousin means well, but nothing will mend their friendship at this point, so I don't even bother trying.

Diesel plasters on the fakest smile, then tells my mom he'd be more than happy to help. He's a suck-up, considering I already know he has a thing for my little sister, and if either of my parents found out, they'd never let her near him again.

"Such a gentleman," my mother praises. "The girls are ready when you are. I've gotta get back to the house to start dinner for your father," she tells me. "You boys are always welcome to come."

Before I can respond, I notice Diesel looking up the staircase as his eyes widen. "Hoooooooly. Shit."

"Language!" my mom scolds in a hushed whisper, but when I follow where he's looking, I have the same reaction.

What the fuck?

Everyone stares up at Zoey, who's walking toward me, looking more gorgeous than ever. Her hair is a tad blonder, and she's a bit tanner, but otherwise, she looks just like she did the minute I left.

"What are you doing here?" I ask when she's in front of me, using a rougher tone than I intended. "I mailed the papers back two weeks ago," I tell her, taking off my baseball cap to brush a hand through my hair before replacing it. It's one of my nervous tells, though she wouldn't know that.

"Oh, I know. My lawyer told me," she explains softly as she folds her hands in front of her. She looks anxious as hell.

"Papers? Lawyer? What is she talkin' about, Riley?" my mother demands. Fisher is now standing next to Diesel, witnessing this shitshow.

I swallow hard, not wanting to lie to my mom. Regardless, now that Zoey's here, everyone is going to find out anyway. Might as well be the one to tell her and introduce them.

"Zoey, this is my mom, River. Mama, this is Zoey. My *wife*."

"What?" she asks in shock.

Fisher is doubled over, laughing his ass off. Kenzie and Elle are standing wide-eyed, and Diesel is grinning like a fool while my mother looks at me in horror.

"Well, not for long. She asked for an annulment," I explain.

"When? How?"

"Vegas," Diesel answers for me, and I glare at him.

With narrowed eyes, she slowly shakes her head. "You're just like your father. I don't even know if I can be mad at you or not."

"Ma, please. Give us a moment, okay?" I beg.

I take Zoey's hand and lead her out of the B&B, making sure no one follows us as I walk her around to the side of the building.

"Sorry about that. My family is…well, they're all fucking crazy. As you can tell." I'm nervous about her being here and rambling, but I can't take my eyes off her. Fuck, she's so beautiful when she looks at me and smiles.

"No, it's okay. I didn't know what to expect, honestly. I spent over twelve hours driving here and rehearsed what would happen when I saw you for the first time, and it wasn't supposed to happen like that." She chews on her bottom lip. In Vegas, I learned it was one of her nervous habits.

"You drove here? Over twelve hours alone?" I ask, surprised.

Zoey nods. "I wanted to clear my head."

"Okay, so…what *are* you doing here then?"

She inhales a deep breath, then looks at me. "I didn't sign the papers."

My brows raise in shock. "I'm going to need more explanation here…" I pinch the back of my neck, reminding myself to breathe. "You sent me the papers and then didn't sign them?"

Zoey fidgets with her shirt, but all I can think about is how I want to kiss those soft lips again.

"I-I thought an annulment was the only option since we don't even live in the same state, but then I started wondering…what if there really was a connection between us? What if we actually gave this a chance instead of calling it quits right away? I couldn't sign those papers without knowing for certain, so I figured I'd come here and stay for a couple of weeks to see if there was something more between us than just one drunken night in Vegas. If so, I'd have to go back home to tell my parents everything first and pack my things, but then after that, I could live here with you. That is, if you wanted to. I mean, you could've met someone since then, so—"

Closing the gap between us, I cup her face, interrupting her words by pressing my mouth to hers. Considering she hasn't signed those papers and wants to see if there's something between us confirms she felt something too. I slide my tongue between her lips, and when she relaxes against me, I deepen the kiss.

Eventually, I pull away, and as we catch our breaths, I rest my forehead against hers. "Sorry, I shouldn't have mauled you like that."

She chuckles and bites down on her lip again. "It's a much better reaction than I was anticipating, so I'm not mad about it."

That makes me smile. "Please tell me I'm not crazy for feeling this way after only spending twenty-four hours with you."

Zoey swallows, then looks up at me. "If you are, then I am too."

"You have no idea how happy I am that you're here." My hand slides around her back, holding her closer.

"I was scared you'd tell me to go the fuck away and push me out on my ass," she admits. "Which I would've deserved."

"Thought about it for a split second, then decided I'd rather kiss you again." I smirk, bringing our mouths back together.

"I'm sorry I didn't call—" she murmurs against my lips.

"Riley Alexander Bishop!" My mother's voice echoes as I hear her stomping down the porch stairs. *Shit.*

She finds us on the side of the B&B and folds her arms over her chest.

"You have some more 'splaining to do." Ma looks at Zoey and smiles. "I'm sure you're a very lovely girl, but can someone enlighten me on how you two ended up married after one night?"

When I see Diesel walking behind her, I point at him. "Why don't you go ask your precious bonus child? The one who *dared* me." I say the words loud enough for him to hear.

"Excuse me? You got married on a dare?" She turns and looks at Diesel, then yells at him, "I told you boys to behave!"

Chuckling, I wrap my arm around Zoey. When my mom faces me again, her expression changes.

"Did you get her pregnant?" she asks firmly.

"Ma! No!" I turn toward Zoey, who looks frightened as hell. "Wait, are you?" My heart stops. We had sex a month ago. That'd be enough time for her to know she's pregnant, right? My parents had me ten months after they met. No wonder my mother's giving me that damn look.

Zoey glances back and forth between us with wide eyes. "What, no! I'm not. That's not why I'm here. I mean, if I was, I'd tell you. But as far as I know, I'm not." Her rambling is adorable, but considering the situation, I don't tell her that. Ma looks like she's about to murder me.

"Your father is going to…hell, your grandmother! You just wait." Mom sighs. "Your father will probably give you a high five." She groans and rolls her eyes because we both know it's true. Dad fell in love with Mom the moment he saw her.

I chuckle and shrug. "Mom, I'm almost twenty-three. Grandma is gonna ask us when we're having babies." I look at Zoey. "She has five kids and twelve grandchildren, yet she's been asking for great-grandchildren since I turned eighteen."

Mom pinches the bridge of her nose, knowing I'm right, and she can't argue it. Grandma might give me shit for not having a proper Southern wedding, but now that I'm married and more Bishop babies are a real possibility, I'll be in the clear for eloping.

"If I were you, Zoey, I'd double up on birth control because these Bishop men knock up their women just by looking at them." And with that, my mother walks away, making me cringe at the thought.

"Nope, she's wrong. Don't need birth control now because that was definitely a boner killer."

Zoey laughs, a blush creeping up her neck and cheeks.

"Well, since you're staying here for a bit, you want a small tour of the ranch?" I ask, taking her hand. "We'll probably find my dad out in one of the pastures."

"Sure, I'd love that. I got in late last night and have only had time to unpack and shower so far," she replies as I lead her to the side-by-side.

"You ever ride in one of these before?" I ask, helping her up and buckling her in.

"Nope. Should I be scared?"

I grip her chin. "Depends." Then I flash her a wink and walk to the driver's side. Seeing and kissing her again have instantly changed my mood. I can't blame her for being scared at first and understand why she thought an annulment was our only option, but now that she's here, I'm not taking this second chance for granted.

CHAPTER EIGHT

Zoey

I've been shaking with nerves since the moment I decided to drive to Texas. What if Riley didn't want me here? What if it was nothing more than a fling, considering how quickly he signed and sent those papers back? What if I walked away from a man who would've truly loved me?

It took me two weeks to finally say to hell with it and pack up my car. My parents know I love being adventurous, I always have. I'm not like my sister, who thrives on stability. I like the unknown, and although that almost made me not come, I was so glad I did the minute Riley kissed me.

I hang on for dear life as he drives us around, showing me the barns, the horse stables, their training facility, and where he mainly works. I looked up the ranch before I arrived, so I know it's huge, but it already looks like a place I could happily wake up to every day.

Riley radios his dad to find out his location and then tells him to stay put. My nervousness increases because the last thing I want to do is piss off both his parents. I know his mom's in shock, and it'll probably take some time for her to warm up to the idea, but having one parent on our side would be nice.

"Good thing you knew to wear boots today," he tells me with a grin. "It's a little muddy out here." He parks the vehicle and takes my hand. Though it's a simple gesture, butterflies flutter in my stomach.

"I hope your dad likes me," I say weakly.

"Well, it can't go any worse than it did with my mom." He chuckles, and I smack his arm with my free hand.

"That's not reassuring!" I scold but laugh at his goofy grin.

"Hey, Dad!" Riley calls, grabbing his attention. The poor guy is standing in mud up to his knees working on a fence. "There's someone I want you to meet."

As soon as his dad turns around and smiles at us, I blink and do a double take. Lord, the two look almost identical. His father's hair isn't as dark, but their facial features are the same. If that's what Riley will look like in twenty years, then I better take his mom's advice to heart. I'm surprised she only had two children.

"Hey, kiddo. What's up?" He steps out of the mud, walking toward us.

"This is Zoey," Riley says, gesturing to me. "Zoey, this is my dad, Alex. But he prefers to be called Old Man."

I snort at his taunting tone, then shake Mr. Bishop's hand. "I'll stick with Alex, don't worry."

"Smart girl." The corner of his lips tilts up, then he glances at Riley. "So by the hand-holding, I take it you're one of Riley's many girlfriends?"

My eyes widen as Riley squeezes my hand in reassurance. "You're an asshole."

I look back and forth between them and can tell Mr. Bishop is giving him a hard time on purpose. "If your mother was here, she'd be yelling at you for that language, son."

"Yeah, yeah." Riley groans. "Now that you've almost scared her off..." He turns and gestures toward me with a grin. "Dad, this is my *wife*."

I hold my breath, waiting for his reaction. It's easy to see they're close, but regardless, this is a pretty big bomb to drop.

Mr. Bishop coughs to cover up his shock, causing Riley to smack him hard on the back. "Breathe, Old Man."

"No, I think you're trying to kill me," he says, swallowing hard.

"Because I heard you say wife, and there's no way my only son would get married without telling me first."

Riley grunts, rolling his eyes. "Now you're being more dramatic than Mom."

"Oh God, your mother knows? Does she still have a pulse?" he asks seriously. "Better yet, how are you still standing after she whipped your ass?"

I can't help it; I start cracking up. This family is so fun, much different from mine, who constantly have a stick up their asses.

"Sorry, I'm not laughing at you. Well, I am. Sorta. It's just you two are hilarious together," I explain, clearing my throat in embarrassment.

"Tell that to my mother because she blames us for giving her gray hair," Riley says. Alex welcomes me to the family, and we chat about how we met and the dare that had us eloping in a Vegas chapel before he has to get back to work.

After we leave his dad, Riley continues driving us around, and I can't help but be amazed by the land.

"It's so open, and the view is breathtaking. No wonder you love it here," I say, unable to take my eyes off the rolling hills and cloudless blue sky.

"Born and raised, can't imagine being anywhere else," he says honestly. "When we need stuff, we drive to San Angelo. That's where my mom works."

"How far away is that?" I ask.

"About forty-five minutes, give or take."

My eyes widen. "Even for groceries?"

"There's a small grocery store in town along with a bank, a bar, and a library. There's a health clinic too, but my mom got hired as a nurse at the San Angelo hospital after she had me since my uncle Evan and aunt Emily worked there as doctors. She's in town several times a week, so if any of us need anything, she can usually grab it."

"So not all of you work on the ranch?" I ask.

"Evan used to when he had time, but since he and my uncle John bought the bar, he's there on his days off to make sure his investment is running properly."

"Wow...your family sure knows how to stay busy. It's like no one slows down."

He shrugs, not disagreeing. "It's all we know. When you're born on a ranch, and you're used to getting up before the sun and working through dusk, you develop a strong work ethic. I could've left after high school and gone to college as most of my cousins did or plan to, but everything I needed to learn about business and management is here on the ranch."

"I didn't go to college either," I admit, and he looks at me with a smile, encouraging me to continue. "I was always passionate about hair and nails, but my mother made it very clear what she thought about that. She said I wasn't using the extent of my intelligence, was wasting my life away, and would always need a man to support me because I wasn't choosing a high-paying career. Blah, blah, blah. But I went for it anyway and did a year of cosmetology school. It might not bring in a million bucks, but every day I worked, I felt like a hero. Someone would come in, not knowing what they wanted, and I'd instantly envision a new look for them. They'd hug me with tears in their eyes because they felt truly beautiful for the first time in their lives. After that happened more and more, I knew I had picked the right direction for me."

"I'm really glad you did," he responds. "There's nothing worse than feeling pushed into a job you're not passionate about. Ranching is hard work, but I love it. Most people think I'm crazy for enjoying it so much, but fuck 'em."

I laugh with him, then blush when he brings my hand to his mouth and kisses my knuckles. "Working in a career you hate isn't worth your happiness, remember that." He flashes me a wink, and I nod, grinning like a fool.

"Speaking of my family..." Riley begins. "We're throwing my little sister, Rowan, a surprise birthday party tomorrow. I'd love to bring you with me. I have a big family, so single introductions could take us a few days, or rather weeks."

I smile nervously, but nod in agreement. "Meeting everyone is a big deal. I'll either be known as the wife who made Riley Bishop the happiest man alive or the one who broke his heart."

He turns and studies my face as if he's wondering the same thing.

"I'd much prefer the former, but we'll cross the bridge of the latter if we need to, but hopefully that won't happen."

We both know I'm only here temporarily. If things work out between us,

I'll still have to go home and confess everything to my parents before I pack up my life and move. It'd be a huge step, but I'm willing to risk it all to see if he's the one.

Riley drives us back to the B&B and comes to my side to help me out. He's a gentleman down to his core, which isn't something I'm used to. The few men I've dated were always so damn self-absorbed and arrogant, but Riley is a different breed.

"So since this is officially your first full night here, what do you say we go out? There's this ridiculous country bar outside of town called the Honky Tonk, and you can't really visit the ranch without experiencing it," he tells me as if he has to sell it to me, but the truth is, I'd go anywhere with him.

"The Honky Tonk? That's the actual name?" I ask, chuckling. "I can only imagine what the inside looks like."

"Well, come with me tonight, sweetheart, and you'll find out."

"I'm in."

"Good. Now, normally I'd walk you to your room and kiss you goodbye until I can pick you up later, but I'm certain half my family is in there waiting to hound us, so it might be best for you to sneak in through the back."

"Ah, good idea." I snicker.

He interlocks his fingers with mine and leads me to the steps of the back porch. "I'll pick you up at eight."

Then he cups my cheek and molds our lips together. My eyes close, inhaling his scent, and being this close to him causes my body to buzz.

He pulls away, and I frown. Riley notices and chuckles at my sad face. "I'll be back. Eight o'clock." He winks, then takes off.

When I walk in, I chuckle because Riley was right. A crowd is in the living room, and somehow, I'm able to sneak upstairs without any of them seeing me. Since I have a few hours before he picks me up, I decide to take a long, hot shower.

At five until eight, there's a knock on my door, and heat coils low in my stomach at the anticipation of seeing him again. As soon as I open the door, my breath hitches at the sight of him. Dark jeans, boots, a plaid button-up, and he's wearing a black cowboy hat.

My eyes linger a little too long because a moment later, he clears his throat, making my gaze shoot back to his.

"I brought you something," he says, holding up a pair of women's cowboy boots.

"For me?" I ask, moving to the side so he can come in.

"Well, my sister said you could borrow them. If you like them, we'll go in to town and buy you a pair." He sets them down, then turns to face me. His eyes wander down my body before he closes the gap between us. "Or perhaps we should just skip tonight altogether because I only have so much willpower..."

The way he eye fucks me causes my cheeks to heat *again*. Riley circles his arms around my waist and pulls us flush together. "You look really beautiful, Zoey. I missed you."

Wrapping my arms around his neck, I tilt my head. "It's only been a few hours," I remind him with a cheeky smile.

"The past month," he confirms, and when his eyes darken, it sends a shiver through me. "I tried to get you out of my head, telling myself I was crazy because we had only known each other less than two days. But my stupid heart wouldn't listen, and anytime Diesel made me listen to his dumb chick playlist, it only made it worse because it'd remind me of dancing with you."

I bite down on my lower lip, his confession taking me off guard. His words come out so smoothly and effortlessly, and I don't know how to respond. "Diesel has a playlist with chick music?"

Riley growls, then slides a hand down to my ass and squeezes me through the denim. "That's the part you're focusing on, huh?"

I chuckle at how easy it is to get him worked up. "I thought about you too. A lot."

"I know I've already said it, but I'm really glad you're here and are giving us a real shot. I promise to take advantage of every day we have together."

"I imagine you will." This time, I pull his mouth to mine and kiss him, letting all my unspoken words tell him just how badly I missed him.

Riley's touch and kisses are what strawberry Starbursts are made of—so damn addicting—and you know if you don't stop, you'll end up devouring the entire bag of candy.

"Fuck, Zoey..." We're both panting as he rests his forehead against mine. "We better go before I rip off those things you call shorts."

Chuckling, I nod in agreement. I dramatically push him away and grab the boots, trying them on. They're a little loose, but they'll work. In fact, they actually look really cute with my denim shorts and tank top.

"How do I look?" I stand in front of him, spinning around. "Like a true Texan?"

Riley shakes his head and laughs. "Not quite, sweetheart. Gotta get that accent down. A hat. And get you on a horse first."

My eyes widen. "A horse?"

He takes my hand and leads me out of the room. I don't bother grabbing my phone because tonight, all of my attention will be on my *husband*.

Considering how much I drank in Vegas with Riley, I decide to take it easy. An hour later, we're at the bar and sticking to beer only. We both know what happens when too much liquor is involved.

The Honky Tonk is exactly what I imagined. People in cowboy boots, taking shots and being loud and obnoxious. Old license plates on the walls complement the rustic décor, and it smells like a barn. A clean one, at least.

And surprisingly, I don't hate it. In fact, I haven't laughed this much in weeks.

"So wife... I think we should have our first dance," Riley says, swiveling our barstools so my legs are between his.

"We danced all night in Vegas," I say. "In fact, I'm pretty sure you went to second base at the third club."

Riley brushes his hand over his facial hair and grins. "You noticed that, did ya?"

I snort, shaking my head. "I doubt they play slow songs here."

He arches a brow as if I just challenged him. "Wait here, my bride." Riley flashes me a wink, then walks over to a jukebox I hadn't realized was there.

Moments later, "A Thousand Years" by Christina Perri starts playing. An oldie but a goodie that I like a lot. He walks back over, all proper, and holds out his hand to me. "May I have this dance?"

"How could I ever deny you?" I place my hand in his, and he leads me to the center of the room.

"Where'd you learn to dance anyway?" I ask after a few moments.

"Bishops don't learn to dance; it's embedded into our DNA," he says firmly.

"Really? Interesting because I'm pretty sure at the final club, you were stepping on my feet."

He gives me a cocky grin. "I was also shit-faced. You're really gonna use that against my dancing skills?" Riley spins me around before I can answer, and when he brings our bodies back together, I have a permanent smile on my face.

"Of course not. You're damn good."

"You're way too good for my ego," he teases. "Could you say it a little louder so the rest of the bar can hear?"

I laugh, my head falling back as he smirks at me. "So you're a Christina Perri fan too? What other things are you going to surprise me with?"

"Well, the fourth movie was my favorite."

I narrow my eyes at him, trying to determine if he's being serious or not. "No way. Are you a *Twilight* fan?"

"What are you trying to say? I'm not cultured enough to love vampire smut?"

Now I'm rolling my eyes at his lousy attempt to feign offense. "Funny. Almost had me there."

He laughs again, bringing his lips to me for a soft kiss. "Rowan, my little sister. She binged all the books in the series, then made me take her to the theater for an anniversary movie marathon. I really had no choice."

"Aww...big brother duty."

"And older cousin. All of the girls were obsessed." He dramatically rolls his eyes.

"So then I guess the true test of our relationship lies on one question..." I say in all seriousness. He furrows his brows, waiting. "Team Jacob or Team Edward?"

"You really expect me to remember who either of them are?"

"I don't think I can do this..." I stop moving. "I can't be married to a man who doesn't know *Twilight*." I shrug, about to walk around him, but he swiftly grabs my waist and pulls me back to him.

"Team Edward...okay. Happy, now? You've officially stolen my man card."

I wrap my arms back around him and smile. "Very."

CHAPTER NINE

Riley

When I closed my eyes last night, Zoey was the only person on my mind. Being with her was magical, and having her here with me on the ranch doesn't seem real. I keep pinching myself to make sure I'm not dreaming.

I roll out of bed before my alarm even goes off. There's too much excitement streaming through me at seeing Zoey again. Not to mention, I have an assload of chores to do before Rowan's surprise party today.

After lunch, the plan is to get Rowan to the bar without suspicion, and I have the perfect idea. What I didn't prepare for was having to introduce Zoey to everyone in the family. I doubt my parents told anyone already, though it's possible, considering the rumor mill in this small town.

I'm not trying to steal Rowan's spotlight, but I know the questions will be never-ending. After I get dressed and make some coffee to go, I burst inside Diesel's room being loud as fuck.

"What's wrong with you, asshole?" He throws a pillow in my direction, groaning. "I still have an hour of sleep. And I was dreaming about your sister. She was just about to—"

"I wouldn't fuckin' finish that sentence," I warn. No matter what time it is, he knows how to aggravate the piss outta me. "I'm getting started early, fuckface. Text me when you're up and ready so I can tell you what I took care of," I say before ripping the covers off his body.

He rolls over without a care and shoos me away. I leave with a grin on my face as I drive to the other side of the ranch and check the water troughs and feed the working horses that the ranch hands ride when they're herding cattle from one pasture to the next. After I quickly muck out the stalls, I stop and take care of the chickens, then drive over to meet up with my dad. Without a doubt, he's already in the office, mapping out what needs to be done for the day before Rowan's party.

Ranchers never stop working. Tasks always need to be done.

As soon as I walk in, Dad's busy drinking his coffee and writing in a notebook. I clear my throat, and he looks up at me. "Mornin'," he says, seeming more tired than usual. "You're here early."

"Just takin' after you." I snicker. He's the best role model I could've ever asked for, and I hope to be exactly like him when I have kids. Mama keeps telling me I'm the spitting image of Dad as if it's a warning, but I see it as a compliment.

"Your mother's still in shock that you're a married man." He gives me a somber expression. "I think I am too," he admits, but then he smiles.

"I know. I blame Diesel, but then again, I'm not mad about it," I say, refilling my mug with coffee.

"Marriage is important, Riley. It's not a game. It's not something you do on a whim." He looks at me with soft eyes.

"I know, Dad. But it could be worse. I could've gotten her pregnant, and she could've shown up at the ranch with a Bishop baby bump," I remind him of his own story. "But I didn't. We're trying to be responsible and see if we should be together. There's something special between us. I knew the moment I met her."

"I felt the same way when I met your mother too. So I get it, more than you know."

His words are comforting.

"Us Bishops have a way of falling head over heels the first time we meet a woman. Guess it runs in the family. And I can't fault you for it. Just be smart. Don't want you getting hurt, son. I saw the way you looked at her." He arches a brow, smirking.

I stare out into the barn, replaying everything that happened in Vegas and how shocked I was to see her at the B&B, but I'm determined to give us a chance.

"Your grandma is gonna be pissed," he warns. "But I'm lettin' you deal with her."

I roll my eyes. "Thanks, Dad. So what's the plan today? I already fed the horses on the north side."

"That's my boy," he says, proudly. "Taking charge. I like that. Since you already took care of the horses, the utility barn is in need of some repairs. I noticed some of the panels were corroding at the bottom, and before it becomes a mess, I thought we'd change 'em out. There's enough time to get it done before ten since you got a head start."

I sip my coffee. "Yep. Shouldn't be a problem. I'll text Diesel and tell him to meet me, and we'll get it done."

"Sounds like a plan," Dad says.

I get up to leave, but he stops me.

"Son."

"Yeah?"

He's smirking.

"Try not to give your grandmother a heart attack today. We did that enough growing up."

I snort and shake my head before walking out. I've heard many stories of how much trouble my dad and uncles would get into, how the sheriff was around regularly, and how they caused mischief everywhere they went.

Before I get in the truck, I text Diesel and tell him our job for the day and where to meet me. I have no doubt we'll be able to finish even sooner than expected.

As I drive over, the early morning sun starts warming everything up. It's going to be a hot one, so I start chugging water because dehydration out here can be deadly. And I don't want my mother to worry.

It's just past seven by the time I make it to the barn, and Diesel's already removed his shirt and is sweating his ass off.

"'Bout time you showed up," he harasses. "I've already got all the metal cut and ready to place if you can just help me get this corroded shit removed. It practically crumbles when it's touched."

"On it," I say, putting on my work gloves. After I carefully remove the sheets, he puts the new ones in place. The bright silver metal is much newer, so the barn's gonna need a fresh coat of paint. We'll have to save that for another day, but I know Grandma Bishop won't allow the eyesore to stay like this for long.

Just as Diesel and I attach the last of the metal, I see long legs heading our way. It's not uncommon for tourists to book the B&B for a real country escape, but I could recognize those legs in the dark. *Zoey.*

I remove my gloves and wipe the sweat from my brow.

"Hey, husband, it looks like you're working hard." She unscrews the top of the bottle of water she's holding and hands it to me. I run my eyes down her body, admiring the tempting curves I haven't been able to stop thinking about. Right now, she's the only thing I want to drink.

"Thanks, wifey." I flash her a wink before removing the steps between us and planting a sweet kiss on her lips. She sinks into me, and I have to force myself to pull away because if I don't, I won't stop.

"Mmm," she hums against my mouth, wrapping her arms around me.

"Arizona!" Diesel calls out with a half-cocked grin. "Where's *my* water?"

I take a sip of the one she gave me and then hand it to Diesel, who drinks it in three gulps.

"We're almost done here. I gotta call my sister and shower, then we can go to the bar where they're setting up," I tell her, my fingers brushing against hers, tempting her to kiss me again.

"I'm really nervous," she admits. "What if they all hate me?"

I snort-laugh because that's not possible. "What if they all love you, then you leave me? That's what you should be more worried about."

The truth seems to fall out. Her smile fades, and she searches my face. "The last thing I want to do is hurt you, Riley."

"Get a room!" Diesel yells, interrupting us. "And come help me finish up this bullshit!"

She leans forward and slides her lips across mine. I love how freely she shows affection. "Better get back to it." She nods at Diesel, who's growing more frustrated.

"I'll pick you up in an hour. Be ready to meet the entire town," I warn with a laugh, but I'm not joking.

"You're not helping my nerves!" she shouts as she walks toward the B&B.

"I'm gonna kick your ass," Diesel tells me.

When she's out of sight, I get back to work, and we finish the task. I suck in a deep breath, realizing I'm anxious to make the announcement. It's scary bringing a girlfriend around everyone, but it's absolutely terrifying to introduce my *wife*. The word almost seems foreign, but damn, it feels so right.

After we're done with the repairs, I text Dad and let him know, then we head straight to the house to shower. While Diesel hogs the hot water, I make a sandwich and call Rowan.

"Whatcha doin?" I ask, purposely not mentioning her birthday. Every year, she thinks I forget, but I never have.

"Nothing much. Putting away some laundry and cleaning. Why? What's up?"

I focus on giving the best performance of my life. "I just finished talking to Uncle John, and he said they were doing inventory for the bar around two since it's a slow time. He mentioned you wanted to learn how to do it, so he told me to let you know."

She laughs. "That means I need to be there."

"You know they don't really give us a choice to do anything, right?" I'm smiling, and I know she can tell.

"Mmhmm. Got nothing better going on other than maybe watching paint dry or something." She sounds somewhat disappointed, but what she doesn't know is fifty people will be waiting for her to show up today.

"I understand. Anyway, I gotta eat. Talk soon, okay?" I make sure to keep my tone chipper.

"See ya," she says, then hangs up.

As I sit at the table and devour my food, I almost feel bad, but then again, I don't because I've never had a surprise party. It was Ma's idea, and she even went through the trouble of secretly inviting some of Rowan's best friends from school. Considering we live in the age of social media, though I'm not on it much, I'm surprised the party hasn't been ruined yet.

After Diesel's out of the shower, I hop in and scrub the sweat and dirt from my body. Though I only worked half a day, I'm tired. Drinking and dancing the night away with Zoey, on top of waking up an hour early, is starting to catch up with me. But I don't regret spending time with her. It was all worth it.

I dress in my favorite jeans and a dressier blue shirt, spray some cologne, and comb my hair before throwing on a baseball cap that's got the Circle B Ranch cattle brand in the middle. I'm proud as hell to be a Bishop.

"So your sister think anything's up yet?" Diesel asks before he chugs a bottle of water.

I shake my head. "Nope. I didn't even tell her happy birthday when we spoke. Didn't want to make her suspicious. She actually sounded sad, so I think when she shows up, she'll be real surprised and happy."

Diesel flashes a mischievous grin. "And you even hired a male stripper!" He undoes his button-up shirt as he thrusts his hips like he did in the Vegas show.

"Oh, really?" I lift a brow. "You'd strip in front of my grandma?" I challenge, knowing he's full of shit.

He instantly starts re-buttoning his shirt. "Damn. Forgot your whole family's gonna be there. Maybe I'll give her a private show instead," he muses.

"Do it and you'll be limping with my foot in your ass," I threaten.

"Fine, fine." He chuckles. "You nervous about bringing Zoey?"

"Yes and no. I think they'll be shocked but will love her," I admit, convinced she'll have no problem fitting in.

Diesel smiles. "You know, she could've at least brought her friend with her for me. Crystal?"

"Chelsea," I correct, snickering. "You ass. You slept with her and don't even remember her name."

His laughter echoes off the walls. "Trust me when I say we didn't do much sleeping."

Shaking my head, I grab my keys and the birthday presents I got for Rowan in Las Vegas, then head over to the B&B to pick up Zoey. She's sitting on the porch in a rocking chair, looking gorgeous as ever.

"Howdy," I say, and she instantly smiles. "Ready to go, wifey?"

"As ready as I'll ever be." I wrap my arms around her as soon as she meets me and take her lips in mine. Is it really possible to feel this way about someone I barely know?

Yes, yes, it fucking is.

"You look stunning. But hell, you always do." I wink, tempted to skip the party and take her to my house even though we're taking it slow.

"Thank you. I need to make a good impression after all. I like how you can go from all sweaty and dirty cowboy to sleek and sexy cowboy in only an hour. It's like being married to two men..." she quips, biting down on her lip.

"Well, I hope you don't mind the dirty one because he's who you'll see more of," I tease.

We climb in the truck, and the conversation flows easily. I tell her more about my sister and how Diesel always taunts me about her. Once we turn onto the main road, I share the ranch's history because the land goes on for miles. She's intrigued by the size and how many generations have kept it alive.

"It's a working ranch too, not just a vacation destination for tourists. We actually raise and herd cattle, brand them, and even train horses."

She grins. "And you guys own a bar, a bed and breakfast, have a massive garden, and your grandma basically runs the town."

I smile with a nod because it's true. My family's well-known 'round here. "Something like that. Grandma Bishop knows everything about everyone. She's active in charitable work too and does a big bachelor auction fundraiser every year for the food bank, has for decades. You only cross her if you have a death wish. The woman's a spitfire, but she's extremely loyal. She also makes the best blueberry muffins I've ever tasted in my life," I tell her random facts, then park the truck a block away from the bar.

I turn and look at Zoey, and she seems more relaxed than before.

"Well, it's now or never. Ready?" I ask, grabbing Rowan's gifts.

We sit in silence for a few seconds before Zoey lets out a laugh. "As ready as I'll ever be."

After we climb out of the truck, I grab her hand and lead her in through the back door. The room is already crowded with people helping decorate with balloons and streamers. As soon as I set the presents down, I run into

Uncle John and Uncle Jackson. They look at me, then at Zoey, mirror images of one another.

She narrows her eyes. "Am I seeing double?"

"They're twins," I say. "And nosy as hell."

I try to walk past them, but Uncle Jackson grabs me by my collar and pulls me back. "Don't be a punk. We deserve a proper introduction to your *new* lady friend."

Zoey snickers, and I know that as soon as I tell them, the entire town will know. Jackson is a loud bastard.

"Uncle John and Uncle Jackass, oh excuse me, I mean Jackson, this is Zoey, my *wife*," I tell them proudly.

They look at each other and shout, *"Wife?"* at the same time. That's when the entire room falls quiet, and I feel all heads turn to look at us.

We're in the spotlight, and I'm about ready to shit myself when Grandma Bishop comes storming through the crowd. "What did y'all say?"

I grab Zoey's hand and bring her forward, and while fifty people are looking at us, it's so quiet one could hear a pin drop. "Zoey, this is everyone. And everyone, this is Zoey, my wife."

My heart pounds hard in my chest when Grandma Bishop bolts toward me. Before she speaks, she stops and addresses those who are staring. "Well, carry on, everyone. We still have a birthday to celebrate."

Then she turns back toward us, a stern expression on her face. "Now, tell me how this happened..." She looks at me, then at Zoey. "You're pregnant, sweetie?"

I burst into laughter as Zoey shakes her head, blushing. Why does everyone think that? As if that'd be the only reason this gorgeous woman would marry me? "No, Grandma. I didn't take after my parents completely."

I explain how we met in Vegas a month ago and had an instant attraction but left the fine details out because that's too awkward to discuss. Then I tell her about the wedding and how Zoey's here to see if we can really make this work.

Zoey smiles and agrees with everything I'm saying. When I'm finished, she meekly speaks. "It's really nice to meet you."

Grandma pulls her into a big hug. "Honey, 'round here, we hug when we meet new people. So you might as well get used to it." She pulls back but grabs Zoey's hands. "Welcome to the family. You caught a good one here." Grandma gives Zoey a wink, causing us to smile. If Grandma accepts Zoey, the rest will, too, because that woman sets the precedent for everything.

We walk away, and Zoey leans in and whispers, "I like her a lot."

"Were you scared?" I tease.

She snickers. "Just a little. The woman is a little intimidating."

I grunt. "You have no idea."

We try to help with decorations but get bombarded at every turn, and I'm forced to personally introduce her. By the time my cousins come over to give me a hard time, there's no way Zoey'll remember anyone's names. Between all the aunts and uncles, cousins, neighbors, family friends, and church members, even I'm a bit overwhelmed. They have no filter and say the first thing that comes to mind, regardless if it's embarrassing or not. It's a relief not to hide being married, but I don't tell anyone it was all based on a dare from Diesel. What they don't know won't hurt them.

Eventually, Diesel arrives with a wrapped present for Rowan, and I'm half-tempted to ask him what it is so I can make sure it's nothing inappropriate she can't open in front of our family.

Someone yells that Rowan's parked in the front, so I grab Zoey, and we hide behind the bar. I lean over and kiss her, not caring who's watching now that people know. When the bell above the door dings, we all pop up and scream, "*Surprise,*" and I watch as my sister beams and shrieks in shock.

I glance over at Zoey, and she's wearing the biggest most genuine smile I've ever seen. She looks so happy here, and everyone loves her just as I knew they would. I know what we have is real, and as crazy as it sounds, I don't want her to leave.

CHAPTER TEN

Zoey

The surprise party for Rowan was amazing, and twenty-four hours later, I'm still buzzing. I was worried I wouldn't fit in, concerned they wouldn't approve of our rushed marriage, but I quickly learned how incredibly supportive Riley's family is. Every person I talked to was so sweet and genuinely interested in learning about me. I chatted about being a hairdresser, and instead of feeling like I wasn't good enough, they were impressed. They accept me for who I am, and that's something I've never really experienced. Even though I've only been here for a day, I already love his family so much.

Last night when Riley dropped me off at the B&B, he reminded me about his grandma's invite to church this morning and lunch at his parents' house afterward. Luckily, I packed a few nice outfits and enjoyed sitting between him and Grandma Bishop at the service. We were both taken by surprise when the pastor asked us to stand as husband and wife so we could be introduced to the congregation as newlyweds. As soon as it was over, Riley apologized like crazy, but all I could do was laugh. However, the hard part isn't over yet. I'm sure lunch with his parents will be interesting since it'll be small and intimate with more questions.

"They don't bite," Riley reassures me as he leads me up the porch.

"I know. I just want them to like me," I admit before we reach the front door.

"Just be yourself. You're amazing." He brings my hand to his mouth and presses a sweet kiss to my knuckles.

I roll my eyes and laugh. "How do you know? I could be a crazy chick who takes advantage of rowdy cowboys."

"Yeah, well, I'm not arguing that. You'd almost have to be to accept one of Diesel's dares, but look where it got us." Before we walk in, he cups my cheeks in his rough palms and leans forward, painting my lips with his. I relax and melt into him until we're lost in each other's touch. When the front door swings open and Rowan clears her throat, we break apart.

"Get. A. Room," she taunts, smirking as she leans against the doorframe with her arms crossed.

A blush covers my cheeks, and I tuck my hair behind my ears. Rowan is only a year younger than me, and just from chatting with her briefly at the party yesterday, I know we could be good friends. She gives no fucks about anything and speaks what's on her mind, something I've quickly learned is a Bishop trait.

"Don't be annoying," Riley scolds, giving her a pointed look as we walk hand in hand into the house.

"Hey, Zoey, have fun at church this morning?" she asks.

"Yeah, it was fine. Kinda embarrassing, though," I admit. I'm not used to so much attention, and it seems I've had a plethora of it since I arrived.

"You'll get used to being called out. Privacy isn't something any of us have around here. Considering the town is so small, everyone is in everyone's business," she explains with a groan. "Makes it pretty hard to do anything I shouldn't because they all talk."

"I can only imagine," I say as Riley watches me intently. Damn, the man leaves me breathless with just one look. He sets my body on fire as he leads me into the dining room where his mother's setting the table.

"Hey, Ma," he says with a lazy grin.

"Oh, you kids made it." She looks down at her watch. "And you're actually on time. See, you're already affecting him in a good way, Zoey," she quips, and all I can do is smile.

Mr. Bishop walks in and gives River a sweet kiss on the cheek. I can't get over how much Riley resembles his dad. They're both so handsome, I'm tempted to ask if there's something in the Texas water.

Rowan plops down at the table. "I'm so hungry I could eat a horse. But not Checkers. He's a sweetie," she says with a giggle.

I sit down next to her as Riley helps his mother bring out the food. My stomach growls as I look at the fried chicken, mashed potatoes with gravy, and green beans. Homemade dinner rolls that smell incredible are set right in front of me with a slab of butter. Riley shoots me a wink and asks me what I'd like to drink. Before we eat, Rowan says the blessing, and then we dig in.

"Oh, honey, you need to put more on your plate than that," Mrs. Bishop orders.

"I'm going to gain twenty pounds being here." I snicker but grab another chicken leg.

River smiles and nods. "I know what you mean. When I first moved here, the big dinners were an adjustment for me, especially since I didn't come from a large family. However, we celebrate everything with a meal," Riley's mom explains.

"Mrs. Bishop," I say, and she interrupts me before I can continue.

"There's only room for one Mama Bishop on this ranch." She chuckles. "But you can call me Ma just like everyone else."

I grin. "Ma." I try it out, and it feels surprisingly natural. "Where are you from?"

"Milwaukee, Wisconsin," she answers and then talks about how she met Riley's dad in Key West and how they fell madly in love. She left everything behind to move to Texas to be with him and start her new life here.

She grabs Alex's hand. "It was the best decision I ever made."

Riley places his hand on my lap, and I thread my fingers through his. It's at that moment I recognize how similar our stories are, minus the being pregnant part.

"Mama Bishop was ready to kill Alex." River chuckles.

"Yeah, Mama can be really scary. You should be glad this one's your mom," Alex tells Riley.

"Oh trust me, I am. Grandma doesn't take no shit from anybody," Riley replies.

"Language," River warns.

"So you're *not* pregnant…" Rowan says it as more of a statement than a question.

I chuckle, my cheeks heating. "No, I'm not."

"You didn't deny that you couldn't be, so that means you two totally did it!" By the smirk on her face, I know she's trying to get under Riley's skin in front of their parents.

He picks up a dinner roll, then chucks it at her. "Shut the hell up!"

"Rowan, that's enough," River snaps, but Rowan's more than amused with herself. The whole dynamic of their family is amazing. There are rules and a lot of work to be done, but just by spending this short amount of time with them, it's easy to see how much they love each other. There are zero doubts about how close they are.

My family is on the other spectrum. First of all, I can name all of my cousins on one hand, and we don't talk so freely around each other. The boundaries are high, but with the Bishops, they say what they mean and mean what they say. And damn, I already love them so much.

After I'm so full that I'm ready to burst, River brings out a homemade apple pie with vanilla ice cream. I don't think I can take another bite, but after she hands me a plate, I shove down a spoonful. As soon as it hits my mouth, I release a moan because I've never tasted anything so good.

"Wow," I say when it's half gone.

"I know, right?" Riley smirks. "You'll never go hungry 'round here."

"I hope you don't expect me to know how to bake," I tell him, and everyone laughs.

"You'll learn real quick, honey. Trust me, the extent of my meals were frozen pizzas and microwavable dinners. Mama Bishop taught me everything I know about Southern cooking. Her recipes are to die for. You'll have to come over and write some of them down. Riley's a great cook, though," his mama brags. "When he wants to be, that is."

"Ma, you can't tell Zoey my secrets," he jokes, but I *do* want to know them all.

"So you gonna tell us about this dare?" Rowan asks, looking at him and then glancing over at me.

I snort, wondering when someone was going to bring it up. "Well…" I turn and look at Riley, not sure how much he really wants them to know, considering it was a payback dare, but he doesn't seem to care. He lays it all out from the strip club, to meeting at brunch, to Diesel being an idiot and daring us to get married.

"Oh, so you're responsible for this, too?" Alex asks me with a cocky grin. "You agreed to this on purpose?"

I shrug, though I know he's only teasing. "I'm often known for my bad decisions." I glance at Riley with a smirk. "But this time, I think it was the right one."

"When you know, you know," his dad says, looking at his wife with so much admiration you'd think they just met yesterday. Their love is undeniable.

"That's true," Riley pipes in. "The moment I saw Zoey, I knew."

"At the strip club?" I ask, searching his face, and he nods.

"So it was like divine intervention?" Rowan asks, giggling.

"We all can't have crushes on people who live in town." Riley cackles, and her face distorts.

"Who? I don't know who you're even talking about." Rowan stands and picks up the pile of dirty plates. She tries to hide her reaction, but I see a hint of blush on her cheeks. Riley doesn't name-drop who he's referring to, which I find cute, but I'm certain it's someone they all know.

"What are your plans for the rest of the day?" Alex asks.

I glance over at Riley, who shrugs.

"I was gonna paint the barn before Grandma has a hissy fit. I know she can't stand things to be out of place, especially since the B&B guests can see it," he says.

"You're right," Alex agrees. "Not a bad idea, and it's not supposed to be as hot this afternoon."

"What about you?" River asks me. "Do you like gardening?"

"Love getting my hands dirty," I admit, smiling.

"Mila's been working at the school all week, so she hasn't had any free time, but she mentioned planting veggies this afternoon if you wanna help," she suggests. "I'm sure she'd love and appreciate the company."

Riley glances at me. "Only if you want to. Don't feel obligated."

"I'd love that, actually. I just need to change first." I'm so damn excited to be involved. I've always wanted a garden but never could have one due to the subdivision we live in, plus our backyard isn't big enough. One time, I planted some herbs, but my mother was annoyed it didn't match her décor, so after we used everything, I didn't continue with it. Most of the time, I try not to get in her way.

After the dining room table is cleared and the dishes are washed, Riley says goodbye, and his mom pulls me into a big hug.

"You come back anytime. Our home is yours," River tells me.

"Lunch was amazing. The pie was to die for," I admit. "Thank you for the invite."

"You're welcome, sweetie. Glad you're a part of the family. Keep this one under control," she tells me, pointing at Riley as we walk out the door.

Guilt surfaces as we walk to the truck. Riley's introducing me to everyone as if I've already moved here permanently. After we climb in, my thoughts take over, and he senses my mood change.

"What's wrong?" he asks, giving me his full attention.

I don't even know how to say what I'm thinking without ruining everything. I blow out a breath and sigh. "I don't want anyone to get too attached to the idea of us," I admit as hard as it is.

He stares intently at me. "Why not?"

I tilt my head. "Because we're in test mode, and nothing is set in stone right now."

Riley grabs my hand and interlocks his fingers with mine, then kisses my knuckles. "I don't want you to leave, Zoey. I know everything is still new, and eloping in Vegas is one of the most insane things I've ever done in my life, but I think what we have is special. The *forever* kind."

I suck in a deep breath, and while I don't disagree, it doesn't stop me from worrying that we're jumping the gun. "But what if it's just the excitement of it all? What happens when the newness wears off? That's the type of thing I think about."

He searches my face, then grins. "Did you notice how my dad still looks at my mom after twenty-three years?"

I think about them and how their love seems to only exist in books. "I did."

"That's going to be us," he says matter-of-factly, then leans over and kisses me. "See?"

"You're presumptuous." I laugh against his lips, enjoying the way he can't seem to stop touching me.

"It's one of my best qualities, baby." Riley winks before starting the truck. He drives to the B&B and waits for me to change. Once I'm ready to go, he guides me to the garden where we find Mila bent over with buckets and small shovels surrounding her.

"Aunt Mila," Riley calls out.

"Over here." She stands and waves. I don't know how it's possible that all these Bishop women are so damn beautiful. I hope when I'm in my late forties, I look half as good as them. She takes off her gloves and goes to the wagon she has with supplies and grabs a jug of water.

"You two coming to help today?" she asks after she takes a long drink and wipes the sweat from her forehead.

"I am!" I say, and it's hard for me to even hold back my excitement.

"Yeah, I'm gonna finish painting the barn before Grandma flips her shit."

Mila gives him a look and grins. "I'm telling your mother you're cursing in front of a lady, mister."

"Aunt Mila. You know you're my favorite aunt for a reason," he tells her, and she laughs.

"True." She hands me an extra set of gloves and a small shovel. "Imma put you to work, Zoey."

"I'm so ready," I admit, excited to play in the dirt.

Riley leans over and gives me a smack on the lips. "See you soon, sweetheart. Mila's gonna kick that city girl right outta you."

"Har, har." I roll my eyes at his dig.

When we pull away, I look at him longingly. It's hard to watch him leave, but damn, the view of him in those tight jeans is nice.

Mila clears her throat, bringing the attention back to her. "Ready?"

I nod, and she gives me instructions on what she's doing, then puts her gloves back on.

"I've already added fertilizer to these two rows here, but now I need to plant seeds all the way down. If you want to start on this side, then I'll start here, and we'll get it done in half the time. Boy, am I happy you're here." She shows me how deep to dig, then sends me on my way.

We're essentially working back to back, and I try to keep up with her as she plants.

"So how do you like it here so far?" she asks.

"Love it. It's hot like Phoenix, but the people here are much nicer," I say.

She chuckles. "Yeah, it is hot as hell here. The winters are nice, though. Still gets cold, and we sometimes get snow, but not often. Gotta love Texas. You'll see what I mean." She scoots down farther on the row. I swear she could run circles around me.

"Yeah," I say, and the guilt comes rushing in again. If the time comes for me to leave, I know it'll be difficult, but I won't go until I know for sure what Riley's and my future holds. I have a feeling I already know the answer to that, but it doesn't make it less scary.

I love the smell of fresh earth and being able to plant something that will grow into food that everyone can enjoy. Plus, it's so peaceful out here. In Arizona, it's so busy, and there's barely any downtime. I need this more than she even knows.

Mila stands and looks at what I've done so far. "You're a natural. I'd totally be okay with you being my official helper if you like gardening."

I nod and can't help the obnoxious smile on my face. "I really do love it. It's relaxing."

"I agree. A decade or so ago, I suggested the ranch start a garden for fresh veggies, and now it's grown into a full greenhouse with several side gardens. I wanted to do something more besides changing dirty diapers and running after toddlers, and the idea came to life. Though sometimes it's hard to grow in this soil because of the rocks, I figured out it's not difficult if you build the ground up with fertilizer first. It's been a great addition, and there's nothing better than fresh tomatoes, squash, and zucchini. Over there, I have tons of different herbs too. Basil, rosemary, cilantro. You name it, we have it," she tells me proudly.

After we finish planting our rows of tomato seeds, we spread more fertilizer and potting soil and continue planting other types of vegetables. Mila asks me questions about my job and home life, and I actually feel comfortable answering.

"Yeah, my dad's a doctor, and I'm the daughter who decided not to go that route." The conversation flows easily, and I can see why Riley says she's his favorite aunt. She actually listens.

Mila lets out a small laugh. "It's almost funny in a way. You know, Riley's Uncle Evan and Aunt Emily are doctors too. I've heard it was a big deal that Evan wanted to go to med school instead of working on the ranch. All the other brothers stayed here, which is what makes this family so special. They'll accept you how you are and only want you to be happy."

I look at her and feel tears well in my eyes. Acceptance is everything to me, considering my own family appears to have lost that ability. The fact that they've known me for two days and have already made me feel at home is almost too much to handle. My emotions threaten to bubble over at the thought of what reaction my parents will have when I'm forced to tell them.

When I came to the ranch, I never expected to fall in love with Riley's family too, yet I am.

CHAPTER ELEVEN

Riley

Yesterday went better than I could've ever imagined. Since Zoey's arrived, I haven't been able to think about doing anything other than spending all my free time with her. Knowing she's here to give us a real shot means everything to me. Not that I'm trying to convince her to stay, because it's a choice she'll have to make, but I want to show her what she'd be missing if she left for good.

I know my family's shocked, but they're the most supportive people I know. Zoey going to church with us yesterday meant a lot to my grandparents. It shows she's trying, and that her reason for being here is legit.

When she's the first thing on my mind when I wake up each morning, I know I have it bad. Hell, I won't even deny it. I just wish she were in my bed with me so I could see her before work, but I don't want to rush this either. Instead, I opt to text her.

RILEY

I'll be at the B&B at 9. Eat breakfast with me?

ZOEY

That depends. Which cowboy is this?

I smirk, knowing damn well she's messing with me.

RILEY

The sexy one. The one you kissed last night. The one you're married to.

ZOEY

Hmm...not ringing any bells. Oh wait, do you wear a cowboy hat? And have a sexy swagger going on?

RILEY

Everyone on this ranch wears a cowboy hat, sweetheart. But I'm the only one with swagger.

ZOEY

Oh good, I picked right. Whew. Then yes, I'll be there at 9. Look for the one who looks completely out of place with shorts and a tank top that says What happens in Vegas, stays in Vegas.

I snort to myself. Zoey makes me smile like a damn fool, but I don't even care. She's beautiful, funny, and I love being around her. She's cute without even having to try.

RILEY

Oh, the irony.

ZOEY

I bought it before the dare. But I kinda like it. Plus, it's pink. My favorite color.

RILEY

Duly noted. Look for the gorgeous lady in pink.

I hold back a groan as I imagine her perfect pink nipples I sucked on.

ZOEY

What's your favorite color?

RILEY

Blue.

ZOEY

Good to know.

I shoot her a winky emoji before sending another message.

RILEY

Save me a spot. See you soon, wife!

I'm cheesing all the way to the shop. She was already up early, which is surprising, but maybe that means she fits in more than she realizes.

"Jesus, it looks like you have a hanger in your mouth." Diesel rolls his eyes as we walk inside the office. Nothing could bring me down from this high. Not even his morning grumpiness.

"Better get used to it," I singsong.

Fisher narrows his eyes the moment he sees me. "Are you still drunk from last night or something?"

Diesel chuckles, shaking his head.

"Nope. Sober as can be. What's on the agenda today?" I ask before taking a sip of coffee.

"Your dad wants you in the shop to help him cut wood for the horse corral," he says.

"What? Jackson's building another one?" I ask because this is news to me.

"Yep. Kiera talked him into adding on."

I smirk. Of course she did. Aunt Kiera could talk Jackson into almost anything.

"And what about me?" Diesel asks, folding his arms over his chest.

"Regular duties, then I need you to run into town for a pickup," Fisher explains, looking down at his planner instead of at Diesel.

"Great. Bye." He's out the door before I've even moved my feet, mainly because he hates being around my cousin.

"You two ever gonna kiss and make up?" I ask Fisher.

"As soon as he pulls that stick out of his ass," he remarks. "He's the one with the problem. Not me."

I roll my eyes. Easy for him to say, I suppose. "Well, you have a few more months here. Might want to find a way to get over your beef."

"Tell that to your boy."

"I bet punching you in the face would make him feel better, but hey, that's just me," I taunt, walking toward the shop. "See ya."

Pulling out the cutter and sawhorses, I set up what we'll need to measure and cut the large pieces for the posts. My dad arrives minutes later with my mom on his heels talking a hundred miles an hour.

Before I can announce I'm here, my dad grabs my mom, cups her face, and kisses her hard. He tilts his head so his hat doesn't smack her as she wraps her arms around his waist. It's adorable how they're still so in love after all these years, and it gives me hope for a long and happy marriage too. However, the second my mother moans, I'm done.

"Excuse me," I say, clearing my throat obnoxiously loud. "This is how childhood traumatic stories are born."

They break apart, not in the least embarrassed as they scowl at me. "You're not a child anymore," my mother retorts.

My dad shamelessly slides his hand down and cups her ass. "How do you think babies are born? Need a demo?" He waggles his brows, which has my mom laughing.

"Oh God. Y'all are too damn much." I groan. "You can do this project alone." I make a big show of ripping off my gloves, but my dad just rolls his eyes.

"And if you do need to know how babies are born, I can give you some pamphlets," my mom adds.

"I went to fifth grade health class. I'm good." I put my gloves back on and walk away. "When you two lovebirds are done making me sick, let's get to work."

"Hey, I'm your boss. Not the other way around," my dad quips.

I wave him off over my shoulder. Perhaps I should be happy they're still together, considering how many of my friends grew up in split households, but I could do without the over-the-top PDA.

My father finally joins me, and we start working. He blasts the radio and starts singing along to the ridiculous country songs. I don't even have it in me to give him shit for it because Diesel does the same thing.

At five until nine, I tell him I'm taking a break to grab a bite to eat at the B&B. He smirks, knowing I'll be meeting Zoey. I know he's still surprised about the marriage, but he understands my situation more than anyone.

I walk into the B&B after cleaning the sawdust off my shirt and jeans, trying not to look like a mess. Zoey's in one of the lounge chairs reading, so I walk up behind her and press my lips to her ear.

"I just found the prettiest woman here. Care to join me for breakfast?"

The woman jumps, nearly smacking me in the face with her book. I stumble back just as she turns and scowls at me. "What the hell do you think you're doing?"

Oh my God. It's not Zoey. Though she has the same hair color and build as her.

"Ma'am, I'm so sorry." I press a hand to my chest, mortified. "I thought you were someone else."

She continues shooting daggers at me, and when I look up, Zoey is standing across the room with an arched brow and a knowing smirk.

"You lost, cowboy?" Zoey saunters toward me as the other woman walks away. I try to apologize to her again before she's out of sight, but she ignores me. No doubt, Uncle John will hear about it.

"I swear, from the back..." I extend my arm to prove that from the angle and the chair, it really looked like her. Defeated, I give up and slump my shoulders. "Fuck it. She was obviously not you."

Zoey chuckles, closing the gap between us and wrapping a hand around my neck. "Well, now that you have the *right* one, what are you gonna do about it?"

Popping a brow, I grab her waist and pull her lips to mine.

"Excuse me?" The sound of my father's voice has us breaking away. Fucking great.

Zoey pinches her lips together, bringing both of her arms behind her as if she's innocent. It makes me chuckle because we're not kids, but to anyone outside the family, my dad looks intimidating as hell. He's stacked like Diesel, but deep down, he's a softy.

"Weren't you just complainin' about me and your mom, and now you're making out in front of the entire place?" He grins at me when Zoey's eyes widen, and she blushes.

"I don't know what you're talkin' about." I grab Zoey's hand and squeeze. "We were just about to eat. Bye, Old Man."

"You be careful with that one," my dad warns when Zoey looks over her shoulder.

She smirks and nods. "Don't worry. I've been fully warned by basically everyone."

My dad laughs, and I hear him call out, "I like this one!"

"Your parents are so cute," Zoey says once we sit down with our plates full of food. "I wish my parents were more easygoing like yours. I can't remember the last time I've felt relaxed around them."

"Maybe they need a trip to the ranch," I tell her, only half-joking. "Everyone who comes here has a good time."

Zoey grins, cutting into her pancakes. "I can see why."

I eat slowly so I can spend as much time with her as possible. My dad will want me back shortly, but I'm not rushing even though I know I'll see her tonight.

"What do you plan to do today? Want to come watch me in the shop while my dad sings off-key?" I ask before shoving more eggs into my mouth.

"As exciting as that sounds, Mackenzie and Elle asked me to hang out, so I think I'm going to do that. Hopefully get back to the greenhouse too." I love how excited she sounds, and the way it promises she'll be staying.

"Whatever you do, don't listen to a word they say about me. It's not true," I say pointedly. "They're all liars."

Zoey nods with her lips tilted to one side. "Right. I'm sure they are."

"I'm glad they're being so welcoming, though, and I'm sure Aunt Mila loves your help with the gardens."

"She'll probably be sick of me soon."

"Doubtful. She's too nice to get sick of anyone."

"I love the idea of growing your own food, and the way you all use it for the B&B and sell the extras to the locals in town. Everyone knows it was grown with care," Zoey says.

"It's how small towns and ranches are around here."

"It's refreshing. Phoenix is great, but there's just something about this place…"

"I've heard that all my life from my mama, who's a Texas transplant. Aunt Mila lived in Georgia before she moved here. My dad's friend, Dylan's wife, moved from Florida. They met on the same trip as my mom and dad. They all moved here, so…"

"So it's a curse?" she teases.

"It's the Bishop genes," my grandmother interrupts, taking a seat next to me. "They pretend to be all macho, but once they find their woman, they turn to mush. Trust me." She winks at Zoey, who smiles in return.

"I believe it. Something about the Southern drawl. I bet it's caused a lot of hearts to break, too."

"Now that would be my son, Jackson. You wouldn't believe what he put Kiera through before he finally got his stubborn ass in gear."

I always laugh when she swears.

"I'm serious…" she continues. "Kiera was engaged to another man before Jackson finally confessed his feelings."

"Oh that's right," I say, remembering this story from years ago.

"All his brothers got their crap together when their special ladies came into their lives, but Jackson? No, he's always been my wild child," Grandma continues, looking at me. "Glad you've decided to take after your father. From the moment your mother came to town, he was attached to her at the hip. Always so protective and caring and making sure she wasn't doing anything strenuous when she was pregnant with you. Wasn't exactly happy they were expecting you before marriage, but he made it right. So that's what counts."

Grandma Bishop is very traditional, but she also knows shit happens.

"And even twenty-three years later, he's still a whipped pussy boy," I blurt out, waiting for the moment my grandma scolds me for my language, but she just narrows her eyes.

"And every Bishop man has been when he finds the one. They don't always fall in love easily, but when they finally do, they fall hard and fast."

"Are you talkin' about me again, Mama?" My dad strolls in and sits next to Zoey. Great, it's a breakfast reunion.

"The one and only."

"What is this?" Uncle John stands at the front of the table. "Y'all on breaks?"

"I'm giving them marriage advice," Grandma responds curtly, arching her brow at him, and he backs off. "And if you'd like some, sit down."

John groans and uncrosses his arms. "Nah, I've had enough of that to last me a lifetime."

"Okay, well I'm very busy today, and Zoey has plans, so we're gonna get going." I stand, and Zoey follows, realizing that I'm trying to get us out of this.

"It was lovely talking with you all," she says politely before we carry our plates to the kitchen.

"So you were saying about there being something special about this place...?" I tease, pulling her back to me.

"I spoke too soon." Zoey tries to fight a smile but fails.

Then I press my lips to hers before reluctantly pulling back. "Let me take you horseback riding tonight. Give you the VIP ranch tour."

Her eyes widen as her lips part. "I've never been riding before, but I'm always up to new adventures."

I smirk at how cute she looks. "And who better to teach you than your cowboy husband?"

The rest of the workday drags on. I'm eager to see Zoey again and actually get some alone time with her. At least while riding, every single family member won't be able to interrupt us.

"What in the world...?" I smile the moment Zoey meets me outside. She's in full getup from the cowboy hat to the plaid shirt tucked into her ripped jeans. As I glance down, I see she's wearing Rowan's cowboy boots too. "Look at you."

"Whatcha think?" She spins when she's in front of me. "Mackenzie said if I was going riding, I needed to look the part."

"Well, she's not wrong." I grab her waist and pull her closer. "You look adorable," I tell her, tugging on one of her pigtail braids. "However, these are giving me bad ideas…" I grin.

"Mackenzie insisted on those too."

"Hmm…she's quickly becoming my favorite cousin."

Zoey smacks my chest with a giggle. "Calm down, cowboy. You have some teaching to do."

We walk hand in hand to the horse barn. It's close to the B&B, and Dad's friend Colton works there mostly. He keeps them fed and groomed for the guests and guides all the riding lessons and tours. Luckily, he's gone for the day by the time we walk in, so we'll have this time to ourselves, completely uninterrupted.

"This one is Sunshine," I tell her. "She'll take good care of you."

Then I show her how to put on the saddle, help her up, and give her a basic rundown. "Don't squeeze your thighs too tight, or she'll think it's time to run."

"I definitely won't."

"Don't worry. She's a good girl." I pet her before getting my horse Gable ready, and soon, we're both riding out to one of the trails behind the B&B.

"It's so pretty out here," she says as we ride farther onto the trail. "No wonder so many come to the B&B. I overheard quite a few people talking about how they visit every single summer."

"Oh yeah, we get a lot of repeat guests. Have for years. It's what helps us stay in business too."

We continue riding, and Zoey stays quiet as I go on about the ranch and the different trails we have. Then I look at her and see her face is expressionless.

"Are you okay?" I move Gable closer to her so I can grab her hand. "You haven't said anything in a while."

Zoey clears her throat before looking at me, and I'm almost certain I see tears in her eyes. "Yeah, I'm fine. Just taking it all in."

"Are you sure?" I squeeze her hand, hoping she'll open up to me. "You can tell me."

She shrugs. "I'm just really glad I came. For days before getting in my car and making the twelve-hour drive, I worried I was making the wrong decision and fought with myself about the *what-ifs* and being a nervous wreck about your reaction. But you and your family have all brought me in with arms wide open. I guess it makes me a little emotional because I know if it were the other way around and you came to me, my family wouldn't be so welcoming."

I nod, wanting to somehow reassure her that I couldn't be happier that she's here. It was a risk for both of our hearts.

"Zoey, come here." I manage to get the horses next to each other so I can cup her face. "If I had it my way, I'd never let you leave. I'm sorry your family isn't very supportive, but you will always have mine, no matter what. Okay?"

She pulls in her bottom lip and nods. Tilting her head up, I press my mouth to hers, and when she opens up for me, I slide my tongue between her lips. When Zoey moans against me, I deepen our kiss, and then she's yelping in the next second.

Sunshine takes off, and Zoey barely has the time to grab on to the saddle horn. Immediately, I kick Gable and chase after them. "Loosen your legs and pull back on the reins!" I yell.

"I can't!" she screams as her hat flies off, her hair blowing in the wind.

Seconds later, I'm next to her again, taking control until Sunshine slows down. I'm trying hard not to laugh at her, but when I see her *holy shit* expression, I can't hold it in.

"Stop laughing at me, asshole!" She swats at my arm. "Your horse nearly killed me!"

I snicker, bringing us closer again. "I told you not to squeeze your legs."

Her eyes widen as a blush creeps up her neck. "Well then, you shouldn't be kissing me like that…"

Chuckling, I hand the reins back to her. "Noted."

CHAPTER TWELVE

Zoey

The past few days with Riley have been nothing short of perfection. We meet for breakfast, sometimes lunch, and then we hang out at night once he's done with work. I've been getting to know his aunts and cousins, helping them in the garden, and even baked cookies with his grandma yesterday afternoon. The Bishops are the kind of family I've never had, and it's making my decision even harder. I have to go back home eventually to confess everything to my parents and face the truth, but I'm not ready to leave yet.

Tonight, Riley insisted on making dinner for me at his house. Every time I come over, he kicks Diesel out, and though I always feel bad about that, he reassures me Diesel will be just fine. It's been fun seeing the dynamic of their friendship too. They're just as obnoxious and playful as they were in Vegas. The closest friend I have in Phoenix is my sister, who's now married and playing the role of the perfect wife.

Before Riley and I part ways each night, he always kisses me good night.

In Vegas, after the alcohol fog cleared, I remembered everything from our amazing night together. My body hasn't forgotten the way he touched me, how he set me on fire, and what it felt like to wake up next to him. I want more than just heated kisses, but I also need confirmation that there's more than just hot sex between us, so we need to resist the urge.

Though it's getting really damn hard when he winks and looks at me with that sexy smirk. It's as if he knows my weaknesses and is just waiting for me to break.

Those dirty thoughts consume me as I stare at his tight ass in those jeans as he stirs something on the stovetop. After work, he showered, and now I'm ready to pounce. The man looks good in literally anything. Tonight he's wearing a ball cap, which I find equally as sexy. Riley's shirt looks painted on, showing off his pecs and biceps, and if the man doesn't put out soon, I might combust.

"Are you enjoying the view?" he asks without looking over his shoulder.

I grab my glass of wine and take a sip. "I thought dinner came with the scenery." Forcing my eyes off him, I look out the window above the kitchen sink.

"You know I can see your reflection, right?"

When I look closer, I see a smirk planted on his lips. "I don't know what you're talking about."

"Mmhmm." He chuckles before turning off one of the burners, then spins around to face me.

"You keep looking at me like that, we won't make it to dessert." He's in front of me in two long strides, planting his feet between my thighs as I sit on the barstool. Riley's kitchen has an island with a breakfast bar, a nice marble countertop, and stainless steel appliances. It looks nothing like what I expected of a ranch cottage, but he told me they remodeled it a few years ago. It's quite impressive.

"Well, it's really not fair. Could you wear a garbage bag or something?"

He pops a brow. "And what? You think you're innocent in all of this?"

"What? I'm just sitting here!" I defend, squeezing my thighs around his legs.

Riley doesn't take his eyes off mine as he grabs my hand and slides it over his jeans. I feel his erection against my palm and hold back a smile, knowing I'm the reason for it.

"Does making pasta always make you this horny?" I quip, keeping a straight face. "Pasta-arousalitis? Is that a thing? You might want to see a doctor about that. Actually, more like a psychiatrist."

"Funny," he says, amused, arching his hips further into my hand. "Pretty sure I've had one since the day I met you."

"Now you *really* might want to see a doctor for that. I imagine it hurts." I lick my lips as I keep my hand on him. *Does he have any idea how much self-control it's taking not to rip off his clothes right now?*

"Same, babe."

I blush. "Shit. I hadn't meant to say that aloud."

"Well…you did," Riley growls deeply. Then he leans down, placing a hand on each side of me on the island counter so our eyes are level. "I haven't forgotten our night together, Zoey. How could I? But we're taking it slow, so that means no more eye fucking me, okay? Otherwise, my willpower will snap."

I inhale a sharp breath at how close he is to me, how much I want to smack my lips to his, and how sexy his voice sounds. God, I'm in so much trouble.

Swallowing hard, I nod, then press my palms to his chest to create some space. I know before we move to the next level, we need to discuss what happened after I left Vegas. "Fine, then you have to do the same."

Riley grins as he shakes his head, moving toward the stove. "Perhaps we both need to wear sunglasses around each other." He turns around and checks the sauce.

I roll my eyes. The man is no fun. "Or you could just take me to your room and fuck me all night long?"

He freezes, his back going stiff as he looks to the side. I watch as he opens his mouth, then slams it shut. The poor guy, I've made him speechless.

Holding back my laughter, I continue, "But if you insist, we can eat dinner."

I help him serve our food. He made a chicken pasta dish that smells delicious. Then he made a side of veggies from the garden, and after taking the first bite, I release an exaggerated moan .

"Where did you learn to cook?" I ask, knowing most men his age have no clue.

"My grandmother. And my mom. After I moved out of the house, I had to fend for myself, so I continued to practice what they had taught me. My mother thinks I'm incapable, though, so she invites me to dinner a few times a week. Of course I don't pass up the opportunity. Diesel usually tags along too."

"So weird question..." I start with a hint of a smile. "Diesel. What's his real name? Does anyone actually know? I've asked all your cousins, and no one seems to have the answer."

Riley starts laughing and nods. "It's because no one ever calls him by it, and after a while, you forget it's not his real name."

"Are you gonna tell me?" I tease. "Or am I supposed to guess?"

Riley smirks. "It's Adam."

"Really?" I shriek. "Wow, I don't see that at all."

We both laugh.

"Yep, but only his mama calls him that."

"I'm going to say it next time I see him just for fun and see if he reacts," I mock. "Considering he teases me every chance he gets."

"That's only because he knows asking about Summer riles you up," Riley tells me.

"She's married!" I protest but chuckle, thinking about it. "He spent the night with Chelsea. She talked about it for a week straight." I roll my eyes because even though I hooked up with Riley, I kept the details to myself.

"Does Summer know you're here?" he asks, which catches me off guard slightly.

I exhale slowly and look down. "No. I didn't tell anyone. She thinks I signed the papers, and everything got taken care of before my parents found out, but..."

"But what?" he pushes.

"They wouldn't approve," I admit softly. "They want a certain lifestyle for me and have been very vocal about that for as long as I can remember, so I knew telling them would only make things worse. Instead, I explained that I needed to clear my head and planned a road trip. I've done it a few times before, so they didn't think anything about it. But the truth is, I needed time away from them and their expectations to really see what it was that *I* wanted."

KENNEDY FOX

I look up and see his stony expression. "And what's that, Zoey? What do you want?" His question comes out harsh, but I don't blame him.

"That's what I'm trying to figure out," I say softly. "This past week has changed a lot for me, and I'm still trying to process it all. Standing up to my parents won't be easy, it never has been, and I don't want to disappoint them. If they knew I was here, they'd find a way to force me to come home."

Riley narrows his eyes at me, dropping his fork. "Zoey, you're twenty-one years old. You're allowed to have your own life and want things for yourself that they might not agree with or condone, but that doesn't mean you can't have them."

This is so not how I wanted our conversation to go. Talking about my overbearing parents always puts me in a sour mood.

"I know that, Riley, but it's easier said than done. I couldn't afford to move out, so I still live with them. And I'm a hairdresser, so it's not like I'm rolling in a lot of money. I save as much as possible so I can escape from time to time, but when I've constantly lived in my sister's shadow, it's hard not to feel like a disappointment. After seeing the way your family is and how everyone loves each other unconditionally, it's a bit much to take in. I wish I had that kind of support, but I don't, so whatever I decide is going to change things. Whether it's deciding to stay here or going home and living life the way they see fit—this trip will change everything."

"What's your heart telling you right now? What is it *you* want, Zoey? Don't think about your parents or the consequences."

This should be an easy answer. Stay here. Be with him. Make a life together.

But I don't say any of those things.

"My heart is torn," I say instead, lowering my eyes because I can't bear to disappoint him.

"Zoey." He says my name firmly, causing me to look at him. "Stay with me tonight."

My lips tilt into a smile at the sweet way he's looking at me. "Okay."

"Sit still," I repeat for the third time, laughing at his eagerness. After dinner, I asked if I could give him a haircut since it was starting to get long on the sides and in the back. Once I confirmed he had a grooming kit, I made him sit on a stool and wrapped a towel around his shoulders. "I'm going to give you a backward mohawk if you keep wiggling."

"Then stop breathing on my neck and making my thoughts turn naughty," he says, side-eyeing me.

"I have no clue what you're talking about, Mr. Bishop." I brush my fingers along his neck to wipe away pieces of hair.

"Really? Do you touch all your clients so seductively?"

"Of course. I work for tips, ya know?" I tease. "Why do you think my hands are so soft? I use lotion daily. It's what keeps them coming back."

"That's not even funny," he hisses.

"You know…" I move between his legs to make sure everything is even in the front and sides. "I wouldn't have thought you'd be the possessive type when I first saw you. But…I can't say I hate it." I smirk, not looking into his eyes as I brush my fingers through his hair.

He grips my waist, then pulls me closer until I cave and bend down. Riley wraps a hand around my neck and brings our mouths together. "Only you've brought that out in me," he says against my lips. "Knew you for a few hours and already wanted to murder any man who dared to look at you. And trust me, at those clubs, they were lookin'."

I smile at his words. I've never met a man who was so open about his feelings and didn't play any childish games, or hell, a man who actually paid attention to me instead of his phone.

"Well, I hadn't noticed because my eyes were only focused on you," I tell him honestly. "I was afraid if I blinked, you'd disappear or something."

Riley grins, grabbing my thighs to pull me down to straddle him. "Are you done with my hair yet?"

Nodding, I wrap my arms around his neck and position myself on top of him. "That'll be three hundred dollars, sir."

Riley chokes, causing me to burst out laughing. "For a trim?"

"You're paying for my upbeat and *very* personal service."

"Oh, of course. How foolish of me not to consider that. Think you could take an IOU? I'm a little short on bullshit this month." He brings our mouths closer.

"Hmm…I think we could arrange something."

CHAPTER THIRTEEN

Riley

Having Zoey here for the past week has been amazing. We've quickly fallen into a routine, and I just wish I had more time. Eventually, she'll decide if she's staying permanently or returning to Arizona. It's something I've tried to push to the back of my mind because losing her for good would be too much. I'm not stupid and understand her whole life is back in Phoenix. We can't last forever the way we are now. Things will have to change.

At first, she was concerned that my family wouldn't like her or accept our marriage, but I knew they'd see what I saw in her the first time we met. However, since we're only testing this out, and they've already fallen in love with her, I won't be the only heartbroken one if she leaves. The thought makes me fucking sick to my stomach.

I take a sip of water and watch my dad, changing the oil in a tractor.

"Wanna give me a hand?" he asks with grease on his face.

I walk over and pick up the spare parts.

"How are things going with the wife?" he asks, grabbing a wrench and removing bolts.

I snort. "Wow, it sounds weird when you ask me questions like that."

"Well, you're a married man now. My little baby boy is all grown up." He chuckles.

"Shut up, Old Man."

"You gonna make me a grandpa already?" He looks up at me with an arched eyebrow.

"Not planning on it yet." This conversation is awkward as hell.

Dad replaces the oil filter and fills the tractor, then goes back to tightening everything the way it was. "Look, son. I know you got it bad when it comes to Zoey, but I want you to be careful. You two rushed into this quite fast, and I don't want you to get hurt." Dad searches my face, wiping his greasy hands on his pants. Mom's gonna kill him. Trying to get stains out of his clothes is one of her pet peeves.

I look out over the horizon and focus on the rolling hills in the distance as I lean against the hot metal of the tractor. "I know."

"You signed the annulment papers. She wouldn't have sent them if she didn't have doubts," he continues. "Her life is in Phoenix. Is she really willing to give that up? Being here on the ranch in the middle of nowhere is a lot to take in. Trust me, it's a huge change for those city girls, and it takes some adjusting. At first, it seems like a vacation, and then the newness wears off. We love it because it's in our genes, but this life isn't for everyone. You know that."

I think back on all the things Zoey and I have talked about over the past week. Her parents, her life, her job, all of it. "If we're meant to be, it will be. I'm not forcing anything, but I know deep in my heart she's the one. The way she makes me feel, Dad. It's real. There's no pretending when we're together. I don't have any doubts."

All he does is nod. I wonder if Ma is worried about me getting hurt too. Being married is a change, for damn sure, but one I'm willing to make. All I want is for Zoey to be happy. We deserve each other in a way that I don't think most people understand. I know that down to the core of my being. Zoey. *My wife*. I'm completely in-fucking-fatuated with her. Though everything happened so quickly, it's already impossible to imagine her not being in my life. I've never met anyone like her before.

"You know, it only took a few days for me to feel the same way about your mother, yet there was a point in my life when I didn't know if I'd ever see her again, and it practically destroyed me. It worked out for us, but not everyone is so lucky. I support you and whatever you do. I know you're smitten, that much is obvious, but marriage isn't easy once the honeymoon phase wears off. There are ups and downs, and you gotta be able to communicate and work through them. Spend this time really getting to know her. Everything about her. The good, the bad, and the ugly. And she needs to know your quirks too."

"Thankfully, I don't have anything to hide. Open book right here." I shrug.

Dad laughs. "Whatever you say."

We finish working on the tractor, and he starts it up, then moves it back into the barn. After he hops off, I look at him.

"Mom put you up to talking to me, didn't she?" I arch a brow at him, suspicious.

The smirk gives him away. "Even though I'm not concerned about you, she is. You're a Bishop, so I know how this works. It's hard for women to walk away from us because we're so damn addicting." He winks, not at all too proud to admit it.

I shake my head, chuckling. "And that's exactly how I was born."

After we're finished, I check my phone and see I have a text from my mother to come over and pick up some leftovers. I show Dad, and he gives me a pointed look. Groaning, I release a slow breath. "Great."

"Might as well call it a day. We're pretty much done anyway. You better not make her wait. She's on the night shift and will be leaving soon," he tells me as I walk toward my truck.

I turn and look at him. "Anything else I need to know?"

"Just tell her you're using protection," he calls out, and I can see he's laughing when he turns around.

"I am!" I yell. I hop in the truck and drive across the property to my parents' house. I walk inside, take off my hat, and see Mom has containers stacked a mile high to the ceiling. Rowan's digging in the fridge, and Mom is nowhere to be found.

"Oh." She turns around and screams. "Who the fuck are you?"

I narrow my eyes at her and shake my head at her dramatics. "What're you talking about?"

"Riley, thank God." She holds her hand to her heart. "Didn't recognize you without your shaggy hair. Looks like your wife is changing you already. Gettin' haircuts and taking showers these days. Damn, ya got hitched and turned into a brand-new man. Who woulda thought?"

"Riley," my mother calls out from behind me. I turn around and see her dressed in scrubs with her hair in a high ponytail. Mom loves her job at the hospital, taking care of premature babies. She gives Rowan a pointed look, and within a few seconds, Rowan slinks out of the kitchen, and it's just us.

"Before you even say anything, we're using protection," I blurt out.

She tilts her head at me, giving me a confused look. "Good for you…"

I groan, realizing Dad set me up. "That's not what you wanted to talk to me about?"

Letting out a soft laugh, she grins. "I didn't want this food to go to waste. But I will admit I'm worried about you falling too hard and too fast, and then things not working out the way you want them to."

Glancing over at her, I scrub my palms over my face and exhale deeply. "Do you like Zoey?" I ask as she places the containers in reusable bags.

I know I'm putting her on the spot, but I have to know.

She moves closer to me, patting my cheek as she's done since I was a young boy. "Yes, I do. I think she's a nice girl."

"That's all I need to know. Ma, I already got the speech from Dad today. I know y'all care about me and think this could end badly, but Zoey's special, and it's all gonna work out."

"I don't think a girl would come all this way for nothing, Riley. It's obvious she genuinely cares about you. I see the way she looks at you. How she laughs at your jokes. There's admiration there, and she respects you. But is it enough to keep her here?"

I nod, halfway wondering that myself but believe it is. "It's enough right now." My phone buzzes in my pocket, and I see it's a text from Zoey telling me to meet her at the B&B in an hour. "I gotta go. I love you, Ma." I give her a kiss on the cheek, grab the extra food, and leave. On the drive home, all I can do is smile, because I know my parents care enough about me to support what makes me happy.

I stack the containers in the fridge, jump in the shower, and wash away the grease and dirt from my day. As I'm leaving, Diesel saunters in looking exhausted as hell. He stupidly volunteered to help brand cattle today, which is hard as fuck, but he loves it.

"Oh look, it's my best friend I never see anymore," he says smugly, walking past me. "Bros before hoes!" He goes to the kitchen and grabs a beer, then plops down on the couch in his dirty, cow shit smelling clothes.

"Dude! You stink like ass, and you're sitting on our furniture." I walk over and kick his muddy boots off the coffee table.

He bursts out into a hefty laugh. "I do, don't I? I should probably shower and call your sister since you won't hang out with me anymore."

Pretty sure he says things like that just to see the steam blow from my ears. "I'll kick your ass!"

He puckers his lip and shrugs as if that consequence isn't a good enough reason to stay away. "I'd deserve it because I don't know boundaries, if you know what I mean." He waggles his eyebrows at me, smirking like a dipshit.

"That's fine. Just let my dad find out. That second son card will be revoked *so* quick," I warn, but he's waving me off and chuckling.

"Seriously, though, I don't blame you for ditching me. If Zoey was here for me, I'd call in sick every day from blue balls." Diesel shakes his head. "Don't know how you're surviving."

"It's only been a week," I retort, though I'm wondering the same thing. "But I gotta run. She's waiting for me. And *stay away* from my sister." I jab my finger hard into his chest. "I'm serious."

"We'll see," he taunts. "Don't you want me as a brother-in-law?" He proceeds to kick off his dirty boots, dried mud falling on the floor.

"Hell no," I say with a smirk. "That'll be the day hell freezes over."

He shrugs. "Imma make you an uncle one day!"

"Fuck off!" I yell before I leave.

Diesel knows exactly what to say to get under my skin. I've always been so damn protective of Rowan and hate that I can't keep her away from all the assholes when she's at college. Protecting her isn't something I can do forever, and even though it might be useless, I can at least try to scare Diesel and any other local guys away. Rowan's a grown ass woman and will do what she wants either way.

I listen to the pop station on the way over to the B&B, which reminds me of when Zoey and I danced in Vegas at the clubs, and when we slow danced at the Honky Tonk. I smile when I see her walking outside as I pull up and park.

"It's almost as if you have a husband tracker on me or something," I say once I pull her into my arms, then slant my mouth over hers. She moans, and I don't know how much longer I can hold back. Just being around her lights a fire inside me, and it's about to burn me alive.

"I missed you," she admits, grinning. Hearing her say that is music to my ears.

I tilt her chin up and smile. "I missed you too, wifey." It's so easy being with her. I wish I could freeze time, and things could always feel this way.

"I really want to show you something!" Excitement fills her voice as she grabs my hand and leads the way.

As I glance over at her, a smile splits my face at how natural this feels as we walk past the horse barn toward the back of the property where Mila's gardens are happily growing. She points to the little sign at the end of the row. I bend down and read it. *Arizona Row.* Zoey points out the three rows of vegetables that she planted and how the seedlings are already growing.

"Look at all of them." She spins around proudly. "They germinated quickly. Mila says I have a green thumb."

I move closer to her, and she wraps her arms around my neck. "That's great, sweetheart. I can't wait to eat them, whatever they are."

She kisses me on my nose before breaking away, pointing out all the different vegetables she planted and how you can tell what it is by the shape of the leaves. Seeing her so happy like this makes me confident that she's not going anywhere. I don't even want to bring it up, but I know the clock is ticking, and soon, a decision will need to be made. I just hope it's the right one for both of us.

CHAPTER FOURTEEN

Zoey

The past two weeks have been magical. I feel as if I'm living someone else's life and can't get over how in love I am with the ranch and how deeply I'm falling for Riley. Every day is different but somewhat the same. It's scorching hot, but the water is cold, and the food is delicious, so I can't even complain. The B&B serves some of the best meals I've ever eaten, and I'm getting spoiled by everyone being so friendly. I know it's not fake either because the Bishops treat anyone who walks through that door like family regardless of their shape, size, or color. If you're on the ranch, you're family.

Earlier this week, Riley took me on a tour of Eldorado. It's so cute and quaint like a town in a country Hallmark movie. I'd seen it once before when we went to the bar, but my nerves were so shot that it was hard to pay attention to anything other than my internal doubts. While we were there, Riley took me to the bakery Mila's cousin, Kat, owns that specializes in all gluten-free pastries. She's an extended part of the Bishop family and welcomed me just like one too. Her shop makes muffins and other treats for the B&B, which I've already tasted from there. Kat refused to let me leave without sending me off with a cupcake, slice of lemon cake, and a pudding pie, all gluten-free. She suggested we hold another ceremony for everyone to attend and even volunteered to bake us a wedding cake. While I couldn't commit to the idea, it was an extremely generous offer because her desserts are to die for.

I've been spending a lot of my time with Mila in the greenhouses, and she's been like an aunt to me who offers advice without judgment. She listens to me discuss my previous adventures, travels, and now being a newlywed. She explained how she met John and how it was awkward for them at first, considering he was a single dad and she was Maize's nanny, but Maize has proudly called her Mom her whole life. Intelligent doesn't even begin to describe Mila. I can't help but wonder if life will always be this easy on the ranch. Could I always be this happy? As long as Riley is with me, I think so.

Last night when we were at the bar drinking and dancing, Riley told me he wanted to take me out today. After I had mentioned how much I loved hitting the trails at home, he insisted that we go, so we made plans to spend the day together since he's off today. This ranch boasts at least twenty miles of trails, mostly for the horses, but they're for hiking too. I'm so damn excited about it that I'm about ready to burst while I get dressed.

As soon as I walk downstairs, I see Riley coming toward me with a grin. He's wearing a baseball hat, shorts, running shoes, and a T-shirt that hugs him in all the right places. I'm not used to seeing him in athletic wear, but it's sexy as hell. In his hands, he's carrying two packs, and when he approaches, he hands me one.

"Thought you'd want a Camelbak full of water. It's gonna get hot out there coming back, and I don't want you to get dehydrated," he tells me, which I find so thoughtful. "I also packed some snacks."

I gawk at him, looking at him like he's a snack, and he notices. As he stands there, all delicious looking, all I think about is eating him up.

"Thanks," I say with a sweet smile. While the sun peeks just barely over the horizon now, I know how hot it gets before lunch, so I'm thankful. I was just going to carry bottles.

"There aren't any bears here, are there?" The concern on my face is evident.

414

He places his hand on my back and shakes his head. "No bears. Should be more concerned about rattlers than anything."

My eyes go wide. "Snakes?"

"Don't worry. I'll protect you, wifey." He winks, sending shivers up my spine—from both his gestures and my fear of getting bit. "I got us some walking sticks, and I'm not afraid to use it. Just be aware. Eyes always open and looking at the ground. You don't want to get bit out here." He leans over and grazes his teeth against the skin of my neck, and I laugh, pushing him away, though I can't deny the goose bumps that surface. All it takes is one touch, and my whole body comes alive, wanting him in every way possible.

We walk out of the B&B and head down the blue trail. Riley and I walk side by side, keeping the same comfortable pace. Neither of us is in any hurry to be anywhere but here, together.

"So since the goal is to get to know each other better while you're here, tell me whatcha wanna know. Ask me anything," he says with a smirk. "Give me your best."

I glance over at him and laugh. "Anything, *anything*?"

"If you have any burning questions"—he shrugs—"I have nothing to hide from you, Zoey. Trust is everything to me." I swallow hard. *Trust is everything.*

"Hmm, okay. When did you lose your virginity?" I throw out. "And to who?"

He snorts. "That's your burning question? I was sixteen, and it was with a girl I dated in high school. Dana Jones."

"Where is she now?" I ask.

"I think she's married with like four kids or something. I dunno, honestly. Didn't keep up with her after we broke up. But I hear some through the town gossip mill."

"Four kids? Geez. Did she start in high school or something? Wait, are they yours?" I tease.

"God, no. She married Billy Barnes right after graduation and basically popped them out one after another."

I laugh, wondering if that's common down here or something. According to his grandmother, women are basically expected to multiply as soon as they get hitched. Or at least that's her philosophy.

"So what about you?" His arm brushes against mine, and I lean into him. "What's your story?"

"Ha! Not much of a story. I was seventeen, and he was a guy I had dated for a short time, mostly to piss off my parents. Don't know what he's up to now. Probably in jail." I laugh, but I'm not joking.

"What type of guys do your parents want you to date? I'm guessing not the bad boys."

I swallow down a giant knot in my throat. "Doctor types."

It feels dirty coming out of my mouth, and I hate that it's even a thing.

"They wouldn't approve of me, then?" he asks straightforwardly.

I glance at him, not wanting to hurt his feelings. "Truthfully?"

The boyish grin doesn't leave his face as he nods.

"Probably not. My father has always wanted my sister and me to marry men who were of a certain prestige. Since he's a doctor, he wanted us to become or marry one and raise them." I groan just thinking about it.

"My mom's a nurse, and my uncle and aunt practice; does that count for anything?" He chuckles, and it's such an easygoing sound.

"If you were their kid, then maybe. But then they'd probably ask why you didn't go to med school too and think something was wrong with you —the same way they treat me." I roll my eyes, releasing a slow breath.

He grabs my hand. "I'm sorry."

"For what?" I ask.

"For feeling like you're not good enough, but honestly, fuck 'em. As long as I'm good enough for you, by your standards, that's all that matters to me. I didn't marry them. I married *you*."

I stop, and so does he. Searching his face, I grab his hands and pull him closer. "You're too good for me, Riley Bishop. I don't deserve you. Or the kindness you or your family has shown me. None of it." Guilt weighs heavy on my chest almost to the point of smothering me. I need to tell him the full truth of why I'm here before it blows up in my face, but I don't want to ruin our time together.

"Why would you say that?" Confusion is written all over his face as he pinches his brows.

I shake my head. "I think about the past two weeks and how incredible and welcoming you've been, and then I think about the future and everything. It's just a little overwhelming."

He sucks in a deep breath and runs his fingers across my cheek. "Then how about we don't? Let's just focus on the now."

Tipping my chin up, he crushes his lips to mine, and I inhale his scent. He's all I can smell. I'm completely and utterly encapsulated by him as he steals my breath away. Nothing else in the entire world matters at this moment. The only thing that pulls us apart is the sound of feet shuffling down the trail, and I see one of the women who's also staying at the B&B.

"Don't mind me, kids," she tells us as she walks past us, and we both hold back our laughter.

Riley leans forward and gives me another peck on the lips, and we continue. "Mrs. Dennison has the worst timing."

"Yeah, she does because if she would've been a minute later, I might've been riding you like a horse," I whisper.

He swallows hard and adjusts himself. "Don't you dare tease me, woman."

My laughter echoes on the path. Our conversation becomes lighthearted as we travel farther down the trail until we end up at a lookout on a hill. The trees are sparse, but we take cover from the brutal sun under one. We're both sweaty, but the smiles on our faces don't falter as we eat the granola bars he packed. Though it's hot, I can't seem to sit close enough to him under the shade. I could stay right here in this spot for the rest of my life. I've found my solace.

Riley and I stay like that for another thirty minutes before it's time to go.

"If you could do or have anything in the world, what would it be?" he asks as we head back.

"Change someone's life for the better," I say without thinking about it.

He falls in line beside me and holds my hand. "You've already done that, Zoey."

A blush hits my cheeks. He knows exactly what to say and when to say it. "I think I'm always searching for happiness. It's one of the reasons I do things on a whim, like travel and hike alone. It's all about the adventure to finding what's missing."

"What about now?"

I glance over at him and smile, not even having to lie. "I'm the happiest I've ever been in my life."

That adorable boyish grin touches his lips as we continue.

"What about you?"

"Now that I have you, I have everything in the world. And as crazy as it sounds, I'm doing exactly what I want to do. I work on the ranch with my family and have a hot wife. My life is made." He snickers, but his sexy smile is genuine.

"Well damn, you're easy to please," I tease. "I like that. A simple life on the ranch."

In the distance, I can see the B&B, and I'm sad our time together is almost up, but the sun has also kicked our asses, and we're sweating like crazy.

Riley brushes his hand over his chin, scrubbing through his facial hair as if he's contemplating his next words. "Could you see yourself spending forever here?" he asks me as we make our way up the back steps of the B&B. I turn around and look out at the land, see the sun high in the sky, and can hear laughter inside. From the corner of the barn, the edge of one of Mila's beautiful gardens is visible, and I think of everything I've experienced so far.

"That's still to be determined. Is there Wi-Fi?" I joke, but deep down, I know I do. The ranch is one of the only places I've ever felt at home and comfortable in my own skin. There isn't another place like it.

With a quick swoop, Riley picks me up and swings me over his shoulder, carrying me inside the B&B like a caveman.

"Oh my God! Put me down!" I can't stop laughing as I try to wiggle free from his strong grasp.

"Riley Bishop," his father says from a table. "Stop acting like that around the guests."

Riley lets out a booming laugh and sets me on my feet, and I playfully slap at him. "Listen to your father!"

"That old man? I'm married now and can do what I want!"

When his father stands and crosses his arms over his chest, glaring at him, Riley backs down quickly.

"That's what I thought," his dad says with a chuckle. "I might be an old man, but I'm not too old to whip your ass."

We sit with Alex and eat lunch as he talks about all the trouble Riley used to get into on the ranch. I laugh until I nearly choke on my food. It's safe to say he was a mischievous little kid, always getting into trouble and finding new ways to scare his parents.

Once our plates are empty, I tell Riley I need a shower. He's yawning and admits he wants to take a nap, which he deserves because he works like crazy. Before we say our goodbyes, we make plans to watch a movie later tonight.

I climb the stairs two at a time and rip my sweaty clothes off as soon as I walk into my room. I soak in the big iron tub and let the hot water soothe my sore muscles. We hiked nearly eight miles today, and my legs and feet feel every step. After I'm done washing my hair and body, I get out and see a missed call from my sister. Knowing I can't avoid her forever, I immediately call her back.

"Summer!" I say as soon as she answers.

"So you're alive?" she says dramatically. "That's good to know!" The sarcasm in her tone is evident, and I feel bad that I haven't stayed in contact with her. "I've been worried about you. Are you making your way back home?"

I stand at the window with a big fluffy towel wrapped around my body and look out at the land. "No, I don't think I am yet."

"What? You said you'd be gone for only two weeks, Zoey. Are you sure you're okay?"

I smile. "Yeah, I'm totally fine. I just decided to stay a little longer."

"Where are you exactly?" She's laying on the questions thick, and I don't want to lie to her, but I also don't want to tell her every detail of what's going on. While she knows about the marriage with Riley, she has no clue I'm here with him, and I'm not so sure she'd approve. This is something I had to do on my own; a decision I have to make without any outside noise —not even hers.

"I'm in Texas, enjoying my life before everything goes back to being so serious," I explain, and while I expect her to scold me, she doesn't, though by her tone, I think she's suspicious.

"Okay, I understand that. Just please take care of yourself. Promise me." She sounds worried, and I hate that I can't tell her the whole truth. I trust my sister, but I don't trust that my parents couldn't get the info out of her.

"I'm having the time of my life, and I've never been happier."

She laughs. "Well as long as you're happy, that's all that matters. And that you're coming home soon. We miss you."

"I miss you too," I tell her before we say our goodbyes. I change into a sundress, then collapse on the bed and close my eyes. Hours later, I'm woken up by the sound of my phone vibrating and see it's a text from Riley, telling me he's making dinner and to come over in thirty.

I get up and look out the window and see the sun has made its way across the sky. When I check the time, it's nearly five.

Pulling my hair into a messy bun, I slip on some flip-flops and hop in my car. I haven't driven anywhere in a couple of weeks since Riley usually drives. When I pull up to his house, it looks like every light is on, and knowing he's planned something for us tonight makes me smile. Instead of knocking, I walk straight into the kitchen and see him adding shredded cheese to the top of a handmade pizza. I wrap my arms around his back, and he jumps, then turns around.

"Holy shit. I thought you were Diesel," he barks out with a laugh.

"Is that how he normally greets you?" I snort, arching a suspicious brow. "Do I have some competition?"

Riley pulls me into his arms, resting his back against the counter. "There'd never be anyone compared to you." He buries his face in my neck. "You smell so fucking good."

"You do too." When he pulls back, I greedily press my lips against his, wanting all of him.

"Whoa, baby. Keep that up, and this pizza won't make it into the oven."

I giggle, shrugging. "I bet you'd taste better anyway."

He growls at my comment, acting tortured. "You're so beautiful," he says, searching my face and running his gaze down my body. "I'm so fucking lucky."

I kiss him again, never wanting this paradise to end. We eventually pull apart, and Riley slides the pizza into the oven. After he starts the timer, he pours us each a glass of wine. As I take a sip, I look at his twinkling blue eyes over the rim of the glass.

"So..." I begin, inhaling a deep breath to collect my thoughts. "I know I said I was staying for two weeks, but I'm thinking of extending my visit. If you'd be okay with that, of—"

"Abso-fucking-lutely," he blurts out before I can finish.

When the words leave his lips, I feel as if I'm floating. The way he looks at me, treats me, kisses me—it's everything I've ever wanted and needed. Life without Riley Bishop wouldn't be worth living, and I had to make sure, though my heart already knew the answer. Once I make an official decision, my entire life will change. For the better.

Riley leads me to the living room, and we take a seat on the couch. "Next week is Independence Day. Grandma and Grandpa Bishop always have a party behind their house with a huge fireworks display. Everyone brings food, and we make a whole day out of it. Come with me."

"That sounds like a blast. I've never really done anything on the Fourth of July," I tell him, setting my wine glass on the coffee table, then I take his and put it next to mine to free his hands.

"I'm so fucking glad you're staying longer," he says with a wide grin.

I take the opportunity to straddle his lap, and when I grind my hips down on him, I feel his hard length. I move forward and capture his lips with mine, wrapping my arms around his neck and rocking my body against his. I need this man like I need air, and the only thing that stops us from continuing is the timer beeping in the kitchen.

"Let the motherfucker burn," Riley whispers against my lips, his palms cupping my ass and pulling me closer.

I let out a laugh. "But I'm starving," I say, my head dizzy from him.

"I'm starving too…for you, but shit, I don't want to set the place on fire." He lets out a frustrated growl as I crawl off him. Standing, he adjusts himself, and I giggle at his scowl. I follow him into the kitchen, and he removes the pizza from the oven, the edges already dark and crisp.

"This is your fault," he says with a smirk.

"It's just a little burnt," I tease.

"I was talking about this." He cups his dick through his jeans, and I laugh, knowing I'm feeling just as sexually frustrated. However, it's probably a good thing we stopped ourselves since we're using this time to get to know each other better. Regardless of how tempting it is.

Riley Bishop's the whole package, and he's mine.

CHAPTER FIFTEEN

Riley

Today's the family's big Fourth of July party, and I'm so excited Zoey decided to stay longer so she wouldn't miss it. These past few weeks have been some of the best of my life, and I want her here permanently. Ever since last weekend, when she said she wasn't leaving just yet, I've been toying with the idea of telling her how I really feel. If she's willing to take the risk, then so am I.

Every morning when I wake up, I'm grateful, but now I have more to look forward to. I love seeing Zoey randomly throughout my day and meeting up with her when I'm able.

When we hung out last Saturday, things heated up between us as they typically do, but this time, we almost didn't stop. The truth is, I'm ready to be one-hundred percent married to her and move her into my house. I want to wake up with her every morning and fall asleep with her in my arms. It's all I think about, and tonight, I'm more determined than ever to tell her. Even if I'm risking my heart, I need to lay it all out there.

Diesel and I are up earlier than normal to get a head start since we'll be cutting our workday short. Though we'll be helping with the party and fireworks, the animals still need to be fed and watered.

"You ready to blow shit up tonight?" Diesel taunts as we make our way back to the shop and wrap everything up for the day. "I overheard Rowan is bringing a guy. You ready for that?"

I snap my head toward him, brows furrowed in confusion. This is news to me. "Who? What guy?"

"I don't know; some dude she met at the bar. Told you it was a bad idea for her to work there," he huffs, and I can't tell if he's genuinely concerned about it or just jealous. My guess is on the latter, but I know every person in this town, so he better be a decent guy, or he's going to be meeting my fist.

"So I guess that means you'll be taking it out on the fireworks tonight?" I snicker, opening up the shop door and walking in.

Fisher's in the office, organizing the desk. "Done already?" he asks, then looks up.

"Yep," I answer.

"Because we fuckin' rock," Diesel adds. "Gotta get ready for the party."

"Is it gonna be a problem that I come tonight?" Fisher asks me, but then his gaze goes to Diesel.

"No, why would it?" I ask, then walk to the fridge for a water.

"Well, I'd be bringing Gretchen. But if it's gonna be a problem, then I won't." Fisher crosses his arms over his chest, but he's not being a dick about it. He's asking because he's honestly trying not to cause issues, so I respect that.

"D?" I ask, tilting my chin at him. "You gonna be on your best behavior later, or am I gonna have to kick my best friend's drunk ass afterward?"

He scoffs, stealing the bottle from my grip. "Like you could." He unscrews the top and gulps half of it down, then turns to Fisher. "Yeah, man, it's fine. I won't say anything."

My brows rise, impressed by how mature he's being. "Good man, Diesel." I pat his shoulder, yanking my water back. "But that doesn't mean you can fuck up whoever Rowan's bringing."

Diesel points at me, his eyes narrowed. "Now that I didn't agree to."

I roll my eyes and wave to Fisher, telling him we'll see him later. Diesel and I head to my truck and drive home to shower and clean up before the party.

While I wait for Diesel's slow ass to get out of the shower, I sit on the couch and take out my phone.

RILEY

You excited to see some real fireworks tonight?

ZOEY

I sure am, cowboy, though I've been feeling sparks for weeks ;)

RILEY

Are you hittin' on me, wife?

ZOEY

Maybe. What if I am?

RILEY

I'd say don't bother wearing any clothes tonight.

ZOEY

Are all cowboys as dirty as you?

RILEY

I wouldn't know...but this one...is only for you.

ZOEY

I like that your grandmother thinks I'm a sweet, innocent angel. She even told me yesterday when I was helping her bake for today. I'd hate to tarnish that image.

RILEY

What my grandma doesn't know won't kill her. It'll be our little secret :)

ZOEY

You're relentless...

RILEY

It's your fault. Stop looking sexy as hell and eye-fucking me every time you see me.

ZOEY

Oh do I? Sorry, that was meant for Diesel. My bad.

I growl even though she can't hear me and send her an unamused emoji face. Immediately, I get a laughing emoji, then two red hearts.

RILEY

I'll kill him.

ZOEY

Turtlenecks and sweatpants from now on. Don't go murdering anyone.

RILEY

Doesn't matter what you wear. I'll be picturing you naked either way.

ZOEY

OMG...you are naughty.

RILEY

I am...you should spank me.

ZOEY

LOL... I'm done with you. BYE.

"You gonna shower, or are ya just gonna sit there with a dumb grin on your face?" Diesel asks as he walks into the living room fully dressed.

"Yeah, might be an extra-long one, though." I chuckle, sliding my phone into my pocket.

"Is this where you tell me to get lost tonight?" He deadpans. "Go find somewhere else to stay?"

"Yep," I say, smiling. "Pack your bag and get the fuck out."

"You could at least have some damn manners, asshole!" he shouts as I make my way down the hallway.

"Pack your bag and get the fuck out, *please*," I repeat.

Less than an hour later, I'm ready, but Diesel drove himself. I feel a tad guilty for kicking him out of his own place, but there's plenty of room at the ranch hand quarters. Plus, if Zoey does stay permanently, he'd have to move out anyway. I wouldn't have my wife move in here with Diesel as our roommate if we're trying to give our marriage a real shot.

I lock the house, then walk out to my truck. Before driving off, I send Zoey a text.

RILEY

Meet me at the horse barn in five.

ZOEY

What are you up to?

RILEY

You'll see.

After parking by the B&B, I walk over to the horses and am getting their saddles ready when Zoey enters, looking sexier than usual. Though that's not really possible because she always looks amazing.

Her golden hair is curled into soft waves and pulled up halfway. Though she usually wears a more natural look, I notice her eyes are darker, and her lipstick is brighter.

"Lookin' quite fancy for a barbecue…" I say, grabbing her hand. Taking a step back, I purposely trail my eyes up and down her body. "Are you tryin' to kill me or something?"

She chuckles, closing the gap between us. "Can't a wife look good for her husband?"

I swallow hard, loving the way that sounds coming from her. "Baby, you *always* look good."

"So why are we in here?" she asks after I press a kiss to her lips. "Isn't the party at your grandma's?"

"Yep, and we're going in style."

"On the horses?"

"Yeah, we'll bring them back before the fireworks show so they don't get spooked, but this way, we can have a fun ride there. Ready?" I ask, then finish tightening the cinch on the saddle.

"As long as the horse doesn't try to kill me again." She deadpans. Her expression makes me laugh.

"If you're gonna live on a ranch, you gotta learn to ride, sweetheart," I say, studying her face.

She inhales a deep breath, then nods. "Okay, fine. But I'm keeping my eye on you, Sunshine." She pets the horse's nose before I help lift her up. After I make sure she's settled and secure, I jump on Gable and lead us out.

"Are you sweatin' yet?" I tease as we ride to the main house.

"I've been sweating since the second I arrived."

I laugh at her dramatic eye roll. "Well, that's why you need a hat."

"Pretty sure it'd mess up my hair," she taunts, keeping her horse steady with mine.

"What happened to you being all adventurous and livin' life on the edge?" I pop a brow at her, grinning.

"I'm a hairstylist..." she reminds me. "Messy hair is a hard limit."

That causes me to bellow out a laugh. "No one cares about hair here, baby. I'm buying you a hat tomorrow."

"Can it at least be a pretty color?"

Shaking my head, I bite down on my lip to keep from laughing at her again. "You've been here for almost three weeks. Have I taught you nothing?"

"Just because I don't dress like a Texan doesn't mean I can't have the spirit of one," she tells me matter-of-factly, and before I can respond, Zoey's digging her heels into Sunshine who bolts into a full gallop.

For a split second, I panic, but then she quickly looks over her shoulder and flashes me a smirk.

There's my adventurous girl.

I kick Gable and rush after her. When I finally catch up, she's laughing and smiling so wide, and it causes me to do the same.

"What the hell was that?" I ask once we both slow down.

"I've been taking some lessons," she admits shyly.

"You have?" My jaw drops. "When?"

"While you're at work. I didn't want to embarrass myself again," she confesses. "But I also really wanted to see the shock on your face, like right now." She chuckles.

"Uh yeah, considered me shocked as hell. I can't believe you did that." I reach and pull her reins until she's close enough for me to touch. Cupping her face, I bring our lips together, tasting her sweetness as she hums against me. "So which bastard gave you lessons behind my back?"

Zoey laughs, pushing against my chest. "I promised I wouldn't rat him out."

"Him?" I raise my brows.

"Calm down, cowboy. He only touched my ass twice, and once was an accident."

My jaw tightens as I narrow my eyes at her. "Not funny, woman."

Zoey is the only woman I've ever felt possessive over, and I'm quite sure she knows it too with the way she taunts me.

"Was it Fisher?" I ask when she repositions herself upright on the saddle, creating space between us. When she doesn't answer, I keep asking. "I doubt it was Diesel; he'd tell me. In fact, he'd brag about it, so it can't be him. One of my uncles? My grandfather?" He's in his sixties and still rides, but he's been pretty quiet, not giving an opinion about the marriage.

Zoey picks up her speed, making me chase after her. "Are you really not gonna tell me?"

She smirks, staying silent. Dammit.

"Colton?" I ask, then feel dumb for not guessing him first, considering he's the one who gives lessons here. She turns toward me with a grin and shrugs. "I'm gonna kill him."

She chuckles and shakes her head. "He was a complete gentleman. His wife even took some pictures for me so I could show my sister. Summer nearly choked when I sent them."

"So Colton and Presley knew? But I didn't?" His wife's a photographer, so it makes sense.

"It was a surprise!"

"Do I get to see these pictures?" I ask as we approach our stop.

"Maybe. If you stop being a baby." The corner of her lips tilts up.

I glower at her. "So you'd be okay with me getting my haircut by the stylist in town? Mary Sue is very flirty."

"Mary Sue?" She snorts loudly. "I'm guessing she's at least sixty and has been cutting your hair since you were a toddler. And you had to be held down because you were a wild child, amiright?"

"I'm gonna kill my mother for telling you that story." I grunt because she already knew the details.

"Actually, it was Rowan." She throws her head back and laughs.

I groan. Too many women in my family love to gossip.

We tie up the horses and walk hand in hand to the large backyard where picnic tables are set up. Grandma always invites half the town, which means a lot of food and people. Zoey immediately walks up and strikes up a conversation with everyone. She fits in so well; it's as if she's lived here all her life.

I leave Zoey with my mom and cousins while I help my uncles and Diesel set up the fireworks. They buy thousands of dollars' worth every year, and this time is no different. A huge trailer is packed with all different types and sizes. Most of them aren't legal, but out here in the middle of nowhere, it isn't an issue. The sheriff and his wife come too.

Once it's time to eat, I return and sit with Zoey, who's talking to Rowan and some guy I don't know.

"Who's this?" I ask, setting a plateful of food in front of me.

"Trace," Rowan answers happily. "He just moved here from Missouri. His parents are friends with the Cottons, and he's living with them until he gets his own place. His job transferred him to San Angelo."

"How old are you?" I ask before taking a bite of my burger. My dad mans the grill each year and does a kick-ass job on the meat.

"Riley!" Rowan scolds. "Be nice."

"I'm just askin'! Geez."

"I'm twenty-seven."

I choke on my food, and Zoey pats me on the back, holding in her laughter. Rowan's face pales because she knows I'm about to lose my shit.

"You're too old to be around my sister," I tell him matter-of-factly. "Best you hang around girls your own age. Try the senior center."

Rowan rolls her eyes, then kicks my leg under the table. "You're not the boss of me."

"Do Mom and Dad know? Or do I get the pleasure of relaying the news?" I smirk, knowing that'll shut her up.

"Mom has no problem with it. Plus, we're just hanging out." She looks at whatever the hell his name is and smiles. Fuckin' great. Now I have to kill him.

"You just turned twenty," I say.

"Really? Damn, I'd forgotten." Her sarcasm isn't lost on me.

When I look up, I see Diesel and wave him over. He'll fix this little issue.

"Riley, don't..." Zoey whispers, but it's too late. He's already heading this way.

CHAPTER SIXTEEN

Zoey

I love how Riley and Rowan are close, and that he's so protective of her. However, I feel bad because he's embarrassed the shit out of her. Rowan and I have grown closer recently, and she mentioned Trace and how excited she was that he was coming today. Now my husband is playing macho big brother, and before I can stop it, Diesel struts over, looking like he wants to crush Trace. He could without even trying.

It's no secret Diesel has a thing for Rowan, but she's off-limits. Riley would never approve, though if Rowan really liked Diesel, she wouldn't care what he thought. But I also think Diesel respects his friendship with Riley too much to push it.

"'Sup?" Diesel sits down on the other side of Rowan, so close their arms touch.

"We're just meeting Rowan's new friend here," Riley says, the sarcasm evident in his tone. "Trace, right?"

"Nice to meet ya," Diesel says, leaning forward and holding his hand

430

out across Rowan. She looks horrified. "I'm Diesel."

Trace shakes his hand, giving him a wary look. "Diesel? Interesting name. Nice to meet you, too."

"Not my real name," he says, sitting back in his seat. "But everyone calls me that and knows not to mess with me."

Oh my God. I see the mortified look on Rowan's face.

"Diesel's like an annoying brother," Rowan explains, swallowing hard. "Which means I have two of them to deal with." She gives Riley a pointed look.

"Wouldn't know much about that," Trace says. "I only had a younger sister, but she's from my dad's second marriage and ten years younger than me."

"So then you know about being a protective big brother," Riley says with an edge to his tone.

Rowan gives me a look, pleading for me to do something.

"Who wants dessert?" I blurt, standing. "Honey, come with me. I told your grandma I'd help cut the pies."

"I'm fine right here."

Leaning down, I press my lips to his ear. "I promise to make it worth your while."

His back stiffens, and I officially have his attention. Riley stands, then gives Rowan one more look before raising his brows to Diesel and tilting his head toward Trace. Diesel grins and gives him a head nod in return.

Once we're far enough away, I grab his arm. "What was that back there? Did you and Diesel just do some bro-code language or something?"

"I was telling him to keep an eye on them and not to let them out of his sight."

I shake my head. "You're too much sometimes."

"Isn't that what you love about me, though?" Riley turns and wraps his arms around me. I can't even be mad about how protective he is of his little sister, especially when he looks at me with lust in his eyes. The way he throws around the L word should scare me, but it doesn't. I've been falling for Riley since the moment we met, and when we're together, I fall harder. I learn something new about him every day, and every day, I find it nearly impossible to leave. I want this relationship to work more than anything, but I have to break the news to my parents first. Somehow.

"She's not a kid anymore, babe. You have to let her make her own decisions, even if you don't agree with them."

He grunts, disagreeing, which makes me laugh. "He's way too old for her. What does a twenty-seven-year-old want with a twenty-year-old anyway? He can't get anyone his own age?"

"Age doesn't matter if he's the right one," I counter. "Are you saying I should've denied you had you been twenty-seven? Rowan and I are nearly the same age, remember."

"That's different." His jaw locks.

I snort, pushing his chest. "That's called being a hypocrite."

As the sun dips below the horizon, everyone lies under the stars, anxiously awaiting the firework display.

At the sound of the first boom, I jump, and Riley holds me tighter. "Whoa, it's really loud!"

He laughs, then presses a kiss to my temple. "Guess that means you better get closer."

The show is amazing, better than I've ever seen. It goes on for over an hour before the grand finale starts. There are dozens of beautiful, glittering bursts that nearly leave me breathless. His uncles laugh as they continuously shoot red, silver, and blue fireworks into the night sky. Eventually, the booms end, and everyone cheers.

"Wow…" I say, impressed as hell. "I can see why so many people come out here." There's not a bad seat in the place.

"I'm so glad you liked it." He bends down and kisses me. "Bishops believe in traditions, and this is one of many."

"I don't doubt it." I sigh. "The only traditions my family have are work related. I'm convinced my parents forgot how to have fun."

"Well, I hope to always be around to remind you." He tilts my chin so our eyes lock. "Will you stay over tonight?"

I chew on my lip to prevent answering too quickly and embarrassing myself. The last time I stayed with him, we fooled around and cuddled. It was amazing, but we didn't cross the line. Though he's looking at me like he wants to now. "Uhh, sure. I mean, your bed's probably more comfortable than the one at the B&B."

He narrows his eyes at me. "I'm gonna need a better response than that, woman."

"Because you'll keep me warm?"

"Try again."

Inhaling a deep breath, the corner of my lips tilts up. "Fine." Then I lean forward and bring my mouth to his ear. "So we can *not* sleep all night."

I pull back to watch his reaction. He's staring as if he's waiting for me to say I'm only kidding. But I'm not.

"Better? Or should I ask some other man around here to—"

Before I can finish, Riley has me on my back with my hands pinned down. He's towering over me with a devilish grin on his face, pressing his hips into mine, and I feel how hard he is. "You have any idea how fuckin' lucky you are that we aren't alone at the moment?" He leans in even closer, and his lips brush mine. "Because I'd be ripping off your clothes and sliding inside you right now."

The deep growl of his voice sends a shiver down my spine. *Yes.* My body is begging for him again.

Swallowing hard, I pull back just enough to look into his eyes. "Then you better take me home, cowboy."

He arches a brow as if he's not sure I'm serious. "I only have so much willpower, so if you aren't ready, I understand, but don't test my self-control and say stuff like that. It's about to fuckin' snap."

I grin, reaching over and finding his thickness between his legs. "Let's test that theory, shall we?"

"Zoey," he warns, his eyes struggling to stay open as I touch him.

"Take. Me. Home," I say slowly, but only loud enough for him to hear as I press my palm harder over his jeans.

"Goddammit," he hisses between his teeth, then he grabs my hands and pulls me up.

The moment we're both standing, he picks up the blankets, then leads us through the crowd of people without saying anything to anyone. Giggling at his eagerness, I quickly wave goodbye to Rowan as he walks faster.

"You're going to make me trip," I say, laughing. Without a response, Riley turns toward me and scoops me up caveman style. He hauls me over his shoulder, then continues walking fast.

"Riley!" I shout, slapping his tight ass. "This wasn't what I meant!"

"Too late, sweetheart." He sets me down on my feet when we arrive at his truck. "Get in. Now."

My eyes widen at his harsh tone, and he jogs to the driver's side and jumps in.

"Don't worry, I told Diesel to get lost tonight."

I chuckle at his smirk and the way he waggles his brows at me. "Oh, so you planned this?"

"Since the moment you arrived." He winks.

On the drive back to his house, I notice he's definitely going faster than usual. The smile on my face is obnoxious, but I can't help it. I've been waiting for this since I arrived, just as eager and anxious as him.

"You lookin' at me like you want to eat me for dessert isn't helping, Zoey," he warns in that deep tone again.

"Now you know what you've been doing to me," I counter, smirking. "Being a gentleman, all considerate and charming, always kissing me so sweetly, and inhaling my scent when you nuzzle my neck. Don't think I haven't noticed."

He shakes his head now, grinning. "That's all it took, huh?"

"Shut up." I chuckle, then turn serious. "It took finding the right one. It's because you're different than any guy I've ever met."

We finally get to his house, and he nearly drags me out of the truck after he parks. Because Riley's in such a hurry, he drops his keys, fumbling to unlock the house. Once we're inside, he backs me up until I'm leaning against the cool wood of the door. His mouth and hands are on me, cupping my face as he slides his tongue between my lips. When my moans turn greedy, he deepens the kiss.

My hands go to the hem of his shirt, lifting it until he gets the hint and pulls it over his head. I kick off my shoes and remove my top. His fingers find the button and zipper of my denim shorts, sliding them down until they reach my ankles, and I kick them away, leaving me standing in only my bra and panties. Our breaths mix in heavy pants, eager to have each other.

It's more than obvious that there's always been more between us. Our conversations are easy, the attraction is mutual, and our chemistry is so hot it could burn. I want nothing more than to be Riley's wife and start our life together here. I know I need to explain what happened after Vegas and why I sent those annulment papers, but right now seems like the worst possible time to tell him.

"Riley..." I moan as he pushes my panties to the side and slides a finger up my slit. "Fuck." My head falls back against the door as his thumb rubs my clit. My arms tighten around his neck as I pull him closer. "Don't stop."

"Hell no. How could I when you sound so goddamn sweet?" He wraps his hand around my throat, and our mouths slam together as he sinks a finger inside me. "You're so wet, baby. You want this?"

My breathing is rapid as my heart tries to catch up with my thoughts that are going a thousand miles an hour. "Yes. God, yes."

"Tell me, Zoey." He sucks my neck before his breath brushes over my ear. Then he adds a second finger, thrusting harder and faster. "Tell me what you want."

"You," I say, digging my nails into his biceps. "I want you."

"Yeah?" I feel him smile against my cheek. "Because I want to fuckin' devour you, sweetheart. I want you fallin' asleep in my bed every night and wakin' up next to me every morning. I want to eat dinner with you, fight over the remote, and take horseback rides at sunset. I want you here—in my life—permanently."

My pulse beats hard in my neck as he says the most perfect things to me. My breath hitches as I take in his words because I want all of that too. I hate leaving at night and not seeing him first thing in the morning even though we spend as much time together as we can. But it's not enough anymore. We both want more.

Heat rushes between my legs as he continues his sweet assault on my pussy. I ache for more of him. I want *all* of him.

"I love you," I whisper, fighting to keep my eyes open so I can look at him. He slows his movements, then pulls back to study me.

"You stole the words right out of my head," he says with a chuckle, smiling as he cups my face and slants his mouth over mine. "I fell in love with you so quick and fast, but I didn't want to scare you away."

"Nothing is scary with you," I admit. "I know this is probably crazy, but I don't care. Falling in love with you was the last thing I expected, but I can't imagine anything else now."

"Does this mean you're staying?" Riley asks, brushing his thumb over my cheek. "Please tell me you are."

Smiling, I nod as tears threaten to fall. "I have to tell my family, in person, but then yes, I'll be back."

"Let me go with you. We can tell them together." My heart races at the thought of them meeting Riley as my husband and having to face the consequences.

"Maybe," I offer. "They'll be in shock."

"Well, I'll come to support you if you want me to, but if not, I understand." Riley tilts my chin, pressing a light kiss to my lips. "As long as you come back to me."

Wrapping my arms around him and pulling him closer, I nod. "Always." I inhale a sharp breath. "Now make love to your wife."

"Jesus fuck, *yes*." He moans as our bodies collide, and he lifts me under my knees until my legs wrap around him. "I've been going through withdrawals."

I giggle as he walks us through the house and into his bedroom. Riley places me on the bed, then removes the rest of his clothing except his boxers. "I'm taking my time with you, baby. No drunken quickies."

My eyes widen. "That was a quickie last time?" I wasn't sober in the least in Vegas, but I'll never forget being with him.

Riley flashes a devilish grin and nods. He kneels on the bed between my legs and cups my ass, dragging me closer to his face. The moment I feel his hot mouth over the thin material of my panties, I'm ready to combust. He slides them down before finding my clit and sucking hard. The way he teases me with his tongue and fingers has me driving closer over the edge, screaming his name and needing relief.

"Riley, please…" I beg, arching my hips and wiggling beneath him. "I'm so close."

He responds by removing his fingers and sinking his tongue inside me while using his thumb to rub circles against my clit. The sensation is enough to drive me insane. I'm so damn close to exploding. I love the way his beard scratches my thighs and pussy as he moves his face around, torturing me in the most pleasurable way.

My fingers tangle in his hair, and I widen my legs for him. When he slides up and circles his tongue against my clit, everything goes black.

"*Yes, yes, yes*…right there."

Riley applies just the right amount of pressure to set me off, causing my body to shake and tremble.

"Oh my God…" I finally manage to say. My chest rises and falls as I catch my breath. I feel him smile against my thigh as he presses a kiss there.

"I can die a happy man now that I've felt you come against my tongue, sweetheart." He towers over me, grinning. "You wanna taste?"

I've never had a man ask me that question before, but from Riley, it's a no-brainer. "Yes."

Putting part of his body weight on top of me, he leans down and slides his eager tongue between my swollen lips and groans when I arch my hips to meet his erection.

"Now let me taste your cock," I say when he settles next to me.

"Fuck, babe. Don't say things like that." He slides his hand over my waist and pulls me closer, groaning at the friction. When I furrow my brows, he continues, "I don't want to come in your mouth, and if your lips are anywhere near my cock, I won't be able to control myself."

"So never?" I pop a brow at him.

"No, not never, but not tonight."

I nod in understanding. "Then you better fuck me soon because I'm dying." I overexaggerate, groaning at the loss of him.

Riley grabs my thigh and wraps it over his hip. "Are you on birth control? I want to make love to my *wife* without a condom, so if you're not, you better tell me now."

I grind myself against him, his throbbing erection teasing my pussy through his boxers. "Yes, I have an IUD."

"Thank fuck. I've always used a condom, but with you, sweetheart, I don't want to."

"I have too. Always," I admit, though I've not had many sexual partners. "I don't want to either."

Riley rolls us until I'm underneath him, and he's between my legs. "We're really doing this, Zoey. Giving our marriage a real chance. You're moving here."

Yes. That's exactly what I want.

I'll figure it all out when I'm in Phoenix, but Riley is who I want regardless of what my parents think or say. Not wanting to ruin the moment, I promise myself I'll tell him all my secrets tomorrow, then make plans to go home so I can tell my family and pack up my things. If he loves me like he says he does, then I know we'll be able to work through anything.

"Yes," I whisper, locking my ankles behind his back.

"Say those three words again, baby." He buries his face into my hair, his mouth slides against my neck.

Smiling, I wrap my fingers around his arms. "I love you."

He grinds against me. Sweet fucking torture.

"Again."

"I love you, Riley."

The sensation of his shorts rubbing against my clit as he positions himself between my legs sends an electric shock through me.

"I love you so fucking much, Zoey."

He captures my mouth as we greedily taste each other, but it never feels like enough. Riley leans back, slides off his boxers, and strokes his length. I suck in my lips, then swallow as he rubs his cock through my arousal before slowly entering.

Finally.

I gasp when he pushes farther inside, my body adjusting to his size as I lift my hips. Wrapping my arms around my back, I unclip my bra and slide it off. The moment I do, he brings a hand to my breast and pinches my nipple. Riley's other hand rubs my clit, and the sensation is like nothing I've experienced before. He jerks his hips, then grips my waist and pounds harder into me. Once he's seated all the way in, my back flies off the bed at how deep he feels inside me.

"Fuck..." I mutter, moving to his rhythm and reaching for him.

"You feel so fuckin' good, sweetheart." He leans down, grabbing my hands and pinning them above my head as he thrusts harder. I lose all train of thought except how much I love this man. He's way too good to be true. I never knew I could be this happy, which is scary, but I'm gambling it'll work out the way it's supposed to.

"Yes...yes..." I lock eyes with him as we both climb toward release.

"You're close. Let go, baby." He takes both of my wrists in one hand and slides his other down my body until it palms my breast, and he squeezes roughly. I love how he loves touching me, even the parts of me I'm insecure about. My breasts aren't huge, never have been, and even though I'm thin, I was always insecure that I didn't have the right curves in the places men seemed to like.

But Riley, he treats me like a fucking queen with his words and his touch.

My eyes flutter closed as my body tightens, and Riley increases his pace, thrusting faster until I'm falling again. This time, I scream his name as I squeeze my thighs around him.

I try to catch my breath because I know Riley's close. Having him bare against me is a first, and it feels so damn amazing. He's thick and hard, and I already know I won't ever get enough of him.

Lifting my hips, I encourage him to go faster. He fills me so full that the moment his body stiffens, I know he's about to explode.

"Come inside me," I tell him breathily.

"Fuck, baby…" he hisses between gritted teeth, removing his hold on my wrists and gripping my hips. I arch them higher as his fingers dig into my skin, chasing his release. He lets out an animalistic groan, the vein in his neck throbbing as he tilts his head back and moans.

A moment later, he collapses on top of me, both of us breathless and sweaty.

"Jesus Christ, Zoey. What have you done to me?" He lies down, brushing his fingers over my cheek and holding me close. "You made me fall in love with you so easily. I've never said those words to a woman before, so I hope you know how much I mean them."

Tears form on the edge of my eyes at how badly I want to give this man everything. He owns my heart and soul, and the only thing holding me back is in Arizona.

"I love you," I tell him, worried he might change his mind when he finds out the truth. "No matter what, please don't ever forget that."

"Never, sweetheart," he reassures me. "Eloping in Vegas was the best dare I've ever done."

I half-chuckle, half-sob at his confession. "Let's not tell our kids that part of the story, though."

A wide grin splits his face. "Kids? You want children someday?"

I shrug because I haven't really thought much about it. I'm still young and have time to decide, but when it comes to Riley, I want it all. "Yeah, I think I'd like having babies with you."

"If I'm dreaming, please don't ever wake me up."

I giggle at his corny line, but hell, I can't help smiling at the truth of his words. "Agreed."

CHAPTER SEVENTEEN

Riley

I wake up with a warm body nestled against mine, and all I can do is grin. Carefully, I roll over and pull Zoey into my arms. Her head rests against my chest, and she lets out a hum. If I could stay here all morning, I'd be the happiest man on earth, but I know I can't. It's times like this, I wish I weren't on such a strenuous schedule. Calling in wouldn't even be a possibility because, ultimately, I'd be letting my family down and they'd have to take up my slack.

"Morning," she says in the sexiest sleepy voice I've ever heard.

Leaning forward, I kiss her forehead and hold her tighter as if she'll slip through my fingers if I let go. "Morning, sweetheart."

She lifts her head, and her eyes flutter open. A small smile touches her lips, and I lean in to press mine against hers.

"You have to go soon, don't you?" she asks, and her eyes close.

"Mmhmm. It's the first time I've considered calling in sick for no reason." I groan, not wanting to leave her warmth.

She sucks in a deep breath and yawns. "We've got forever, Riley."

I remember last night when she told me she *loved* me, and I smile like an idiot. After she tells her family, she's really coming back to live here with me. We'll fall asleep together every night and wake up in each other's arms.

"We do, baby." I kiss her cheek. "I'm going to make some coffee, and it'll be waiting for you in the kitchen when you decide to get up."

"Okay," she says, her breathing becoming more steady.

I slip out from under her and lean over and kiss her again. I can't seem to stop. "Meet me at the barn behind the B&B after you wake up."

Zoey lets out a sigh, and she's soon falling back asleep. She's not used to my alarm clock yet, so I know it woke her.

"I'll text you," I whisper, then get dressed. As I sit on the edge of the bed and slip on my work boots, I glance over my shoulder at her, sleeping so peacefully. I'm three seconds away from hopping back into bed, but my dad would know, and he'd bust up in here to kick my ass. Being love-sick isn't a proper excuse. Not one he'd accept anyway.

On the way over to the office, my smile doesn't falter. Zoey's made me the happiest I've ever been, and to know she's going to stay with me and be my wife just feels unreal. When I walk into the shop, Diesel is already there with a smug look on his face.

"Oh, guess you didn't die from sex overload," he jokes, checking his watch.

I look up at the clock over the door. "I'm five minutes late."

"Which still makes you late and now behind," Fisher says, and I glance over, rolling my eyes. Nothing they say will spoil my good mood this morning. Life is too fucking perfect.

"I've already fed the animals," Diesel says.

"Your hustle's been quite impressive lately," Fisher tells him, and I nearly die of a stroke that he gave Diesel a compliment. It's kinda scary how they're getting along. Maybe they've turned a new leaf, or maybe Diesel's more concerned with Rowan dating an older man and has forgotten about Fisher stealing Gretchen. Though I don't really want him thinking about my little sister either.

"Grandma said she wanted a new garden shed built for all of Mila's tools. Right now, she's keeping them in the barn with all the side-by-sides, and it's becoming too crowded."

Diesel huffs, crossing his arms. "A few shovels don't take up that much space."

"She has eighteen bags of fertilizer and forty bags of soil, six shovels, a cart, three wheelbarrows, and a dozen water hoses," Fisher corrects.

"Fuck. She's serious about this gardening, isn't she?" Diesel eyes go wide. "I had no idea."

Fisher gives us the plans for the building, and I study it. "I think we can have it framed by this afternoon."

Diesel looks over my shoulder. "We're pouring concrete for this? Seriously?"

"It won't be that bad," I encourage, though I can tell he's already in one of his moods. Fisher sends us on our way, and we start loading the supplies in the back of the old work truck—hand mixers, a dozen bags of cement, and extra shovels.

"You survive last night after I left the show?" I ask him as we drive across the ranch.

He looks at me with a lifted eyebrow. "I should be asking you the same thing."

I chuckle. "I survived just fine."

"I want to bash that Trace guy's head in. What the actual fuck?" Diesel is livid all over again, and I can feel my blood pressure rising at the thought of it.

"I want him to stay away from her," I admit as we pull up to the garden. The area where Mila wants the shed is already staked out, so it makes our job a lot easier.

Diesel continues talking shit about this Trace guy as we start unloading everything. "He's too fucking old for her and knows exactly what he's doing with a girl that young. I don't want her to get taken advantage of," Diesel admits. "Because then I'll have to bash his ugly face in."

"Spoken like a second older brother," I tell him, chuckling.

He stiffens, then changes the subject. "Has Zoey made up her mind yet? I imagine you two didn't do a whole lot of talking last night." He sets the bags of cement down and then pulls out the mixer.

I want to scream out so everyone can hear the good news, but I somehow contain my excitement. My smile's so wide it nearly hurts. "Yeah, she's decided to stay and be my wife. We're gonna make it work for the long haul."

"You're welcome," Diesel says proudly. "If it weren't for me..."

"Oh, don't even give me that bullshit. But since it worked out, I guess I can thank you now." I snicker. Grabbing the two-by-fours, I check the specs Fisher gave me this morning, then remeasure our cuts before we build the form for the concrete slab. After everything is set, Diesel and I nearly break our backs mixing the crushed rock and water.

"So I get to name your first kid, right?" he teases. "Wait, does she want to have kids? A boy named Adam?"

I laugh. "Yeah, she does eventually. I'd seriously have a million babies with that woman." Hell, I'd knock her up now if she were ready. Imagining her carrying my child with a cute round belly makes my cock twitch.

"Maybe I should dare you to get her pregnant now." He smirks. I wouldn't put it past him, though. The asshole.

"I still owe you one first," I remind him. Smirking, I remember all the stories my uncles have told me about how their dares got them into a ton of trouble growing up. Specifically uncle Jackson. "Maybe I'll dare *you* to stay away from my sister for good," I threaten. "Or maybe dare you to go find that Chelsea chick. Have you even called her since Vegas?"

"What the hell? How'd we get on this subject?" He grunts. "Whatever dare you pick better be mild, considering you got the girl."

Checking the time, I realize it's a quarter past nine and text Zoey; however, I bet she's still asleep. We didn't get much rest last night. I mentioned we should meet for lunch at the B&B and to keep an hour free afterward. As long as we can get this framing done today, Diesel won't mind the unplanned break.

"What the fuck you cheesin' about?" he teases when I stuff my phone back in my pocket.

I waggle my eyebrows.

"You're gross," he says.

"You're just pissed because your relationship status is basically nonexistent." Sometimes it's fun to poke the bear.

"Well, if your bitch ass cousin wouldn't have stolen my girlfriend, and if you'd get the stick out of your ass about me fucking your sister, then it wouldn't be so nonexistent now, would it?" he snaps as we continue adding cement.

I'm two seconds from throwing a shovel at his head, but all he does is laugh. "My sister wouldn't fuck you if you were the last man on earth," I say confidently, but I'm not so sure. Sometimes, I see Rowan staring at him, but then she turns her head and pretends she wasn't.

"I bet she would. She'd love it. Probably beg for more." He's determined to agitate the piss outta me today.

"Fuck off!" I yell, splashing concrete on his boots. "I don't want to think about Rowan being with any guy, especially you."

"I knew that'd get you all worked up. It's sexy," he taunts just as my dad walks over and inspects what we've accomplished.

"Nice work. Lookin' good so far. Mila's gonna be real happy with this," he says, glancing down at the concrete on Diesel's boots. "Y'all try not to make a mess out here."

"Yes, sir," Diesel says, glaring at me, and I shoot him a smirk. Once we're alone again, Diesel reminds me that we can't start framing until the concrete has cured for at least twenty-four hours. Considering I forgot about that fact and so did Fisher, I text him and let him know we're at a standstill until tomorrow. He reminds us to deliver more hay to the training barns, so we go pick up the lowboy.

"I know I've been giving you shit for the last month and a half, but I'm really happy for you," Diesel admits as we enter the storage barn.

"Thanks, man. Really means a lot to me. I know it's gonna be a big change and all, for you too, but for the first time in my life, I'm truly happy."

He climbs up the ladder to the loft and starts throwing down bales as I load them onto the trailer. We discuss how he'll need to move out once she's back for good, and he surprisingly doesn't give me shit for it. Once we're full, we drive to the B&B to start unloading at the main horse barn. The dinner bell rings on the back porch, and I know it's eleven. Diesel looks at me longingly like he hasn't eaten in five years, and as soon as he sees Zoey walking toward us, he takes the opportunity to break for lunch.

"Hey, Arizona," he tells her as they pass.

"Hey, Adam."

He spins around on his heels and glares at her. She's bent over gasping for air, laughing at his reaction. "Diesel. I mean Diesel," she corrects.

"I'm gonna kill you, Bishop!" he shouts, flipping me off as he storms off to the B&B. He hates it when anyone uses his real name, but I find it hilarious. Grandma calls him Adam all the time, and he just grins and takes it like a champ.

Zoey closes the gap between us and nearly falls into my arms. Her hair is down, and she smells delicious as if she just got out of the shower. After I remove my gloves, I lead her into the barn where the hay is stacked. I want to devour her but manage to refrain because too many guests frequent the area. The last thing I need is for my grandma to find out I was fucking in the horse barn. That's the type of embarrassment I can live without, though I've heard stories from my uncles who didn't care as much about getting caught.

I grab her hand, and that's when I notice Zoey's wearing the cowboy boots I bought her when we went into town. "You look sexy as fuck in those," I tell her.

"I was thinking the same thing about you, cowboy." Her sultry voice has my dick springing to life, and I move forward, pushing her against one of the stall doors. In one swift movement, she wraps her legs around my waist, and I cup her ass, our tongues twisting together. I don't think I'll be able to stop myself this time because I need her like I need water on a hot summer day.

"Riley," she whispers, panting. "Fuck me."

And I'm two seconds away from doing that very thing when I hear an unfamiliar male voice behind me calling Zoey's name. Immediately she stiffens, her eyes bolt open, and she pulls away. After I set her down, she looks at me with worry in her eyes.

"Zoey, what the fuck are you doing?" he asks, and I turn around and catch a glimpse of an older man wearing a sport coat and slacks, looking out of place.

"Excuse the fuck outta me," I say, placing my arm around her waist to protect her from this dickhead.

He strides toward us and reaches for her arm, pulling Zoey away. "You need to get over here right now." He jerks her toward him as if she's a child, causing my blood to boil. Zoey looks back at me with tears in her eyes.

"Get your hands off her," I warn, feeling my anger take over as he looks at her with disdain.

The douchebag glares. "You're nothing but Southern trash," he spits out.

"Benjamin, don't," Zoey demands. Who the fuck is Benjamin?

My heart races and pounds, and I don't understand what's going on. A minute ago, we were making out. "Who is this?" I look at her and then glare at him. "Explain, Zoey."

"I'm her fiancé," he answers, wrapping his arm tightly around her as if he's claiming his prize. "And we're leaving."

Fiancé? That can't be right. How can you be engaged to someone if you're married to another person? I look at Zoey, who's shaking her head with tears streaming down her cheeks.

"Is that true?" I ask, begging her to tell me what the hell is going on, but she pinches her lips together tightly. Her silence is all I need to know.

I take a step forward, coming face to face with him, not scared in the least bit even though he's taller than me. The guy looks like he has his balls waxed and nails done once a week. "Yeah, well, you've got your hands on my *wife,* and you're going to let go of her before I beat the shit outta you."

Benjamin laughs in my face and jerks Zoey closer to him. Instead of doing what I say, he pushes me, but I barely stumble back. This guy is a grade A pussy.

"Zoey. Get your shit. We're leaving," he demands, and in one quick movement, my fist connects with his face.

CHAPTER EIGHTEEN

Zoey

"You motherfucker," Riley says as he throws another punch.

I scream as soon as I see Riley push Benjamin to the ground and jump on top of him, fists being thrown left and right. Benjamin covers his face with his arms, trying to defend himself, but he's never fought anyone in his entire life. Riley's destroying him, and I'm not sure who I should feel sorry for at this moment. If Riley continues, Benjamin will get hurt and get his lawyers involved, taking it to a level it doesn't need to go. I already know how this will end if Riley doesn't gain control, but I can't blame him. This is all my fault.

I beg him to stop, screaming and crying, grabbing at his arm before he can take another swing at Benjamin's face. Somehow, I get through to him, and he stops, but he looks at me with hurt in his eyes, breathing hard. Seeing Riley so upset destroys me.

Riley stands as Benjamin tries to get a hold of reality, cursing and spitting out blood. He looks like total shit, and I know I won't hear the last of this anytime soon.

Before more words are exchanged, Riley walks away, shaking his hand out as he bends his fingers back and forth. I scream his name, following and not wanting him to go because it feels so final. He turns on his heels and glares at me as if I'm a stranger, someone he doesn't care to know, and it's more hurtful than any words he could ever speak.

I wish I could go back and tell him all of my secrets, tell him about Benjamin and the engagement I didn't want.

"Is it true? You're engaged to marry *him*?" he quietly questions me, but he's heaving with anger. His jaw is so tight, I'm afraid it'll break.

"I wanted to tell you. I planned to..." I say, but he shakes his head, not having any part of this conversation or me.

"You betrayed me, Zoey. You betrayed me and my family in ways I can't even begin to describe." His sad eyes meet mine, and I know nothing I can say or do will fix any of this right now. Riley gives me one last glance, his nostrils flare, then walks away.

"You have twenty minutes, and we're fucking leaving. I'm not playing these games with you," Benjamin barks, and I run out of the barn toward Riley, who's already made his way to the side of the B&B. I yell his name again, wanting him to stop so I can explain everything, but he ignores me. Before he climbs in his truck, I grab his hand and force him to look at me.

"Please," I beg. "Let me explain everything to you." Before he can respond, Benjamin calls my name.

"Go back to your fiancé," he snaps, jerking his hand from mine. Riley gets into his truck, not giving me another look, and backs out of the driveway, spitting up rocks as he leaves. I watch until I can no longer see his truck. Sobs escape me at the reality of the shitstorm I've created.

What have I done?

Benjamin comes up behind me, and that's when I notice the Mercedes parked nearby. Of course he'd rent a flashy luxury car. He sticks out like a sore thumb in his business casual, Rolex, and slicked back hair.

"I've called you, and you've done nothing but ignore me. What the fuck do you think you're doing, Zoey? I am your fiancé. You belong to *me*."

All I can do is scowl at him—the man who thought proposing at my sister's wedding was a genius idea, the man who I said yes to because I had no other choice. With my parents and every person in their social circle there, I was put on the spot. Embarrassing them would've garnered lifelong consequences, and at the time, I didn't know what to do. I knew it was what my parents wanted, and at that moment of weakness, I crumpled to their wishes. Coming to Texas and being with Riley grounded me for the first time in years. I found out who I was, the part of me that I almost lost.

"We're leaving in the morning," Benjamin hisses. "Your parents are expecting us at dinner tomorrow night to discuss wedding plans," he says it as if it were some business meeting for work that's nothing more than an inconvenience. I look at him like he's lost his fucking mind, but it doesn't faze him in the least. For a man who asked me to marry him, he doesn't even ask about who I was kissing before he showed up. That's because he doesn't care. I'm only a piece of property to him.

"What are you doing here?" I ask, finally able to find my words.

He takes a step forward, his eye already starting to bruise. With a busted lip and rustled hair, he looks like complete shit. My parents will definitely notice and ask questions.

"I came to get my goddamn fiancée from this shithole. I seriously don't understand why you've been here for so long." Benjamin makes a disgusted expression. "Look at this place." He places his hands on his hips and looks at the B&B as if it were a fallen down shack.

When I look around, all I see is heaven on earth, a treasure of a place where social status and the amount in the bank doesn't mean anything, something Benjamin wouldn't understand. He wants the best of the best and only cares about appearances, just like my parents.

Studying his hands, I can see he's seething. "Do you have any idea what would've happened if these were damaged? I'd sue the living fuck out of this ranch. I'd take them for every penny they're worth and finish this place. We'd rename it Benjamin's B&B." He laughs at his joke and thinks he's so damn clever.

I try to steady my breathing, but my entire body shakes from the inside out, knowing that I might've lost the man I love forever.

Benjamin stares at me. "You'll need to fully explain yourself on the plane ride home tomorrow. I really don't have time to be rescuing you, Zoey. This is childish and immature, and your parents aren't happy. I may have never found you if it weren't for Summer."

"Summer?" I ask in disbelief.

"She told your parents you were staying at a B&B in Texas. I had my assistant looking for you for the past week. It wasn't easy to track you down." He takes a step forward. "You've embarrassed me."

His eyes grow dark and dangerous, and I step back to create some space between us before he hurts me. I wish Riley hadn't left me with him, but I don't blame him for it. "I'm sorry." I swallow down my pride and say what he wants to hear.

Shaking his head, he waves off my apology.

"What about my car?" I ask, considering I drove. I need it to come back here once everything clears up.

"I've already planned for it to be shipped back to Phoenix. I hired a company to pick it up before the end of the month. Enough slumming in this shithole."

"It's not a shithole," I spit back at him. I find a little courage to mutter my next words. "And I'm not going with you, Benjamin."

He remote starts the Mercedes. "Darling, you don't really have a choice. Your parents want you home immediately. You're about to lose the space for your job. Plus, we have a wedding to plan. Quit pretending your life is here, Zoey. It's not, and you're on the path to lose everything and everyone who cares about you. So let's snap back to real life, okay? Playtime is over."

Just as he finishes his speech, my phone rings, and I see it's my mother. I ignore it, but then she calls Benjamin, which he answers with a grin.

"Hi, Mrs. Mitchell." He pauses as I faintly hear my mom's voice. "Yes, I found her. I know. I was worried as well. Yes, she'll be on the plane with me tomorrow, and we'll be there for dinner. She's safe. I'll pass on the message. Alrighty, bye." He ends the call and glares at me. "She said she misses and loves you. So do you really want to ruin your mother's happiness?"

I resist the urge to roll my eyes at his manipulation. "I'm already married, Benjamin. You're too late," I throw at him, shrugging so he knows the wedding is off, but instead, he laughs.

"A few thousand dollars can fix anything. It can get annulled in a few days. So, be a good little daughter for your mother and grab your things. We're staying in San Angelo tonight."

I look at him and feel sick to my stomach because I know I'd just be another thing added to his collection. All of this is a political move, and if my parents think I don't realize that, then they're the stupid ones. My happiness doesn't matter, and being with Benjamin would be repulsive. Before Riley, I considered the idea for a minute, but I felt nothing for Benjamin. There's no connection, no chemistry between us, and I have no desire to see him. I continued going on dates with him to appease my parents, but I was ready to call it quits before I even went to Vegas. Once I returned, and we got busy with the final details of Summer's wedding, I didn't get the chance to break it off for good. Then he put me on the spot with the proposal, and that was when I knew I had to get away from all of the bullshit.

Even if I liked him enough to actually marry him, I'd be nothing more than a trophy wife, and if we had kids, they'd just add to his list of accomplishments. Bile rises in my throat at the thought, but I swallow it down and try to figure out how I can appease him enough to go on without me. The way he's looking at me tells me he won't allow that to happen.

"Benjamin, I'm not going to San Angelo with you. I'll check out in the morning, and you can pick me up here before the flight. It's the only way I'm getting on that plane," I counter, wanting to give myself just a little more time to clean up this mess of a situation I've created.

Blood drips from his nose, and when he gets it on his hands, he opens the car door and pulls out a box of tissues and hand sanitizer. A few guests exit the B&B and look at my tear-streaked face and then at Benjamin. There's too much attention on the two of us, and he notices. I'm known for being stubborn, and if he wants his way, he'll play by my rules even though I know I don't really have a choice. If I'm not back in Phoenix tomorrow, my parents will come for me next. Handling this is something I have to do before it's too late to fight for Riley. I have too many fires to put out right now and not enough water.

Between my parents, sister, job, Benjamin, and Riley, the stress and anxiety are real, and I don't know how I'm going to solve any of these issues without hurting people.

After Benjamin's cleaned himself up, he grabs my arm and jerks me closer to him. The pain of his tight grip shoots through me, and I try to pull away, but all he does is squeeze harder.

"I will do what you want this one fucking time, but when I come to pick you up tomorrow, you better not resist, Zoey."

I stare out into the pasture, the rolling hills, wishing the land would swallow me whole, wishing he'd disappear.

"Pay attention," he barks, pulling me back to reality, to the nightmare I'm living.

"Okay. No argument. I'll go willingly in the morning." As much as it pains me, I agree. I swallow hard, knowing if I don't get on that plane, I'll have more to deal with than just him. My parents will want an explanation, and so will Summer, considering she's believed all this time that the annulment was processed weeks ago. I couldn't find the strength to admit my doubts. I didn't want to hear her try to convince me that marrying Benjamin was the right thing to do because I knew deep down it wasn't. The pressure from it all was too much, and I made one bad decision after another. All of my secrets, everything I've been hiding, will have to come out in the open, and it scares me to death. Getting married in Vegas on a dare? It's irresponsible, I know, but it was one of the best decisions I've ever made.

I think about Riley, and my heart lurches forward, wishing I could go back and tell him everything from the beginning. He may never forgive me for this, considering I know exactly how this looks from the outside.

Benjamin pulls me into his arms, forcing his lips against mine. I can't even find the strength to kiss him back, but it's not like he notices. He's just going through the motions of being in a relationship. Turning around, he gives me one last glare before he gets into the car and drives away. The tears come in streams as my world crumbles around me.

"What the hell?" Diesel shouts from the porch. "Who the fuck is that? And why were you kissing him?"

When I turn to face him, Diesel shoots daggers in my direction with his arms crossed. I open my mouth to explain, but my words escape me again. Shaking his head, he turns and walks away.

The last thirty minutes feel like a blur, and it's hard for me to even comprehend what's happened. I went from being on cloud nine to being forced into the pits of hell. I've really messed up this time, and I'm not sure I can fix it without a small miracle and some grace.

I was willing to risk my heart, but it seems as if I've risked everything. And lost.

CHAPTER NINETEEN

Riley

I've never felt anger or pain on such an intense level. As soon as I walk inside my house, my body begins to shake, my knuckles bloody and sore, as the adrenaline rush finally catches up to me. It's been a long while since I lost control like that. I probably shouldn't have taken it out on him because he seemed just as oblivious as me, but the way he grabbed Zoey and jerked her around like she was a child, pissed me off. No man will ever touch her like that in front of me, regardless of the situation.

Fiancé? How could this happen? How could she not tell me?

Why the fuck did she lie?

She's the one who came here, searching for me, so this makes no goddamn sense. Now, I'm not sure what was real between us and what was an act, considering she had another man waiting for her back in Phoenix. The betrayal runs deep.

Zoey was supposed to be mine and *only mine*, and I truly thought she was. Until I realized she wasn't. She belongs to another man, and I feel like a fucking fool, played like a fiddle. My heart is throbbing so hard and fast, I can feel it in my neck. I know I need to calm down, but I can't. There's too much anger streaming through me.

"Fuck," I yell, pacing through my empty house that was supposed to be our home. Yesterday was one of the best days of my life, hell, even today was up until the minute her fiancé showed up and turned my world upside down.

Why didn't she file the papers as soon as I sent them back to her? Why tell me she wanted to see if we had something real if she was already with someone? What the fuck?

Too many questions stream through me that I may never get the answers to. Maybe I should've stayed to hear her explanation, but truthfully, it hurt too much to look at her once everything unfolded.

My mind wanders, and I know I need to relax before I give myself a heart attack, so I go into the kitchen and pour a double scotch. After shooting it down in one big gulp, I then sit on the couch and stare at the wall. It's going to take more than that to ease my mind. Scotch and sleep sound like the perfect combination.

A heavy weight sits on my chest, and it's making it hard to concentrate on anything as my mind takes over, creating ridiculous scenarios involving that douchebag and her. Has she been intimate with him? Do they live together? How long has she been engaged?

A minute later, the front door swings open, and Diesel charges through with fury in every single step. If anyone is in my corner, it's him, always. Even though we give each other shit on a daily basis, he really is like a brother. We've been through the wringer together, and nothing will change that. Diesel sits next to me on the couch, and while he waits for an explanation, I don't even know where to begin because I don't have all the pieces to the puzzle.

"What happened?" he finally asks, breaking the silence. "I saw her with the dickhead in the Mercedes. I almost took a crowbar to it and then kicked his teeth in."

"You should have." Just the thought of her being with that asshole who treated her with zero respect has me seething all over again. He looked old as hell too, at least in his mid-thirties.

"I saw them kissing," Diesel says, the dagger driving deeper into my heart.

"That's her fiancé," I say, swallowing down the words that taste like poison.

He looks just as confused as I feel. "How's that even possible? She's married. To *you.*"

"Means nothing, apparently." Saying it out loud makes it seem more real. More painful, too.

Diesel looks at me and shakes his head. "I'm so sorry, man. I know how much you really cared for her. Never in my life did I think something like this would happen. Especially with Zoey."

"Thanks. I didn't either. I do care about her; that's why it hurts so goddamn much. Maybe my parents were right after all." I think back to the conversation I had with them when they warned me to be careful. Falling fast has its consequences. "Maybe they knew something like this would happen. Maybe it was all fake for Zoey. Coming here was a last hoorah before she got married to a man who seems to be what her parents want for her." Self-doubt is beginning to settle in, and I question if I really was good enough. I replay every conversation we've had since she arrived, and it all seems so obvious now.

Diesel shakes his head. "No. Zoey cares about you, too. There's no faking that. It was real. Trust me."

"I'd like to think it was," I say, but I'm second-guessing everything right now. "Not so sure anymore."

"We should go out," he says, standing. "Visit the bar and get shit-faced. Forget about it all."

I look at him, defeated. "I don't feel like being around people. I wouldn't be good company right now. I just need to figure all this clusterfuck out."

Diesel sucks in a breath and looks at me with pity in his eyes. I stand and walk to my room, grateful that he doesn't follow me. He knows when I want to be alone, it's best to just let me. I close the door and lie back on my bed. My pillow still smells like her, the sweetness a cruel reminder of our incredible night together. Squeezing my eyes tight, I try to forget the shitstorm that's my reality, but it's impossible.

After an hour passes, I realize I'm starving. I didn't eat lunch because it was interrupted. Opening the fridge, I decide to pull out some leftovers Mom sent home with me a few days ago. I pop a container in the microwave and sit at the table, reminiscing over the past few weeks, pissed I let her in so willingly. I keep wondering what the point of her coming here was? To run away from it all? Too bad it followed her.

Once my food is warm, I take a few bites, and though my stomach is growling, I don't have an appetite. As I push the plate away, I hear a few light knocks on the front door. I don't have the strength to deal or talk to anyone right now. However, news travels fast around here, so I'm sure everyone knows what happened by now, and considering we were at the B&B when I slammed my fist into her fiancé's face, people were looking. I'm almost certain it's my dad coming to bitch me out for not controlling my temper. Dread washes over me with each step, but when I open the door, Zoey stands there with swollen eyes and a red nose. She's been crying, but I keep my emotions buried inside, protecting what little piece of my heart I have left.

Though I'm tempted to slam the door in her face, I don't.

"What do you want?" My words come out harsh, but she just broke my fucking heart, so I don't apologize.

"Can we talk? Please?" She bites her lower lip, something I've come to adore, but now it pisses me off.

"You should probably leave," I snap, not wanting to hear the details of her and the asshole she's engaged to.

Zoey crosses her arms and takes a step forward. "I'm not leaving until we talk. I know I'm the last person on earth you want to see right now, but you deserve answers, and I want to give you at least that."

Though I want to push her away, I can't find the strength to do so. Stepping aside, I let her in and suck in a deep breath as I shut the door. I need to gain my composure and not wear my emotions on my sleeve, but it's so hard when she's here in the flesh looking so goddamn beautiful.

"You have five minutes." Just being around her is driving me absolutely crazy, and when she sits on the couch, I sit as far away from her as possible. She notices but doesn't say anything.

"I'm sorry, Riley. I'm so fucking sorry. I never wanted to hurt you, and I never imagined he'd show up here like this," she begins, not denying the fact that she's engaged to another man.

"You never thought you'd get busted, is what you mean, right?" I glare at her as I sit stiff as a board.

She shifts in her seat, frowning. "No, it's not like that at all."

"So please enlighten me. Please tell me what it's like because, right now, none of it is adding up, Zoey. None of it. The past three weeks have been the best time of my life, and for it to end like this? It's completely fucked up."

"Riley, I know. I should've told you as soon as I got here, but I was scared you wouldn't give us a chance. I never meant for it to get to this level. Benjamin proposed to me after Vegas."

"So you were dating someone during Vegas? Just wondering if you're a cheater or a liar, or both." I'm growing more frustrated with every passing second.

Shaking her head, she opens her mouth, then closes it, trying to find her words. I don't rush her, giving her all the time she needs for now, but the clock is ticking.

"Kinda. No. We weren't official. We had gone out on a couple of dates, but we weren't together. I only went to amuse my mom and dad because they're friends with Benjamin's parents. Each date was worse than the one before, and I hadn't planned on going out with him again. But then he shocked the shit outta me when he proposed at Summer's wedding. Everyone in the family and our social circles were there, smiling at me, and I was expected to accept. It all happened too fast, and I said yes. Even though I had doubts, I was terrified of disappointing my parents in front of so many people."

At the mention of her folks, everything she's told me about them makes sense. Always living in her sister's shadow and wanting to impress them, though I can't understand why. They all sound horrible.

"So you said yes and filed for an annulment soon after..." I clarify.

Zoey nods. "I had my lawyer send the papers for you to sign, and when you sent them back, it didn't feel right. So a couple of weeks later, I came here to find out if you'd felt the same or not."

I let her words soak in, understanding the situation she was put in, but that doesn't explain why she felt like lying to me was her only option.

"We talked about honesty. At any point over the past three weeks, you could've told me the whole story. We could've figured it out together, as husband and wife. You talked about your parents and their expectations, but somehow, you forgot to mention Benjamin was what they wanted for you too. You lied to my face and hurt me. You betrayed my trust and my family's trust too. I feel used, like you came here to take advantage of me, like an excuse you needed to get out of your proposal, and it's a dirty feeling. I thought I knew you, but I'm not so sure anymore." My heart pounds rapidly while I'm harsh and to the point. I look up at the clock, and though she opens her mouth to more than likely refute everything I've pointed out, I interrupt her. "Your time is up, Zoey."

She stands, wiping tears from her cheeks. "I'm leaving with Benjamin first thing in the morning. My car will be picked up before the end of the month."

I stand, frowning. "So that's it? You're going back to Phoenix with him?" I search her face, knowing it's not what she wants.

"I have to," she says, shrugging. I want to tell her it's bullshit, that she doesn't have to leave, and remind her that she can stay here with me forever. I'm tempted to mention that we can get through this because even though I'm hurt, I'd be willing to fight if she is. She's *my* wife, married to me, but I don't say any of that. Instead, I stare at the wall, replaying everything that's happened. The question of if she plans on returning lingers in the room. Though I want to ask, I don't think I'll be able to take the truth if her answer is no.

At my silence, she walks toward the door, and I follow. She turns and looks at me before opening it. "I know I hurt you, but please know I never intended to, Riley. I really am sorry."

"I have to believe you didn't, or I'll drive myself crazy. However, you need to figure out what you want in life, Zoey. I love you, but is it enough for you? Will living on the ranch make you happy? Small towns aren't for everyone, and I understand that, so you need to decide," I tell her, the look on her face tempting me to kiss the fuck out of her. "Decide so we can both move on with our lives—either together or apart. The ball's in your court. You already have the papers with my signature on it, so make your decision and let me know when you have it."

Zoey stays silent as we stare at each other. Her expression's unreadable. I want her to respond, to say something, to tell me that she's coming back and not marrying that asshole, but she doesn't say anything. She doesn't reinforce the way she feels about me or how the past three weeks were amazing, and it destroys me.

Instead, she walks out without muttering anything.

I refuse to beg her to stay because, at the end of the day, I only care about her happiness, unlike her fucking family. And if he makes her happy, though I don't think he does or ever could, then that's who she needs to be with. I'll always cherish the time we spent together. It will be a time in my life that I'll never forget, not even if I wanted to.

I stand at the door and watch until I can no longer see the taillights of her car, and that's when reality hits that she's really gone. Closing it, I let out a deep breath, then turn around and see Diesel standing there.

"What the fuck are you doing here?" He nearly scares the shit out of me because I thought I was alone.

"I fell asleep in my room." He brushes his fingers through his hair. "I really miss my bed."

"Yeah, sorry about kicking your ass to the curb," I say, going back to the kitchen and cleaning up my mess. I just need to keep my mind busy.

"I know it's gonna happen eventually, so it's not a big deal." He continues to watch me. "Why the hell did you let her leave?"

I look at him like he's lost his mind. "Why wouldn't I?"

"I dunno, because you're supposed to fight for the woman you love? That's the Bishop way, isn't it?" He smirks.

Shaking my head, I roll my eyes and finish wiping off the counter. "If she wants to be with me, she knows where I live. The last thing I want to do is beg her to stay when she doesn't want to. She's an adult. She can make her own choices without me influencing her decision. Her family does that for her enough."

"You're stubborn as fuck," he quips.

"Now that's the Bishop way," I retort.

Diesel opens the fridge and grabs a beer. "We're going out tonight. Honky Tonk has ladies' night, or we can go to the Circle B Saloon and play a round of pool."

"You're relentless as hell," I tell him, shaking my head.

"You need to get out of here. You need to get your mind on something else, or you're going to drive yourself mad. Whiskey makes everything better, and I'll even volunteer to be your designated driver so you can get trashed." I hesitate, not feeling right about going out, but fuck, I need a drink. Before I can answer, he continues, "Dare ya."

I narrow my eyes at him. "You would, you bastard."

CHAPTER TWENTY

Zoey

"**G**ood morning," Benjamin says as he takes my suitcase from my hand and pops the trunk.

"Fuck off," I mutter, walking past him to the passenger's side.

"Now, now. Don't be upset, Zoey. You'll get back into your routine at home and forget all about this place," he tells me before we both get into the car.

"How about we just don't talk until we land in Phoenix?" I glower, narrowing my eyes at him, daring him to push me. I'm exhausted and cranky, and I'm not in the mood for his shit. I hardly slept last night, wishing I was in Riley's arms again, but instead, I slept alone.

"Whatever you want, darling," he says as he drives away from the B&B. Glancing over my shoulder, I watch until the large house is out of sight. Sadness washes over me.

After leaving Riley's house last night, I went back to my room and started packing. Shamelessly, I had to let John know that I'd be checking out

460

in the morning, and he stayed professional, giving me my invoice and wishing me a safe trip home. I'm not sure how long it'll take before his whole family finds out what happened between us, but I know it'll disappoint them all. I'm disappointed in myself.

I didn't even get the chance to say goodbye to Rowan or their parents. Or Aunt Mila and his cousins.

All the memories we made, all the laughing we did, and the stories we shared. They'll be in my heart forever, and no one can take those from me. I know Riley is heartbroken right now, so am I, but I hope one day he'll understand why I didn't tell him right away and will eventually forgive me.

The flight back home is short, and I'm relieved when Benjamin takes me home because I want distance from him. I'm pissed I don't have my car and will have to rely on the bus or someone to drive me around. I know he said it's being delivered, but I would've preferred to have driven it back myself. Of course, I didn't get an option, though.

The moment Benjamin hands me my luggage, the front door flies open, and my mother rushes toward me.

"Zoey Marie! Oh my God, you're finally home!" She wraps her arms around me. "I was so worried about you," she scolds, pulling back to frown at me. "You didn't answer any of my phone calls."

I immediately feel guilty for making her worry. It wasn't my intention, but I knew she'd ask too many questions. "Sorry, Mom. The reception wasn't great where I was," I tell her, which is mostly true.

"Well, come in. We can talk inside."

Great.

Benjamin follows, and I groan, feeling like an adolescent who's about to get disciplined.

"I told you I'd get her back safely," he says, gloating, as if I'm his bounty, and he's waiting for his reward. "Even if it ended up a bit difficult."

My mom pats his cheek with a concerning grin. His eye bruised more overnight, and I know she's wondering what happened. "Thank you, dear. I know you'll always protect my little Zoey."

"Can you stop talking about me as if I'm not here?" I sit on a stool at the breakfast bar. "I didn't need his protection."

Benjamin crosses his arms, giving me a pointed look. "Maybe when you're done acting like a child, we'll have a proper discussion about what the hell you were doing in Texas."

I narrow my eyes at him, wishing I had the power to blow him up with my fury. If my mother wasn't present, I'd give him a piece of my mind with a side of junk punch.

"Dinner is at six," my mother tells him, ignoring the silent exchange between us, and thankfully, she doesn't ask any questions.

"I'll be back then," he says sweetly, kissing her cheek.

Benjamin walks to me and places his lips on my forehead. "Take a nap, darling. You'll feel better."

Breaking his nose would make me feel better.

Once he's gone, my mother smiles at me. "I'm so glad you're back so we can really start planning the wedding. Everyone's still gushing about your proposal, and we're so excited about your big day."

Though I force a smile to appease her, I remain silent at her words.

"Where's your ring, sweetie?" she asks, glancing down at my hand.

"I left it in my jewelry box so I wouldn't lose it on my trip," I tell her honestly.

"Oh, okay. Well, when you freshen up for dinner, make sure to put it on." She pats my hand.

I hop off the stool and grab my bag. "I'm going to my room for a bit."

"Alrighty. Get some rest. Lots to do!" she singsongs as I make my way upstairs.

I wish Summer still lived at home so I could crawl into her bed, and we could talk like before. She'd pet my hair and help me talk through my issues, but I know I need to figure this out on my own. Though I do decide to text her so she knows I'm back.

ZOEY

Back in Phoenix. Mom's having dinner at 6 and Benjamin's coming.

SUMMER

Thank God! I was so worried about you.

ZOEY

Why? You knew where I was. Speaking of which, thanks for telling them where I was...

SUMMER

Babe, I'm sorry. You know how Mom gets when she worries, and she was calling me twice a day, then Benjamin came over, and he knew I was lying when I told him I didn't know.

ZOEY

He's such an ass.

SUMMER

He's your fiancé.

I roll my eyes. That doesn't excuse his behavior.

ZOEY

Can we plan a sister date tomorrow?

SUMMER

Of course! Let's meet for lunch.

ZOEY

Okay, see you then.

Before unpacking my bag, I decide to text Riley.

ZOEY

Just letting you know I made it back to Phoenix.

I watch as the dots bounce on the screen a moment later.

RILEY

Okay. Good to know.

My heart sinks. I don't know what I expected, but I don't have anyone to blame but myself.

As I take out my clothes, I hold back the tears. The smell of dirt and muffins immediately hits my senses, and I laugh. It smells like the B&B. And him.

God. The way he looked at me—with pure disappointment and heartbreak—is an image that'll forever be imbedded into my mind. I wish I would've had enough strength to tell Benjamin to go to hell when he showed up, but I knew he wouldn't have left. His head is so far up my father's ass, I would've been dragged out kicking and screaming. Riley already punched his face in, so there's no telling what would've happened had I resisted.

Benjamin and I have one thing in common, and that's money. Well, my parents' money. They would've done whatever it took to get me out of there and back on Benjamin's arm, looking like the proper fiancée. The whole charade is disgusting, and it sickens me that my parents believe I want that. For my entire life, I've followed a certain set of rules while bending just enough not to get into trouble. Traveling and exploring new places are what I love to do, and as long as I always returned and plastered a smile on my face around my family, they never asked any questions. However, now they've demanded I start thinking about my future, which involves being Benjamin's arm candy. They probably expect me to have kids right away, too, since I don't have a prominent career. Then I'll have the picture-perfect family.

By a quarter till six, I'm rested, showered, and dressed for what is going to be the worst dinner in history. Benjamin might have my parents fooled, but not me. I see straight through his bullshit.

"You look beautiful," he says after I meet everyone downstairs. He's early, of course. Leaning in and kissing my cheek, he acts as the perfect gentleman. I watch as my parents beam with pride. I suck in a breath, resisting the urge to slap him.

"Such a gorgeous couple," my mom gushes, clasping her hands together as Benjamin wraps his arm around me. "Come sit. Dinner's ready."

Benjamin holds out my chair for me, and I take my seat. Dad immediately talks about work as Mom brings out the final dish.

"Time for grace, dear," Mom tells Dad, and we all hold hands. My mother speaks, and once she says, "*Amen*," we all repeat it, and I immediately yank my hand from Benjamin's.

Shortly after we pass around all the food and our plates are full, my mom leads the conversation to the wedding, just as I suspected she would.

"So what time of year are you two thinking? We could do a gorgeous spring wedding," she suggests. "Though if you two can't wait that long, a fall themed one would be amazing, too."

"The sooner, the better," Benjamin says, winking at my mom, which makes her blush.

Oh, give me a fucking break.

"What about you, Zoey?" my father asks as if they just realized I was in the room. "What time of year were you thinking?"

"Oh, um. I was thinking about the season of never." I flash a smile, then dive into my potatoes.

"Zoey." My father's warning tone makes me look up at him. "What's going on?"

I drop my fork, deciding now's the time. "I'm already married, so marrying Benjamin isn't going to be possible." I shrug. "Also, I hate him."

"What do you mean you're already married?" My mother gasps, pressing a hand to her chest over her heart as if I've given her the worst news of her life.

"It's nothing we can't take care of," Benjamin intervenes, plastering on a confident grin and completely ignoring my comment about him.

"Who? When?" Finally. My father asks good questions.

"His name is Riley Bishop," I tell them, but saying his name aloud causes my stomach to flip. "We met in Vegas, and he's who I went to visit in Texas these past few weeks."

"Why would you marry a stranger?" my father asks, his face distorted. "What does he do?" Of course he'd ask about his career.

I shrug, not wanting to give him the details of our drunken dare to elope. "He's a rancher. His family owns a huge cattle and horse ranch in Eldorado, Texas. They own a bed and breakfast on the land and a bar in town."

"It's Southern white trash," Benjamin hisses. "The place is filthy."

I snap my gaze to his. "You're just pissed Riley kicked your ass," I say without thinking.

"What?" my parents both say.

"I'm *not* marrying Benjamin."

"Zoey..." Dad warns. "Whatever this is, whatever it is you're going through, we'll figure it out. File the annulment papers, and we can cover it up. No big deal." He fans out his napkin, then places it gently on his lap. "Can you pass the salt, please?"

He ends the conversation as if my words meant nothing to him. I just said I'm not marrying Benjamin, and my father asks me to pass the *fucking* salt? What is wrong with my goddamn family?

"Did you hear what I said?" I ask him pointedly as he waits for the shaker.

"I did, but you don't know what you're talking about. Stop acting like a child. Salt, *now*."

My blood boils as years of pent-up aggravation hit the surface at the realization that I'm nothing more than a political ploy to them. Marry off their daughter to a hotshot doctor and basically change everything about myself to make them happy.

It stops *now*. My chair scrapes against the floor as I push away from the table, the three of them looking up at me wide-eyed as I stand. I toss my napkin down on my plate and scowl. "I'm done. Excuse me."

"Zoey!" Benjamin shouts, standing as I move toward the door. "Do not walk away from me! You're my fiancée. You're *mine*."

"No…" I say comically, turning around and facing him. "I was never yours. Proposing to me in front of a room filled with family and knowing I'd have no choice but to agree makes you a coward. We went on a handful of dates, and you never once asked me any important questions. You don't even know who I really am. What I like. What makes me happy. You don't give a fuck about me." Then I face my parents, who look as if they've seen a ghost. "And shame on you, Mom and Dad. You'd rather marry me off to some man you approve of than ask me what I want. I've only ever wanted to make you proud, but I've finally realized it's not worth my own happiness to live the life you want for me. So I hope it was worth it…risking never seeing me again because you've pushed me too far this time."

I slide off the engagement ring and slam it down on the table. "Wedding is off. Goodbye, Benjamin. Forever. Eat shit."

With my head held high and my heart racing, I stomp up the stairs and don't breathe until I'm locked inside my bedroom. I've never stood up to my parents like that before, but it's been a long time coming.

No one bothers me the rest of the night, and I manage to sneak out the next day without anyone noticing. I take an Uber and meet Summer for lunch at a nearby cafe. I know she's dying to know all the details.

As soon as we spot each other, I stand, and she pulls me into her arms. "Zoey! I missed you." She squeezes harder, and I choke out for air.

"You act like I went to the moon or something," I tease as we sit.

"Three weeks is a long time for us not to hang out or at least chat," she says before the waitress arrives and takes our drink order.

"Have you talked to Mom or Dad today?" I ask.

"No, why? Everything okay?"

I look down at the table, feeling like everything's about to change. "I don't think so. Benjamin came over for dinner last night, and I told him I wasn't marrying him. Told Mom and Dad I was already married, and he's who I went to visit in Texas."

Her eyebrows fly to her hairline. "Oh." Summer blinks a few times and clears her throat. "I imagine that didn't go over very well. What did they say?"

"That I was a child...Benjamin said he'd pay to get it taken care of... basically to sit down and shut up."

"Zoey..."

"I didn't file the annulment papers," I blurt out. "That's why I left. I needed to see if Riley and I had a true connection or not. I knew marrying Benjamin would be a mistake either way, but I needed confirmation."

"Was Riley surprised to see you?" she asks as our drinks are delivered. The waitress takes our order and then leaves us to continue our conversation.

"Yeah, at first. Then once I explained why I was there—minus the Benjamin part—it was like we just continued right where we left off in Vegas. I don't know...it felt so right. So natural. I didn't have to pretend to be anyone. He likes me just the way I am," I say with a sad smile.

Summer nods, but I know her mind is racing at my confession. "So everyone lost their shit at dinner, I suspect?" She takes a sip from her drink as if we're discussing the weather. Summer's proper most of the time, especially in public, but I know the real her. The one she let loose in Vegas. "How'd the night end?"

"With me telling them all off and leaving the room. Haven't talked to any of them since," I reply, shrugging.

"So where does this leave you? What are you gonna do?" she asks, narrowing her eyes as if she's trying to figure me out.

"I'm not sure, honestly. Benjamin came to the ranch, Riley punched him, then Benjamin hauled my ass back home. I didn't want to leave Texas, but I knew I had to make things right here first. I had just told him the night before that I loved him and wanted to stay there. He said he loved me too." I choke back tears and sigh. "Then I broke his heart."

467

I close my eyes, not wanting to get emotional, but it's no use. I miss him so much already.

"Wow…" Summer inhales a deep breath. "Did you talk to Riley and explain your situation?"

"Yes, I told him everything. He basically told me the ball was in my court, and that I knew where he lived. I explained I had to go and straighten things out with my parents, but you should've seen his face. I hurt him. Betrayed his trust. His family was so wonderful to me, Summer. Showed me what it was like to have people in your life who support and love you unconditionally."

"I support you," she counters. "You're my sister, and I love you so much."

"I know you do. But for the most part, I've done what's been expected of me my whole life. I didn't want to go to med school, and I don't want to marry a doctor. I'm a huge failure in their eyes. But I can't live my life for them anymore."

"Exactly," she states. "You cannot live your life for anyone except you. I've loved Owen since I was fifteen. The fact that he wanted to be a doctor had nothing to do with me wanting to marry him. Sure, it made our parents happier than a pig in mud, but if he had wanted to do something else, that wouldn't have changed the way I feel about him. Mom and Dad would've had to get over it. I know you think you're a disappointment, but I also know they care about your happiness. They push you because they think it's what they're supposed to do instead of just supporting you in whatever it is you want."

"Well, they could've fooled me for the past twenty-one years." I scoff. "They always made me feel like I embarrassed them for being a hairdresser and wanting to explore everything and anything. They wanted a cookie-cutter daughter, but they got me instead."

Summer reaches across the table and places her hand on top of mine. "They'll come around, Zoey. They won't risk not having a relationship with you and know they can't push you to do something you don't want. If Riley's *the one*, they'll just have to accept it."

"I'm not even sure if what Riley and I had can be fixed at this point. He said it was my decision, but I'm afraid I'm just going to hurt him more."

"Follow your heart, Zoey. It'll always lead you in the right direction."

CHAPTER TWENTY-ONE

Riley

It's been a week since Zoey left and took my heart with her. She texted me once to say she made it back home, but we haven't talked since. I've been tempted a dozen times to reach out because I miss her so much, but then I decide not to and delete my message.

The worst fucking week of my life.

I told her the ball was in her court, knowing she had a big decision to make. I don't want to be anyone's second choice, and I thought it was different with Zoey. The betrayal I feel for not knowing the whole truth of why she was here still weighs heavy on my heart. Even though I believed her when she told me she loved me, I couldn't beg her to stay or force her to choose me. Part of me wanted to, but the other part knew letting her go was the right thing to do. Her life was never here.

"Turn that frown upside down, Birthday Boy!" Diesel singsongs as he pours shots of tequila. "The ladies are gonna be here any second to pregame, and then we're hitting the bar!"

Groaning, I take the shot from him and swallow it down. This wasn't my idea, but after telling Diesel I didn't want to celebrate and wanted to just spend the night alone, he made plans for the both of us. I don't have enough energy to argue anymore.

"Cheers to twenty-three, you old fart!" He hands me another, and again, I swallow it down. Maybe it'll numb me long enough to stop thinking about Zoey for more than ten seconds.

The doorbell rings, and Diesel claps. "They're here! Get ready! Your birthday gifts have arrived…"

Grunting, I shake my head. I have zero interest in any woman who isn't my wife.

Diesel lets them in and blasts the music.

Just fucking shoot me already.

"Alright, quit being a miserable bastard." Diesel grabs my arm and lifts me to my feet before setting me down on a barstool. It's the one from the kitchen that Zoey and I fooled around on. *Great.*

"Ladies, ladies…" Diesel says. "Lookin' fine as hell. Let's make the man of the hour feel better, shall we?"

Diesel changes the music, and soon, the girls are dancing in front of me. I have no idea who they are, but knowing my best friend, they've been bought for the night. Asshole.

I drink a beer while they strut their stuff, trying to tempt me to dance with them, but I push them away. A *thanks, but no thanks* approach and directed them toward Diesel instead.

"I'm getting a refill," I tell him and leave the room before he can stop me. He has one girl on his lap while the other dances around them.

As I grab another beer from the fridge, I hear the doorbell ring again and shake my head. Who knows who else he invited? Probably more women. I'm going to need to be way drunker if Diesel has more shenanigans up his sleeve. So I grab two beers before walking back into the living room. It's then I hear her voice.

"Oh, hi. Um. I'm looking for Riley, but it looks like I came at a bad time. I'll come back…"

"Zoey?" Diesel says, standing and going to the door. I stand frozen, watching it all unfold, too shocked to move my damn feet. "What're you doing here?"

"I came to talk to Riley…" Her sweet voice rings out, but I hear the devastation in her tone. Fuck, this looks really bad. "But never mind. You're busy. I'll go."

Setting the bottles down, I rush through the room and push through Diesel and the girl. Zoey is already rushing down the stairs and back to her car.

"Zoey, wait…" I call out, following behind her. "It's not what it looks like."

She spins around and faces me, her expression unreadable as I approach her. "You don't owe me an explanation, Riley."

"You came back?" I ask on a breath.

"I'm sorry I showed up uninvited, but I wanted to give you these…" She hands me a manila folder. I watch as she chews on her lip—her nervous tic —as I open it and see it's the annulment papers I first signed. *Son of a bitch.* "Hurting you will always be my biggest regret, Riley. I'm sorry for not telling you the whole truth sooner, but—"

"Do you still love me?" I interrupt, my heart throbs in my chest at seeing her and these fucking documents.

She blinks up at me and nods. "Yes, it's why I—"

My jaw tightens, and I step closer. "Then why are you doing this?" I ask, shaking the folder in my hand.

"Riley, I'm trying—"

"Why are you walking away?" I take another step closer. "Don't you feel how right this is?" I grab her hand. "How perfect we could be together?" I place her palm over my pounding heart and close the gap between us until she's against the car door.

Our closeness causes her breath to hitch. With my eyes locked on hers, she whispers, "Yes, I do."

"Then why did you sign the fucking papers, Zoey? Please tell me why," I ask, squeezing her hand tighter.

She swallows, then looks up at me. "I didn't."

I lean back as if she'd just slapped me. "What? But you brought them here and gave them to me." I drop her hand. "Or you wanted me to witness you signing them instead?"

She winces, and I immediately regret the words. "Guess I deserved that."

"Shit, I'm sorry." I shake my head, setting the folder on top of the car.

"Then, please explain what it is you're doing here because my mind is going fucking crazy."

Zoey inhales a deep breath and smiles at me. Fuck, I've missed her smile. "I came here to say that I want you. *Only you.* I brought the papers so we could burn them together. I don't want an annulment. On the chance that you still want to be married to me, that is."

"Are you serious?" How could she even second-guess that she's all I want?

Well, the two half naked girls in my house probably don't help.

She nods. "I never had feelings for Benjamin or anything my parents pictured for me, but I tried for so long to make them happy that the lines began to blur between living my life and living for them. I decided life wasn't worth living if you weren't in it."

I can't help the smile on my face as I take in her words. "Really? You want to stay married then?" Caging her against the car, I lean forward, waiting for her to say the words.

"Yes, dummy!" She swats at my chest, laughing. "Had you not interrupted me a dozen times, I could've said that sooner."

Wrapping a hand around her neck, I pull her mouth to mine and press our bodies together. Zoey immediately relaxes against me, looping her arms around my waist and pulling me tighter. I can't believe she's really here.

"You're staying..." I whisper against her lips.

"Yes," she replies.

"You're mine."

"Yes." She slides her tongue between my lips. "Only yours."

"Always."

Zoey grins against me. "Yes."

Hesitantly, I pull back as we both catch our breaths. "Tell me what happened," I say, and she immediately knows what I'm referring to.

"I told my parents the truth, and that I refused to marry someone just to appease them. They weren't happy about it, but once the initial shock wore off, they accepted that my happiness was more important. They apologized for making me feel pressured, and as soon as I was able to get things in order at my job and pack up, I grabbed a flight out here. Summer said she'd ship me the rest of my things, assuming you didn't kick me out on my ass."

I smirk. "I'm crazy in love with you, Zoey. I'd never kick you anywhere, except maybe into my bed."

She brings our lips back together before pulling apart and grinning. "So you want to explain the two strippers in your house, or are we just going to ignore that?"

Chuckling, I shake my head. "Fucking Diesel. It's his birthday gift to me." I roll my eyes with a sigh. "Told him I didn't want him to do anything, but you know how well he listens."

She furrows her brows at me, frowning. "I'm sorry I missed your birthday. I'm the worst wife ever."

I look at my new watch—a gift from my parents and Rowan—and grin. "It's not over yet. Plenty of time to make it up to me." I waggle my brows.

"Well, in that case…let's go inside."

"I like that idea much better." I wink.

After I grab the folder and her luggage, we walk back into the house and go straight into my bedroom. The moment the door is shut, I drop everything and wrap Zoey into my arms.

"I think it's time we take a proper honeymoon, wife. What do you think?" I suck on her neck, brushing my facial hair against her skin because I know it drives her insane.

She arches, giving me better access. "Mmm…I like that idea very much."

"Let's start now." My hands slide around her back and up her tank top. "We'll call it a pre-honeymoon."

She chuckles and raises her arms so I can take it off. "What about your company?"

"Meh. Let Diesel have fun with them. It'll keep him away from my sister, at least."

Zoey laughs, reaching for my shirt and lifting it over my head. "You won't be able to forever, you know."

"Yes, I will," I state matter-of-factly, pulling her closer. "And that Trace douche? Pretty sure Diesel scared him away for good."

"Poor Rowan," she says.

Wrapping a hand around her, I unclasp her bra and toss it. "Can we not talk about my sister right now?"

"Would you rather talk about mine?" she counters, smirking.

"That's…" I shake my head. "You're weird. Clothes. Off. Now."

Zoey laughs, unbuttoning her shorts. "Hey, you married me."

"And I'd do it again," I say without hesitation, undoing my jeans and kicking them off with my boxers.

"No regrets?" she asks as she slides her panties down.

"Fucking never." I growl, launching myself toward her until she's back in my arms. I cup her ass as she wraps her legs around me. "This just became the best birthday of my life."

"Does this mean I have to put out for every birthday from now on?" she taunts as I place her on the bed and tower over her.

"You've set a precedent now," I tell her. "Birthday sex is now a thing."

She crosses her ankles behind my back, pushing me against her gorgeous naked body. "Okay. Sex on your birthday, breakfast in bed for mine."

I smile against her collarbone as I feather kisses down her body. Lifting my head, I meet her eyes. "Wait, that sounds good. I want that too."

"Nope, you only get one," she says, then releases a moan when my erection brushes against her pussy.

"How about we both get breakfast in bed and sex on our birthdays, so really we get to celebrate twice?"

"Hmm...okay, deal." She arches her back as I wrap my mouth around her peaked nipple.

"Look at us." I flatten my tongue between her breasts. "Already making compromises as a married couple."

"I'm nothing if not agreeable," she hums. "Unless you think we're moving too fast?"

Lifting up on my palms, I tower over her beautiful face. "I'm quite sure that ship sailed within the first twenty-four hours of meeting." I lift my hips toward hers, letting her feel how hard I am. "I knew I wanted you the moment I saw you and fell head over heels in love with you within two weeks of you being here. There's no slowin' down, baby. Except when I'm devouring you...because I'll take my time doing that."

Leaning down on one elbow, I tilt up her chin and bring her mouth to mine.

"I don't deserve you," she says softly, dropping her legs on either side of me. "The way I hurt you...I'll regret it forever."

Brushing hair from her cheeks, I kiss her sad lips. "That's something you'll learn about the Bishops. We fall fast and love hard. You made a mistake, but that's what makes you human, so forgive yourself, sweetheart. Because I already have."

"I love you," she whispers, capturing my mouth with hers. "I'll spend the rest of my life proving that to you."

Grabbing her thigh, I hitch it over my hip and squeeze her ass, before slapping it. "And I'll enjoy every goddamn minute of it."

Zoey pushes me down and straddles my waist with a shit-eating smirk on her face. "Then hang on, cowboy. It's gonna be a bumpy ride."

She presses her palms to my chest and lifts herself up. I grip her waist as she takes my cock and strokes it.

"Fuck..." I groan as my head falls back. A moment later, she positions it at her entrance, then slowly slides her body down. "Jesus Christ, Zoey."

She feels so goddamn amazing that I can barely breathe. As Zoey rocks her hips against me, she leans over, allowing me to cup her breast.

"You feel so good," she whispers against my mouth, squeezing her eyes shut.

"Look at me, sweetheart," I demand, then slide my hand to her neck. When she opens them, I flick my tongue out and lick her lips. "It feels so fucking right."

She nods, releasing a moan so sweet, it nearly sends me straight to heaven. I bring my hand back to her ass and slap it. Zoey yelps and laughs, pushing up on my chest and increasing her pace.

Arching my back, I jerk my hips up and meet her thrusts. They're frantic and greedy, both of us wanting more of each other with no desire to stop anytime soon.

I can tell she's about to come when her pussy tightens around my dick, so I circle my thumb over her clit and pinch her nipple.

"Oh my God..." she pants, throwing her head back. I love the way her hair falls, begging to be pulled.

"Yes, baby. Keep goin'. You're so close." I add more pressure, rubbing her sensitive spot faster. Sliding my hand up between her breasts, I grip my fingers around her throat and lightly squeeze.

"Fuck, *yes, yes, yes*..." Zoey unravels, her body shaking with convulsions as she moans and rides out her release. "Oh. My. God," she says, panting. "That was intense." Blinking, she looks down at me, and I chuckle at the way she's trying to catch her breath. Her tits bounce in front of me, and I push myself up until I can capture one in my mouth.

A moment later, I flip her over until she's underneath me. She yelps and laughs, keeping our bodies molded together. Grabbing her leg, I prop her ankle up on my shoulder and close the gap between us.

"I'd hang on to the headboard if I were you." I flash her a wink, slowly pulling out before quickly thrusting back inside.

"Jesus," she says, reaching above her head and grabbing the rails.

When I lean down, her knee nearly touches her chest, allowing me to go even deeper. She grips me so damn tight that I know I won't last long if she keeps doing that.

Her other leg snakes around my waist, and when she begs for more, I know I can't deny her. I lean back slightly and grip her hips, driving into her as fast as I can. She screams my name, rocking her body against mine, and as soon as I feel her tighten around my dick, I'm fucking gone.

With a loud growl, I unleash into her. We please each other until we're both spent and gasping for air.

"I hope Diesel didn't hear that," she says, her chest rising and falling after I collapsed next to her. "I'm already gonna have a hard time looking him in the eyes. He probably hates me."

"Is that who you were thinking of this whole time?" I tease. "Should I ask him to join us?"

She snaps her face to mine in horror. "Is that something you…do? I mean, no judging, but…"

"Zoey." I burst out laughing. "No! God, no. I was joking."

She smacks me before rolling over and resting her head on my chest. "You're the worst."

"Yeah, well you married me, so now you gotta deal with me." I brush the hair off her sweaty face, which causes me to smile.

"I know…but at least the sex is good." She shrugs.

"Good?" I ask, feigning offense and arching a brow.

"Pretty good?"

I move my hand down and smack her ass, harder this time.

"Okay, geez!" She laughs. "You sure like your ego stroked."

"Not just my ego…"

She rolls her eyes. "Lord, I'm done."

Zoey tries to roll over, but I wrap my legs around her and pin her to my body. "Not so fast, Mrs. Bishop." She tries to hold back a grin, but I see it. "We have some making up to do."

She furrows her brows. "Isn't that what we just did?"

"That was birthday sex," I tell her. "Now it's makeup sex time."

Zoey bites down on her lower lip. "Does that include bending me over and telling me I've been a very bad girl?"

"Jesus, fuck..." My cock hardens, and I groan at her dirty words. "I'm about to throw you over my shoulder and take you in the shower."

"It's good to be back," she whispers with a cheeky grin, letting out a hum.

"I'm glad you're home, wifey."

CHAPTER TWENTY-TWO

Zoey

FIVE MONTHS LATER

Christmas on the ranch is something I've looked forward to for months, and now that the temperature has significantly dropped, I'm even more excited. The B&B is decorated with colorful lights, candy canes, and fake snow, and I adore it so much. Not to mention the holiday music and eggnog available at all hours of the day. The Bishop women got together and strung lights, made homemade cookies, and put up the famous twelve-foot tree. It was the most fun I've had during the holidays since I was a kid.

When I moved to Texas, my parents were pissed, but I didn't care. I'd embarrassed them for calling off the wedding with Benjamin, and I refused to apologize for it because my heart knew what was right. The day I packed my shit and left, their hold on me was released. It took all of three weeks for

Benjamin to find another victim, and he's now already married and expecting a baby.

Before Thanksgiving, my folks flew here to talk to me because every phone call ended with one of us hanging up on the other, and I was exhausted from dealing with them. As soon as they showed up, they apologized, and after meeting the Bishops, they fully understood why I loved being here so much. I was shocked, but they finally accepted me and my decisions.

I roll over and feel the bed is empty, but it's still warm from Riley. Putting on my slippers and robe, I head out to find my husband. He's in the kitchen dressed in layers, sipping his coffee. The longer scruff on his chin suits him, which I've always loved. I take a few steps forward and plant a kiss on his lips, telling him good morning.

"You're gonna be so damn excited," he tells me with a smirk.

"Why?"

"Go look outside." He tilts his head toward the door.

"No..." I gasp. "No way!"

He nods and follows me to the big double windows in the living room. The sun hasn't risen yet, but the moonlight makes it visible. Outside, a thin layer of snow coats the grass, something that doesn't happen too often in Texas.

"It's a Christmas miracle!" I shout, so excited to see the white-covered ground. Without thinking, I go outside and immediately regret it because it's freezing, but I scoop up some snow that almost immediately melts when I grab it. I hurry and mold it into a ball, then throw it at Riley. He chuckles, closes the space between us, and pulls me into his arms. His soft lips gently paint mine, and I sigh against him. To think, I almost lost him, and at moments like this, I'm so grateful I didn't.

"I love you so damn much," he whispers.

"I love you more," I say, pouring everything I have into him. A shiver courses through me, and Riley leads me back inside.

"The last thing I need is you getting sick," he says, pouring me a cup of coffee. "I'm gonna feed the animals, and then I'll be back to get you for lunch at Grandma's."

I walk over to him, sitting on his lap. "But don't you want your Christmas present now? It's not suitable for your parents to see."

His eyebrows perk up. "Uhh. Fuck yes."

"One second," I tell him and rush into the bedroom, pulling a sexy set of red lingerie that I bought online from my dresser. After I change, I walk back into the kitchen in panties and a bra that leaves no room for the imagination with a ribbon tied around my stomach.

"Merry fuckin' Christmas to me." He beams, untying my makeshift bow. Riley picks me up in one swift movement and carries me to the bedroom.

"You have time, right?" I ask, knowing he has a list of things to do before the sun rises.

"I'll always have time for you, sweetheart. No matter what," he murmurs. Laying me down on the bed, he takes his time admiring me as he removes all of his clothes. "I'm the luckiest man in the world."

He still has the ability to make me blush. "Come here," I demand.

Our lips crash together, and I wish we could spend all day rolling under the sheets as the snow falls outside, but I'll take him whenever I can get him. Riley wastes no time, looping his fingers in the lace of my panties and sliding them down before removing my bra and taking each nipple in his mouth.

I let out a moan, needing him more than I need warmth on this cold winter day.

"Shit, you're ready for me, baby," he hums, sliding his fingers between my legs. "I have to taste you first. Christmas breakfast." He winks, which makes me chuckle. The man has no shame.

As he drags his lips down my stomach and kisses between my thighs, I nearly beg him to stop teasing me. But when his tongue flicks against my clit, I see stars. Riley knows how to please me in ways no one has ever been able to, making sure I come at least once before he does. As I lose myself in the moment, he hovers above me, carefully filling me with his length. Placing my palms on each side of his face, I pull his mouth to mine, allowing our tongues to dance as our bodies move together in perfect rhythm.

"You're so damn beautiful." He grins, panting as he speeds up the pace. His words are so heartfelt and make me feel like I'm his whole world.

My body tightens, shaking as he brings me over the edge. I moan his name, digging my nails into his back. His body seizes, latching his lips to mine as he releases inside me. Riley topples over, pulling me with him, and I laugh.

"Best Christmas morning I've ever had," he teases, and I can't help but agree.

Soon, we're cleaning up, and he's putting on his layers of clothes so he can get the day started. I frown because I already miss him.

"I'll pick you up around eleven for lunch." He gives me a goodbye kiss, and I want to pull him back into bed with me, but I know I can't. I yawn, and once he's out the door, I easily fall back to sleep.

I wake to Riley plopping down on the bed next to me, brushing his fingers over my cheek. I reach for him with sleepy eyes and a smile.

"You know we can't be late," he reminds me, but there's no way I'd forget. Grandma Bishop invented punctuality.

"Is the snow still there?" I lift my head and try to catch a glimpse out the window but fail miserably.

"No, as soon as the sun came up, it pretty much all melted. Usually doesn't stick." He leans down to give me a kiss, which I happily accept. "It's half past ten," he tells me, playfully pushing me, and I lazily roll out of bed, still naked, and go to our closet.

"Damn, am I glad I made Diesel move out." Riley groans with a smirk, fully taking me in, and it causes me to laugh.

I slip on a sweater and some jeans, then put on some boots that go halfway up my calves, and throw my hair into a messy bun.

"Don't forget to grab the Christmas gifts for Grandma and Grandpa," I remind Riley.

"Good call," he tells me with a grin, pulling the presents from under the tree.

Yesterday, we celebrated at his parents' house, exchanging gifts and eating a ton of food and sweets. Riley's parents told me stories about him as a kid, and Rowan didn't let them hold back anything. She and I have become really close friends, and I can tell her almost anything, though I leave out all the sex because it's her brother, and she'll roll her eyes with a gag. I adore his parents so much, and they've quickly accepted me as their second daughter, a title I'm proud to have earned.

Riley and I climb into the truck and head to the other side of the ranch where his grandparents live. The yard is full of trucks, and I know the house is going to be crammed full of all the kids and grandkids.

We walk inside, and everyone instantly starts shouting their hellos. No one with the last name of Bishop is remotely quiet. I think it's because they've always had to talk over each other to be heard, which I find hilarious.

Before we make our way to the kitchen, Riley points above the entrance where mistletoe is haphazardly hung. With a swift movement, he pulls me into his arms and captures my lips with his. The aww's and a few gagging noises from his younger cousins fill the space because, of course, we have an audience.

"Gotta kiss my wife under the mistletoe," he exclaims. "Bishop tradition."

I laugh and grab his hand and look around at all the love in the room. Grandma Bishop comes up and pulls us into a big hug and gives us kisses. She's wearing the cutest Santa Claus apron and looks like Mrs. Claus. "So glad you kids could make it."

"Wouldn't miss it for the world," I say, and she gives me a soft pat on the cheek.

"We're getting ready to say grace so we can eat," Grandma Bishop announces, speaking loud enough for everyone to get the message. The men remove their ball caps and cowboy hats before their grandfather says the blessing. He ends it with a big, "Let's eat!"

All the adults sit at the main table to eat, and in the other room, a kiddie table is set up. Since we're married, we get to sit with the grown-ups, which has Riley gloating as the others shoot daggers at him. We fill our plates high from the mounds of food. By the time we're done eating, we're so miserable from stuffing ourselves to the max. I take our plates to the kitchen and set them in the sink when Grandma Bishop thanks me.

"So when are you and Riley going to make me some great-grandchildren?" she asks pointedly.

My eyes go wide, and Riley's mama walks up and clears her throat. "I'm not ready to be a grandma just yet."

"Well, I'm not gettin' any younger," Grandma Bishop hints, giving me a sweet smile. The woman loves her kids, grandchildren, and I've heard stories about how much pressure she puts on everyone. Needless to say, we're in the hot seat. I laugh, excusing myself, and rush back to Riley.

"Your grandma just cornered me about having kids," I tell him as he leads me into the living room.

"Well?" he pushes. "Did you tell her we're trying?"

"No!" I release a nervous laugh. "Your mom walked up, and needless to say, it was awkward."

"Get used to it. Grandma's relentless," he says into my neck.

"I heard that!" she scolds, walking around with a plate of cookies. I take one, but I'm not sure I can even eat it. I might not be pregnant, but I definitely have a food baby. But you never deny Grandma Bishop's food. I learned that the hard way. She rounds us all up, and we somehow manage to all fit in the living room. Once she hands out presents to her kids and grandkids, we open them, chatting and laughing. It's not until everyone's done that she and Grandpa unwrap theirs. I can't help but look around the room and feel so damn grateful for getting to be a part of this family, one so welcoming and loving, I can't imagine life without them all.

Just as his grandparents finish thanking everyone for their gifts, Riley stands and says he has an announcement to make. I look at him curiously because I have no idea what he's going to say. All eyes are on him, which makes me nervous as hell.

"So everyone knows that Zoey and I eloped in Vegas, thanks to my best friend who dared us to get married..." He smirks, and laughter fills the room. "Come up here, my gorgeous bride." Riley grabs my hand and pulls me up so we're face to face. I furrow my brows at him, my heart racing at the unwanted attention.

"What are you doing?" I whisper, but he just winks before dropping to one knee. He opens a black velvet box with a beautiful diamond ring inside. Then he takes my hand, and we lock eyes.

"You're already my wife, the best thing that has ever happened to me by far. I know you risked so much to be with me, and I'm glad you did. I love you so damn much, baby. Will you marry me...*again*?"

I glance down at the cheap novelty ring he bought me at the chapel in Vegas and haven't been able to part with it.

"Well?" he nervously asks when I don't respond.

Blinking, I smile wide. "Yes, absolutely!" I take off my old ring, one I'll still treasure forever, and allow him to slip on the new one. It's absolutely stunning; I can hardly believe it. "It's so beautiful," I murmur.

"You're beautiful," he counters. "I want to give you the wedding you deserve, baby."

Nodding and holding back tears, I nearly knock him down as I lean forward to kiss him. He falls on the floor with me in his arms, and I can't stop kissing him regardless of all the people watching.

"I said I wanted great-grandkids, but I don't want to witness them being made," Grandma Bishop blurts out, and the room bursts into laughter.

We pull apart, and I can't stop staring at this perfect man who's changed my entire life. Everyone goes back to their own conversations, and I look down at the ring, then glance at him.

"Are you sure you want to marry me again?" I ask with a smirk.

"I'd marry you a million times, Zoey." The passion in his voice is prevalent.

"Same," I say, the grin covering my face. "Guess I'll be getting hitched to the cowboy *again*."

"And damn, I can't wait for the honeymoon."

EPILOGUE

Riley

TWO AND A HALF YEARS LATER

I help carry boxes into Rowan's bedroom, and I'm pissed because it feels as if she's packed them full of textbooks. And possibly rocks. "What the hell do you have in here?" I groan, setting one down with a thud.

"Lots of stuff," she singsongs. "I accumulated a ton of shit after four years of college," Rowan tells me matter-of-factly. She graduated with her bachelor's degree in finance a few weeks ago and had to have everything out of her place by this weekend. Dad voluntold Diesel and me to help, which meant we didn't have a choice. So we drove six hours to Houston, loaded up all her boxes, drove six hours back and have been unloading for the past half hour. It's been a long fuckin' day considering we left at four a.m.

Honestly, I'd rather have shoveled horse shit for a week.

But she's my baby sister, and now that she's done with school, she's back permanently. I'm happy she's home, but now that means keeping an eye on her, especially when my best friend is always drooling over her.

"You better be glad I love you. That's all I have to say. I wouldn't have done this for anyone else." I laugh, but I'm not kidding.

Rowan sits on her childhood bed and looks around. "It's going to be weird living back with Mom and Dad, but I'm excited to be close to you, Zoey, and the new baby!" She does a little squeal, and I flinch at her high-pitched tone.

"Me too, sis. Auntie Rowan will be on babysitting duty every weekend, right?" I tease.

"I plan to have a life, thank you very much."

"Yeah, hanging out with me," Diesel interrupts, hauling a box in and dropping it.

"Hey! That could've been fragile!" Rowan stands and scowls.

"Relax, princess. I looked inside, and it wasn't." He flashes a shit-eating grin as if he'd been digging into the cookie jar.

"Don't look through my things, you weirdo!" She pushes his chest, but Diesel doesn't budge.

"She literally just moved back. Can't you two be adults and stop antagonizing one another?" I ask, then laugh, knowing they've been at each other's throats for as long as I can remember. Diesel's a year older than Rowan and has been taunting her since grade school. At this point, it's his life's mission.

"Between me and Diesel, there's only one adult here," Rowan jabs, narrowing her eyes at him.

Diesel presses a palm to his chest and frowns. "Now that just hurts. You wound me."

Rowan rolls her eyes and pushes past him toward the door.

"Alright, children. Let's get this shit done so I can go back to my *pregnant* wife." Zoey's eight months pregnant and ready to burst any day. She's been miserable in this Texas heat and having my sister close will be helpful, even though Rowan will be spending most of her time managing the bar and getting some business experience under her belt.

"I can't wait to meet my nephew!" Rowan looks over her shoulder with a wide smile as I follow her out into the hallway.

"I'm over the moon excited." I grin.

"You know that means you'll need to give him a little sister right away? Just like Mom and Dad. They had you and realized they needed me to complete their family." She turns around and smirks.

"Har, har. You were a whoops baby."

"Liar! You were!"

We laugh all the way back to the trailer and grab another round of her stuff.

When Zoey told me she was pregnant, I cried tears of joy. We'd been trying for months, and while we didn't want to rush into having kids, we took the *if it happens, it happens* approach, but I was more than ready to start a family with her. After she moved here permanently, Mary Sue gave her a part-time position at the salon and Zoey had been working three to four days a week until a month ago when her feet couldn't take it any longer. She was happy she was able to continue cutting hair here and loved meeting new people in town. She'll eventually go back to work, but for now we're staying focused on the baby.

Zoey has made me the happiest man on the planet, and just when I think our life together can't get any better, something else amazing happens and proves me wrong.

Grandma Bishop nearly fell to her knees because she was so damn excited about the news. After we told our parents, she was the first up on the list and probably the most thrilled. She's told everyone at church; hell, she's announced it to the whole town that she's gonna be a great-grandmother. Being the first grandkid to have a baby and giving her the first great-grandchild is one of my proudest moments. All of my aunts and uncles have been celebrating the new Bishop addition and have gone above and beyond with buying gifts and making Zoey and me feel loved. It's been so long since there was a baby Bishop that they're borderline going overboard, but I can't complain. That's just how my family is.

But more than anything, I'm excited our little family is growing, and if I have it my way, we'll have a house full of kids sooner than later. Growing up on the ranch shaped who I am, and I'm excited to share this life with my son and wife, keeping the Bishop traditions alive.

Diesel walks into Rowan's room, carrying a box that has the word *clothes* written in black Sharpie on the side. "I went through this one too." He shoots me a smirk. "You have a thing for red thongs, huh?"

"You ever gonna grow up?" Rowan snaps at him.

I sure as hell could've gone my entire life without knowing that information.

He shakes his head and shoots her a wink. "Never, baby."

"Why is he here again?" she asks as we walk outside to the lowboy that's still stacked full of boxes. Diesel lingers a little too long just so he can check out my sister's ass, which infuriates me to no end. He's relentless and has kept this act going for years, making me wonder if he's serious. Better not be because Rowan is off-limits. Though she's turning twenty-three soon and is a grown ass woman, she'll always be my little sister. I will stand up and protect her no matter what. Even when she doesn't think she needs it.

"Because Mom and Dad love him for some reason," I say sarcastically, but I have to give credit where credit is due. "He has grown up some since he got promoted, though." I give her a smile, pretty damn proud of my best friend. "Overseeing the cattle operation is a big job. Lots of horseback riding, fence fixin', branding, and all the other stuff that goes along with it. One of the reasons he got the old cabin to fix up too. He's really stepped up," I remind her. Diesel has been busting his ass over the past two years, showing that he was ready for more responsibility. Everyone's impressed, even me, though it still hasn't stopped his shenanigans and relentless flirting with my sister.

"He's still immature," she retorts, but her voice is much softer when she speaks.

A chuckle escapes me. "Okay, well I can't deny that."

After we help her move every single box, she thanks me with a hug. Then she turns to Diesel and gives him a handshake and a glare.

"I'll take a kiss as a thank you." He leans down, pointing at his cheek.

"Will you turn back into a toad if I do?" she jokes, playfully slapping his arm.

"No, sweetheart, I'm already your prince." He puckers his lips, which only causes Rowan to groan and walk away.

I get in my truck, and Diesel climbs in the passenger side so we can drop off the trailer, and I can head back home.

"I think she likes me." He beams.

I snort. "I think you're still drunk from last night."

"Nope, totally sober," he taunts, touching the tip of his nose with his right finger then his left.

"Don't forget I'll kick your ass if you fuck with my sister. She's off-limits," I warn, completely serious. Diesel is a great guy, but he's known for one-night stands and partying. Rowan just graduated and is focused on her future. No guy will ever be good enough for her in my eyes, not even Diesel.

"What you don't know won't hurt ya, Daddy." He snickers.

"Dude! It's sick when you call me that."

Diesel's mood shifts, and he frowns as I start the truck. "I might've seen who she was texting earlier," he states, and when I look at him, he continues. "You're not gonna like it."

"Who was it?"

"Trace. That guy she hung around a couple of years ago."

Snarling, I ask, "That fucking thirty-year-old?" I remember him from the Fourth of July party she invited him to and didn't like him then.

"I think he was twenty-seven at the time, so almost, I guess."

I growl just thinking about it as I drive over to Diesel's truck.

"What the fuck is he doing texting her?"

"The message said 'Can't wait!' so it sounds like they're planning to meet up," Diesel explains, but I can tell he's agitated as hell over it.

"Over my dead body," I hiss. "No good can come from her dating an old fart like him, especially after the last guy who cheated on her." My jaw tenses just thinking about that Nick asshole she dated her last year in college. "She told me she wasn't interested in anyone," I say. After she got her heart broken a couple of months ago, she swore off men and has been pretty vocal about it.

I park next to his Chevy, and after he hops out, he leans back in and smirks. "I'm lookin' quite good now, aren't I?" He waggles his brows. "At least you know I wouldn't cheat on her."

My brows furrow as my body tenses. "No, because you don't date. You just bang 'em and bail," I retort. "And I'd really hate to have to kick your sorry ass if you touch my sister. So, don't even think about it."

Diesel gives me a cocky salute, and as he walks to his truck, I honk my horn at him. When he looks, I flip him off, then drive away, amused with myself. I drop off the trailer in the old barn by the B&B and then make my way home where Zoey's waiting impatiently.

As soon as I walk in, she smiles but doesn't get off the couch. Her feet are propped up on the coffee table, and there's a towel on her forehead. I lean down and kiss her before sitting next to her. "You feeling okay?"

"It's torture in here. How is it possible for Texas to be hotter than Phoenix? It's shit!" She groans.

I try not to laugh, though she's so damn adorable when she's mad. It's pitiful. The air is on, but it can't keep up in this heat or with a pregnant woman's hormones.

"Is there anything I can do for you?" I grab Zoey's hand and weave her fingers through mine.

"Pull this baby out? I've tried to coax him. Even made some insane deals that I promise to God I will keep, but he refuses to take the bait. He's stubborn!"

I snort, knowing Zoey can be the same way. The past three years together have been amazing, and I wouldn't change them for anything, but we've done our fair share of bickering. You learn a lot about a person you married on a whim when they move in with you. All the quirks and bad habits come to light.

"What kind of deals?" I grin, loving her crazy pregnancy antics.

She readjusts the pillow that she uses to support her back. "I told him if he decided to come out within the next twenty-four hours, I'd buy him a brand-new Mustang convertible when he turns sixteen. What kid turns that down?" she shouts.

I lean forward, rub her belly, and speak to him. "Zach? You hear that? You'll be a chick magnet with a convertible. You'll pull all the hoes. I'd take that deal!"

I place my ear to her stomach, waiting for a response. I don't hear a thing, not even a tummy growl. Sitting up, I look at her. "I don't think he's going for it, baby. Might want to sweeten the pot."

She groans again, leaning her head against the couch and readjusts the cold cloth on her head. "I think I want to take a bath in ice cubes," she says, grunting. "I'm literally sweating in places I didn't know could sweat, and this is *all* your fault."

My eyes go wide. "It takes two to tango, honey. And you don't seem to take no for an answer! Even when I'm sleeping!"

She laughs, a smile finally splitting her cheeks. "You're right. But you didn't warn me that all the Bishop babies have been giants. *No*, you conveniently left that part out, and Rowan had to share that lovely news with me, and then your mother confirmed. If I would've known that—"

I press my lips against hers, stopping her rant. "You still would've wanted all my babies."

"Ugh." She rolls her eyes. "You're right, but dammit, I hate you right now."

I pull her legs into my lap, and she repositions herself so I can gently massage her swollen feet. "It could be worse, though," I tell her.

She leans up and scowls at me. "How so?"

"You could be having twins. Or hell, triplets. Runs in the family," I remind her, smirking.

"Multiple ten-pound babies?" Her eyes widen as she falls back. "That sounds like divorce to me."

I grin at her dramatics. "There's always next time. Twin siblings would be cool, wouldn't it, Zach?"

She grabs her stomach. "Oh my God! He kicked like he was answering you."

Roaring laughter escapes me. "That's my kid."

"What am I gonna do with you two?" She beams, and I notice the sparkle in her eyes. It's been there since the moment she found out she was pregnant.

"Love us unconditionally?"

She repositions herself and moves closer so she can kiss me, slow and passionately. "I already do, cowboy. And always will, for the rest of my life. Even when you knock me up with giant babies."

"I love you so much," I tell her, knowing my words will never be able to fully explain how much she means to me. Our relationship may have started with a dare, but it didn't end in divorce. Zoey's my everything, and though we had a rocky start, it was all worth it, and I wouldn't change a thing.

**Continue reading for Diesel & Rowan's story
in *Catching the Cowboy***

Catching the Cowboy
DIESEL & ROWAN

Settling down and starting a family is something Diesel has considered, regardless of his one-night stand reputation. However, he just might be single forever since who he wants is off-limits—his best friend's little sister.

He's been in love with her for years, but betraying his friendship could ruin everything.

Rowan Bishop is over men, especially after finding out her boyfriend cheated and left her heartbroken. After graduating from college, she's back home and has to face the one guy who purposely gets under her skin—her older brother's best friend.

She hates that she's attracted to him, but she's willing to fight for who she wants.

Spending time together is a bad idea, but neither can deny the chemistry sizzling between them. Late night talks turn into spontaneous adventures and just when Rowan's willing to admit how she truly feels, Diesel's past catches up with him and ruins their picture perfect romance.

One secret turns into another and before either can grasp their new reality, more truths unravel—threatening to expose their forbidden relationship.

I love it when you just don't care
I love it when you dance like there's nobody there
So when it gets hard, don't be afraid
We don't care what them people say

"Life of the Party"
-Shawn Mendes

Diesel

TEN YEARS AGO

I stare at her.

I stare at her *a lot*, actually. An embarrassing amount of time.

But Rowan doesn't notice. She hardly acknowledges me, except for when she brushes me off and rolls her eyes at my lame attempts to flirt. I *shouldn't* be flirting with her, considering she's my best friend's little sister. Riley's three years older than her, which makes him even more protective. She's only a year younger than me, though.

Tonight's her eighth grade winter formal, and since I'm a freshman in high school, I can't go to protect her from those little pricks. They mindlessly stare at her tits and long, tanned legs and aren't subtle about it. I spent the better part of middle school giving them threatening glares. And even though I told myself it was for Riley's sake—as his friend—that was mostly a lie. I did it because none of them deserved her, and I wanted her for myself. Still do.

Given that she pays no mind to me, I've resorted to making fun of her instead. It's not the type of attention I want, but for a moment, it means I have hers, even if she's telling me off or smacking me. It's childish—like a boy chasing a girl to pull on her pigtails on the playground—but it's the only way Rowan will actually look at me or speak to me.

Pathetic as hell, I know.

One of these days, Rowan Bishop will notice me as more than a nuisance or her brother's best friend. Guaranteed.

"Boys!" their mother screams out the second-story window. River's like a mom to me, considering how long I've known the Bishops and how much time I spend on the ranch. "Hurry up! She's ready to go, and I need to take pictures!"

Riley and I jump out of his dad Alex's truck and rush toward the house. Even though we're still dirty from the day's work, we try to brush off as we head up the steps to the porch. I help on their family ranch on the weekends and during the summer. It's my own personal escape, and I can't wait until school's over so I can be here every day. It's much different here than in town where I live, and I never want to leave.

The front door whips open, and we enter. I wait with bated breath for Rowan's grand entrance down the staircase. My clothes and hair are a mess, and I'm embarrassed by how much of a disaster I must look, but when Rowan rounds the corner in a bright pink gown, my throat goes dry. Even if I were dressed in my Sunday best, I'd still be out of her league.

She smiles wide, her adorable dimples peeking through, as she holds the railing and walks down. Alex and River wait by the bottom step with pride filling their faces. Pulling out her phone, River begins taking pictures, then demands a daddy-daughter photo. Alex is wearing his typical cowboy hat, Wranglers, and work T-shirt and smiles next to Rowan who looks like royalty.

"Get in the picture, Riley," River orders, waving him over after she gets a few good ones of just the two of them. She snaps several more, and then I step in.

"You need a family photo with all of you," I tell her, reaching for her cell. "Get in the picture, Mrs. Bishop."

She hands it over. "Oh, you're a gem, Adam!" Aside from my mother and grandmother, River's the only other person who uses my real name. I've repeatedly told her to call me Diesel—a nickname I've had for as long as I can remember—but she insists I'll always be Adam to her.

"No problem, Mrs. B."

River stands on one side of Rowan, and Riley and Alex are on the other. I step back, then click a few shots. Aside from their different hair color, Rowan looks identical to her mother. Riley's always resembled his dad, even when he was younger.

"One more," I say, then motion for them to move closer and tell them to smile wider.

Rowan doesn't look at the camera. Rather, she flicks her eyes to mine, and when the corner of her lips tilts up, I imagine that smile is for me. A grin fills my face, and my imagination goes wild with thoughts on how I'd make this night memorable for her if I were her date. It'd be nothing short of perfection as we danced to her favorite songs, drank punch, then ended the evening with a quiet stroll under the stars.

"Alright, I'm gonna be late!" Rowan lifts the front of her ball gown, revealing cowboy boots, then walks out of the group. I smirk at her shoes, knowing she'd never wear heels unless she was forced. Hell, I'm surprised she's even wearing such a poofy dress. She's worn sundresses to church before, but never something this fancy. She's a natural tomboy, born and raised on a ranch, and has always preferred getting dirty over pompoms. Riding horses is second nature to her, and she often gives me a run for my money when it comes to hard work and getting chores done. It makes me like her even more.

"You sure you don't want a picture of you shoveling shit in the barn? You in your natural habitat?" I tease, knowing it'll annoy the hell out of her.

"Now, now, Adam. Be nice and watch your language." River steps forward, grabbing her phone from my grip, and gently pats my cheek.

"Yeah, *Adam*." Rowan huffs and crosses her arms over her chest, which was a really bad thing to do. The movement pushes up her tits, and I immediately avert my gaze, trying not to stare. "Maybe you should go back into *your* natural habitat, in the mud, with the *pigs*."

Riley howls, cracking up so hard, I'm worried he'll piss himself. This is an ongoing thing in the Bishop house. Me teasing Rowan, her throwing it right back, and Riley laughing at my expense.

"You ready to go, princess?" Alex asks, digging his keys out of his pocket.

"You sure you don't want me to take her?" Riley interjects. "I'm her big brother after all and way cooler than you."

"Excuse me?" Alex nudges Riley in the arm, wearing a playful grin. "I managed to land your mother, didn't I? I smooth-talked her into moving to Texas, after all. She had it *bad*."

"According to my math," Rowan chimes in, "and my sources, Mom was knocked up with Riley and came back to tell you, which means y'all had sex before marriage."

My cheeks heat at Rowan's bold words, but honestly, I expect nothing less from her.

"Rowan Rose Bishop!" River scolds. "Who told you that?"

"Grandma," she reveals. "Like it's a secret? Riley was born *before* your wedding date."

"So Riley's a bastard. What else is new?" I tease.

"Language, Adam." River gives me a firm look before turning to Riley. I can't help but laugh, considering the conversation. "We're taking Rowan to the dance, but I need you to pick her up at midnight. I'm trusting you to be there *on time*."

It's Saturday night, and knowing Riley as well as I do, he's not gonna like this.

"Ma, what? Why do I have to pick up the little rug rat?"

"Because you're *so cool*. Also, your father and I are going to bed early so we can *all* get up for church in the morning," she says pointedly. "I expect you to be there tomorrow, too."

Riley groans with an eye roll, which causes me to snort.

"Yes, ma'am," he begrudgingly mutters.

"Good boy." She sweetly pats his head like he's a five-year-old.

The three of them leave, and I'm anxious the moment Rowan's out of sight.

"Thank God, they're gone. Let's go drink in the barn!" Riley shouts, pushing me toward his room. "I'm gonna shower first, though."

"Did you suffer a blow to the head?" I ask as he follows me down the hallway. "You have to pick Rowan up in four hours."

"So?" He shrugs without a care in the world.

"So you shouldn't be drinkin', smartass."

"I'll be fiiiiiine. Quit worryin', pretty boy." He slaps my shoulder. "You can be my DD."

He knows damn well I'm only fourteen and don't have my license, but that hasn't stopped me from driving his drunk ass around before. I drive around the ranch sometimes, and I've had to take him home from partying in town a couple of times but never with Rowan in the truck.

Over three hours pass, and I'm stuck dealing with a shit-faced Riley in the barn we hang out in on the weekends. He invited a few friends who brought an ice chest full of their parents' booze. I tried to slow Riley down, but he downed six beers and four shots of bourbon like there were no consequences. Now he's three sheets to the wind.

"Dude, you're supposed to pick up Rowan in forty-five minutes. You need to start chugging water," I tell him. My last beer was over an hour ago, and I only had two total.

"Stop being a pussy," Riley slurs.

I check my watch. By the time I manage to get him into the back seat and drive into town, it'll be close to midnight. I don't want to keep Rowan waiting around by herself or worse, with those little dicks from her class.

"Say goodbye. We're going." I stand and tower over him. Riley might be muscular from working on the ranch, but I have a good four inches and fifty pounds on him. Grabbing his arm, I lift him to his wobbly feet. "You're gonna be puking your fuckin' guts out."

"Whatever you say, *Dad*," he mocks, and the other guys laugh. If he wasn't my best friend and a decent human—sober—I'd leave his ass out here for his parents to find in the morning.

With fifteen minutes to spare, I pull into the parking lot. Since Riley's passed out in the back seat, I leave the truck running and hop out. Parents are already starting to arrive to pick up their kids, so instead of waiting out here, I go inside to check on Rowan.

I spot her under the disco ball dancing with a bunch of girls. She's smiling, but it seems forced. Her cousin Mackenzie is with her, drawing tons of attention, as usual. Ten minutes later, the DJ announces the final slow song of the night. He then tells the guys to find their sweetheart, and one approaches their circle but grabs Kenzie's hand. She grins wide, and the two of them walk away. I watch Rowan's fake smile drop as do her eyes before wrapping her arms around her waist and leaving the dance floor.

What the fuck?

As much as I don't want guys near her, I don't understand why the hell none of them at least asked her to dance.

I warned most of them off last year, so it must've actually worked.

After thirty seconds of watching her stand alone with that sad expression, I can't stand it. Suddenly, I'm halfway across the gym, moving toward her.

"Row..." I grab her attention, and she looks shocked as hell.

"What are you—?"

I tilt my head toward the dance floor. "C'mon. Let's dance." Holding out my hand, I nod for her to take it.

When she finally does, I don't even try to contain my smile. I lead her out into the middle under the sparkling disco ball, then pull her into my chest and wrap my arms around her.

"What're you doing here?" she asks, holding my shoulders because she's too short to place her arms around my neck. But holding her this way is perfect.

"Your idiot brother is as drunk as a skunk, so I drove us here. Came inside to check on you and didn't want you to miss out on dancing to the last song."

She licks her lips and swallows. "The boys here don't like me. They say I'm too much. Too loud. Too—"

"They're fuckin' morons," I interject.

Rowan looks down and shrugs. "Oh well."

I tilt up her chin and gaze into her gorgeous brown eyes. "Trust me, none of them are good enough for you."

"You *have* to say that." She sighs, her shoulders rising and falling. "You're my brother's best friend."

I scoff. "No, I don't. I'm not *your* brother."

She shrugs casually. "Close enough. You pick on me worse than him. Always around. I'm surprised you haven't tried to pants me in public yet."

Our laughter eases the tension. "That's Riley's specialty," I tease, remembering the time he did it to Rowan a few years ago at one of their family's picnics. She was livid and ended up sucker punching him between the legs.

"Middle school boys are dumb," she states.

A smile spreads across my face. "High school ones are too. Don't forget that."

When she's a freshman next fall, I'm going to have to try not to be so overbearing. I'll be a sophomore, and we'll be on opposite sides of the building, but I'll still keep my eye on her. It'll be better than her attending another school altogether. Hopefully, I'll see her around after class, considering I play football and baseball, and she'll probably try out for the softball team.

Everyone in this town is well aware of my family ties with the Bishops. I make sure Rowan and her cousins aren't messed with, especially when Riley isn't around.

"I love this song," she says softly.

I know she does. She plays it on repeat in her room. I've noticed she likes listening to slower songs while she studies and does homework.

"Who's the singer?" I ask as if I'm clueless.

"Shawn Mendes," she tells me and I nod, pretending it's brand-new information. If Rowan knew how much I watched and obsessed over her, she'd think I was batshit crazy. Hell, when it comes to her, there's no doubt I am.

Riley would kick my ass if he ever found out.

As the music begins to fade, I frown at the anticipation of losing her touch. She blinks up at me, and a small smile plays on her lips that are only inches from mine. Forgetting where we are, *who* we are, I slide my hand up her arm and cup her cheek. I study her expression, waiting to see if she pushes me away, and when she doesn't, I lean in closer.

She inhales sharply as my lips softly brush hers. I taste the fruit punch she must've drunk earlier, but we're harshly interrupted before I can deepen the kiss. We pull apart when a loud commotion echoes through the gym.

"Fuck," I mutter under my breath as I see Riley staggering toward the middle where we're standing. "C'mon, we gotta go."

I reach for her hand, but then think better of it and drop my arm. Riley's wasted, bumping into tables and students as he nearly falls on his ass.

"What the hell?" I steady him, grabbing his arms. "Why didn't you stay in the truck?"

"I couldn't find you," he stutters loudly. "You left me."

Everyone stares, and when I look at Rowan, her cheeks are beet red. She's embarrassed as hell, and it's all my fault. If I had just waited outside for her, Riley would've never stumbled in here looking like a fool.

"You were passed out," I tell him between gritted teeth. "I came in to grab Rowan."

He blinks, looking around me as if he just realized his sister was next to me. "Oh." He wobbles from side to side, and his eyes are in slits as he stares at us.

Ignoring his suspicious look, I straighten my shoulders and try to get us out of here fast. "Let's go."

I turn Riley around and walk him to the exit, hoping no one gives her shit for this later. While he picks on his sister regularly and has zero qualms about embarassing her in front of family, he'd never intentionally humiliate her in front of her classmates.

"Shotgun!" Riley shouts once we're outside. How the hell he's still standing is beyond me. He's plastered, and if he doesn't sit the fuck down, he's going to vomit all over his truck.

I manage to get him into the passenger seat, and Rowan follows me to the driver's side. She gets in the back, and I sit behind the wheel. Once we're all buckled, I glance up in the rearview mirror and see her stunning brown eyes. We barely kissed, but I felt it all over. I wonder if she did too, but now isn't the time to bring it up.

We're halfway to the ranch when Riley perks up and looks over at me.

"I know I'm a little drunk..." he begins, slouching. "But did I see you kissing my sister in the gym?"

My eyes round, and I swallow down the panic streaming through my veins. He's too drunk to really kick my ass at the moment, but that doesn't mean I won't pay for it tomorrow.

"Dude, what?" I contort my face. "You must be more hammered than I thought if you're seeing me lock lips with your kid sister."

He leans back against the seat. "I know what I saw," he grumbles.

"You're wrong," I tell him flatly. "You must've seen another couple."

Riley turns just enough to look at his sister. "Rowan?"

"What?" she asks as if she's annoyed.

"Were you kissing my best friend?"

Without any hesitation, she replies, "Gross, no. He offered to dance with me, and that's it."

Riley scoffs, not believing her. "Then why was his mouth so close to yours?"

"Do you really think I'd waste my first kiss on him?" she spits out.

Jesus fuck.

That was her first kiss?

"He's your annoying best friend who follows me around like a sad puppy," she adds. "The *last* person on earth I'd ever want to kiss. If his mouth ever touched mine, I'd knee him in the jewels."

Ouch.

Her words hurt like a thousand needle pricks. If her plan was to convince him it wasn't real, she's golden. If it was to hurt me in the process, then mission fucking accomplished.

"*Dayum.*" Riley whistles, slapping his knee.

I glance up into the mirror, seeing her narrowed eyes and tense jaw. *What the hell*? I denied it to save my friendship, but she went a step further, dragging me through the mud in the process. Did she expect me to tell him? Is she pissed I didn't?

Silence draws on until we pull up to their house. Riley passed out against the window, and drool is sliding down his chin.

"Can you cover for your brother?" I ask Rowan when I open the back door and hold out my hand to help her out. She dismisses me and jumps down. "Tell your parents he's sleeping over at my house tonight?"

She shrugs, then nods. "Alright, fine."

I shut the door and follow her to the porch. "Rowan, wait."

She spins around, her face emotionless.

"You know I only denied it so he wouldn't beat my face in, right?" My eyes plead with her to believe me.

"It doesn't matter, *Adam.* I don't care."

I flinch at her harsh words. She leaned into me, I know she did, so why is she acting as if I'm the biggest inconvenience of her life?

Furrowing my brows, I step closer. "Was that really your first kiss?"

She bursts out laughing, crossing her arms. "Yeah right."

"What the hell is your problem?" I finally ask.

Before she can respond, the front door swings open. "I thought I heard voices out here." Alex looks at the two of us, squinting. "Where's Riley?"

"We're gonna hang out at my house if that's alright?" I step away from Rowan. "I'll make sure he's at church tomorrow, though, sir."

Alex nods, then looks at Rowan, smiling. "Did you have fun at the dance?"

Rowan glances at me before climbing the steps and nods. "It was fine, Dad. I'm tired, though."

"Okay, kiddo. Let's get you to bed then."

"Good night," I call out, waving to both of them. Alex waves, then shuts the door.

I drive Riley to my house in town and hope I don't get pulled over in the process. My parents are asleep, so I quietly help him to the couch in my room. The asshole can sleep there without a pillow and blanket for putting me through this shit tonight. Hopefully, he'll forget what he saw between his sister and me.

It seems as though Rowan already has, so perhaps I should too.

Though there's really no way I can.

What she doesn't know is that was my first kiss too, and I've been waiting for her.

I don't understand why she's so pissed, but I'll do whatever it takes to figure it out.

CHAPTER ONE

Diesel

PRESENT DAY

"**D**amn," I mutter as I roll out of bed, realizing I'm late as fuck for work. I probably shouldn't have stayed up until two drinking, and I sure as hell shouldn't have made out with that woman at the bar. I don't remember her name, just her long legs and revealing neckline. As quickly as I can, I rush to the bathroom to piss, then brush my teeth, and that's when I see the dark purple hickeys on my neck. Not one or two, but three are in plain sight. I should've called her Hoover, considering they're the size of a vacuum hose.

"Shit," I say after spitting out the toothpaste because I know I can't cover them up. Wearing a turtleneck sweater in June might be more of a red flag than just owning up to my stupid mistake. I shrug, then rinse my mouth, and hurry to get dressed. This is why I stopped staying out late and drinking so much, but sometimes, those old habits reappear. Before leaving my modest cabin located on the Bishop Ranch, I text my boss, Alex, and let him know I'm running late.

ALEX

I knew that an hour ago. Hurry your ass up.

DIESEL

Yes, sir. I'll be right there.

With a smile, I crank my truck and rush down the long dirt road toward the shop where we do our morning roundups. Riley's dad holds staff meetings every morning so we're on the same page. What's needed around the ranch often changes for reasons like the weather or emergency repairs, so doing this each day is necessary. About six months ago, I was promoted to help manage a group of ranch hands, and together, we tend to the cattle. It's a group effort, considering how large the property is, and while it's a lot of hard work, I nearly sold my soul for this opportunity. There are days when all I do is sit in a saddle in the hot, blazing sun, sweating my ass off, but I wouldn't have it any other way. The Circle B Ranch is my home, and I don't plan to ever leave. I could be shoveling shit and be as happy as a hog here because this place is my own personal heaven on earth. I've grown up here, and the Bishops are my chosen family.

Trust me, I've done my fair share of bitch work over the years because nothing is handed to anyone. Everything here is earned, which I respect and appreciate.

I pull up to the metal building and see no other vehicles except for Alex's old beat-up truck he drives around the ranch. The bumper is dented from dumbasses backing into random things, and there are scratches all over the paint. Honestly, I don't blame him for using it because I've done my fair share of damaging it, too.

Before I get out, I grab my cowboy hat and place it on my head, then take in a long, deep breath. When I walk inside, he's drinking a cup of coffee and gives me a smug look. He's like my second dad, but I'm actually afraid of Alex's repercussions. The man could kick my ass all the way to the border of Texas and back. I'd never want to intentionally cross him.

His steel blue eyes glance up at the clock on the wall, then pierce through me. "One hour and twenty-three minutes *late*."

"Sorry," I say. Walking over, I grab a cup and pour some steaming hot coffee into it. "I..."

"Don't lie to me," he snaps.

"I wasn't going to. I drank too much and—"

"What's on your damn neck?" Riley asks. I didn't even realize he'd walked in. I glare at him as he wears the cheesiest expression ever. He comes closer and tugs on my shirt to fully reveal the marks. All I can do is smirk.

"That's how you get a disease," he explains. "Lettin' strange women suck all over ya." Riley chuckles, but Alex shakes his head, unamused.

"Well, not all of us went to Vegas and came back with a wife," I throw at him. Three years ago, as a twenty-first birthday present, Riley took me on a surprise trip to Las Vegas. When I think about it now, I smile because it was a weekend to remember. Riley found Zoey, and I ended up hooking up with one of her friends. The only difference is I didn't put a ring on it, and I don't even remember her name. However, a lot has changed since then because while I go to the Circle B Saloon often and have a few drinks, I'm not into the one-night stands like I was years ago. That's why Ms. Hoover Vacuum didn't come home with me last night, which is probably for the best. I might not have survived her sucking powers.

The Circle B Saloon is also owned by the Bishops. Riley's uncles John and Evan invested in the property and fully remodeled an old building downtown. It now consists of a large beer and liquor selection, a pool table, and a quaint seating area. Before the Saloon opened, there were zero places for people to hang out at after dark, so it became an instant moneymaker. It's done really well, and everyone in the family helps run it, especially Rowan, who's taking over now that she's graduated. Their cousins Ethan and Kenzie bartend a few nights a week when they're home during college breaks.

"It looks like she bruised you from the inside out," Riley taunts with a grin. "You might wanna get that checked out."

"I'll live." I glower, ready to give him a snide comment about wishing it was his sister who marked me. But since their dad is within earshot, I hold my tongue. I'm already in the hot seat with him for being late so I don't push my luck. These Bishops aren't always mild mannered—the men or the women—if I'm being honest.

"Anyway," Alex drawls, "it's supposed to start raining this afternoon, so

I'm not sure how much you'll be able to get done, but you can try. I had Grayson start since you were nowhere to be found."

Grayson was hired this past year to help with the cattle. He's my right-hand man and super dependable, so it doesn't surprise me that he stepped up today. He saves my ass when needed, which is great, considering Riley and I work in different areas now and can't cover for each other anymore.

"Sorry about that, sir," I apologize again, taking a sip of coffee because I need to wake up. "Won't happen again."

Riley chuckles. "Yeah right."

"Shut the hell up." I punch his shoulder, then look at his dad. "It won't."

"Since it's getting hot out there, ya need to ride around and check the wells and make sure the water troughs are full. I know the pond out in the far pasture is drying up, and we can't have those cows getting dehydrated. It's so dry the rain ain't gonna do nothin' but evaporate as soon as it lands. Not much shade after all. Can't afford to lose any of them due to the heat," Alex explains.

"I'll get right on it," I tell him, finishing every hot drop of coffee, then head out.

Riley follows behind me, laughing his ass off.

"Way to make me look bad in front of your old man." I scowl, narrowing my eyes.

"He already knows how you are, Big D." He waggles his brows. "Don't forget, we gotta drive to Houston tomorrow and help my sister with all her stupid shit."

I grin at him with a smug expression. "You know I won't."

He shakes his head. "Oh God. Don't you be gettin' that look in your eyes like that. You know she hates you."

"I think that means she's got the hots for me. Maybe you can put in a good word and have her start calling me Big D, too?" Just seeing him squirm is worth every second.

"Shut your damn mouth, you dumbass." He groans. "Tomorrow morning, we leave before the sun rises. Four o'clock sharp. It's a long ass drive, and I wanna get there and back as fast as possible."

I know it's because he wants to be with Zoey, and I can't blame him, considering she's eight months pregnant. He's supposed to be on pre-baby duty right now, but he can't seem to stay away from the ranch life, even if it means meeting at the shop for ten minutes. He's addicted to this, just like the rest of us. Tomorrow, we'll be on a tight schedule, and I'm sure he'll be in a mood. If Zoey goes into labor while we're gone, I'm not sure he'll ever forgive Rowan or his dad since we were voluntold to help.

I throw him a grin. "Whatever you say, *Daddy*."

He pretends to gag as I hop in my truck and crank it. I roll the window down and holler at him. "See you in the morning after I dream about your sister sittin' on my face."

As expected, he flips me off and walks away, but it's all in good fun. Though when it comes to Rowan, I'm never joking. If she'd let me, I'd hang the damn moon for her. We haven't spent much time together because she's been at the University of Houston for the past four years and only comes home during her breaks, but it doesn't matter. My feelings for her haven't changed.

Something about Rowan makes my blood pump a little faster and my adrenaline rush. Rowan Bishop's a goddamn firecracker, sassy as can be, and Southern to the core with her values. One day, I'm going to make her mine, and I've been telling Riley that since we were kids, even if he's been warning me away from her for that long too. He thinks I'm too unreliable and unable to settle down, but he's wrong. She may be dead set on loathing me, but I'm still convinced she'll eventually get on board. *Hopefully*.

I drive out to the old barn where Grayson is busy saddling the horses. He looks at me over his shoulder and shakes his head before tightening the strap. Hopping out of the truck, I walk over to him.

"Where the fuck have you been?" he asks.

"That is no way to talk to your boss," I snap, then grin. "Overslept."

"You dumbass. I already sent the boys out to the far pasture to round up the cows and move them. Saddled Meadow for you so we could ride over to the wells and make sure they're good. I think the pump on the east side needs to be rewired. It was making a noise a week ago."

"A noise?" I prompt. "And you decided to say something *now*?" Releasing a deep breath, I shake my head and walk over to Meadow and climb on. He's a red quarter horse who loves to run and ride through the mud. We've had some great days together even though he's young, spunky, and doesn't always listen.

Once my feet are in the stirrups and Grayson is on his horse, we take off down one of the yellow trails that shortcuts over to the little water shack we need to check. Looking up at the sky, I see the dark clouds in the distance and know we don't have much time.

"Should we take the four-wheelers instead?" Grayson asks, looking out over the horizon.

"Nah, I think we'll be okay if we get going and don't lollygag any longer. We're already halfway there."

"Alright. You're the boss." He snickers and follows me as we continue forward.

The temperature is dropping, and the wind is picking up, but I focus on the task at hand so we can get it done before getting dumped on.

"You gonna talk about those bruises on your neck?" Grayson finally asks, trotting up beside me.

"God, not you too," I huff. "Riley's ragged on me enough this morning for it. In front of Alex, too."

"Well, it's impossible to ignore it when they're like beacons in the night." He chuckles.

"I drank too much, but luckily, I wasn't drunk. One more beer and I might've gone home with her, but I've had enough one-night stands to last me a lifetime," I admit.

"And it's not because Rowan's coming home tomorrow?" He arches a brow.

All I can do is smirk. "Maybe I'm not as transparent as I thought."

"Better get something to cover up those marks, or she'll notice."

I nod, agreeing. I honestly didn't think about it. Rowan will use every opportunity to bust my balls, and these stupid hickeys will be enough to get her wrath for a month.

We continue riding until we arrive at the water well. We dismount and tie the horses to a fence post before walking over. Grayson was right; it's making a noise, but I'm not sure what it is exactly.

"Go check the water trough and turn on the water so I can hear this pump kick on and off," I order, and he jogs across the pasture. I take the casing off the pump and continue to listen closer. After everything is filled, Grayson joins me in the small shed.

"I'm pretty sure it's the bearings. They need to be replaced before this thing burns up. We'll need to look in the supply room and see if we have a few extra." I pull out my cell phone and take pictures of the model number and type of pump it is. "And we're gonna have to hurry. This storm's movin' in quickly."

Grayson unties the horses as thunder rumbles in the distance. After hopping on, we decide to gallop for a while and run into my ranch hands, who are moving the cattle to where we just were. We don't have time to stop and chat but exchange words in passing.

"I'll catch y'all at the B&B for lunch," I yell, and several of them give me a thumbs-up. The Circle B Bed & Breakfast has been around for decades on the Bishop's ranch. It's an old farmhouse Riley's grandparents converted into a secluded Southern getaway. It's known for many things: the rooms are named after colors, they serve the best damn food in this part of Texas, and horseback riding lessons are offered. Riley and Rowan's cousin Maize is the chef now. She uses all of Grandma Bishop's homemade recipes, and a kitchen staff prepares every meal fresh. John has been in charge of it for years and gets his panties in a knot anytime us ranch workers come in and overstay our welcome. But just thinkin' about Maize's buttermilk biscuits makes my mouth water. The B&B's booked year-round with repeat guests who love visiting the ranch and animals.

I can't blame anyone for wanting to return because I've been obsessed with this place since I met Riley. During my high school summers, I started at the bottom of the barrel doing grunt work and all the shit assignments. I hoped after years of busting my ass, I'd get promoted, and once Herbert announced his retirement, Alex offered me the job.

The only thing that would've made things better is getting promoted earlier so I could rub it in Fisher's face. He's Riley's cousin who lives in California and worked on the ranch during the summers and busted my balls on a daily basis. He conveniently started dating my ex Gretchen and constantly pissed me off and pushed my buttons. While we had a small rivalry for years, we ended our feud and became friends. After Fisher got married, he took a full-time job in Sacramento and stopped working here. If only he could see me now.

"What're you smiling about?" Grayson asks when we climb off the horses.

"Nothing." I quickly change the subject. "I'm gonna run to the shop and see if I can find the parts we need. We'll take the side-by-side so we can get out there quicker if you wanna put the horses up before the storm hits."

"Sounds good," he says, leading them into the barn.

Running to my truck, I haul ass to the storage building where the spare parts are kept. After digging around, I find an extra pump that's the same model and quickly disassemble the housing and remove the bearings. I stuff them in my pockets and head back. By the time I meet Grayson, he's finished and waiting for me. We hop in the side-by-side and take off.

Less than ten minutes later, the bottom falls out of the sky, and when we finally make it to the pump house, we're both soaked. Grayson isn't amused as he parks and follows me inside. I pull some tools from my pocket, turn off the pump, and change the bearings as fast as I can because lightning's striking too close for comfort. Thunder booms, making us both jump.

"Hurry the hell up," Grayson urges, looking out the door as the rain pours down around the little shack we're standing in. It takes every bit of strength I have to loosen the bolts, and the constant rumbles have my nerves on edge. For us to be out here like this is dangerous, and I can tell Grayson is just as unhinged as I am. The storm seems to have stalled right above us, and we're already soaked from head to toe, but in this part of Texas, we pray for rain, especially during the brutal summer months. There have been too many years when we've suffered droughts, so we never take it for granted. After tightening everything and replacing the casing, I start the pump and thankfully, the loud squealing noise is gone when it comes on.

"Thank fuck," I mutter, wiping my greasy hands on my jeans. "Let's get the fuck outta here."

We run to the side-by-side and hope we don't get struck by lightning as we rush to the barn. Though it's nearly impossible to see the trail, when the building comes into view, I let out a sigh of relief and feel better once we're inside. Grayson turns off the engine and shakes his head at me.

"If you wouldn't have been late this morning, then we would've finished earlier."

"And if you would've told me that shit was rattling like that last week, we wouldn't have had to do it in the rain."

Grayson rolls his eyes. "Yeah, yeah. Whatever," he mutters, knowing I'm right.

Lightning cracks in the distance, and we leave. Once we're inside my truck, I pull out my phone and text Bradley, one of the guys who works for me, to check in with him. Considering it's pouring, I don't expect a text back anytime soon, but I hope he and the other ranch hands are being safe. While I'd never admit that Grayson is right, I am actually annoyed I overslept because it really did fuck up our schedule.

Instead of immediately pulling away and heading to the B&B, I tell Grayson I want to wait a few minutes to see if the guys come back. He doesn't care because he's getting paid either way, so he pulls out his cell and scrolls through his phone. After thirty minutes, they ride up on horses and once they're in the barn, I get a call from Bradley.

"Hey boss, first herd of cows are moved. What do ya want us to do now?"

"Thanks. Unsaddle the horses and I'll call Alex. Don't want you out there with all that lightning. Meet you at the B&B once y'all are done."

"Yes, sir. See you there," he tells me, and I end the call.

"See, now that's what you call respect. He called me sir." I crank the truck and glance at Grayson.

He rolls his eyes. "I'm not really into stroking your ego. It's big enough."

On the way there, Grayson does nothing but chat about Maize's cooking, and it makes me even more hungry. We park on the side of the large house and walk up the steps of the porch. As soon as we enter, John shakes his head when he sees us dripping wet. We should've changed clothes, but my stomach is rumbling, and I didn't want to wait.

I suck in a deep breath, and the hearty smell fills my nose. I can't grab a plate fast enough. Grayson and I sit and immediately dig in. I look around, and laugh because there are more ranch hands than guests in the dining area. If Maize comes out and sees us eating up all her food, she's gonna lose her shit. Honestly, though, she should be used to it by now. It's been a longtime tradition among the workers, which was started by John, Jackson, and Alex themselves, not to mention it's Grandma Bishop approved.

The next morning, I'm up before I get a text from Riley because I'm so damn nervous to be around Rowan. It's time for us to drive to Houston to help her move all of the shit she's accumulated while at college back home. The last time she was in town was spring break two months ago, and even then, we both worked, so I didn't actually see her that much. I'd be lying if I said I wasn't excited for her to be here permanently.

I meet him at the B&B, then we hook up the lowboy and get going. It's a six-hour drive to the campus, and Riley calls Zoey almost every hour to check on her. It's disgustingly cute.

After all the boxes are loaded, we immediately drive back. Rowan's following us, and Riley notices the smug grin on my face. If looks could kill, I'd be six feet under.

We don't stop to eat a proper lunch, just some shitty fast food to go because Riley wants to get home before dark.

"You know this ain't gonna tame the beast," I tell him, unwrapping and nearly devouring the burger within three bites. I can barely hear him scolding me for making a mess as I sip my Coke.

Though we're not supposed to speed while hauling a trailer, Riley doesn't follow the rules. He goes as fast as he wants and takes curves like a bat outta hell. Rowan's boxes are sliding around, and I know if any of them fall off, she'll kick someone's ass. And for once, it won't be mine.

We finally make it back to Eldorado, and Riley nearly flies down the long dirt road that leads to his parents' house. He parks, hops out, and already has a box in his hands by the time Rowan catches up with us and gets out of her car.

"Seriously? I'm telling Zoey how you were driving." She throws Riley a glare with a hand on her curvy hip. Soon, the two of them are going back and forth as we carry the boxes. Rowan's trying her hardest to ignore me, but each time I pass her, our eyes meet.

After thirty minutes, we're still unloading. Her shit is heavy, as if she packed the boxes with bricks, so I peek inside one and see a few romance books and souvenirs from her college life. I walk into her bedroom she had when we were kids, and it brings me back in time. The walls are still purple, and some posters of her favorite boy bands are still hung. It's like a time capsule of Rowan's teenage years.

"I plan to have a life, thank you very much," I hear her say.

"Yeah, hanging out with me," I interrupt, hauling in an oversized box and dropping it.

"Hey! That could've been fragile!" She stands and gives me a scowl. She's so cute when she's mad.

"Relax, princess. I looked inside, and it wasn't." I flash her a shit-eating grin.

She pushes her finger into my chest, but I don't move an inch. "Don't look through my things, you weirdo!"

I chuckle as Riley interrupts our moment. "She literally just moved back. Can't you two be adults and stop antagonizing one another?" he asks, then laughs.

"Between Diesel and me, there's only one adult here," she says, narrowing her eyes at me.

I press a palm to my chest. "Now that just hurts. You wound me."

She rolls her eyes and pushes past me, all worked up.

"Alright, children. Let's get this shit done so I can get back to my pregnant wife." Riley scolds, following her. By the smile on his face, I can tell he's thinking about Zoey. I take a few minutes to look around her room and remember coming in here when we were kids. Before she gets weirded out that I'm lingering, I leave and pass them as they continue bickering.

I look at the boxes and see one has clothes written on it in black Sharpie. If she was worried about me looking through her romance books and pictures, this will really get her fired up. Happily, I grab it, walk inside, then set it down.

"I went through this one too." I smirk at Riley, knowing he's going to be annoyed at our banter, but I don't care. "You have a thing for red thongs, huh?" I tease Rowan.

"You ever gonna grow up?" she snaps at me.

Shaking my head, I shoot her a wink and grin. "Never, baby."

Rowan heads outside, and we're on her tail. As she bends over, I stare at her plump ass, imagining her completely naked and in my bed. Riley's glaring at me, and I can tell he's getting pissed, but I just can't help it. For years, he's warned me how off-limits his sister is, but it hasn't stopped me from finding ways to antagonize him. They walk past me and continue their conversation, but I'm too busy laughing to care.

It takes nearly an hour for us to put all of Rowan's stuff in her room. She gives her brother a hug and me a firm handshake accompanied by a glare.

I lean down and point at my cheek. "I'll take a kiss and a thank you."

"Will you turn back into a toad if I do?" She playfully slaps my arm, and a jolt of electricity streams through where she touched me.

"No, sweetheart. I'm already your prince." I pucker my lips, which only causes her to groan and walk away. I deserve a medal for trying.

As we climb into the truck, I'm beaming with joy. Once we're inside, I turn to Riley. "I think she likes me."

He snorts. "I think you're still drunk from last night."

"Nope, totally sober," I say, giving him my mini version of a sobriety test by touching my nose with the tip of my finger.

"Don't forget I'll kick your ass if you fuck with my sister. She's off-limits," he warns, being completely serious. Rowan deserves the world, and I wish I could be the one to give it to her.

I snicker. "What you don't know won't hurt ya, Daddy."

"Dude! It's sick when you call me that."

When I start the engine, my mood shifts, and Riley notices my frown. I'm trying not to sound like a jealous stalker, but I'm not happy. "I might've seen who she was texting earlier."

Riley looks at me.

"You're not gonna like it." Hell, I don't either.

"Who was it?"

"Trace. That guy she hung around a couple of years ago." Just knowing Rowan is chatting with him again makes my stomach turn. He's old as dirt, at least ten years older than her, and I hated when she hung out with him.

"That fucking thirty-year-old?" Riley's livid, and as I recall the memory of when she brought him to the Fourth of July party, it has me seething all over again. At least Riley hates the guy as much as I do.

"I think he was twenty-seven at the time, so almost, I guess."

Riley lets out a growl and grips the steering wheel even tighter as he drives me to my truck that's parked at the B&B. "What the fuck is he doing texting her?"

I suck in a deep breath, growing more agitated with every passing minute, but Riley needed to know. She won't listen to me if I say anything, but she might listen to Riley if he tells her he doesn't approve of him. "The message said 'Can't wait!' so it sounds like they're planning to meet up," I explain, agitated as hell over it.

"Over my dead body," Riley hisses. "No good can come from her dating an old fart like him, especially after the last guy cheated on her."

The thought of any man using Rowan in the way Nick did has me ready to bust my knuckles against his face. The thought of Rowan being with another man drives me insane, and it's something I try to ignore, though it's hard as hell. No one will ever be good enough for her. At times, I don't think even I can spoil and treat her the way she deserves, but I'd damn sure try.

He parks next to my Chevy and hops out, still thinking about Trace. "I'm lookin' quite good now, aren't I?" I waggle my brows, knowing I'm a better fit for Rowan than Trace or any man in a five hundred mile radius could ever be. "At least you know I wouldn't cheat on her."

With furrowed brows, he tenses. "No, because you don't date. You just bang 'em and bail. And I'd really hate to kick your sorry ass if you touch my sister. So, don't even think about it."

After I give him a cocky salute, I walk to my truck. Riley honks his horn, grabbing my attention long enough to see him shooting me the bird. He's more than amused with himself over it too. I expect nothing less from my best friend, an asshole extraordinaire who's determined to protect his little sister.

Riley Bishop has no idea how much I want and have always wanted Rowan, and I need to figure out how to keep that shit to myself, which may be more challenging than even I realize. Especially now that she's home, looking so goddamn beautiful, giving me all of her sass and side glances. It's not the attention I want, but hell, I'll take anything from her.

Flirting with Rowan might be a death wish from Riley, but damn, she's more than worth the risk.

CHAPTER TWO

Rowan

Graduating from college was a dream come true, and I learned a lot that'll help with the family bar and ranch. It's been a week since I moved home, and I'm still trying to get used to it. It's been weird living back with my parents and staying in the bedroom I had growing up. The walls are the bright purple we painted them when I was thirteen, and all my old posters are still hung, just a tad faded by the sun. I'm temporarily brought back to being a kid without a care in the world.

While I've come home during my breaks to visit and help out, I wasn't here long enough to want to redecorate. Now that I'm staying with my parents until I get my own place, I might change it up a bit, make it more stylish. It'd be for no reason, though, because I won't be bringing a man home with me. My dad would murder him, and not to mention, I'm more single than a dollar bill.

My parents haven't enforced a curfew yet because I'm helping at the bar, which closes at two a.m. on the weekends, but it doesn't mean they haven't been in my business. While they mean well, I'm ready to have some privacy outside this house.

Mom knows Nick and I broke up, but I didn't give her the details about how dirty he did me. Cheating bastard. Just the thought of him has me raging all over again. I suck in a deep breath and exhale slowly, trying to calm down.

Nick never liked a woman who didn't know her place. I was always too much sass and dominance for him to handle, so he found a replacement—a woman who'd do whatever he said. The moment I caught them in bed together, it took everything I had not to murder them both. All I remember was walking across the room and pulling the bimbo by her hair before Nick hopped out of bed and rushed toward me. With all my strength, I pushed him, nearly knocking him down on his bare, cheating ass before leaving.

He immediately apologized, making up some stupid excuse for his mistake, but I told him to go fuck himself. I hate liars. A man who can't be truthful, especially one I loved and trusted with my whole being, has no business being in my life. I don't do second chances when it comes to cheating. After graduation, I was more than ready to come home even though I knew Nick was moving back to San Angelo, which is only an hour away. I'm grateful Dad made Riley and Diesel help me because I would've had to hire a company. It wouldn't have been cheap, but I would've paid any amount to get the hell away. Over the past four years of being in Houston, I've accumulated way too much stuff.

I look around my bedroom and see boxes stacked against the wall. Each one is marked with what's inside, but I'm not feeling motivated to unpack. I've put up all my clothes and attempted to go through my things, but I can't bring myself to do it. My heart still hurts from what Nick did a month ago and many pieces of our life together are packed in those boxes. I'd almost rather the memories of him stay there for eternity. While I'd love to forget about him, he's moving back to San Angelo to help with his family's business. Unfortunately, I won't be able to erase his dumbass from my life soon enough because he's literally forty-five minutes away from me. Running into him is still an unfortunate possibility.

A knock rings out on my door, and I roll over and check the time on my phone. It's nearly nine in the morning, and I've been up for a while, just thinking about how strange life is at the moment.

Another knock taps out. "Rowan?" my mother says from the other side. "I'm awake."

The door cracks open, and I sit up.

"I made breakfast. Come eat before I put everything up." She gives me a smile, and I nod, twisting my hair into a high bun.

"You don't have to tell me twice." I put my feet on the floor and follow her into the kitchen. Mom doesn't disappoint and has a whole spread of food on the table. I know she probably got up early and had breakfast with Dad, then made this for me. After I fill my plate with bacon, eggs, and a biscuit with a huge scoop of gravy, I smile.

"You've outdone yourself, Ma," I tell her around a mouthful.

She shrugs. "I'm off work today, so I thought I'd spoil you a bit." She works as a nurse at the hospital in San Angelo, and her shifts are typically long.

Before I can say another word, Dad walks through the door. He goes straight to Mom and pulls her into his arms and kisses her. Their love is beautiful, and even though I've been burned, I hope one day I find what they have.

"Okay, gross," I say as the kiss deepens. "I don't want breakfast and a show."

Dad laughs. "You do know how you were made, don't you?"

I put my fingers in my ears. "I was delivered by a stork."

The last thing I want to think about this morning is my parents doing it. That's a visual I can live without for the rest of my life.

Mom giggles, but I've known how babies were made since I was ten. Considering her job, she was determined to give Riley and me the sex talk as soon as puberty hit. Then we both proceeded to tell all the other kids at school, which got back to Grandma Bishop, who was ready to kick our asses. She was so embarrassed, but I've never seen Dad laugh so hard.

Dad talks about the ranch and his daily duties as I finish eating. "You workin' tonight?

"Mm-hmm." I finish chewing. "I'm supposed to meet Uncle John around five. I should be finished learning everything within the next month, and then he's gonna let me loose."

"Oh lord," Dad says. "Well just know if running the bar doesn't work out, you can always help Maize in the kitchen at the B&B." He grins.

"Hard pass. I didn't go to business school to cook. Not to mention, I'm horrible in the kitchen. Plus, Maize is a hard-ass perfectionist. One time, we made cupcakes, and she nearly had a hissy fit because of how I iced one. No thanks!"

Dad chuckles and shrugs. "Don't know where she would've gotten that trait from."

His sarcasm isn't lost on me.

"Not from Uncle John," I say, and we both laugh because Maize's exactly like him—meticulous to a T. He follows all the rules unlike his twin brother, Uncle Jackson. The two are complete opposites.

Mom fills a mug full of coffee and blows on it before taking a sip. "What are your plans today?"

I shrug. "Not much going on other than hoping Zoey has that baby before I have to go to work."

Mom and Dad both grin. We've been eager and waiting for Zach to be born, and after her last appointment, we were told it could happen at any moment. I'm just ready to become an aunt so I can spoil my nephew rotten. Grandma Bishop is growing impatient too because it's her first great-grandchild.

"Mama's been praying about it all morning," Dad says with a wink.

"You know when Grandma sends messages to God, things happen." I laugh, but I'm not wrong.

Dad checks the time and tells us he has to get back to work before anyone notices he's gone. We say our goodbyes, and I finish my bacon.

Once I'm done eating, I help clean the kitchen. Afterward, I hop in the shower and get dressed, then go to the B&B to see what's going on today. It's weird being home, and it'll take some getting used to after juggling a hectic schedule in college.

When I walk inside, Uncle John is sitting behind the counter and Maize is leaned over talking to him. Her dark hair is pulled back into a bun, which is normally covered in a hair net when she's in the kitchen. They're chatting about something and laughing their asses off. When I clear my throat, she turns around, and I smirk. They have a special connection, especially considering Maize's biological mother passed away soon after she was born, and he became a single dad overnight. John's wife, Mila, raised Maize as her own, and most don't know because they're so close.

"Hey, kiddo," Uncle John greets me just as Kenzie bursts through the back door being her usual loud self. She's majoring in education and is home for the summer. As soon as she has her degree, she'll be here permanently, following in Aunt Mila's footsteps—like mother, like daughter. She opened a daycare years ago, and it eventually transitioned to a private school. While our town isn't big at all, many of her students are from the surrounding areas. When more teachers are hired, they can accept more kids off the waitlist, so it's a big deal for Kenzie to get her degree.

"I'm starving," Kenzie says, glancing at her sister. "Did you make banana bread today?"

Maize gives her an incredulous look, narrowing her blue eyes. "Yes, for the *guests*."

"I'm a guest all summer," Kenzie quickly retorts.

When I chuckle, Kenzie just shrugs, then goes to Maize and wraps her arms around her and squeezes. "Come on, sis. You love me soooooo much. You can't deny my love for your banana bread."

Uncle John grins at his daughters the entire time. "She does have a point. It's really good."

"Fine!" Maize says, knowing she won't win.

"Well, if you're serving up slices, I want one too! And don't be stingy," I say.

"Same!" Uncle John adds.

Maize pretends to be annoyed, but I know how much she loves cooking and finds joy in us being obsessed with her food. Five minutes later, she's walking into the main area carrying three small plates.

"It's still warm," I say excitedly, noticing steam rising from the top. Kenzie doesn't wait before she's stuffing her mouth full. I take a bite, and it's so delicious that I quickly devour it regardless of the big breakfast I just ate. Maize happily snickers.

"So yummy and addicting. I think I need three more slices. How is this even legal?" I say, tempted to lick the crumbs from my plate. Kenzie and Uncle John nod in agreement.

"Y'all are just saying that."

I roll my eyes because she knows better. "Not many people can cook as good as Grandma. So shut the hell up."

That makes her laugh. "I mean, I don't wanna low-key brag or anything, but I know it's delicious."

"Of course you do," Uncle John says. "Good job!"

A guest walks up, and we move out of the way. I follow Maize and Kenzie onto the back porch, giving the lady privacy to speak with Uncle John.

"So, next weekend is your twenty-third birthday..." Kenzie glances at me. "We're going out, right?"

"I'm sure I have to work." I walk to the edge of the porch and look out at the rolling hills.

Maize interrupts my thoughts. "Nope. I'll take care of Dad. We're celebrating instead. I mean, when's the last time the three of us got together?" She loops her arm in mine.

Kenzie comes to the other side. "It's been a while, Rowan. Let's drink and dance the night away."

"I honestly forgot about it. I totally would if I can get off work."

Immediately, Kenzie walks inside, causing Maize to shake her head. She turns to me. "You doin' okay with everything?"

A ragged breath escapes me because I know she's referring to the breakup. I texted her soon after it happened because while she's my cousin, she's also one of my best friends. Always has been. We're close in age, only a year and a half apart, and grew up doing all sorts of stuff together.

"I'm making it."

"You're better off without that douche in the long run. Seriously, I don't know what you saw in that polo-wearing pretty boy anyway. You need a *real* man. A cowboy. Someone who can fit in with the fam."

I suck in a deep breath, chuckling at her description of Nick. She's not wrong, though. "Sometimes love is blind."

"That's what they say," she sing-songs. Soon, Kenzie is bursting through the back door.

"You're off next weekend," she states matter-of-factly.

"Really?" I'm actually kinda shocked because I've only been home for a week.

"Dad was cool with it. You only get to celebrate your birthday once a year," she tells me. "I'm gonna get with Elle too and tell her to cancel all her plans next weekend and meet us. It'll be just like old times with all of us girls together!"

Maize squeals, and we're all giddy with excitement. I would love for Elizabeth to join us. Elle's in her last year of veterinary school and is interning at a local office, but she's been so busy with work this week, I've barely gotten to see her. Our schedules are completely opposite these days, but I hope that changes now that I'm here for good. Before I can say another word, my phone rings with a call from Riley.

"Zoey's going into labor!" he shouts, not even giving me a chance to say hello.

"OH MY GOD! Right now?" I yell.

"Yep, her water broke. No baby yet, but Zach will be here soon! We're going to the hospital. Gotta go. Calling everyone else."

He immediately hangs up, not waiting for a response. Maize and Kenzie impatiently wait for me to explain.

"I'm gonna be an aunt today! Oh my God! I gotta go." I give them both hugs.

"Should we come with you?" Kenzie asks.

"Only if you want to sit in the waiting room for hours," I say.

Kenzie laughs. "How about you tell us when Zoey starts pushing and then we'll come up?"

"Sounds great!" I'm overjoyed as I tell them goodbye.

I rush through the back door, letting Uncle John know the good news on my way out. He's just as ecstatic about it as I am. "I'll be up there later! Don't worry about going to work tonight. I'll get Ethan to cover for you."

"Okay! Thank you!" I yell through the common area and hurry home where I know Mom and Dad are eagerly waiting for me.

"Let's go!" Dad rushes as soon as I walk in. We're giddy as can be as we drive to the hospital in San Angelo. The hour drive feels like an eternity. By the time we make it into the parking lot, I'm ready to hop out before Dad parks the truck. Once we're inside, Mom leads the way to the delivery floor, and her co-workers congratulate her as we pass them.

"You're gonna be a grandma, River! Feelin' old yet?" Amelia asks.

They've been friends since Mom started working at the hospital after Riley was born. Mom laughs and tells me and Dad to stay in the waiting area as she checks on Riley and Zoey. We sit, and the anticipation nearly kills me. Dad's a bundle of nerves too.

Moments later, Mom returns. "They're checking to see how dilated she is. She's having some intense contractions already, so it shouldn't be too long."

I let out a sigh. "She needs to hurry up and push that baby out already."

"Rowan, it's barely been two hours since her water broke. They're not going to pull the baby out by his head. He'll come when he's ready."

Patience isn't one of my strong suits. I try to busy myself and play on my phone, and text Riley every twenty minutes until he tells me to stop bothering him. Instead of listening, I keep up my annoying little sister act that I've perfected over the years, but he straight up ignores me. It's deserved, though, because I'm sure he's helping Zoey with whatever she needs.

More family members arrive until the entire waiting room is full of Bishops. All I know is I'm going in and seeing my nephew first or I'll be throwing fists. After four hours, Riley comes out, and he's grinning wide. Pretty sure he's shedding some tears too. He tells us everything went great, and they've moved Zoey into a regular room so we can visit now.

I quickly text my cousins and let them know the baby is here. Riley's bombarded by everyone, but I hurry and follow my parents through the hall to see Zoey while he explains that all went perfect with no complications.

When we enter the room, she's nothing but smiles as she holds her little bundle of joy. I rush over to her, and my emotions get the best of me when I see Zach for the first time.

"Oh, Zoey," I whisper. "He's beautiful."

She sees my eyes well with tears and chuckles. When she looks down at his sweet little face, it's obvious how much love she already has for him. "Do you want to hold him?"

Mom and Dad stand behind me, and we all admire this adorable tiny human in my arms.

"Hey, buddy," I say. "I'm your aunt Rowan, and I'm going to spoil you so much."

Though I want to be greedy with him all day, I eventually pass him to Dad. Riley enters, and we're all beaming. Considering there are so many family members here, I give my brother a congratulatory hug, then tell Zoey and Zach how much I love them before leaving so others can visit. As soon as I make it to the waiting room, Grandma and Grandpa excuse themselves to go in next.

"So?" Kenzie prompts as Maize stands next to her. "How are they doing?"

"They're great! But I don't know how my brother made such a cute baby." I chuckle. "Newborns typically look weird, but not Zach. He's absolute perfection," I tell her. "Where's Elle?" I look around.

"She said she got stuck at work and would be here as soon as she could," Kenzie explains.

"You got baby fever yet?" Maize pops an eyebrow.

"You kinda need a partner to have baby fever," I retort.

"That is true," I hear a husky deep voice say over my shoulder. Turning, I see Diesel's wide grin. I give him my well-practiced groan and go to hell look.

"Mind your own business," I mutter and ignore him. Maize tilts her head as Diesel moves closer to us, forcing himself into our conversation. I turn and look at him. "What?" I challenge, needing him to go away.

He shrugs and tilts his cowboy hat toward me. "If you really want a baby...I can help you with that. Big D is at your service."

I look at him like he's lost his mind, then roll my eyes. "What's wrong with you? Do you have brain damage or something? Eat too many paint chips as a kid?"

Kenzie snickers. "It's all the cow shit he's sniffed over the years. Affected his critical thinking skills."

Diesel arches a brow, smirking. "Man, are all the Bishop women this quick on their feet? Hopefully that means the same under the sheets." His eyes pierce through me, and I'm ready to clock him right in the jaw as a blush hits my cheeks.

Uncle John walks up, and my other uncles Evan and Jackson are behind him with their wives. Usually, when all the Bishop brothers are together, it means trouble or a celebration. Thankfully, this time, it's the latter. As soon as he sees all of my uncles, I see the fear of God in Diesel's eyes as he wonders if they overheard him or not. He quickly leaves and sits in a chair against the wall on the other side. It takes everything I have not to laugh at how quickly he cowered. My uncles are mighty intimidating, especially Uncle Evan, but I think it's because he's a doctor and has an arrogant air about him.

Kenzie and Maize go with their parents to see the new addition to our family, and I pull out my phone and sit, trying to busy myself while everyone takes their turn visiting. Diesel gets up and moves close to me, taking a seat next to mine. I ignore him the best I can, but it's nearly impossible when I can smell the fresh scent of his body wash and cologne. I try my damnedest to breathe in the other direction, but it's so obvious, he notices.

He clears his throat, trying to get my attention. Diesel's being so obnoxious as he shakes his leg and taps his foot. I turn my head and glare at him.

"What do you want?" I look into his green eyes.

He pops an eyebrow. His gaze meets mine, then trails down to my lips, my breast, and further before he shrugs.

"You're an animal."

When he leans over, his lips are mere inches from my ear, and his warm breath brushes against my skin. "Only in the bedroom. Care to find out for yourself?"

Diesel is undeniably attractive and has muscles for days, but I also know his history. He's known for banging women's brains out and then not calling them the next day. While there have been times in my life when I may have gone for something like that, I don't find that appealing anymore.

After my heart was used and abused by a cheating bastard, I need something more than to be dicked down by a manwhore. I need someone I can trust and who will treat me right. I have more respect for myself than a one-night stand with someone like Diesel, who I'll have to see every day for the rest of my life. Plus, there's no doubt Riley would murder him. The thought makes me grin, and he notices.

"What?" he asks.

"Oh nothing," I sing-song and lean further back in my seat.

Seeing baby Zach, and my brother so happy with his family, I've realized that's what's really missing in my life. I want a forever relationship, not one that's just temporary, but after Nick smashed those dreams, I'm starting to think it's not in my future.

Almost as if it's a divine intervention, I get a text message from Trace, a guy I sorta dated for a short time two and a half years ago. When we first met, he'd just moved here because his job transferred him to San Angelo. He's older than me, nearly thirty now, but mature and well established in his life, which is a change from the guys my age. Things ended mutually when I left to go back to college, and we kept in touch as friends.

My smile grows even larger.

> **TRACE**
> Welcome back to Nowhere, Texas! I didn't forget to text you when I got back in town, but wanted to give you some time to settle back home. Hope we can get together soon!

> **ROWAN**
> I'm ready when you are! When are you free?

> **TRACE**
> Next weekend?

I think about my plans with my cousins and know I can't cancel on them. I wouldn't anyway, especially not for a guy, but Trace is one of the good ones. He's also not bad to look at either.

> **ROWAN**
> Dang! I'm busy next weekend. What about the one after?

> **TRACE**
> I'll be traveling that weekend. Hmm...we'll have to reconvene again ;)

Diesel shifts in his seat. "Are you talking to that old asshole again?"

Frustration is written all over his face, and I find it adorable he's so damn jealous. When I first introduced Trace to everyone at the Bishop's traditional Fourth of July party, Diesel and Riley nearly lost their minds. They don't like the fact that Trace is so much older than me, but I am a grown ass woman and will do whatever I want. The last thing I need is their permission or approval.

"What's it to you, *Adam*?" I say his real name and watch him stiffen even more.

"It's nothing to me. When you're in public, though, everyone's gonna wonder why you're dating your dad. That's all." The snark in his tone isn't lost on me.

"My dad?" I laugh. "Trace isn't much older than us," I remind him.

"Nearly ten years, Rowan."

"Seven," I correct.

He scoffs. "You need someone who won't pull their back out to keep up with you." He tilts his head. "Someone who's used to working hard and not sitting behind a computer all day."

"Oh really? Someone like you?" I snort. "No, thank you."

"Don't knock it until you've tried it." He waggles his brows.

I think back to when he kissed me when I was thirteen, then I remember how he denied it, and I hated him for ruining the memory. All night I'd been rejected, and it was just another reminder that I wasn't good enough to be claimed by anyone, not even *him*.

My phone vibrates in my palm as I watch Diesel from my peripheral. He's trying to play it off like he doesn't care, but it's more than obvious he does.

I look around, making sure none of my family is close, and it seems most of them have cleared out. They're probably all stuffed in Zoey's tiny little room or waiting in the hallway to go inside. "I'd rather be alone for the rest of my life than *try it*. I don't want to catch a disease. I have no idea where you or your traveling dick have been."

"You can only deny me so much before you jump on board, Row."

I scoff. "I'm not jumping on anything, especially you."

"We'll see," he says confidently.

"Whatever. Shit in one hand and wish in the other. See what happens quicker." I shake my head, knowing he's trying to get under my skin. At times, I think he might really have a thing for me, but I'm convinced he flirts just to aggravate the piss out of my brother and me.

Instead of giving him any more attention, I unlock my phone and reply to Trace. We decide to play it by ear and plan something another time. A smile touches my lips, and Diesel tightens his fist as uneasiness drifts from him.

Knowing he's jealous as hell only encourages me to keep chatting with Trace because poking the beast and watching him squirm is fun. If Diesel wants to play games, maybe I'll appease him, but it doesn't mean I'll ever be crawling under the sheets with him. I don't care about his cute, boyish grin or how great he smells; he's off-limits. The last thing I need is my brother punching Diesel in the face, but I do smirk at the thought.

CHAPTER THREE

Diesel

Two weeks have passed since Rowan moved back, and as much as I try, I can't seem to get her off my mind. It's nearly impossible, especially when she's working at the Circle B Saloon nearly every night. Hanging out at that bar is one of my favorite pastimes, and knowing I'll see her has me putting on cologne and taking showers twice a day. When I get off work, I just want to have a beer and relax, but now, I'm changing into nice clothes as if I'm going on a date. "Dress to impress" is one of my mama's favorite sayings.

After work, I do exactly that, then sit at the bar for hours. I was actually kind of disappointed when I arrived and didn't see Rowan there. Apparently, she had the night off, or at least that's what Kenzie told me after giving me shit for asking. They all think it's just an act, but I'm gonna prove to her and everyone else that it's not.

I've had a thing for her since we were kids, but knowing she was Riley's little sister has always deterred me. Thinking back on my past relationships though, the reason I haven't settled down is because they weren't Rowan. The heart knows what it wants, and while Rowan's favorite hobby is pushing me away, I'm confident that one day she'll see what's always been right in front of her.

Saturday's her birthday, and I got her something she'd never guess. She probably doesn't think I remembered, but I'll never forget her special day.

I thought she'd be working tonight, but she's spending time with her nephew, so I'll have to give it to her some other time. With her name on my tongue and thoughts of her dancing in my head, I start taking shots. It doesn't take long before I drink too much and have Grayson taking me home. He's a good, responsible sidekick while Riley's busy with his family.

"Want me to pick you up in the mornin'?" he asks, my vision slightly blurring.

"Yeah, don't be late, though, because Alex will chew me up and spit me out."

"Yep, will do, but remember all this when it comes time for a raise," he tells me, grinning. "Need help gettin' inside?"

"Imma big boy. I can handle it." When I open the door to the truck and step out, I nearly lose my balance and laugh. Grayson waits for me to make it on the porch before he backs out of the driveway and leaves. It's really dark out and idiot me forgot to turn on the porch light, so I end up tripping over the mat in front of the door. I catch myself before falling and lean against the wood for a second, noticing my mail haphazardly sticking out of the box. I reach over and grab it, then walk inside and plop on the couch.

Most of it is nothing but stupid fliers and junk, but one envelope grabs my attention. The handwriting is neat and is addressed to my nickname instead of my formal name.

I open it and pull out a single sheet of paper. The curly handwriting matches the front.

Diesel,

My sister, Chelsea, didn't want me to contact you, but I feel it's your right to know that she gave birth to a little boy named Dawson, and I believe he's yours. She could really use your help right now. If you could, please call me.

-Laurel

There's a phone number and name at the bottom, and all I can do is laugh. I'm ready to throw it in the trash because this seems like something Riley would do, especially after I bragged about how cute his son is to everyone. Word around the ranch travels fast, and I wouldn't be surprised if he's trying to pull my leg or something.

I set it on the coffee table, kick off my boots, and end up falling asleep on the couch. Hours later, I wake up to pounding on my front door. Disoriented and a bit confused, I roll over and land on the hardwood floor, then look up and realize I'm home. When the knocking continues, I stand, unsteady on my feet, and open the door to see Grayson's smiling face.

"What?" I ask.

"It's time to go to work, ya big dumbass. It's five," he says, pulling his phone from his pocket and shining the bright screen in my face. "And you look like shit."

"I drank too much...*again*," I mutter, needing to brush my teeth because the nasty taste in my mouth makes me want to vomit.

"I know, I was there. You have five minutes. We gotta go, or Alex is gonna be pissed." Grayson snaps his fingers, and I'm two seconds from shutting the door in his face and going back to sleep. Instead, I get dressed and cleaned up, take some headache meds, and before I follow him out, I grab the letter from the coffee table and shove it into my pocket. I thought I'd imagined it all but guess not.

I need a gallon of coffee and a bottle of ibuprofen, and the sun hasn't even risen yet.

When we pull up to the B&B, I say a little prayer that today won't be too hard. I should learn my lesson about not going to the bar on a weeknight, but until I start dry-heaving next to the boss, I might not.

"Damn, Diesel. You sure you're okay?" Grayson asks, actually looking worried.

Wiping my mouth with the back of my hand, I suck in a deep breath. "Yep. I'm good," I lie. I feel like a giant sack of shit, and considering it's supposed to be well over a hundred degrees today, it's not gonna get any better. The heat always makes my hangovers worse.

Grayson pats me on the back, and we walk inside the shop. Alex is kicked back in a chair with his feet on the desk, sipping his coffee.

"Mornin'," Alex greets. He's had a permanent grin on his face since becoming a pawpaw. If I wanted to try to get away with anything, now would be the time because he's been in such a good mood. I break out into a cold sweat.

Alex notices as he goes through our schedule today. "You okay?"

I nod, walking to the fridge and grabbing a cold bottle of water and taking a long sip. "Yeah, I think I'm just hungry." I can't remember the last time I ate, which might legitimately be a part of the problem.

"Well shit, go to the B&B and eat. You know what needs to be done now."

Grayson agrees. "Yeah, and if you don't feel any better, I can take over and let everyone know."

"Hell no. Duties need to be done, rain or shine," I argue.

"Hungover or not." Alex shrugs. "Been there. Sucks, but all of our choices have consequences. I gotta hand it to you, though, at least you were on time."

Grayson looks at me. "You're welcome."

"Shut the hell up." I grunt.

Alex glances back and forth between us. "You better get going before I change my mind and give you tomorrow's chore list too."

"Not needed," Grayson says as we leave.

When we get into the truck, Grayson cranks it and backs out. "Maybe next time you're on beer eight, you'll stop drinking before ordering two shots. Don't you know the rule? Beer before liquor, never been sicker."

I close my eyes. "Once I eat, I'll be good to go."

As soon as we arrive at the B&B and walk inside, I smell the homemade bread. My mouth waters as we help ourselves to the buffet. Before I sit with my plate stacked high, Maize comes around the corner glaring at me.

"That's for the guests," she says with her arms crossed.

"I'm a guest. I'm just visiting until my plate is empty," I taunt, shoveling food into my mouth like I'll never see a biscuit again.

Grayson doesn't say a word while she's around, and eventually, she walks off, muttering some cuss words. I shrug, completely unbothered by her. He picks up his fork and begins eating.

"So, boss, where do you want me to start today?"

We're digging a trench to place pipe so we can get water to a new area on the property that has more shade for the cows. It'll take us at least a week to complete, which is okay.

"I was thinking maybe a few of you can mark the area first, then half of you start on the east side. Eventually, we'll meet in the middle."

"Sounds like a good plan," he says. I've had some time to think about it because Alex had mentioned it last week in passing.

"You think you can get everyone started? I wanna go check on Riley after breakfast. I'll grab some keys to a side-by-side and meet you out there when I'm done."

"Sure thing," Grayson says around a mouthful.

Once we finish eating, Grayson sits back and pats his stomach. "Damn, that woman can cook."

"Right?" I grin. "She should open a restaurant, but this is much better because then I can eat for free."

Grayson chuckles. "If we keep eating triple amounts of food, she might start charging us or really kickin' our asses. The woman hates us."

"Comes with the territory." I shrug, not that worried. "But if she did that, I'd call her grandma and snitch because Mrs. B told me I could eat here anytime I wanted," I explain. "And no one crosses Grandma Bishop. Not even her own kids and especially not her grandkids."

I stand and pick up our extra plates and place them in the dirty dish tub. We say good morning to John and walk out the back door before he has the chance to give us a hard time.

"See you in an hour?" Grayson asks as I look out at the rolling hills, feeling slightly human again after eating some carbs.

"Yep, an hour should be good. Hey, after work, can you take me to the bar to get my truck?"

"Yeah, not a problem, boss." He nods, and we go our separate ways.

Walking to the shed, I grab the keys to a four-wheeler and climb on. It takes no time to get to Riley's house. Even though he's not working at the moment, he keeps his early morning schedule to help take care of the baby or spoil his wife with breakfast. We've been waking up at the butt crack of dawn since we were teenagers. Chores had to be done, which meant rising early, and it's hard to reset an internal clock after that long.

I lightly knock on his front door, and within seconds, Riley opens it and lets me in. He rushes back to the kitchen where he's cooking. I glance around and notice all the lights in the house are off except in this room, which means he's the only one awake. Every move we make seems amplified, or maybe that's just my hangover.

"So what's up? You're visitin' early," Riley says as he pours oatmeal into a boiling pot of water.

I pull the letter from my pocket, grinning like an idiot before I sit. "You almost got me."

Riley looks confused. "What're you talkin' about?"

I pick up the envelope and tap it against the table. "This."

His forehead creases. "I really don't know what that is."

Riley comes over, and I hand it over. He takes the paper out and reads it. "I didn't send you this."

"Shut up." I laugh. "You really don't have to keep up the act."

The look on his face is pure seriousness. "I swear to you on my great-grandfather's grave, Diesel. I didn't send it."

It only takes seconds for my smile to fade. Riley never jokes around about family like that. I take off my cowboy hat and set it down before running my fingers through my hair.

"You want something to drink?" he asks as the blood drains from my face.

"Is it too early for whiskey?" I glance up at him.

He pulls out a bottle of Jack Daniel's from the cabinet, and I shake my head, wanting to puke just from looking at the liquid. "I'll take some coffee instead."

A mug is set in front of me, and Riley hands the envelope back. "Did you call the number?"

"No, because I thought this shit was a joke," I admit.

"Chelsea. Chelsea," Riley repeats. "Wasn't that the chick's name from Vegas?"

I think back to my birthday nearly two and a half years ago and try to refresh my memory. "I don't remember." Sadly, I don't even remember what she looks like either, but I don't say that out loud.

He begins plating food. "Did you wear protection?"

"I always wear protection. There's no doubt about that."

Riley shrugs. "If you know for a fact you wore protection, then I wouldn't worry about it until she comes knocking on your door with a kid in tow. You know? If she'd have sex with you after one night, then you probably weren't the only person she slept with at the time she got pregnant. You weren't exclusive or anything. Hell, you didn't even exchange numbers."

"Right," I agree, tucking the letter back in my pocket.

"I'm sure it's nothing," Riley encourages. I push the thoughts away and refuse to give it any more of my attention.

"How's the dad life so far?" I ask with a grin, changing the subject.

"Feels like a dream," he admits. "I can't believe I have a son. It's everything I've ever wanted."

"I'm happy for you, man. And envious as fuck," I say, wishing I had what he has.

"You'll find someone. She might be an idiot for gettin' with ya, though," he teases.

"Shut the hell up. That's no way to talk about your sister," I add and then hightail my ass out of his house before he beats the shit outta me. I tell him goodbye and ask him to give Zoey and Zach my love before I hop on the four-wheeler and head to the east side of the land where my ranch hands are hard at work.

By the time I make it to where the guys are working, my stomach has settled. The food I ate and coffee I drank made me feel like a million bucks.

After parking, I walk toward them and look over what they've accomplished so far. The area where we need to dig is marked with spray paint, and they're spaced out in twenty-foot sections with shovels. Working with them makes my life easy because I don't have to micromanage anything they do, and they're self-sufficient.

"Make sure y'all are drinkin' plenty of water. Don't need anyone gettin' heatstroke out here," I tell them.

I look at Grayson, who's wiping sweat from his brow. "I'm gonna drive around to the other side of the property and check on the cattle we moved last week. If you need anything, call me."

He nods before going back to digging, and I make my way across the pasture on the four-wheeler. Though I run the cattle operation, we have to do backbreaking tasks at times so the cows will survive the intense heat waves. Making sure they get water is the number one priority in the hotter months.

It takes me nearly thirty minutes to drive to the far pasture. I go down a large hill and start counting the herd to make sure none are lost. There's a lot of land fenced off, so it takes me a while, but each one is accounted for. It's easy for them to get lost, and I've heard rumors of thieves cutting barbed wire and stealing entire herds at dark. It's one reason we spend weeks branding in the summer. If I ever catch anyone stealing from the Bishops, my fists would have a long conversation with their face.

By the time I make it back, it's well after lunch. They took a break to eat, but since I ate a large breakfast, I decided to skip. For the rest of the afternoon, I help lay the pipe and am sweaty and starving by the time our shift is over. Grayson and I decide to stop at the B&B to see what Maize cooked for dinner before going to get my truck from the bar.

As soon as I walk up the steps to the porch, Rowan, Maize, and Kenzie walk out dressed in short skirts that leave absolutely nothing to the imagination. My jaw hits the floor as my eyes trail up Rowan's long legs until I meet her gaze.

"Take a picture, why dontcha?" she barks, and her cousins laugh.

"Where the hell are you goin'? I ask. "Especially looking like *that*."

"We're going out," Maize says.

"For Rowan's birthday," Kenzie adds. The two of them look at me before walking down the steps in their high heels, but Rowan lingers for just a moment, and I notice she's wearing cowboy boots with her skirt.

"Damn. You look really nice," I tell her, smiling.

"Thanks, *Adam*. That was the goal," she gloats.

If she only knew what I really want to say to her right now, but instead, I keep my feelings for her tucked deep inside. I suck in a deep breath. "Stay out of trouble tonight. You need a real man to save you, call me."

She laughs. "Trouble's my middle name, and I'm more than capable of taking care of myself, thank you very much."

And I don't doubt her one bit. All I want to do right now is pull her into my arms and kiss the fire out of her, but the way she's looking at me tells me I'd only get burned.

"You got a designated driver?" I ask.

"Shit, you're worse than my parents."

"Rowan," I warn, crossing my arms over my chest.

"We're staying at a hotel all weekend. We don't need a DD. Any more questions? " She runs her fingers through her dark brown hair, and I watch her tongue dart out and lick her ruby red lips.

If asking her questions would keep her here all night, I'd keep going.

"Come on!" Kenzie yells from her Jeep.

Rowan looks at her, then back at me but doesn't say a word.

"Hope you have a happy birthday," I say, lowering my voice. She looks as if she wants to say something but doesn't. Instead, she walks away.

"And be careful," I say even louder. She glances at me over her shoulder and smirks.

"We'll see," she says. I swear Rowan's shaking her hips just to drive me fucking crazy. She climbs into the Jeep and mumbles something to Maize before Kenzie backs out of the driveway. The dust kicks up in the air, and I watch until they're out of view.

I'm half-tempted to go home, take a shower, and follow them, but I didn't ask enough questions. They could be going to San Angelo, or hell, knowing them, they might've even gone to the River Walk in San Antonio. The Bishop girls are unpredictable.

Though I'm full of disappointment because Rowan won't be here for her birthday, and I left her gift at my house, I push it away and go into the B&B with Grayson trailing me.

"What?" I look at him.

"Nothing," he says. "Just seems you've met your match."

"With who?" I ask and notice John's sitting behind the counter reading a magazine. Instead of giving me shit, he just throws us a head nod and a grin.

"Rowan. I saw the way she was lookin' at you."

I smile as I help myself to the beef tips and mashed potatoes they're serving tonight. Maybe I wasn't imagining the look in her eye, after all, or maybe Grayson is just fucking with me, but either way, I'll take it.

As I sit down and eat, Rowan's long legs fill my mind. After I get my truck, I'll be taking a cold shower with hopes of pushing the thoughts of her away. But I'll fail miserably because I always do when it comes to Rowan Bishop and what she does to me even if she doesn't realize it.

CHAPTER FOUR

Rowan

Kenzie turns the volume up on the radio, and we blare Garth Brooks. We sing along about friends in low places like stupid teenagers as we make our way to San Angelo for the weekend. I thought it would be more difficult to get off work since I've only been back for two weeks, but Uncle John wasn't too much of a hard-ass about it. As Kenzie said, the four of us haven't been together in ages and deserve a girls' night out.

When we make it to town, I can't stop thinking about how Diesel looked at me. Not often do I catch the seriousness in his eye that says I'm more than his best friend's little sister. The reality is that line can't be crossed, even if Diesel was the first man I ever kissed. Not even my cousins know that secret.

"What's on your mind?" Maize asks me as we park and walk toward the entrance of the hotel.

I hurry and smile. "My eighth grade winter formal."

Maize laughs her ass off.

"Why?" Kenzie chuckles as she opens the door, allowing us past her.

"I dunno, just a random thought."

She looks at me as though I've lost my mind, and a part of me thinks I have. Eighth grade wasn't that important. It's not like it was high school prom or senior formal. It was a stupid dance where the boys were too embarrassed to be close to the girls.

After we check into the hotel, the three of us wait for Elle to arrive. She's been super busy with work and assisting Dr. Wallen but said she could use some fun and decided to join us after her shift. I'm so damn excited to get to hang out with my cousins this weekend. The four of us used to get into so much trouble growing up.

A light knock on the door grabs our attention, and Maize gets up to answer it. Elle walks inside, looking pretty as ever with her dirty blond hair pulled up and bright green eyes behind black-rimmed glasses. She's all smiles as she gives us hugs.

"Look at you, birthday girl!" she says, noticing my outfit. "You're gorgeous as ever!"

I willingly take the compliment. It's the first time I've seen her since I moved back.

"We look like trouble." I giggle. We grab our purses and head to the Honkey Tonk bar down the road. Kenzie doesn't turn twenty-one for a few more weeks, so she's our designated driver, which is a good thing because honestly, getting drunk is the only thing on my to-do list tonight.

We immediately walk up to the bar, and I order a soda for Kenzie and three shots.

"To Rowan turning the big two-three and all of us celebrating together!" Maize says, and we all clink our glasses together. I smile wide, then shoot the tequila down. It's smooth and goes down like water, which is dangerous as hell. Moments later, Maize orders another round.

"I'm not going to have any more," Elle tells us after the second one. She's always been the responsible one and follows the rules. "I don't want to drive back home tomorrow with a hangover." She winks.

Once the liquor is flowing through my veins, we sashay onto the dance floor and shake our asses. Martina McBride blares through the room, and we sing along to an oldie but a goodie as loud as we can. The music fades, and a slow song comes on, and I'm brought back to being that girl who isn't asked to dance as Maize and Kenzie go off with two guys. Instead of letting it get to me, I go back to the bar with Elle and order a cocktail as I get lost in my thoughts on being single forever.

"How's work going?" I ask her.

She groans. "Busy, as usual. I work nonstop."

I chuckle. "Well, your boss is drop-dead gorgeous, so it can't be that bad to be around him all the time."

"True. He's a walking, talking wet dream. I think people feed their dogs chocolate just so they can get an emergency home visit from him. It's pathetic. I mean, I get the allure, but he's kinda an asshole, which is a total turn-off." She smiles, but there's something more behind her tone.

"Who's an asshole?" Kenzie walks up and asks as Maize continues dancing with this tall, good-looking fellow.

"Dr. Connor Wallen." Elle says his full name with an eye roll. "He's good with animals and turns on the charm with their owners, but behind closed doors, he's brooding and snappy," she explains. "And that's *after* he's had his morning coffee."

"Oh damn." I chuckle, thinking how it sounds like Dr. Wallen needs to get laid and how long it's been since Elle's been in a relationship. She could probably help turn his attitude around.

"The things I'd let him do to me." Kenzie releases a dreamy sigh, elbowing Elle in the arm.

"Before I forget, who's that guy who works with Diesel again?" Elle asks, noticeably changing the subject away from her boss. I glance out on the dance floor and notice Maize still's shaking her ass with a guy who seems super interested in her.

"You're probably talking about Grayson. A little shorter than Diesel, sandy brown hair," I describe him and watch as Kenzie tenses. We make eye contact, but she tucks her bleach blond hair behind her ear and pretends it's nothing, but I saw her reaction.

"Yeah, that sounds like him. Is he new? I saw Diesel with him the other day when I was dropping something off for Uncle John." Elle glances at Kenzie.

"What? I don't know anything about Grayson." Kenzie sucks on her straw, checking out of the conversation, which causes me to laugh. I've noticed she snaps at him any chance they're in the same room together, though she's never given us a reason. She only says he's annoying and leaves it at that.

"He's been around for five or six months. I think he's Kenzie's age," I tell Elle, glancing at Kenzie.

She shrugs with a look of indifference. "So? Doesn't mean I know anything about him."

I laugh at her expression, but I see something in her eyes. She's not telling us something, but I don't push her on it.

A few minutes later, Maize joins us and orders a drink too. We all turn and look at her.

"Please tell me you got his number," I say, looking past her at the sexy guy across the room she was grinding against the last few songs.

She shakes her head. "He didn't ask me for mine, and I wasn't gonna dare to make the first move. It's all the validation I need to know I'll end up a nun or single forever with forty-seven cats. There are no good-looking, single men around here."

I stand, lifting my hand, and Maize gives me a high-five. "Same, sis. Same."

A few more slow songs play, and eventually, the mood in the room changes as Shania Twain blasts out about men not impressing her very much. I'm pretty sure this is my theme song. One reason this country bar stands out above the others is they always play old-school country songs. It brings me back to being a kid and the music my grandparents always have playing in their house.

I know I need to stop drinking, or I'll be trashed before midnight. I order a glass of water and chug it so I don't have a hangover tomorrow. When I'd go out with my friends in college, it was the only way I wouldn't be sick the next day.

As soon as Rednex comes on, the entire room starts line dancing. I'm honestly having an amazing time with my cousins. The four of us can't stop laughing as we nearly trip on each other to "Cotton Eye Joe." Drunk people were not taken into consideration when this dance was invented, but it's another reason I love to wear my cowboy boots. Heels are just too dangerous. Kenzie and I stumble around and nearly take Maize and Elle down with us. We are those basic girls wearing skirts and being obnoxious at the bar, but I don't care what anyone thinks. Maize encourages me to take more shots with her and to keep dancing. She's the life of the party right now, and I'm living for it.

After we've nearly tired ourselves out, we find a table in the corner, then sit and catch our breaths. My face hurts from laughing so much, and I honestly can't remember the last time I had this much fun. Damn, I love being home. These girls are my best friends and practically like my sisters.

While I'm at the table, I pull my phone from my purse and ask the waitress to snap a picture of us. We smile wide, wrapping our arms around each other. Once we check the photo, I post it to Facebook with a sappy post about being out with my cousins. *Grateful these three are in my life. Happy Birthday to me!*

After it's live, I scroll through my feed, and that's when I see a picture of Nick and the skank he cheated on me with. She has a big diamond ring on her finger and looking at it makes me want to puke. The ring, the man, the future—all of it was supposed to be mine, but it was stolen from me in a blink from a man who never deserved me in the first place.

"What the fuck!" I shout and show Maize my screen. Immediately, her reaction changes, and she shakes her head.

"He's a bastard," Maize says.

Elle adds, "A *cheating* bastard, at that."

"I guess we'll join the convent together," Maize continues. "Won't be so bad if we're both there, right?"

I snicker, regardless of how frustrated I am. "You know what I want right now?"

All eyes are on me, waiting for me to continue.

"I want *revenge*."

Kenzie rubs her hands together. "Are you thinking what I'm thinking?"

By the evil look on her face, I'm not sure I am. "I'm scared to know what's going through your mind right now."

"Bishop women don't get back, they get even." Maize has always been Team Rowan, and even from the very beginning, she didn't like Nick that much. She said there was a *vibe* about him. I never saw it, but should have. I was blinded by his good looks and made excuses for his arrogance.

Never again.

Elle looks back and forth between us. "Oh lord. You're gonna make me be an accomplice, aren't you?"

"I just need you to drive by his place for me."

"He's back in town?" Kenzie asks.

I suck in a deep breath, then blow it out. "Yes, he moved back with his ho in tow last week. Trust me, I wasn't thrilled about it. Out of all the men in the entire state of Texas going to the University of Houston, I had to date some asshole who only lived an hour away from home."

"You were happy about that when you thought it was going to work out," Elle reminds me.

"Yeah, I honestly thought it'd be great because I always planned to come back after graduation. No man was going to keep me away from home. I don't care how sexy or rich he was. It was a compromise. Have a handful of kids. I'd work on the ranch and help with the bar, and he'd continue running his family's business. We'd had our entire future planned out," I explain with a frown. "Until he fucking ruined it. I'm not sure I'll ever be able to forgive him for what he did to me."

"I might become a nun with y'all," Elle says, causing the three of us to laugh.

"Are you sure about this?" Elle hesitates.

"Abso-fucking-lutely," I tell her and walk toward the exit, leading the way.

We hop in the Jeep. I sit in the front while Maize and Kenzie sit in the back. Elle starts the engine, and we turn out of the parking lot, then I give her directions to Nick's house. A part of me feels like a loser for keeping tabs on him, but we dated for a little over a year. I can't just snap my fingers and make my heart forget the way he made me feel when things between us were good. We shared some happy memories, but he was so willing to throw it all away.

Elle turns down his street, and my heart races a million miles per hour. My throat goes dry, and I'm unsure of what I'll see when we pass. Thanks to Facebook and his willingness to brag about everything, I knew exactly what house he'd bought. We'd looked at it together online once, but when I said we'd need to compromise and live between San Angelo and Eldorado so it'd be convenient for us both, he closed out of the webpage, then told me to forget about it and changed the subject.

She slows in front of the house, and that's when I see his Mercedes parked next to a Corvette. I bite my bottom lip so hard, I'm shocked I'm not bleeding.

"Stop," I tell her, my blood pressure rising as I think about everything that's happened over the past couple of months. I get out of the Jeep and open the back door to the hatch and find a tire iron. Before I even know what I'm doing, I'm marching down the driveway on a mission and take all of my frustrations out on his beautiful bright yellow Corvette. With every bit of strength I have, I swing the cool iron against the windshield. Watching it shatter gives me so much fucking satisfaction that I don't stop. I go to every side window and even the back before I take my anger out on the hood of the car.

Maize whisper-shouts my name. "Rowan, come on!"

Looking up at her, I make one final blow to the taillight. I'm sure if she wouldn't have stopped me, I'd have kept going too. Before walking back to the Jeep, I look at all the damage I've caused and don't feel an ounce of regret. Actually, I feel better. Though I'm still not over being cheated on, I'll sleep great tonight knowing tomorrow morning when that prick gets up to go to work, his prized possession won't be so immaculate.

I climb inside the Jeep, setting the tire iron in the back seat between Maize and Kenzie. They look at me with wide eyes and their jaws dropped.

"That was badass," Kenzie eventually says, breaking the silence.

"I'm in shock," Elle tells me, chuckling. "I can't believe you fucked up his car like that."

"Thousands in damage, without a doubt," Kenzie says.

"Yep!" Adrenaline rushes through my body as we head back to the bar. "Oh wait, can we just go back to the hotel? I think I've had enough fun for the night."

"Only if we can stop and get double cheeseburgers first. Do you know how badly I'm craving McDonald's?" Kenzie says. "Sometimes it's hard living so far away from greasy food."

"I'm convinced you're really a raccoon," Maize teases. "Mischievous, messy, and eats everything in sight."

I burst into laughter. "That's the best thing I've heard all day. Kenzie, the trash panda. I think we might've found a new nickname for you."

Kenzie rolls her eyes. "Oh my gosh, y'all. I'm not *that* bad!"

"You are," Elle speaks up as she pulls into the drive-through. "You totally are."

After she's ordered nearly four of everything on the menu, she pays, and then we're handed three bags filled with chicken nuggets, double cheeseburgers, and a ridiculous amount of salty french fries. Living in the country does have its disadvantages, but I'm grateful not to have any of this conveniently close to home. In Houston, there was a fast food place on every corner.

Kenzie has a bag opened and is stuffing her mouth before we even make it out of the parking lot. I honestly didn't realize how hungry I was until Maize hands me a box of chicken nuggets. I feel like I swallowed them whole and didn't even chew them. Elle drives us to the hotel, and once we're in our room, we finish eating. I continue to devour food until I'm stupidly full, then kick off my boots and lie back on the bed with a smile on my face.

While I may not have gotten completely even because bashing in a car doesn't fix a broken heart, damn, it felt good to get him back. If only I could see Nick's face in the morning when he notices his expensive toy is now damaged goods. I'd pay good money for that. I hope he learns his lesson, but men like him never do.

A part of me wonders if he'll even suspect it's me, but the other part doesn't care. He never could handle me, not when we were dating and especially not now. One thing's for certain, I might be a Southern woman, but I still have a temper at times. He's underestimated what happens when you cheat on a Bishop.

CHAPTER FIVE

Diesel

I'm soaking wet, covered in nasty water from head to toe. A calf walked into the pond and couldn't get out because of the mud, which meant Grayson and I had to perform an impromptu rescue mission. There was no time to think about taking off our boots or anything before we were hopping into the water and walking through mush.

It's common for cows to stand in the bodies of water during the hot months since it helps them cool off, but the babies are sometimes the worst because they go out too far and can't get back to the bank. The little bastard was screaming at the top of his lungs, and we just so happened to be doing our afternoon checks. Together, Grayson and I carried the little asshole to the grass and made sure he was okay before driving off. Doesn't help our situation, though. We officially smell like cow slobber, pond mush, and sweat.

By the time we make it back to the shop, we both stink, my feet are soaked, and I'm ready for a drink.

"Wanna go to the bar tonight?"

Grayson looks at me. "Like this?"

"Hell no! I need a shower," I tell him, taking off my hat and setting it on my lap.

"I think I'm gonna take a rain check. It's been a hectic fuckin' day, and I'm exhausted. Gotta love Mondays."

I give him a smile and look down at my boots and pants. "Yeah, I totally understand. Never expected to be doing half that shit today. Every day's an adventure on the ranch," I remind him. The unpredictability is one of the things I love the most about my job. There's no monotony. Honestly, I don't know how people sit behind a computer at a desk all day. It sounds like eternal hell. I'd go crazy not being in the country.

We give Alex the rundown of what happened, then I hop in my truck and drive home. At times like this, I wished I carried an extra set of clothes around. I'm forced to drive back with the windows down because I can't stand the smell of myself. Once I'm home, I see Rowan's gift on the counter and smile before going to the bathroom. She's working tonight. I made sure to find out this morning from John. I've been waiting all weekend to see her to give her that present.

I take off my clothes and turn on the hot water. Stepping inside, I allow the warmth to soothe my sore muscles from carrying a one hundred pound calf today.

After I'm done washing every inch of my body, I brush my teeth and get dressed. I run my fingers through my hair and throw on a baseball cap, then spray on some cologne because I know it drives Rowan wild. It always has, ever since we were teenagers. She pretends to be immune, but I've noticed her reactions. The thought of seeing her tonight causes excitement to bubble inside me. No woman has ever made me feel like this, and as much as I try to shake it, I can't. Rowan Bishop has been in my veins since I was fourteen years old and tasted her lips against mine. Even though we were so young, I've never been able to forget the electricity that streamed between us. It's still there too.

Before leaving, I grab the gift along with my keys and head into town. I couldn't stop thinking about her the entire weekend. I saw a picture she posted on Facebook of her and her cousins at the Honky Tonk in San Angelo and thought about making the drive, but I knew better. The last thing I'd want to do is ruin her birthday by showing up unannounced. She looked beautiful as can be, though, and I know all eyes were on her at the bar. There's no doubt she was the prettiest woman there.

When I park in front of the Circle B Saloon, I see Rowan's car on the side. I sit and stare inside the building, watching as she pours a beer for an older guy and then smiles sweetly as she sets it down on a napkin. She laughs at something he says and just looking at her nearly takes my breath away. Without even trying, she's as pretty as can be with her hair pulled up into a tight ponytail on top of her head.

Knowing I can't watch her from my truck all night, I turn off the ignition, grab the present, and go inside. As soon as I walk in and sit at the bar, our gazes lock. I smile, and she narrows her eyes at me, then at the bright-colored wrapping paper. A moment later, she walks over, places a napkin in front of me, and treats me like every other customer.

"Hi, would you like a drink menu?" she asks, properly batting her eyelashes.

I snort at her sarcastic tone. "Give me a Bud."

She glances down at the box. "What's that?"

I push it toward her, grinning wide. "I got you something."

"Why?" She tilts her head. "Is it a gag gift?"

"You'll see," I challenge, moving it closer to her.

"I trust you as far as I can throw you, and we both know how much that is," Rowan retorts as she walks away and grabs a frosty mug from the cooler. She sets down an ice-cold beer in front of me before snagging the box.

I gently grab her hand before she can walk away and meet her deep brown gaze. "Don't open it around anyone."

"Oh God. Now I'm really scared."

I shrug and take a sip of my beer, the smile meeting my eyes as she walks away.

A second later, I watch a preppy ass guy enter and forcefully move the stool from in front of the bar next to me, making all sorts of noise. He stands tall like he owns the place, but everyone in here knows better. He's a puny little runt wearing a polo tucked into well-pressed khaki pants with a belt. Rowan notices him and tenses fiercely. Alarm bells go off in my head as he barks her name. Something isn't right with this guy, but he needs to watch his goddamn tone when speaking to her.

Rowan rushes over to him and lowers her voice, and I try not to pry. I try to keep my eyes locked on the TV on the back wall, but I can't tell what's on right now, though.

"What're you doing here?" she asks in a hushed tone, trying not to draw more attention.

"You know why I'm fucking here," he hisses.

I suck in a deep breath, trying to control my temper while staying out of her business. Truthfully, it's damn hard.

Rowan laughs. "Because you miss me?"

It takes everything I have not to roll my eyes because I know exactly who this prick is now—her cheating ex-boyfriend, Nick. Granted, the way he's looking at her, though, isn't with love but hate.

"Miss you? Miss *you*?" His voice grows louder. "Not quite. I'm here because you're a stupid bitch."

I jump to my feet so fast, the barstool falls to the ground with a loud crash. "You need to watch your language when speaking to a lady."

"Lady?" He snarls. "She's no fucking lady. She's a jealous whore who destroyed my Corvette."

Rowan pipes in. "I did not touch your *precious* car. Why would I do that?" She crosses her arms over her chest, challenging him.

"Because you're a goddamn cunt," he snaps.

Taking a step forward, I'm mere inches from him and ready to punch his face in. "I've already warned ya once. Don't call her names again. I don't care what the fuck she did to your car. And trust me, it won't be anything compared to what I do to your goddamn face if you keep disrespecting her like that."

"You need to leave, Nick," Rowan demands, pointing at the door, but something in her expression tells me she really did fuck up his car.

"Leave? How about you make me?"

Seconds later, his stark white polo is in my fist, and I'm ready to beat his face in when Rowan quickly comes around the bar and breaks us up. She softly places her hands on my chest and begs me to calm down. "Please, Diesel," she whispers. "He's not worth it."

I take a step back and try to chill out. No one's going to talk to her like that in front of me—not an ex, not even a family member, and especially not in *her* bar while she's working. He's trying to humiliate her, and I won't tolerate it.

"You're gonna pay for this, Rowan," Nick threatens.

"For what, exactly?" she questions.

He takes his cell phone from his pocket and plays a video, turning it around for her to watch. Considering I'm so much taller than she is, I can see it perfectly. She's got a tire iron in her hand, and she's destroying his car. With every swing she takes, I can feel the anger buried deep inside her. Damn. Remind me never to piss her off. She's a goddamn savage. Without realizing it, I start laughing my ass off, which nearly makes her ex spontaneously combust. He's not stupid enough to threaten me, though he gives me a dirty ass look.

I hear Rowan suck in a deep breath and groan. "Cameras."

"You're a fucking idiot," he tells her.

I move Rowan to the side and step closer to Nick. "I warned you about your language," I tell him. Before he can move, my fist meets his nose, and he falls down hard on his ass as the other customers watch the commotion.

"Motherfucker!" He covers his face with his hands.

"I think it's time for you to leave," I demand, pulling him up by his shirt and pushing him toward the door.

"You're gonna pay for every fucking dent and scratch you made," he shouts at Rowan, spitting out blood. "I'll be back if you don't."

"You're done, asshole," I tell him, basically throwing him outside. I stand in front of the entrance with my arms crossed over my chest and watch him storm off to his sparkly Mercedes. If he doesn't watch out, she might destroy that one too.

After he peels out, kicking up dirt and rock, I go back inside. Rowan is nowhere to be found. Kenzie is helping customers and refilling drinks. Honestly, I didn't even notice she was here until now. She helps at the bar but assists her mom at the daycare during her college breaks. She has a couple of years left before she graduates. Though she plans to work with kids, she does a good job bartending too. That natural people-person personality comes in handy in a small town like this. I sit and finish my beer, hoping Rowan returns soon. I order another drink and bide my time, but I still don't see her. Soon, it's closing time, and Kenzie locks the front door, then proceeds to clean. Considering I'm kinda part of the family, she doesn't force me to leave but rather lets me sit there even though I'm stalling.

"Hey, is Rowan still here?" I ask as she grabs her purse from under the counter.

"Yeah, she's in the office. You can go back there if you want. I won't tell anyone." Kenzie shoots me a wink. I walk her to the door, let her out, then relock the entrance.

When I go to the back, I see Rowan sitting in the office with her head down on the desk.

"Rowan?" I ask softly.

"Yeah?" She turns around, and I can tell she's been crying by how puffy her eyes are. It hurts my heart to see her like this.

"You okay?"

She nods and forces a smile, wiping her cheeks. "I'll be fine."

Shaking my head, I walk toward her, and she stands.

"Thanks for sticking up for me. I appreciate it."

"I'd punch him for you any day of the week," I tell her with a grin.

A chuckle escapes her. "You'd protect any woman who was being called names like that. He's such a dick."

I shrug. "Not sure what you saw in him, honestly."

"Me either." Rowan glances at me before moving past me. "I need to close out the drawers."

I follow her, going behind the bar as she takes out the money. "So…" I laugh, trying to lighten the mood. "I didn't realize you were the batshit crazy ex-girlfriend type who seeks revenge on luxury cars."

She eyes me. "It was a moment of weakness."

"Didn't look too weak to me with the way you were swinging that tire iron. I guess all those years of playing softball in high school did you some good."

Rowan grins, then scoffs, trying to blow me off, but I'm standing way too close to her to be ignored. I can tell she doesn't want to talk about this, but something in the way she looks at me says more than her words ever could. That familiar spark I saw when I kissed her the first time returns and dances behind her eyes.

As she sucks in a ragged breath and her lips part, I have the urge to kiss her again. We're too close, and I can smell the sweetness of her skin and the flowery scent of her shampoo. Loose strands of her dark hair fall from her ponytail, and I reach over and tuck them behind her ear. Her chest rises and falls when I place my thumb under her chin, hoping she gives me permission to move in.

The world around us seems to fade away as I lean closer. My heart is galloping in my chest as Rowan's eyes flutter closed. I lick my lips, and then as if someone turned on the lights, she moves away from me and denies our kiss. Shattered is the only way I can describe how I feel, but it also gives me hope. We were so close, but I understand her hesitancy.

She just went through a major breakup, one that had her beating the shit out of his car, so it might seem too soon. Having her almost give in to me, though, is all the encouragement I need to know that not all hope is lost between us. That fire is still burning bright, and I'll do whatever I need to help it blaze.

"You should open your gift," I say, swallowing hard around a large lump in my throat.

"Okay." She nods.

I gain my courage after being rejected and follow her back to the office. She rips off the paper on the small box and looks at me with happiness as she holds a mood ring between her fingers.

"Where did you find this?" she asks, grinning.

I lean against the doorframe, soaking in her beautiful features. "You lost it when we were younger."

"Yeah, I remember. Me, you, Riley, and Elle were playing tag, and it fell off," she reminds me.

I nod. "I spent an entire week looking for it out in the pasture."

"And you actually found it?" She seems shocked.

"I refused to give up because I knew how much you loved it," I admit.

"Why didn't you give it back to me then?" Rowan's eyes meet mine as she adjusts the sizing and slips it on her finger.

"Because you hated me, and I didn't want you to think I was weird or something."

She lets out a holler of a laugh. "You'll always be weird to me, Adam. But thank you. It really means a lot."

"So what color is it?" I step inside the office and look down at the ring.

"Pink," she says, and I watch her cheeks heat.

"Which means what exactly?" I'm actually curious. She had all the meanings for the colors memorized when we were younger.

Rowan shakes her head and playfully tucks her plump bottom lip inside her mouth.

"Come on, tell me," I urge. "I promise I won't laugh."

She sighs, inhaling a deep breath. "Fine. It means feeling flirty or romantic," she tells me with a chuckle, and my eyebrows rise.

"I think it's spot-on," I tease, and I'm damn happy about that.

CHAPTER SIX

Rowan

It's been two weeks since Nick showed his ugly face while I was working and threatened me. I know I acted irrationally, but considering he's stupid rich and doesn't need the money, it grates on my nerves. He could easily afford to pay for the damage or report an insurance claim, but to appease him and save my ass from him reporting me, I'll pay to get him out of my life for good.

The way Diesel stepped in and protected me hasn't left my mind either. We shared a moment and almost kissed, but I got cold feet and turned away. He's always been that annoying brother type who picks on me and drives me crazy for shits and giggles, but that doesn't mean I haven't noticed how he's changed over the years. He's huge—muscular and tall—dark and handsome. It'd be impossible not to notice.

Although it's Friday and Ethan doesn't normally work, he'll be here tonight for a few hours. Kenzie is coming in soon to help with the late rush. Once the ranchers finish their shifts and have dinner with their families, they'll come down and drink for a few hours. The weekends are definitely busier, and having an extra set of hands is always nice so I can focus on manager duties too.

"Another cold one..." George holds up and waves his empty beer bottle at me. In his mid-fifties, he's one of our regular customers and drinks like his stomach is never-ending. At least he's a decent tipper, though.

"Coming right up," I tell him, walking toward the cooler to grab him a new one. His wife, Mary, comes in with him sometimes, but he's riding solo tonight. "Where's the missus?" I ask when I swap out the bottles.

"Her sister is visiting this weekend. Hence why I'm here and not at home." He tilts the corner of his lips before taking a sip.

"Ah..." I say with a smirk. "Not a fan, huh?"

"Oh, they cluck like hens all night long. It gives me a headache, so I come here to look at your pretty face instead."

"Be careful now, George. Your compliments might go straight to my head."

"And trust me, she doesn't need a confidence boost," Ethan adds, coming up to my side. "She's already full of herself."

I jab my elbow into his ribs, causing him to let out a harsh breath. "Look who's talking, Mr. Suave. I could smell your cologne the second you walked in. Who're you tryin' to impress?"

"The ladies, duh." He chuckles, moving around me.

"You mean Harper." I cackle, and he gives me a dirty look. They've been best friends since they were in diapers, but he'll never make a move. She's the daughter of my dad's best friend, Dylan. We're all friends and grew up together, but she's currently dating some asshole they went to high school with. "Stop being a chickenshit," I tease.

"Look who's talkin'." He gives me a pointed look, then flashes a cocky smile. "Plus, I'm too young to settle down. Gotta play the field a bit."

Shaking my head, I hold up my palm toward Ethan and look at George. "See? This is why I'm single. Men are just too annoying and full of themselves."

Speaking of which...

The door opens, catching my attention, and Diesel walks in with Grayson and Wyatt, one of his townie friends. He laughs and playfully pushes Wyatt before our eyes lock, and his smile deepens.

"You were sayin'?" George taunts, chuckling around the neck of his beer before he takes a long sip.

Blinking, I clear my throat and grab a rag, needing to stay busy. It's not uncommon for Diesel to hang out and drink after work, but ever since he put Nick in his place, I can't stop thinking about him.

"Hey, *Row*," he says, taking a seat next to George, and the other two follow suit, sitting down on the other side of Diesel. He knows I hate that nickname, yet he says it to annoy me anyway.

"Hey, *Adam*." I flash a smug grin, knowing he hates it when people use his real name especially in public settings.

The corner of his lips tilts up into a shit-eating smirk. "You know, it only makes my dick harder when you call me that."

I gulp, then glare at him as I shake my head. "Pretty big talker there."

He winks, then continues, "Didn't know you'd be workin' tonight."

Liar. Yes, he did. With the exception of my birthday weekend, I've worked every Friday night since I moved back a month ago.

"Yep, I'm closing. Putting my big fancy finance degree to work." I chuckle because this was the plan after graduation. Maybe not bartending per se but being involved in the family's businesses and training to handle all the financial accounts. It'll be a while before I completely take over, so I'm managing the bar for now. "What can I get y'all?"

Diesel looks at them before glancing back at me. "Three beers to start. We'll save the shots for right before I kick their asses in pool."

"Pretty cocky for someone who almost broke their neck earlier," Grayson teases.

"Cocky is his middle name," I interject before I grab their drinks and set them down in front of them.

"Got that right," Wyatt adds.

"So how were you a dumbass today?" I ask, holding back my worries.

"They're being dramatic," he states calmly before bringing the beer to his mouth. The mouth I shouldn't be fantasizing about.

"This motherfucker..." Grayson starts, shaking his head. "He's on a tractor, and instead of parking it where it *belongs*, he wedges the damn thing between two others with no space to actually get down. So he decides to *jump* to the one next to him and nearly misses. Then he does it again and falls on his damn head."

"It was my shoulder," Diesel corrects. "And I'm fine, by the way. Thanks for your concern." He narrows his eyes at them, and I snort at their interactions, shaking my head at the way they give him shit. It's too easy, though. Diesel's a big kid in a grown man's body.

A really sexy body.

"You poor thing," I sing-song, resting a hand on my chest. "I'll keep you in my thoughts and prayers."

He cocks a brow. "I like you thinkin' about me."

My eyes slide to George, who's shooting a half grin. "Told you," I tell him.

George laughs, and Diesel furrows his brow, clearly not amused he's not in on the inside joke.

"Told him what?" he asks. "That I'm charming? Good-looking? Your future baby daddy?"

I nearly choke as a blush creeps up my neck and cheeks.

"That men are annoying. You just proved my point."

"You wound me, Row." Diesel sticks out his lower lip, pouting.

"Sorry to burst your *enormous* ego, but men like you are the worst ones out there," I say matter-of-factly.

"Gentlemanly? Kind? Willing to punch an ex-boyfriend for their best friend's little sister?" he challenges, raising his eyebrows and clenching his jaw. The scruff on his face is a little thicker than usual, and a fantasy of his facial hair brushing against my inner thighs emerges into my head. I immediately blink the vision away.

"He's gotcha there," Grayson chimes in.

I roll my eyes, no longer wanting to give this conversation any more attention. Luckily, more customers enter and order drinks.

Ethan and I take turns with the customers, mixing cocktails while making sure the place stays clean. Kenzie shows up for her shift and replaces Ethan, and before long, it's nearly closing time. Diesel, Grayson, and Wyatt played pool and darts, taking shots after each game. I watched them silently, forcing my eyes away before Diesel could catch me staring, and have started wondering what the hell's wrong with me. Diesel's been like an annoying brother to me most of my life, and now whatever is sparking between us is freaking me the fuck out. I know I'm not imagining it.

"Diesel, we're heading out," Grayson says.

"You better not be driving," I tell him sternly.

"They're not," Diesel reassures me. "We're staying at Wyatt's apartment tonight. It's just down the block. We walked."

"Ah, okay. Good," I say as I turn toward the register to grab their tab so they can cash out.

"I'll meet you guys there in a bit," Diesel tells them after they pay.

Grayson and Wyatt stumble out, leaving Diesel and me alone with a couple of regulars on the opposite end of the bar. Kenzie is busy wiping down tables and sweeping, not paying any attention to anything else.

"Here," he says, grabbing my attention with his signed receipt.

I grab it from him and go to input it into the system when I read the tip amount he wrote.

"Diesel, I think you made a mistake and added too many zeros," I say, chuckling and glancing over my shoulder at him. He looks sober as hell, which is crazy, considering the amount he drank tonight. His lips are in a firm line, and his eyes pierce through me.

"No, that's right."

My face falls, and I think I'm in shock. "You don't have to tip me that much."

"I know, but I wanted to, so let me."

"No."

"Yes. I'm the customer, and I'm *always* right," he fires back.

I snort, shaking my head. "I can't allow you to do that."

"And why not?" he challenges.

I slump my shoulders in embarrassment. "Because I need to earn the money to pay Nick back without it being given to me. You did enough, and I already feel guilty you got involved."

"It's not a handout. That tip was hard-earned."

"You're full of shit, and you know it."

"Just take it, Row. It's not like I have a wife and six kids to support. I can afford it."

"I wasn't saying you couldn't," I quickly defend. "I just don't want your pity."

"I'd never pity you, Rowan," he says sincerely.

"Fine," I say in defeat, but quickly add, "Just this once. Don't get used to me giving in so easily when you try to overtip again. Got it?"

He chuckles, enjoying this way too much. "Sure, whatever you say."

I groan with a smile. He's so damn stubborn sometimes.

"Do you remember the night of your eighth grade winter formal?" he asks after I input the tip amount and take out the cash, stuffing it into my apron.

"What?" I ask, scrunching my nose. "That was like…ten years ago. Why do you ask?"

"Because I remember it like it was yesterday and wondered if you did too."

I swallow hard because I *do* remember and even found myself recalling it not too long ago. How could I forget my first kiss? Or that it was with Diesel.

"Um…yeah, kinda. I guess." I blush, thinking about it.

Before he can continue, Kenzie comes up to me. "All done. Chairs are up, floors are swept, garnishes are stocked. Do you need me to do anything else?" she asks.

I think about the closing checklist, but I can't really concentrate on anything other than the fact that Diesel has chosen tonight to bring up a memory that's haunted me for years. "Nope, I think that's all. Once I cash those guys out, I'll just have receipts to go through, and then I'll close up."

"Do you mind if I go? I know I'm supposed to so you aren't alone, but—"

"I'll stay with her," Diesel interjects. "That way you don't have to wait, and Rowan doesn't have to close alone."

"Are you sure?" Kenzie asks eagerly. She must have plans, but it's almost two a.m., so I can't imagine she'd be doing anything this late. Then again, she is almost twenty-one and on her college summer break, so anything's possible.

"I was gonna stay anyway, so go right ahead," he tells her. The two of them don't even ask what I think about it, but honestly, I'm glad they don't because my throat has suddenly gone dry.

The final patrons pay their bill, and I follow them to the door so I can lock it and flip over the *open* sign. Nerves tickle my skin as I walk back around the bar and feel his eyes on me. We've been around each other for most of our lives but hardly ever alone. And never in this kind of situation.

Honestly, most of my memories with Diesel are of him aggravating the shit outta me. He finds ways to tease me, and I always ignore him the best I can. But ever since I've moved back and he threatened Nick, there's been a shift between us.

An indescribable one.

"I remember the exact dress you wore that night," he says, my back turned to him as I print out the end of day reports. "Probably makes me sound like a creep, but—"

"A little." I chuckle. "But I remember the song we danced to, so it's not any less creepy than that, I suppose."

Turning around, I see his intense gaze on me. Butterflies swarm my stomach as I watch his expression.

"Why are you asking about that night?" My voice is soft.

Diesel shrugs. "I actually heard that song on the radio recently, and it reminded me of my first kiss."

I blink hard and retreat a step. "Wait, what?" Tilting my head, I study his face and then my eyes lock on his. "That...that wasn't your first kiss."

The corner of his lips tilts, amusement written all over his face. "Actually, it was." He furrows his brows. "Why's that so surprising?"

"Well, considering your history..." I chuckle anxiously. "I just assumed you started kissing girls in kindergarten or something."

He laughs, his shoulders relaxing. "I probably did, but those don't count. Our kiss that night..."

"That counted?" I ask, my cheeks flush by the direction our conversation went. Diesel's rarely serious, and things feel different with him tonight. That kiss affected me, more than I was willing to admit at the time, but nevertheless, it sparked numerous fantasies as I bloomed into a teenager.

"It did," he states honestly. "But I thought maybe it didn't mean as much to you since you seemed to hate me after that."

"I didn't *hate* you," I blurt out. "I was thirteen and...awkward."

"Then why'd you lash out at me after I took you home?"

"I don't know." I suck in my lower lip, shrugging. "After Riley suspected us, I guess I figured that if I pushed you away first, then you couldn't reject me." I shrug again, embarrassed. "Teenage girl insecurities."

Narrowing his eyes, he rests his forearms on the bar. "You're the one who called me gross," he reminds me. "I denied it so Riley wouldn't punch me in the face, and afterward, you avoided me like a bad haircut."

"It was *ten* years ago, Diesel," I emphasize. "We were kids."

He leans back against the stool and stares at me before speaking. "I guess you're right."

Needing to end this unpleasant conversation, I grab my store keys from my pocket and shake them in my fingers. "I better close up."

Diesel nods, staying silent as I walk to the office. My nerves are in overdrive, like I'm thirteen all over again, and it takes me three times to input the right safe code before it successfully opens. I grab the log notebook and sit at the desk, writing in the total amounts for the day. Once I'm done, I walk back to the register and take out the cash to put in the zipper pouch for a bank drop afterward.

One of the reports I printed calculates our inventory and how many cases I need to restock, so I do that next.

"Can I help with anything?" Diesel asks when I return in front of him.

"Sure." I smile and hand him the list of what I need.

He follows me to the stock room, and we make trips back and forth until the beer fridges are stocked full. I look around a final time, double-checking Kenzie's work and wiping down a few stools before I spot clean behind the bar. She took care of most of it, but missed some small things.

"Would you mind wiping down the liquor bottles while I finish up in the office? I have just a couple more things to do," I say.

Diesel nods with a grin. "Can do."

"Thanks."

We've been working in silence, the tension between us thick and electric. I input some information into the computer, then sign off. I tidy up the desk and double-check the safe is locked. I'm stalling, too nervous to face Diesel, and I hope he doesn't call me out for my weird behavior.

The sound of glass breaking draws my attention, and I shoot out of the chair, then rush to the bar. "Are you okay?" I ask when I see a shattered beer mug on the floor.

"Don't come over. I'll sweep it up." He walks around the mess. "Where's the broom?"

"It's in the storage room. I'll grab it."

"No, let me. You finish what you're doing." He walks toward me, closing the gap between us. I swallow hard as my gaze lowers down his body, taking in how good he looks in his tight jeans and boots.

"If John asks, tell him Kenzie did it," he teases, and we both laugh, which eases the tension some.

"She dropped an entire bottle of tequila once, so trust me, one mug doesn't even put a dent in the amount of shit workers have broken around here," I reassure him.

Diesel walks around me to get to the cleaning supplies, and I head back into the office, needing the space to clear my head for a moment. I don't know what's happening right now, but I've never felt this nervous around him, and now suddenly, I'm worrying if I have food in my teeth and if I remembered to pluck my eyebrows this morning.

I leave myself a few Post-it reminders, then do one final glance around the bar. Closing never takes me this long, but Diesel has me completely distracted and on edge. But I need to face him, lock up, and get out of here. I square my shoulders and walk out to where he's waiting.

"All good?" I ask casually.

"Yep, everything on my end anyway."

I snort. "Thanks for your help," I tell him, swallowing down the large knot in my throat. "Although you *did* volunteer so…"

He chuckles, nodding. "That I did." Then he walks toward me with a shrug. "Hope you didn't mind the company?"

Diesel searches my face as the space between us gets smaller and smaller. "Uh, no. Not at all. You're a lot easier to boss around than Kenzie," I tease, taking a small step back.

"I don't know about that…" He lifts his baseball cap, an old one he's worn for years, and brushes a hand through his messy hair.

"I think that hat is on its last leg," I say, dragging out the conversation for whatever reason I can't figure out yet.

"You think so?" The corner of his lips tilts into an amused smirk. "I've had this since I was—"

"Fifteen," I answer without thinking. I'm not sure why I just blurted that out or how I even remember, but the memory resurfaces of the first time he wore it. He'd been working on the ranch all summer, which meant I saw him almost every day. I was horseback riding when he and Riley drove up on a four-wheeler, and I couldn't stop staring at him. The boys typically wore things to keep the sun out of their eyes while working—either their Stetsons or baseball caps—but this one fit him like a glove, and it stood out to me for some reason.

He puts it back on his head and nods. "Yeah, a gift from my grandfather."

It's a beaten-up bluish gray color with a silver embroidered Texas state on the front. Nothing fancy, but I always liked the way it looked on him.

"I can't believe it hasn't unraveled yet, honestly." I lick my lips, willing myself to stop talking. This is the most normal conversation Diesel and I have had in ages, maybe ever. He's usually poking fun at me, and I'm typically telling him to fuck off.

Get out! Time to leave! Walk away and drive home!

Diesel chuckles, nodding in agreement. "Same. It's my favorite one, though, so hopefully it'll last forever." He takes a step toward me, nearly caging me in against the bar top. "So, I have another question for you."

"Okay." I swallow hard.

"About that night…" he reiterates.

"What about it?"

Diesel's in front of me, our bodies so close our feet touch. "Was it your first kiss?"

Inhaling a sharp breath, I can't seem to get enough oxygen. Why is he asking me this?

I remember how he asked that night too.

Blushing, I nod. "Yeah, it most definitely was."

He cocks a brow, entertained. "Really? Because I remember a sassy brat who told me 'yeah, right' and then stomped away."

My chest deflates as I exhale. "Like I said, thirteen-year-old insecurities…I wasn't exactly an expert on boys. Hell, I didn't even have a *real* boyfriend until my junior year of high school."

"Chad was a tool bag," he states. "Edward too. Your history ain't lookin' too good."

"*Mine?*" My voice raises an octave. "Let's discuss your lineup of Southern belles then, shall we?"

"Actually, I was hoping to have a repeat of our first kiss instead." He leans down, pinning me with his hard stare.

The casual way he throws that request out has me blinking, slow and hard. "What?"

"Can I kiss you, Rowan?" His deep Southern drawl sends shivers right between my legs.

What the hell is happening?

Swallowing hard, I inhale a deep breath, trying to find my courage. "You didn't ask that night so…"

"I'm a gentleman now," he retorts with a cocky grin. "Do I need to ask a second time?"

Biting my lip, I chew it for a moment before releasing it and sliding my tongue across it. "Yes."

"Yes, I need to ask again, or yes, I can kiss you?"

The smug look on his face tells me he knows exactly which question I was responding to. He's such an arrogant jerk sometimes.

Deciding to give him a little taste of his own medicine, I wrap my arms around his neck and pull his face to mine but not all the way. I stop when our lips are merely centimeters apart, and I can feel his ragged breathing against my mouth.

His strong hands grip my waist, and he squeezes my hips, waiting for permission. "Yes," I whisper. "Kiss me."

CHAPTER SEVEN

Diesel

A s soon as the words leave her mouth, I wrap my hand around her neck and pull her lips to mine.

Sweet and soft.

Just as I remembered.

But this kiss is electric. Intense. A decade in the making.

My other hand squeezes her hip, and she arches her back, pressing herself into me. Rowan moans when I slide my tongue inside and taste her deliciousness. My fingers grab her two french braids, and I roughly pull on them like I used to when we were kids. Her head falls back, and our kiss deepens; our tongues fight for control as eagerness takes over.

"Fuck, Row," I growl, sweeping my tongue along her bottom lip. "I've been waiting ten years to do that."

Her breathing is ragged as we make eye contact. "I was only thirteen. That would've been highly inappropriate."

"Most of my fantasies about you were," I admit, shrugging.

"Oh really?" She cocks a brow. "Care to elaborate?"

My eyes gaze down her body, admiring every curve. "Hell yeah."

Before she can protest, I grab under her ass and lift her. She squeals as she locks her hands around my neck and wraps her legs around my waist. I walk us around the bar and set her down on one of the stools so we're eye level. Cupping her cheek, I bring our mouths together and savor her taste.

"I always liked when you did your hair like this," I taunt, pulling on one of her braids again. "You have no idea what they did to my teenage boy hormones. Then you'd put on a cowboy hat, and I'd nearly nut in my jeans at the thought of how I'd yank on them as I bent you over."

Rowan bursts out laughing, tightening her thighs around me. "That's quite the imagination for a teenager."

I flash a half grin. "That was in my thoughts just last week."

She swats at my chest, but I grab her wrist, pulling her closer. "Did you wear them for me?"

"Do you think everything is about you?" she retorts. "How does that ball cap even fit with that big head of yours?"

"Answer the question, Row."

"I've been fixin' my hair like this for years," she tells me. "You'd chase me and pull on them, then tease me and say I looked like Little Red Riding Hood."

I chuckle at the memory and shrug. "Well, your hair does have a red tint in the sun."

"And you'd say how you were the Big Bad Wolf, and that if you caught me, you were going to eat me," she adds, unamused.

I burst out laughing again. "I was a little shit."

"So I'd run, and of course, you were always faster than me," she deadpans, tilting her head. "Now I remember why I hated you so much."

My mouth tips into a grin. She's trying so hard to be upset with me, crossing her arms and putting space between us. After a decade, I finally kissed her again and am not wasting another opportunity.

"That was just foreplay," I taunt, leaning closer. "All these years of pent-up sexual frustration...stop fightin' it, Row."

"And what were all the one-nighters and hookups? Practice?"

I arch a brow. "Were you jealous?"

She gives me her famous eye roll. "No."

I tilt her chin up until our gazes meet. "Let me kiss you again."

"You gonna ask every time?" I can tell she's holding back a smile.

"You gonna stop being stubborn?" I counter, plucking her bottom lip from her teeth. "Because I have plans for this sassy mouth."

"Is that how you win all the girls over? Skip over the dating and get-to-know-yous and go straight for the panty-dropping one-liners?"

"I know everything about you, Rowan. At this rate, we've been datin' for years because there isn't anything I don't already know or haven't observed."

She scoffs. "You don't know *everything*."

I close the gap between us until my mouth hovers over hers. "Try me," I challenge. "I bet if I slid my hand between your legs, you'd be wet. Am I right?"

She swallows. "Wrong."

I smirk. "And I bet if I rubbed my thumb over your nipple, it'd be hard."

"It's chilly in here."

"That right? So I have no effect on you? Is that what you're sayin'?"

Rowan shrugs, unfazed.

"You're bruising my heart here, woman. Throw me a bone or something," I plead. "I won't kiss you again until I know where your head's at."

I refuse to screw this moment up by thinking with my dick. As much as I want her, I won't go into this one-sided. She'll have to tell me she wants me just as much, or she'll need to stop this before it can even start.

"Alright," she says, sitting straighter. "Can I show you?"

I wave my hand out, motioning for her to proceed.

Rowan grabs my wrist and places my palm against her chest. "You feel that?" she asks. I close my eyes and feel her heart rapidly pounding.

"Yes," I tell her.

"That's *you*," she says softly. "Something changed between us, and now when you're near, my body reacts to your presence." She exhales sharply. "Even more with your touch."

"What changed?" I open my eyes and ask, sliding my hand up to her face.

"I started seeing *you*." Rowan looks up at me, her expression soft and vulnerable. "You still annoy the shit outta me, but now I see a man I want to spend more time with than away from."

Chuckling, I brush my thumb over her flushed cheek. "Took you long enough to get here." I cover her mouth with mine, sliding my tongue between her lips, and give in to the desire I've held back for so long.

We battle with our bodies, touching, sucking, pushing, pulling. I can't get enough of the woman I've wanted since I was a teen, and it feels too good to be true.

"What does this mean for us, Row?" I ask, leaning my forehead against hers. "The ball's in your court."

I watch as she licks her lips and blows out a shallow breath. "I think it'd be best if we just take it slow and see where things go before announcing anything."

"You're afraid of what Riley will do?" I cock a brow.

"Well, yes," she admits, then smirks. "Plus, sneaking around could be kinda fun. Gives us a chance to explore our feelings before the whole town's in our business. Because they will be."

She's right. The moment the news is out, everyone will have an opinion about it. "Alright, I'm good with that."

Rowan smiles, then nervously chews on her bottom lip. "Now what?"

"Now I walk out of here with blue balls, and we try this secret dating thing until we're ready to tell people, which means we have to keep up the act of only being friends in public."

"Does that mean you'll be dating other people in the meantime?" she asks. "You know...to keep up *appearances*."

"Hell no and neither will you. I'm not screwing up the best thing to ever happen to me."

Rowan's who I've always wanted anyway, and I'll do everything I can to prove that to her.

She chuckles, then nods. "Okay."

"Rowan Bishop, are you blushing?" I tease, pulling on one of her braids.

"Oh my God, I hate you!" She punches my arm, laughing.

"See? People will be none the wiser that we're dancing between the sheets behind closed doors." I waggle my brows, and she pushes me back, jumping off the stool.

"I'm already regretting this decision," she states, walking away, but I quickly grab her arm and pull her back into my chest.

"I've always adored that smart mouth of yours," I tell her, bringing my lips to hers. "I can't wait to see what else you can do with it."

DIESEL

You're lookin' pretty sexy in those jean shorts. Especially when you bend over.

ROWAN

Stop staring at my ass.

DIESEL

Never. I've been staring at it since I was ten.

ROWAN

OMG! You were a little perv.

DIESEL

Says the girl who wore bikinis around all summer. Would you rather I stared at your chest?

ROWAN

I'm almost certain I did catch you looking a few times…

DIESEL

Well, I only had so much willpower. Teenage hormones won nine times out of ten.

ROWAN

Go away.

DIESEL

Come home with me tonight.

ROWAN

I can't. I'm trying to work, and you're distracting me.

I chuckle, unable to hide how happy bantering with Rowan makes me. She's working till close, and I've been here for two hours, purposely ordering expensive beer that she has to get from the bottom of the cooler. Though she's trying to act unaffected by me, she's doing a shit job with her hidden glances and flushed cheeks. We're supposed to be acting normal so no one notices, but considering Riley and Grayson both asked why I've been smiling all day, I know I'm not doing a great job at it either.

So far, we only get moments together at closing time when I stay behind and help her. Once her duties are complete, we make out in the office until she tells me to go home. I've been fucking exhausted for four days, but it's been so goddamn worth it. However, I crashed right after work tonight so I didn't get to the bar until ten. Staying up until three a.m., then having to be up at six to work a nine-hour day is quickly catching up to me. Rowan's told me I don't have to come in and visit every night, but it's the only time we get between our work schedules. I have off on Saturdays, so I'm hoping she'll have some time to spare for us to really hang out privately.

My place is still being fixed up, but we can still hang out in my living room. Of course she's hesitant because Riley or any of the other ranch hands could come over and bust us being together. Keeping our relationship to ourselves isn't an ideal situation, but it's what we have to do right now until we figure out this new territory together.

DIESEL

You should meet me in the equipment barn tomorrow during my lunch break.

ROWAN

What time? I have a couple of errands to run for my dad in the morning.

DIESEL

I'd make any time work for you.

ROWAN

I should be done by noon.

DIESEL

It's a date, baby. Wear your hair in those braids I like.

ROWAN

Get your mind out of the gutter! No getting handsy.

DIESEL

Absolutely no promises...In fact, wear a skirt too.

She knows I'm joking, but just to be sure, I send her a winking emoji. We're taking things slow, something I'm constantly having to remind myself, but it's for the best. As much as I want to explore every inch of Rowan, I want to give this a real shot. No hopping into bed and screwing shit up. Though I know a lot about her, she's slowly been opening up, and I've seen another side of her. Rowan confessed last night that she's hesitant about jumping into a relationship after the way her last one ended. I assured her we'd go at her pace, and I'm not pressuring her to do anything she doesn't want to. I'll be one hundred percent patient for her. I've waited this long, and I'll wait as long as needed until she's ready to take a leap.

ROWAN

SMH. You're relentless.

DIESEL

I can lift it again like I did at the church picnic when everyone saw your Barbie underwear.

ROWAN

Another reason I hated you growing up.

DIESEL

Lies. You adored me.

ROWAN

That really was a cruel prank. I should get you back for that.

DIESEL

What'd you have in mind? Handcuffs? Blindfolds? Maybe a whip?

ROWAN

That's a GREAT idea! Once you're all tied up, I'll take a picture and send it to all your exes, and they'll realize they dodged a bullet.

DIESEL

Man. You're evil. Pure evil.

ROWAN

You started it!

DIESEL

I was eight!

I hear her cackling in the office and know she's laughing at our conversation. She pretends to be annoyed by me, but by the way her mouth attacks mine, it's more than obvious she's putting up a front. Whether she's holding back because she's worried how everyone will react once we announce it or that she'll get hurt, my goal will always be to make her laugh. I'll prove to her I'm nothing like any man she's ever dated, especially her douchebag ex-boyfriends. I'd take a gunshot to the heart before I hurt Rowan.

She returns to the bar moments later and tells Claire, one of the other bartenders, to start on some of their closing duties. There's two hours left, but it's been slow, which means she might actually be finished earlier than usual.

"I can start grabbing cases and restocking for you," I tell her before finishing off my beer.

She rests her arms on the bar and leans close to me. "You should go home and sleep. Those bags under your eyes make you look old."

"I hear chicks dig older guys." I shrug.

"Really? What chicks are you referring to?" She makes a show of looking around at the near empty room. George is on the far end of the bar, and another couple are on the other side.

"The only chick I care about is right in front of me." I smirk, knowing that'll get me an eye roll because if I mention Trace, I might get slapped upside the head.

"Are you always a smooth talker, or do you just turn it on when it suits you?" she taunts.

"Oh, always. You were just too busy being a brat to notice."

"A brat?" She scoffs, pulling back. "You constantly picked on me!"

My face splits into a knowing grin. "Because I liked your attention."

I see the way her cheeks tint, and I crave more of it. Before I can open my mouth again, the door opens, and we both look.

"Uncle Evan," Rowan says, surprised to see him here this late. We both are. I notice he's still wearing scrubs too.

"Hey, kiddo." He gives me a firm nod when our eyes meet. "Diesel."

"What's up, man? You're comin' in late."

He takes a seat next to me. "Just getting off a thirty-six-hour shift."

"Geez," Rowan says. "Want a beer?"

"Yes, please, and an inventory report when you get the chance."

"Sure thing."

Evan and his wife, Emily, are both doctors and work in San Angelo an hour away, but he's always found a way to stay involved as much as he can with his hectic schedule. John handled the bar between his duties at the B&B, but now that Rowan is back for good, they're handing her the reins.

I'm proud of her because I know how hard she worked in school. She loves numbers and accounting, which is great for staying involved in their family businesses. Though we didn't talk much when she was away, I always made it a point to see her when she was home for breaks. She was smart in high school too, and I had no doubt she'd make perfect grades in college.

"You're here late," Evan states when Rowan heads to the office. "Don't you work in the morning?"

I nod, unsure how to approach this conversation. Most ranch hands don't drink or party during the week, considering we have to be up early and work long hours, so he'd be suspicious no matter what I tell him.

"Yeah, but I thought I'd keep Rowan company since it's a slow night," I say, but he doesn't look convinced. "Everyone else was busy," I add.

"Hmm," he says, then takes a long sip. Thankfully, Rowan returns with the reports he wanted, and his attention turns to the papers in front of him. "Thanks. I'll bring these back in a day or two." He stands, puts a ten on the counter, then says goodbye.

"Now you should really go home," Rowan tells me once he leaves. "There's no way he's going to think you're just keeping me company for no reason."

I know she's right, but I argue anyway. "Well, he already saw me, so what's the point of leaving now?" I flash her an arrogant smirk.

"Then go home and sleep so you don't break your neck for real by being too exhausted tomorrow. If something happens to you, I'll have to find someone else to annoy me at work all night."

"Aww…you worried about me, Row?"

She groans. "George keeps me plenty company, so *go*," she urges, giving me a pointed look.

Claire returns, so I can't be sneaky and kiss Rowan goodbye even though she's not paying any attention to us. I take Rowan's hand in mine and bring it to my mouth, pressing my lips to her knuckles. "I'll see you tomorrow. Noon. Barn. Skirt and braids." I flash her a wink before standing and pull my wallet from my back pocket.

I set down two twenties and tell her to keep the rest. I only had a few beers tonight, so I know she's going to give me the death stare about over-tipping.

"Good night, Cowboy." She slaps her hand over the money and drags it off the bar. "Sweet dreams."

"Don't you worry about that." I waggle my brows, then reluctantly turn and walk away.

Tomorrow can't come soon enough.

CHAPTER EIGHT

Rowan

My heart hammers in my chest at the reality of what I'm doing. *What am I doing?*

I never thought in a million years I'd be sneaking into the barn to meet up with Diesel. If we'd been friends, it wouldn't look so suspicious, but everyone on the ranch knows I'd never give him the time of day.

Now, he's consuming my every thought, and it scares me. But his confessions, the way his smile gives me butterflies, and the nervousness I suddenly feel when I'm around him confirm that something has drastically changed between us.

And I don't want to ignore it. I can't.

After Nick left my heart in shambles, I should be running the other way at the prospect of dating another man, but I've known Diesel my whole life. He's not just a random guy I met at a bar, and I know the true intentions of his heart aren't to hurt or use me. If we're going to see where this goes, then I need to put in the effort and give it my all.

Goose bumps cover my arms as I make my way from the B&B where I stopped to meet with Maize for a quick chat and walk over to the equipment barn. It takes me a good ten minutes to get there, but since I don't want anyone to see my truck, I have to be sneaky. I could take one of the four-wheelers, but if someone catches me, I'd have no excuse as to what I was doing.

I step inside, looking around for him, but it's dead quiet. Perhaps he's not here yet, so I decide to text him.

ROWAN

I'm here. Where are you?

After two minutes and no response, I'm ready to call his ass for not being on time, but before I can, a hand wraps around my mouth and I'm being hauled into a hard chest. I immediately know it's him when his lips brush against my ear.

"I missed you," he whispers.

Spinning around in his arms, I glare at him. "What the hell?"

He puts a finger to his lips, motioning for me to be quiet. "C'mon, I'm taking you somewhere."

Diesel grabs my hand and leads me around the tractors and gardening equipment until we're at the back of the barn. "What are you doing?" I whisper-hiss as he opens the side door.

"Sneaking you into my truck." He looks back at me and smirks. "Stay down."

I see his Chevy close by, and we quickly run together toward it. He helps me into the passenger side and then rushes to the other.

"Crouch down," he orders, then hits the gas.

"Where are we going?" I ask, feeling completely out of the loop.

"It's a surprise."

"This can't be good." I laugh. "I thought you only had a half-hour break?"

"I'm taking an extended lunch." He chuckles, making a sharp turn. "Don't worry, they won't even notice I'm gone."

"Mm-hmm, right." I lick my lips as I lower my eyes down his body. Even after working all morning, he still looks good enough to eat. "Can I sit up yet?"

"One second…"

I feel the truck drive up a hill and look through the window. Trees and overgrown brush line the dirt road.

"Okay, you're good to go now." He gives me his hand, and I grab it, hoisting myself up in the seat.

Looking around, I notice we're on one of the trails leading to an area we sometimes partied in high school and have the occasional bonfire.

"What do you have up your sleeve, mister?"

He waggles his brows with a mischievous smirk on his face. "I packed us a lunch."

My eyes widen in surprise. "Really? You packed us *edible* food?"

He rests a hand on his chest. "Why are you so shocked? I'm very capable of asking Grandma Bishop to make her famous chicken and biscuits."

I snort out a laugh as my head falls back against the seat. "You're slick, I'll give you that."

Diesel drives us to a place that's been named the "Bishop spot" over the years. Apparently, my uncles brought their dates up here, and they'd party and drink. It became something rather special and meaningful for a lot of them and even for Riley and his wife, Zoey.

"You know everyone who brings their crushes here end up married," he tells me smoothly as he parks the truck.

"I've heard," I say, fighting back a smile. "Except I'm pretty sure my uncles and even Riley brought a lot of women they ended up not marrying here too. Even you, probably."

"Nope. Been waiting for the right one." He flashes me a shiver-inducing wink, and I'm nearly melting in my seat before he rounds the front and escorts me out. He grabs the cooler, then takes my hand to the back of the cab.

There's a sleeping bag unzipped and spread out with blankets and pillows all around. It looks cozy, and I'm shocked as hell he thought of something this sweet.

"Wow…" I say when he helps me up, and he makes his way to my side. "You've never done this before?" I ask.

"Never had a relationship, Row," he says.

"Seems you know what you're doing," I tell him when he hands me a plate covered in foil.

Diesel shrugs as if he doesn't agree. "Guess we'll see, huh?"

I smile when he does, and it warms my entire body. Adam Hayes is someone I never knew I needed.

We talk and laugh all through our lunch. The food is delicious, no surprise there, but the company and scenery are even better. Once we've finished, he wraps me in his arms, and we lie on the blankets.

"You can see the stars out here for miles at night. It's my favorite part of living on the ranch. You don't get that in Houston," I say as I wrap my arm over his chest and hold him close to me.

"There's just something special about living out here, and I'd never want to be anywhere else." His arm is around my shoulders, and he tightens his hold, sending warmth all down my body.

We continue talking and admiring the view for over an hour. Much longer than Diesel is allowed to take for his break, and after his phone starts going off, I know our time is over.

"Shit," he hisses when he pulls it from his pocket and sees all his missed calls and texts.

"You're gonna get in trouble," I tease.

He leans in and presses his lips to mine. "It'll be worth it."

"You better go back."

"But being here is *so* much better." He turns so we're face to face and lifts my chin. "I feel like I'm dreaming."

"And what are you gonna tell them when they ask where you were?"

"Tell them to mind their damn business." He flashes an evil grin. "Or that I had some hot chick in the back of my truck I was trying to seduce."

"Oh God." I groan. "Please don't tell them that. I think Uncle Evan is already suspicious now."

"Nah. If he mentions anything, just say he was sleep deprived and has no idea what he's talking about."

I snort, lifting myself on my elbows. "That'd go over well, I'm sure."

I'm close to all my uncles, but Evan is the most protective over me. I spent a lot of time at Emily's and his house hanging out with Elle. She's over a year older than me, but we were close growing up until she left for college. We always stayed in touch, but between me moving to Houston and her demanding job, it doesn't give us time to hang out as much.

Grabbing the cooler and blankets, we finally get into the truck and make our way back to the ranch. He manages to bring me back without anyone noticing.

"Thank you for lunch," I tell him before he leaves. "I could get used to that kind of company."

"You're very welcome." He lowers his eyes down my body, not even trying to hide his gawking anymore. "I could get used to the view."

"At least you're persistent," I say, laughing. "As usual."

"But now I can be even more so without you threatening to cut off my balls." He wraps his arms around my waist and snuggles me against his chest.

"Don't get cocky." I pull his face down and cover his mouth with mine. His tongue slides between my lips, and soon, we're panting for air as we battle with our desire for more. He slides his hands down to my ass, then back up to my neck where his fingers tangle in my hair. Every spot he touches burns with an intensity I hadn't known existed. I want more of it, more of him, and I'll take anything he's willing to give.

"Okay, now you really need to go," I say against his lips, neither of us moving. "Text me later, okay?"

"You workin' till close?"

"Yep. But maybe bring Wyatt this time so it doesn't look suspicious." He doesn't work on the ranch and has no idea we typically didn't get along.

"Damn. I was hoping to have you all to myself." He smirks.

"In a bar filled with drunks? Good luck."

Diesel pats my ass one more time and presses a quick kiss to my lips before he takes off and runs to his truck. "Dammit, now you got my dick all worked up!" he yells from the window, and I see him adjusting his jeans.

"Sorry 'bout that!" I chuckle, waving him away.

It's been a week since Diesel kissed me in the bar office, and it's been the best seven days I've had in a long ass time. We sneak around to find time to hang out, even if it's for thirty minutes or during my shift at work. He comes in every night and then stays late until I'm done. I know he's tired as hell, so on our days off, I make him sleep in or tell him to take a nap so he doesn't end up killing himself on the ranch equipment.

My adrenaline high crashes and burns the moment I wake up to a text from Nick the Asshole.

NICK

You better get me that money, or I'm taking the security footage to the cops.

ROWAN

I told you I was working on it. I don't have a million-dollar trust fund like you to just write a check.

NICK

Should've thought about that before you took a crowbar to my car, you bitch.

ROWAN

Wow, do you feel like a man calling me that?

NICK

Better watch that filthy mouth of yours, unless you want me to report you for vandalism? I wonder how your hick family would take that kind of news?

ROWAN

Kiss my ass, you dickless cocksucker. I said I'd get you the money, and I will.

NICK

You better.

I'm on the verge of tears by the time I read his final text, then toss my phone aside.

God, what I ever saw in him is beyond me. He's such an arrogant tool bag, and I wish I'd never given him the time of day. I know he's probably already gotten the stupid car repaired and is just using this opportunity to have something to hold over me and piss me off. He didn't like that *I* broke up with him after he cheated.

Instead of eating my feelings like I want to, I take a thirty-minute hot shower. Though it feels good, it doesn't stop my anger from brewing over. Knowing Maize is probably working at the B&B, I decide to head over there after I get dressed and ready for the day.

"Oh my God! We should've cut him when we had the chance!" she squeals after I read her the texts.

I snort at her dramatics. "You and me both."

"Who are we cutting?" Elle walks into the kitchen with a perched brow.

"My stupid ex-boyfriend. Look what he sent me this morning."

She looks over my shoulder as I show her the screen and scroll down.

"Wow. Douchebag needs to get the stick out of his ass." She leans down and grabs a muffin, then stuffs it into her mouth. Maize doesn't say a word surprisingly.

"Tell me about it. *Why* did I date him?" I groan, collapsing on top of the counter with my head in my hands.

"You don't always see someone's true colors until it's too late," she tells me, rubbing my back. "The important thing is that you learned before you got in too deep."

"And even that was too long. I want that time back." I growl.

"You very well coulda married the dickwad. Yikes! Thank the Lord ya didn't," Maize says.

They both chuckle, and we end up hanging out for the next hour before Elle has to go back to work. She stops in from time to time like most of my family does. The B&B's a social spot for us to eat and gossip.

After saying goodbye and walking out of the kitchen, I head through the main sitting area and wave at the guests. Most are regulars who come every year, but some are new and just driving through, needing a place to stay for the night. Some love the atmosphere so much that they book a room to stay every few months. Can't say I blame them, though. The ranch offers horseback riding, four-wheeling adventures, trail walking, and true Southern meals. We host weddings and honeymoons here too.

DIESEL

You okay? Grayson said he saw you at the B&B looking like someone kicked your dog.

I snort. We have lots of dogs on the ranch, but none that stay in the house.

ROWAN

You two always gossip about me?

DIESEL

Only every day of my existence. Don't you know by now my world revolves around you?

ROWAN

Stop being overly sweet.

DIESEL

Can't help it, baby. Charming is my middle name.

ROWAN

It's Christopher, but close enough.

I giggle because our conversation easily puts me in a good mood again.

DIESEL

So c'mon, tell me. What's going on?

I get into my car, then text him back.

ROWAN

I woke up to a very nice message from my ex who reminded me that I'm under the gun to pay him back, and that if I don't soon, he'll report me for vandalism. I told him I was working on it, but he was being his normal asshole self.

DIESEL

Let me take care of him and pay your debt so he goes away for good.

ROWAN

No and definitely not! I'm not allowing you to get involved any more than you already have. I'm saving up and will give it to him.

ROWAN

But thank you for offering. I do appreciate you wanting to help.

DIESEL

Should let me punch his face in again to send him a not-so-nice message in return.

ROWAN

Then he'd probably sue you for wrecking his pretty boy face.

DIESEL

It'd be worth every penny to smash it in, though. ;)

ROWAN

Okay, Cowboy. Hold back before you get arrested for assault. We can't sneak around when you're behind bars.

DIESEL

You're right. I'll just have to be smug in the fact that I have you now, and he doesn't.

ROWAN

Works for me :)

DIESEL

Why don't you come over tonight since you work a short shift, and I'll show you all the ways I can console you?

ROWAN

Hmm...you paint a tempting picture. You think that's a good idea?

DIESEL

Park at the B&B and take a four-wheeler over to the equipment barn, and I'll pick you up there.

ROWAN

Okay, I'll be done here in two hours and will text you when I'm leaving so you can meet me.

DIESEL

I'll be waiting!

His eagerness always makes me smile. It'll be the first time visiting his house, and I'm not quite sure what to expect. I know he's been fixing it up since he basically got kicked out of the cabin he and Riley shared. Once Zoey came to town, and they decided to try to make things work, Diesel moved into one of the ranch hand cabins that needed a lot of work. I know he's been remodeling it in his spare time, which I'm learning isn't very much. Probably even less now that he's spending it with me instead.

Ethan's working till close tonight and knows how to do the reports and safe, so I don't worry about it when I decide to dip out early. Claire will arrive at eight, and since we aren't that busy, I decide to leave a half hour early.

I take the extra time to freshen up and change before heading to Diesel's. Before I can leave the house, my mother walks in the door and asks where I'm going so late. I hold back any comments on how it's barely dark outside, and that I'm twenty-three years old.

"Maize and I are meeting up for a girls' night. Nothing special." I smile, hoping she believes me. I hate lying to my mom. We're close, and she trusts me, but I can't tell her this secret. At least not yet.

"Oh, alright. Tell her I said hi. You two have fun." She gives me a kiss on the cheek and a hug, and my soul dies a little at how easily the lie spilled from my lips.

By the time Diesel picks me up, I'm in a sour mood, and I hate that I can't be more excited to see him tonight. My eyes water, and I wipe away the tears before they can fall.

"Looks like someone needs cheering up," he says, guiding me through the front door. "Wanna start with a tour?"

"Sure." He takes my hand and shows me around, telling me how he plans to fix it up. Some of the things include: knocking out walls to open up the living room, adding a kitchen island for more storage space, replacing a window with patio doors, and then building on a huge deck.

"Wow…that all sounds amazing. I bet it's going to be gorgeous once you're done." I look around and see empty spaces with tarps and paint cans. He's done some stuff already but has quite a bit to finish.

"I hope so. Riley was supposed to help me, but now that he's on permanent Dad duty, I may have Grayson and Wyatt help too. Maybe Ethan."

I snort at the mention of my cousin. "Ethan barely wants to get his hands dirty as it is, so good luck." His parents are both doctors so he was never forced to do chores until my other uncles got a hold of him and basically threw him in the dirt. So now he's going to school for agricultural science and has one year left, but since he's home for the summer, he helps at the bar or anywhere he's needed on the ranch. Once he graduates, he'll work on the ranch full-time and plans to help find ways to expand.

"Maybe I'll bribe him with a few beers to help." He grins. "Maybe I can bribe *you*?"

"That wouldn't look suspicious at all," I mock.

"We'll say you owed me."

My jaw drops. "Owe you for what?"

"For kicking your ex's ass," he states proudly.

"Mm-hmm, right. Not sure what I can do anyway, besides paint maybe."

"Perfect. Sounds like a date."

"You really are relentless, aren't you?"

"All part of my charm."

When I smile, he lifts my chin and softly presses his lips to mine. "There's that gorgeous smile I love so much. My plan worked after all."

Nick is officially off my mind, and all I can think about is Diesel.

"Guess it did." I fist my hands in his shirt and bring his mouth back to mine, and soon we're making out like a couple of teenagers who have a curfew.

Diesel leads me to the couch and sets me on his lap without even breaking the kiss. His fingers thread in my hair, cupping the back of my head and pulling it back slightly so his tongue can slide in deeper. Hot electricity sparks between us, and it takes all the energy I have to pull away.

"If you don't stop doing that, we're going to violate our 'going slow' rule," I tell him.

He squints one eye and tilts the corner of his lips. "Pretty sure that was just your rule."

I playfully smack him and get off his lap, then sit down next to him. "I had to lie to my mother tonight, and it sucked."

He reaches over and grabs my hand. "We don't have to, you know? I can take care of whatever backlash Riley gives me. Or hell, your father. They'll probably both want their turn to knock me on my ass individually, but it'd be one hundred percent worth it."

Groaning, I throw my head back on the couch. "Don't say that. I'd just like to explore this without everyone's comments. I recently got out of a relationship, and I'm sure my mom and cousins will have something to say about it."

"What are you afraid of?"

"I'm worried they'll put doubt in my head about dating someone so soon, being with you, or that we're moving too fast."

"Okay…" He nods, then brings our hands up to his lips and sweetly kisses my knuckles. "Then we'll keep it our secret for now. I'm sure it's not the worst thing you've lied to your mother about." He flashes a devilish grin, knowing damn well he's right.

"Well, no. But that's besides the point. I don't like violating the trust between us."

"I'm sure once it's out there, she'll understand why you did."

I inhale slowly and sigh. "I hope so."

"Until then, we'll secretly make out in the back of my truck."

I laugh at how smooth he tries to be, but I don't exactly hate the idea either.

"So I know I wanted to take your mind off your ex, but can you tell me what happened between you two? How long did you date? How'd you meet?"

"You really wanna know that stuff?"

"Only if you feel comfortable telling me, but I want to know everything about you. The good, the bad, and even the ugly."

"And Nick is definitely the ugly part."

He chuckles, brushing his hand over his scruffy chin. I love that he leaves it just long enough for me to scratch my nails through it.

"We met at a college party and were actually friends for a few months before he asked me out. We dated for a total of fourteen months. It was after I hung out with Trace a few times."

Diesel audibly groans, and I smirk at how jealous he gets.

"Do you still talk to him?" he asks.

"Just as friends," I reassure him. "That's all we ever were, so don't get your panties in a bunch."

"He sure as fuck didn't look at you like y'all were only friends."

"You met him one time," I remind him, smirking. "Calm your tits."

"As long as when our secret is out, he knows it too."

"It's a small town. Everyone will know within twenty minutes."

He grunts, squeezing my hand tighter. "Good."

"Anyway…" I grin. "When I found out Nick had cheated on me, he apologized and begged me to give him another chance. He promised over and over he'd never do it again and tried to win me back. I told him there was no chance in hell because he'd broken our trust, and I couldn't forgive a man who did that to me. Being honest and having open communication are two of the most important things to me, and he violated them both."

"Well, I'm truly sorry he did that, but I'm also thankful as fuck because it brought you to me."

Diesel and I talk for hours. Even though we seem to know a lot about the other, we share more intimate and personal things. We laugh and tease each other, and before the night is over, I feel closer than ever to him.

It's just what I needed after the shitty way my day started.

CHAPTER NINE

Diesel

Ever since that night a week ago when Rowan came over almost in tears, we've grown closer both physically and emotionally. We're still taking things slow and sneaking around, but after years of pining for her, it feels amazing to have my feelings for her reciprocated. Though I'm not getting much sleep, every second I spend with her is well worth the three hours I do get.

"You wake up gettin' your dick sucked or something?" Riley taunts as we walk out of the shop.

"That or he's gettin' it regularly," Grayson adds.

"How about y'all mind ya damn business," I say smugly, flashing my teeth.

"Shoulda seen him in Vegas," Riley tells Grayson. "Could barely handle himself around all the blondes."

"Look who's talkin'? You married one of them."

He points at me, smirking. "True, but she wasn't blond."

594

Riley's back to working full-time, which means he's returned to giving me shit as much as possible. Baby Zach was born over a month ago, and even though he was a little early, he's doing great.

"Probably some town skank," Grayson adds.

"Don't worry, I was thinkin' about your sister the whole time," I spit out and immediately move out of Riley's punching range. Rowan made a good point the other day that it'll raise red flags if my normal teasing about her disappears. She insists that we need to keep arguing around people.

"Dude, I swear to God," Riley growls, running after me as I rush toward the B&B and fly up the steps. He knows once we're inside, he can't try to kick my ass around the guests. As soon as I whip open the door and go in, he pushes my back and has me nearly flying into John. And he doesn't look happy.

"Guys." He steadies me, then steps back. "Behave or leave."

"Sorry." I swallow hard and hold back my smile. "I tripped."

John snaps his eyes to Riley who's giving him his best innocent look while Grayson covers his mouth with his hand, trying not to laugh.

"Hurry and eat so you can get out," John tells us before walking away.

The three of us make our way to the breakfast buffet and fill our plates full before taking a seat at one of the tables. We're chatting about what we need to do the rest of the day when Maize, Kenzie, Elle, and Rowan all walk out of the kitchen.

Shit.

"Oh, if it isn't the morning freeloader crew," Maize says smugly as she holds a plate of fresh muffins.

"Got a blueberry one?" Grayson asks, ignoring her snide comment.

"Not for you, asshole," Kenzie replies before Maize can.

Riley and I burst out laughing as Grayson narrows his eyes at her. "Pretty sure I didn't ask you."

"Okay, children. There are guests around." Maize grabs one of the muffins from the tray and hands it to Grayson. "Can I personally serve anyone else?" She flashes a condescending grin, unamused with us being here.

"Well, if you're offering—" I grin, knowing it'll piss off Riley or Maize.

"Not that kind of serving," Rowan interrupts, flashing me a glare that could kill. I know she's not really mad, but she's damn good at putting on an act.

"Shit." Riley shakes his head, stabbing his fork into his eggs. "How you two manage to always piss off all the Bishop chicks is beyond me."

"I'm pretty sure Diesel's been doing it since I was born." Rowan rolls her eyes, then stalks away.

"I think she likes you," Grayson mocks, and I kick him under the table.

"Don't worry, Diesel. I don't hate you," Kenzie says with a cheeky grin, then adds, "as much as Rowan."

"No, you just act like a spoiled brat," Grayson mutters.

Before Grayson can react, Kenzie grabs the muffin from his hand and smashes it against the table, digging her palm into it. The thing is nothing but a pile of crumbs.

Riley and I are nearly doubled over at Grayson's shell-shocked expression.

"What the hell?" He scowls at her.

"Enjoy your breakfast, *boys*," she says sweetly before walking away.

"You better clean that up," Maize tells him before leaving.

Grayson grunts, wiping up the mushy mess.

"You two need to just fuck it out, for Christ's sake," I tell him. Their rivalry started months ago, and no one really knows the reason. "Why does she hate you anyway?"

"Good fuckin' question."

"Probably calling her a brat doesn't help your case," Riley taunts.

"Well, am I wrong? Look at what she just did!" He holds out his hands, motioning to the table.

Laughing, I shake my head and continue eating. I'm almost certain there's gonna come a time when they finally bang it out. It makes me think about Rowan and how far we've come in such a short amount of time. It gives me hope that someday we'll be able to tell everyone, and they'll support us being together.

Once the three of us are done eating, Grayson and I go off to work in the cattle barn while Riley does other maintenance shit.

"So, tell me honestly," Grayson says when we're knee-deep in cow shit. "You've been different the past week or so. What's goin' on?"

Fuck my life. He chooses to ask me this now?

"Nothing's goin' on," I lie, shrugging so he doesn't notice any of my tells. "Can't a guy just be in a good mood?"

He narrows his eyes as if he's trying to read my mind. "I don't know. Something is up with you, and I'm gonna figure it out."

Laughing, I keep my eyes down and continue shoveling to avoid his hard gaze. "Why don't you worry about yourself instead of me? Actually, go figure out why Kenzie hates your guts so much."

"Dude, she's hated me since the second I got here, I swear. I breathed, and she decided I was the devil."

I snort at his remark. Kenzie wouldn't just hate someone for no reason, but honestly, there's no telling. She's three years younger than me, and I didn't talk to her a lot in high school. It wasn't until I started working here full-time that I did.

"I'm sure there's a reason you haven't thought of yet. Did you run over her dog or something? Call her ugly? Fuck her best friend?"

He pinches his lips, shifting them side to side. "Not that I can recall." Then he shrugs and drops the conversation.

Thank fuck.

After three hours, we're finally done in the cattle barn and stop at the shop for a quick water break. I check my phone and see a message from Rowan.

> **ROWAN**
>
> Sorry about earlier. My cousins are all getting suspicious and keep asking me why I'm so happy lately, so I was trying to keep up appearances. I wish I could tell them, but I keep denying anything's going on. Well, now they're certain it's because of Trace, because they know he's been texting me. But even though I tell them we're only friends, they don't believe it.

> **DIESEL**
>
> Don't worry, baby. I figured as much. In fact, the guys have been on my ass about what's going on with me all day. Guess it's been a little obvious how happy you make me ;)

> **ROWAN**
>
> Did you just call me baby?

DIESEL

Yes?

ROWAN

That's kinda...sexy. I like it.

DIESEL

Is that so? I'll make sure to whisper it in your ear later.

ROWAN

Did we have plans for...later?

DIESEL

Damn right. I'll come in tonight around 10. That okay?

ROWAN

That's perfect. Ethan's shift ends at 9:30, and Kenzie's off. Claire works with me, and she won't know any better.

It's a weekday, so it'll be slow after ten anyway, which means I might actually get to sneak her into the office and kiss her for more than five seconds. Claire isn't from around here and doesn't know our history, so it's a little easier to talk when we don't have to worry about prying ears.

DIESEL

It's a date, baby.

"We're supposed to get some heavy rain and wind tonight," Riley says as he walks into the shop with Ethan. "I need all hands on deck to bring in the horses."

"Don't you work at the bar tonight?" I ask Ethan, curious as to why he's here.

"Yeah." He tilts his head. "How do you know my work schedule?"

Fuck, fuck, fuck. That slipped out way too easily.

I shrug, trying to act indifferent. "Just a guess. You work most weeknights, don't you?"

Ethan blinks, then nods. "Yeah, I gotta head in soon but thought I'd help before I go."

We pile into the back of Alex's truck, and when I look up, I notice how dark one side of the sky is already. We can always use the rain, especially in the middle of summer, but it sucks when we have to rush around the ranch and do things around the weather's schedule.

An hour later, I'm drenched with sweat and cussing out Riley for making me tag along. They could've handled it, but he has learned I won't say no and enjoys making me do extra shit.

"Quit scowlin'," he blurts out when we ride back to the shop. "Doesn't look good on your ugly mug."

Ethan and Grayson laugh at my expense, and he's damn lucky I hold back on pushing him out of the cab.

"Pretty cocky there, Bishop," I taunt. "You've gone soft since you became a dad, so I wouldn't poke the bear that's already bigger than you."

Riley laughs, kicking his foot out toward me. "I don't know. Those dark bags under your eyes imply you ain't gettin' much sleep, so I think we're pretty equal in that department."

"The difference is, my lack of sleep isn't due to changing dirty diapers and spit up." I flash a cocky grin.

"So it *is* a chick keeping you up," Grayson adds with satisfaction. "I fuckin' knew it!"

"Yeah right," Riley drawls. "He's drinking alone and jerking off to fetish porn."

Ethan chokes out a laugh. "Huh. What's your fetish?"

I grin, knowing Riley's about to kill me. "Best friend's little sisters."

"Goddammit, Diesel. That's getting old." Riley rolls his eyes with a deep groan. "Like ten years' worth old. Time to find a new fantasy."

"No can do, Daddy."

Alex parks the truck, and we all haul out.

"Told ya I'm gonna marry her someday."

"Not on my watch. You don't settle down for shit. You'll get your fix, then leave her brokenhearted like you do every other woman you bang." He pushes his finger into my chest. "Back off already."

"For your information, the last one-night stand I had was in Vegas," I tell him, reminding me of the letter I received weeks ago, but then I immediately push that thought away. Her name was Chelsea, and the only reason I remember that is because of Riley. Not my proudest moment, honestly.

"Oh, my bad. You buy them dinner and drinks first, then wait until after the second date to ghost them."

I shake my head, my jaw tensing as my anger rises. He's wrong.

"Actually, the last chick I took on a date told me she didn't see us having a future together, and we mutually broke it off before the second date ended." Which is true. We met through a friend and didn't even sleep together. My dating life has been pretty much nonexistent.

Riley slow claps as if he's supposed to be impressed, and it pisses me off further.

"Whatever." I walk away, finished with this fucking conversation.

"Yeah, whatever. Stay away from my sister!" he howls at my back.

"I'm pretty sure Riley's gonna kill me," I tell Rowan, then chug my glass of whiskey. "Like actually stab me, cut out my heart, and then display it on a wall like a deer head."

Rowan looks at me wide-eyed in horror. "That's quite graphic."

"I know he's been telling me for years that you were off-limits, but he's been extra asshole-ish about it lately."

"He's also sleep deprived and taking care of a newborn. He's probably just edgier because of that," she explains with a sad smile. "At least, let's hope that's what it is."

I take off my cap, brush a hand through my hair, then replace it. "I don't know. It's like he's determined to make my life a living hell right now." I rub my eyes, inhaling slowly as I think about the consequences of Riley finding out the truth. It'd suck if being with Rowan ruined my lifelong friendship with him.

Thankfully, Riley hasn't come in the bar since Zoey found out she was pregnant, so I know we're at least safe in here for now. But if he catches us even remotely being friendly, there's no way he won't figure it out.

"Well, I think we both need to get better at hiding our happiness so everyone stops asking. It'll calm down, and we can just go back to hanging out without guilt." She refills my glass.

I pick it up and take a sip. "Do you feel guilty?"

She shrugs, lowering her eyes before meeting mine again. "Only about lying, not that we're dating."

That makes me smile. "Good. Because even with all the outside noise bullshit, I've never been happier."

Rowan leans against the bar, placing her hand over mine. "Me too."

I could stare into her gorgeous brown eyes for hours. "I wish I could kiss you right now…" I whisper.

The corner of her lips tilts up mischievously as she looks around the bar and checks to make sure everyone's drinks are still full. "Come to the office in one minute."

She tells Claire she's going on a short break and then walks away. Luckily, she's been too busy to notice how close the two of us have been all night. I'm completely under her radar when I follow Rowan to the back a moment later.

As soon as I shut the door, I pin her against the cool wood and bring my mouth to hers. I wrap my arms around her body and hoist her closer as she loops hers around my neck. She slides her legs around my waist, rocking against the hard-on I can't contain.

"Fuck, baby," I whisper. "You're driving me wild."

"Mmm…that sounds even sexier in person."

"Yeah?" I slide my mouth against the softness of her neck

Rowan releases her thighs and lands on her feet. "We have at least fifteen minutes before Claire even notices I'm still gone." She locks the door, then gives me a devilish look.

"What're you up to?" I taunt, watching her and admiring how beautiful she looks. Some strands of her reddish brown hair have fallen loose from her half ponytail, and she tucks it behind her ear. Her jean shorts show off her long legs, and her band T-shirt hugs her in all the right places. Rowan's curves are what my wet dreams are made of.

"Let me fix that problem for you," she says confidently, tilting her head toward my groin. "You want to stand or sit?"

I blink. "*What?*"

She asks so casually as if we're talking about the weather.

"I want to get on my knees for you." She licks her plump lips.

My eyes widen in shock, certain she's joking. "Here? Are you serious? Don't fuck with me."

She chuckles, then nods eagerly. "Yes and we're gonna run out of time if you don't tell me. So sitting or standing?"

"I-I, uh…" I'm tripping over my words like a teenage boy about to get head for the first time. "Baby, you don't have to. Not here."

She comes closer, moving her hands to my belt buckle. "Adam…" She says my name seductively, and I melt into a puddle. "Let me suck you off and send you home a happy man, okay?"

"Jesus fuck, Row." My throat goes dry. She's the only chick who's ever managed to nearly put me into cardiac arrest. I must hesitate too long because she drops to her knees in front of me and torturously unzips my jeans.

The moment I feel her hand around my shaft, my eyes roll to the back of my head. I can hardly believe this is happening. I've fantasized about it a million times but never dreamed it'd be a reality.

Forcing my eyes open because I don't want to miss a second of this, I look down and watch as she peeks up at me like a seductress eating her last meal. The moment her tongue glides from the bottom of my cock to the tip, I'm about to explode.

"*Christ*, baby." I lean against the door and wrap my fist around her long hair. "This room soundproof?" I half-tease, though I really wish we could be loud without the entire bar hearing.

"No, so keep it down." She smirks before wrapping her lips over the crown of my length and sucks hard.

Fuck. She nearly swallows me whole, and when she pulls me to the back of her throat, I'm five seconds from prematurely shooting my load. Though I don't want to rush, we can't take our time like I'd want to.

"Rowan, shit." I cup the back of her head and help guide her mouth deeper and harder. She rotates and strokes her hand on the base of my cock as she continues sucking on the tip. Her hot mouth feels goddamn amazing, and when she blinks up at me again, my balls tighten, and I know I'm close.

Groaning, I watch as she pumps me faster, and then I quickly pull out and release in my palm. I stroke myself as she leans up, and I grab her chin, fusing our mouths together.

"You didn't have to do that," she says as we break apart. "I wanted to taste all of you."

"Then I'll have something to look forward to next time." I flash her a wink, then help her to her feet with my free hand.

"Let me grab you some paper towels." She snickers when she sees my mess.

Rowan goes to the storage closet and returns within a minute, and once I'm fully clean, I zip my jeans and redo my buckle. "You think anyone heard us?"

"Nah, the TVs are on, so if anything, they'll just think it's from the show," she explains, but I know she's full of shit.

I pull her into my arms and smile. "I'd stay and help you close tonight, but you've made me quite relaxed now."

"That was my goal the whole time. You need to get some sleep."

"Mm-hmm. I know, but I can't help wanting to spend all my time with you," I admit. "Does that scare you?"

She licks her lips before biting on her bottom one. "A little, but not because you want to be around me. Rather, it's how much I want to spend time with you too."

"You're not used to being on this side of things, are you?" I flash her a smug grin. "You're too used to running away while calling me an asshole."

She groans as her head falls back slightly. "You better pull that ego back, or I'll go tell Riley right now that you touched his little sister."

"Is that supposed to be a threat? I can take him." I puff out my chest, which causes her to laugh, and seeing the way her cheeks heat causes intense electricity to shoot through my body.

"Well, you just might need to start honing your fighting skills. I have no doubt Riley's gonna think you corrupted me."

"He thinks I'm going to use you, that I can't manage a real relationship, and that I'll break your heart."

Her face drops. "Are you?"

I tilt her chin up to look at me so she can see how serious I am. "Not a chance in hell, Rowan. I'm risking everything because if I lose you, I lose a best friend and a family I've known my whole life, too. I've waited for you, and I'm not gonna fuck up this chance you're giving me. Don't think for one second I don't know how lucky I am. I'm not taking a second of it for granted. You hear me?"

"You are risking a lot," she says softly. "It's only been a couple of weeks, and I'm already losing sleep thinking about you. The last thing I want is for our relationship to break apart friendships or cause any awkwardness in my family."

"I'll do whatever it takes to make this work, and if sneaking around is the only way I can have you right now, then I'll take it. We'll wait until you're comfortable or when you think everyone else can handle the good news."

She gives me an expression that makes me laugh. "We might be sneaking around a while then. Riley might never be ready."

"Maybe after we move in together, get hitched, and you get pregnant with my baby, he'll finally accept it. We wouldn't have to make a big ordeal about it then because everyone would eventually just figure it out." I shrug nonchalantly.

She snorts, laughing at my antics. "The *never announcing it* method. Sure, that oughta work. After the third baby, they might start putting the puzzle pieces together."

I brush the wild strands of her hair off her face and tuck them behind her ear before leaning down and kissing her forehead. "We'll figure it out."

Rowan reminds me that she has to get back to work before Claire comes looking for her. We kiss goodbye, then I casually make my way out the side door. I wish I could stay and talk to her all night, but we both know I need the sleep.

Hopefully one day—one day *soon*—I'll be able to go to bed and wake up with her in my arms, and we won't have to hide our relationship. I'm falling harder for her every day, and it almost doesn't seem real how strong my feelings already are. Then again, they've been lingering for years, waiting to be unleashed when she finally saw who was right in front of her the whole time.

CHAPTER TEN

Rowan

I actually have the day off, so I'm killing time at the B&B with hopes to see Diesel later. Three weeks have passed since we've started sneaking around, and as much fun as it's been, I'm constantly on edge and worried we'll get caught.

It still doesn't feel real. These feelings seem as if they've come out of nowhere, but Diesel acts like he's been waiting his whole life for me. All the shit I used to give him now makes me feel guilty, though I keep telling myself it's just a part of our history. Perhaps if I had seen him differently years ago, we wouldn't be where we are now. I know us being together is still so new and early, but the timing seems right, and everything is so good. Trying to navigate a long-distance relationship while I was at college wouldn't have been ideal for either of us. We both had some growing up to do.

"So how's it feel to be back for good? Think you'll miss going to Houston?" Maize asks as we hang out in the B&B kitchen. She's making one of her Southern specialities for the guests and putting her amazing cooking skills to good use. Maize graduated from culinary school a couple of years ago and became the head chef at the bed and breakfast. It happened at a good time too since the previous cook in charge was retiring.

"Nah, I don't think so. Actually, it's not as bad as I was anticipating," I say honestly, reaching for one of the paninis. "After Nick the Dick ruined my life, I thought life would suck."

She perks up a brow, knowing there's more to the story. *More* that I can't tell her. "But it doesn't?"

I shrug, purposely not making eye contact with her. If I do, she'll know I'm keeping something from her. She's two years older, and we've always been close. She knows all my tells, and I hate having to lie to her.

"Nah, I guess not. It's nice to be back home and working for the fam. At least I'm not having to help with ranch chores." I chuckle with relief. When I was still in high school, I would do whatever was needed during weekends and summers, which meant a slew of bitch work. Didn't matter that I was a girl and half the weight of the guys, my dad made sure I had a good work ethic.

"You have been in a pretty chipper mood," she states as if she's implying there's a reason, but I play dumb.

"I'm not gonna let some cheating asshole bring me down." I take a large bite of my sandwich so I can't speak.

"Too bad there are no men around here for you to rebound with," she taunts, waggling her brows. "In fact, there are no men here period. We're all gonna be alone with a handful of horses. Horse ladies."

I snort and cover my mouth with my hand to prevent food from spewing all over her. After I chew and swallow, I laugh. "Well, you need to get out of the kitchen every once in a while to find someone. All you do is cook."

She shoots me a deadpan expression. "It's my job, brat."

"I'm working tomorrow night. You should stop in. It'll be busy," I tell her.

"And do what? Be the loser in the corner drinking alone?"

"Well, with that charming attitude, I'm shocked you're still single!" I gasp dramatically, placing a hand over my chest.

She grins and throws a piece of bread at me. "I hate you."

I scoff, waving her off. "There are like two dozen ranch hands. Pick one and make him your sex slave for the night."

Maize makes a gagging noise that has me doubling over. "Oh my God. I'm related to like half of them. Plus, I don't shit where I eat, okay? "

"Gross." I stick out my tongue.

"You don't mess around with men you can't escape from, which means all guys on the property are off-limits. That's my one rule," she explains.

"Oh really? So if a superhot and charming cowboy starts working here and is sweet-talking your panties off, you'd still say no?" I challenge, raising a brow.

"Well..." She hesitates a moment. "I didn't say it was a *hard* rule."

We're both laughing when my mother walks into the kitchen wearing her scrubs. She must be heading into work soon. "I thought I heard some giggling in here." She smiles, then comes over and kisses my cheek. "What're you girls talkin' about?"

"Boys," I tell her.

"Or lack thereof," Maize adds with a groan. "We're staying single forever and joining a convent."

"That is not going to give me or your mother—" She points at Maize. "Grandchildren."

"Riley and Zoey just gave you a grandson!" I remind her. "Shouldn't that hold you off for a while?"

"Nope. He only made me want more," she retorts with a smug grin.

"Well, don't look at me!" I tease. "I'm not like Riley who just goes out for a weekend and finds someone to marry."

My mom snorts, shaking her head. "Your father too," she reminds me. I think it's adorable how they met, but that'll never be me. "It's the Bishop male gene. Too bad you weren't a boy. You'd be married with a baby already. Maybe even two."

I roll my eyes. "Thanks for the reminder that my biological clock is ticking, Mom."

"Oh, you have time, sweetheart. Ten years or so. But the sooner, the better." She shrugs. "Especially if you want more than one."

"Alright, got it. Find a husband, then get knocked up ASAP."

"Your words, not mine." She smirks. "But your grandmother did say she was hoping to have another great-grandchild before she kicks the bucket."

"Oh my God, Mom!" I scowl at her. "Grandma isn't dying for a long, long time." Although she is in her mid-seventies, she still has a lot of life left in her. She's too stubborn. The woman will probably live until she's a hundred and twenty.

"Okay, girls. You two be good. I gotta get to work." She gives me a hug, and we say our goodbyes.

Once she's out the door and out of earshot, Maize speaks up. "Guess you better find yourself a ranch hand to procreate with very soon." She smirks.

I narrow my eyes at her and walk toward the door, flipping her the bird. "Fuck off." Then I turn around before leaving. "Tomorrow night. Come and hang out. Drinks are on me."

Maize breathes in sharply through her nose, then exhales. "Fine. But you promised me fresh man meat, so you better deliver."

I snort and wave goodbye.

Checking my phone as I walk to my car, I shoot Diesel a text.

ROWAN

My mother wants more grandchildren.

DIESEL

Now? Meet me in the barn. Haystacks.

ROWAN

OMG, you animal!

DIESEL

Only for you, baby ;)

ROWAN

You're lame.

DIESEL

You adore me.

ROWAN

Sometimes.

DIESEL

You gonna come visit me or what?

ROWAN

Where are you?

DIESEL

Just got out of the shower.

ROWAN

You're done with work?

DIESEL

We had extra hands on deck today, so I bailed early since someone's been keeping me up all hours of the night.

ROWAN

Then you should take a nap. I can come over later since I have the day off.

DIESEL

Hell no! Get your luscious ass over here right now.

ROWAN

On one condition...

DIESEL

...what?

ROWAN

You actually go to bed early. No more working on three hours of sleep.

DIESEL

I'd sleep a helluva lot better if you were in my bed with me.

ROWAN

Play your cards right, Cowboy and MAYBE.

DIESEL

DEAL.

Though we're not rushing into sex, there are times I'm tempted to rip off our clothes and give in to the emotions swirling between us. I gave in to my desires last week when I got down on my knees in the bar office. It was hot as hell and perhaps a little reckless, but the memory of it makes it hard for me to continue to take things slow. It's not that I don't trust him or my feelings, but once we cross those lines, there's no going back. If something bad happens, and we break up, it'd be impossible to be just "friends" and pretend nothing ever happened. I know I'm over Nick, but it doesn't mean I'm over how he violated my trust. Diesel would never intentionally hurt me like Nick did, but I still need to be cautious. My heart is still fragile.

I also know the moment Riley finds out, he's going to be red-hot angry. Even though Diesel's reassured me he'll get over it, I don't want to be the reason their friendship blows up. Since we were younger, Riley's been clear about me being "off-limits" to his friends. While I'm not a child anymore and can make my own decisions, I only hope he's not as mad as I think he'll be when he finds out.

I drive toward Diesel's house but don't park in front of his cabin. Instead, I leave my car near one of the barns, then walk the rest of the way. Before I go up his porch steps, I look around and make sure none of the ranch hands are working close and can see me. There's no doubt it's weird for me to be at his house.

Once the coast is clear, I knock, and within seconds, he whips it open.

"Hey—" Before I can finish my sentence, Diesel has me wrapped in his arms and shuts the door behind me. Then he pushes me against it and covers my mouth with his. After a moment, I suck in a breath and laugh. "What the hell was that?"

He flashes a lopsided grin. "Didn't want anyone to see you."

"I checked before I walked up the porch," I tell him, smiling. "Mmm... you smell good." I clench my fingers in his shirt and pull him closer, inhaling his scent. "*Really* good."

"Fresh outta the shower." He winks, sliding his hand down to squeeze my ass. "I missed you today."

"You just saw me last night," I remind him.

"With a bar between us and a dozen pair of eyes on you." He growls. "I hate that all the guys stare at you."

"They do not."

"Trust me, they do. I want to go all caveman on their asses and claim you publicly so they know you're mine." He holds me tighter.

"Oh yeah? And then what?"

"Then we get hitched, knock you up, and raise our ten kids on the ranch."

My eyes go wide at the seriousness of his tone. Pulling back, I look at him wide-eyed. "Okay, that's my cue…"

He grabs my wrist before I can slide out of his grip. "Okay, fine. I'll compromise. Five kids." Then he winks, and I burst out laughing.

"Why do I feel like you're actually serious but downplaying it for my sake?"

"I don't wanna scare you off, so…" He casually shrugs.

"Have you ever done this before?" I ask as he leads me into his living room. It's half covered with tarps from his remodel.

"Done…what?" he asks, pulling me onto his lap when he sits on the sofa.

"A relationship. Commitment. Dated someone longer than one night," I reiterate.

"Well, there was Billie Sue in fifth grade. She told everyone she was my girlfriend and made me hold her hand at recess."

I arch a brow, amused. "That skank. How dare she!"

"I broke it off during the second recess."

Chuckling, I wrap my arms around his neck as I straddle his lap. "So what makes you think you know how to be a boyfriend?"

"Is that what I am?"

"I don't know. Do you wanna be?"

He blinks hard. "You have me going in circles here."

We both laugh, and I blush at the direction this conversation is going.

"What if I said I've considered it?" I shyly admit.

"I'd say…is it too early to propose?"

I throw my head back with a groan. "How can you just throw those kinds of lines out when you've never had a girlfriend before? Aren't you like, terrified of commitment and shit?"

"Nope," he says immediately and with certainty.

"You're strange." I lean in closer. "You've pushed my buttons for as long as I can remember, and then you'd hook up with my friends." I pop a brow, waiting to hear how he explains himself.

"You—" He punches the word, gripping my hips tighter. "Wouldn't give me the time of day."

"That's your excuse?"

"If memory serves me right, and I'm sure that it does, you weren't so nice to me either. *Even* when I was nothing but sweet to you." He tilts his head, daring me to argue, but he's right. We've been going back and forth for years.

"You're obnoxious sometimes!" I admit, chuckling, then biting my lip. "I could never take you seriously, and you liked making me uncomfortable. Or like last month…" I throw up my hand. "You went through my boxes and brought up my red thongs in front of my brother!"

His head falls back with loud laughter, and I swat his chest.

"See!"

"Alright, so I'm not the subtle type." He shrugs unapologetically. "Most chicks dig that, by the way. In fact, a lot of girls in high school always commented on how much attention I gave you, but you wouldn't have any of it. Instead, you found ways to get rid of me."

Rolling my eyes, I shake my head. "Not true. You're so full of shit."

"Right. So me going out of my way to do things for you was for what? Shits and giggles? Boredom? It's not like I had any motive to be nice to you unless I wanted to be."

His words hit me hard as I think back to all the ways he did do things for me during middle and high school. "I thought it was because Riley told you to," I admit. "Or you had some best friend's sister code."

"The only rule he had was not to touch you, so…"

"So I was the shiny forbidden toy that made you want it even more?" I mock.

"If you mean the smart-mouthed, sassy pain in the ass, then yes." He wraps an around my waist and hoists me up higher until I feel his erection between my legs. "You gonna be my girl, or do I need to get a plane to spell it out in the sky?"

I arch a brow, confused.

"You're not as subtle as you think you are, Rowan Bishop. I knew exactly where this conversation was going, and if you need to throw a bunch of questions at me to make sure I'm ready to be in a relationship with you, then go ahead because I've been waiting years for this. I'm not gonna be the dumbass who lets the girl of his dreams slip through his fingers."

My breathing quickens at his unexpected confession, but it's one I'll replay in my head over and over again. Adam Hayes officially has my heart.

"Okay," I whisper, then bite my lip. For whatever reason, my nerves are shot, and I can feel my cheeks heating.

"Okay what?"

"You're gonna make me say it, aren't you?"

The smirk on his face tells me his answer.

"I'm gonna need to hear you say it just so there's nothing lost in translation," he states, clearly loving how nervous I am. I rock my hips against him, and he groans. "Better stop that."

"Or what?"

"Or you better be prepared to finish what you start, sweetheart."

My eyes lower down his sculpted body. He's large, and I feel small next to him. Everything on him screams man—his large hands, long legs, and toned arms.

"You're the one who pulled me onto your lap," I remind him.

I screech when he shoots off the couch and lays me down on my back, then towers over me. "Answer my question, Row. Are you mine?"

Licking my lips, I nod. "Yes, I'm yours."

He grins, shaking his head in disbelief. "About goddamn time."

Diesel crashes his mouth to mine, sliding his hand up and around my neck. My legs wrap around his waist, wanting him against me. I grind against his obvious erection, which causes him to growl against my lips. "Fuck, don't do that. I only have so much willpower when it comes to you."

"I said I wanted to go slow, not that we had to withhold from *everything*," I reiterate, grabbing his hand and placing it on my breast.

Without another word, he leans back, then lifts up my shirt until it flies off. He presses kisses on my chest and wraps a hand around my back to unclasp my bra. I flash him a suspicious look. "Did you just undo my bra with one hand?"

He shrugs, undoing my bra and flinging it off. "I'm good with my hands, baby."

I roll my eyes and laugh. "I'm sure you are."

He cups my breast and wraps his lips around one of my nipples. My eyes close at how good it feels. His hot mouth and his eager tongue have my entire body on fire.

"Adam," I cry out, arching my back to give him more of me.

"Jesus fuck," he hisses. "I love hearing you moan my name."

He moves his mouth to my other breast, giving it the same amount of attention. I'm smacking myself in the face for telling him we needed to go slow because right now, I'm craving more of him.

Diesel has wedged himself into my head and heart so quickly that if I'm not careful, I'm gonna get whiplash. All of my assumptions about him hit me in the gut because I was so damn wrong.

"I'm sorry," I tell him softly, and he lifts his eyes up to mine. "I never should've treated you the way I did growing up."

He brings his finger up to my face, brushing back the strands of hair that fell from my ponytail. "Don't be. It's a part of our story."

"I don't deserve you."

"I've told myself that for so long, and I started to believe it, but you know what? It didn't stop me from going after what I wanted anyway. And now look?"

"Your persistence paid off," I say, chuckling at his honesty.

"Damn straight." He smirks, bringing his mouth back to mine. "You have the sexiest tits, by the way."

I snort, blushing. "Wow. There's that romantic side of you."

"I'm romantic as fuck! Just wait until I can take you out on *real* dates."

"Oh, really? What would a real date with Diesel be like?" I taunt as my fingers play with his belt buckle. The damn thing must come with a combination because it's impossible to undo with one hand.

"You will find out *very* soon, sweet Rowan. Now get your hands away from my dick before I throw your rule out the goddamn window and fuck you against my couch."

I groan loudly, tempted to rub my thighs together for relief. Sticking out my lower lip, I give him my best pouty look. "That's not fair. You took off my shirt."

"Okay, fine." He leans back and wraps a hand behind his neck, pulling off his. "There, we're even."

"Hardly," I say with a deadpan expression. "Now, your pants."

"No, ma'am." He swats away my eager hands. "I'm not just a play toy."

I scoff, chuckling at him feigning offense. "Then tell your cock that because it's begging to come out and *play*."

Diesel chuckles, leaning over me. He tilts my chin up and brings our lips together, soft and slow. "Let me take you out. We'll leave town and see where the night goes."

"You really take this whole dating thing seriously, don't you?" I tease, capturing his bottom lip with my teeth.

"I take you being my girl seriously."

We continue making out, his rough hands massaging my breasts while heat pools between my thighs. He's working me up but not willing to do anything about it.

"You need to stop, or I'm going to combust." I grind against him, needing the friction to relieve myself.

"Let me help with that..." He shifts our bodies so we're chest to chest. Sliding his hands down my body, he slips beneath my shorts and into my panties. His fingers find my clit, and soon, he's rubbing circles, and I'm gasping for air. "Better?" His voice is taunting, but I nod, arching my hips for more.

"Don't stop," I beg. I wrap my hand around his bicep, squeezing hard as he increases his pace. "Oh my God..." My eyes roll to the back of my head as he slides two fingers inside me while his thumb rubs against me.

"You have any idea how many wet dreams I've had of this exact moment," he murmurs against my lips, and I can tell he's smiling. "So fuckin' many, Row."

"Sounds like you needed a hobby," I tease, bucking my hips.

He chuckles. "I did. You're it now."

As I get closer to the ledge, his mouth sucks on my neck, and he kisses my jawline before sliding his tongue between my lips. The heat between us is so intense, and I know I'm about to explode at any moment.

"Let go, sweetheart. Come on my fingers," he demands. "I wanna taste you."

My legs shake, my back arches, my spine tingles. So. Damn. Close.

"Diesel!" Two hard knocks sound at the door, and we both freeze. "Open the door!"

"You gotta be fuckin' kidding me." He growls.

The doorknob jiggles, and that's when I push him off me. "Shit, I need my bra and shirt!" I fly off the couch, gathering my things, and once I cover myself, I rush toward the bathroom.

Diesel grabs my arm and stops me before I make it down the hall. "Stay in there, and I'll come get you when they leave."

I nod. "Don't forget your shirt." Then I lower my gaze to his groin. "Might wanna adjust that…"

He curses under his breath, then walks back to the living room while I go and hide.

Like a dirty mistress.

After ten minutes of waiting, I start to worry. I heard voices at the front, but he didn't let them in. I don't know what excuse he gave them, but after a while, it goes eerily quiet, and I worry he left me in here.

Another five minutes pass, and I grow more annoyed. "Fuck this shit."

Slowly, I undo the lock and poke my head out. I don't hear a thing and decide to chance it.

The moment I open the door wider and step out into the hallway, a hand covers my mouth, and I'm slammed into a hard body.

"Shh…" Diesel whispers into my ear, then pushes me back inside the bathroom. After he shuts the door, he twists me in his arms, then lifts me up under my thighs.

"What the hell are you doing?" I squeal and wrap my arms around his shoulders as he carries me to the sink counter. "Who's here?"

"Your dad."

My eyes widen. "What? Why?"

"And Riley."

"Oh hell. That can't be good." My head falls back against the mirror.

"Nah, it's fine. They were looking for something I had in my truck. They're gone now."

I straighten and look at him. "Then why did you—" I wave my arm out. "Basically shove me back in here like we were gonna get caught."

The corner of his lips tilts up. "To fuck with you."

I narrow my eyes at him and growl. "That was mean! Asshole."

He laughs, showing off his perfect white teeth. "I'm getting revenge for all those years you tortured me with these delicious tits and long, tan legs you always showed off but never let me touch. And now that I know what they feel like against my skin and tongue, don't expect me to be able to keep my hands off."

I can't even be mad at his little stunt because hearing those words from him—a guy who annoyed me for years but managed to turn what I thought about him around—changes everything. I love that no one knows about us, and we can be completely honest with one another without any outside noise.

"Not sure I can get used to this charming side of yours..." I lift a brow. "But I kinda adore it."

He presses a hand to his chest. "Because I'm fuckin' adorable."

I shake my head. "You're too much sometimes."

"And I'm all yours, baby."

CHAPTER ELEVEN

Diesel

It's been two days since Rowan came to my house and we almost got caught by her brother and dad. Luckily, they didn't ask to come in, and they only talked to me for a few minutes outside, but it was another reminder of how careful we have to be.

Grabbing Rowan's arm before she walks past me, I guide her into one of the tack rooms in the horse barn and bring her against my chest.

"Jesus!" she whisper-hisses. "You're gonna give me a heart attack one of these days." She playfully swats at my chest. "Why can't we sneak around without you scaring the shit outta me every damn time?"

I cup her face and lower my mouth, brushing my lips against hers. "I like getting your blood pumping." Waggling my brows, I slide my other hand down her back and squeeze her ass. "Now let me do dirty things to you."

Rowan's eyes widen, pulling away. "What if someone walks in?" she asks as I slowly move her backward until the saddle stand stops her.

"They're free to watch me pleasure you." I flash her a cocky smile as I grip her hips. "Everyone went to the diner for lunch today," I tell her. "We have an hour, at least."

She perks an eyebrow. "And you didn't go with them? Aren't you hungry?" The way she so sweetly asks gets my dick hard.

"Oh, sweet Rowan." My gaze rolls down her tempting body. "Starving."

My fingers reach for the top of her jean shorts, and she watches as I slowly unbutton them, then lower the zipper.

"What are you doin'?" she asks with a grin.

"I told you...I'm hungry." I throw her a wink, then drop to my knees. "And you're just what I'm craving."

As I slide her shorts down, my cock throbs at the sight. I look up as Rowan snags her bottom lip between her teeth while keeping her hands steadily planted on the saddle behind her.

"You okay with this, Row?" I ask, digging my boots into the floor as I balance my weight in front of her.

She nods with a half-smile. "No one's ever..." Rowan nervously clears her throat. "But I want you to."

I tilt my head at her, wondering if she's fucking with me or not. "What do you mean, no one's ever...?"

"The few guys I've dated didn't do *that*."

"Wait. Are you kiddin'? That's what they told you, or they never offered?"

"Both." She shrugs as if she's embarrassed.

Standing to my feet, I hold her face in my hands and press my lips to hers. She melts against me, wrapping her fingers around my wrists as I slide my tongue inside her mouth.

"That's because before me, you were with *boys*, not a man." I smirk, excited I'll be the first and *only* to taste her that intimately. "Another first kiss of yours I get."

Rowan chuckles, then nods. "I'm glad it's you."

I press a quick kiss to her mouth before lowering my body again. Not knowing how soon the rest of the workers will return, we don't have a lot of time to waste.

When I brushing my lips to the inside of her thigh, she shudders. I've barely touched her, but she's so goddamn responsive; it won't be long before she's coming on my tongue.

"Widen your legs, baby," I tell her. She obliges, and I tease her first, kissing her skin and sliding my tongue on her clit over her panties.

She arches her hips toward me, groaning and holding my head in place. I love how vocal she is, and the way she responds to my touch sends a jolt of electricity through me. I want to please her more than anything, but I also want to taste her.

Pulling back slightly, I gaze up at her and watch as she licks her lips. Her eyes burn into mine, and I know she's ready.

I slide her thong down, and she steps out of it, baring herself for me. She watches as I tuck it into my pocket, giving me a teasing side-eye.

"What do you think you're doing with that?"

"Keepin' my prize."

"And what do you plan to do with it?"

I lean in close, then rub the tip of my nose along her thigh, inching toward her pussy. "Savor it till the day I die."

She chuckles, spreading her legs in response.

"Fuck, Row." I slide my tongue up her slit and circle her clit. "I can't get enough of you."

"Mmm…" Her sweet voice vibrates. "More. We're on a time limit here," she reminds me.

I laugh at her urgency, then dive in.

Licking, sucking, fucking her with my tongue.

It's better than I could've ever imagined.

Her moans echo through the room, burning a fire within me so deep, I'm not sure how to control myself when I'm this worked up around her. The desire to be near her, touch her, kiss, and love her hits me so strong, I want her to feel me for days.

Gripping the back of her thighs, I squeeze hard as I feast on her like my last meal. Sliding a finger inside her tight cunt, I thrust in and out as I suck on her clit. She grinds against my tongue as she throws off my hat and digs her nails into my hair. I smile in amusement as I feel her buildup start to soar.

"Oh my God. I'm so close."

"Yes, baby. Just like that." I flick my tongue and increase my pace, finger fucking her harder and faster until she jerks her body and shakes against me. She unravels, hissing through her teeth as I relentlessly taste her.

I adjust my body between her legs and spread her pussy wider, not wanting to let her go just yet.

"Adam..." she whispers. "You're going to get us caught."

Sliding my tongue up her slit, I taste her arousal, sucking on her clit. Rowan rides my face as I drive her to another orgasm. Her hands shake as they rest on my shoulders, and she's only seconds away from giving me more of what I want.

The moment she claws her nails into my skin, I know she's there. Her body jerks as I release her clit, then press a kiss above it.

"I'm a selfish man. I wanted more." I wink, licking my lips.

With a satisfied smirk, she shakes her head at me. "That was...crazy."

Knowing I was her first fills me with pride and possession. I want to be the only one to ever touch and taste her down there forever.

"Best damn lunch break I've ever had," I tease. "Same time tomorrow?"

Rowan laughs, then rolls her eyes. "I need to get out of here before someone catches us."

I help her back into her shorts, then stand. "You should let me take you out this weekend. I'm off on Saturday and work Sunday evening. We can plan a sleepover since I know you're not working," I tease.

She retreats a step and side-eyes me. "Take me out? Like on a *date?*"

"Yes, ma'am. Dinner, dessert, a walk under the stars."

She snorts. "You and me?"

Tilting my head, I hold back a smirk. "You gonna make me beg, woman?"

"I'm just trying to imagine *you*, Adam Hayes, taking a girl out on a romantic date, and...I'm just not seeing it." Rowan shrugs with a grin.

"That's because you haven't experienced it yet." I pull her back to me, wrapping my arms around her waist. "So whaddya say? We'll go into San Angelo and stay at a hotel. It'll be romantic as fuck."

She laughs, and I beam with excitement when she finally agrees. "Okay, I suppose I could spare a night."

"And the morning after." I wink.

Before Rowan leaves, I peek outside the barn to make sure the coast is clear. The guys aren't back yet, but our time together is coming to an end. They'll be here any minute.

"Alright, I think you're good to go," I tell her, then give her one last kiss. "Text me later tonight."

"What are you talkin' about? I'm gonna text you in five minutes."

She chuckles as she walks backward out of the barn, looking at me, then spins around and goes out the side door.

I wait a few minutes before leaving, staring at my phone at a text Riley sent, then stop in my tracks when I see Rowan and Maize are talking outside.

They both stop and look at me.

"What?" I blink.

"What are you doing?" Maize asks.

"Going to my truck. What are you doin'?"

"I meant, what are you doing in there?" She points at the barn behind me.

"I was putting some shit away. That okay, nosy?" I taunt, walking toward them while trying to act normal. "What's it to you?"

"Because I watched Rowan coming out of there, and when I asked her if she saw you, she said she hadn't..." Maize looks at Rowan, then to me.

I shrug. "I was in the tack room."

"Hmm." She folds her arms, narrowing her eyes.

Glancing at Rowan, I can see her cheeks heat and her nostrils flare, which means she's nervous.

"Why were you lookin' for me anyway?"

"Oh, right." She clears her throat. "I need some muscles to help me lift a large box of flour, and it looks like you're the only one around. Literally everyone's gone."

I chuckle and raise my arm, showing off my bicep. "By help, you mean, do it for you?"

Maize rolls her eyes. "Never mind. Put your ego away. I bet Rowan and I can handle it."

Shrugging casually, I walk around them. "Alright." Then I look over my shoulder and grin. "Remember to lift with your legs."

"Asshole," I hear Rowan mutter, then smirk when Maize looks away.

DIESEL

Are you packed?

ROWAN

If by packed you mean a bag of Starbursts and my cowboy boots, then I'm good to go!

DIESEL

Well, darlin', you won't be needing much else anyway :) I'm almost to Wyatt's. You leaving soon?

I'm driving us to San Angelo, but since her parents think she's staying with a friend, she can't leave her truck at home or anywhere they'll see it. But since Wyatt lives in Eldorado, he's letting her park it in his garage. He's the only person who knows about us, and I trust he'll keep it that way until we're ready to announce it.

ROWAN

Be there in 10! Had to find my lucky thong.

DIESEL

The red one, I hope?

ROWAN

You'll have to wait and see ;)

I love the way she always makes me laugh. Chuckling, I shake my head and park my truck on the street outside Wyatt's apartment. I send him a text so he knows I'm here and can give me his garage opener.

"You two gonna finally bang tonight?" he asks the moment he comes up to my window.

"Shut the hell up and give me the opener," I say, holding out my palm.

"I've had to listen to you talk about Rowan Bishop for months, so the least you could do is give me the details."

I roll my eyes, ready to sucker punch the idiot. "Not happenin'. Go back to your Pornhub."

"Just fuckin' with ya. Relax." He digs into his pocket, then hands it over to me. "Tell her to park it in nice and slow…"

"For fuck's sake, don't make me kick your ass."

Wyatt laughs, and when I try to smack him, he retreats. "Okay, for real, though. Have fun. Wear a condom."

He waves when Rowan's car comes into view, and I open the garage for her. She turns in, and I go and meet her.

"Hey, Cowboy." She hops out and immediately wraps her arms around me.

"Hello, yourself." I pull her closer and press my lips to hers. "I'll grab your stuff so we can get outta here."

I put her bag in my truck next to mine, then open the passenger door for her.

"So gentlemanly," she teases as she sits and fixes her sundress.

"My thoughts are anything but *gentlemanly*." I waggle my brows as I stare at her bare legs. "Especially with you wearing that."

She blushes and shakes her head at me.

"Ready?" I ask after I get in the driver's side.

"Yep! If anyone asks, I'm visiting my friend Camila this weekend."

"Camila? Got it." I smirk.

"Do you remember in high school when Thomas Blake asked me to junior prom?" she asks as I turn on the main road that leads out of town.

I look at her confused. "Huh?"

"Thomas Blake," she repeats. "The quarterback of the football team," she clarifies, though I know exactly who she's talking about. The asshole I nearly punched in the face after I found out he'd asked her.

"What about him?" I tighten my grip on the steering wheel, hoping she's not about to confront me about something in the past.

"I've just been doing some thinking lately and wondering why no guys asked me out until my senior year because the day after Thomas did, he canceled."

I feel her staring at me.

"Huh. Weird."

"Yeah," she draws out the word. "*Weird*."

I finally look at her. "You think I had something to do with it?" I lift a brow, feigning innocence.

"I'd be willing to bet money you did." She crosses her arms, glaring. "I started to put it together the other day, especially when I asked Riley about it, and he looked at me like I'd grown a second head. So that only leaves one other option..."

"That you just weren't that nice in high school, and no guy wanted to date you?"

She smacks my arm so hard, I actually groan and pull away from her. "See?"

"Don't play dumb!" She points her finger and narrows her eyes at me. "I know you must've said or done something to make sure no one ever asked me out. It's no coincidence that once you graduated, a few guys finally did."

I inhale a deep breath and readjust myself in the seat. "It was for your own good, Rowan."

"Oh my God!" she screeches. "I knew it!"

"Okay, geez. Take it down an octave, babe."

"I can't believe you..." She pouts and looks out the window.

Reaching over, I grab her hand and thread my fingers through hers. "You can't be mad. That was years ago, and we're together now, so...you're welcome."

Slowly, she turns her head toward me as though she's possessed. Her eyes are squinted so tight that I'm waiting for her to blow me up with her lazers.

"You're really mad I told some punks to stay away from you?" I pop a brow.

She continues glaring, but it's so damn cute, and I can't help but laugh at how adorable she acts when she's upset.

"This isn't funny!"

"Alright, fine." I bring our locked hands to my lips and press a kiss to her knuckles. "Let me make it up to you this weekend, and you'll be glad I kept those little dickheads away. Otherwise, the alternative would've been you dating some tool bag who would've broken your heart. And you were going off to college anyway." I flash the most charming smile I can.

"Well, we could've gone to the same college together..." she counters.

"Name one guy in our high school who went to the University of Houston," I challenge.

"If I had dated someone, and it was serious, he might've followed me. Or I could've followed him to another school. You don't know!"

I snicker at how serious she is about this. "But aren't you glad you came back to me?"

Rowan rolls her eyes as she struggles to fight a smile.

"You forgive me?"

"No," she says dryly. "But maybe you're right about the long-distance thing. Nick and I went to the same school, and it still didn't work out."

The corner of my lips tilts up. "That's because he's a fucking asshole. It's no coincidence y'all broke up before you moved back home. It just allowed me to give you everything you've ever dreamed of having in a man."

"Don't be smug! This doesn't mean you're off the hook."

"I'm about to romance your pants off this weekend, and you'll forget all about those lame high school boys."

She snorts, then starts chuckling. The sound is contagious, and soon, we're both laughing our asses off.

"I really should've suspected something when no one would dance with me in middle school."

"Exactly!" I say proudly. "Now we can tell our kids we were each other's first kiss."

Rowan blushes, then smiles. "You got lucky that after years of tormenting me, I actually did end up liking you." She pinches her thumb and finger together. "Just a little."

"I think you mean a lot," I mock.

She shrugs casually. "Nothing else to do, so…"

My eyes widen.

She bursts out laughing. "Relax, geez! I'm kidding."

"Now you have to make it up to *me*…" I tell her. "I expect full service treatment too."

"You ruined all my teenage dating opportunities," she reiterates. "You have *years* of making it up to me."

"Oh, sweet Rowan. Don't fuckin' tempt me."

CHAPTER TWELVE

Rowan

Arguing and laughing with Diesel makes the drive to San Angelo fly by. A part of me worried that if we weren't sneaking around, being alone would be awkward, or that our relationship was only built on the excitement of hiding, but it's not been the case at all. If anything, I've felt more comfortable with him, and it makes me want to tell the world that somehow, someway I'm falling for Diesel.

I'm falling hard and fast for him.

This weekend, we won't have to hide, and in some odd way, it feels so damn right.

We'll get to hold hands and have dinner in a restaurant and act like a normal couple out on a date.

"Wow…this room is so nice," I say, noticing how fancy our hotel room is.

Walking in farther with Diesel behind me carrying our bags, I spot a large bouquet of roses on a table, an ice bucket with a bottle of champagne, and a platter of chocolate covered strawberries. He wasn't joking when he said he'd pull out all the stops to make this romantic and perfect for us.

It's a scene straight from a Hallmark movie, but I love it all the same. So very *not* Diesel, but very much him trying to be sweet.

"You planned quite the night," I hum, turning around with a smile.

He drops our bags, then pulls me into his chest. "I told you I was turning on the charm."

"I'm gonna be really mad if there isn't a violinist at our table or it doesn't rain when you kiss me outside," I tease, biting my lower lip. The anticipation of what's to come gives me butterflies.

"You don't give me enough credit," he mocks with a wink.

"It's very sweet," I tell him. "Thank you for doing this."

"I would've done it much sooner, but you were too busy hating my guts."

"That's because you were too immature to tell me you liked me."

He chuckles, and a grin spreads across his face that has my entire body fluttering. "Well, you calling me an asshole every other day didn't convince me you'd reciprocate the feelings…"

I roll my eyes and squeal when he lowers his hands and smacks my ass. "But we're here now, so let's not waste another minute…"

Before I can respond, Diesel lifts me over his shoulder caveman style. I squeal as I hang down his back, yelling at him to put me down.

He smacks my ass before tossing me on the bed. "You still think I'm *sweet*?" he mocks.

I laugh, wrapping my legs around his waist and pulling him on top of me. "I didn't mean it as a bad thing."

"Mm-hmm…" He smirks before cupping my face and pressing his lips to mine.

Arching my back, I lean my hips into him, feeling how hard he is against his jeans. Grinning, I inhale the scent of his cologne and groan at the anticipation of getting to be with him all night long—without worrying we'll get caught.

"I don't want to wait, Adam," I tell him, sliding my hands up his chest and undoing a button. "I'm dying and want you inside me."

"Fuck, Row," he growls against my mouth. "I have a whole night planned out for us…but shit."

I chuckle, and when he leans back, we lock eyes. Sucking in my lips, I reach for his belt buckle and zipper. He's hard, and when I slide my hand into his jeans, I wrap my palm around his cock through his boxers.

Stroking him, I watch as he unbuttons his shirt as we keep our gazes on one another. My heart pounds hard in my chest as the reality of what's about to happen seeps in. Even though he's been "Diesel" to me my whole life, Adam makes me anxious by how quickly we're growing close. I want to give him all of me, but I'm so scared of giving my heart away again.

Once his shirt is off, I help him remove my sundress and bra. "You're so beautiful, Row. I'm one lucky man."

I swallow hard and smile. "You're not so bad to look at either."

"I've caught you checking me out a few times." He winks with a smug grin. "Drooling over the eight-pack."

"Oh my God!" I burst out laughing. "Just like when you drool over my ass."

"Damn straight!"

I wrap my legs around his waist and move his lips back to mine. Rocking my hips against his, I moan at the friction our bodies create, so damn eager for more.

Diesel pushes his cock against my pussy, and I'm desperate to tear off our remaining clothes and climb him like a damn tree. "Boxers. Off. Now," I demand, panting.

He moves back slightly, grabbing both of my wrists and putting them above my head. "Not so fast, baby."

I'm seconds away from begging. "What? Why?"

"Because I've been waiting years for this, and I'm not about to rush my time with you." He wraps one hand around both my wrists and moves his free hand down between my breasts. "I'm taking it nice and slow. Gonna devour every inch of your soft skin and make sure I mark every part of you properly."

Shivers run down my spine at the anticipation and desperation for everything he's willing to give me. I want it all.

"Adam...don't tease me," I plead.

"Oh, I'm going to have you beggin', sweet Row." The corner of his lips tilts up in a cocky, assured smirk as he circles my nipple with the pad of his finger. "It's the only way I'll know you really want me as much as I want you."

"You know I do," I tell him. "I'm going insane!"

"Let me taste you first."

He guides himself down my body and widens my legs as he settles between them, peeking up at me with a knowing grin. Then he kisses the sensitive part of my thigh, and my eyes roll to the back of my head.

Switching to my other thigh, he does the same and shoves his hands under my ass, pulling me closer to his mouth.

"Fuck," he mutters as he nuzzles his nose against my clit. "Hope you aren't attached to this."

Before I can respond, he grabs both sides of my thong and rips it completely off my body.

Holy. Fucking. *Shit.*

My eyes widen in shock, and without another word, he slides his tongue up my slit and buries his face in my pussy. I don't have anything to compare his skills to, but he's a fucking pro. His mouth and tongue feel amazing as he drives me closer to the edge.

"Adam...*yes, yes, yes,*" I pant as my fingers tug his hair, and my back arches. "Don't stop."

He pushes a finger inside, and when he sucks my clit, I unravel against his mouth. It's intense, and I'm still flying high when he adds a second finger.

Diesel's groans are such a turn-on. Knowing he's feasting on me like his favorite meal, I want more of him, and I don't ever want him to stop.

My hands fist the blankets as I jerk my hips up and down, so close to another release. My body responds to him so strongly and it drives me wild every time he touches me.

"That's my girl," he praises as another orgasm rocks through my core.

"Please don't stop," I plead. "I want you inside me, *now.*"

"Patience..." He presses his lips to my stomach. "I'm just getting started with you."

Diesel's hot mouth kisses up my body and cups my breast before sucking on my nipple. He gives them equal attention, massaging and licking each one. Every inch of me is on fire, desperate and greedy for all of him.

My arms wrap around his body, being as close to him as I can. He's muscular and hard, but he touches me so softly and sweet.

Diesel roll his hips, grinding his dick harder against me, and I groan. "That's not fair." My head falls to the side as he kisses up my neck.

"This is what you do to me, Row," he whispers in my ear. "You make me crazy. For *years*. I couldn't stop wanting you even when I fuckin' tried."

"*Adam...*"

He moves his mouth to mine. "I tried to get over you. Tried to date other women. Tried to have feelings for someone else so I could erase the ones I had for you."

My eyes water at his confession. "I'm so happy you didn't..." I say softly.

"It never worked anyway. My heart is yours. Always has been. I was just waiting for you to catch me."

I palm his cheeks and hold his face. I never thought I'd say these words to him, but I mean them wholeheartedly. "You have mine too. I'm falling for you faster than I could've ever imagined, but I'm not going anywhere now that I know these feelings are real."

"I've been falling for you for years, baby, but harder than I could've predicted."

Diesel kisses me passionately, pressing our bodies together as our hands explore each other. He pulls back and stands, removing his jeans and boxers. My breathing increases as I watch him grab a condom from his wallet, then strokes himself and slides it on.

He stares at me, moving his eyes down my chest, stomach, legs. Then he meets my gaze with a smirk. "So fucking gorgeous."

"You better get over here before I do the job for you..." I tease, sliding my hand down to my clit. It's been throbbing since the second he touched me.

"Like hell you will, woman." Approaching the edge of the bed, he wraps his hands around each of my ankles, then gently yanks me down until my ass is nearly hanging off the mattress.

I squeal, hanging onto the covers. "What're you doing?"

"Making sure my hands are the only ones pleasuring you."

He strokes his cock a few times before lining it up to my entrance. My chest rises and falls faster; the anticipation mixes with desire as he pushes inside.

Diesel grips my thigh and pulls it up around his waist as he goes deeper. He feels so thick and hard as I widen my hips and take all of him.

"Oh my God…" My head rolls back, the sensation already too much.

"Jesus, Row," he groans, slowly sliding out before returning. I dig my nails into his biceps, enjoying how tight he feels inside me. "So goddamn wet."

My other leg wraps around him, and I lock my ankles behind him. He places a hand on the bed next to me while his other cups my breast and squeezes. "You feel amazing."

I can't even form words around my heavy breathing and moaning, but I smile when our lips meet.

As I rock my hips against him, our bodies form a perfect rhythm as our hands and lips touch and kiss everywhere we can. Diesel increases his pace, grabbing my waist and controlling the speed. He's sculpted to pure perfection, and I could stare at him all day as he drives us further to the ledge.

He brings his hand between us and rubs my clit. It's the sweetest torture I've ever felt, and even though I'm close, I don't want this to end.

"That feels so good," I moan, pinching my nipples. "I'm so close…"

"Yes, baby. I wanna feel you come on my dick," he says, his voice rough and deep, almost sliding all the way out before he drives back in. He's so deep, my legs shake at how hard he's fucking me.

Diesel continues circling my clit, and when my back flies off the bed, he slows his pace and whispers sweet things as I ride out my climax.

"Not gonna lie, that was fuckin' sexy."

His cocky smile makes me laugh.

Pulling out, he nods toward the headboard. "Scoot up."

Once I'm settled in the middle of the bed, he climbs up my body and lifts my leg to his shoulder. When he's back inside me, I gasp for air as he thrusts harder.

"Faster," I beg.

Moments later, my body tightens and shakes as another orgasm rocks through me. I've never had more than one during sex, but Diesel's changed the game for me in more ways than one. He's changed *everything*.

It's not long before Diesel's groaning out his release and burying his face in my neck.

"Jesus fuck," he grunts with a laugh. He falls to my side, and we look at each other with big, satisfied smiles on our faces. Leaning in, he brushes the hair out of my face with a grin. "Wow. That was…incredible."

"My thoughts exactly." I chuckle while trying to catch my breath. The way he looks at me has my heart pounding, but not because of what we just did. Diesel stares at me as though he actually sees the real me.

I wish I knew where we go from here, how we'll announce the news, and what it'll mean for his friendship with my brother. Diesel's been a part of my life for years, and I can't imagine him not in it.

Leaning forward, I brush my lips against his, and we kiss slowly. He lets me take the lead as I slide my tongue inside and capture his with my teeth, smiling as his hand moves down to my ass, then smacks it.

"I think we're gonna be late for our reservations if we don't get out of this bed," I tell him after twenty minutes of us making out and teasing each other. He got up to dispose of the condom, but then climbed right back into bed next to me.

"Probably," he says, shifting our bodies until I'm straddling and leaning over him. "But knowing how you look underneath me will distract me too much, so you better ride me to help me focus."

"I don't think that's how that works…" I mock, grinding my pussy against his bare cock between us.

"Or we could just order room service and stay naked the rest of the night," he counters.

"Now that's a deal I'm willing to accept."

By the next morning, my entire body feels like I've run a marathon. Every inch of me is sore but in the most delicious way. Knowing it's from having sex with Diesel all night and into the early morning has me smiling like a damn fool. The man is insatiable, and I've never experienced anything like it before.

After I rode him for our second round, we ordered food and ate while talking and laughing in bed. It was actually quite sweet how attentive he was and all the memories he recounted of us as kids.

Our third round was him bending me over, but when my legs gave out, he slid behind me so my back was to his chest, then fucked me until I nearly went blind.

We finally passed out sometime after three a.m., and our fourth round was in the shower before we had to check out at noon. The entire night feels like a dream come true, one I wish didn't have to end, but when Diesel drives us back to Wyatt's house, I know we're back to hiding and sneaking around.

"Say something to piss me off," I tell him after he opens the door to my car.

"What?" He laughs, putting my bag inside.

"If I go back all euphoric and happy, my cousins and parents will start asking questions. So I need a reason to wipe this smile off my face," I explain, knowing how ridiculous I sound, but it's true. "They're already suspicious, and I won't be able to hide the way I feel unless I lock myself in my room all week."

"Guess that makes two of us. The guys will be all over my ass. You're better at telling me off, so you say something to piss me off instead."

I groan. "We're not gonna be convincing at all."

He closes the gap between us, brushing his finger over my cheek to fix my hair. "It'll be alright. If they find out, they find out. I can handle Riley."

"And my dad?" I add.

"He loves me!" We both laugh because it's true. My dad treats Diesel like a second son, but he wouldn't think twice about hounding Diesel for dating his only daughter.

"And my grandma, my cousins, and my uncles. All their opinions and comments."

"Don't care." He shrugs. "I've been telling them for years I'd finally get you."

Wrapping my arms around his waist, I rest my chin on his chest. "That's true, you did. Kinda like a stalker."

He kisses the tip of my nose. "Stalkers need love too."

I snort, and we break apart, knowing I have to get home before my mom and dad send out a search party for me.

"I'm gonna hang out with Wyatt for a bit so we don't arrive at the ranch at the same time," he tells me as I sit in the driver's seat of my car. "Text me when you're back home."

"I will." I start the engine and stick out my lower lip, pouting that our weekend's over.

"Don't be sad. I'll see you soon," he promises. Then he kisses me one final time before I leave, my heart racing as I think about what an amazing night we had and how I hope this never ends.

It's one thirty when I finally make it home. I missed church and know my mom is gonna give me shit for it, but luckily, no one's at the house yet. Diesel and I showered this morning, but I go ahead and take another one with my fruity body wash to make sure his scent doesn't linger on my skin. Though I love the way he smells after he showers.

Once I'm dressed and make a cup of coffee, I check my phone and see a message from him and a group text message from Elle and Maize.

DIESEL

Confession: I stole your ripped thong for my spank bank.

ROWAN

You're really adding to your stalker resume.

DIESEL

I'm also sniffing them while picturing your tits bouncing in my face.

My cheeks heat at his words. He's so blunt, and it turns me on. I've not really sexted before. Nick could hardly perform in the bedroom, and his skills didn't land in texting either.

ROWAN

Oh yeah? I'd shove them into your mouth while riding your cock so you could taste and feel me at the same time.

DIESEL

Jesus, now I'm hard as fuck again. Which is really awkward with Wyatt playing video games next to me. He's already giving me shit for looking like a stoned-out rodeo clown.

I giggle as I imagine how uncomfortable he must be not being able to take care of himself right now.

ROWAN

It wasn't awkward before with you sniffing my panties?

DIESEL

He wasn't looking then.

ROWAN

Mm-hmm. Well, good luck with that. It's safe for you to come back now and touch yourself in the shower.

DIESEL

Don't give me any more ideas…though I've been jerking off to thoughts of you since I was a teenager, so it'd be nothing new.

ROWAN

You just went from sexy stalker to weird creeper.

DIESEL

So I shouldn't tell you about the love letter I wrote you when I was in eighth grade?

ROWAN

You did not!

DIESEL

I swear! I was infatuated with you. Still am ;)

ROWAN

Stop being so damn sweet when I was such a brat to you. I feel so bad when I think about all the times I was mean to you.

DIESEL

Don't worry...I took it as flirting. You just weren't very good at it :)

I snort, chuckling in relief. He's the easiest person to talk to and always knows what to say to keep me laughing.

ROWAN

Har har. You're seriously ridiculous sometimes.

DIESEL

You've always adored me, admit it.

ROWAN

Ha! Gotta go! Elle and Maize want me to hang out, so I gotta put my game face on.

DIESEL

If it helps, I'm picturing you naked right now.

ROWAN

That absolutely does not help. Asshole.

I click to the group message so they don't think I'm ignoring them.

ELIZABETH

I gotta help birth a calf. The mama is having some complications. You two wanna come and help?

MAIZE

Where's Dr. VetDreamy?

ELIZABETH

On another job, which is why I gotta go solo.

ROWAN

I just took a shower...

MAIZE

I'm hungover from last night.

ELIZABETH

OMG you guys suck! I just need some extra hands.

MAIZE

Take Ethan.

ROWAN

Or Kenzie.

ELIZABETH

Meet me at the B&B in 10 minutes. Both of you!

I laugh because Maize and I were only joking. She knows we'll come. Grabbing my rubber boots and keys, I head to my car and drive over.

"You nervous or something?" I ask when I see Elle in her truck. "You're sweating."

"It's hot."

"Mm-hmm." I snicker, hopping into the passenger's seat. "Maize coming?"

Before she can answer, we see her walking down the steps of the B&B porch looking like she got hit by a bus.

"Oh my God..." I laugh when she opens the back door. Turning, I raise my brows at the dark circles under her eyes and the messy bun on top of her head. "What the hell happened to you?"

Elle starts driving, and Maize groans at the bumpy road.

"I went to the bar last night to keep Kenzie company, and well..." She sighs. "Do either of you know a Gavin?"

I purse my lips, thinking about all the regulars and townies who come into the bar. "No, doesn't ring a bell," I tell her.

"Thank God. I hope he was just passing through."

"Maize..." The corner of my lips tilts up. "What'd you do?"

"I think the question is *who* did you do?" Elle mocks.

"You hooked up with a stranger!" I laugh, shocked and kinda impressed. Maize doesn't do hookups.

"Don't talk so loud!" she scolds. "My head's still pounding."

"Go figure, the one night I'm not working you find a hottie to bang. What'd he look like?"

"Like all the other cowboys in this damn state. Ugh, fuck my life. I'm gonna be so embarrassed if I run into him again after being a sloppy drunk and probably a horrible lay." She hangs her head in shame. Elle and I try to hide our laughter, but it doesn't work.

"Stop worrying. I doubt he's from here."

"So…how was it?" Elle asks.

"Yes, do tell."

She rolls her eyes, but I see a half-smile on her face, which is enough for me to know she had a good night.

"Even drunk, he was good. Like *really* good."

"Did you get his number?" I ask.

"No! I didn't even get his last name. And to make matters worse, I left before he woke up."

"What?" I screech. "You didn't!"

She buries her head in her hands. "I was embarrassed! I didn't want to be the one he bailed on, so I got dressed and got the fuck out."

Her face is so red, I'm tempted to ask if she's running a fever, but then I think better of it when she smacks her forehead against the window.

"I can't believe you left…" I chuckle to myself.

"I wanna meet this guy," Elle adds. "He's got you all kinds of flustered."

Maize turns and glares.

"Do you remember anything else about him?" I ask as Elle turns into a gravel driveway.

"I think he mentioned something about bull riding…like he used to or something."

I snap my fingers. "I bet that's why he's just passing through town. Probably on the way to a competition or something."

"Wait, where did y'all hook up?" Elle asks.

"At some apartment but he said it wasn't his."

"So he must be visiting a friend," I say, trying to put the pieces together. "Did you see anyone else there?"

"No, but it was like two in the morning, and I was on the tipsy side," she states dryly. "This is humiliating. What was I thinking?"

"You were thinking you needed some dick." I snort.

"I hate you. If you'd been working, you could've stopped me from making a fool out of myself."

"Oh, this is *my* fault?" I ask, amused.

"Yes," she states firmly. "Where were you anyway?"

"Visiting my friend, Camila," I tell her, the guilt immediately creeping in as I lie right to her face.

"Alright, we're here. Think you two can manage to help me so I don't fuck this up?"

"You've done this dozens of times. Why are you so nervous now?" I ask as we all get out of the truck, and she grabs her bag of supplies.

"Connor made it very clear these were very close friends of his and to treat them well." She shrugs when I pop a brow at her, not buying it. "I don't want to disappoint him, okay?"

"Because you *love* him," Maize teases. "I wouldn't mind having one night with him."

"Alright, drunky, you stay in the truck," Elle orders.

"Oh c'mon, I'm fine! I just know you have a thing for your boss, and you're too chicken to tell him."

"How could you not, though? He's ridiculously sexy!" I fan my face when Elle glowers at me.

"You two are hopeless." Elle starts walking toward the barn, and Maize and I follow. "Y'all gonna get me fired."

CHAPTER THIRTEEN

Diesel

I've had a permanent smile on my face ever since I got back from San Angelo with Rowan. Being with her has been a dream come true and something I've always fantasized about but never imagined would happen. After I got home, I almost told her we needed to just tell her family. I'm tired of hiding the way I feel, and considering the way she looked at me when we last saw each other, I know she is too. Riley would get over it, and then she could move in with me. Every night and morning, I'd make sure to pleasure her in all the right ways. I'd treat her like the queen she is and prove to her I was the right choice.

"What the hell are you smiling about now?" Riley looks at me as he stuffs his face with sausage. I actually didn't realize I was cheesing so much. It's hard to hide happiness like this.

"Just thinkin' about your sister," I tease, but I'm being truthful, which is even more funny to me. If only he knew I wasn't joking this time. Rowan.

Damn, just thinking about her causes my temperature to rise as memories of this weekend cause heat to shoot through my veins.

A biscuit flies toward my head, and I quickly move out of the way only for it to swiftly hit one of the guests. Riley immediately stands and goes to her.

"I am so sorry, ma'am. I was just horseplayin' and didn't mean to hit ya," he tells her.

She smiles. "It's okay, honey. I have grandkids your age, so I understand."

A clearing of a throat comes from the doorway, and I see John looking at us incredulously. "Riley!" he snaps, curling his finger. "Come over here, boy."

I snicker and pull my phone out of my pocket to see a text from Rowan.

> **ROWAN**
> I miss sitting on your face in the mornings.

> **DIESEL**
> And I miss having you for breakfast. I mean, Maize's cooking is great, but it's nothing compared to eating you.

> **ROWAN**
> You're bad, but in a way I love, Cowboy.

> **DIESEL**
> Did you just say you love me?

I smirk, knowing it's way too early to exchange those words, but there's no other way to describe the way I've always felt about Rowan Bishop. Now that I have the chance of a lifetime with the woman my fifteen-year-old self jerked off to nearly every night in the shower, there's no way in hell I'm fucking it up.

> **DIESEL**
> I'm just kidding.

> **ROWAN**
> Shut the hell up.

DIESEL

Why don't you make me? I can think of a few ways.

Riley returns, and I tuck my phone in my pocket and stuff my mouth with food so I don't have to talk. The smirk isn't lost on him, though.

"You're a dickhead," he murmurs, keeping his head low.

"Surprised John didn't murder you back there," I tell him.

Riley glares at me. "If I wasn't family, he probably would've. Just picked up extra chores for hitting a woman with a biscuit because you don't know how to shut the fuck up."

I shrug. "And you don't know how to control your temper."

A few seconds later, Riley takes his attention from his plate and glances behind me. I turn around and see a blonde walking toward us, but I don't recognize her, so I go back to my breakfast.

"Diesel?" she asks when she gets closer, looking directly at me.

"Howdy," I greet. "Can I help you?"

I wonder if I've met her before, but she doesn't look too familiar, so I'm fairly certain I haven't.

She looks at me, then at Riley. "Is there any way we can chat in private?"

Riley shoos me away.

"Sure, no problem." Though I'm curious as to what she has to say.

Looking around, I lead her out onto the back porch because it's fairly empty. Once we're outside, she turns to me.

"I'm sorry for showing up unannounced." She hesitates as if she's waiting for a reaction.

I give her a grin and shrug. "It's no problem, ma'am. What can I help you with?"

She sucks in a deep breath, and I can tell she's nervous. I wish she'd just spit it out, though. "I wrote you a letter a couple of months back…"

It takes me a minute to comprehend what she's talking about. "Letter?"

…but I know exactly what she's referring to.

"Yeah, my name is Laurel. You didn't call me even though I left my number so you left me no choice but to come here. My sister, Chelsea, needs your help, even if she's too proud to ask for it."

I blink hard. "Chelsea?"

She nods. "Chelsea's my sister. You two hooked up in Vegas three years ago. She gave birth to your son nine months after." Laurel grabs her cell phone and swipes through her photos, then turns it around and shows me the screen.

"There he is. Just look at him. There's no doubt he's your son. I knew the moment I saw your Facebook photos that you were his daddy."

I look down at the picture of the beautiful boy who's a spitting image of me when I was that age. He has my mouth, nose, and even my green eyes. Learning I have a son that Chelsea never told me about makes me sick to my goddamn stomach.

"Why would she keep this from me?" I search Laurel's face. Her cheeks flush, and her pink lips tuck inside her mouth.

"I have no idea. Anytime I brought it up, she'd tell me to mind my own business. But now—"

"But now you're not?" I stare at her.

She shrugs, unapologetically. "Not when it comes to my nephew. I love him more than anything."

My heart races, and I don't know how to feel or what to think. I take one last look at the boy's photo, a toddler at this point, and allow the image of him to burn into my memory. Then I walk off the back of the porch.

"Where are you going?" she asks, trailing me.

"I got some thinkin' to do," I tell her without turning around. Right now, I need to be alone, but she doesn't take the hint. The only thing that stops me is her grabbing my hand and spinning me around.

"Can you at least give me your number? I want to stay in contact with you."

I study her, then swallow hard. "Tell me what you hoped to accomplish by coming here, Laurel. Chelsea obviously doesn't want me involved so what can I really do?"

She tilts her head and looks at me. "You can be a father to your son. It's your right." She digs in her purse and hands me a business card. "My cell is on there. If you change your mind about wanting more information, call or text me. I did my part. I can't make either of you do the right thing for Dawson, but I can sleep better at night knowing I told you. The ball's in your court now."

After she's finished, she turns on her heels and walks toward the B&B.

Once she's out of sight, I go to my truck, crank the engine, and mindlessly drive around.

Never would I have imagined that today I'd wake up and discover I'm a dad. This news was so unpredictable, I feel as if I'm living in an alternate universe. Of course, it'd come when Rowan and I took the next step in our relationship.

This could change everything.

The plane lands on the runway in sunny Phoenix with my heart lodged in my throat. All I can think about is how Rowan will react to me being a dad and the fact that my son lives hundreds of miles away from me. I took off work, needing some emergency vacation days, but couldn't bring myself to tell Rowan I was going out of town. How do I even explain this to her when I barely understand it myself?

Regardless, as soon as I have all the details, she'll be the first to know. While Dawson bears an uncanny resemblance to me, it's important to have proof that he's mine. Once I have that, I'll figure out my next steps.

Chelsea has no idea I'm here, and my nerves get the best of me as I'm handed the keys to a rental car. Showing up unexpectedly is not what I wanted to do, but after I spoke to Laurel two days ago, she suggested it'd be better to blindside Chelsea because she'd never agree to meet me otherwise. I'm not the type of man who gets a woman pregnant and walks out on my kid, and even though I didn't know, I can't help feeling guilty for missing Dawson's first two years of life. After seeing how much Riley's in love with his kid and how much pride he takes in being a dad, it's a dagger straight to the heart.

Considering my life was finally going in the right direction with Rowan, I feel like the universe is laughing at me. Riley always said I'd hurt his sister, and though I'd never do it intentionally, this could be what it takes to screw things up.

I feel uneasy as I drive to Chelsea's apartment. I've never felt this level of anxiety before, but it's like my mind can't stop racing, and my heart is pumping in overdrive.

I park, wondering if this is the right decision, but my mama raised me better than to be a coward. My conscience couldn't handle not stepping up, and running away from my problems isn't a way to solve them. Not to mention, if she does need help supporting my son, I want to contribute any way I can.

After a deep breath, I get out of the car and walk down the sidewalk until I see her duplex. I take the stairs two at a time, and when I get to her door, I hesitate for a moment. I can hear cartoons playing and child's laughter on the other side. Sucking in another breath, I tap on the door.

The handle jiggles, and the hard wood swings open. Our eyes meet for the first time in three years.

"Diesel," she gasps, then swallows hard. "W-what are you doing here?" she stutters, looking around until she realizes I'm alone.

"I'm askin' myself the same question," I say honestly.

Her brows furrow, but she keeps her voice in a hushed tone. "How'd you get my address?"

"Laurel found me."

"Fuck," she whisper-hisses. "I told her to stay out of this." Chelsea looks over her shoulder. "I'll be right back, sweetie," she says before stepping outside, but leaving the door cracked open.

"Look." I keep my voice as calm as I can. "She told me about Dawson. I felt it was my duty to come here and see for myself. If he's my kid, it's my right to know."

Her face softens, and she looks up at the sky, releasing a slow breath. Tears well on the rims of her eyes, and she tries to play it off, but I notice her wiping her cheeks.

"I'm sorry for showing up unannounced. Laurel has Dawson's and your best interest in mind. She cares about you, but I gotta admit, you've got a lot of explainin' to do." I pause briefly until our eyes meet. "Like why it wasn't you tellin' me."

Chelsea looks around as if she doesn't want any of her neighbors to hear us. "Would you like to come in?"

Shaking my head, I rub my palms down my jeans. This whole situation is making me sweat.

Chelsea gives me a small smile and tilts her head toward the inside of her apartment. "I think it's time you met your son, Diesel."

My mouth falls open, and I lick my dry lips. "Okay," I muster, but my emotions are going haywire, a convoluted internal mess.

She opens the door, stepping aside for me to enter. I see my son sitting on the couch with a toy tractor in his hand, watching TV. He smiles at me but has no idea who I am.

"Hi," he says in a small voice. When he grins, an overwhelming amount of joy and fear rushes through me. I'm his dad. *Holy fuck.*

"Hey," I say, then look back at Chelsea who's standing with her hands in her pocket, but she seems happy. She nods for me to move closer to him, so I do. "What kinda toy do you have there?"

"This is my favorite tractor," he says, raising it up high where I can see it better. Then he waves it proudly, giggling as he hands it to me.

I sit down next to him on the couch, angling my body toward his. "You know, I have one like this at my house. A real one. A big green John Deere."

"You do?" he asks with wide eyes.

"Yep. I have lots of tractors actually." I pause briefly, then continue, "Maybe I can show you someday?"

He smiles when I hand it back.

"Yeah!" he shouts loudly, causing Chelsea and me to laugh. "I'm thirsty."

I swallow hard, not sure how to interact with a two-and-a-half-year-old. This feels like some weird reality show, and I'm waiting for Ashton Kutcher to come out and say "You just got punk'd!" But now that I see Dawson, as scary as it sounds, a part of me wants it to be true.

Chelsea walks into the kitchen, then returns with a sippy cup of water and hands it to Dawson.

"What do you say?" She gives him a pointed look.

"Thank you, Mommy."

"You're welcome, baby." She glances at me, then lowers herself to Dawson's eye level. "My friend and I are going to talk in the other room. Can you be a good boy for me and stay here for a bit?"

"Okay, Mommy," he says, then sits back with his cup.

I stand and follow her to a small breakfast nook. It's hard not to look around her quaint home where she's raising our son. While it's small, it's clean and perfect for them.

"You want some coffee?" she asks as she pours water into the top of the maker.

"Sure, that'd be great."

Chelsea's stalling, that's more than obvious, but I'm happy for it. Once the drip is finished, she grabs two mugs from the cabinet and fills them.

"Cream?" she asks.

"Nah, I'm good."

She hands it over, then sits in front of me once she's added milk and sugar to hers.

We sigh in unison, which causes us both to let out our nervous laughter.

"I don't really know what to say." Her words break through the silence. "Except that I'm pissed off at my sister."

"Why?" I ask.

"Because it wasn't my plan to ever find you. I didn't know anything about you except that you lived in Texas. You were a complete stranger to me, and it made the most sense to keep it that way given we only hooked up once. Guys like you have handfuls of one-night stands, and it's not like it meant anything to either of us. It was purely physical, and I was being realistic with my expectations of a twenty-one-year-old."

"Realistic?" My nostrils flare at her assumptions. "You were being *selfish*, Chelsea. I have a son—who's had birthdays and celebrated holidays—and I didn't get to take part in that. I don't care what your preconceived notions about me were, didn't you think it was my right to know? What about his right to know his father?" I lean over the table, keeping my voice low so I don't alarm Dawson.

She stares down at her coffee, not making eye contact with me. I can tell she's trying to find her words, and I understand me barging into her life isn't the easiest thing to deal with. Not to mention, I'm pretty fired up now that I'm here and see he's real.

"I don't know what my reaction would've been three years ago, but I deserved a choice at least," I add. "Instead, you made it for me."

"Diesel, I'm sorry." Chelsea's eyes finally meet mine, and I see a tinge of regret. "You have to put yourself in my shoes for a minute. I'm not the type of girl who meets a guy on vacation and hooks up with him. When I got home, I went on about my life and realized I missed my period. My sister forced me to take a pregnancy test; though after being sick for a week, I had a feeling I was. When it was positive, I had an ultrasound to confirm it. I saw the little flutter on the screen, and my entire life changed." She chews her bottom lip and shrugs. "I was scared."

"And you're sure I'm the father?" I ask gently.

"I hadn't been with anyone else but you at that time. The last guy I was with was over six months before we met in Vegas. I knew for a fact it was your baby, but all I had was a stupid nickname because we didn't share personal details about ourselves. I thought about asking Zoey since I knew she ended up with Riley, but then I started second-guessing myself. I didn't know how you'd react or if you'd care, and my heart wouldn't be able to handle it if you wanted me to abort or give up the baby. I also didn't want to be forced to co-parent with a complete stranger who I knew nothing about. So instead of risking it, I didn't say anything at all. I guess at the time, being a single mom was easier than the what-ifs of telling you. You living in Texas meant sharing him would be super complicated, not to mention confusing since you'd be in and out of his life, assuming you'd even want to be in it. I know I'm rambling, but I did what I thought was best for Dawson and being shipped between states wasn't the right thing for a little kid."

I put myself in her situation and think about how we'd only hooked up that one time and didn't know each other. I really do get why she'd have concerns about telling me.

"I can understand your situation, Chelsea. It must've been hard for you to make that decision, and while I wish you'd told me sooner, I can't fault you for putting his needs first "

"I'm not saying what I did is inexcusable, but I'm relieved you know now and can accept *why* I didn't reach out. I love Dawson more than anything—more than life itself—and the thought of a stranger taking him from me was terrifying. I didn't want to be something you *had* to deal with."

Nodding, I take a sip of my coffee, happy it's cooled some. "I'd never think that, but there was no way of you knowing that. It takes two to tango, but I'd never *take* him from you. If anything, at least, Dawson deserves financial support. Laurel said you're strugglin' to make ends meet."

She groans and shakes her head. "And I hate that she told you that too. The last thing that I'd ever do is come to you for money."

"I know, but if he's mine—"

"You doubt he is?" She pops a brow. "He's your mini twin, down to your cocky attitude too." She chuckles, and I laugh with her, remembering I was quite arrogant the night we met.

"I'd still like to get a paternity test done so there's no doubt in either of our minds. That way it's a fact, and he can legally get my support and benefits.."

"Alright, then what?" she asks calmly.

"Then I'll help support Dawson and find a way to see him more. If he's my son, I'd love to form a relationship with him. It won't be easy being in two different states, but we'll come up with some sort of arrangement, even if we have to wing it. I can fly here, and you can fly there. We'll take turns."

She immediately starts shaking her head. "I can't afford that, Diesel."

"I'll take care of it." I smile genuinely. "Seems like we're both in a predicament. You don't want to leave here, and I can't leave my home either. So we'll have to make do the best we can."

A long breath escapes her. "Okay."

"My return flight is in two days. If we can get the test done before I leave, then we can move forward together and figure out the details of what to do next."

She nods, and I feel good we've found common ground, regardless if it's still shaky. We don't make small talk, but instead, I finish my coffee and then stand to leave. I thank her for the hospitality, and we exchange contact information. After her number is saved in my phone, I tell her I'll look into a testing facility and send all the details as soon as I have them.

"I'm staying in a hotel down the road, so I'm not far if you need anything…" I say when she walks me to the door.

"Thanks."

Turning, I smile at Dawson who's happily bouncing around the living room to the music playing on the TV. "Bye, Dawson. See you soon!" I wave, and my heart melts a little when he waves in return.

The next two days fly by. We go to the lab for the blood tests, have lunch and dinner, and try to get to know each other between all the craziness. My thoughts are all over the place, and I can't seem to focus past the fact that in a week I'll find out for sure if Dawson's my kid or not. Though a part of me is hoping he is because after spending time with him, I'm already wondering when I'll get to see him again.

I'm grateful for the five a.m. flight because I need to get back to work and more importantly, back to Rowan. She's texted and called, but I haven't figured out a way to tell her this yet. I'm nervous about what she'll say, but mostly what this'll mean for our relationship. No doubt she's asked Riley and he told her I had an emergency. I just hope he didn't tell her everything.

As the plane takes off, my nerves get the best of me as reality sets in that I will have a lot of explaining to do. Telling her I got a random woman I met in Vegas pregnant three years ago and it's quite possible I'm his dad. It'll take a week for the results to come in, however, after seeing Dawson in the flesh, and hearing Chelsea wasn't with anyone else, there's really no doubt. Hopefully, Rowan will understand, and she doesn't think less of me for something I did years ago. I told her that wasn't my lifestyle anymore, and I'm ready to prove that, but now I'm worried she'll think the worst.

I can't even be that surprised this happened. Riley always warned me that my party life would catch up with me someday. I haven't been that reckless since I was twenty-one, but it doesn't change anything now. Once I was promoted to oversee the cattle operation, I realized there was no room for that type of lifestyle anymore. Kicking women out of my bed at four a.m. was no fun when I had to be at work at the butt crack of dawn.

All I've wanted since discovering my feelings for Rowan weren't one-sided and that she had them too was to settle down with one woman and build a family with her someday. I just never imagined it'd be like this. It's as if the universe gave me an Uno reverse card as soon as things got serious.

Rowan deserves to be more than my best-kept secret, and I want the whole world to know we're together and that she's mine. But after she finds out the news of my new reality, she may write me off completely. I'm not sure my heart would ever be able to recover from losing Rowan Bishop, especially when there's no doubt she's my past, present, and future.

CHAPTER FOURTEEN

Rowan

I look down at my phone, turn it off, then turn it back on to make sure it's still working. After I go into my messages, I see the last one Diesel sent, which was yesterday morning. Since then, he's been eerily quiet and not responded to anything I've texted. They've all gone unanswered. Every. Single. One.

Alarm bells go off in my head, and I can't help but feel doubt creep in. My heart tells me something's wrong, but I tell myself he's probably just busy on a job. There are times when he doesn't have his cell phone on him, so I try not to overreact, especially after the amazing weekend we just had, but my thirteen-year-old insecurities are resurfacing after not hearing from him. He already thinks I'm a crazy ex-girlfriend, considering what I did to Nick's Corvette, which has proven to be a big mistake. No taking it back now, though. What's done is done.

The next morning, I still have zero text messages from Diesel. While I'm concerned something happened to him, all I can think is if I said or did something wrong. We shared an amazing night away, and now he's basically ghosted me. It's exactly what Diesel promised never to do and everything my brother said he does. Unable to lie in bed any longer, I sit up and pull my hair into a high bun. I can hear Mom chatting with someone in the kitchen. *Riley.*

I jump out of bed and rush through the hallway because if anyone knows where Diesel is, it's him. Once they're done with their conversation, and Mom briefly walks away, I glance at my brother who's looking more grown up with every passing day. Dad life is being good to him, which is nice to see.

"Hey," I say, casually. I don't know how to even start the conversation without him getting suspicious, but I go for it anyway. "I haven't seen your stupid best friend around lately. Where's he been?"

He looks at me incredulously. "Why do you care?"

I clear my throat, finding my courage. "Well, Maize needed him to help her yesterday and couldn't get in touch with him, so I texted him this morning and got no reply too. Just wondering if he's being his typical asshole self when a lady needs a hand. It wouldn't be the first time." A part of me feels guilty as hell for making up another story, but it's the most believable thing I could come up with on the spot. Also, I can't blow my cover.

Riley picks up his coffee cup and takes a sip. "He's in Arizona seeing his kid, apparently."

I glare at Riley, who laughs, but I'm almost certain I heard him wrong. "What'd you say?"

He shakes his head, grinning as if he's about to tell me a hilarious story. "It's a crazy story. Remember when I brought him to Vegas for his birthday?"

I nod, trying to keep a straight face, not wanting to react, but my temperature feels as if it's rising. "What about it?"

"He hooked up with a chick while we were there, and her sister came to the ranch the other day and told him he had a kid. Showed proof or whatever. So yesterday he went to Phoenix to figure it all out. What a total fucking shitshow!" He continues laughing. "I've been joking with him about having baby fever since Zoey got pregnant. Who would've ever thought he'd actually have his own?"

I feel sick to my goddamn stomach, and I'm actually happy I haven't had the chance to eat anything yet. Undoubtedly, it would've come up. My world feels like it's spinning out of control.

Why the fuck wouldn't Diesel tell me this? Why wouldn't he share something so personal and intimate, something that will most definitely affect our current relationship? I spilled my heart to him, and this is what he does to me?

"You okay?" Riley looks at me, and I know I've gone pale.

"Yeah, I'm perfectly fine. Also, your friend's a dumbass, so it doesn't surprise me one bit he knocked someone up. That's what he gets for sticking his dick in random pussy. Probably has a handful of other children out there too."

Riley shrugs. "That's what I said. He said he'd be back in two days. Wouldn't shock me if he marries the girl and returns with a wife and a kid. He'd consider it doing the right thing, then they'll probably have another right away."

I really wish Riley would shut the hell up. "Gross."

Mom walks back in the kitchen and looks back and forth between us. My emotions are unstable, so I take the opportunity to leave the room. "Gonna go shower," I say, not giving them a second glance.

Scalding hot water actually sounds great right about now and will give me the privacy I need. I go to the bathroom, turn on the shower, and step inside after I undress. The streams pound against my skin as the tears roll down my cheeks. I lean against the wall, pissed at myself for falling so quick and hard.

Is that why Diesel didn't tell me? Does he plan to come back with a wife, but more importantly, what does this mean for us? Our future? I let out a ragged sob, realizing that maybe we never had one to begin with. My broken heart almost felt whole, but now it's shattering all over again.

I knew something wasn't right when he didn't answer my texts yesterday or send me one before he went to work this morning. In the end, I guess he got what he wanted, another mark on his bedpost with my name all over it. He's officially at the top of my shit list, right above Nick.

Two days have passed since my world turned upside down, and I know Diesel's supposed to return today. He still hasn't responded to me, and I refuse to be the fool who reaches out again. I'm hurt that he didn't feel like he could tell me what was going on in his life and left me hanging. Diesel's lost my trust, and I'm not sure he'll ever be able to get it back.

I go to work, and Kenzie immediately notices I'm in a bad mood.

"Oh shit," she mumbles when I knock over a full bottle of beer, and it spills everywhere. George isn't upset and laughs it off, but I soaked him.

"I'm so sorry," I tell him. "I'm not myself today."

"It's okay, honey. Just get me another one quick." He throws me a wink, and I do and don't even charge him for the next one either. It's the least I can do, considering his crotch will be wet for the next few hours.

"You okay?" Kenzie asks me when I walk into the office. "You've been acting weird for the past few days." She looks at me concerned.

"Yeah, just a lot going through my head right now. Nick wants his money for the damage I did to his car. Like now. And I'm just not feeling like myself today."

"I've heard Mercury's in retrograde." She laughs and glances down at the mood ring I've kept on my finger since Diesel gave it back to me.

I take it off and tuck it in my pocket. I'm pretty sure it's broken anyway, considering it's been stuck on the "in love" color for weeks. Or maybe I'm broken.

For the rest of my shift, I try to keep myself busy and clean every single nook and cranny I can while Kenzie works the bar top. Wednesdays are typically a slow night, but thankfully, the time passes by quickly.

After all the customers pay their tabs, Kenzie mops and wipes everything down as I finish counting the money and closing the drawers. "How'd you do tonight?" I ask her.

"Okay. Fifty bucks is better than zero because that's what I walked in with." She gives me a smile. "Becoming a stripper seems like a better gig every single day."

"Your parents would murder you, and Grandma Bishop would turn your body into a rug."

She chuckles, then shrugs. "Oh well. I'd be walking out with thousands right now."

Now I'm laughing. "No, you wouldn't. The guys around here are cheap. But becoming a nun seems like a real possibility these days, plus no bills. So there's that."

"Do you think nuns masturbate?" She's grinning so wide, I can't help the burst of laughter that escapes from me. She's definitely put me in a better mood without even trying.

"Oh my God. I have no idea. Probably not. But then again, maybe?"

I grab the deposit bag, lock up, and we walk outside together. She follows me to the bank drop, and then we go our separate ways. On the whole drive home, all I can think about is Diesel and how it's been radio silence between us. He has to know I'm concerned by my messages, and still, he doesn't respond or give me reassurance on anything.

Bastard.

I pull into the driveway, then get out of my car. As I'm walking to the front door, a dark shadow comes toward me, and I immediately open my mouth to scream, but he comes into view as I retreat a step.

"I'm sorry, Rowan. I didn't mean to scare you," Diesel says softly, coming closer.

With all the pent-up frustration and anger from the past seventy-two hours, I close the gap between us and push him. He's a marble statue compared to me and barely budges.

"I'm sorry," he whispers, defeated.

"You're sorry for a lot of fucking things, aren't you?" I glare at him, and he tilts his head, almost as if he's confused. "Riley told me, dumbass."

I'm brought back to eighth grade again when he denied me, but this is that on crack. Right now, I just want to go inside, shower off the night, and go to bed. I need to forget about him, about us, though I have a feeling it won't be so easy.

"Can we talk at least?" he asks.

"Oh..." I sarcastically laugh. "Now you want to talk after blowing me off for two days? Wow, how convenient for you. Hmm, let me think about it. No." I walk around him, but he grabs my hand, pulling me back toward him. His warmth sends swarms of butterflies through my body. My head's saying no, but my body's saying yes. I have to be strong, though. There's no excuse for him ignoring me, regardless of the situation. I'd never do that to him, especially after the intimate moments and open conversations we've shared.

"Please, Row…" He drops down on his knees and begs.

I frown at his pitiful expression. "You do realize that if my dad comes out here, you're gonna be a dead man, right?"

"It's worth the risk to explain myself to you."

I let out a sigh. "You've got ten minutes of my time, then that's it. I'm leaving."

He looks around, the porch light casting a warm glow on his face. Diesel stands, and I take a step back before he grabs my hand and leads me down one of the trails behind my parents' house.

In the distance, there's a clearing where a four-wheeler is parked. No wonder I didn't see his truck. The moonlight splashes shadows on the ground, and the warm summer breeze brushes against my cheeks. I try to keep my attention from him and look up at the moon.

"Rowan," he whispers. "I have a lot to tell you."

"You better get to talkin' because your time is running out," I snap, finally gazing into his eyes, seeing the hurt and frustration in them. "Riley told me you got one of your random Vegas hookups pregnant. So how about we start from there?"

He nods. "Her name is Chelsea. Her sister, Laurel, wrote me a letter saying I had a son, but I ignored it and brushed it off as a joke."

My eyes widen with shock.

"I know, I know. I should've reached out to her, but I didn't. Not much I can do about that now. Anyway, Laurel showed up at the ranch a few days ago and explained her sister had a baby, and is certain it's mine. She's struggling financially to raise him, but thought I deserved to know I have a son."

I watch him fidget with the hem of his shirt. "Okay, then what?"

"I got her address and flew to Phoenix to figure it all out. It didn't seem like a conversation to have over the phone, especially if she didn't want me knowing in the first place."

"And? How'd that go?" My heart hammers in my chest.

"She wasn't happy to see me at first and was annoyed that Laurel reached out to me, but she came around to the idea of knowing. I told her I wanted to take responsibility if he was mine, so I took a paternity test while I was there. The results won't be back for a week, so I won't know for sure, but he's the spitting image of me."

Diesel's words gut me. As crazy as it sounds, a part of me wanted to be the only woman who gave him a child. I've thought about what it would be like to start a family with him. How many kids we'd have. How me and Riley's children would grow up together. It's almost as if I'm mourning my fantasy, something I thought about once I realized my feelings for him. Those dreams feel demolished now.

I nod, trying to keep my emotions from spilling out. If it's his son, I don't want to be negative about it and make him choose between a new relationship and being a dad. "Maybe it's better that it happened this way, you know? Maybe we were never meant to last, and it was another shitty way for me to learn that I shouldn't trust men and the empty promises they give me. Or maybe it's the whole better to have loved and lost than to have never loved at all kind of situation. Either way, you have a child and a family to take care of now, Diesel. I think it's best if you focus on that right now instead of us."

Diesel grimaces and shakes his head, actually looking hurt and surprised by my words. "Are you serious, Rowan? You're just gonna walk away?"

"Why wouldn't I be?" I glare at him. "You have a family to focus on now. There's no point in starting something new when you have unfinished business to take care of." I'm so hurt that nothing he could say right now could mend my heart.

"A *family*? I have a kid, not a wife. I don't want Chelsea. You know who I want? Who I've always fucking wanted? You, Rowan. *You.* You're the woman I dream about every single night and have since I was a teenager. I just finally got you, and there's no way I'm going to allow this to wreck what we have. I'm not giving up on you or us. I won't."

I cross my arms over my chest, retreating a step. While I appreciate his effort, it's not enough right now. "I'm not getting in the middle of this, Diesel. You need to be there for your son. You need to build a bond with him because you haven't been in his life. And who knows, maybe once you and Chelsea are around each other, sparks will fly again. There must've been an attraction between you, or you would've never fucked her in Vegas. I'm not stupid, okay? Y'all connected enough to make a baby, so you need to focus on getting to know the mother of your child and co-parenting. Trust me when I say I'll only get in the way, and I don't want to live with that." The tears build, but I push them away. I will not allow him to see how much this actually pains me. I can't.

"I can do both, Row. I can be a father, and I can be with you." He inches closer. "Please, let me prove it to you."

I tighten my jaw, wishing he would allow me to just walk away. I knew it wouldn't be easy, but he's making this much harder than it should be. I know I'm doing the right thing, even if it's breaking me in the process, and he doesn't agree.

"I'm not sure about that. You never replied back to my messages, Diesel. You ignored me for nearly three days after the most amazing night we had together. That meant something to me, and then you basically ghosted me. If it hadn't been for my brother telling me, I would've thought something horrible happened to you. It made me feel like I was just another hookup, and it meant nothing to you. For hours, I racked my brain on what went wrong, but all along, it was you being selfish. I poured my heart out to you, which you know wasn't easy for me, yet you still didn't feel the need to tell me what was going on. The moment I found out the truth, from someone who wasn't you, is the moment *you* walked away. And that's okay. I'll be just fine, and so will you."

"I should've told you," he says. "For that, I'm so goddamn sorry. I was so scared this would ruin us, and it looks like I fucked it up anyway." He lifts his hat, runs his fingers through his hair, then sets it back on. "I'll spend the rest of my life making it up to you. What can I do to fix this?"

Blinking, I stare at his lips, then back to his green eyes. "At this point? Nothing." My mind's made up. "If he's your son, you'll be talking to her all the time, and what if you start seeing her differently or she starts having feelings for you? I'd constantly feel like I'm getting in the way of you being with your son and you two being a family. Then we all risk getting hurt, and I won't be the other woman in this scenario. I'm sorry, Adam." I turn and begin walking down the trail.

"Row," I hear him say, but I don't stop. "Rowan, please give me another chance." I keep moving forward, knowing I can't turn around because I may not be strong enough to deny his pleas. This is the right thing to do with what's going on in his life. Leaving him before he can leave me is what has to happen because deep down, it feels inevitable.

As I continue putting one foot in front of the other, tears begin to fall in streams. A week ago, I would've never imagined I'd be breaking it off with him, but here we are. From now on, I'll guard my heart with everything I am and not trust men so easily. Not even those who I've known nearly all my life.

CHAPTER FIFTEEN

Diesel

I t's been one week since the paternity test, and the results come right on time. I call Chelsea when I receive them to let her know. Dawson's mine, but after seeing him in the flesh, there were no doubts. He's a mini version of me, down to his eye color. When she gets off work later in the day, she calls me back.

"I was thinking that maybe you and Dawson could come out and visit the ranch soon," I suggest.

There's silence on the other line.

"Ya there?" I ask.

There's hesitation in her voice. "Yeah, I just don't know if that's a good idea."

"Chelsea, it's really important to me. I want him to know my roots, where I grew up, what I do for a living. Who knows, he might enjoy the ranch life much better than the city life anyway."

"No," she snaps. "See, this is what I was afraid of, that you'd expect me to uproot my entire life and move away from my family to Texas. Maybe this—"

"Hey. I'm not asking you to move here. I just want you to visit for the weekend. I have a spare bedroom you two can stay in. I'll show you around the ranch and introduce you to my family and friends. I haven't told my parents yet, but I know they're gonna be super excited to know they're grandparents. They'll want to spoil him rotten."

She lets out a ragged breath. "Okay, but we can really only come for a weekend. I'll have to fly out late Friday afternoon after I get off work and leave Sunday. I don't have many vacation days left."

"I understand. Let me know the details, and I'll be happy to book it for you. And Chelsea?"

"Yeah?"

"Thanks for giving me a chance to be his father," I tell her.

"You're welcome. Thank you for wanting to be. He deserves a good man in his life."

"I know you're concerned about it and probably think me finding out is a mistake, but I'm gonna do the best I can. I really don't know how to be a parent, but I want my son to know me, and my life, and where he comes from. The last thing I want is for Dawson to grow up thinking he has a deadbeat dad who didn't want him." Because I most definitely do.

"I don't think it was a mistake. But it's still new for all of us, and I was blindsided by you just showing up. While I want Dawson to get to know you, I need to as well. There's so much that's in the dark right now. You're a stranger to me, Diesel. We had sex three years ago and haven't spoken or seen each other since. I don't even remember what we talked about beforehand."

I laugh. "So you're saying it wasn't monumental?"

She snorts. "Oh my God. Men. I'll look up the flights and let you know."

"Sounds good," I tell her. We say our goodbyes, and I end the call, then stare up at the ceiling of the kitchen. My life is a goddamn mess.

Instead of staying home, I decide to go to the B&B and see what Maize cooked for dinner. I'm starving, and her food is the best in all of Eldorado. Well, after Grandma Bishop's.

When I walk in, I spot Rowan who looks at me and immediately turns. She's still being distant and pretending I don't exist. If it weren't such a serious matter, I'd say it's cute, but I know better. I hurt her, and just as I promised, I'll spend the rest of my life trying to make it up to her, as long as she doesn't move on before I can.

The night we had together in San Angelo was unforgettable. Being with her in such an intimate way was everything I ever dreamed it would be and more, then in a snap, it was ruined. I should've told her what was going on as soon as I found out, but I didn't know where to begin. Would it have changed anything? I'm not so sure. Rowan acted like she was a homewrecker or something, which is insane because I don't even know Chelsea or want her. Rowan's the only woman I've ever wanted, and now she's slipped through my fingers.

"Hey," I say, looking at Maize, then glancing at Rowan.

"What're you doing here?" Maize asks with judgment in her eyes.

"Thought I'd stop and grab some dinner," I say truthfully.

Rowan continues on as if I'm invisible and speaks directly to Maize. "Well, I gotta go to work. I'll see you tomorrow." She walks away, and I can smell the hint of her shampoo as she leaves.

I try to act as if I'm not gutted, but it's hard as hell. I don't know what to say or do. No one besides Wyatt knew we were together, and if I acted any other way, they'd all become overly suspicious.

Maize glares at me as she tucks loose strands of hair behind her ear. Flour is on the sleeves of her shirt, and she looks like she's had a rough day. "Don't you know how to cook?"

"Grandma B told me I could help myself anytime I wanted. Should I call her and ask?" I taunt. Maize knows her grandma gave an open invitation to all of the workers on the ranch.

She groans and walks away, mumbling something under her breath. I grab a plate, fill it full of beef tips, rice, and brown gravy, then I stack a roll on top of my delicious pile and find a seat. Riley walks in and looks at me. I tell him hey, but my mouth is full, and it comes out garbled.

He sits and glares at me. "You know why my sister's pissed all the time?"

I nod and swallow. "Maybe she's on her period?"

"Dude." He groans, but his eyes don't leave mine. It's more than obvious he's suspicious. "You sure you don't know?"

"Yeah, I'm sure. Why?" I press, taking a huge bite of meat.

"Last week, I told her where you were, that you had a kid and all of that, and she's been moody and strange ever since. I started piecing some things together." He leans forward. "Diesel, I swear to fucking God if you messed with my sister, I will chop off your dick and shove it down your throat."

"Jesus…" I say, not having the words to be able to deny it. "Why the hell are you threatenin' my junk?"

He narrows his gaze at me, looking as though he's ready to murder me and hide my body. "I'm serious. She was upset and distant. She's been so freaking odd since you got back, and I have a feeling the common denominator here is you. If I find out you touched her, I will kick your ass to San Antonio and back. I'm not even kidding."

"Riley. You need to chill out. Geez. First of all, Rowan is a grown ass woman who doesn't need you making rules for her. Second, I don't know what's going through her head right now. I try to talk to her, and she ignores me, but then again, what else is new?" I leave out the part where I've texted her every single day since our chat on the trail, and she's ignored all of them. Nothing can shake her stance on this, but I'm determined to break her down. I've done it once, and I know I can do it again. Rowan's gonna have to try a lot harder to keep me away because I'm not giving up on her or *us*, ever. What we have is real, and we both know it.

He glares at me just as his uncle Jackson walks through the back door, causing a much-needed distraction from this conversation. "What're you boys doin'?"

"Eatin'," I say, but that much is obvious as I stuff another spoonful into my mouth.

"Don't tell Maize, but I came to get a few slices of apple pie. Mama told me she baked a few for the guests tonight, and I haven't been able to stop thinkin' about it." He grins, walks over to the buffet, and grabs an *entire* pan, not just a few pieces like he said. When he turns around, Maize is standing there with her hands on her hips and nostrils flared. She's actually pretty damn scary when she's in a mood.

"What do you think you're doing, Uncle Jackson?"

I snort, but she's seriously pissed.

"That's no way to speak to your most favorite uncle now, is it?" He gives her a wink, then walks past her and leaves.

Maize's mouth falls open, then she turns and looks at us. "This—all of this—is for the guests. I don't need y'all eatin' everything when we have a full house. I'm gonna have to start making double."

Riley snickers. "I don't know why you haven't done that already. Nothing's changed, Maze."

"Shut. Up," she barks, then storms into the kitchen.

"I'm telling you, they're all experiencing the time of month at the same time," I quip, and Riley shakes his head before standing.

"Guess I should get going. Honestly, I came to get one of those apple pies too." He walks over and grabs one, leaving only one for the guests. Maize comes around the corner, and Riley takes off running with her right behind him. I can hear commotion through the living room, and eventually, she comes back huffing and puffing.

"At least I'm not *that* bad," I tell her as she walks by.

"I'd murder you if you were. I deal with them because I have to," she says matter-of-factly before disappearing out of sight.

I chuckle, finish eating, and set my perfectly cleaned plate in the dish tub before leaving. On my way out to the truck, I decide to go home, take a shower, and go to bed early. I have a ton of shit to do at work tomorrow, and though it's hard, I'm trying to give Rowan some space.

The next day, I'm in the saddle all day long rounding up cattle and moving them to another pasture. It might be late August, but it's still hot as hell outside. The temperature isn't expected to drop for a few more months, but we're prepping for winter already. Barns are full of hay, and I've made sure to get extra grain for the cows for when the grass completely dies. Today, Riley didn't ride my ass or even mention his sister, so I'm hoping the conversation we had yesterday eased his mind. Though I didn't completely lie to him, it wasn't the whole truth, which I hate, but he can't find out yet.

While I don't want Rowan and me to stay a secret, if she refuses to give me another chance, that might be how it goes. Though it'll be extremely hard for me to accept.

After work, I go home to clean up, then head up to the bar. Rowan may not want to see me, but it's killing me not to see her. Even if she gives me shit or ignores me, it's better than nothing at all. I put on the baseball cap I know she loves, spray some cologne I also know she loves, and dress in a T-shirt, jeans, and boots.

As I pull into the parking lot, the thought of seeing her has my heart hammering in my chest. I wish things weren't like this, and we could go back to the way we were, but it feels impossible now. My life has changed indefinitely, and all I can do is take it one day at a time.

When I walk in, she's smiling and talking to George, and that pretty grin immediately fades when she sees me.

"Well, hello to you too, beautiful," I say, sitting at the end of the bar.

Kenzie walks up, wearing a cheesy grin. "Hey, stranger. Where ya been?"

I lift an eyebrow at her. "What's up with the act?"

She leans closer. "Rowan said she doesn't want to talk to you, so I'll be helping you tonight."

"Seriously?" I can tell Kenzie has this all figured out, but she doesn't say anything. Damn, maybe we're more transparent than either one of us thought. "Rowan!" I yell across the bar. "Hey!" I wave, making a scene.

"Go away, Diesel," she says before turning around and going to the office. I let out a huff.

"Told ya," Kenzie gloats. "Want your usual?"

"I guess." Within a few seconds, she pops the cap off a Bud and sets it in front of me. I try to pay attention to the preseason football game on the TV screen, but it's so hard to focus when the woman I'm in love with is dead set on erasing our existence together. I order another beer and wait around until closing time. Rowan peeks around to see if I'm still at the end of the bar and rolls her eyes when I smile at her. I feel as if we're back to square one, right where we were when she moved home in May. There's no way she could so easily forget everything we shared together. I refuse to accept that one bit.

Kenzie finishes cleaning, and I close out my tab, tipping her nicely for putting up with me all night. She tells Rowan she's leaving and smiles before walking out. Rowan comes from the office and looks at me.

"You need to leave," she says, and I can tell she's not playing around.

"No can do. You'll be here alone." I just look at her, taking the final sip of my beer. "Are you gonna ignore me for the rest of my life?"

"That's the plan," she snaps.

"Row," I whisper.

"*Don't* call me that."

I stand and walk around the bar until I'm mere inches from her. Resting my hands on her shoulders, I stare into her beautiful brown eyes. She tucks her bottom lip into her mouth, and I want nothing more than to pluck it from her teeth.

"I've missed you so fucking much," I tell her, gently lifting her chin. "I can't stop thinking about you."

She lets out a ragged breath, and it causes my heart to race. Without hesitation, I lean forward and gently slide my lips against hers. Instead of fighting it like I thought she would, or pulling away, she sinks into me. Our tongues twist as the kiss deepens, and I feel as if the world has tilted on its axis.

Rowan grabs the hem of my T-shirt, and we're so goddamn ravenous for one another, by the time she pulls away, we're breathless. She places her fingers on her swollen lips, and I swallow as I move loose strands of hair from her face. "I know you're scared, and you think walkin' away from me is the right thing to do, but it feels so fucking wrong."

"Diesel…"

"I'm not letting you go without a fight, Row. Never."

It's been a few days since I kissed Rowan at the bar, but it was all the encouragement I needed to know that not all is lost. She kissed me back without a fight, which means I still have a chance with her.

After work, I send her a text, telling her I'm coming to the bar, and she sends me a thumbs-up emoji in response. Not quite the attention I was aiming for, but it's better than her ignoring me completely.

She's started responding and has been supportive for the most part, though she's still guarded.

I walk in, and she tries to hold back a smile. There's hardly anyone at the bar tonight because it's been raining all day. Honestly, I'd swim here if it meant getting to see Rowan. Kenzie's no longer in town because she went back to college to finish her last year, but things typically slow down when school starts anyway.

Rowan sets a beer down in front of me, then looks past me out the large front windows where the rain is pounding against the glass.

"It's still raining?"

"Yep, not supposed to stop until the morning," I tell her, taking a swig. I place my hand on top of hers and gently brush my thumb against the softness of her skin.

"I was thinking maybe we should tell everyone we're together." I'm being dead serious, and she knows it.

Rowan hesitates. "It's a bad idea."

"It's the *best* idea," I quickly say.

She nervously shifts on her feet because I've put her on the spot. "Diesel. I need more time. I'm sorry. I can't just jump into bed with you again because you kissed me."

"You mean, just because I took your breath away?" I smirk.

She rolls her eyes. "I can't. Not right now. You need to get adjusted to everything that's going on in your life. Learn to be a dad. Then if there's still room in your heart for me, we can talk about it."

I tilt my head, grab her hand, and press it against my chest. "My whole heart is yours, Rowan Bishop. It always has been and always will be. I want the whole fucking world to know you're mine and only mine, regardless of everything else going on in my life."

A blush hits her cheeks before she moves away from me. I am relentless and will always be when it comes to her. I stay the entire shift and help her clean up before we walk out. On the way out, I tell her about Chelsea and Dawson coming to visit, and she gives me a small smile. I want to kiss her goodbye, but I'm hesitant to cross that line again. I'd wait an eternity for her if that's what she wanted.

That night, I go to sleep with a smile on my face, hoping she truly understands what she means to me.

The next morning, I get to work early. Riley calls me out on the way I'm acting, and he thinks it's because I'm picking up Chelsea and Dawson from the airport this afternoon. Little does he know it's because his sister makes me the happiest fucking man on the planet. But I am also very excited about showing off my son.

I asked Chelsea what kind of car seat I needed to buy because I'm seriously bad at this parenting thing. There are too many choices, and I had no clue where to start, but she happily guided me. Knowing they were coming, I tried to do as many of the repairs to the house as I could to childproof the place better. The spare room is ready for them with clean sheets and freshly painted walls. I've worked hard to get it all together, and I hope she appreciates it. I want her to trust me so she thinks I'm suitable enough to be Dawson's dad. Even though I have proof he's mine, I'd never fight her for custody, knowing what she's done to support him on her own. I can only hope one day we'll be able to co-parent properly and both have time with him.

On the way to the airport, my nerves get the best of me. Chelsea's right; we're practically strangers, so introducing her and Dawson to my parents will undoubtedly be awkward. Last night, I told them about how I met Chelsea and her getting pregnant. I gave them all the details, and at first, they were upset she didn't tell me, but I explained why Chelsea felt that way. I do wish she would've told me as soon as she knew, but there's no point in being mad about the past. What's done is done, so all I can do is try to make up for the lost time.

When I arrive, I wait for ten minutes before I see her and my son. As soon as Dawson sees me, he smiles, which makes me do the same as I grab all of their bags. He's such a cute kid and well mannered, even for a two-and-a-half-year-old. I just hope he's nothing like I was as a teenager, or we'll both have our hands full. I gave my parents a run for their money, and they always said I'd have a payback kid who did the same to me. Hopefully, Dawson isn't it, but he does have his dad's good looks, so I'm not holding my breath.

Once we get to my truck, Chelsea shows me how to buckle him into the car seat.

"Dawson?" She looks at him. "Do you know who this man is?"

"Mommy's friend, Diesel." He grins proudly.

"Yes, baby, but remember when I said he was someone very special? He's your daddy," she explains.

Dawson blinks up at me, then giggles. "Nuh-uh." I chuckle at his expression.

The amount of happiness I feel is unfathomable. I didn't expect for her to tell him right then, but I'm glad she did so I could be here for it. "Yep, it's true. What do you think about that?"

All he does is laugh about it, which makes us both chuckle too.

After he's buckled in with his toy tractor in his hand, Chelsea and I climb in the truck. We head back to the ranch, and I explain some of the details of the area to her. The sun is barely setting over the horizon, and the sky has long whips of purple and pink. It doesn't take long before Dawson is happily asleep. I can't stop glancing at him in the rearview mirror, feeling overwhelmingly protective of him. I'm still in shock he's really mine.

When we make it to my cabin, Chelsea gets out and gently carries Dawson as I grab their luggage. I unlock the door and usher her inside. Chelsea looks around with a smile on her face. "Wow. This is not what I expected at all."

"You like it?" I ask. "It's not completely finished. I still have a lot to do, but I've been remodeling here and there on my days off."

There's a sparkle in her eye as she follows me to the spare bedroom. "It's really homey. I like the colors."

"Thanks." I set their bags down. "If you need anything, please let me know. The bed and breakfast is just down the road if you want a home-cooked meal, and I can borrow extra blankets if needed."

She sets Dawson on the bed, and he doesn't even stir. "I think everything is perfect. Really."

"Great. You hungry?" I ask.

"Nah, I ate before the flight. Just want a shower and to probably go to bed. I think the time change is going to catch up with me."

I nod and show her where the bathroom is and give her a mini tour of the place. When she goes to take a shower, I sit in the rocking chair I put in the corner of the spare bedroom and watch Dawson sleeping peacefully. My heart swells watching him, and I already don't know how I'm going to continue without getting to see him. I just hope everyone falls in love with him as quickly as I have, especially Rowan, because I know she's gonna be in both of our lives forever. Even if she's not convinced at the moment, she will be.

CHAPTER SIXTEEN

Rowan

I t's insane to think that Diesel has a son. He asked everyone to meet at the B&B so he could introduce the group of us to Chelsea and Dawson. I'm nothing but a ball of nerves, and I thought about not going. Seeing the woman he had a one-night stand with isn't really on my to-do list, but it's important to him, so I suck it up and push my feelings to the side.

"You coming?" my mother asks as she peeks into my room.

I shrug. "Do I really have to?" I'm only half-joking.

"Rowan, you better get in that car. You know Adam is a part of the family, and we have to be supportive of him."

"Fine," I say between gritted teeth. "But I don't wanna go."

She gives me a stern look, and I know better than to cross her, so I get up and follow her to the car. I hate the unknown of what it's going to be like, seeing him with his son and Chelsea or how seeing them around each other will feel like. What if they're flirty? Or worse, what if they look really good together? I don't want my jealousy to get in the way, though it undoubtedly will. The five-minute drive to the B&B has my stomach in knots, but I play it off as if I'm bored as hell instead.

I get out of the car, make my way up the steps, and walk inside to see Diesel holding a toddler who looks just like him. My mouth falls open, and my heart instantly swells when I see him. He hasn't noticed me yet because my uncles and aunts have his full attention.

Riley walks in behind me as Mom rushes forward.

"Isn't this some crazy shit?" He nudges me.

"Uh, yeah. Can't believe he reproduced."

"Reproduced or that someone actually slept with him?" Riley jokes, but I'm not laughing because at that moment I see her. *Chelsea*. And she's pretty. Blond with a perfect smile and bright blue eyes. There's a softness to her, and I see what Diesel saw, even if it was a random hookup. Immediately, a pang of envy and guilt rushes through me.

I watch the way they interact, and it's friendly, not crossing any lines beyond friendship. She says something, and he laughs as his little boy shows everyone his toy tractor. Grandma Bishop's tickled to death over him, and it's only going to get her started on wanting more great-grandkids. *Great.*

Mom waves Riley and me forward, and for the first time all day, Diesel sees me. He swallows, and it feels as if all the air in the room escapes, and I can't breathe.

"Rowan," he says, knowing my entire family is around and watching. So is his baby mama. "Come and meet Mr. Dawson."

I follow and tilt my head at one of the cutest little boys I've ever seen. "Hi, Dawson," I say, and he hides his face in Diesel's shoulder.

"Pretty ladies make him shy."

I shake my head and roll my eyes at him even though my heart's actually bursting. Seeing him being all fatherly is actually pretty sexy, but then I turn my head and notice Chelsea staring at our interaction.

"Oh hi," I say. "I'm Rowan." I hold out my hand and shake hers.

"Nice to meet you." She's polite and grins. I can only imagine how awkward this is for her to be around so many strangers, and I really try to imagine myself in her place.

I get out of the way and let my mom and dad visit. Not wanting to draw any attention to myself, I sit on the couch on the other side of the room and listen to everyone talk.

"Was your mama excited to meet him?" Grandma asks Diesel.

He laughs. "Oh, of course. She's been on me like white on rice to give her some grandchildren. Little did any of us know, I already had." He's making jokes, and I hear my parents' laughter because it's actually not too different from their story. My mouth goes dry because my parents are still insanely in love with each other.

It literally feels like it's one hundred degrees in here, so I get up and step outside, needing the fresh air before I suffocate. Right now, I feel like the other woman, the mistress who has to hide her relationship.

My mom told us she and Dad had to really get to know each other after finding out she was pregnant with Riley even though they knew immediately when they met in Key West that they had an undeniable connection. Is this the same? Is it only a matter of time before Diesel and Chelsea's spark reignites and those old feelings are brought back to the surface? It's not out of the realm of possibilities regardless of what Diesel says. He hasn't spent enough time with her to know and surely hasn't given it a chance.

I lean against the railing of the front porch and look out at the bright blue sky and fluffy cotton-looking clouds.

My phone vibrates in my pocket, and I see it's a text from Trace. We had planned a few months ago to get together and our schedules never really synced. I appreciate how he's not so pushy and gives me my space. Then again, I do like a pushy man. Diesel's a prime example of that.

TRACE

Hey you! You got plans this weekend?

I laugh and shake my head. Is this the way it's supposed to be? I look up at the sky again, waiting for some sort of sign, but I'm given nothing. Maybe I'm supposed to be with Trace, and Diesel's supposed to be with Chelsea, or maybe I've quite possibly completely lost my mind over all of this.

Maize comes outside, looking at me incredulously. "You good?"

She's suspected something has been going on between Diesel and me for a while but hasn't asked about it.

"Why wouldn't I be?"

673

She shrugs and doesn't push the conversation, thankfully.

"I need to get ready for work tonight, so Mom needs to stop gabbing and take me home."

"Good luck with that," Maize says, and before walking back inside, she stops. "You know you can tell me anything. I won't judge you or say a peep."

I search her face, and my expression softens. "I know. Thanks."

"I've noticed how different you've been. I saw you leaving the barn with Diesel, and I can't deny how things changed between you two. You're one of my very best friends, Rowan. I know you inside and out."

I let out a ragged breath, not wanting to completely crumple, but I don't feel like I can hold it in anymore. "I'm in love with him. Stupidly in love with him. And now he has a kid and might as well have a wife. They already look like the perfect little family."

She searches my face but doesn't seem shocked. "Does he know this? Have you told him?"

"I mean, sorta. Not in those exact words, but he knows I have feelings for him. We were sneaking around before the news broke about Dawson and Chelsea," I admit.

Maize sighs and frowns. "He's been in love with you since the beginning of time, Rowan. Everyone knows this. Even Riley as much as he wants to deny it. I'm actually relieved you have finally pulled the blinders back and see what's been right in front of you for so damn long." She smiles.

I'm shocked. Speechless, actually. I open my mouth and close it, which causes Maize to laugh.

"All those years, he threatened every guy to stay away from you, and you never noticed he wasn't interested in anyone else. He's been waiting for *you* for years," Maize tells me.

I adjust my ponytail. "I don't know what to do, Maze. I have no idea. I feel completely lost even though he's spilled his heart to me and told me how he feels. He wants us to be together forever and already talks about what our future will be. "

She places her hand on my back. "Then what the hell are you waiting for? Sounds like everything you've ever wanted."

I shrug and laugh as a tear falls down my cheek. "A sign?"

"If you're looking for a sign, you found it. Here it is." She places her palm over my racing heart. "You need to go for it so you don't look back years from now and regret not being with a man who will treat you like the queen you are and worship the ground you walk on. Hell, he already does that," Maize says matter-of-factly. "I'm actually quite jealous." She smirks.

Before I can respond, my mother opens the door and steps outside. "Ready?"

"Yep, sure am." I wipe my face and tuck my emotions back inside.

Maize gives me a big hug and whispers in my ear, "Follow your instincts. They'll always lead you to where you're supposed to go."

I pull away from her and smile appreciatively. "I love you."

"I am your favorite cousin for a reason, you know." She snickers, then walks inside.

Mom and I get into the car, then she drives us home. "Apparently, Maize is making homemade blueberry pies tonight. You should ask her to make an extra one for you and bring it home for me and your dad," Mom suggests with a wink.

"Nope. I'm not gonna make her head explode. You'll have to ask her yourself," I tell her as we park in the driveway. I get out and walk to my room, then send Diesel a text.

ROWAN

Your kid is the cutest. He must take after his dad.

I don't expect him to reply immediately because he's currently being Bishop bombarded, but I know he will later. I change into something more comfortable and get ready for my shift tonight with a totally different outlook on this situation. Maybe I should've opened up to Maize much sooner instead of keeping it a secret. Or maybe I had to realize how much Diesel really meant to me before I could accept that we really have a future together. Either way, I'm looking forward to telling him exactly how I feel and apologizing for ever doubting him. Then again, that's what a broken heart will do to a woman.

The next morning when I wake up, I smile at the text Diesel sent me late last night.

DIESEL

I knew you thought I was cute. Just imagine what our kids will look like :)

With a smile on my face, I climb out of bed and get dressed. I know Chelsea's leaving today because yesterday before I walked out, I overheard someone ask her when she was headed back to Phoenix.

After speaking with Maize yesterday, the conversation has been on my mind. For most of my life, one of my hobbies was ignoring Diesel and all his glory, regardless of how much he encouraged me to give him attention. I realize now what I've been missing. I have to give it to him for never giving up on me.

Excitement and nerves fill me as I pull my hair into a high ponytail. I need to talk to him right now and let him know how I feel. If he wants to be with me, and I want to be with him, then I don't give two shits what anyone thinks or says about it. If Riley knows what's good for him, he'll keep his opinions to himself. I'm a grown ass woman who's more than capable of choosing who I want to date, even if it is his best friend. If what Diesel says is true, then he deserves a second chance to prove he won't break my heart.

The smile that's planted on my face nearly hurts as I drive over to Diesel's house. All the memories from the last time I was here begin to surface. The way he roughly said my name as he kissed me causes goose bumps to trail up my arm. Damn. How could I be so blind?

I park behind his truck and walk up the steps to his house. He's done an amazing job with the place, and I think about all the future plans we made together. I lightly tap on the door, not wanting to disturb his guests because it's still early in the morning. I wait, but he doesn't answer.

My heart is like a ticking time bomb in my chest as I knock again, but still nothing. I go to the front window and peek inside and that's when the blood rushes from my face.

Diesel's sitting at a barstool in the kitchen, and Chelsea is between his legs, nearly ready to climb on his lap. He's saying something to her with his hands firmly wrapped around her waist. I nearly choke on my thoughts, on my words, and feel like the biggest idiot in the entire world for believing that nothing was between them. Not able to keep watching, I turn and rush to my car, then back out of the driveway. I know I can't go home like this. Tears stream like a river down my face, and I'm so damn mad at myself for believing him.

I drive around for twenty minutes in an effort to calm down, needing to push the thoughts of him and her together out of my head. Their faces were inches apart, and Chelsea was leaning forward as if they were going to kiss. Maybe they already have? Maybe the two of them just had a morning quickie as their kid slept in the next room. The thoughts gut me and cut me straight to the bone.

I pull over at one of the lookouts and stare at the rolling hills until my vision blurs. Sucking in a deep breath, I wipe the tears away and text Maize.

ROWAN

I was wrong about everything. Seeing Chelsea all over Diesel was the biggest sign of all.

Text bubbles immediately pop up, but I set my phone down and decide to finally go home. Thankfully, I'll have the house to myself because right now, I need to be alone.

CHAPTER SEVENTEEN

Diesel

Having my son on the ranch with me has been everything I've ever dreamed of. Chelsea has been kind enough to let me have some time with him while she supervised from a distance. I showed him the big John Deere tractor, which he got a complete kick out of because it looked just like his favorite toy. I sat him on the seat, and he screamed with excitement. I made sure to snap a picture with plans to frame it. When I looked over my shoulder at Chelsea, she was smiling wide.

Even if he's a little shy, he has the same little quirks I did when I was a kid, but I think over time, he'll get to know me better and will open up more. Maybe even call me dad one day. So far, he hasn't, but that's okay. I'm sure he's just as confused as to what's going on as I am. Everyone knows where he came from, and that's enough right now.

I'm stuck between a rock and a hard place because I want to be involved in his life as much as I can, but Phoenix is too far to drive every weekend. Chelsea agreed to FaceTime me after work throughout the week so Dawson and I can talk regularly. I've also decided to try to visit him at least once a month if I can get off one weekend a month for the twelve-hour drive.

The second night Chelsea was here, I finally got her to open up about what she needed so I can help support Dawson. I'll do whatever she needs to make sure Dawson doesn't go without.

My parents were over the moon excited about having a grandkid, and I saw the instant love in my mother's eyes. She called me later that day with all sorts of stories about how I acted when I was Dawson's age.

Chelsea and I have found common ground and get along quite well, so I'm hopeful it'll be easy to work together. I've gotten to know her a little better and found out she works as a teller at a bank and hopes to one day become a loan officer. Most of the time, she's living paycheck to paycheck but has somehow made it work. I guaranteed her she'd no longer have to worry about buying whatever he needs.

The next morning, I wake up and go to the kitchen to make coffee. I have the day off and want to spend as much time with Dawson as possible before I have to take them to the airport this afternoon. As the maker stops dripping, Chelsea comes into the kitchen and pours herself a mug and leans against the counter.

"Mornin'. You sleep okay?" I ask.

She nods, then saunters closer.

She parts my legs and stands between them, leaning forward with lust in her eyes. There's nowhere for me to go, so instead, I firmly place my hands on her hips to stop this from going anywhere.

"Chelsea…" I quietly say, not wanting to disturb Dawson sleeping.

She gives me a side grin and bats her long lashes at me. "What?" she purrs. "We're both single."

"No." I shake my head. "I'm dating someone, and even if I weren't, I don't think it'd be a good idea. The last thing I want to do is confuse our son while trying to build a solid relationship with him. It's important to me. Plus, you and I hardly know each other and look at what happened the last time we jumped into bed together."

Defeat washes over her face. "Ouch. That hurts."

"I'm sorry," I tell her, hoping she understands. "I think you're nice and very pretty, but even if I were available, I wouldn't want to cross that line."

Chelsea backs away, creating the much-needed space between us. "Who is she? Why isn't she around then?" I try to keep my voice calm as I explain. "It's a new relationship, and we're keeping it under wraps at the moment. We haven't told anyone yet."

She rolls her eyes. "You don't have to lie."

"I'm *not* lying, but it doesn't matter anyway. I've grown up, Chelsea. I don't sleep with women just to do it. There has to be some sort of spark there. Any man would be lucky to have you, but it can't be me because I don't have feelings for you that way. I'm madly in love with someone else."

She releases a long, deep breath. "I can respect that, Diesel. Most guys would just use me. Sorry. I must look so desperate. I just thought things were going well, and there was a connection between us, but I shouldn't have assumed."

"There *was* a connection three years ago, and we made a beautiful kid, but being friends and raising our son is all that can be between us now."

She walks to the fridge, grabs some milk, and pours it into her coffee. "Do you have sugar?"

I know she's trying to change the subject, so I give her the escape. The last thing I wanted to do was embarrass her, but I can't cross that line, not when Rowan means so much to me. What I said to Chelsea is true—I'm in love with another woman. I'll be damned if I let my dick fuck that up any more than it already has.

Chelsea excuses herself and takes a shower. Once she's out and dressed, she brings Dawson into the living room. I make him scrambled eggs and add some fruit to his plate. Chelsea puts milk in a small cup, and he sits at the table in a booster chair like a big boy. He's talkative this morning, which I find adorable.

After he's done and Chelsea has changed his clothes, I ask if I can take him to the horse barn, just me and him.

She looks at me as if she's contemplating it but is still hesitant.

"Pretty please?" I beg with a grin. "I swear on my life that I won't let anything happen to him. It's safe as can be, and we're not going too far. Just to the horse barn at the B&B, right up the road."

She forces a smile and nods. "Okay, but only for a couple of hours. He'll need a nap before we travel. Otherwise, he'll be cranky on the flight, and I don't want anyone throwing me dirty looks."

I can't stop grinning. "Yes, of course. Thank you!"

Chelsea gives me a list of things to do. "Make sure he's buckled in the car seat really well. Don't let him out of your sight because he will take off running. If he—"

"Hey," I say, calmly. "He's gonna be fine. I won't let him run wild. I promise. Trust me, okay?"

"I have issues with trust. I'm sorry," she admits, and I feel for her in the same way that I feel for Rowan.

"I understand, completely."

She picks up Dawson and explains to him what's happening, and for the first time, he reaches for me. I hold him into my arms, and we go outside. Chelsea decides to help me buckle him in and continues with instructions. I squeeze her shoulder and grin. "He's in great hands."

"Not the first time I've heard that from you." She laughs, our eyes meet, and then she takes a step back, allowing me to shut the door.

I climb inside the truck and wave bye before backing out of the driveway. During the ten-minute drive to the B&B, I chat with Dawson about ranch life. I tell him about the horses and then find myself talking about Rowan. He listens carefully, though I know he has no idea what I'm saying, but that's okay. One day, he will.

I park in front of the B&B, and I take him straight to the barn where the lessons for the guests are held. There are several horses saddled, which means Colton, one of the instructors, probably has some scheduled for the ten o'clock hour.

Carefully, I set Dawson on one of the ponies and support him so he won't fall. These horses are for beginners, so they're very gentle. He giggles and keeps leaning forward to pet the horse. It's the cutest thing ever. This is a part of his heritage, and I'm determined for him to know that. It hurts my heart that he won't get to grow up on the ranch, something I always wished I had. Seems he might get the city life too, unless I can somehow convince Chelsea to give Texas a chance, but as of now, she's not on board. I'll have to do what I can with what she's willing to give.

After we've been outside for an hour, I notice Dawson is sweating, so I bring him inside the B&B to cool off. I place him in one of the high chairs, grab some water, and then snag one of Maize's incredible chocolate chip cookies. I hold the cup for him so he can drink, then he gobbles the cookie with a smile on his face.

Feeling parched as well, I pour some water for myself but don't take my eyes off Dawson. An older lady chats with him, and he brags about the pony he rode, pointing outside. My heart's overflowing, that is, until someone smacks me in the back of her head with their hand. When I turn and see Maize, she gives me a scowl.

"What the fuck is wrong with you?" she whisper-hisses, trying not to draw attention to herself.

"What?" I lift my ball cap and rub over the spot she smacked. "Why'd you hit me?"

"You're an idiot, Diesel," she says between gritted teeth.

"What else is new?" I ask with a shrug, but I have no idea what she's referring to this time. Then again, it's not uncommon for her to call me names.

"Rowan told me everything. *Everything*. And then you went and messed things up. She told me what she saw this morning." She cocks her hip, placing her hands on them.

I search her face, confused. Rowan told her about us? "What are you talkin' about? Saw what?"

"Rowan went to your house this morning to talk to you. You didn't answer the door so she looked through the window and saw Chelsea wrapped up in your arms." Maize shakes her head, grimacing. "I was rooting for you, too." She sarcastically laughs. "Riley's gonna lose his shit. I ought to kick your ass myself for leading her on."

My eyes go wide, and I start to panic at what Rowan must've seen before I pushed Chelsea away. "It wasn't like that. I *swear*."

"And to think Rowan wanted to come clean to everyone about your relationship, too. But you fucked it up," Maize grits. "You ruined *everything*."

"Come clean about what relationship?" Riley asks from behind, and I close my eyes, wishing this wasn't happening right now. I turn around and see him and John staring like they're ready to murder me.

"Please let me explain…" I hold up my hands, hoping he'll take mercy on me since I'm here with my son and there are guests around.

Riley's tight jaw and daggers tell me he doesn't give any fucks about that. "I warned you, Diesel." He fists his hands in my shirt and pushes me against the wall. Maize squeals, telling Riley to take it outside, but he's too pissed to listen. "I warned you to stay the fuck away from my sister. And now I'm gonna punch your pretty face in for hurting her. I knew you'd do this. You just couldn't stay away, could you? Just wouldn't feel content until you hurt my sister, the way I always knew you would." Before I can get a word in, Riley rears back and punches me in the face. I try to block it, but he's too fast. If it were any other person in the world, I would've laid them out flat, but I don't fight him back. I can't.

"Hey!" I hear a woman's voice shout.

"Mama," Dawson says, holding his arms out. She takes him from the high chair and kisses his cheek.

"What's going on here?" Chelsea asks, walking toward the group of us, and Riley retreats, putting space between us.

"What are you doin' here?" I ask, holding a hand to my face. I'm gonna have a black eye now. "And *how* did you get here?" I'm actually shocked to see her. I hope she didn't walk because that's miles down a dirt road, and it's hot outside.

"I might be from the city, but I know how to drive a four-wheeler, Diesel." She laughs. "Truthfully, I got nervous. This is new territory for me, and I just wanted to check on Dawson for my own sanity."

She notices my face fall, but I don't blame her. This is new territory for us all.

"It's nothing against you. He's around strangers and an unknown environment, and I started to worry. I just needed to see him and make sure he was safe."

I nod. "I understand, it's okay. He was having a good time. He saw the horses, and then we stopped in here for a snack and water."

Dawson begins to tell her about the pony. "Hold on, baby, one second." Chelsea looks at all of us.

Maize is annoyed and crosses her arms over her chest. "Glad your girlfriend could show up and save your ass."

Riley is ready to beat me to a pulp, and John is overly annoyed because we caused a scene...*again*.

I look at Chelsea. "Rowan saw us together this morning."

Her face drops. "Oh no. I'm so sorry," she says to me, then looks at everyone. "Whatever you think happened between Diesel and me this morning didn't and was one hundred percent my fault," she explains. "I made a move, but he stopped me, then admitted he was dating someone. It's all a really big misunderstanding, honestly. There's nothing between us," she says, and I'm so damn thankful she's here because they wouldn't have believed me, thanks to my past. Riley's still tense and so is John. Maize's eyes soften, though.

Silence cuts through the room as my heart erratically beats. I never thought Rowan's and my relationship would be announced like this, especially since she's not even here, but I'm glad the news is out there finally. Assuming she'll give us another chance, I'll fight to prove how much she means to me.

"Is that the truth?" Riley asks me.

"I swear. I would never do anything to hurt Rowan, man. I'm in love with her and have been for years. She's the only woman I've ever felt that way for. I love her," I confess, then wait for Riley to say something. But the only sound heard is a loud gasp behind us.

We turn around, and that's when I see Rowan standing at the top of the staircase, looking as beautiful as ever with her hair down and pushed to the side. Her eyes are bloodshot, like she's been crying. I fucking hate knowing I upset her. She stares at us, and I know she heard what I said by the shocked expression on her face. I'm not sure if it's because of what I just said or the fact Riley knows about us now. Either way, I'm in love with her, and I want the whole goddamn world to know.

CHAPTER EIGHTEEN

Rowan

Maize refused to let me go home to an empty house for the rest of the morning, though I had every intention of doing so. She threatened to come over, but she had work to do. So instead, she suggested I hang out at the B&B and even bribed me with my own personal breakfast full of strawberry pancakes, bacon, eggs, and homemade hash browns.

One thing's for certain—if Maize Bishop ever volunteers to cook something special for you, you do not deny her. It'll be one of the best meals of your life. She should open her own restaurant but enjoys working for the family too much. Maize acts modest, but she one hundred percent knows she could win contests with her food, and people drive over an hour away to eat it.

When I arrive, she's wearing an apron with her name embroidered across the chest. Her dark hair's in a high bun, and though she's smiling, there's also a sad look in her eyes. She pulls a tall barstool up to the prep table and pats it for me to sit as she prepares my breakfast. She listens to me spill my truths as she shreds a potato, mushes fresh strawberries into the batter, and warms the skillet. It doesn't take long before I have a beautiful picture-worthy plate of yummy food to eat. I didn't realize how hungry I was until she put it in front of me. I'm happy we're alone, and I can speak so candidly about what's happened over the past few months. It feels good to tell someone because I've kept this tucked deep inside for way too long.

"I'm so upset, Maze. Diesel hurt me more than Nick ever could, and I think it's because I didn't actually love Nick. I was just infatuated with the thought of us being together, though he never treated me right. I was always too much for him to handle, and he tried to mold me into something I wasn't—a housewife. I've never felt so defeated in my life. Diesel likes me for who I authentically am. I didn't have to pretend to be anyone other than myself around him. Do you have any idea how that feels? To be yourself in front of a man because that's what he loves about you? I actually feel sick talking about it," I explain. She pushes my plate closer and hands me some syrup she hand mixed.

I force a smile and take a bite. It's comfort food at its finest.

"I'm gonna chop off his balls and make a gumbo out of them, then I'm gonna make him eat the whole damn pot."

I snort. "You wouldn't."

"I would, and I am. He better not show his stupid face in the B&B for the rest of his life, or we're gonna have words," she threatens, snagging a piece of my bacon, but I can't even be mad about it. She made way too much anyway, but that's just how it is here. Full plates are an everyday occurrence.

"First, he strings you along and gets you to have sex with him. Then his baby mama just shows up with his kid in tow, and he screws her too? This is such bullshit. I'm livid right now." She grabs a butter knife and holds it in her fist. I take it from her hand and set it down on the table.

"Has anyone ever told you how scary you are?" I giggle-snort, and I'm so happy to be spending time with her. She's right, going home would've done me no good. I would've just sulked and felt like total shit the rest of the day. Maize makes me feel a little better about the whole situation.

She shrugs. "A few times. Just don't mess with my feelings, food, or my family, and everything will be just fine."

"Noted, but you not wanting us to eat the food at the B&B really isn't fair. You know it's addicting, but then you don't want us to eat it. Pretty mean if you ask me," I say, stuffing my mouth full.

"Says the person who got their own personal breakfast buffet this morning." She snickers.

"Also, you make it sound like Diesel made me sleep with him. It takes two to tango, and trust me when I say I'll be thinking about the times I had with him for the rest of my life—even if I hate him. No man has ever..." I whisper, keeping my voice low. "Pleasured me the way he did."

She blushes. "It was that good?"

"Better than good. Mind-blowing. So I can see why Chelsea came back." I frown, swallowing down my food. "I really thought what we had was more than that. I believed we had something special. Maybe I was nothing more than a forbidden fuck," I tell her.

"You're much more than that, Rowan. I honestly can't believe any of this because of the way he's always acted when it comes to you. Something isn't right, but if you saw them together, I will believe you any day of the week."

"I know. It doesn't add up, especially when he was dead set on announcing to everyone we're together just a few days ago. Maybe it's my fault? Maybe I pushed him away?"

Maize shakes her head. "No, he's just a man slut. That's all."

I yawn and realize I'm still tired from last night, plus I'm emotionally drained from what I witnessed today. I need a nap.

"Why don't you go upstairs and rest? Our favorite room has no guests in it right now," she suggests.

"The purple room?" I laugh.

"Mm-hmm. Bed's made and waitin' for ya. I'm gonna have to start preparing lunch soon."

"Whatcha making?" I ask as I finish picking at my plate until it's nearly empty, but I literally can't take another bite, or she'll have to roll me up the stairs.

"Grandma's Southern chicken salad sandwiches."

My eyes go wide. "With homemade sourdough bread?"

"Yep." She nods and laughs. "I'll make extra for you."

"You love me so much," I tell her, standing.

We exchange a hug. "I do, and it's not just because we're gonna become nuns together."

I roll my eyes, thank her for listening to me, then head upstairs. When we were kids, we'd get lost playing in the B&B. It holds so much history and happy memories. We'd use to take our Barbies in here and pretend it was our house. It's almost fitting that it's the only room available at the moment.

I walk inside and lie on the tall four-poster bed. My heart hurts, and I'm not sure anything could heal it at this point. After rolling over onto my side and staring out at the blue sky for nearly an hour, tears well and then fall in streams. I really thought we had a future together, but I was so wrong. My eyes feel heavy from crying, and somehow, I eventually fall asleep. When I wake up, I smell the bread Maize's baking, and though I'm still full from earlier, I could eat her cooking again.

I step into the hallway and immediately hear commotion at the bottom of the stairs. My pulse races when I see Riley reach back and sock Diesel right in the jaw. Surprisingly, Diesel doesn't try to retaliate against him. Though if I were willing to bet, I think he could take Riley. He's nearly double his size, but then again, Riley does have some strength behind him.

Before I can break it up, Chelsea walks in and admits what happened this morning. She made a move on him, and he denied her. I must've walked away before that happened, too upset to continue spying.

"Is that the truth?" Riley asks.

"I swear. I would never do anything to hurt Rowan, man. I'm in love with her and have been for years. She's the only woman I've ever felt that way for. I love her," Diesel admits.

All I can do is gasp, then cover my mouth. They turn and look at me before I can disappear. My timing is terrible today. My words and thoughts, everything has completely escaped me.

"Rowan?" Diesel says, walking toward me and searching my face. He feels the same way I feel about him, and I'm so fucking happy that I could cry *again*.

He stalks toward me, climbing the stairs two at a time until he's a step below me. "Hey." He grabs my hand. "I'm so sorry you saw that. It's not what—"

"Did you mean it?" I whisper, interrupting.

That boyish grin that I love so much sweeps across his perfect lips. "I've been in love with you for quite some time now, baby."

I wrap my arms around his neck, and our lips crash together. At this moment, I want to devour him as we lose ourselves in each other's touch, taste, and kiss. The only thing that stops us from a full-blown make-out session is a deep clearing of a throat. I pull away to see my uncle John standing there with his arms crossed over his chest, but he's smiling.

"Do you mind? Some of us are about to lose our stomachs here," he says from across the room, and I see everyone staring at us.

I laugh as happy tears spill from my eyes. Diesel wipes them away with his thumbs and holds my cheeks with his warm hands. "I love you so much, Rowan Bishop."

"I love you too," I confess, and I feel those words in every fiber of my being. Finally, our relationship is out in the open. It's not how I expected any of this to happen, but it feels like a giant weight has been lifted off my shoulders. No more hiding and no more sneaking. Now we can just be together and openly love each other. It doesn't mean I won't get shit from my family—nothing would allow me to escape that—but it's okay. I just hope Grandma doesn't start talking about me giving her a handful of great-grandkids anytime soon. I don't want to rush this and want to savor every second with him.

Diesel laughs, grabs my hand, then leads me down the stairs. Riley scowls, and I lift my eyebrows at him, daring him to say a word. The boys in school weren't scared of me for no reason. I pack a punch hard enough to knock a man down.

Chelsea walks up to me with Dawson in her arms, and I can see the embarrassment written all over her face. Diesel takes Dawson from her arms for just a moment so the two of us can have some alone time.

"Rowan...I owe you an apology," she says.

I give her a smile. "Really, don't worry about it. You didn't know."

"I know, but I just don't want you to think I was trying to steal him. I would've never crossed that line if I'd known. Neither of us talked about our relationship status, but I also didn't ask. If I could take it all back, I would."

I try to imagine being a single mom for the past two and a half years without a partner. She went through the delivery and raised a newborn all on her own. This woman is strong as hell, and I have so much respect for her, and even more now because she can admit her mistakes. "Listen. I'm not upset with you, Chelsea. Not at all. I should've asked Diesel what was going on. I shouldn't have just assumed."

"I know what it looked like and what you saw, and that's not your fault," she insists.

I search her face and notice how sincere her words are. "Diesel really loves his son, and I really love him, so that means we're gonna be in each other's lives for a long time. Maybe it started off on the wrong foot, but that's okay. We understand each other more and the whole situation. It seems just like a big misunderstanding." I laugh. "And I have really bad timing."

She grins. "I'd like that…being friends, at least. I know this probably hasn't been easy for you. Diesel told me your relationship was new, and no one really knew about it, and then I roll up here with a kid. Trust me when I say it wasn't my idea, but it's for the best for Dawson."

"I agree one hundred percent. They both deserve the opportunity to form a relationship, and I have so much respect for you for allowing that."

I can see she's getting emotional, and we both laugh as I pull her in for a hug. "Hormones are such a bitch," I say.

Diesel walks up, breaking up the moment because Dawson starts getting fussy. She turns and takes him from Diesel. "Told you he needed a nap or he'd be cranky."

"Mama knows best," Diesel says. "If you wanna wait in the truck, I can bring you home in just a few minutes."

Chelsea nods. "Actually, would you mind if I grabbed some lunch? It smells delicious."

Diesel chuckles. "Help yourself. Might have a wheelbarrow in the back after you're done because Maize's cookin' is the best in the area."

Chelsea laughs and walks to the dining area as Riley moves toward us.

"This is really gonna be a thing? You two all lovey-dovey, smoochin' in front of everyone, and causin' a show?"

"Riley," I warn. "Mind your own damn business. You don't get to tell me what to do, who to date, or any of those things. And if you do have a problem with it…" I take a step forward, ready to knock him down, but he takes a step back.

"Hey…" He lifts his hands. "I know I can't control you. I just don't want you gettin' hurt, Rowan. I've only wanted the best for you, my only little sister, even if it means you choosing this dickhead."

"I'm your best friend in the entire world!" Diesel argues. "Don't you trust me?" He places a hand to his chest, pretending to be insulted.

Riley gives him a pointed look and tilts his head.

"If anyone's gonna treat your sister right…" Diesel thrusts his hips, and Riley groans, grinding his teeth. I can't help but laugh because through all of this, the man still has jokes.

"If you hurt her, I won't think twice about punching you again," Riley warns.

"And when he's done with you, I'll chop off your dick," Maize adds, walking up to us.

I glance at Diesel, and he winks at me, and I know this is what true happiness feels like. Maize tells Riley to stop causing a scene and pulls him away. I wrap my arms around Diesel's neck, finally getting a tad bit of privacy.

"It's gonna take him some time to get used to this, Cowboy," I say. His strong hands rest on my hips, and he pulls me even closer to him. "I'm sorry for assuming the worst. I should've known better, but my emotions had me thinking back on my past when I caught Nick cheating."

"No, I get it. This is new for all of us, and I probably would've thought the same thing had I seen another man's hands on you. Except I would've barged in and flattened him out."

I chuckle, knowing he definitely would have. I nearly get lost in his eyes before mine flutter closed, and I'm ready to taste him. Before our lips can touch, the door slams, and I pull away. My eyes go wide, and I can't believe who's standing in the living room of the B&B.

Trace, and my ex, Nick.

My mouth falls open, and the only thought that runs through my mind is *what the actual fuck?*

CHAPTER NINETEEN

Diesel

I see red the minute my eyes land on the two guys standing in front of me.

Rowan's tool bag ex-boyfriend and Trace.

Why the fuck are they here?

Better yet, why are they here together?

Rowan pulls away and steps toward them before they can come any farther into the B&B. "What's going on?"

"You know why I'm here—" Nick stands taller. The cocky son of a bitch is about to meet my fist, more personally this time.

"I just came to check on you," Trace interrupts. "You seemed upset this morning and stopped responding to my messages."

My jaw clenches. I glance at Rowan who's fidgeting with the hem of her shirt.

"You texted him?" I ask.

"I was upset…it was after I saw you and Chelsea and wanted someone to talk to."

"I thought you talked with Maize?"

She turns toward me, her eyes wandering before they land on mine. "I did, but I needed a guy's perspective too. I was only reaching out for a friend…" she reassures, but it doesn't make me any less annoyed.

Rowan faces Trace, who looks confused as hell. "I'm so sorry, Trace. I didn't mean to leave you hanging or have you worry about me. I really appreciate that you care, but it was all a misunderstanding and things are fine now."

"That's good to hear," he says. "Sorry I just showed up unannounced."

"Nah, man, it's fine," I chime in, wrapping my arm around her waist so both of them know she's mine. "I appreciate you coming to check on her."

"Of course."

"Lovely…" Nick interjects. "If this cheesy Hallmark moment is over, can we get back to the money you owe me?"

I swallow hard, trying like hell to contain myself in a room filled with Bishops and guests.

Snapping my eyes to Trace, I smile. "Why don't you go into the dining area and help yourself? My son's mother is in there and a few of Rowan's family members."

"Alright, sure. Thanks." Trace walks around me, and then I turn to Rowan. "I'm going to take Nick outside for a little chat."

Her eyes widen in fear, but I flash her a wink. Then I stalk toward Nick and nod toward the back door. He follows, and once we're off the porch, I turn around and cross my arms. Nick matches my stance, and his smug frat boy look has me wanting to punch him in the face.

"You're brave comin' here like this, especially after the last time."

"She owes me money," he counters.

I bring a finger to my lips and tap twice. "You broke her heart, and she broke your car in return. Sounds even to me, so ya need to go back to where you came from and never step your preppy ass on this property again."

"This doesn't involve you." He scowls.

I squint and tilt my head at the dumb motherfucker. "See, that's where you're wrong." Stepping forward, I push his chest, and he stumbles back, losing his balance. "Anything involving my girl involves *me*."

He pushes back. "She owes me money, and I'm not leaving till she pays."

This little cocky fucker. "Perhaps you didn't hear me the first time?" I crack my knuckles. "No one's paying you a dime."

"Then I'll report that whore for vandalizing my property. I have the video and will hand it over to the cops." He flashes an arrogant grin and spins around.

I quickly grab his collar before he can walk away. Fisting his shirt in my fingers, I rear back and deck him in the face. His hands cover his nose as he hunches over.

"I warned you," I remind him. "You threaten her with that video or the money, I'll fuckin' hit you. Your stupid ass didn't believe me."

"You broke my nose!" he whines, moving his hands away to reveal blood.

"It won't be the only thing I break if you don't stop harassing Rowan. But if you be a good little boy and stay the fuck away, I won't break any more of your bones. Deal?"

"Fuck you," he spits, blood dripping from his chin.

I pat his shoulder with a smirk. "Good. Glad we had this nice chat. Should I walk you to your car?"

He shoves me away, then makes his way around the B&B to the parking lot. Looking at my knuckles, I see they're already red and starting to swell.

The asshole better stay away this time.

I walk back into the B&B and smile when I see Rowan sitting with Dawson on her lap. My whole world in one beautiful view.

Chelsea and Trace are in the middle of a conversation, so I sit on the other side and grab Rowan's hand.

"He likes you," I tell her.

"He's a toddler. He'll like anyone who plays with him," she retorts.

"I doubt that." I laugh. "It means a lot that you still want to be in my life after everything I've put you through. I didn't exactly handle it in the best way and—"

"Adam," she says my name, stopping me. "Yes, you should've told me what was going on sooner, and I should've confronted you about Chelsea. We're gonna need to work on communicating if we want this to work long-term."

I nod in agreement. Rowan's my everything and future. The last thing I want is to fuck it all up. "Definitely. Complete transparency from now on, Scout's honor."

She snorts. "You weren't a Boy Scout."

"I totally could've been!"

Dawson starts giggling at our laughter. "You think I'm funny, right?" I smirk.

He nods and starts talking. I love hearing him ask questions and point at things.

"He's precious," Rowan swoons. "Definitely your mini."

I hate that they have to leave today. "I'm gonna miss him."

Chelsea stands and frowns. "He's gonna miss you, too."

Holding back my emotions, my throat goes dry, but I nod. This is all so new, yet it feels natural. I was meant to be Dawson's dad.

DIESEL

Hey, I'm back. Wanna sneak over here? ;)

After everything that went down at the B&B, it was time to take Chelsea and Dawson to the airport. I hated saying goodbye, but I made plans to visit in a few weeks. Until then, we'll FaceTime, and she promised to send me daily pictures of him.

ROWAN

You know we don't have to hide anymore, though it was kinda fun...maybe you should leave your window open for me, and I'll crawl in.

DIESEL

You know the entire town knows by now anyway.

ROWAN

Yep. My parents already had "the talk" with me after you left. Then my grandma. It was embarrassing...I had to keep reminding them I was twenty-three years old and not a child anymore.

DIESEL

They think I corrupted you now, don't they?

ROWAN

Ooooh yeah. Riley's still walking around with a pissed-off expression. I hope I didn't ruin your friendship.

DIESEL

Nah, he'll get over it. We'll be laughing over beers in no time.

ROWAN

I hope so. Zoey already texted me and said he was grunting around the house.

I shake my head as I envision my best friend having a fit. He should know by now that I'd never intentionally hurt Rowan, but I can't fault him for being protective. I am too.

DIESEL

I'll see him tomorrow and clear the air. He already got one hit in, so we should be even.

ROWAN

Okay, good. Then I don't feel so bad coming over.

DIESEL

Well, I did punch your ex for you. Again. You kinda owe me...

She sends me an eye-roll emoji, and I laugh.

ROWAN

Be right there.

696

We haven't been alone since our date two weekends ago, and I'm dying to have her all to myself again.

When I hear her car pull up, I rush to the door and whip it open. I don't bother waiting for her to get to the house before I walk toward her. As soon as she parks and gets out, I pin her to the side and claim her mouth.

Rowan wraps her arms and legs around me as I press my body into hers. She groans against my mouth as I slide my tongue between her soft lips.

"I missed you so fuckin' much," I tell her. We hardly talked or saw each other for a week, and it was miserable. "I was devastated when you wouldn't answer my calls or messages."

"I missed you too," she admits. "I needed time to process it all."

Setting her back on her feet, I tilt her chin, and she meets my eyes. "I know. We both did. But I want you in my life and hopefully Dawson's too."

"I'm not goin' anywhere, Cowboy." She smiles wide.

I blow out a relieved breath. "Thank fuck."

"When will you see him again?" she asks as I take her hand and guide her into the house.

"Hopefully in three or four weeks. I'd like to go visit for a few days. After that, I'm not sure. We're playing it by ear."

"Maybe she'll decide to move here."

We walk to the kitchen so I can get her something to drink. "Doubtful. She sounded pretty hell-bent on staying in Phoenix."

"I don't know…" Rowan sing-songs when I hand her a bottle of Bud. "She and Trace were hitting it off at the B&B."

"Trace?" I muse.

"Yep," she says with a smile, popping the p. "Trace was smooth-talking her, and she was eating it up like candy."

"I better not have to punch his face in," I growl.

"Trust me, Chelsea was *all* over it. You wouldn't have to worry about Trace. He's really one of the good ones around." I give her a pointed look. "We're only friends!" she reiterates, chuckling. "The most we ever did was kiss, but there was no real spark between us."

"He does seem nice, so I'll give him the benefit of the doubt. However, it's unlikely she'd move here just for a guy. She won't for her son's father."

"Maybe she'll surprise you and do it for all three of you."

"I'd love having Dawson around all the time. Show him the real ranch lifestyle and watch him grow up here. Then we can give him a few siblings along the way."

Rowan chokes as she takes a sip and starts coughing.

"Too soon?" I tease.

"Not according to Grandma Bishop."

I waggle my brows, getting a giggle out of her. "Back up, Cowboy. You're a few years too soon."

"*Years?*" I frown.

"Just because Riley jumped into marriage and having a kid doesn't mean you should," she scolds. "Well, besides the kid you already have, but you know what I mean."

I cup her face and smirk. "Alright, got it. Make you my wife before knocking you up, just like Grandma B said."

"Precisely." The blush on her cheeks is adorable, though I know she tries to hide it. Talking about our future doesn't scare me in the least. I've been ready for Rowan for as long as I can remember.

"Then right now, I'll make sure to enjoy having you all to myself." I grab her hips and lift her body until she wraps her legs around me.

"Yes, please." She laughs when I trip over the stool as I rush out of the kitchen and into my bedroom. "If you don't kill us in the process."

Once I successfully set her down on the bed, I tower over her and crash my lips to hers. Settling between her legs, she arches her back. Rowan rubs against me, and while my cock's already hard, she's making it harder.

"Shit...that already feels amazing." I chuckle.

Her hands slide beneath my shirt, and she scratches her nails down my chest. I want to take things slow and really show her how much I love her, but she's just as ravenous as I am.

Groaning, I try to hold on to my willpower, but it's a losing battle with her. Rowan's skin is so soft, and all I want to do is touch and kiss her all night long.

"Fuck it." I lean back and grip my shirt behind my neck, then pull it off.

Rowan giggles and openly gawks at me. "I could stare at that eight-pack all damn day." She licks her lips and waggles her brows.

"You're gonna be doing a lot more than just starin'."

"Arrogant," she mocks. "But yes, take off those jeans."

I hurriedly undress, then help her out of her shorts and top. Staring down at her, I'm still so amazed she's mine. Shocked, really.

"Why are you looking at me like that?" The corner of her lips tilts up.

"Feels surreal."

"What does?"

"You being mine, and the world finally knowing." I rub my thumb along her cheek. "Being able to tell you how much I love you."

She leans up on her elbows, then cups the back of my neck until my face is close to hers. Rowan's lips crash into mine, and she releases a low hum when our tongues dance together.

"I love you, too," she whispers as we rest our foreheads together. "I'm gonna try really hard not to let my issues with my past relationships mess this up. It almost did already."

"Between me having no relationship experience and the douchebags you've dated, we're a match made in heaven," I tease, tipping her chin up. "Don't worry. We've got this, baby."

I pull her in for a deep kiss, and when she moans, I shift our bodies until she's on top of me.

"I wanna watch you ride me." I fist my dick and pump it a couple of times.

Rowan pops a brow. "Ride your cock or your face?"

"Shit. *Both*."

She laughs, placing her palms on my chest to lift herself. Slowly, she slides down my length, and with every inch, I smile wider at the vision in front of me. Rowan's a gorgeous woman, but she's also stunning inside. Once you get through her hard exterior, she really shows who she is. Funny, hard-working, loyal as hell. Sometimes a little crazy, but those are all the qualities I love about her.

Even at thirteen, she was beating all the guys at barrel racing.

"Jesus," I hiss between gritted teeth, grabbing one of her breasts. "Your tits bouncing in my face is hot as fuck."

Rowan rotates her hips, taking me even deeper as she increases her pace. She leans back, and I nearly come at the sight of her body on display for me. Her adorable braids, her smooth, soft skin, the cute freckles on her shoulders—I can't fucking get enough.

I bring the pad of my thumb between us and rub her clit in quick circles until her back straightens, and she moans out my name.

"That was sexy as hell," I tell her, wrapping an arm around her waist to flip us over.

She squeals, hanging on before I drop her underneath me.

"Bend over. You and those braids are driving me insane."

Rowan turns, and I immediately grip her hips, positioning her into place. I line us up and slowly re-enter her, feeling her tight walls around me. She feels so damn good, and my heart nearly bursts at the emotions bubbling inside me. I've never made love to a woman before Rowan.

Once I'm deeper inside her, I thrust my hips and move us into a steady rhythm. I watch as she fists the sheets, moaning and moving her body with mine. I reach up and grab the ends of her braids, then tug until her head falls back toward me.

"You feel this, baby?" I growl against her ear. "You and me."

"Yes," she whispers. "*So* good."

Squeezing her hip with my other hand, I pick up my speed, knowing she's close. Soon she's whimpering, begging me to let her come.

Releasing her hair, I slide my hand down her stomach and rub between her legs. "Enjoy it, baby."

She grips my wrist and squeezes as I bring her over the edge, thrusting deeper as she throws her head back and moans out my name.

"Fuck, Row…" I grit between my teeth as her pussy tightens around my dick.

Her chest rises and falls as she pants, and when I release her, she lays flat with her ass up. I smack a cheek, and I smirk when she lets out a little squeal.

"Hang on, sweet Rowan," I warn, gripping her hips and driving into her hard and fast. The sounds of our skin slapping together and heavy breathing echo throughout the room as I come undone and release inside her.

My arms are jelly, and I quickly roll over so I don't crush her. Rowan's legs fall with a grunt.

"See whatcha been missin' out on?" I smirk at her.

"I don't even have the energy to scold you for being a smug asshole."

Chuckling, I turn on my side and wrap my arm around her, moving her closer to me. "Thanks for giving us a chance. I promise I won't let you down."

Rowan blinks and looks at me. "Stop acting like you don't deserve to be happy. I'm the lucky one."

With a grin, I shrug. "Agree to disagree."

Last night and a quickie this morning with Rowan were pure perfection, and I can't remember a time I was ever this damn happy. Between having Dawson here over the weekend and working things out with Rowan, I'm on cloud nine. Though I'm exhausted as hell working on only an hour of sleep, every second with her was worth it.

"Hey, dipshit. Quit smilin' like a moron," Riley harasses when we meet in the shop for our daily list.

I can't help it. It's just too easy to piss him off. "Can't help it when I'm thinkin' about your sister."

"I swear to God, Diesel…" He grits his teeth.

"Oh, c'mon. You can't be *that* mad. I've been telling you I liked Rowan for years. You just didn't listen."

"And I told you to stay away. *You* didn't listen."

"What's more important? Her happiness or being pissed at your best friend?" I challenge, knowing he'll cave. "You know I'm not gonna hurt her. I love her."

"You've never had a relationship."

"You didn't either until Zoey!" I remind him. "And you went and married her on a dare."

"He's gotcha there," Alex walks in and adds. "You two seriously having a pissing contest about this right now?"

I open my arms. "I'm ready to kiss and make up."

Riley rolls his eyes at my laughter.

"Well, you better soon because I have a new guy I wanna introduce you to. So hug it out or whatever you kids do."

"I promised Rowan I'd clear the air with you today, so whaddya say?" I arch a brow, waiting. "Gonna make me a liar already, or realize I'm the only one who can make her happy?"

"Some big words there, Diesel," Alex says. "I see Riley already gave you a shiner."

"Yes, sir. Only because I let him."

"God, you're such a fuckin' smartass," Riley hisses.

"And you owe me, so just quit being bitter so we can move on."

"Owe you for what exactly?"

"I could think about a hundred things, but specifically, the night of Rowan's formal dance in eighth grade. Remember?"

"What about that night?" Alex asks, looking back and forth between us.

It takes Riley a minute to realize what I'm talking about. The night he got so shit-faced, I had to drive his truck at only fourteen years old to pick up Rowan from school. "I hate you."

I snicker, shaking my head. "So, we good now or what?" I prompt, holding out my hand and knowing he'll take it.

After a moment, Riley grabs it, and I pull him in for a hug. "You should be excited to have me as a brother-in-law someday."

He laughs, adjusting his hat. "I wouldn't go *that* far."

"Our kids will be cousins."

"Alright, if you ladies are done, Gavin's here," Alex says, interrupting us.

We both turn to a hulk of a man, tall and chiseled. He's stacked like me but bulkier. I have no idea who he is, but he looks like he's ready for a fight. He's at least ten years older than me.

"Gavin, this is my son, Riley," he introduces them, and they shake hands. "This is Diesel, he runs the cattle operation."

"Nice to meet you," I tell him, taking his hand.

"He's new to Eldorado and will be staying in one of the ranch hand cabins. He'll be working with Jackson on breaking in the wild horses. He has bull riding experience and trains riders too."

"Bull riding?" My brows shoot up. "Impressive."

"Thanks. It was dangerous work, won some competitions, got some trophies, but I'm retired now."

"I bet you have some insane stories about traveling to rodeos and competing, huh?" Riley asks.

"Or how much ass you got?" I taunt.

The corner of Gavin's lips tilts up as if he could tell us crazy shit for days. "You could say that." He strokes his fingers over his scruffy jawline, smirking. "On both accounts."

"Maybe over a round of beers," I suggest. "My girlfriend works at the Circle B Saloon in town and will hook us up. We could meet up after work."

Riley groans at the mention of me calling his sister my girlfriend, but I hid it for too long to keep on for his sake. I'm gonna tell everyone and anyone I want now.

"Uh, sure. I've been there a couple of times." He pinches the back of his neck. "How about nine?"

"Sounds good."

"Alright, now that our *team meeting* is over…" Alex snickers. "I'm gonna give Gavin a tour of the property and get him settled in with Jackson and Kiera."

"Your cousins are gonna lose their shit over him…" I say once Alex and Gavin leave.

"Great, another guy I have to threaten to stay away from my family."

I pat him on his shoulder. "Good luck, bro. You'll be fighting *them* off him."

CHAPTER TWENTY

Rowan

DIESEL

I'm meeting your brother and a new worker at the bar at 9 tonight.

ROWAN

Does this mean Riley doesn't want to kill you anymore?

DIESEL

Told you he'd get over it...I'm very convincing ;)

ROWAN

Yeah, I'm sure...

DIESEL

Can't wait to see you. Wear those cowboy boots I like. And pigtails.

ROWAN

With the jean skirt?

DIESEL

HELL YES!

ROWAN

You know every guy will see me wearing it in the bar, not just you...

DIESEL

I've been scaring men away from you since we were in middle school. I'm a pro at this.

ROWAN

Oh my God, you're so possessive.

DIESEL

Damn right. And it worked :)

ROWAN

...ten years later.

DIESEL

Love's a marathon, not a sprint.

ROWAN

Ha! Says the guy who was talking about marriage and babies last night.

DIESEL

Shh...don't say that in front of your brother. He really will kill me.

ROWAN

It'll be our little secret.

My cheeks hurt from smiling so much. Ever since leaving his house this morning, I just can't stop. I'm so happy I don't have to hide my feelings anymore. Especially when my cousins are making faces at me.

"Bite me," I say at their expressions.

Kenzie and I met at the B&B to hang out with Maize while she cooks. I don't work till later, so hanging out with them means we can officially catch up since Kenzie decided to come home from the weekend, considering her university is only a few hours away.

"So how's the sex?" Kenzie blurts out.

"Kenzie!" Maize scolds.

"What?" She takes a bite of her omelet. "You were thinking it too. I just care enough to ask."

"When it's with the right person…" I let out a dreamy sigh. "It's perfect."

Maize makes a gagging noise, and we all laugh.

"Don't be a love hater. Someday, Maze…you're gonna find the one."

She rolls her eyes as she beats her fist into a ball of bread dough.

"Speaking of which, Diesel and Riley are coming to the bar tonight with the new guy who just got hired. You should come. Kenzie and I are working."

"Hells yes, you should!" Kenzie's face lights up. "Stay until after my shift so I can use my newfound drinking freedom to do it legally." She turned twenty-one a month ago and has been using any opportunity to remind us all.

"I'm busy tonight," Maize says.

"Doing what?" I ask doubtfully. "Bingeing *Love is Blind* and shoving dark chocolate into your mouth doesn't qualify as busy."

Maize glares at me, knowing I'm right.

"But you gotta admit, it's a train wreck you can't look away from…" Kenzie says about Netflix's new reality show. "Cameron's my favorite. I'd marry him in a heartbeat."

"See?" Maize holds a hand out toward Kenzie. "I need to catch up." I've always admired Maize and Mackenzie's sisterly relationship. Though I'm close with both of them, I've always wondered what it'd be like to have a sister.

"You can do it tomorrow. Tonight, you're coming to the bar! No arguing!"

"Damn, I thought getting laid would make you nicer," Maize mutters with a smirk.

"Maybe you're the one who needs to get laid, meanie," I retort.

"I *definitely* need to get laid," Kenzie adds, and the three of us burst out laughing.

"What's all the noise I'm hearing in here?" Uncle John enters the kitchen, and I hope he didn't just hear his daughters talking about needing to get some.

"None of your business," Maize smarts off. "Girl talk. No boys allowed."

"Pretty sassy for someone who still lives under my roof," he teases.

"Kenzie and I are gonna get an apartment in the city," she says casually, knowing damn well her father will blow a gasket at the idea.

"Not a chance in hell," he states firmly. "Nice try, though." Uncle John reaches over and steals one of the apple turnovers that Kat delivered this morning.

"Dad..." Maize begins. "I'm almost twenty-five and live at home. Do you know how pathetic I sound? I need my own place."

"You can move out when you get married."

Maize snorts loudly. "And did you and Mom wait till marriage to move in with each other?"

We all know the answer to that one. No.

"Do as I say..."

"Not as I do," Kenzie finishes for him.

"That's right." He kisses Kenzie on the head. "Your mom isn't ready to be an empty nester yet, and frankly, I think she'll go crazy without you two there, so until you're in a serious relationship, no talk of moving out."

"My parents are halfway there. I wonder if they'll get all sappy on me when I move out?" I question.

"Knowing your mom and dad, they're ready to relive their youth days and have their privacy back." Uncle John chuckles. "They didn't exactly take the slow and steady route."

"Thanks for that visual..." I groan. "Now I need to throw up my breakfast."

After another couple of hours of hanging out at the B&B, I head home and do some house chores with Mom. She talks my ear off about Diesel and how she just knew we'd eventually get together.

"Adam's so sweet," she gushes. "Reminds me a lot of your father."

"Ugh, Mom. Don't say that." I shiver, trying to push the comparison out of my head. "That's really the last thing you wanna hear about your boyfriend."

Boyfriend.

It's still weird to call Diesel that. But also amazing.

"I just meant how attentive and loyal he is. Your dad was ready to fight anyone who came near me or threatened our relationship. As soon as I moved here, he jumped in with two feet, eager to make us work no matter what. I was expecting the worst when I told him I was pregnant, but he fell to his knees and almost cried. He was so happy."

"Do you ever think back and wish you'd gone a little slower? Like enjoyed the honeymoon phase a bit longer? Or are you glad you guys had a baby and got married right away?" I ask as we fold a basket of towels.

"I've thought a lot about that over the years, and I can honestly say it all worked out the way it was supposed to. It's never ideal to get pregnant that soon, especially when we weren't technically even dating, but it brought two people from different parts of the country together, and we formed an undeniable connection. I fell in love with him within a matter of weeks. He's always been my rock."

"Why do you ask, sweetie?" she asks.

I shrug, not making eye contact. "You said Diesel reminds you of Dad, and it just had me thinking about these early dating years and how we should enjoy them before all the marriage and baby stuff happens."

"Are you pregnant?" she rushes out.

"Ma! No!" I burst out laughing when she tilts her head, doubtfully. "I swear!"

"Well, I can't say I'd be mad about the idea. Even though you two have known each other for most of your lives, not rushing is smart. Get to know each other on a more personal and deeper level before you bring in more responsibility. I love your brother, but he was a helluva lotta work."

I chuckle. "He still is."

I'm ecstatic when Diesel shows up at the bar earlier than he said. He's not with Riley or the new guy, so I get to steal a few private moments with him.

"Hey, Cowboy," I say, wrapping my arms around his neck. He's wearing his black hat, which I love.

"Howdy, cowgirl." He pulls on one of my french braids. "You fulfilled my requests." He eyes my outfit with an arrogant smirk.

"Of course..." I squeeze him tighter. "Only because I'm hoping you'll take it all off later."

"Goddammit, woman." He brings a hand down to his groin. "Don't talk like that here or I'm gonna have to excuse myself."

"You asked for it," I remind him of his earlier text messages.

"Listen, lovebirds..." Maize groans from one of the stools. "I agreed to come hang out, not watch you two make out."

"Stop being a grump." Kenzie sets a shot glass in front of her. "Blow jobs on me!"

"What?" Riley enters the bar at that precise moment with another guy behind him. "That's the very last thing I *ever* wanna hear from my cousin."

"Shots, perv!" Kenzie pours the liquor and then tops it with whipped cream. "Now, Maze. Take it without using your hands."

"Seriously? This is dumb."

I stand behind the bar next to Kenzie and laugh at her sour mood. "Be glad she didn't top it with a cherry. I nearly choked on the stem the last time she made me do one!"

Maize furrows her brows, then sighs. "Fine." With a groan, she leans down, wraps her mouth around the shot, then tilts her head all the way back. Once the liquid slides down her throat, she drops the glass down.

There's whipped cream all over her face, which has us laughing.

"You. All. Suck." She points at us as I hand her a napkin.

"But it's good, right?" Kenzie teases.

"Uh...anyway." Riley clears his throat, directing our attention to him. "This is Gavin. He'll be working with Jackson training horses."

Kenzie's eyes widen as her face lights up. Gavin looks like sex on a stick, so it's no surprise she's seconds away from jumping his bones.

"You already met Diesel," Riley says, waving his hand toward him. "That one behind the bar is my pain in the ass little sister, Rowan..."

"Just call me Rowan. Hold the 'pain in the ass' part," I mock.

Gavin flashes the smallest of smiles. "Nice to meet you."

"Then my cousin, Kenzie, who works here sometimes. Also a pain in the ass."

"Excuse you?" Kenzie places her hands on her hips. "If anyone's a ginormous ass, it's Riley."

"Noted," Gavin says.

Riley chuckles, moving on. "This is my other cousin, Maize. She's the cook at the B&B."

"Ooh, the one who makes amazing pancakes," Gavin states. They must've gone there this morning when we were busy talking in the kitchen.

Maize turns slightly to shake his hand and then quickly retreats.

"So Gavin…" I say, bringing the attention to me instead of Maize's sudden inability to speak. "Where're you from?"

"Houston," he says in a thick drawl. "But I've traveled a lot in the past twelve years or so. I've been all over the state."

"Gavin's a retired bull rider," Riley explains. "Trains riders now on the side."

"Oh my God," Kenzie gushes. "That is so cool. I would love to see you ride."

I'm five seconds away from pouring a glass of cold water over her because she's about to internally combust.

"Told ya…" Diesel says to Riley. I'm not sure what he's referring to, but they both start cracking up.

"Told him what?" I ask, stepping closer.

Diesel leans into my ear, and whispers, "That your cousins would act like cats in heat around him."

I snort, shaking my head.

Maize looks pale as hell. "You okay, Maze?"

She blinks, then licks her lips. "Um, yeah. I'm just gonna run to the bathroom real quick." Then she shifts her eyes and moves them to the side, motioning for me to follow her.

After she hops off the stool and walks toward the back, I wait a few seconds before excusing myself from the conversation and then meet Maize in the single-stall bathroom.

"Hey, what's goin' on?" I ask, shutting the door behind me. "You look like you've seen a ghost."

"That guy…"

"Gavin? What about him?"

"That's *Gavin*."

I blink. "Right, I just said that."

"No, I mean, yes. That's the Gavin I slept with a few weeks ago."

"Wait…" I rack my brain. "The guy you bailed on the next morning?"

"Yes!"

I quickly cover my mouth with my hands, trying to hold back my laughter. "Oh my God, Maze!"

"Shut up!" She smacks my arm. "This is humiliating!"

"This is freaking awesome." I chuckle. "Did he recognize you?"

"I don't know. I recognized him right away. That's why I quickly turned away."

"Well, go out there and say hi!" I push her toward the door, and she digs her heels in, not budging.

"Hell. No!" She frantically shakes her head.

"Weren't you just tellin' your daddy you were almost twenty-five years old and old enough to move out?" I cock my hip and place my hand on it. "This isn't very mature." I snicker, knowing she's growing more agitated by me.

"I didn't realize how much older than me he was. He looks older, right?"

I nod, agreeing. "He definitely does. Probably ten years older?"

"Oh my God." She drops her face into her hands. "I'm leaving through the back."

"I don't think so."

"Fine, then I'm staying in here."

"The bathroom?"

She drops her arms. "Rowan, please! Help me."

I sigh. "Alright, fine. I'll make sure the coast is clear." Slowly, I open the door and peek around.

"Okay, you're good," I say. Turning to face her, I wave her on, and she rushes for the employees' only exit.

"Thank you!" she whispers.

As soon as she's gone, I quickly wash my hands, then return to the bar.

Kenzie furrows her brows as she looks at me. "Where's Maze?"

"She left. Wasn't feeling well." I shrug.

"What a lightweight." Kenzie laughs. "She had one beer and a shot."

"She throwing up after only that?" Riley cackles.

"Right?" Kenzie adds as I turn around and wipe down the counters. "Maybe she's pregnant."

My eyes widen at the thought. She did look awfully pale tonight. Could she be?

She said they hooked up a few weeks ago. I grab my phone from my pocket and text her.

ROWAN

Totally random question for no reason, but when was your last period?

She doesn't respond until she's back home twenty minutes later.

MAIZE

Uh…I don't know? Why?

ROWAN

Well, any chance you could be pregnant?

MAIZE

WHAT? No!

ROWAN

Are you sure? Like 100%?

MAIZE

I'm on the pill, and we used a condom.

ROWAN

Did you remember to take your pill?

MAIZE

I think so…I mean, sometimes I forget, but typically I do!

ROWAN

Oh my God…

MAIZE

Shut up. I swear. I'm not pregnant.

ROWAN

Then take a test.

MAIZE

We hooked up like three weeks ago. It'd be too soon to know anyway.

ROWAN

Maybe. I'm buying you a test, though, just to be sure.

MAIZE

And when I prove to you I'm NOT, you owe me $100!

ROWAN

Ha! You better cross your fingers and toes you aren't. Unless you want Mr. Brooding Cowboy as your baby daddy ;)

MAIZE

I hate you so much.

"What are you laughin' about?" Diesel grabs my attention and asks. I slide my phone back into my pocket so he doesn't see the conversation.

"Just checking on Maize."

"She okay?"

"Yeah, I think so."

"You gonna come over tonight?" he asks, bringing the conversation back to him.

"Hmm…that depends. You gonna make it worth my while?" I taunt, willingly giving him all my attention.

"Oh hell yes, you know I will."

Once my shift is over, I follow Diesel back to his place, and though it's almost three a.m., neither of us is tired enough to go to bed.

"I think I'm gonna take a shower and wash the bar smell off me." I kick off my boots. "You wanna join me?"

"You even gotta ask?"

We race to the bathroom, and Diesel wraps me in his arms. Our lips fuse as we frantically undress each other. Diesel turns on the water, and once it's hot, we both step in and mold our bodies together.

"So there's a fundraiser hoedown in San Angelo next month."

"Really?" I slide my palms over his hard chest, then down his rock-hard abs.

"I was thinking of taking my best girl and dancing with her all night long. Whaddya think?"

I pinch my lips together, teasingly. "Hmm…I bet she'd like that."

"Maybe relive our first kiss."

I smile, raising my brows. "Hopefully not the 'getting interrupted by my brother' part."

He shakes his head, groaning. "That asshole. I was just about to stick my tongue in your mouth too."

Bursting into laughter, I wrap my palm around his cock. "I'm sure you were."

"Mm-hmm. Then I was gonna slide into second base."

"Right there on the dance floor, huh?"

"Yep. Make sure everyone there knew you were mine and only mine. Forever."

"Fourteen-year-old boys must have wild imaginations," I taunt, stroking him faster.

He releases a moan. "You have no idea, baby."

Diesel cups my breasts and squeezes before leaning down to take a nipple into his mouth. His rough hands rub over my skin, grabbing my ass and pulling me closer to his chest. "I loved you then, and I love you now. Even if you hated me." He winks, then brushes his lips over mine.

"It took me a while to see who was right in front of me, but I'm glad I caught you when I did." I have no doubt Chelsea would've climbed in his lap had he let her and he'd been single. I'm still getting used to the idea that he has a son and will have contact with Dawson's mom on a regular basis. I don't want to be the jealous girlfriend, but I see what a catch Diesel is, and I'm not about to let him go.

"I see the wheels spinning in your head," he says. "Stop overthinking."

"I'm not," I lie.

He chuckles, then slides his hand between my legs. "I'm about to make sure of that."

CHAPTER TWENTY-ONE

Diesel

Rowan and I stand at the gate hand in hand as we wait for Chelsea's and Dawson's arrival. It's been four long weeks since I've seen him, and I can't believe how much I missed the little guy. Chelsea has sent me pictures nearly every day, and we see each other on FaceTime a few times a week.

The moment Chelsea spots me, she sets Dawson down, and he comes running toward me. Kneeling, I open my arms and wait for him. He tackles me, and we both go down laughing.

"Hey, buddy." I hug him, then bring him back to his feet. "I missed you." I stand, then pick him up.

"Hey." Rowan waves.

"Hi, guys," Chelsea says as she catches up to him.

"How was the flight?"

"He talked everyone's ear off." She chuckles. "And besides trying to potty-train a toddler during a flight, it was fine."

"Oh no," Rowan says. "Did he have an accident?"

"No, he's wearing a pull-up, but he likes to sit on the potty forever, and those plane bathrooms are so tiny, and some people aren't very patient."

"I'll teach him how to stand and pee," I say proudly.

Chelsea gives me a look.

"What? It'll be my contribution. I have some makin' up to do."

"Throw Cheerios or Froot Loops in the toilet and tell him to aim for them," Rowan says with a laugh. "That's how my mom said they trained Riley." She shrugs.

"I'll keep that in mind," Chelsea responds, chuckling.

We all walk together to the baggage claim, and once we have their luggage, we take my truck back to the ranch. It's an hour drive, so we use that time to catch up.

"So, there's something I wanted to talk to you about…" Chelsea says when we get into the house.

"Spill it."

I look over at Dawson, who's playing with Rowan on the couch. Hearing their laughter is music to my ears.

"Well, okay, don't freak out." She bites her bottom lip.

"Oh hell, Chelsea. Don't say that." I remove my cowboy hat, brush a hand through my hair, then put it back. I'm already starting to sweat.

"Sorry, it's not bad. I swear."

I release a breath. "Alright, good. Then tell me."

"I had a phone interview at a bank in San Angelo last week, and I'm going in for a second one while I'm here."

"Wait. What?" I tilt my head, confused. "You're movin' here?"

"Well, we'd move to San Angelo so the commute wouldn't be too long, but—"

"You'd be close!" I exclaim before she can finish.

She laughs, nodding. "Yes, we'd be really close."

I lean down so I'm eye to eye with Dawson. "You hear that? We'll get to see each other more than once a month!" I pick him up and pull him to my chest, then I turn to Chelsea and smile. "Thank you."

"Dawson deserves to have a dad," she simply says with a shrug. I would've never asked her to move here for me, but the fact that she made this decision on her own has me so damn excited.

"Can I ask you something?" I say to Chelsea, and she nods. Swallowing hard, I look at Dawson and then back at her. "I'd really like him to have my last name."

She nods again. "I'm already working on it. I planned on changing it before we move here."

"Dawson Hayes..." I say aloud with pride.

"He's gonna be a heartbreaker," Rowan chimes in. "Especially with his father's genes."

"Hey!"

Chelsea and Rowan both laugh.

"Daddy!"

The three of us go quiet and look at Dawson.

"Did he...?" I point at him.

Rowan's eyes light up. "He did!"

"You just called me daddy?" My heart is about to burst, and tears well in my eyes. I can't help it; this is one of the happiest moments of my life.

Dawson giggles when I tickle him. "I love being your dad, kid."

"This is the right decision," Chelsea says. "Plus, it'll give Trace and me a chance to get to know each other."

Rowan's jaw drops. "I knew it!" She points at me. "I told you!"

I snort at her dramatics. "You did."

"Told you what?" Chelsea asks.

Dawson gets restless on my hip, so I set him down and watch him carefully as he wanders around the room. If he's going to be here more often, I'll have to toddler-proof the house a lot better. There are too many things he could get into.

"That you two were totally flirting at the B&B that one day," Rowan explains.

Chelsea blushes, and I couldn't be happier that she's interested in someone. "We exchanged numbers and have been *casually* talking. I knew there was no point if we were in different states, but then a bank job opened, and Dawson's been asking to visit you more, and it just felt like all the pieces were coming together for us to move here."

"So...it wasn't just for me?" I tease, popping a brow.

"Oh, shut up." Chelsea throws a pillow at me.

I'm so relieved that things aren't awkward between us, especially with

Rowan and her, and that the three of us get along. We're going to be co-parenting, and though I'm still new to it, I'm excited to spend time with him and teach him everything I know about country living. Rowan's been patient and understanding, and we've grown even closer.

"When's the interview?" I ask.

"It's tomorrow, so I was hoping you'd be able to watch him."

"What time? I have to work in the morning, but I can in the afternoon," I tell her.

"Otherwise, I can help," Rowan adds. "I have off tomorrow. I'll take him to Grandma Bishop's, and she'll just die over him while spoiling him properly."

I laugh, knowing she's right. "If that's okay with Chelsea? I'll come over as soon as I'm done."

"I mean, yeah, that's fine as long as Rowan doesn't mind. Dawson can be a handful."

"Absolutely! My cousins are looking forward to playing with him too," Rowan reassures her.

"Okay, thank you. I appreciate it. I'm not used to getting much help and always feel like a burden when someone offers. When I'm at work, he goes to daycare, and my sister's shifts are the same as mine so I didn't have extra hands." She blows out a breath as if the whole world isn't all on her shoulders now.

"I'm here, Chelsea. You don't have to do this alone anymore. When you move here, we'll come up with a schedule so you have some nights to yourself. You deserve it."

"I can't remember the last time I had an entire night to myself," she says with a laugh. "Or an uninterrupted bath."

Dawson grabs my cowboy hat off the coffee table and puts it on his head, covering his eyes and nose. He starts giggling, which makes the three of us burst out laughing too.

"How ya doing over there?" Rowan asks from the doorway, leaning against it with her arms crossed. The smartass look on her face tells me she knows damn well how things are going.

"Half his dinner is on the floor, so…not great."

She walks toward me with a smile, then she looks at the table. "Did you try to feed him spinach?" She wrinkles her nose.

"It's healthy for him," I retort.

"Only if it makes it into his mouth," she teases.

"Daddy, no!" He swipes my hand again when I hand him a fork. "I want candy!"

"You can't have candy, buddy. How about some fruit?"

He nods and shoves a piece of hot dog in his mouth. Of course he'll eat that, but nothing with actual nutrients.

"Don't get discouraged," Rowan tells me as I cut up an apple and banana. "Toddlers are picky shits."

"How did Chelsea do this by herself for so long?" I ask, setting the slices in a bowl. "He's been here for three hours, and I'm exhausted. I chased him all over the house, put him on the potty ten billion times, and then he screamed for food but won't eat."

"Is that why he's not wearing any pants?" Rowan chuckles, and the sound causes me to smile. I lower my gaze down her body and appreciate her curves.

"Yep," I say. "He's wearing his big boy underwear because it's faster to get him on the toilet without removing the extra layers."

"Did you try the cereal trick?"

"Also, yep. He grabbed the Cheerio out of the water and then popped it into his mouth before I could stop him."

Rowan covers her mouth to hold back her laughter, but I see the corner of her lips tilts up.

"Oh my God…" She pats my arm. "He's as much work as you were, I'm sure."

"My mother's already confirmed that as true when I called and asked for advice." I grunt.

It's been a few weeks since Chelsea and Dawson moved to Texas for good. It's the first night he's sleeping over, and while I'm happy to have him here and give his mother a break, I'm nervous as hell. I've been getting the spare room ready for him, but I have a feeling he's not going to stay in his toddler bed without a fight. Chelsea's already warned me he likes to get out.

"Well, maybe once he's asleep, I can help ease some of your tension," Rowan says seductively.

I pop a brow. "I might be down for that…" Grinning, I take the bowl of sliced fruit and set it down in front of Dawson. I don't even bother with the fork this time. He's flung it four times already.

After dinner, we give Dawson a bath, get him into his pajamas, and then read him two bedtime stories. Just as Chelsea warned, he snuck out of his bed, and I repeatedly tucked him back in. After the seventh time, he wore himself out and finally fell asleep.

"I am *so* tired…" I groan as I collapse on the bed next to Rowan. She's been watching TV while she waits for me. "Any chance I can just lie here while you pleasure me? I don't think I can move."

Rowan grabs the remote and turns it off. Then she straddles my lap and wraps her arms around my neck. "You did good," she praises. "And I gotta admit, watching you be a dad is sexy as hell."

I arch a brow. "Oh, really? How sexy are we talkin'?"

"Mmm…like blow job sexy. Slide your cock between my breasts and let you come all over my chest sexy."

"Don't fuck with me, woman," I warn. "My dick is already hard."

She rocks her hips and grins when she feels me between her legs. "Or you can just lie there while I ride you. Your pick."

"Pick?" I huff. "I choose all three. Blow job. Ride me. Fuck your tits. In that order."

Her head falls back as she releases a deep laugh, and I lean forward, kissing her neck and sucking hard. She rocks her hips against me, and I groan at the friction.

"Christ…" I hiss. "Take off your clothes right now."

Within seconds, we're undressed, tripping over ourselves before falling back on the bed. Rowan pushes me down and eagerly slides over my length, and I grip her thighs, moving her against me faster.

I fucking love the way she looks on top of me. It's not just sex, it never has been, but making love to my dream girl and knowing someday I'm going to marry her have me craving more of her every day.

"Should we make him a little sister?" she taunts as she leans closer.

"Don't even joke," I say seriously. "I'll knock you up right now."

She grins wide. "Not yet, Cowboy. Dawson gets you to himself for a while."

"Okay, that's fair." I smirk.

Rowan brings her mouth to mine, and I cup the back of her head, deepening our kiss. "I love you," I whisper against her lips.

"I love you, too," she whispers back as I slide my other hand down her body, then smack her ass.

She squeals, and we pull apart. Quickly, I flip us over and lift her leg until her calf rests on my shoulder. Rocking harder, she arches her back, then covers both of her hands over her mouth as she screams out her orgasm. I follow behind her moments later, burying my face in her neck as we fall over the edge.

We lie in bed with my arms wrapped around her. My body feels like jelly, but I want to absorb every tender moment with Rowan.

"So how are things going with the new guy around the ranch?" she asks after we catch our breaths.

"Gavin?" I furrow my brows, and she nods. He's been working with Jackson for almost a month now. "I guess fine. I don't see him much. Why do you ask?"

"Just wondered if he's said anything about Maize."

"No, not to me. What would he say about her?" I'm confused as hell as to where this conversation is going. "Rowan..."

"What?"

"What aren't you telling me?"

"Um...it's just girl stuff. Nothing. Forget I said anything." She waves me off, and it's cute she thinks I'm just going to so easily *forget*.

I tilt her chin up and arch a brow. "It's nothing like actually *nothing* or nothing like I need to punch him in the face?"

She squints her eyes and twists her lips. "Neither?"

"So it's something..."

She sighs, rolling her eyes. "They might've hooked up when he first arrived."

"No fucking way."

"It was the night you and I went to San Angelo actually. They met at the bar, and of course it was a night I wasn't working."

"Holy shit."

"I know…" She inhales. "She took a pregnancy test."

"Jesus, Row." I blink hard. "Please tell me she's not—"

"It was negative," she interjects. "Then I had to pay her a hundred bucks for losing the bet."

I breathe out a sigh of relief, my brain still spinning from this news. "So they hooked up, and then what?"

"Then nothing. She avoids him at all costs, which is why I asked if he's ever brought her up. 'Cause if he did, I thought maybe he was thinking about her."

"I don't see him that much. When I'm not working, I'm with you and Dawson. But I have a feeling even if I did, he wouldn't say a damn thing. In fact, he doesn't talk that much. He looks pissed off most of the time."

Rowan snorts, giggling. "Yeah, it's always the quiet ones you have to worry about. He does have that whole sexy, brooding thing goin' on, too."

My brows shoot up. "'Scuse me?"

"Not to mention, he's way older. Probably more experienced."

"I'm older," I remind her.

"By one year!" She chuckles, climbing on top of me. "Aww…is someone jealous?"

"Is someone tryin' to *make* me jealous?" I brush loose strands of hair behind her ear and smile at her.

"I didn't even have to try in school. You scared every guy away who breathed in my direction."

I puff out my chest. "Damn straight."

"We better get to sleep. Dawson will probably be up in four hours," she tells me. "And he'll want your full attention."

"I plan to take him out to see the cows after breakfast anyway. They'll burn him out, or he'll burn them out. Win-win either way."

Rowan leans down and softly kisses my lips. "You're a great dad."

"I'm trying to be." I wrap my arms around her. "Hopefully, a great husband one day, too." When I waggle my brows, she rolls her eyes at me, but she knows I'll put a ring on her finger one day.

"Gonna finish fixing up this place this winter, and then you won't be able to resist movin' in with me."

"Alright, Cowboy. Challenge accepted."

CHAPTER TWENTY-TWO

Rowan

FOUR MONTHS LATER

DIESEL
You wearing that sexy red thong I like?

ROWAN
I was thinking commando might be more your style?

DIESEL
Screw dinner. Gonna fuck you against the table instead.

ROWAN
That is not the romance package I signed up for on our first Valentine's Day.

DIESEL

Okay, fair point. I'll wine and dine you, then fuck you senseless.

ROWAN

Deal.

"You sure you're okay babysitting?" I ask Elle who's sitting on my bed, waiting for me to finish getting ready for my hot date tonight.

"I think I can handle a three-year-old," she states. "Plus, Kenzie and I are having a singles-only party after Dawson goes to bed, so she'll be there to help me."

It's been a crazy five months since Chelsea and Dawson moved to Texas. In fact, it's been quite the adventure since the night Diesel kissed me in the bar office.

But I wouldn't change it for the world. I've never been happier and love seeing this side of Diesel.

"Alright, I'm ready," I tell Elle, staring into the mirror and inhaling a deep breath. I'm dressed up more than usual, and I hope I knock Diesel on his ass when he sees me. "How do I look?" I spin around for her to get a good look.

She examines me from head to toe with a cheeky grin. "Like you're about to get laid six ways to Sunday."

"Well, then I guess that's perfect!" I chuckle, brushing my hands down my skintight dress. "Though I'm like ninety-percent positive I won't be able to sit in this thing without it splitting at the ass."

"I'm wondering how you're going to even walk in those shoes…" She raises her brows at my five-inch platforms. I've worn heels less than five times in my whole life, and it's possible I might trip and break my neck.

I walk around my bed, and my ankle jerks, making me stumble. "Dammit. How do women wear these things?"

"You should've practiced," she scolds.

"No, no. I think I have this…" I straighten my back and walk around my room. "I'll be fine."

"You're walking in slow motion," Elle deadpans.

"It's the only way."

She snickers, shaking her head at me.

"You're basically a doctor, so if I twist something, you can fix me up!" I grin.

"A *vet*," she emphasizes. "An animal doctor."

"Potato, *potahto*."

"No, ma'am. Now, if you're birthing a calf or a foal, then I'm your girl. Otherwise, you'd be going to see my parents at the ER." Both my uncle Evan and aunt Emily would no doubt give me a hard time for wearing these, especially if they saw me at the hospital banged up.

"Yeah, I don't want that. Would kinda ruin my whole rough sex plans for tonight."

Elle gags, making me laugh.

"Please, let's go before you hurt something." She stands, and we head for the door.

We drive to Diesel's house where Dawson's staying tonight. He wanted to give Chelsea and Trace a chance to have a romantic night without worrying about getting up with a toddler in the morning. They've been seriously dating for the past few months, and they're great together. Trace adores Dawson and is great with him. He's surrounded by so much love and is the luckiest little kid to have four adults who get along and can co-parent together.

Elle parks her truck, and I slowly get out, adjusting my dress before making my way to the door. As soon as it opens and he sees me walking up his steps, his jaw drops.

"Hooooly fuck."

Seeing Diesel's face was totally worth it.

"You like?" I ask, swallowing hard.

Elle comes to my side. "He better, considering what it took to get you in that thing."

"I definitely do, but now I don't want anyone else to see you…" He pulls me into his arms and slides one hand down my back. "Especially with your legs and ass on display. Hell, you're tryin' to kill me, aren't you?"

"She's gonna kill herself in those heels," Elle says, snickering as she walks into the house, and Dawson comes running toward her.

"I don't think I've ever seen you wear those before." His gaze lowers, admiring every inch of me.

"Nope, but I wanted to wear them for a special occasion."

"Then we better get going because my mind is running wild with ideas…" He closes the gap between us and kisses me. "Like right now, I'm envisioning you bent over wearing *only* those heels."

"Mmm…now that I can probably arrange," I whisper, brushing my lips against his again.

"Daddy!" Dawson interrupts, tugging on his jeans.

We quickly pull apart. I forgot we had an audience.

"What is it, bud?" Diesel kneels, removing his cowboy hat.

"Aunt Ellie said I could have cereal for supper!" His smile's so wide and genuine, it's impossible to tell him no.

"Is that so?"

I crack up laughing because Dawson's obsessed with cereal. Ever since we tried that potty training trick, it's all he wants to eat.

"Would you rather I feed him something I make? Because trust me, it won't be good. That's Maize's area."

Elizabeth Bishop is smart as a whip, but her cooking skills are null.

Diesel picks him up and stands. "Alright, buddy. You have fun with Aunt Ellie." He kisses his head, then hands him off to Elle. "In bed by eight," he reminds her.

"This isn't my first babysitting rodeo," she mocks. "I have this. We're gonna get high on sugar, run a mile, then crash out. Easy peasy."

Diesel groans.

"Bye, lovebirds!" Elle all but pushes us out the door, and Diesel takes my hand, threading our fingers together as we walk to his truck.

"Can you actually walk in those things?" he asks, opening the passenger side for me.

"Where's your confidence in me?"

He lifts me, and I settle into the seat.

"About three inches lower." He snickers.

I glare at him, buckling in. "We're on a date, mister. You're supposed to be charming and romantic, remember?"

Diesel clears his throat and slides his hands down his dressy button-up shirt. "Startin' now." He throws me a wink, then shuts the door and runs to his side.

As soon as we're on the road, he grabs my hand and presses his lips to my knuckles, planting a sweet kiss there.

"In case I wasn't clear, you look gorgeous."

"You look quite handsome yourself. That shirt is making me want to rip off the buttons and slide my tongue up your abs."

"You better watch that naughty mouth."

"My mouth most definitely wants to be on you."

"Rowan…" he warns in a deep drawl. "Getting my dick hard in these jeans is uncomfortable, so start talkin' about something else."

I grin, tightening my grip on his hand. "So I shouldn't tell you I'm wearing a new black thong and bra set tonight?"

"Goddammit, woman." His jaw tenses. "That black piece of fabric you call a dress is already drivin' me insane."

Although we spend as much time together as we can between our work schedules, we don't always get nights alone, so after fourteen days of no sex, I'm dying for him. He gets Dawson three to four times a week, and by the end of the night, Diesel's usually so exhausted he falls asleep the second his head hits the pillow. I'm still working late at the bar, so I need to make tonight count.

"Or that I haven't touched myself since you last did, and I'm so wet right now."

"Row…I won't hesitate to pull this truck over and put you up on my lap, so unless you want us to miss our dinner reservations, you better stop."

I know he wants this to be super special, but all I want is him.

"I think you should do just that…"

Diesel jerks the steering wheel to the right until we're off the road. Gravel spits up under the tires as he takes a hidden path, and I squeal, hanging on tight as he laughs.

"What're you doing?" I shout. "You tryin' to kill us?"

"Hang on, sweetheart."

It's been raining for three days straight, which is more than we typically get in an entire month this time of year, but it means it's muddy as hell. The truck dips into a deep puddle and then water rises and splashes against the side.

"Adam!" I shriek through my laughter.

He quickly turns the wheel again, and we drive through another muddy puddle. Dirty water flies everywhere, covering my window.

Diesel looks over at me with a shit-eating grin on his adorable face before he does another donut, and the truck spins in circles.

I hang on for dear life, gripping the safety handle, and can't stop smiling and laughing. I've gone mudding on four-wheelers through the woods before, but nothing like this.

After ten minutes, Diesel finds a dry spot and parks the truck.

"What the hell was that?" I ask, still trying to catch my breath from the rush of adrenaline.

"That was the equivalent of me dumping a bucket of cold water over your head so you'd stop looking at me like I was your next meal."

"But that's all I want," I pout, sticking out my lower lip.

He adjusts his seat so it slides all the way back and then grabs my hand and helps me climb over the middle console. My dress is too tight to straddle his lap, so I sit on his legs.

"Why do I even bother trying to plan a romantic night for you?" he asks, brushing a strand of hair behind my ear.

I shrug, grinning. "Good question. You know I'm not high maintenance."

"One of these days, I'm gonna try to propose, and you're gonna jump me before I even get the chance to ask."

Smiling wide at the thought of him putting a ring on my finger, I nod in agreement. "Probably. So you might wanna ask me when I'm least expecting it."

"Duly noted." He winks. "But I actually have something for you."

"A gift?" I prompt.

"Perhaps." He stretches back and reaches for a small box behind him. "This is one of them. The other is at the house."

"You really didn't have to get me anything," I tell him. "I just wanted to spend time with you."

He grabs my chin. "I know. But this gift is a little selfish."

I narrow my eyes as he sets it in my palm. "What do you mean?"

"It's for both of us," he clarifies.

"Oh God. Is it one of those remote vibrators?"

"Huh?"

"Like I put it inside me, and you have the remote to control the speed…"

Diesel furrows his brows, looking at me like I've lost my mind.

"Okay, so by your expression, I'm gonna say no."

He smirks. "Rowan, just open it."

My heart races as I lift the top and unwrap the tissue paper. Whatever it is feels light. My fingers rub against metal, and when I pull it out, I narrow my eyes in confusion. "A key?"

"Yep," he says.

I hesitate. "Because I have the key to your heart?"

He releases a laugh. "Well, yes. But this is the key to my cabin."

"You're giving me a key to your house?" I ask. Is this the next part of a relationship? Exchanging house keys?

"I am."

"Oh." I flip the key and study it. "Thank you."

"But I'm also giving you the key to *your* house."

My eyes meet his, and I frown. "Wait. What?"

Diesel grabs my hand and rubs the pad of his thumb over my knuckles. "I want you to move in with me."

With wide eyes I blink, and my throat goes dry.

"I want to wake up with you every morning and go to bed with you every night. I'm tired of cramming time with you between our work schedules and hectic lives. Now that the cabin is all fixed up, I want it to be *our* home. Decorate the walls. Fill it with pictures and candles. Pick out new pillows and blankets in your favorite color. Hell, new china and silverware. I've been ready for the next step with you for months but didn't want to rush you. However, I know I want you in my life forever."

Diesel's looking at me as though I'm his whole world with his cowboy hat sitting just right and his green eyes sparkling at me. The scruff on his chin is newly trimmed. He's my everything.

There's no doubt in my heart that I want him.

"Rowan, what do you say? Do you want to live together?"

My eyes swell with happy tears. I frantically nod and wrap my arms around his neck. "Yes, absolutely!"

I pull his lips to mine, and he tightens his hold on me. "I love you," I murmur.

"I love you more." His hands slide up my thighs, moving my dress up to my waist, and he shifts my body until I'm straddling him. Rocking my hips,

I feel him harden between my thighs. Diesel groans as I rub his cock against me.

"You want to take another one of my firsts?" I whisper.

He pulls back slightly, furrowing his brows. "What's that?"

"Sex in a truck," I explain. "I've never."

The corner of his lips tilts up into a wide grin. "Good, neither have I."

Leaning back, I flash him a skeptical look. "Really?"

"Serious! I was saving all the fun places for you."

I snort, laughing. "I'm sure."

He manages to undo his buckle and jeans, sliding them down until I palm his cock and stroke him.

"Fuck…" he hisses. "Why does it feel like it's been too damn long?"

"Because it has!"

Sliding my panties to the side, he pushes a finger inside me. "Now you'll have me all the time."

"Finally," I say, gasping as he adds a second finger. When Dawson sleeps over, we have to be quiet since his room isn't far from the master, but now that we're in his truck, we can be as loud as we want. "I need you inside me."

He lifts me slightly to position himself against me, and I slowly slide down his length. I wrap my arms around his shoulders, and my head falls back as we rock in unison and come together.

It's the best Valentine's Day ever.

"You're what?" Riley shouts as I tape up the boxes in my room.

"You heard me." I smirk.

"You and Diesel are moving in together? Like…legit?"

I nod.

"No one asked me."

Snorting, I laugh. "Why does this surprise you so much? We've been dating for six months. You married Zoey after twelve hours," I remind him with a shit-eating grin.

"Am I ever gonna live that down?" he huffs.

"Nope," Diesel answers, rounding the door and walking in.

"That's different. You're moving in with my best friend," Riley retorts, then points at Diesel. "And you…"

Diesel holds up his hands in surrender. "What now?"

"You know the rules. You break her heart; I break your neck."

Diesel smirks. "Crystal clear, boss."

"Relax." I stand and pat Riley's shoulder. "We're living in sin, not getting hitched in Vegas."

Riley groans, and without another word, he turns around and leaves.

"You'd think he'd be used to us dating by now," I say, wrapping my arms around his waist.

Diesel leans down and gently presses his lips to mine.

"I could be the King of England, and I still wouldn't be good enough for his little sister." He shrugs, knowing there's no use in worrying about it.

"Would that make me your queen?"

"You are most definitely my queen. Royal title or not."

I smile. "Ready to be roomies with me?"

"Ready to have a three-year-old around half the time?"

"Well, I grew up with Riley so…" We both laugh, and we hear him shout from the room across the hall.

"I heard that!"

"Dawson's a good kid. I love watching you be a dad and getting to experience him learning something new. Do you think Chelsea will be okay with me being around more?"

"Of course. I told her so she's aware, but Trace is around him all the time too. As long as his parents are happy, he'll be happy."

"And that's all that matters, right?"

"All that matters to me is you, my son, and this ranch. I don't think I could be happier if I tried." He cups my face, and our lips merge.

A throat clearing from behind interrupts us, and we pull apart. "Y'all can't wait till you're under your own roof to make out?" my mother scolds. Then she looks at Diesel. "I hope you take good care of her. You hear me?" She steps in and hugs me. "This is my baby."

"Mom." I grin. "I'm not going very far," I remind her.

"But still. I wasn't ready for this. Seems too soon."

"If it helps, I'll still come over and raid the fridge while you do my laundry."

"Nice try." She pats my butt.

Like clockwork, my father enters. He's been working all morning and gives Diesel a curt nod. "You're really leavin'?" he asks, crossing his arms over his chest.

"Five minutes away," I say. "You won't even notice I'm gone."

He pulls me in for a long hug. "I'll always notice the absence of your bobby pins lying around the house and tripping over your boots you never put away."

"Geez, it's like you two want me to be here until I'm eighty."

He pulls back and kisses the top of my head. "We're gonna miss you. You know we will."

"I'll miss you guys too. As soon as I figure out how to cook, we'll have you over for dinner."

They both laugh and nod. I'll have Maize help me.

"Well, we're burning daylight. Let's get your stuff loaded up and outta here," my dad says and recruits Riley to help.

It only takes one trip to bring my essential boxes over. Since Dawson needs room for his things too, I left some of my stuff at my parents. Most of it I need to go through and toss or donate anyway. I don't want to crowd the house with all my useless crap.

After everything is unloaded, I say goodbye to my parents and Riley, and then it's just Diesel and me in a house surrounded by boxes.

"Well, this is it. No turning back now," I tease as he wraps me up in his arms, and we fall onto the couch.

"You wouldn't get very far. I'd chase you."

I sit on his lap. "Ahh, yes. The stalker is back."

"Always and forever, baby." He cups my ass. "You're mine."

Smiling, I bring our lips together. "And I couldn't be happier about it."

Diesel

FIVE MONTHS LATER

I can't believe Rowan and I have been together for almost a year. Knowing that she took a chance on me and loves my son as much as I do is everything I could've ever wished for. Today's the big Fourth of July party at the Bishop Ranch, but it's also going to be a day to remember for everyone, especially Rowan.

John and Jackson are busy grilling burgers and hot dogs while the other men are setting up the firework display. Alex takes me off to the side, and Riley follows suit. "You ready for this?"

Riley looks at me, smiling. He's finally somewhat used to me being with his sister, which is a relief.

I glance over my shoulder and see Chelsea sitting on a blanket next to Trace. Elle and Kenzie chat with Rowan as Dawson sits on her lap. I'm so goddamn lucky.

"Yeah, I'm ready," I tell him without hesitation. Riley calls one of his friends on the phone and makes sure all of my plans are in place. "You've got ten minutes."

Alex gives me a side hug and grins. "Mama B is gonna start asking about babies."

A chuckle escapes me. "She already has! What are you talkin' about?"

"Before marriage?" Alex asks with his eyebrows raised.

I shake my head. "She said ring first, five babies second. In that order."

"Of course she did." Alex snickers before we go our separate ways.

Five minutes later, Alex turns on the stereo and blasts it while everyone sits on blankets and picnic tables, waiting for the sun to set so we can start popping fireworks.

"Life of the Party" by Shawn Mendes blasts through the speakers, and I walk across the pasture and mouth the words to Rowan. Her eyes widen with recognition and shock.

"What're you doin'?" she mouths back.

Chelsea takes Dawson as I grab Rowan's hand and pull her to her feet. I start dancing with her in front of everyone, re-creating the night of her winter formal when we first danced to her favorite song. I spin her around and dip her a few times until the airplane flies overhead. It's low in the sky, and the engine's loud, grabbing the entire town's attention. Behind it flies a sign that reads: "Will You Marry Me, Rowan Bishop?"

Everyone in a fifty-mile radius can read it without a doubt. She looks up, then glances back at me, her lips parted.

"What does that say?" she asks just as I drop down on one knee.

I'm nervous as hell, knowing all eyes are watching us, but I try to focus on the beautiful woman in front of me who I'm going to make my wife. I fidget and pull the ring box from my pocket and flip it open. Rowan's eyes are full of tears, but the smile hasn't left her face.

"I knew when we were kids that you were the only woman for me. So many people have told me that when you know, you *know*, and I knew you were meant to be mine when we danced and shared our first kiss that night. Somehow, I've always known." She covers her mouth with her hands, tears sliding down her cheeks and fingers. "Rowan, you make me the happiest man alive. You've taught me so much in so little time, and I can't imagine a life without you. You love me wholeheartedly. You love and welcome my son in your life. I love you more than words can express. You're everything I've ever wanted." I reach up and grab her hand. "Sweetheart, will you marry me?"

Rowan nearly knocks me down as she wraps her arms around my neck. The ring goes flying as she kisses me in front of her whole family.

"Rowan Bishop," her grandma says. "You better give that man an answer and not keep him and the rest of us waitin'."

Rowan

Everyone surrounding us laughs at Grandma Bishop's outburst. She has her hand on her hips, impatiently waiting.

"Yes, yes, yes! I will marry you." I scream out for the whole town to hear.

I'm nearly straddling him in front of God and country, but all I want to do is kiss his soft, perfect lips. Eventually, we break apart, and he helps me back to my feet.

"Oh, the ring," he says, seeing the box on the ground. Neither of us cared about it and were too caught up in the moment of being together for the rest of our lives. He pulls the sparkling diamond out and slips it on my finger. I can't help but gasp at how stunning it looks on me.

"This is too much," I whisper, looking down at the rock.

"You deserve it all, baby," he says, just loud enough for me to hear. "So let's get you knocked up."

I smack him across the chest, but the truth is, I have my own secret to tell. After everyone has given us a stupid amount of hugs and congratulations, Diesel takes me off to the side, away from everyone so we can have some privacy for the first time all day.

"Are you happy, Row?"

I look at him, feeling the tears creeping in my eyes. "You have no idea. I...I...didn't expect any of this. Not today. I don't know how you managed to buy a ring and plan all of this without me knowing."

A sneaky grin sweeps across his lips. "You think all we do all day is work on the ranch? You're sadly mistaken."

I shake my head. "You're so bad."

He leans over, and I press my lips against his and melt into him. By the time we pull apart, we're both breathless, and I'm more than ready to get out of here and consummate this proposal, but not before I say what I need to.

"Adam," I say seriously, looking up into his eyes.

He tilts his head, furrowing his brows. "Yes?"

"I don't know how to say this without just telling you...." I hesitate.

He searches my face and looks alarmed, so I give him a reassuring smile.

"I'm pregnant," I say, swallowing hard, watching him process what I just said.

He blinks hard. "Wait, what?"

"I found out a few days ago. I was feeling weird at the bar and picked up a handful of tests from the store after work. They were all positive." I shrug.

His mouth falls open before cups my face and smashes his lips against mine. "Really? We're having a baby?"

The excitement in his voice is so damn contagious that I can barely contain my happiness. "Yes, really. It's happening. I mean, I didn't expect it so soon, but Dawson is gonna have a brother or sister next year." Though we joked about having babies and making a big family, I was on the pill, and we weren't trying. However, it looks like the universe had other plans for us.

Tears well in his eyes, and seeing him overjoyed with emotion has me crying too. We kiss and laugh, and he holds me as though he's never letting me go. I know he won't. I'm his forever.

"You've truly made me the happiest man in the world," he says. "You have no idea. I didn't get to experience all the baby things with Dawson. I love my son more than life itself, but I missed out on a lot. I'm so damn excited right now. I just can't even explain myself. My words seem like pig mush."

I giggle at his analogy. "I can wait to grow our family, babe. This is everything I ever wanted."

"Me too, Row. A houseful of kids who get to grow up on the ranch while I grow old with you." Diesel leans over and nuzzles against my neck.

Butterflies stream through me as I lean into his touch. "Same, Cowboy. Also, can we wait a while before we tell everyone our news? Keep it our little secret for old times' sake?" Truthfully, I just want confirmation from my doctor first before we tell our parents. The moment they know, the entire town will know.

He chuckles. "I'm good with that. You know we're gonna get bombarded with questions and loads of baby stuff."

"I know." I sigh with an enthusiastic smile. "That's why I kinda just wanna enjoy the news with you for a while before we share it with our families."

"Our relationship started out a secret, so we might as well have another." He winks with a mischievous smirk.

I kiss him deeply, and we both smile before walking back to the group. They're happily eating and goofing off. The ring shines and sparkles, and I can't stop staring at it as I interlock my fingers with Diesel's. After we grab a burger and chips, we sit on a big blanket, and I lean against his chest, waiting for the firework show to begin. Fourth of July is my favorite holiday, and each year the show gets bigger and better because my uncles act like they're trying to set a Guinness Record or something.

Looking around, I'm so grateful to be able to raise a child on the ranch with my family close by. I know it's exactly what Diesel wants, and it's been my dream for as long as I can remember.

Before the first explosion goes off, I see Maize standing off to the side with her arms crossed, looking pissed as ever. I tell Diesel I'm gonna grab something to drink and go over to her. When I move closer, I notice how tense her jaw is and narrowed her eyes are. Holding her temper is not her strong suit.

"Everything okay?" I ask, grabbing her hand and pulling her away from Uncle Evan, who's too close for this conversation.

She lets out a huff. "No, it's not."

I search her face. "What's going on?"

"Did you see who Gavin brought with him to the party?" she asks, more irritated than when the ranch hands steal food off the buffet table.

"So? You haven't given him a lick of attention since he moved here," I tell her.

"That is Sarah Cooke, Rowan. She was such a bitch to me in high school. Made fun of me every single chance she got. Seeing her flirt with him makes me want to break her skull in," she says between gritted teeth.

"Whoa there, Maze. You gotta calm your tits, or you'll stroke out or something. Let's get something to drink. If I didn't know better, I'd say you were envious," I tell her with a wink, going to the lemonade and punch table. Before I can grab a cup for Maize and me, Gavin walks up. I pretend to contemplate what I want to drink as he leads Maize to the side. They're far enough away to have some privacy, but still close enough for me to eavesdrop.

"I've put the pieces together, Maize," he says in a hushed tone.

"What're you talkin' about exactly?" Maize asks, playing dumb. Even I know what he's referring to. They had a one-night stand, she spent the last year avoiding him like an STD, and now that he's brought another girl around, she's jealous as hell.

For a moment, silence draws on between them, and I can imagine Maize's staring him down like he's grown a third eye. I slowly put ice cubes in some cups, taking my sweet time. It's too easy to be nosy when they're right there.

He chuckles, unfazed by her antics. "I've tamed wild horses, Maize Bishop, and I'll tame your *attitude* too. I like a good challenge."

She scoffs. "Is that a threat or somethin'?" Maybe she doesn't notice, but I can hear the shakiness in her voice as I pour my punch.

"Not a threat, sweetheart. That's a damn promise," Gavin keeps his voice low, but the confidence oozes off his words before he walks away. Maize comes up to me completely infuriated.

My eyes are as wide as saucers as I glance at her, and she groans before pulling a flask from her back pocket and taking a long swig. "I hate him. I hate him *so* much! Egotistical, bigheaded, tight blue jean wearing bastard!"

"You forgot to say brooding and sexy as sin in there somewhere," I say, snorting at how annoyed she is.

"He just needs to go away. I don't shit where I eat for a damn reason, yet here I am," she says as Gavin walks back to Sarah with a cocky grin. Maize watches them for a minute, and I swear laser beams are going to shoot from her eyes at any moment. It has me holding back laughter.

"Come on, ignore them," I say and grab our drinks and meet Diesel back on the blanket. Maize follows me, bitching under her breath as she plops down next to Kenzie with her arms crossed.

"I thought you got lost or something. What took so long?" he asks, kissing me right behind the ear, causing me to squirm.

I giggle and turn toward him, whispering. "Oh nothing other than Maize and Gavin exchanging words. He *totally* confronted her."

His stares at me, and his mouth falls open. "No way."

"Yep, and she's ready to murder him and his date," I explain.

He laughs. "Welp, my money's on her. She's scary as hell."

"I guess we'll see," I say, chuckling, then lean over and plant kisses on his mouth. "That was us at one point."

Diesel grins. "It was, and now look whatcha've gone and done."

"What's that?" I ask.

"You roped Big D," he gloats. "You actually caught the uncatchable cowboy."

I shake my head and slide my lips across his as our kiss deepens. "No, Cowboy, you're wrong. You caught me."

Continue reading for Gavin & Maize's story in *Wrangling the Cowboy* or read *Evan & Emily*, Bishop Family Origin, #2

About the Author

Brooke Cumberland and Lyra Parish are a duo of romance authors under the *USA Today* pseudonym, Kennedy Fox. Their characters will make you blush and your heart melt. Cowboys in tight jeans are their kryptonite. They always guarantee a happily ever after!

Connect with Us

Find us on our website:

kennedyfoxbooks.com

Subscribe to our newsletter:

kennedyfoxbooks.com/newsletter

- facebook.com/kennedyfoxbooks
- twitter.com/kennedyfoxbooks
- instagram.com/kennedyfoxduo
- amazon.com/author/kennedyfoxbooks
- goodreads.com/kennedyfox
- bookbub.com/authors/kennedy-fox

Books by Kennedy Fox

CONNECTED DUET SERIES

CHECKMATE DUET SERIES

ROOMMATE DUET SERIES

LAWTON RIDGE DUET SERIES

INTERCONNECTED STAND-ALONES

BISHOP BROTHERS SERIES

CIRCLE B RANCH SERIES

BISHOP FAMILY ORIGIN

LOVE IN ISOLATION SERIES

ONLY ONE SERIES

MAKE ME SERIES

Find the entire Kennedy Fox reading order at
Kennedyfoxbooks.com / reading-order

Find all of our current freebies at
Kennedyfoxbooks.com / freeromance